THE MAMMOTH BOOK OF PULP FICTION

Also available

The Mammoth Book of Classic Science Fiction
The Mammoth Book of Golden Age Science Fiction
The Mammoth Book of Vintage Science Fiction
The Mammoth Book of New Age Science Fiction
The Mammoth Book of Fantastic Science Fiction
The Mammoth Book of Modern Science Fiction
The Mammoth Book of Private Eye Stories
The Mammoth Book of Great Detective Stories
The Mammoth Book of Spy Thrillers
The Mammoth Book of True Murder
The Mammoth Book of True Crime
The Mammoth Book of True Crime 2
The Mammoth Book of Short Horror Novels
The Mammoth Book of True War Stories
The Mammoth Book of Modern War Stories
The Mammoth Book of the Western
The Mammoth Book of Ghost Stories
The Mammoth Book of Ghost Stories 2
The Mammoth Book of the Supernatural
The Mammoth Book of Astounding Puzzles
The Mammoth Book of Terror
The Mammoth Book of Vampires
The Mammoth Book of Killer Women
The Mammoth Book of Zombies
The Mammoth Book of Historical Whodunnits
The Mammoth Book of Werewolves
The Mammoth Book of Golden Age Detective Stories
The Mammoth Book of Contemporary SF Masters
The Mammoth Book of Erotica
The Mammoth Book of Frankenstein
The Mammoth Book of Battles
The Mammoth Book of Astounding Word Games
The Mammoth Book of Mindbending Puzzles
The Mammoth Book of Historical Detectives
The Mammoth Book of Victorian & Edwardian Ghost Stories
The Mammoth Book of Dreams
The Mammoth Book of Symbols
The Mammoth Book of Brainstorming Puzzles
The Mammoth Book of 1000 Great Lives

The Mammoth Book of

PULP FICTION

Edited by
Maxim Jakubowski

Carroll & Graf Publishers, Inc.
New York

Carroll & Graf Publishers, Inc.
260 Fifth Avenue
New York
NY 10001

This collection published in the UK by Robinson Publishing 1996

First Carroll & Graf edition 1996

ISBN 0–7867–0300–8

Typeset by Hewer Text Composition Services, Edinburgh
Printed and bound in the United Kingdom

10 9 8 7 6 5 4 3 2 1

CONTENTS

ACKNOWLEDGEMENTS

Introduction and collection © 1996 by Maxim Jakubowski.

TOO MANY HAVE LIVED by Dashiell Hammett, © 1933 by Dashiell Hammett. First appeared in *American Magazine*. Reproduced by permission of The Robert Lantz-Joy Harris Literary Agency, Inc. and the Dashiell Hammett Estate.

FLIGHT TO NOWHERE by Charles Williams, © 1955 by Charles Williams. First appeared in *Manhunt*. Reproduced by permission of Abner Stein.

BLACK by Paul Cain, © 1932 by Paul Cain. First appeared in *Black Mask Magazine*. Reproduced by permission of No Exit Press.

FINDERS KILLERS! by John D. MacDonald, © 1953 by John D. MacDonald. First appeared in *Detective Story Magazine*. Reproduced by permission of Vanessa Holt Ltd.

MURDER'S MANDATE by W. T. Ballard, © 1946 by Better Books, Inc. Copyright renewed 1974 by Willis Todhunter Ballard. First appeared in *Thrilling Detective Magazine*. Reproduced by permission of Golden West Literary Agency.

CIGARETTE GIRL by James M. Cain, © 1952 by Flying Eagle Publications, Inc. First published in *Manhunt*. Reprinted by permission of Harold Ober Associates.

THE GETAWAY by Gil Brewer, © 1976 by Gil Brewer. First appeared in *Mystery*. Reproduced by permission of A. M. Heath & Co. Ltd.

PREVIEW OF MURDER by Robert Leslie Bellem, © 1949 by Robert Leslie Bellem. First appeared in *Thrilling Detective Magazine*.

FOREVER AFTER by Jim Thompson, © 1960 by Jim Thompson. First appeared in *Shock*. Reproduced by permission of Vanessa Holt Ltd.

THE BLOODY TIDE by Day Keene, © 1950 by Day Keene. First appeared in *Black Mask Magazine*. Reproduced by permission of Al James on behalf of the Estate of Day Keene.

DEATH COMES GIFT-WRAPPED by William P. McGivern, © 1950 by William P. McGivern. First appeared in *Black Mask Magazine*. Reproduced by permission of Maureen Daly McGivern on behalf of the Estate of William P. McGivern.

THE GIRL BEHIND THE HEDGE by Mickey Spillane, © 1954 by Mickey Spillane. First appeared in *Manhunt*. Reproduced by permission of the author.

ENTER SCARFACE by Armitage Trail, © 1930 by Armitage Trail. First appeared in *Scarface*.

A CANDLE FOR THE BAG LADY by Lawrence Block, © 1968 by Lawrence Block. First appeared in *Alfred Hitchcock's Mystery Magazine*. Reproduced by permission of the author.

BLACK PUDDING by David Goodis, © 1954 by David Goodis. First appeared in *Manhunt*. Reproduced by permission of A. M. Heath & Co. Ltd.

A MATTER OF PRINCIPAL by Max Allan Collins, © 1989 by Max Allan Collins. First appeared in *Stalkers*. Reproduced by permission of the author.

CITIZEN'S ARREST by Charles Willeford, © 1966 by Charles Willeford. First appeared in *Alfred Hitchcock's Mystery Magazine*. Reproduced by permission of Abner Stein.

SLEEPING DOG by Ross Macdonald, © 1965 by Ross Macdonald. First appeared in *Argosy*. Reproduced by permission of David Higham Associates.

THE WENCH IS DEAD by Fredric Brown, © 1953 by Fredric Brown. First appeared in *Manhunt*. Reproduced by permission of A. M. Heath & Co. Ltd.

SO DARK FOR APRIL by Howard Browne, © 1953 by Howard Browne. First appeared in *Manhunt*. Reproduced by permission of the author.

WE ARE ALL DEAD by Bruno Fischer, © 1955 by Bruno Fischer. First appeared in *Manhunt*. Reproduced by permission of Ruth Fischer on behalf of the Estate of Bruno Fischer.

DEATH IS A VAMPIRE by Robert Bloch, © 1944 by Robert Bloch. First appeared in *Thrilling Mystery Magazine*. Reproduced by permission of A. M. Heath & Co. Ltd.

DIVIDE AND CONQUER by Jack Ritchie, © 1957 by Jack Ritchie. First appeared in *Manhunt*. Reproduced by permission of the Larry Sternig & Jack Byrne Literary Agency.

A REAL NICE GUY by William F. Nolan, © 1980 by William F. Nolan. First appeared in *Mike Shayne Mystery Magazine*. Reproduced by permission of the author.

STACKED DECK by Bill Pronzini, © 1987 by Bill Pronzini. First appeared in *New Black Mask Magazine*. Reproduced by permission of the author.

SO YOUNG, SO FAIR, SO DEAD by John Lutz, © 1973 by John Lutz. First appeared in *Mike Shayne Mystery Magazine*. Reproduced by permission of the author.

EFFECTIVE MEDICINE by B. Traven, © 1954 by B. Traven. First appeared in *Manhunt*. Reproduced by permission of A. M. Heath & Co. Ltd.

KILLING BERNSTEIN by Harlan Ellison, © 1976 by Harlan Ellison. First appeared in 1976 in *Mystery*. Reprinted with permission of, and by arrangement with, the Author and the Author's agent, Richard Curtis Associates, Inc., New York, USA. All rights reserved.

THE SECOND COMING by Joe Gores, © 1966 by Joe Gores. First appeared in *Adam's Best Fiction*. Reproduced by permission of the author.

HIBISCUS AND HOMICIDE by William Campbell Gault, © 1948 by William Campbell Gault. First appeared in *Thrilling Detective Magazine*. Reproduced by permission of the author.

HELL ON WHEELS by Thomas S. Roche, © 1996 by Thomas S. Roche. Reproduced by permission of the author.

ORDO by Donald E. Westlake, © 1977 by Donald E. Westlake. First appeared in *Enough*. Reproduced by permission of James Hale Literary Agency.

All efforts have been made to contact the respective copyright holders. In some cases, it has not proven possible to ascertain the whereabouts of authors, agents or estates. They are welcome to write to us c/o the book's publishers.

I owe a particular vote of thanks to various authors and editors who provided invaluable assistance in tracing copyright holders and living relatives and recommended particular stories. A bow of the fedora, then, to Max Allan Collins, Ed Gorman, Martin H. Greenberg, Gary Lovisi, William F. Nolan and Bill Pronzini.

INTRODUCTION

Maxim Jakubowski

THERE IS NO such thing as pulp fiction.

Sweeping assertion, hey?

And, I suppose, a perfect touch of controversy to open a volume which I hope you will find full of surprise, action, shocks galore, sound and fury, pages bursting with all the exhilarating speed and bumps of a rollercoaster ride.

Which is what all the best storytelling provides.

So long live pulp fiction!

First, let's bury the myth that pulp fiction is a lower form of art, the reverse side of literature as we know it. Until pyrotechnic film director Quentin Tarantino spectacularly hijacked the expression, most ignorant observers and accredited denizens of the literary establishment relegated pulp writing to a dubious cupboard where we parked the guilty pleasures we were too ashamed to display in public. Pulp was equated with rubbish. Crap of the basest nature. How arrogant of them to dismiss thus what, for many, was a perfect form of entertainment!

What we have come to call, to know as pulp writing came about from the magazines where much of its early gems first appeared: the colorful publications, so often afflicted with endearing but terrible names, which cheapskate publishers insisted on printing on the cheapest available form of paper, pulp paper; sadly this is another reason for the aura that now surrounds them as so few have survived the onslaught of time and decay, and the rare remaining examples have become increasingly collectable, albeit all too often in crumbling form on the shelves.

Many of the names have gone down in legend: *Black Mask, Amazing, Astounding, Spicy Stories, Ace-High, Detective Magazine, Dare-Devil Aces,*

Thrills of the Jungle, *High Seas Adventures*, *Fighting Aces*, *Secret Service Operator #5*, etc ... to the nth degree. There were literally hundreds of such often live-by-night magazines with wildly exotic and frequently misleading names from their initial appearance at the beginning of the 1920s in America. And I would not pretend that everything they published was made of gold. Far from it. We are talking commercial fiction, mostly catering to the lowest common denominator. But then do our modern paperbacks have loftier ambitions and a superior hit-rate, quality-wise?

But what makes them stand out is the fact that the pulps had one golden rule which unsung editors insisted upon and good and bad writers alike religiously followed: adherence to the art of storytelling. Every story in the pulps had a beginning and an end, sharply-etched economical characterization, action, emotions, plenty going on. The mission was to keep the reader hooked, to transport him into a more interesting world of fantasy and make-believe, spiriting him away from the drab horizons of everyday life (remember, there was no television in those very early days, or CDs or other modern leisure addictions).

This compact with the consumer might appear self-evident, and was indeed very much a continuation of the Victorian penny dreadfuls and novels written by instalments in newspapers and magazines by the likes of Conan Doyle, Charles Dickens and so many other overlooked pioneer scribes just a few decades earlier, but it is a tradition that has sadly since been lost to the trappings of Literature with a capital L and pretension. We now have partly forgotten the pleasures of old-time radio but at least the pulp magazines have left us with millions of words of splendid, lurid, cheap and exciting writing. And not only does this inheritance still afford much pleasure but it can also be said to have influenced many commercial writers practising their art long after the literal disappearance of the pulp magazines due to wartime paper shortages. The spirit of pulp continued unabated after the war and ended in the pages of the paperback books that took over the literacy baton in England and America. The 1950s was in fact a further golden age for pulp writing, with the exploding paperback market opening opportunities by the dozen as imprints mushroomed and thrived, providing fertile ground for the remaining pulp survivors and newer generations of popular writers, many of whom, particularly in the fields of mystery and science fiction writing, would go on to better things and, eventually, to the respectability of the hardcover book. Many of these authors were also busy contributing to the renaissance of popular genre magazines now in digest format, with tales that often echoed or prefigured their novels, and are represented in this selection.

This anthology restricts itself to crime and mystery stories in the pulp tradition. Strictly speaking, of course, the pulp magazines ventured further afield, encompassing science fiction, fantasy, horror, spy tales, aviation yarns, spicy stories (that would not make even a maiden blush today), jungle capers, westerns and a pleasing variety of super heroes like The Shadow, Doc Savage, the Spider and other masked and unmasked crusaders. But tales of noir streets, gorgeous molls and shady villains fighting ambiguous sleuths and dubious heroes are the archetypes that represent pulp writing at its best.

There are very few popular fiction magazines left alive today and those there are tend to prefer a more refined type of tale, but still pulp fiction survives in the writings of many authors. Because pulp fiction is a state of mind, a mission to entertain, and literature would be so much poorer without it, its zest, its speed and rhythm, its unashamed verve and straightforward approach to storytelling.

However long the present anthology might be, I regret it couldn't be ten times longer. The pulp magazines and writers and their successors are still unknown territory and the brave researcher with time on his hands could, I am confident, mine so much more from these yellowing pages and honour even more forgotten writers and give them their five minutes in the sun. As it is there are so many writers it wasn't possible to include here, for reasons of space or availability of rights. In no particular order: Ed McBain (as Evan Hunter and Richard Marsten), Raymond Chandler, Cornell Woolrich, Andrew Vachss, Loren D. Estleman, Carroll John Daly, Brett Halliday, Raoul Whitfield, Mark Timlin, Richard Prather, Leigh Brackett, Erle Stanley Gardner (pre Perry Mason), James Ellroy, Clark Howard, Max Brand. In addition, rising paper costs prevented me from making this volume even heavier, as I had to withdraw material by Ed Gorman, James Reasoner, Ed Lacy, Frank Gruber, Loren D. Estleman, Derek Raymond, Robert Edmond Alter, Frederick C. Davis, Jonathan Craig and Roger Torrey – so look out for these names elsewhere. They are certainly worth a detour. But the list could be endless. Check them all out. Thrills absolutely guaranteed.

The stories selected span seven decades of popular writing, from the now-forgotten pseudonymous Armitage Trail whose *Scarface* (the opening chapter of which is excerpted here) inspired the early days of film noir and an initial appearance from Dashiell Hammett's Sam Spade to current masters like Donald E. Westlake, Lawrence Block and brand newcomers like Thomas S. Roche. In between you will find the great names of yesteryear and familiar bylines from the paperback world. Enjoy the forbidden thrills. And when you have turned over the final page, I just know you will repeat after me: pulp fiction will never die.

THE MAMMOTH BOOK OF PULP FICTION

TOO MANY HAVE LIVED

Dashiell Hammett

THE MAN'S TIE was as orange as a sunset. He was a large man, tall and meaty, without softness. The dark hair parted in the middle, flattened to his scalp, his firm, full cheeks, the clothes that fit him with noticeable snugness, even the small, pink ears flat against the sides of his head – each of these seemed but a differently colored part of one same, smooth surface. His age could have been thirty-five or forty-five.

He sat beside Samuel Spade's desk, leaning forward a little over his Malacca stick, and said, "No. I want you to find out what happened to him. I hope you never find him." His protuberant green eyes stared solemnly at Spade.

Spade rocked back in his chair. His face – given a not unpleasantly satanic cast by the v's of his bony chin, mouth, nostrils, and thickish brows – was as politely interested as his voice. "Why?"

The green-eyed man spoke quietly, with assurance: "I can talk to you, Spade. You've the sort of reputation I want in a private detective. That's why I'm here."

Spade's nod committed him to nothing.

The green-eyed man said, "And any fair price is all right with me."

Spade nodded as before. "And with me," he said, "but I've got to know what you want to buy. You want to find out what's happened to this – uh – Eli Haven, but you don't care what it is?"

The green-eyed man lowered his voice, but there was no other change in his mien: "In a way I do. For instance, if you found him and fixed it so he stayed away for good, it might be worth more money to me."

"You mean even if he didn't want to stay away?"

The green-eyed man said, "Especially."

Spade smiled and shook his head. "Probably not enough more money

– the way you mean it." He took his long, thick-fingered hands from the arms of his chair and turned their palms up. "Well, what's it all about, Colyer?"

Colyer's face reddened a little, but his eyes maintained their unblinking cold stare. "This man's got a wife. I like her. They had a row last week and he blew. If I can convince her he's gone for good, there's a chance she'll divorce him."

"I'd want to talk to her," Spade said. "Who is this Eli Haven? What does he do?"

"He's a bad egg. He doesn't do anything. Writes poetry or something."

"What can you tell me about him that'll help?"

"Nothing Julia, his wife, can't tell you. You're going to talk to her." Colyer stood up. "I've got connections. Maybe I can get something for you through them later . . ."

A small-boned woman of twenty-five or -six opened the apartment door. Her powder-blue dress was trimmed with silver buttons. She was full-bosomed but slim, with straight shoulders and narrow hips, and she carried herself with a pride that would have been cockiness in one less graceful.

Spade said, "Mrs Haven?"

She hesitated before saying "Yes."

"Gene Colyer sent me to see you. My name's Spade. I'm a private detective. He wants me to find your husband."

"And have you found him?"

"I told him I'd have to talk to you first."

Her smile went away. She studied his face gravely, feature by feature, then she said, "Certainly," and stepped back, drawing the door back with her.

When they were seated in facing chairs in a cheaply furnished room overlooking a playground where children were noisy, she asked, "Did Gene tell you why he wanted Eli found?"

"He said if you knew he was gone for good maybe you'd listen to reason."

She said nothing.

"Has he ever gone off like this before?"

"Often."

"What's he like?"

"He's a swell man," she said dispassionately, "when he's sober; and when he's drinking he's all right except with women and money."

"That leaves him a lot of room to be all right in. What does he do for a living?"

"He's a poet," she replied, "but nobody makes a living at that."

"Well?"

"Oh, he pops in with a little money now and then. Poker, races, he says. I don't know."

"How long've you been married?"

"Four years, almost" – she smiled mockingly.

"San Francisco all the time?"

"No, we lived in Seattle the first year and then came here."

"He from Seattle?"

She shook her head. "Some place in Delaware."

"What place?"

"I don't know."

Spade drew his thickish brows together a little. "Where are you from?"

She said sweetly, "You're not hunting for me."

"You act like it," he grumbled. "Well, who are his friends?"

"Don't ask me!"

He made an impatient grimace. "You know some of them," he insisted.

"Sure. There's a fellow named Minera and a Louis James and somebody he calls Conny."

"Who are they?"

"Men," she replied blandly. "I don't know anything about them. They phone or drop by to pick him up, or I see him around town with them. That's all I know."

"What do they do for a living? They can't all write poetry."

She laughed. "They could try. One of them, Louis James, is a – a member of Gene's staff, I think. I honestly don't know any more about them than I've told you."

"Think they'd know where your husband is?"

She shrugged. "They're kidding me if they do. They still call up once in a while to see if he's turned up."

"And these women you mentioned?"

"They're not people I know."

Spade scowled thoughtfully at the floor, asked, "What'd he do before he started not making a living writing poetry?"

"Anything – sold vacuum cleaners, hoboed, went to sea, dealt blackjack, railroaded, canning houses, lumber camps, carnivals, worked on a news-paper – anything."

"Have any money when he left?"

"Three dollars he borrowed from me."

"What'd he say?"

She laughed. "Said if I used whatever influence I had with God while he was gone he'd be back at dinnertime with a surprise for me."

Spade raised his eyebrows. "You were on good terms?"

"Oh, yes. Our last fight had been patched up a couple of days before."

"When did he leave?"

"Thursday afternoon; three o'clock, I guess."

"Got any photographs of him?"

"Yes." She went to a table by one of the windows, pulled a drawer out, and turned towards Spade again with a photograph in her hand.

Spade looked at the picture of a thin face with deep-set eyes, a sensual mouth, and a heavily lined forehead topped by a disorderly mop of coarse blond hair.

He put Haven's photograph in his pocket and picked up his hat. He turned towards the door, halted. "What kind of poet is he? Pretty good?"

She shrugged. "That depends on who you ask."

"Any of it around here?"

"No." She smiled. "Think he's hiding between pages?"

"You never can tell what'll lead to what. I'll be back some time. Think things over and see if you can't find some way of loosening up a little more. 'By."

He walked down Post Street to Mulford's book store and asked for a volume of Haven's poetry.

"I'm sorry," the girl said. "I sold my last copy last week" – she smiled – "to Mr Haven himself. I can order it for you."

"You know him?"

"Only through selling his books."

Spade pursed his lips, asked, "What day was it?" He gave her one of his business cards. "Please. It's important."

She went to a desk, turned the pages of a red-bound sales-book, and came back to him with the book open in her hand. "It was last Wednesday," she said, "and we delivered it to a Mr Roger Ferris, 1981 Pacific Avenue."

"Thanks a lot," he said.

Outside, he hailed a taxicab and gave the driver Mr Roger Ferris's address . . .

The Pacific Avenue house was a four-story, graystone one set behind a narrow strip of lawn. The room into which a plump-faced maid ushered Spade was large and high-ceiled.

Spade sat down, but when the maid had gone away he rose and began to walk around the room. He halted at a table where there were three books. One of them had a salmon-colored jacket on which was printed in red an outline drawing of a bolt of lightning striking the ground between a man and a woman, and in black the words *Colored Light, by Eli Haven.*

Spade picked up the book and went back to his chair.

There was an inscription on the flyleaf – heavy, irregular characters written with blue ink:

> *To good old Buck, who knew his colored lights,*
> *in memory of them there days.*
>
> > *Eli*

Spade turned pages at random and idly read a verse:

STATEMENT
Too many have lived
As we live
For our lives to be
Proof of our living.
Too many have died
As we die
For their deaths to be
Proof of our dying.

He looked up from the book as a man in dinner clothes came into the room. He was not a tall man, but his erectness made him seem tall even when Spade's six feet and a fraction of an inch were standing before him. He had bright blue eyes undimmed by his fifty-some years, a sunburned face in which no muscle sagged, a smooth, broad forehead, and thick, short, nearly white hair. There was dignity in his countenance, and amiability.

He nodded at the book Spade still held. "How do you like it?"

Spade grinned, said, "I guess I'm just a mug," and put the book down. "That's what I came to see you about, though, Mr Ferris. You know Haven?"

"Yes, certainly. Sit down, Mr Spade." He sat in a chair not far from Spade's. "I knew him as a kid. He's not in trouble, is he?"

Spade said, "I don't know. I'm trying to find him."

Ferris spoke hesitantly: "Can I ask why?"

"You know Gene Colyer?"

"Yes." Ferris hesitated again, then said, "This is in confidence. I've a chain of picture houses through northern California, you know, and a couple of years ago when I had some labor trouble I was told that Colyer was the man to get in touch with to have it straightened out. That's how I happened to meet him."

"Yes," Spade said dryly. "A lot of people happen to meet Gene that way."

"But what's he got to do with Eli?"

"Wants him found. How long since you've seen him?"

"Last Thursday he was here."

"What time did he leave?"

"Midnight – a little after. He came over in the afternoon around half past three. We hadn't seen each other for years. I persuaded him to stay for dinner – he looked pretty seedy – and lent him some money."

"How much?"

"A hundred and fifty – all I had in the house."

"Say where he was going when he left?"

Ferris shook his head. "He said he'd phone me the next day."

"Did he phone you the next day?"

"No."

"And you've known him all his life?"

"Not exactly, but he worked for me fifteen or sixteen years ago when I had a carnival company – Great Eastern and Western Combined Shows – with a partner for a while and then by myself, and I always liked the kid."

"How long before Thursday since you'd seen him?"

"Lord knows," Ferris replied. "I'd lost track of him for years. Then, Wednesday, out of a clear sky, that book came, with no address or anything, just that stuff written in the front, and the next morning he called me up. I was tickled to death to know he was still alive and doing something with himself. So he came over that afternoon and we put in about nine hours straight talking about old times."

"Tell you much about what he'd been doing since then?"

"Just that he'd been knocking around, doing one thing and another, taking the breaks as they came. He didn't complain much; I had to make him take the hundred and fifty."

Spade stood up. "Thanks ever so much, Mr Ferris. I – "

Ferris interrupted him: "Not at all, and if there's anything I can do, call on me."

Spade looked at his watch. "Can I phone my office to see if anything's turned up?"

"Certainly; there's a phone in the next room, to the right."

Spade said "Thanks" and went out. When he returned he was rolling a cigarette. His face was wooden.

"Any news?" Ferris asked.

"Yes. Colyer's called the job off. He says Haven's body's been found in some bushes on the other side of San Jose, with three bullets in it." He smiled, adding mildly, "He *told* me he might be able to find out something through his connections . . ."

Morning sunshine, coming through the curtains that screened Spade's office windows, put two fat, yellow rectangles on the floor and gave everything in the room a yellow tint.

He sat at his desk, staring meditatively at a newspaper. He did not look up when Effie Perine came in from the outer office.

She said, "Mrs Haven is here."

He raised his head then and said, "That's better. Push her in."

Mrs Haven came in quickly. Her face was white and she was shivering in spite of her fur coat and the warmth of the day. She came straight to Spade and asked, "Did Gene kill him?"

Spade said, "I don't know."

"I've got to know," she cried.

Spade took her hands. "Here, sit down." He led her to a chair. He asked, "Colyer tell you he'd called the job off?"

She stared at him in amazement. "He what?"

"He left word here last night that your husband had been found and he wouldn't need me any more."

She hung her head and her words were barely audible. "Then he did."

Spade shrugged. "Maybe only an innocent man could've afforded to call it off then, or maybe he was guilty, but had brains enough and nerve enough to – "

She was not listening to him. She was leaning towards him, speaking earnestly: "But, Mr Spade, you're not going to drop it like that? You're not going to let him stop you?"

While she was speaking his telephone bell rang. He said, "Excuse me," and picked up the receiver. "Yes? . . . Uh-huh . . . So?" He pursed his lips. "I'll let you know." He pushed the telephone aside slowly and faced Mrs Haven again. "Colyer's outside."

"Does he know I'm here?" she asked quickly.

"Couldn't say." He stood up, pretending he was not watching her closely. "Do you care?"

She pinched her lower lip between her teeth, said "No" hesitantly.

"Fine. I'll have him in."

She raised a hand as if in protest, then let it drop, and her white face was composed. "Whatever you want," she said.

Spade opened the door, said, "Hello, Colyer. Come on in. We were just talking about you."

Colyer nodded and came into the office holding his stick in one hand, his hat in the other. "How are you this morning, Julia? You ought to've phoned me. I'd've driven you back to town."

"I – I didn't know what I was doing."

Colyer looked at her for a moment longer, then shifted the focus of his expressionless green eyes to Spade's face. "Well, have you been able to convince her I didn't do it?"

"We hadn't got around to that," Spade said. "I was just trying to find out how much reason there was for suspecting you. Sit down."

Colyer sat down somewhat carefully, asked, "And?"

"And then you arrived."

Colyer nodded gravely. "All right, Spade," he said; "you're hired again to prove to Mrs Haven that I didn't have anything to do with it."

"Gene!" she exclaimed in a choked voice and held her hands out toward him appealingly. "I don't think you did – I don't want to think you did – but I'm so afraid." She put her hands to her face and began to cry.

Colyer went over to the woman. "Take it easy," he said. "We'll kick it out together."

Spade went into the outer office, shutting the door behind him.

Effie Perine stopped typing a letter.

He grinned at her, said, "Somebody ought to write a book about people sometime – they're peculiar," and went over to the water bottle. "You've got Wally Kellogg's number. Call him up and ask him where I can find Tom Minera."

He returned to the inner office.

Mrs Haven had stopped crying. She said, "I'm sorry."

Spade said, "It's all right." He looked sidewise at Colyer. "I still got my job?"

"Yes." Colyer cleared his throat. "But if there's nothing special right now, I'd better take Mrs Haven home."

"OK, but there's one thing: According to the *Chronicle*, you identified him. How come you were down there?"

"I went down when I heard they'd found a body," Colyer replied deliberately. "I told you I had connections. I heard about the body through them."

Spade said, "All right; be seeing you," and opened the door for them.

When the corridor door closed behind them, Effie Perine said, "Minera's at the Buxton on Army Street."

Spade said, "Thanks." He went into the inner office to get his hat. On his way out he said, "If I'm not back in a couple of months tell them to look for my body there . . ."

Spade walked down a shabby corridor to a battered green door marked "411." The murmur of voices came through the door, but no words could be distinguished. He stopped listening and knocked.

An obviously disguised male voice asked, "What is it?"

"I want to see Tom. This is Sam Spade."

A pause, then: "Tom ain't here."

Spade put a hand on the knob and shook the frail door. "Come on, open up," he growled.

Presently the door was opened by a thin, dark man of twenty-five or -six who tried to make his beady dark eyes guileless while saying, "I didn't think it was your voice at first." The slackness of his mouth made his chin seem even smaller than it was. His green-striped shirt, open at the neck, was not clean. His gray pants were carefully pressed.

"You've got to be careful these days," Spade said solemnly, and went through the doorway into a room where two men were trying to seem uninterested in his arrival.

One of them leaned against the window sill filing his fingernails. The other was tilted back in a chair with his feet on the edge of a table and a newspaper spread between his hands. They glanced at Spade in unison and went on with their occupations.

Spade said cheerfully, "Always glad to meet any friends of Tom Minera's."

Minera finished shutting the door and said awkwardly, "Uh – yes – Mr Spade, meet Mr Conrad and Mr James."

Conrad, the man at the window, made a vaguely polite gesture with the nail file in his hand. He was a few years older than Minera, of average height, sturdily built, with a thick-featured, dull-eyed face.

James lowered his paper for an instant to look coolly, appraisingly at Spade and say, "How'r'ye, brother?" Then he returned to his reading. He was as sturdily built as Conrad, but taller, and his face had a shrewdness the other's lacked.

"Ah," Spade said, "and friends of the late Eli Haven."

The man at the window jabbed a finger with his nail file, and cursed it bitterly. Minera moistened his lips, and then spoke rapidly, with a whining note in his voice: "But on the level, Spade, we hadn't none of us seen him for a week."

Spade seemed mildly amused by the dark man's manner.

"What do you think he was killed for?"

"All I know is what the paper says: His pockets was all turned inside out and there wasn't as much as a match on him." He drew down the ends of his mouth. "But far as I know he didn't have no dough. He didn't have none Tuesday night."

Spade, speaking softly, said, "I hear he got some Thursday night."

Minera, behind Spade, caught his breath audibly.

James said, "I guess you ought to know. I don't."

"He ever work with you boys?"

James slowly put aside his newspaper and took his feet off the table. His interest in Spade's question seemed great enough, but almost impersonal. "Now what do you mean by that?"

Spade pretended surprise. "But you boys must work at something?"

Minera came around to Spade's side. "Aw, listen, Spade," he said. "This guy Haven was just a guy we knew. We didn't have nothing to do with rubbing him out; we don't know nothing about it. You know we – "

Three deliberate knocks sounded at the door.

Minera and Conrad looked at James, who nodded, but by then Spade, moving swiftly, had reached the door and was opening it.

Roger Ferris was there.

Spade blinked at Ferris, Ferris at Spade. Then Ferris put out his hand and said, "I *am* glad to see you."

"Come on in," Spade said.

"Look at this, Mr Spade." Ferris's hand trembled as he took a slightly soiled envelope from his pocket.

Ferris's name and address were typewritten on the envelope. There was no postage stamp on it. Spade took out the enclosure, a narrow slip of cheap white paper, and unfolded it. On it was typewritten:

You had better come to Room No 411 Buxton Hotel on Army St at 5 p.m. this afternoon on account of Thursday night.

There was no signature.

Spade said, "It's a long time before five o'clock."

"It is," Ferris agreed with emphasis. "I came as soon as I got that. It was Thursday night Eli was at my house."

Minera was jostling Spade, asking, "What is all this?"

Spade held the note up for the dark man to read. He read it and yelled, "Honest, Spade, I don't know nothing about that letter."

"Does anybody?" Spade asked.

Conrad said "No" hastily.

James said, "What letter?"

Spade looked dreamily at Ferris for a moment, then said, as if speaking to himself, "Of course, Haven was trying to shake you down."

Ferris's face reddened. "What?"

"Shake-down," Spade repeated patiently; "money, blackmail."

"Look here, Spade," Ferris said earnestly; "you don't really believe what you said? What would he have to blackmail me on?"

"'To good old Buck'" – Spade quoted the dead poet's inscription – "'who knew his colored lights, in memory of them there days.'" He looked somberly at Ferris from beneath slightly raised brows. "What colored lights? What's the circus and carnival slang term for kicking a guy off a train while it's going? Red-lighting. Sure, that's it – red lights. Who'd you red-light, Ferris, that Haven knew about?"

Minera went over to a chair, sat down, put his elbows on his knees, his head between his hands, and stared blankly at the floor. Conrad was breathing as if he had been running.

Spade addressed Ferris: "Well?"

Ferris wiped his face with a handkerchief, put the handkerchief in his pocket, and said simply, "It was a shake-down."

"And you killed him."

Ferris's blue eyes, looking into Spade's yellow-gray ones, were clear and steady, as was his voice. "I did not," he said. "I swear I did not. Let me tell you what happened. He sent me the book, as I told you, and I knew right away what that joke he wrote in the front meant. So the next day, when he phoned me and said he was coming over to talk over old times and to try to borrow some money for old times' sake, I knew what he meant again, and I went down to the bank and drew out ten thousand dollars. You can check that up. It's the Seamen's National."

"I will," Spade said.

"As it turned out, I didn't need that much. He wasn't very big-time, and I talked him into taking five thousand. I put the other five back in the bank next day. You can check that up."

"I will," Spade said.

"I told him I wasn't going to stand for any more taps, this five thousand was the first and last. I made him sign a paper saying he'd helped in the

– in what I'd done – and he signed it. He left sometime around midnight, and that's the last I ever saw of him."

Spade tapped the envelope Ferris had given him. "And how about this note?"

"A messenger boy brought it at noon, and I came right over. Eli had assured me he hadn't said anything to anybody, but I didn't know. I had to face it, whatever it was."

Spade turned to the others, his face wooden. "Well?"

Minera and Conrad looked at James, who made an impatient grimace and said, "Oh, sure, we sent him the letter. Why not? We was friends of Eli's, and we hadn't been able to find him since he went to put the squeeze to this baby, and then he turns up dead, so we kind of like to have the gent come over and explain things."

"You knew about the squeeze?"

"Sure. We was all together when he got the idea."

"How'd he happen to get the idea?" Spade asked.

James spread the fingers of his left hand. "We'd been drinking and talking – you know the way a bunch of guys will, about all they'd seen and done – and he told a yarn about once seeing a guy boot another off a train into a cañon, and he happens to mention the name of the guy that done the booting – Buck Ferris. And somebody says, 'What's this Ferris look like?' Eli tells him what he looked like then, saying he ain't seen him for fifteen years; and whoever it is whistles and says, 'I bet that's the Ferris that owns about half the movie joints in the state. I bet you he'd give something to keep that back trail covered!'

"Well, the idea kind of hit Eli. You could see that. He thought a little while and then he got cagey. He asked what this movie Ferris's first name is, and when the other guy tells him, 'Roger,' he makes out he's disappointed and says, 'No, it ain't him. His first name was Martin.' We all give him the ha-ha and he finally admits he's thinking of seeing the gent, and when he called me up Thursday around noon and says he's throwing a party at Pogey Hecker's that night, it ain't no trouble to figure out what's what."

"What was the name of the gentleman who was red-lighted?"

"He wouldn't say. He shut up tight. You couldn't blame him."

"Uh-huh," Spade agreed.

"Then nothing. He never showed up at Pogey's. We tried to get him on the phone around two o'clock in the morning, but his wife said he hadn't been home, so we stuck around till four or five and then decided he had given us a run-around, and made Pogey charge the bill to him, and beat it. I ain't seen him since – dead or alive."

Spade said mildly, "Maybe. Sure you didn't find Eli later that morning, take him riding, swap him bullets for Ferris's five thou, dump him in the – ?"

A sharp double knock sounded on the door.

Spade's face brightened. He went to the door and opened it.

A young man came in. He was very dapper, and very well proportioned. He wore a light topcoat and his hands were in its pockets. Just inside the door he stepped to the right, and stood with his back to the wall. By that time another young man was coming in. He stepped to the left. Though they did not actually look alike, their common dapperness, the similar trimness of their bodies, and their almost identical positions – backs to wall, hands in pockets, cold, bright eyes studying the occupants of the room – gave them, for an instant, the appearance of twins.

Then Gene Colyer came in. He nodded at Spade, but paid no attention to the others in the room, though James said, "Hello, Gene."

"Anything new?" Colyer asked Spade.

Spade nodded. "It seems this gentleman" – he jerked a thumb at Ferris – "was – "

"Any place we can talk?"

"There's a kitchen back here."

Colyer snapped a "Smear anybody that pops" over his shoulder at the two dapper young men and followed Spade into the kitchen. He sat on the one kitchen chair and stared with unblinking green eyes at Spade while Spade told him what he had learned.

When the private detective had finished, the green-eyed man asked, "Well, what do you make of it?"

Spade looked thoughtfully at the other. "You've picked up something. I'd like to know what it is."

Colyer said, "They found the gun in a stream a quarter of a mile from where they found him. It's James's – got the mark on it where it was shot out of his hand once in Vallejo."

"That's nice," Spade said.

"Listen. A kid named Thurber says James comes to him last Wednesday and gets him to tail Haven. Thurber picks him up Thursday afternoon, puts him in at Ferris's, and phones James. James tells him to take a plant on the place and let him know where Haven goes when he leaves, but some nervous woman in the neighborhood puts in a rumble about the kid hanging around, and the cops chase him along about ten o'clock."

Spade pursed his lips and stared thoughtfully at the ceiling.

Colyer's eyes were expressionless, but sweat made his round face shiny, and his voice was hoarse. "Spade," he said, "I'm going to turn him in."

Spade switched his gaze from the ceiling to the protuberant green eyes.

"I've never turned in one of my people before," Colyer said, "but this one goes. Julia's *got* to believe I hadn't anything to do with it if it's one of my people and I turn him in, hasn't she?"

Spade nodded slowly. "I think so."

Colyer suddenly averted his eyes and cleared his throat. When he spoke again it was curtly: "Well, he goes."

Minera, James, and Conrad were seated when Spade and Colyer came out of the kitchen. Ferris was walking the floor. The two dapper young men had not moved.

Colyer went over to James. "Where's your gun, Louis?" he asked.

James moved his right hand a few inches towards his left breast, stopped it, and said, "Oh, I didn't bring it."

With his gloved hand – open – Colyer struck James on the side of the face, knocking him out of his chair.

James straightened up, mumbling, "I didn't mean nothing." He put a hand to the side of his face. "I know I oughtn't've done it, Chief, but when he called up and said he didn't like to go up against Ferris without something and didn't have any of his own, I said, 'All right,' and sent it over to him."

Colyer said, "And you sent Thurber over to him, too."

"We were just kind of interested in seeing if he did go through with it," James mumbled.

"And you couldn't've gone there yourself, or sent somebody else?"

"After Thurber had stirred up the whole neighborhood?"

Colyer turned to Spade. "Want us to help you take them in, or want to call the wagon?"

"We'll do it regular," Spade said, and went to the wall telephone. When he turned away from it his face was wooden, his eyes dreamy. He made a cigarette, lit it, and said to Colyer, "I'm silly enough to think your Louis has got a lot of right answers in that story of his."

James took his hand down from his bruised cheek and stared at Spade with astonished eyes.

Colyer growled, "What's the matter with you?"

"Nothing," Spade said softly, "except I think you're a little too anxious to slam it on him." He blew smoke out. "Why, for instance, should he drop his gun there when it had marks on it that people knew?"

Colyer said, "You think he's got brains."

"If these boys killed him, knew he was dead, why do they wait till the body's found and things are stirred up before they go after Ferris again? What'd they turn his pockets inside out for if they hijacked him? That's a lot of trouble and only done by folks that kill for some other reason and want to make it look like robbery." He shook his head. "You're too anxious to slam it on them. Why should they – ?"

"That's not the point right now," Colyer said. "The point is, why do you keep saying I'm too anxious to slam it on him?"

Spade shrugged. "Maybe to clear yourself with Julia as soon as possible and as clear as possible, maybe even to clear yourself with the police, and then you've got clients."

Colyer said, "What?"

Spade made a careless gesture with his cigarette. "Ferris," he said blandly. "He killed him, of course."

Colyer's eyelids quivered, though he did not actually blink.

Spade said, "First, he's the last person we know of who saw Eli alive, and that's always a good bet. Second, he's the only person I talked to before Eli's body turned up who cared whether I thought they were holding out on me or not. The rest of you just thought I was hunting for a guy who'd gone away. He knew I was hunting for a man he'd killed, so he had to put himself in the clear. He was even afraid to throw that book away, because it had been sent up by the book store and could be traced, and there might be clerks who'd seen the inscription. Third, he was the only one who thought Eli was just a sweet, clean, lovable boy – for the same reasons. Fourth, that story about a blackmailer showing up at three o'clock in the afternoon, making an easy touch for five grand, and then sticking around till midnight is just silly, no matter how good the booze was. Fifth, the story about the paper Eli signed is still worse, though a forged one could be fixed up easy enough. Sixth, he's got the best reason of anybody we know for wanting Eli dead."

Colyer nodded slowly. "Still – "

"Still nothing," Spade said. "Maybe he did the ten-thousand-out-five-thousand-back trick with his bank, but that was easy. Then he got this feeble-minded blackmailer in his house, stalled him along until the servants had gone to bed, took the borrowed gun away from him, shoved him downstairs into his car, took him for a ride – maybe took him already dead, maybe shot him down there by the bushes – frisked him clean to make identification harder and to make it look like robbery, tossed the gun in the water, and came home – "

He broke off to listen to the sound of a siren in the street. He looked then, for the first time since he had begun to talk, at Ferris.

Ferris's face was ghastly white, but he held his eyes steady.

Spade said, "I've got a hunch, Ferris, that we're going to find out about that red-lighting job, too. You told me you had your carnival company with a partner for a while when Eli was working for you, and then by yourself. We oughtn't to have a lot of trouble finding out about your partner – whether he disappeared, or died a natural death, or is still alive."

Ferris had lost some of his erectness. He wet his lips and said, "I want to see my lawyer. I don't want to talk till I've seen my lawyer."

Spade said, "It's all right with me. You're up against it, but I don't like blackmailers myself. I think Eli wrote a good epitaph for them in that book back there – 'Too many have lived.'"

FLIGHT TO NOWHERE

Charles Williams

1

IT WAS INCREDIBLE. There were no signs of violence or even sickness aboard the ship, and the Gulf itself had been calm for weeks. Her sails were set and drawing gently in the faint airs of sunset, her tiller lashed, and she was gliding along on a southeasterly course which would have taken her into the Yucatan Channel. Her dinghy was still there, atop the cabin, and everything was shipshape and in order except that there was not a soul on board.

She was well provisioned, and she had water. The two bunks were made and the cabin swept. Dungarees and foul weather gear hung about the bulkheads, and in one of the bunks was the halter of a woman's two-piece bathing suit. And, subtly underlying the bilge and salt-water smells, there still clung to the deserted cabin just the faintest suspicion of perfume. It would have gone unnoticed except that it was so completely out of place.

The table was not laid, but there were two mugs on it, and one of them was still full of coffee. When the hard-bitten old mate in charge of the boarding party walked over and put his hand against the coffee pot sitting on one burner of the primus stove it was slightly warm. There had been somebody here less than an hour ago.

He went over to the small table where the charts were and opened what he took to be the log book, flipping hurriedly through to the last page on which anything was written. He studied it for a moment, and then shook his head. In forty years at sea he had never encountered a log entry quite like it.

". . . the blue, and that last, haunting flash of silver, gesturing as it died. It was beckoning. Toward the rapture. The rapture . . ."

Before he closed the book he took something from between the pages and stared at it. It was a single long strand of ash blonde hair. He shook his head again.

Putting the book under his arm, he picked up the small satchel which had been lying in the other bunk and jerked his head for the two seamen to follow him back on deck.

A few yards away in the red sunset the master of the American tanker *Joseph H. Hallock* waited on her bridge for the mate to come aboard.

Freya, of San Juan, P. R., it said under her stern, and the master of the tanker studied her curiously while he waited for the mate. She was a long way from home. He wondered what she was doing this far to the westward, in the Gulf of Mexico, and why a small boat from Spanish Puerto Rico should have been named after a Norse goddess.

The mate came up on the bridge carrying the big ledger and the satchel. "Sick?" the captain asked. "Or dead?"

"Gone," the mate said, with the air of a man who has been talking to ghosts without believing in them. "Just gone. Like that.

"Two of 'em, as near as I can figure it," he went on, sketching it tersely. "A man and a woman, though there wasn't much in the way of women's clothes except half a bathing suit. One or both of 'em was there not over an hour ago."

"Well, as soon as you get that line on her we'd better go back and see," the captain said. "Anything in the log?"

"Gibberish," the older man replied. He passed over the book, and then the satchel. "Cap, you ought to be thankful you've got an honest mate," he said, nodding toward the little bag. "Just guessing, I'd say there's about fifty thousand dollars in there."

The captain pursed his lips in a silent whistle as he opened the bag to stare briefly at the bundles of American currency. He looked outward at the *Freya*, where the men were making the towline fast, and frowned thoughtfully. Then he opened the big journal at the page the mate indicated and read the last entry.

He frowned again.

The rapture . . .

When there was no longer any light at all and they had given up the search for any possible survivors and resumed their course, the captain counted the money in the presence of two of the ship's officers and locked it in the safe. It came to eighty-three thousand dollars. Then he sat down alone in his office and opened the journal again . . .

2

It was a hot, Gulf Coast morning in early June. The barge was moored out on the T-head of the old Parker Mill dock near the west end of the waterway. Carter had gone to New Orleans to bid on a salvage job and I was living on board alone. I was checking over some diving gear when a car rolled out of the end of the shed and stopped beside mine. It was a couple of tons of shining Cadillac, and there was a girl in it.

She got out and closed the door and walked over to the edge of the pier with the unhurried smoothness of poured honey.

"Good morning," she said. "You're Mr Manning, I hope?"

I straightened. "That's right," I said, wondering what she wanted.

She smiled. "I'd like to talk to you. Could I come aboard?"

I glanced at the spike heels and then at the ladder leaning against the pier, and shook my head. "I'll come up."

I did, and the minute I was up there facing her I was struck by the size of her. She was a cathedral of a girl. In the high heels she must have been close to six feet. I'm six-two, and I could barely see over the top of the smooth ash blonde head.

Her hair was gathered in a roll very low on the back of her neck and she was wearing a short-sleeved summery dress the color of cinnamon which intensified the fairness of her skin and did her no harm at all in the other departments.

Her face was wide at the cheek-bones in a way that was suggestively Scandinavian, and her complexion matched it perfectly. She had the smoothest skin I'd ever seen. The mouth was a little wide, too, and full lipped. It wasn't a classic face at all, but still lovely to look at and perhaps a little sexy. Her eyes were large and gray, and they said she was nice.

It was hot in the sun, and quite still, and I was a little uncomfortable, aware I'd probably been staring at her. "What can I do for you?" I asked.

"Perhaps I'd better introduce myself," she said. "I'm Mrs Wayne. Shannon Wayne. I wanted to talk to you about a job."

"What kind of job?" I asked.

"Recovering a shotgun that was lost out of a boat."

"Where?" I asked.

"In a lake, about a hundred miles north of here – ."

I shook my head. "It would cost you more than it's worth."

"But – ," she protested, the gray eyes deadly serious. "You wouldn't have to take a diving suit and air pump and all that stuff. I thought perhaps you had one of those aqualung outfits."

"We do," I said. "In fact, I've got one of my own. But it would still be cheaper to buy a new shotgun."

"No," she said. "Perhaps I'd better explain. It's quite an expensive one.

A single-barreled trap gun with a lot of engraving and a custom stock. I think it cost around seven hundred dollars."

I whistled. "How'd a gun like that ever fall in a lake?"

"My husband was going out to the duck blind one morning and it accidentally fell out of the skiff."

I looked at her for a moment, not saying anything. There was something odd about it. What kind of fool would be silly enough to take a $700 trap gun into a duck blind? And even if he had money enough to buy them by the dozen, a single-barreled gun was a poor thing to hunt ducks with.

"How deep is the water?" I asked.

"Ten or twelve feet, I think."

"Well, look. I'll tell you how to get your gun back. Any neighborhood kid can do it, for five dollars. Get a pair of goggles, or a diving mask. You can buy them at any dime store. Go out and anchor your skiff where the gun went overboard and send the kid down to look for it. Take a piece of fishline to haul it up with when he locates it."

"It's not quite that simple," she said. "You see, it's about three hundred yards from the houseboat to where the duck blind is, and we're not sure where it fell out."

"Why?" I asked.

"It was early in the morning, and still dark."

"Didn't he hear it?"

"No. I think he said there was quite a wind blowing."

It made a little sense. "All right," I said. "I'll find it for you. When do we start?"

"Right now," she said. "Unless you have another job."

"No. I'm not doing anything."

She smiled again. "That's fine. We'll go in my car, if it's all right with you. Will your equipment fit in back?"

"Sure," I said.

I got my gear and changed into some sports clothes. She handed me the car keys and I put everything in the trunk.

As soon as we were out the gate she fumbled in her bag for a cigarette. I lit one for her, and another for myself. She drove well in traffic, but seemed to do an unnecessary amount of winding around to get out on the right highway. She kept checking the rear-view mirror, too, but I didn't pay much attention to that. I did it myself when I was driving. You never knew when some meathead might try to climb over your bumper.

When we were out on the highway at last she settled a little in the seat and unleashed a few more horses. We rolled smoothly along at 60. It was a fine machine, a 1954 hardtop convertible. I looked around the inside of it. She had beautiful legs. I looked back at the road.

"Bill Manning, isn't it?" she asked. "That wouldn't be William Stacey Manning, by any chance?"

I looked around quickly. "How did you know?" Then I remembered. "Oh. You read that wheeze about me in the paper?"

It had appeared a few days ago, one of those interesting-character-about-the-waterfront sort of things. It had started with the fact that I'd won a couple of star class races out at the yacht club; that I'd deck-handed a couple of times on that run down to Bermuda and was a sailing nut; that I'd gone to M.I.T. for three years before the war. It was a good thing I hadn't said anything about the four or five stories I'd sold. I'd have been Somerset Maugham, with flippers.

Then an odd thought struck me. I hadn't used my middle name during that interview. In fact, I hadn't used it since I'd left New England.

She nodded. "Yes. I read it. And I was sure you must be the same Manning who'd written those sea stories. Why haven't you done any more?"

"I wasn't a very successful writer," I said.

She was looking ahead at the road. "Are you married?"

"I was," I said. "Divorced. Three years ago."

"Oh," she said. "I'm sorry. I mean, I didn't intend to pry – ."

"It's all right," I said. I didn't want to talk about it.

It was just a mess but it was over and finished. A lot of it had been my fault, and knowing it didn't help much. Catherine and I hadn't agreed about my job, my interests in boating or writing – or anything. She'd wanted me to play office politics and golf. We finally divided everything and quit.

I had learned diving and salvage work in the Navy during the war, and after the wreckage settled I drifted back into it, moving around morosely from job to job and going farther south all the time. If you were going to dive you might as well do it in warm water. It was that aimless.

She looked at me and said, "I gathered you've had lots of experience with boats?"

I nodded. "I was brought up around them. My father sailed, and belonged to a yacht club. I was sailing a dinghy by the time I started to school. After the war I did quite a bit of ocean yacht racing, as a crew member. And a friend and I cruised the Caribbean in an old yawl for about eight months in 1946."

"I see," she said thoughtfully. "Do you know navigation?"

"Yes," I said. "Though I'm probably pretty rusty at it. I haven't used it for a long time."

I had an odd impression she was pumping me, for some reason. It didn't make much sense. Why all this interest in boats? I couldn't see what blue-water sailing and celestial navigation had to do with finding a shotgun lost overboard in some piddling lake.

3

She never did say anything about herself, I noticed, and I didn't ask. She always kept working the conversation around to me, and inside an hour she had most of the story without ever seeming actually to be nosy.

We went through another small town stacked along the highway in the hot sun. A few miles beyond the town she turned off the pavement onto a dirt road going up over a hill between some cotton fields. We passed a few dilapidated farmhouses at first, but then they began to thin out. It was desolate country, mostly sand and scrub pine, and we met no one else at all. After about four miles we turned off this onto a private road which was only a pair of ruts running off through the trees. I got out to open the gate. There was a sign nailed to it which read: *Posted. Keep Out.* I gathered it was a private gun club her husband belonged to, but she didn't say. Another car had been through recently, probably within the last day or two, breaking the crust in the ruts.

We went on for about a mile and then the road ended abruptly. She stopped. "Here we are," she said.

It was a beautiful place, and almost ringingly silent the minute the car stopped. The houseboat was moored to a pier in the shade of big moss-draped trees at the water's edge, and beyond it I could see the flat surface of the lake burning like a mirror in the sun.

She unlocked the trunk and I took my gear out. "I have a key to the houseboat," she said. "You can change in there."

She led the way, disturbingly out of place in this wilderness with her smooth blonde head and smart grooming, the slim spikes of her heels tapping against the planks. I noticed the pier ran on around the end of the scow at right angles and out into the lake.

"I'll take the gear on out there," I said. "I'd like to have a look at it."

She came with me. We rounded the corner of the houseboat and I could see the whole arm of the lake. This section of the pier ran out into it about thirty feet, with two skiffs tied up at the end. The lake was about a hundred yards wide, glassy and shining in the sun between its walls of trees, and some two hundred yards ahead it turned around a point.

"The duck blind is just around that point, on the left," she said.

I looked at it appraisingly. "And he doesn't have any idea at all where the gun fell out?"

She shook her head. "No. It could have been anywhere between here and the point."

It still sounded a little odd, but I merely shrugged. "All right. We might as well get started. I'd like you to come along to guide me from the surface. You'd better change into something. Those skiffs are dirty and wet."

"I think I've got an old swimsuit in the houseboat. I could change into that."

"All right," I said. We went back around to the gangplank and walked aboard. She unlocked the door. It was a comfortably furnished five-room affair. She pointed out a room and I went in to change. She disappeared into another room. She was a cool one, with too damned much confidence in herself, coming out to this remote place with a man she didn't even know.

Cool wasn't the word for it. I could see that a few minutes later when she came out on the dock while I was getting the skiff ready. She could make your breath catch in your throat. The bathing suit was black, and she didn't have a vestige of a tan; the clear, smooth blondeness of her hit you almost physically. There was something regal about her – like a goddess. I looked down uncomfortably and went on bailing. She was completely unconcerned, and her eyes held only that same open friendliness.

I fitted the oarlocks and held the boat while she got in and sat down amidships. Setting the aqualung and mask in the stern, I shoved off.

We couldn't have been over seventy-five yards off the pier when I found the gun. If I'd been looking ahead instead of staring so intently at the bottom I'd have seen it even sooner. It was slanting into the mud, barrel down, with the stock up in plain sight. I pulled it out, kicked to the surface and swam to the skiff.

Her eyes went wide and she smiled when she saw the gun. "That was fast, wasn't it?" she said.

I set it in the bottom of the boat, stripped off the diving gear, and heaved that in too. "Nothing to it," I said. "It was sticking up in plain sight."

She watched me quietly as I pulled myself in over the stern. I picked up the gun. It was a beautiful trap model with ventilated sighting ramp and a lot of engraving. I broke it, swishing it back and forth to get the mud out of the barrel and from under the ramp. Then I held it up and looked at it. She was still watching me.

The barrel could conceivably have stayed free of rust for a long time, stuck in the mud like that where there was little or no oxygen, but the wood was something else. It should have been waterlogged. It wasn't. Water still stood up on it in drops, the way it does on a freshly waxed car. It hadn't been in the water 24 hours.

I thought of that other set of car tracks, and wondered how bored and how cheap you could get.

4

She pulled us back to the pier. I made the skiff fast and followed her silently back to the car, carrying the diving gear and the gun. The trunk was still open. I put the stuff in, slammed the lid, and gave her the key.

Why not, I thought savagely. If this was good clean fun in her crowd, what did I have to kick about? Maybe the commercial approach made the whole thing a little greasy, and maybe she could have been a little less cynical about waving that wedding ring in your face while she beat you over the head with the stuff that stuck out of her bathing suit in every direction, but still it was nothing to blow your top about, was it? I didn't have to tear her head off.

"You're awfully quiet," she said, the gray eyes faintly puzzled.

This was the goddess again. She was cute.

"Am I?" I asked.

We walked back to the pier and went into the living room of the houseboat. She stopped in front of the fireplace and stood facing me a little awkwardly, as if I still puzzled her.

She smiled tentatively. "You really found it quickly, didn't you?"

"Yes," I said. I was standing right in front of her. Our eyes met. "If you'd gone further up the lake before you threw it in it might have taken a little longer."

She gasped.

I was angry and I stuck my neck out another foot.

"Things must be pretty tough when a woman with your looks has to go this far into left field – "

It rocked me, and my eyes stung; a solid hundred and fifty pounds of flaming, outraged girl was leaning on the other end of the arm. I turned around, leaving her standing there, and walked into the bedroom before she decided to pull my head off and hand it to me. She was big enough, and angry enough.

I dressed and was reaching for a cigarette when I suddenly heard footsteps outside on the pier. I held still and listened. They couldn't be hers. She was barefoot. It was a man. Or men, I thought. It sounded as if there were two of them. They came aboard and into the living room, the scraping of their shoes loud and distinct in the hush. I stiffened, hardly breathing now.

Detectives? Wayne himself? Suddenly I remembered the way she'd doubled all over town getting out on the highway and how she'd kept watching the rear-view mirror. I cursed her bitterly and silently. This was wonderful. This was all I lacked – getting myself shot, or named co-respondent in a divorce suit. And for nothing, except having my face slapped around under my ear.

I looked swiftly around the room. There was no way out. The window was too small. I eased across the carpet until I was against the door, listening.

"All right, Mrs Macaulay," a man's voice said. "Where is he?"

Mrs Macaulay? But that was what he'd said.

"What do you want now?" Her voice was a scared whisper. "Can't you ever understand that I don't know where he is? He's gone. He left me. I don't know where he went. I haven't heard from him – "

"We've heard that before. You've made two trips out here in 24 hours. Is Macaulay here?"

"He's not up here, and I don't know where he is – "

Her voice cut off with a gasp, and then I heard the slap. It came again. And then again. She apparently tried to hold on, but she began to break after the third one and the sob which was wrung from her wasn't a cry of pain but of utter hopelessness. I gave it up then too, and came out.

There were two of them. The one to my left lounged on an armchair, lighting a cigarette as I charged into the room. I saw him only out of the corners of my eyes because it was the other one I wanted. He was turned the other way. He had her down on the sofa and off balance with a knee pressed into her thighs while he held her left wrist and the front of her bathing suit with one hand and hit her with the other. He wasn't as tall as she was, but he was big across the shoulders.

I caught the arm just as he drew it back again. He let her go. Even taken by surprise that way, he was falling into a crouch and bringing his left up as he stepped back. But I was already swinging, and it was too sudden and unexpected for even a pug to get covered in time. He went down and stayed down.

I started for him again, but something made me jerk my eyes around to the other one. Maybe it was just a flicker of movement. It couldn't have been any more than that, but now instead of a cigarette lighter in his hand there was a gun.

He gestured casually with the muzzle of it for me to move back and stay there. I moved.

I was ten feet from him. He was safe enough, and knew it. I watched him, still angry but beginning to get control of myself now. I didn't have the faintest idea what I'd walked into, except that it looked dangerous. I couldn't place them. They weren't police. And they obviously weren't private detectives hired by her husband, because it was her husband they were looking for. Somebody named Macaulay, and she'd told me her name was Wayne. It was a total blank.

The one I'd hit was getting up. Pug was written all over him. He moved in on me clearing his head, catlike, ready. He was a good six inches shorter than I was, but he had cocky shoulders and big arms, and I could see the bright, eager malice with which he sized me up. He was a tough little man who was going to cut a bigger one down to size.

"Drop it," the lounging one said.

"Let me take him." The plea was harsh and urgent.

The other shook his head indifferently. He was long, looselimbed, and casual, dressed in a tweed jacket and flannels. I couldn't tab him. He might have been a college miler or a minor poet, except for the cool and unruffled deadliness in the eyes. He had something about him which told me he knew his business.

"All right," the pug said reluctantly. He looked hungrily at me, and then at the girl. "You want me to ask her some more?"

I waited, feeling the hot tension in the room. It was going to be rough if he started asking her some more. I wasn't any hero, and didn't want to be one, but it wasn't the sort of thing you could watch for very long without losing your head, and with Tweed Jacket you probably never lost it more than once.

Tweed Jacket's eyes flicked from me to the girl and he shook his head again. "Waste of time," he said. "He'd scarcely be here, not with her boyfriend. Check the rooms, though; look at the ashtrays. You know his cigarettes."

The pug went out, bumping me off balance with a hard shoulder as he went past. I said nothing. He turned his face a little and we looked at each other. I remembered the obscene brutality of the way he was holding and hitting her, and the yearning in the stare was mutual.

There was silence in the room except for Shannon Wayne's stirring on the sofa. She sat up, her face puffed and inflamed; her eyes wet with involuntary tears. She clutched the torn strap of her bathing suit, fumblingly, watching Tweed Jacket with fear in her eyes. Tweed Jacket ignored us. The pug came back.

"Nothing. Nobody here for a long time, from the looks of it."

He looked at me hopefully. "How about Big Boy? Let's ask him."

"Forget it. Stick to business."

There was no longer any doubt as to who was boss, but the pug wanted me so badly he tried once more. "This is a quiet place to ask, and he might know Macaulay."

Tweed Jacket waved him toward the door. "No," he said. His eyes flicked over the girl's figure again coolly. "It's Mrs Macaulay he's interested in." They left.

In the dead silence I could hear their footsteps retreating along the pier, and in a moment the car started. I breathed deeply. Tweed Jacket's manner covered a very professional sort of deadliness, and it could easily have gone the other way. Only the profit motive was lacking. He simply didn't believe Macaulay was here.

I turned. She was still holding the front of the bathing suit. "Thank you," she said, without any emotion whatever, and looked away from me. "I'm sorry you had to become involved. As soon as I can change, I'll drive you back to town."

5

It wasn't until ten, that night, that I said goodbye to Shannon Macaulay. We'd driven back to town and stopped at a cocktail lounge. She'd cleared up some of the questions that had been hanging in my mind. She did know where her husband was. He had been an insurance executive for a marine underwriters outfit in New York. He wasn't in trouble with his firm or the police. I could check that by calling them, she said. The Tweed Jacket, whose name was Barclay, represented some syndicate who were looking for her husband. Why? She evaded that one. I wasn't satisfied with that, but I went along.

And where did I come in? Easy. The phony dive act was necessary because Shannon had to sound me out. See what kind of a guy I was. Check my experience against that article she'd read about me.

They needed more than a diver. Specifically, they wanted me to buy and outfit a boat and take them off the Yucatan coast to recover something from a sunken plane. Then I was to land them secretly in Central America. That explained her questions about my navigational experiences in the Gulf and the Caribbean. What was in it for me? She'd said, "The boat is yours. Plus five thousand dollars."

I'd whistled softly. There was nothing cheap about this deal. I could see myself cruising the world in the *Ballerina*. She was a beautiful auxiliary sloop. I'd wanted her even before she'd been put up for sale. With the *Ballerina* and five thousand bucks I could live the kind of life I always wanted. I could work and play as I pleased. Manning of the *Ballerina*.

That about clinched it. That and Shannon Macaulay. She'd been awfully good about my misunderstanding of her motives that afternoon and grateful for what I'd done.

Look, I asked myself, what was with Shannon Macaulay? I didn't know anything about her. Except that she was married. And her husband was on the lam from a bunch of mobsters. So she was tall. So she was nice-looking. So something said sexy when you looked at her body and her face, and sweet when you looked at her eyes. I *had* seen women before, hadn't I? I must have. They couldn't be something entirely new to a man 33 years old, who'd been married once for four years. So relax.

I tried to relax walking back to the pier, but it wasn't easy. I couldn't figure the Macaulay guy. What was he mixed up with? Why was he so sure he could spot the plane? How did he figure he could shake this mob with something as easy to spot as this big beautiful blonde wife of his? I knew landing them secretly in a foreign country wasn't legal. And I didn't like the possibilities of tangling with "Tweed Jacket" and his buddy again, but those were risks I'd have to take.

Relax? Hell, I'd wanted to drive her home, but I knew how stupid that was the minute I'd said it. She gave me her number and told me to watch what I said, to make it sound like a lovers' meeting in case Tweed Jacket was tapped in. We'd arrange to meet once more to give me the money I'd need. Just before she drove away, she'd thanked me, saying, "You've got to help me, Bill, I can't let him down."

6

It was about 10:30 when I walked up to the shack at the pier.

Old Christiansen, the watchman, came out. "Fellow was here to see you, Mr Manning," he said. "He's still out there."

"Thanks," I answered, not paying much attention. "Good-night." It was late for anybody to be coming around about a job. I entered the long shed running out on the pier. It was velvety black inside, and hot. Up ahead I could see the faint illumination which came from the opened doors at the other end. There was a small light above them on the outside.

I started over toward the ladder to the barge and then remembered that old Chris had said somebody was waiting out here to see me. I looked around, puzzled. My own car was sitting there beside the shed doors, but there was no other. Well, maybe he'd gone. But Chris would have seen him. The gate was the only way out.

I saw it then – the glowing end of a cigarette in the shadows inside my car.

The door swung open and he got out. It was the pug. There was enough light to see the hard, beat-up, fight-hungry face. He lazily crushed out his cigarette against the paint on the side of my car.

"Been waiting for you, Big Boy," he said.

"All right, friend," I said. "I've heard the one about the good little man. A lot of good little men are in the hospital. Hadn't you better run along?"

Then, suddenly, I saw him holding and hitting her again and I was glad he'd come. Rage pushed up in my chest. I went for him.

He was a pro, all right, and he was fast. He hit me three times before I touched him. None of the punches hurt very much, but they sobered me a little. He'd cut me to pieces this way. He'd close my eyes and then take his own sweet time chopping me down to a bloody pulp. My wild swings were just his meat; they'd only pull me off balance so he could jab me.

His left probed for my face again. I raised my hands, and the right slammed into my body. He danced back. "Duck soup," he said contemptuously.

He put the left out again. I caught the wrist in my hand, locked it, and yanked him toward me. This was unorthodox. He sucked air when my right came slamming into his belly. I set a hundred and ninety-five pounds on the arch of his foot, and ground my heel.

He tried to get a knee into me. I pushed him back with another right in his stomach. He dropped automatically into his crouch, weaving and trying to suck me out of position. He'd been hurt, but the hard grin was still there and his eyes were wicked. All he had to do was get me to play his way.

He was six or eight feet in front of the pier, with his back toward it. I went along with him, lunging at him with a right. It connected.

He shot backward, trying to get his feet under him. His heels struck the big 12-by-12 stringer running along the edge of the pier and he fell outward into the darkness, cartwheeling. I heard a sound like a dropped canteloupe and jumped to the edge to look down. The deck of the barge lay in deep shadow. I couldn't see anything. I heard a splash. He had landed on the after deck and then slid off into the water.

I went after him, wild with the necessity to hurry. But the minutes it took me to break out the big underwater light and a diving mask made the difference. The ebbing tide had carried him under the pilings supporting the pier and by the time I got to him he was dead. He was caught there, his skull crushed by the fall on the deck. His eyes were open staring at me. I fought the sickness. If I gagged, I'd drown.

7

The next thing I was conscious of was hanging to the wooden ladder on the side of the barge, being sick. I'd left him there. The police could get him out; I didn't want to touch him. I climbed up to the deck and collapsed, exhausted. I was winded, soaked and the cut places on my face were stinging with salt. My right hand was hurt and swollen.

I had to get out to the watchman's shanty and call the police. But then the whole thing caught up with me. This wasn't an accident I had to report. I'd killed him in a fight. I'd hit him and knocked him off the pier, and now he was dead. It wasn't murder, probably, but they'd have a name for it – and a sentence.

Well, there was no help for it. I started wearily to get up, and then stopped. The police were only part of it. *What about Barclay?* And the others I didn't even know? This was one of their boys.

Suddenly, I wasn't thinking of the police any more, or of Barclay's hoodlums, but of Shannon Macaulay. And the *Ballerina.* Of course, the whole thing was off now. Even if I didn't get sent to prison, with those mobsters after me and convinced I had some connection with Macaulay I was no longer of any use to her.

No, the hell with reporting it. Sure, I regretted the whole thing. But I was damned if I was going to ruin everything just because some vicious little egomaniac couldn't leave well enough alone. Leave him down there. Say nothing about it – I stopped.

How? Christiansen knew he was in here. I was all marked up. In a few days, in this warm water, the body would come to the surface, with the back of his head caved in and bruises all over his face. I didn't have a chance in the world. He'd merely come in here to see me, and had never come out. That would be a tough one for the police to solve.

Of all the places in the world, it had to happen on a pier to which there was only one entrance and where everybody was checked in and out by a watchman – No. Wait. Not checked in and out. Just questioned as they came in. No books, no passes. And the watchman only waved them by as they went out.

It collapsed. It didn't mean anything at all, because *nobody* had gone out. Christiansen would never have any trouble remembering that when the police came checking.

There *had* to be a way out of it. I looked across the dark waterway. Everything was quiet along the other side; there was nothing except an empty warehouse, a deserted dock. Nobody had seen it. Barclay probably didn't even know the pug had come out here. He'd done it on his own because he couldn't rest until he'd humiliated a bigger man who'd knocked him down. There was nothing whatever to connect me with it except the simple but inescapable fact he'd driven in here to see me and had never driven out again – . I stopped. *Driven?* No. I hadn't seen any car. But how did I know there wasn't one out there? The shed was dark. I got a flashlight and checked. There it was in the corner of the shed. All I had to do was drive it out past the watchman, and the pug had left here alive. It was as simple as that.

Out at the gate the light was overhead, and the interior of the car would be in partial shadow. The watchman's shack would be on the right. I could hunch down in the seat until I was about the pug's size. All the watchman ever did was glance up from his magazine and wave. He wouldn't see my face; nor remember afterward that he hadn't. It was the same car, wasn't it? The man had driven in, and after a while he had driven out.

Wait. I'd still have to get back inside without Christiansen's seeing me. But that was easy too. It must be nearly eleven now. Chris went off duty at midnight. All I had to do was wait until after twelve and come back in on the next man's shift. He wouldn't know where I was supposed to be, or care.

I walked over to the car, flashed the light in, and saw there were no keys. I leaned wearily against the door. I knew where the keys were, didn't I? It would take only a minute. Revulsion swept me.

But I knew it had to be done. I dove down, emptied his pockets, and came up to surface again. I hadn't looked at his face. It took me a few minutes to clear the gear I'd used. Then I tried to fix up my face with hot water applications. After that I changed into dry clothes that were similar in color to the ones he'd been wearing. I dried his keys and started his car.

I hunched down in the seat and drove up to the gate slowly. Chris was in the shack, pouring coffee out of a thermos. He looked over casually, waved a hand, and turned back to his coffee.

I drove the car uptown – away from the waterfront, parked it on a quiet street, and threw the key far into a vacant lot. I was free of him now, the poor little punk. *Why* couldn't he have stayed away?

8

At twelve-thirty I stepped into an all-night drugstore and called a cab. I hoped the driver couldn't see my face.

We passed the last street and were approaching the gate.

He braked to a stop in front of the shanty. The 12-to-8 watchman was looking out the window. "Manning," I called out, keeping my face in shadow. He lifted a hand.

"All right, Mr Manning."

The cab started to move ahead, then stopped. Somebody was calling out from the shack. "Mr Manning! Just a minute – "

I looked around. The watchman was coming out. "I almost forgot to tell you. A woman called about ten minutes ago – "

I wasn't listening. I stared at the window of the shack. Old Chris was looking out, a puzzled frown on his face.

The other watchman was still talking. "– Chris was just about to walk out and tell you. He said you was on the barge."

I couldn't move, or speak. Chris was standing beside him now, looking in at me. "Son of a gun, Mr Manning. I didn't see you go out."

I fought to get my tongue broken loose from the roof of my mouth. "Why – I – " It was impossible to think. "Why, I came out a while ago. Remember? When my friend left. We drove out to have a couple of beers. It must have been a little before twelve – "

"You was in that car?" He peered at me dubiously. "I looked right at it, too, and didn't even see you. I must be getting absent-minded. I was about to walk all the way out there to the barge and tell you that woman called – "

He broke off suddenly, concerned. "Why, Mr Manning. What's wrong with your face?"

I was rattled now, but I tried not to show it to these two old men who meant well, but who would remember everything they saw later on.

"Oh," I mumbled, feeling my face as if I were surprised at the fact of having one. "I – uh – I was getting something out of the storeroom and fell."

"Well, that's too bad," he answered solicitously. "But you ought to put something on them cut places. Might get infected. You never know. I think it's the climate around here, the muggy air, sort of – "

"Yes," I said. "Yes. Thanks."

I got rid of the cabbie, who'd be the third guy to answer any questions asked by the police – or Barclay's bunch of killers.

I tried to think. How much chance did I have now? In a few days he'd float up, somewhere along the waterfront, and the police would start looking. One of the first things they'd do would be to question all the guards along the piers.

Float up? That was it. He couldn't float up. I had to stop it. I looked downward again, and shuddered. Could I go back into that place once more? *Once?* It would take at least a half dozen dives to do it, to make him fast with wire to the bottom of one of those pilings. Too much precious time and breath were wasted in going down and coming up.

There was just one more thing, I thought, and then we had it all. Carter would be back from New Orleans sometime this morning, here aboard the barge, and I wouldn't be able even to look.

I fought with panic. I still had a chance, I told myself. They might never connect me with it. After all, there was no identification on him now that I'd shoved the wallet into the muck. They wouldn't have a picture of him, except possibly one taken as he looked when he came up. Chris might not have had a good look at him when he came in the gate.

But I wouldn't know. That was the terrible part of it. I'd never have any idea at all what was happening until the hour they came after me.

I had to get out of here. I was thinking swiftly now. Quit, and tell Carter I was going to New York. Sell my car, buy a bus ticket, get off the bus somewhere up the line, and come back. Buy the boat, under another name, of course. In three days I could have it ready for sea. We'd be gone before they even came looking for me. If they did.

It didn't occur to me until afterward that never once in all of it did I ever consider the possibility of not buying the boat and not taking Shannon Macaulay.

Suddenly, I had to see her. For the first time in a self-sufficient life I was all at once terribly alone, and I didn't know why, but I had to see her.

That reminded me. The watchman had said that a woman had called. I was still holding in my hand the slip of paper he had given me. It was a telephone number, the same one she had given me in the bar. Maybe something had happened to her. I ran toward the car.

Calling from the watchman's shack would be quicker, but I didn't want the audience. I slowed going through the gate, and the graveyard watchman lifted a hand and nodded. I noted bitterly that old Chris had gone home at last.

I pulled up at the nearest bar and called her. She answered, finally, her voice tense. We put on the lovers' rendezvous tone to take care of possible listeners. She arranged to meet me at the cocktail joint we'd drunk at earlier in the day.

I was sitting in the car in front of it when she pulled up and parked her Caddy. If she were being followed I didn't want to go inside where they might get a look at my marked-up face. I eased alongside. She saw me, and slipped out on the street side and got in. It had taken only seconds.

I shot ahead, watching the mirror. There were cars behind us, but there was no way to tell. There are always cars behind you. I was conscious of the gleam of the blonde head beside me, and a faint fragrance of perfume.

She noticed my face and gasped. *Tell her?* What kind of fool would tell anybody? I had known her less than twenty-four hours; I knew practically nothing about her; I knew she had gotten me into this mess; yet I would have trusted her with anything. I told her. I brushed off her sympathetic offerings, but I didn't find them unpleasant.

I had been watching the mirror carefully. By this time we were well out on the beach highway and traffic had thinned out considerably. There were three cars behind us. One of them stopped. I shot ahead fast, dropping the other two well behind me. As they disappeared momentarily behind some dunes, I slowed abruptly and swung away from the beach. We were some 50 yards from the road, well out of range of passing highlights. I shut the headlights before we stopped rolling.

She started to light a cigarette. "Not yet," I said. Both cars went by, their tail-lights slowly receding down the road.

I lit her cigarette.

"All right, listen," I said. I told her what I was going to do. "There's only one catch to it," I finished. "You'll have to give me the money for that boat with no guarantee you'll ever hear from me again. The word of a man you've known for one day isn't much of a receipt."

"It's good enough for me," she said quietly. "If I hadn't trusted you I would never have opened the subject in the first place. How much shall I make the check?"

"Fifteen thousand," I said. "The boat is going to be at least ten, and there's a lot of stuff to buy. When we get aboard I'll give you an itemized statement and return what's left."

"All right," she said.

"Pick a name," I said. "How about Burton? Harold E. Burton."

She wrote out the check. I held it until it dried, and put it in my wallet. "Now. What's your address?"

"106 Fontaine Drive."

"All right," I said, talking fast. "I should be back here early the third day. This is Tuesday now, so that'll be Thursday morning. The minute the purchase of the boat goes through and I'm aboard I'll mail you an anniversary greeting in a plain envelope, just one of those dime-store cards. I don't see how they could get at your mail, but there's no use taking chances. Other than that I won't get in touch with you. I'll be down there at the boat yard all the time. It's in another part of the city, and I won't come into town at all. I've only been around Sanport for about six months, but still there are a few people I know and I might bump into one of them. I'll already have everything bought and with me except the stores, and I'll order them through a ship chandler's runner – "

"But," she interrupted, "how are we going to arrange getting him aboard?"

"I'm coming to that," I said. "After you get the card, you can get in touch with me, from a pay phone. It's Michaelson's Boat Yard; the name of the sloop is *Ballerina*. I'm just hoping I can get her. She was still for sale last night. But if something happens and she's already sold by the time I get back, I'll make that card a birth announcement instead of an anniversary greeting, and give you the name of the one I actually do buy. All straight?"

"Yes," she said. She turned a little and I could see the blur of her face and the pale gleam of the blonde head. "I like the whole plan, and I like the way your mind works." She paused for a moment, and then added quietly. "You'll never know how glad I am I ran into you. I don't feel so helpless now. Or alone."

I was conscious of the same thing, but probably in a different way than she'd meant it. There was something wonderful about being with her. For a moment the whole mess was gone from my mind.

"You were good on the phone, too," she said. "Thanks for understanding."

In other words, *keep your distance, Buster*. I wondered why she thought she had to warn me. We both knew it was only an act, didn't we? Maybe I was always too aware of her, and she could sense it. "All right. Now," I said curtly. "That leaves the problem of getting him aboard. I'll have to work on that. He's in the house, isn't he?"

"Yes," she said, surprised. "How did you know?"

"Guessing, mostly. You said they'd searched it while you were gone. They wouldn't have had to tear it up much, looking for a grown man. So maybe he told you they had."

"You're very alert. He heard them and told me."

"Why is he hiding there? And how?"

She leaned forward a little and continued. "I've been wanting to get to this. Here's the whole story, briefly.

"About three weeks ago my husband spotted them on the street and knew they'd caught up with us again. He had a plan for getting to Central America and losing them completely, for the last time. It was about completed. It involved a man who'd been a close friend of my husband's in college. He lives in Honduras and is a wealthy plantation owner with considerable political influence. He's also a rather passionate flying fan. He's always buying planes in the States and having them flown down to him, and my husband was to take this one to him. It would get him out of the country without any trail they could follow, you see? He'd merely take off without filing a flight plan, and disappear. It would be illegal, but as I say this friend of his had political connections.

"However, he had to go alone. It was a light plane and its cruising radius with the maximum amount of fuel was still a little short, so he'd added an extra tank. I was to come later, making sure I wasn't followed. I was to do it over the Memorial Day weekend, and it involved about five different zigzagging commercial flights with the reservations made considerably ahead of time. On a long holiday like that they'd be sold out, you see? Anyone trying to follow me might catch a no-show at one or even two of the airports, but not all of them.

"Two days before I was to leave, my husband came back. He crashed off the Yucatan coast, but got into a life raft and was picked up by a Sanport fishing boat. They docked at night and he got home unseen.

"But now they've found out where we live, and they have the place surrounded. Barclay rented the house right across the street, and they watch me all the time, waiting for me to lead them to him – "

"And they don't know he's inside?"

"I don't think so. You see, they searched it the first time while he was actually gone. They made it look like burglary."

"But didn't you say they'd searched it again today? Yesterday, I mean?"

She nodded. "He's in a sealed-off portion of the attic, and the only way into it is through the ceiling of a second-floor closet. He stays up there nearly all the time. All the time when I'm out of the house. I think they're pretty sure he's gone, but they know if they keep watching me I'll lead them to him sooner or later. I hadn't realized until what happened up at the lake that they might try beating me up. That scares me, because frankly I don't know how much of it I could take."

That angered me and made me realize how much more there was to this girl than her looks. No whining, no heroics – she simply said she didn't know how much of it she could take and went right on with what she had to do. The next time that pug looked at me, I'd look back.

She went on. "And as to what's in the plane, it's money. About eighty thousand dollars. All he has left. He can't take much more, Bill. That plane crash did something to him – and being brought back to Sanport after he thought he had gotten away. And losing the money on top of it, so he couldn't even run any more."

"But you just wrote a check for fifteen thousand – "

"I know. Naturally, he left me some so I could follow him. I sold my jewelry, and borrowed on the car."

I began to catch on then. She was merely handing me the last chance they'd ever have. This girl was a plunger, and when she said she trusted you she trusted you all over.

"Well, wait," I said. "I can probably find a cheaper boat – "

She shook her head. "I don't want to go to sea in a cheap boat. And we'll recover the money from the plane, anyway."

"Do you realize the jam you'll be in if I turn out to be a phony?"

"That was the general idea, Bill, when I said I wanted time to make up my mind about you. Remember?"

"I remember," I said. "Do you mind if I get a little personal? I've been feeling sorry for Macaulay because he was up against a rough proposition alone. I'd like to amend that; I don't know of anybody who's less alone."

She didn't answer for a moment, and I wondered if I'd gotten it off as lightly as I intended. After all, this was an awkward situation for her, and she'd already shown me the road signs once.

It was almost too fast for me then. She slid toward me on the seat, murmuring, "Bill . . . *Bill!*" her face lifted to mine and her arms slipping up around my neck, and then I was overboard in a sea of Shannon Macaulay. Yet even as I swam into that sea, my mind was trying to tell me it was an act and that the reason she was saying my name over and over was to keep me from having my head blown off. And that's what it was.

A voice said, "All right, Jack. Break it up and turn around."

I turned. A light burst in my face, and another voice I recognized as Barclay's said, "You people are oversexed, aren't you?"

Two thoughts caught up with me at once. The first was that they hadn't heard us and didn't suspect anything. Her reaction time had been so fast they'd caught us kissing, just as you'd have expected of two people in a parked car along the beach. That was good.

But it was the second one that pulled the ground from under me. They had that light right in my face, and they'd be blind if they didn't see the marks that pug had left on it.

I had never been more right. "Hmmmmm," Barclay said softly. "So that's where he went."

"Who?" I asked, just stalling for time. I had to think of something. "What are you talking about?"

"Don't be stupid. The guy you hit, up at the lake."

If I denied it they wouldn't believe me anyway, and when he didn't show up they'd go out there and ask the watchmen. They'd know then I'd done something to him. There was a better way: talk like a loud-mouthed fool, and admit it. It didn't have much chance, but at least it had more than the other.

"If that's who you mean," I said. "He did. I guess you haven't seen *his* face. Keep him out of my hair or he's going to be bent worse than that the next time you get him back."

"Where is he now?"

"How would I know?" I said. "Was he supposed to tell me his plans?"

"Skip it, wise guy," he said. "And get out of town. We're too busy to be chasing around after your love instincts. Get out of the car."

I didn't want to, but I got out. I heard her shaky indrawn breath as I closed the door. "*No. No. No – .*"

It was a good, cold-blooded, professional job. Nobody said anything. Nobody became excited. I never did even know for sure how many there were besides Barclay. I swung at the first dark shape I saw, because I had to do something; the blackjack sliced down across the muscles of my upper arm and it became a dangling, inert sausage stuffed with pain.

They gave me a good working over. The last thing I heard was Shannon's screams.

When I came to, she was there on her knees beside me, helping. My arm was numb and I felt sick, but she rested there until the pain subsided.

9

Driving back to town, neither of us said anything about the way she'd put on the kissing act to keep my head from being blown up.

Finally, I asked, "What did Macaulay do to them?"

She hesitated.

"It's all right," I said. "If it's none of my business – ."

"No," she said slowly, staring ahead at the headlights probing the edge of the surf. "It isn't that. It's just that I don't know the whole story myself."

"Didn't he tell you?"

"Most of it. But not all. He says I'll be safer if I never know. It happened about three months ago. He had to go to the Coast on business, for about a week, he said. But three days later he called me late one night, from San Antonio, Texas. I could tell he was under a bad strain. He said for me to pack some bags, and leave right away for Denver. He didn't explain; he just said he was in trouble and for me to get out of New York fast.

"He met me in Denver. It was something that happened at a party he went to, in some suburb of Los Angeles. He didn't want to talk about it, but he finally admitted a man had been killed, and he had seen it."

"But," I said, "All he has to do is go to the police. They'll protect him. He's a material witness."

"It's not that simple," she said. "One of the people involved is a police captain."

"Oh," I said.

It sounded too easy and too pat, but on the other hand there wasn't any doubt she was telling the truth. But what about Macaulay himself?

"How long have you been married?" I asked.

"Eight years."

"And he's been with that marine insurance firm all the time?"

"Yes," she said. "He's been with them ever since he came out of law school, back in the thirties, except for three years in the service during the war."

I shook my head. There was nothing in that. We came into the almost deserted town. I stopped beside her car and got out with her. She put out her hand. "Thanks," she said. "It'll be bad, waiting for that card."

There was nobody on the street. I was still holding her hand, hating to see her leave. But all I said was, "Don't go out of the house at night while I'm gone. If you have to come downtown, do it during rush hours when there are lots of people on the streets."

"I'll be all right," she said.

"If you see a car behind you on the way home, don't worry about it. It'll be mine. That's all." I followed her out. It was an upper-bracket suburb out near the country club. She pulled into a drive and stopped under a carport beside a two-storied Mediterranean house with a tile roof and ironwork balconies. I stared at the house across the street. The windows were all dark. But they were in there, watching her as she got out of the car and fumbled in her bag for the key. She waved a white-gloved hand, and went inside.

I went on, looking the place over. It was the second house from the corner. I turned at the intersection and drove slowly down the side street. There was an alley behind the house. A car was parked diagonally across the street from the mouth of it in the shadows under the trees, and as I went past I saw a man's elbow move slightly in the window. They had it covered front and back. There'd be one at the other end of the alley.

All I had to do was get Macaulay out of there alive. And by that time they'd be after me too.

I made my plans quickly. I drove back to the barge, packed my stuff, cleaned my face up as well as I could. It was morning when I started into town. I thought about the guy under the pier and then tried to dismiss him from my mind. Shannon helped. I couldn't push her out of the picture at all – nor could I forget Macaulay. His story didn't jell. I knew something about that tricky coastline off Central America. He'd have to be a superb navigator to find that spot again.

I sold my Oldsmobile for half of what it was worth and bought a bus ticket to New York. Before I got on the bus, I sent a telegram to Carter explaining that I had to see sick relatives in New York and that he'd have to get a new diver. It was the least I could do.

I fell asleep the minute I hit the seat.

10

We came into New Orleans at ten-fifteen p.m. Through passengers going east were scheduled to change buses, with a layover of forty minutes. I got my bag, ducked out a side door, and caught a cab. I registered as James R. Madigan at a little hotel and went to work on the marks on my face. Another few hours and they'd hardly be noticed.

They might find out I'd left the bus, and they might even trail me to this hotel and eventually start looking for somebody named Madigan, but there the whole thing would end. Harold E. Burton was only a check for

$15,000, and the last place they'd ever expect me to go would be back to Sanport.

I studied the rest of it. There'd be the station wagon I had to buy to get back to Sanport with all the gear. I'd store it in a garage after we sailed. After a year or so they'd probably sell it for the storage charges, and if anybody ever bothered to look into it all he'd find would be that it had been left there by a man named Burton who'd sailed for Boston in a small boat and never been heard of again. People had been lost at sea before, especially sailing alone.

After I'd landed them on the Central American coast, I'd return to Florida and could lose myself among the thousands who made a living along the edge of the sea in one way or another, gradually building up a whole new identity. I burned my identification. I fell asleep thinking of Shannon.

It was a little after eight when I awoke. I shaved hurriedly, noting my face was almost back to normal now, and dressed in a clean white linen suit.

A little later, I put in a long distance call to Sanport, to the yacht broker. I told him I was interested in the *Ballerina*. He said it was available at eleven thousand dollars. I arranged to meet him at Michaelson's yard in Sanport at nine the next morning.

When the banks opened I went into the first one I came to, endorsed the check for deposit, and opened an account, asking them to clear it with the Sanport bank by wire. They said they should have an answer on it by a little after noon.

The used car lots were next. Part of my mind had been occupied with the problem of getting Macaulay out of that house, and now I was starting to see at least part of the answer. I didn't want a station wagon; I wanted a black panel truck. I found one in the next lot. After trying it out, I told the salesman I'd come back later and let him know. I couldn't buy it until the check cleared.

The wire came back from the Sanport bank a little after one. I cashed a check for three thousand, picked up the truck, and drove over to a nautical supply store. It took nearly two hours to get everything I needed here, chronometer, sextant, azimuth tables, nautical almanacs, charts, and so on, right down to a pair of 7×50 glasses and a marine radio receiver. That left the diving gear. Of course there was still the aqualung in the back of her car, but the coast of Yucatan was too far to come back for spare equipment if anything went wrong. I bought another, and some extra cylinders which I had filled. At five o'clock the truck was full of gear, and nothing remained but to check out of the hotel and start back.

No, there was one thing more. I went into a dime store and bought an anniversary greeting card.

I drove all night.

At dawn, I hit the outskirts of Sanport where Michaelson's Boat yard was located. I parked the car and went into a diner for breakfast. When the workmen started to drift into the yard, I walked in and got a look at the *Ballerina*. She was a beauty.

The yacht broker showed up and we closed the deal for $10,500. I checked the work list with the foreman and arranged for a shakedown cruise the following morning. She was in such good shape that he guaranteed she'd be ready for me that same afternoon. Looking her over, I agreed.

Just then the telephone rang. The girl at the desk said, "Just a minute, please." She looked inquiringly at the super. "A Mr Burton – ?"

"Here," I said. "Thank you."

"Burton speaking," I said.

"Can you talk all right from there?" she asked softly.

I couldn't, so I got her number, walked down to a pay booth and dialed, fumbling in my eagerness. She answered immediately.

"Bill! I'm so glad to hear you – "

It struck me suddenly she didn't have to act now, as she had the other night, because there was no chance anybody could be listening. Then I shrugged it off. Of course she was glad. She was in a bad jam, and she'd had two days of just waiting, biting her nails.

"I didn't do wrong, did I?" she went on hurriedly. "But I just couldn't stand it any longer. The suspense was driving me crazy."

"No," I said. "I'm glad you didn't wait for the card. I was worried about you, too. Has anything happened?"

"No. They're still watching me, but I've been home nearly all the time. But tell me about you. And when can we start?"

"Here's the story," I said, and I told her. We set the sailing date for Saturday night.

And then she asked the big question.

"Have you thought of anything yet? I mean for getting Francis aboard?"

"Yes," I said. "I've got an idea. But something else has occurred to me."

"What's that, Bill?"

"Sneaking him aboard isn't the big job. Getting you here is going to be the tough one."

"Why?"

"They're not sure where he is. But they're covering you every minute."

I went on, talking fast, checking with her about the layout of the house and the streets in the neighborhood.

Finally, I said, "All right. That's about all I needed to know. I think we can pull it off, but I want to work on it a little more. And I've still got to figure out a way to get you."

"And your diving equipment," she said. "It's still in the back of the car."

"I know," I said. "I was just coming to that. There won't be time to fool with it, either, when I come to get you, no matter what kind of plan we work out. Anyway, put that aqualung in a cardboard carton and tie it. Pack what clothes and toilet articles you can get into another carton, and put both of them in the trunk of your car. Around noon tomorrow call Broussard & Sons, the ship chandlers, and ask if they'll deliver a couple of packages to the *Ballerina*, along with the stores. They will, of course. But don't take them to Broussard's yourself.

"Take the car to the Cadillac agency for a supposed repair. As soon as you get inside on the service floor, call a parcel delivery service to come after the cartons. Whoever's following you will be outside and won't see the things come out of your car. If he did they'd be hot on the trail in nothing flat to see where they went. All straight?"

"Yes. Now, when will I call you again?"

"Saturday afternoon about five, unless something happens and you have to get in touch with me sooner."

It took the rest of the morning to check the gear on the sloop and make out a stores list. Broussard's runner came down in the afternoon and picked it up. The yard closed at five. I drove the truck inside and parked it. The night watchman was another problem; as fast as I solved one I had two more to take its place. I had to get them aboard without his seeing them.

I studied the layout of the yard. The driveway came in through the gate where the office and the shops were located, and went straight back to the pier running out at the end of the spit. The *Ballerina*, of course, would be out on the pier after I brought her back in from the shakedown. If I backed the truck up to the pier and left the lights on he wouldn't be able to see them come out the rear doors.

I cleaned the cabin of the boat that night and got a good night's sleep.

The *Ballerina* checked out beautifully the next morning and the yardwork was done. I paid the bill and spent the afternoon checking and stowing all the gear aboard her. Later, I bought a paper, but there was nothing about his body's being found.

With nothing to do, I began thinking of her again. I still hadn't figured a way of getting her aboard. Finally I hit on an idea. If it worked, this time tomorrow we'd be at sea.

11

The stores came down in a truck at a little after nine. I looked quickly for the two cartons, took them aboard, and started checking stores with the driver. When he had it all on the end of the pier I wrote out a check and started carrying it aboard.

I was still at it at eleven o'clock when two strange men came into the yard.

They were dressed in seersucker suits and panama hats, and were smoking cigars. They started around the yard, talking to each of the workmen for a minute or two.

Then they were coming toward me. I was just picking up a coil of line; I straightened, watching them. I'd never seen them before as far as I could tell. They showed me a photograph, questioned me briefly, and left.

They worked fast. It couldn't possibly have been more than a few hours since they'd found him, and already they had a picture. Not *a* picture, I thought. Probably dozens of them, being carried all over the waterfront. And it was a photograph of him as he was alive, not swollen and unrecognizable in death.

Anybody but a fool would have known it, I thought. The pug would have a criminal record, and when they have records they have pictures. Maybe they had identified him from his fingerprints. But that made no difference now. The thing was that Christiansen would recognize him instantly.

I shook it off. They'd still be looking for Manning, who had gone to New York. And we'd be gone from here in another twelve hours. I was still tense and uneasy. It was Saturday afternoon, and it grew worse as the afternoon wore along.

It was exactly five o'clock when the telephone rang inside the booth at the gate.

"Bill," she said softly, "I'm getting really scared now. Are we all ready?"

"We're all ready," I said. "Listen. I've got to get Macaulay first. They're not sure where he is, and if it works right they won't even know he's gone. They won't suspect anything's happening. But when you disappear, everything's going to hit the fan."

"I understand," she said.

I went on, "Tell him to dress in dark clothes and wear soft-soled shoes. He's to come out the back door at around 9:10. That'll give him plenty of time to get his eyes accustomed to the darkness and make sure there's nobody in the alley itself. I don't think there will be, because they're too smart to be loitering where somebody might see them and call the police. They're watching the ends of it, sitting in cars. I'll come down Brandon Way and stop at the mouth of the alley at exactly 9:20 – "

"But, Bill, you can't stop there. He'll know what you're doing. He'll kill you."

"He'll be busy," I said. "I've got a diversion for him, and I think it'll work. Now, the truck will be between him and the mouth of the alley. Tell Macaulay to come fast the minute the truck stops. And if anything goes wrong he's to *keep coming* toward *the truck*. If he breaks and goes back he hasn't got a chance. Tell him when he reaches it to stand a little behind the door and just put his hand up on the frame of the window, near the corner. He's not to get in or open the door, until the truck starts moving.

If he even puts his weight on the running board while it's stopped, that guy may hear it. Got all that?"

"Yes," she said. "Then what?"

"You're next. Have you ever been to a drive-in movie?"

"Yes. Several times."

"All right. As soon as he leaves the house at 9:10 you lock all the doors. Be standing right by the phone at 9:20. If you hear any commotion or gunshots, call the cops and hide, fast. A prowl car will get there before they can get to you. But if you don't hear anything, you'll know he got away. Leave the house at 9:30. Some of them will follow you, of course. Go to the Starlite drive-in, out near the beach on Centennial Avenue. Centennial runs north and south. Approach from the north, and try to time it so you get there at ten minutes before ten. If you look you'll see a black panel truck parked somewhere in the last block before you get to the entrance. That'll be me. Drive on in.

"Now, all this is important. Be sure you get it right. This is Saturday night, so it'll be pretty full. But you know how they're laid out, fan-wise, spreading out from the screen, and there are always a few parking places along the edge because the angle's poor out there. Enter one of the rows and drive across to the exit, slowly, looking for a good spot. But there aren't any. So you wind up clear over at the end. Sit there twenty minutes, and then back out. You've decided you don't like that, and there must be something better further back. So drop back a row and go back to the entrance side again. Park there for five or ten minutes, and then get out and walk down to the ladies' room in the building where the projector is. Kill about five minutes and then come back to the car. The minute you get in, back out and drive toward the exit. Before you get to it, pull into one of the parking places along the edge, and step out, on the right-hand side. Don't scream when a hand grabs your arm. It'll be mine."

"Won't they still be following me?"

"Not any more," I said. "By the time you come back from the ladies' room I'll know who he is."

"You think he'll get out of his car too?"

"Yes. It's like this. There'll probably be two cars trailing you. When they see you go into a drive-in theatre one man will follow you in to be sure it's not a dodge for you to transfer to some other car. And the other bunch will stay outside near the exit to pick you up coming out, because there's a hellish jam of cars fighting for the exit when the movie breaks up and they could lose you if they both went inside. There's just one thing more. If an intermission comes along, sit tight where you are. You've got to make those two moves and that trip to the powder room while the picture's running and not many people are wandering around. It's darker then too; nobody has his lights on."

"Yes, but how are you going to stop him from following me the second time? Bill, they're dangerous."

"It's all right," I said. "He won't even see me. When he gets out to follow you on foot I'll fix his ignition wires. By the time he tumbles to the fact his car's not going to start, you'll already be down at the other end of the row and in my truck. When the picture's over, we just drive out, along with everybody else."

"All right. But you'll be careful, won't you?"

"Why?" I asked. I couldn't help it.

"Couldn't we put it this way – if anything happens to you we wouldn't get away."

"We'll call it that."

"Yes," she said. Then she added, "That, at the very least."

She hung up.

12

I sweated it out. It was eight-fifty when I reached the neighborhood and cruised slowly to time it right. I was betting a lot on just a flashlight and a black panel truck. The thing was to give him just a little time to look it over, so I wouldn't spring it on him too suddenly. He'd be able to see what I was doing, and as I passed under the street light at the intersection of Fontaine Drive he'd see the black sides of the truck. My headlights would cover the Louisiana license plate. At 9:18 I eased away from the curb.

Switching on the flashlight, I held it in my left hand and shot the beam into dark places under the trees and back among the hedges as I came slowly down the street. After I crossed Fontaine I could see him. He was in the same place, facing this way. I flashed the light into another hedge.

I had to calculate the angles fast now. I was well out in the center of the street, watching the mouth of the alley on his side. He was parked just beyond it. I stopped with my window opposite his, and at the same time I threw the light against the side of his car but not quite in his face.

"You seen anything of a stray kid?" I asked, as casually as I could with that dryness in my mouth. "Boy, about four, carrying a pup – "

It worked.

I could feel the breath ooze out of me as a tough voice growled from just above the light. "Nah. I haven't seen any kid."

"Okay. Thanks," I said. I felt along the edge of the window frame in the opposite door. *Hurry. For the love of God, hurry.*

My fingertips brushed across a hand. I inhaled again.

I let the truck roll slowly ahead three or four feet, and said, "If you see a kid like that, call the station, will you? We'd thank you for it."

I moved the light away from him. He wouldn't be able to see anything for twenty or thirty seconds, and Macaulay was on the far side of the truck, walking along with me. But he had to be in it before we hit the street below Fontaine, under the light. I slipped the clutch and hit the accelerator a couple of times, shooting the flashlight beam along the sidewalk. The door opened soundlessly, and he was sitting beside me. He closed it gently.

There was no outcry behind us. I wanted to step on the gas. Not yet, I thought. Easy. I still hadn't seen him at all. He was only a dark shadow beside me as we rolled on toward the intersection. Then a cigarette lighter flared.

I jerked my face around, whispering fiercely. *"Put that – "*

"It's all right," a smooth voice said. "Just turn at the corner and go around the block."

I saw a lean face, and tweed, and the gun held carelessly in his lap. It was Barclay.

We turned. I was numb all over and there was nothing else to do.

"Park at the mouth of the alley, and do it quietly," Barclay said.

"Mrs Macaulay?" I asked mechanically.

"She's in the house."

"Is she all right?"

"Yes."

I swung around the next corner, and we were on Fontaine, under the big, peaceful trees. "Then you finally killed him didn't you?"

"Oh. Yes," he replied, almost as if talking to himself. "Too bad."

There was no point in asking what he meant. I was too far behind now to catch up in a week. We parked at the mouth of the alley. Across the street I could see the red tip of a cigarette in the other car. Bitterness welled up in me. I'd fooled them, hadn't I?

Barclay opened the door on his side. "Go in. We'll be leaving soon."

"Leave?"

"Sail. *Ballerina* sleeps four, right?"

He stepped aside in the darkness and followed closely behind me. My mind turned the parts of it over and over with no more comprehension than a washing-machine tumbling clothes. Sail? Four of us? Macaulay was already dead, that was what they'd wanted, wasn't it?

It was – unless she had been lying all the time. I tried to shove the thought out of my mind. It came back. How would they have known I was coming by in the truck unless she had told them?

Maybe I could have got away from him in the alley, but I didn't even try. The whole thing had fallen in on me, and I didn't have anywhere to go. I wanted to see her, anyway. She had lied about it, or she hadn't lied about it. I had to know.

I had wanted to see Macaulay and when I finally saw him he was a corpse on the floor of his living room. He'd been dressed according to the instructions I'd given Shannon. She was there, shocked and speechless,

barely able to keep herself together when Barclay escorted me in. Two of
his friends were there, too. He gave his instructions tersely.

"Very well. We're finished here," he said. "Who has the keys to
her car?"

"Here." The big blond guy fished them from his pocket.

"Give them to Carl," Barclay directed crisply. "You'll go with us in the
truck."

He shifted his gaze to the other man. "Take the Cadillac downtown and
park it. Meet us on the south-east corner of Second and Lindsay. We'll
be going east, in a black panel truck, Manning driving. Get in the front
seat with him. When we go in the gate at the boat yard Manning will tell
the watchman you've come along to drive the truck back to a garage. If
Manning tries any tricks, don't shoot him; kill the watchman. As soon as
we're all aboard the boat, take the truck to some all-night storage garage
and leave it, under the name of Harold E. Burton, and pay six months'
storage charges in advance. Then pick up the Cadillac, drive it to the
airport, and leave it. Take a plane to New York, and tell them we should
be in Tampa in three weeks to a month. Tell them about Macaulay, but
that we have her and it's under control. You got that?"

"Check," Carl said. He took the keys and went out.

I could see a little of it now. They were hanging it on her quite neatly.
The police already wanted me, and they'd be after her now too, for killing
Macaulay. I didn't know what Barclay wanted with her, but he had her
from every angle. There was nowhere we could run.

13

We boarded the *Ballerina* the way Barclay scheduled it and he used my
loading plan perfectly. The watchman never suspected a thing. Carl drove
the truck off the pier and that was it. I could have jumped over the side
and possibly escaped, but he knew I wouldn't. I had nowhere to go, with
the police looking for me, and I couldn't leave her. The big one helped
her down into the cockpit.

On deck, Barclay said, "Let's sail."

"Where?" I asked.

"I'll give you a course when we're outside. Now, step on it."

"I'll have to light the running lights first. Is that all right with you?"

"Certainly."

"I just wanted to be sure I had your permission."

He sighed in the darkness. "This is no game, Manning. You and
Mrs Macaulay are in a bad spot. What happens to her depends on
the way the two of you coöperate. Now, get this sloop away before the
watchman hears us and comes snooping."

Getting the watchman killed would accomplish nothing. "All right," I said. We moved slowly away from the pier, out toward the channel, going seaward. There was no other traffic.

Barclay sat down across from me in the cockpit, smoking. "Very neat," he congratulated himself above the noise of the engine.

"I suppose so," I said. "If killing people is your idea of neatness."

"Macaulay? We couldn't help it."

"Of course," I said coldly. "It was an accident."

"No. Not an accident. Call it calculated risk." He paused for a moment, the cigarette glowing, and then he went on. "And speaking of that, here's where you fit in. You're also a calculated risk. I can handle small boats well enough to take this sloop across the Gulf, but I couldn't find the place we're looking for. We need you. We won't kill you unless we have to. Score yourself a point.

"But before you start anything, imagine a bullet-shattered knee, with gangrene, and only aspirin tablets or iodine to treat it. And figure what we could do to Mrs Macaulay if you don't play ball.

"One of us will be watching you every minute. Do as you're told, and there'll be no trouble. Is it all clear, Manning?"

"Yes," I said. "Except you keep telling me this is no game, so there must be some point to it. Would you mind telling me where you think you're going, and what you're after?"

"Certainly. We're looking for an airplane."

"You mean the one Macaulay crashed in? You're going to try to find it after you've killed the one person on earth who knew where it is?"

"She knows," he said calmly. "Why do you think we brought her?"

"Look," I said. "He was alone in it when it crashed. How could she possibly know?"

"He told her."

"You'll never find it in a million years."

"We will. He knew where it was, and was certain he could go back to it, or he wouldn't have hired you. So it has to be near some definite location, a reef or something. And if he knew, he could tell her. She's already given me the general location. It's to the westward of Scorpion Reef. You know the spot?"

"It's on the chart," I said curtly. "Listen, Barclay. You're stupid as hell. Even if you found the plane, that money's not recoverable. I didn't tell her, because the main thing they wanted was to get away from your bunch, but that currency's pulp by now. It's been submerged for weeks – ,"

"Money?" he asked. There was faint surprise in his voice.

"Don't be cute. You're not looking for that plane just to recover the ham sandwich he probably had with him."

"She told you there was money on the plane? Is that it?"

"Of course that's it. What else? They were trying to get to some

place in Central America so they could quit running from you and
your gorillas – "

"I wondered what she told you."

"What do you mean?"

"You're nuts, Manning. We're not looking for any money. We're after
something he stole from us."

"I don't believe it."

"It's not important what you believe. But what makes you so sure, when
you'd never met him and knew nothing about him at all?"

"I know her. She wouldn't lie about it."

He chuckled. "Wouldn't she?"

The *Ballerina* began lifting slowly on the long groundswell running in
through the mouth of the jetties. I searched the darkness ahead and could
see the seabuoy winking on and off. I wondered why Barclay had tried to get
off a cock-and-bull story like that. He was in control; why bother to lie?

"I found their bag, the one she sent aboard."

I looked around. It was the voice of George Barfield, down below.

"Any chart in it?" Barclay asked.

"No." Barfield came out carrying something in one hand and sat down
beside Barclay. "The satchel was in it, all right. About eighty thousand,
roughly. But no chart, none at all."

"*What?*" It exploded from me.

"What's the matter with Don Quixote?" Barfield asked. "Somebody
goose him?"

"Could be he just got the point," Barclay murmured. "She told him
that money was in the plane."

"Oh," Barfield said. "Well, I wanted to see everything before I died,
and now I have. A man over thirty who still believes women."

I felt sick. "Shut up, you punk." I said. "Put that bag down and throw
a flashlight on it. There's one on the starboard bunk."

"I've got it here." Barfield put the bag down, flipped on the light and I
looked at bundle after bundle of twenties, fifties, and hundreds.

*I sold my jewelry and borrowed what I could on the car. It's the last chance
we'll ever have. I don't know why they're trying to kill him; it was something
that happened at a party –*

"All right," I said. "Turn it off, Barfield."

"You're supposed to say, 'turn it off, you punk.' "

"Shut up," I said.

"How long would it take you to learn enough navigation, Joey?"

"Too long," Barclay answered. "Leave him alone."

"I was pretty good at math." Barfield said. "Want me to try it? I could
get sick of this guy."

"Stop it," Barclay ordered curtly. "Even if we could find the place alone,
we still need a diver."

"Anybody with an aqualung."

"George," Barclay said softly.

"All right. All right."

"What's in the plane?" I asked.

"Diamonds," Barclay answered. "Lots of diamonds."

"Whose?"

"Ours."

"And she knows about it?"

"Yes."

I wanted to hear it all. "And they weren't trying to get to Central America?"

"Yes, they were, at first. But Macaulay couldn't take her in the plane because he had to take a diver."

I was a chump. A sucker. I'd believed her. Even when I'd had intelligence enough to realize the story sounded fishy I'd still believed it. She wouldn't lie. Oh, no, of course not. Hell, how stupid could you get? She couldn't go in the plane because he'd had to add a fuel tank to stretch out its cruising radius. I was their last chance to escape; she had trusted me with all the money they had left – She must have been laughing herself sick all the time. I even imagined her telling her husband about it. *Dear, this poor sap will believe anything.*

And because I'd believed it I had killed that poor vicious little gunman and now the police would be looking for me as long as I lived. Only I wasn't going to be living very long. I was scheduled for extinction when I found Macaulay's plane and brought up what they wanted.

So was she. And wasn't that too bad? I wondered if she realized just what her chances were of selling Barclay and that big thug a sob-story of some kind. As soon as she told them where to look for that plane she was through. There should have been some satisfaction in knowing her double-crossing had got her killed as well as me, but when I looked for it it wasn't there.

So I was going back to feeling sorry for her? I was like hell. The dirty, lying, double-crossing – I stopped, puzzled. If she knew what was in the plane and where it was, why hadn't they grabbed her off long ago? Why had they kept trying to sweat Macaulay out of hiding so they could take him alive and make him tell, when they could have picked her up any time they pleased?

What the hell, was I still trying to find a way out for her? Of course they hadn't wanted her as long as there was a chance she would lead them to Macaulay. Her information about the plane would be second-hand, and they'd only taken her as second choice after Macaulay was dead. She was all they had left.

Well, I thought, they didn't have much.

14

Barclay had me set a course for west of Scorpion Reef. Barfield watched me plot it in the chartroom.

I gave Barclay the corrected course, and he let her fall off another point.

"Now," he said, "ever handle a sailboat, George?"

"No," Barfield replied, across from me. "But if your nipple-headed friend can do it, anybody can."

"Well, you won't have to," Barclay said. "Manning and I will split the watches. You'll be on deck when he has it and I'm asleep. Mrs Macaulay can have the forward part of the cabin; you, I, and Manning can sleep in the two bunks in the after part. And Manning won't go down there when one of us is asleep.

"It's after twelve now," he went on. "Get some sleep, George. Manning can stretch out here in the cockpit and I'll take the first watch, until six. When Manning relieves me, you'll have to come on deck."

I sat down, as near Barclay as I dared, and lit a cigarette. "It would be tragic," I said, "if he blew his stack and killed me before I found your lousy plane for you and the two of you could take turns at it."

"Why should we kill you?"

"Save it," I said. "I knew all along you wouldn't. Just give me a letter of recommendation. You know, something like: 'This will introduce Mr Manning, the only living witness to the fact that we killed Macaulay and that his widow is innocent – '"

"Not necessarily," he said. "You can't go to the police. You're wanted for murder yourself."

He knew I'd have everything to lose and nothing to gain. But if I were dead and lying somewhere in two hundred fathoms of water there was no chance at all. And .45 cartridges were cheap.

I moved a little nearer, watching his face. It was calm and imperturbable in the faint glow from the binnacle. I could almost reach him.

The eyes were suddenly full of a mocking humor. "Here," he said. He handed the .45 automatic to me butt first. "Is this what you want?"

For a fraction of a second I was too startled to do anything. Then I recovered myself and grabbed it out of his hand.

"You really wanted it?" he asked solicitously.

"Come about," I said. "Take her back to the seabuoy."

"What an actor!" His voice was amused.

"You don't think I'd kill you?"

"No."

"So it's not loaded?" Completely deflated, I pulled the slide back. I stared. It *was* loaded.

"You won't pull the trigger," he said, "for several reasons. You can't go back to Sanport, because of the police. You couldn't shoot a man in cold blood. You aren't the type – "

"Go on," I said.

"The third reason is that Barfield is down there in the cabin with another gun, with Mrs Macaulay. If you try anything, she gets it."

"I don't give a damn what happens to Mrs Macaulay," I said.

He smiled. "You think you don't, but that would change with the first scream. You don't have the stomach for that either."

"I'm the original gutless wonder. Is that it?"

"No. You're just weak in a couple of spots where you can't be in a business like this. I've sized you up since that afternoon at the lake."

"Then you knew what she was up to? That's the reason you shoved off and left us?"

"Naturally. Also the reason we roughed you up without really hurting you, that night on the beach. We wanted you to hurry and get this boat for them so we could find where Macaulay was hiding. It worked, except that he forced us to kill him. That's that, and now I'll take my gun back."

Sweat broke out on my face. I had only to squeeze the trigger, ever so gently, and there would be only one of them. He watched me coolly, mockingly.

My finger tightened. I didn't care what happened to her, did I? I cursed her silently, bitterly, hating her for being alive, for being here.

"George," Barclay said quietly.

I went limp. I handed the gun to him, feeling sick and weak all over.

"What is it?" Barfield's voice asked from the companionway.

"Nothing," Barclay said.

I lit a cigarette. My hands shook.

He had wanted me to realize the futility of jumping one of them to get his gun as long as she was where the other could get her. I detested her. Maybe I even actively hated her. She and her lying had ruined everything for me, I was sick with contempt when I thought of her, and yet he'd known he could tie my hands completely by threatening her with violence. I was "weak" all right.

"The hell with Mrs Macaulay," I said. "What did Macaulay do?"

"He stole three-quarters of a million dollars worth of diamonds from us. Since you were in the salvage business," he went on, "you must have known the *Shetland Queen*."

I looked up suddenly. "Sure. I remember her."

She had gone down in about ten fathoms, off Campeche Bank last fall, and the underwriters had let a contractor salvage as much of the cargo as wasn't ruined. They had saved some machinery and several thousand cases of whiskey that somehow hadn't been smashed. The crew had been saved.

"So that's the first time your diamonds were dunked," I said. "But where does Macaulay fit in?"

I began to get the connection. Salvage – underwriters; the part about his being in the marine insurance business was true.

"They were aboard the *Shetland Queen*," continued Barclay. "But they didn't appear on the cargo manifest or any of the Customs lists. They were in some cases of tinned cocoa which were going to a small importing firm in New Orleans. A cheap way to ship diamonds but tough to explain if something happens to the ship, as in this case. The cocoa was insured, for two or three hundred dollars. We would have looked stupid trying to collect three-quarters of a million dollars from the underwriters when we'd paid a premium on a valuation of three hundred dollars. We couldn't explain that to Customs either.

"Benson & Teen had paid off all claims, including ours, and were salvaging what they could, but they weren't going to waste time bringing up a few dollars worth of tinned cocoa. They paid, and wrote it off. We made a few feelers. Since they were working inside the ship anyway, why not bring up our cocoa and let us drop our claim? They brushed us. We let it drop, before they got suspicious. We had to wait until they were finished and then do our own salvaging.

"But then some – uh – competitors of ours got wise and also tried to buy the cocoa from Benson & Teen. This was a little too much for Macaulay, who was in charge of the operation. He sent a confidential agent down to the salvage operations to look into this chocolate business on the quiet. This guy asked to have the cocoa brought up and, since he was acting for Benson & Teen through Macaulay, they brought it up. He found out what made it so valuable, devalued it, and phoned Macaulay.

"They had two problems. The first was getting the stones into the States without paying duty or answering any embarrassing questions as to where they had come from. The second was to keep us from getting them. We had two men in the Mexican port keeping an eye on the cargo that was brought in. Macaulay solved both problems at once. He'd been a bomber pilot in the Second World War, and held a pilot's license. He came down to the Gulf Coast, chartered a big amphibian, and came after his agent and the stones. They were to meet in a laguna some ten or fifteen miles east of the Mexican port. They did, but our men were there too. They'd followed Macaulay's man and lost him in the jungle, but saw the plane coming in and got there just as the man was climbing aboard. They recognized Macaulay and opened fire, killing the other man, but Macaulay got away in the plane."

"With your stupid diamonds," I said.

He nodded. "We thought so. Macaulay didn't go back to New York, knowing what he was up against now. His wife disappeared also. The firm said he had suffered a heart attack and resigned. He'd told them, earlier, that he had to go to the Coast because of illness in the family. We almost caught up to him two or three times. He never tried to sell any of the diamonds. We figured that, just about the time we ran him down in Sanport. He hadn't sold them because he didn't have them.

"He escaped us in Sanport, taking off in a plane with a man carrying an aqualung diving outfit. Macaulay, by the way, couldn't swim. When we learned about the diver, we knew what had happened. The metal box with the diamonds had fallen into the water when Macaulay's friend was killed.

"We stuck close to Mrs Macaulay, knowing she'd soon lead us to him. But just about that time we suspected he was back in Sanport because of a little story in the paper. About five days after Macaulay took off, a fishing boat docked with a man it had picked up in a rubber liferaft on the Campeche Bank. He told them he was a pilot for some Mexican company and had crashed while going from Tampico to Progreso alone in a seaplane. He took off the minute the fishing boat docked."

"I get it now," I said. "As soon as she got in touch with me you knew the castaway was Macaulay. And you realized he had crashed out there somewhere, but that he knew exactly where the plane was and could find it again, or he wouldn't have been trying to hire a diver."

Barclay nodded. "Correct. We also suspected he was in the house, but taking him alive wasn't going to be easy. He was armed and panicky."

"The thing that puzzles me," I said, "is that you and your meat-headed thugs never did put the arm on her to find out where the plane was. You're convinced now she knows where it is, but you let her come and go there for a week or more right under your noses."

"We weren't certain she knew *then*."

"But you are now. Why?"

He lit a cigarette. Sanport's lights were fading on the horizon.

"It's simple," he explained. "I wrote Macaulay a letter two days ago advising him to tell her."

I shook my head. "Say that again. You wrote him a letter – where?"

"To his house. Even if he weren't there she would get it to him."

"And he'd be sure to tell her, just because you suggested it? Why?"

He smiled again. "Sure, he was an insurance man, wasn't he? I just pointed out that there was always the chance something might happen to him and he ought to protect her."

"By telling her where the plane was?" I asked incredulously. "So he could guarantee her being put through the wringer by you – .""

He shook his head gently. "You still don't see Macaulay's point of view. He knew she'd be questioned. But suppose she *didn't* know where the plane was?"

I saw the bastard's logic. "Good God – "

"Right. Life insurance. He was leaving her the only thing that could stop the interrogation."

I saw then what Macaulay must have gone through in those last few hours. He had to tell her.

I leaned my elbows on my knees and looked at him. "*You dirty son – *" I stopped. I'd forgotten him. She'd been telling the truth. Barclay had sent that letter to Macaulay only two days ago. I had to talk to her.

Barclay let me, too. He knew he was tying me tighter to Shannon and that I'd be easier to handle that way, so he called Barfield up. Barfield liked his sleep a lot more than he liked me. I could see his face burning as I went below.

She was lying on the starboard bunk with her face in her arms.

15

"Shannon," I said.

"What, Bill?" Her voice was muffled.

"How long have you known what these gorillas are after?"

She turned slowly and looked up with listless gray eyes.

"Since three this afternoon," she said.

I felt weak with relief or joy, or both of them. I'd been right. All the bitterness was gone and I wanted to take her in my arms. Instead I lit a cigarette. "I want to apologize," I said.

She shook her head. "Don't. I sold you out, Bill."

"No," I whispered. "You didn't know. I thought you had lied, but you hadn't. It doesn't matter that he was lying to you."

"Don't make it any worse, Bill. I had six hours to call you, and you could have got away. I tried to, but I couldn't. I thought I owed him that, in spite of what he did. Maybe I was wrong, but I think I'd still do it the same way. I don't know how to explain – "

"You don't have to," I said. "You were telling the truth all the time. That's all that matters."

She stared up at me. "Why does it?"

"I don't know," I said.

I wanted to shout it out to her, or sing it, but I kept my face blank and lit a cigarette for myself.

"I'm sorry about it," I said gently.

She didn't answer for a moment. Then she said, "It's all right. He didn't have a chance, anyway. I think they knew he was in the house, and anything we tried would have failed."

"Why hadn't he ever told you?" I asked.

"Ashamed, I think. He wasn't really a criminal, Bill. There was just too much of it, and it was too easy, and no one would ever know."

"It's too bad," I said. "It's a dirty shame."

She turned her face a little, and her eyes met mine squarely. "You know I must have suspected it, don't you? Nobody could be stupid enough not to guess there must be more to it than he told me. I did suspect it. I can't deny it. I was cheating when I told you what he told me, because I was afraid it wasn't the truth, or not all the truth. But what could I do? Tell you I thought my husband was lying? Did I owe you more than I did him? Doesn't eight years of time mean anything, or the fact he had never lied to me before, or that he'd always been wonderful to me? I'd do it again. You'll just have to think what you will."

"You know what I think? I'll tell you about it some day."

"Wait, Bill," she whispered. "You don't know all of it yet. When you do, you'll think I'm a fool. He was going to leave me. He wasn't on his way to Honduras when he crashed. He was going to destroy the plane and disappear somewhere on the Florida coast."

I got it then. "And you'd have gone on to Honduras, thinking he would be there? And when he wasn't, you'd have been certain he was dead? Down somewhere in the Gulf, or in the jungle?"

"Yes," she said. Then she smiled a little bitterly. "But I wasn't the one he wanted to convince. If Barclay and his men had managed to follow me down there, they'd give him up as dead too."

"But running out on you? Deserting you, leaving you stranded in a foreign country?"

"Not quite stranded, if you mean money," she said. "You see, it wasn't in the plane. I thought it was, but it was in a bag of his I was supposed to bring down with me. None of it's clear-cut, Bill. He was leaving me, and he had to double-cross his friend who bought the plane, but he wanted me to have the money."

Conscience money, I thought.

Suddenly she was crying silently. "Does it make much sense to you that I still didn't call and tell you, after that?"

"Does it have to?" I asked.

She put both hands alongside her face and said slowly, around the tightness in her throat, "I don't know how to explain it. When he told me that, I knew I would leave him, but I couldn't run out on him until he was safe."

I tried to see Macaulay, and failed again. How could he inspire that kind of loyalty on one hand and be capable of the things he had done, on the other? I said nothing about it because it might not have occurred to her and it would only hurt her, but he had killed that diver, or intended to until the airplane crash saved him the trouble. The way he had it planned, there couldn't be any second person who knew he was still alive. He'd probably killed him as soon as the poor devil brought up the box in that Mexican laguna. And he would have killed me, in some way.

Then I thought of something else. "Do you really know where that plane is?" I asked.

She nodded. "Yes. He told me very carefully. And I memorized everything he said."

I wondered. She thought she did. Barclay was convinced she did. But apparently I was the only one aboard who had any idea of the immensity of the Gulf of Mexico and the smallness of an airplane. If you didn't know within a few hundred yards you could drag for a thousand years and never find it.

Not that I cared if they found their stupid diamonds or not. It was something else. If they didn't, Barclay would think she was stalling. " – suppose she *didn't* know," he'd said softly. The implication was sickening.

"He didn't show you on a chart?" I asked. "Or make a drawing?"

"No," she said. "But it's near a shoal about fifty miles north-north-east of Scorpion Reef. It's around a half mile long, running north and south. The plane sank two miles due east of it."

"Was there white water, or did he just see the shoal from the air before he crashed?"

"He didn't say."

That wasn't good. You had to assume too many things. You had to assume that Macaulay had known where he was himself and that the water was shallow enough at that spot to cause surf, so we could find it. If he'd merely seen a difference in the coloration of the water from above, we didn't have a chance. Then you had to have faith in his ability to estimate his bearing and distance from the shoal in the wild scramble to launch the rubber raft.

I tried to reassure myself. He could navigate, or he wouldn't have tried to fly the Gulf in the first place. He gave the location in reference to Scorpion Reef, so he must have sighted Scorpion. Fifty miles was only a few minutes in a plane, so he couldn't have gone far wrong in that distance. And there had to be visible white water. He'd been intending to go back to it in a boat, hadn't he? He must have known what he was doing.

Then something else struck me. "Wait," I said. "Barclay told me to set a course to the *west* of Scorpion Reef. Are you sure you said east?"

"Yes. He must have misunderstood. I said north-north-east."

"Just a minute," I said. I went out into the after part of the cabin and leaned over the chart. With the parallel rulers I laid down a line 33 degrees from Scorpion Reef, picked fifty miles off the edge of the chart with the dividers, and set them on the line. I stared. There was no shoal there.

Beyond, another 20 or 25 miles, lay the Northern Shelves, a wide area of shoaling water and one notation that three fathoms had been reported in 1907. Could he have meant that? But if he had, we didn't have a chance. Not a chance in the world.

In the first place, if he couldn't fix his estimated position within twenty-five miles that short a time after having sighted Scorpion Reef his navigation was so sloppy you had to throw it all out. There went your first assumption, the one you *had* to have even to start: that Macaulay had known where he was himself. And in the second place, that whole area was shoal. God knew how many places you might find white water at dead low tide with a heavy sea running. Trying to find an airplane with no more than that to go on was so absurd it was fantastic.

Fumbling a little with nervousness, I swung the rulers around and ran out a line NNW from Scorpion Reef. Barclay said she had told him that direction. I looked at it and shook my head. That was out over the hundred fathom curve. Nothing there at all. And if he'd been headed for the Florida coast he wouldn't have been over there in the first place.

I thought swiftly. We'd never find that plane. To anybody even remotely acquainted with salvage work the whole thing was farcical except there was nothing funny about it here, under the circumstances. They were going to think she was stalling. She'd already contradicted herself once, or Barclay had misunderstood her.

Three-quarters of a million dollars was the prize. Brutality was their profession. I thought of it and felt chilly along the back.

16

I was still looking at the chart when the idea began to come to me. I looked at my watch. It was just a little less than two hours since we'd cleared the seabuoy. Guessing our speed at five knots would put us ten miles down that line. Growing excited now, I marked the estimated position and spanned the distance to the beach westward of us with the dividers. I measured it off against the edge of the chart. It was a little less than nine miles.

Hope surged up in me. We could do it. There was still enough glow in the sky over Sanport to guide us, and if there weren't all we had to do was keep the sea behind us and go downwind. The water was warm. You could stay in it all day without losing too much body heat.

I hurried back through the curtain and told her my idea.

She was scared. She couldn't swim very well, but when I told her there wasn't a chance in the world of finding that plane and that they'd kill us anyway, she agreed.

I told her to play sick, grab the belt as she got past Barfield, and go overboard holding it while I handled Barclay.

She nodded. "Thank you for everything," she said softly. She thought we were going to drown.

I put my hand against her cheek. "We'll make it," I said. Just touching her brought back that intense longing to take her in my arms. I stood up abruptly and went back on deck. It was very dark. Barfield growled something and went below. I sat down in the cockpit, on Barclay's right and as near him as I dared.

"Nice talk?" he asked.

"Very nice," I answered.

"She really didn't know what he was doing, did she?"

"No."

"Could be," he said.

My eyes were becoming accustomed to the darkness now. I looked astern and could still see the faint glow over the city. Involuntarily, I shuddered. There was a lot of dark water between here and the shore.

"Did she tell you where the plane was?" Barclay asked.

"Yes," I said. I repeated what she had said, and asked, "Where did you get the impression it was west of Scorpion Reef?"

"That's what she said," Barclay answered. "She said NNW."

"She was suffering from shock," I said coldly. "I believe she had just seen her husband butchered in cold blood. And, anyway, it's a cinch he wouldn't have been to the westward of Scorpion Reef if he'd been heading for the Florida coast."

"Maybe," he said. "We'll see about it after breakfast. Get some sleep and don't try anything stupid."

I started to say something, but at that moment I heard voices in the cabin. She had started up.

"Where do you think you're going?" Barfield's voice growled.

"I – feel nauseated," she said. I could barely hear her. " – fresh air – "

"Hey, Joey," Barfield called out. "All right to let her up?"

I waited, holding my breath.

"No," Barclay said. "Find her a pail."

If she hadn't passed him we had no chance at all, but it was now or never. I swung. My fist crashed into the blurred whiteness of Barclay's face, and at the same time I yelled, "Run!"

Barclay fell back, clawing in his pocket for the gun. She came up through the hatch, moving fast, with Barfield shouting behind her. I could see her for a brief second, standing erect on the deck at the forward end of the cockpit with the bulky life-preserver clutched to her breast. Then she was lunging and falling outward, splashing somewhere in the darkness. I grabbed Barclay's jacket and pushed him into Barfield as he came lunging up. I slid over the rail, and water closed over me. Even as I was going down I tried to keep myself oriented.

The *Ballerina* was off course now, all of its angles gone. I started to swim back hoping to spot her blonde head or the white of the life belt, but the whitecaps were confusing.

When the sloop was some 75 yards away, I lifted my head and called out,

not too loudly, "Shannon. Shannon!" There was no answer. I wondered if
I had gone beyond her. I began to be afraid, and called out again.

This time I heard her. "Here," she said. "Over this – " The voice cut
off, and I knew she had gone under. She was off to the left, downwind.
I turned.

Another sea broke over me. Then I was floundering in the trough. The
blonde head broke surface right beside me. "Thank God," I said silently,
and grabbed her dress. She clasped her arms tightly about my neck and
tried to pull herself up. We went under. I felt suddenly cold in water that
was warm as tea. She had *both* arms about me.

Our heads came out. I shook water from my face. "Shannon! Where's
the lifebelt?"

She sputtered and fought for breath. "It – I – " she said, and gasped
again. "I lost it."

17

It was the bright sunlight streaming into the cabin that brought me out
of it slowly. And then the wonderful nightmare of the night in the water
came back to me. The lifebelt was gone, and she knew we couldn't make it.
Yet she'd ignored Barclay's hailing from the *Ballerina* as he tried to locate
us in the darkness. She'd been wonderful. Scared, but she'd followed my
directions fully. Stripped for buoyancy, we tried the hopeless push toward
Sanport, orienting on the stars.

It was dawn and we hadn't covered a third of the way, when I choked
up enough breath to tell her.

"I couldn't tell you before," I said. "Even – if he had run out on you.
But doesn't matter now. Have to tell you. I love you. You've never been
out of my mind since you walked out on the edge of that pier – "

She didn't say anything. She brought her arms up very slowly and put
them about my neck. We went under, our lips together, arms tight about
each other. It was like falling endlessly through a warm, rosy cloud. I seemed
to realize, very dimly, that it was water we were sinking through and that if
we didn't stop it and swim up we'd drown right there, but apparently there
was nothing I could do about it. I didn't want to turn her loose long enough
to swim up. We went on falling, through warmth and ecstasy and colors.

We'd broken surface again, and then I'd seen the masts of the sloop.
They were still looking for us. Suddenly I realized she'd let go, voluntarily.
I'd gotten to her, even as I realized that the sloop was bearing down on us.
Barclay'd made good use of those 7 × 50 binoculars. I remember Barfield's
whistling as he dragged her aboard. Then I'd blacked out.

It was four in the afternoon when Barfield shook me awake. The husky
guy hated my guts all right, but evidently Barclay had told him to lay off.

He told me to make some sandwiches and coffee, wake Shannon, and get up on deck. It was while she was dressing and I was preparing the food that the idea came to me. If we could shake these two, all problems were solved. Why go back? Here was the *Ballerina*, the girl I knew I wanted, and eighty thousand dollars. We could change our names, get married in one of those little Carribean ports. We'd change the name of the boat and its Port of Registry. We'd stay away from the big ports, cruise the world, and they'd never find us.

The dream faded abruptly. My two friends upstairs were calling from on deck. You couldn't dream them away.

I had five days, maybe a week. They had to slip up sometime – I hoped. Shannon helped me bring the food.

Barclay was at the tiller, and Barfield lounged on the port side, his legs outstretched. He drew them in, and grinned. "Going for a swim, honey?" he asked.

She glanced briefly at him as if he were something that had crawled out of a ditch after a rain, and sat down on the starboard side holding the plate of sandwiches in her lap.

He looked to me. "Take the helm."

He took a sandwich, glanced at me and then at Shannon. "We're about fifty miles from land. Don't try any more swimming stunts and forget about the dinghy. I've thrown away the oars. We'll pistol whip you, Blondie, if either of you tries anything again.

"Now let's get down to business. Tell us exactly what your husband said about that plane crash."

Shannon stared at him, contemptuously.

"All right. It was late in the afternoon, he said, near sunset, when he picked up Scorpion Reef. He was heading for the Florida coast somewhere above Fort Myers. A few minutes later his starboard engine caught fire. He couldn't put it out, and knew he was going to crash. He had noticed a reef or shoal below him just a minute or two before, and tried to get to the downwind side of it, where the sea wouldn't be so rough, but he couldn't make it. He crashed on the east side of it, about two miles off, and the plane sank almost immediately. He just had time to climb out on a wing and throw the raft in the water. As you probably know, he couldn't swim at all."

"Why didn't he try to get the diamonds off with him?"

"He had stowed the box in a locker so it wouldn't go flying around in rough weather. The locker was aft, already under water."

"What about the diver?"

That hurt her. She hesitated, sickness in her eyes. "He said the man didn't have his belt fastened, and was killed in the crash."

Barclay lashed it at her suddenly, "Why was he so sure of his exact bearing from that reef? He didn't have time to take a compass reading before the plane went down, and he didn't have a compass on the raft."

She was quite calm. "It was late afternoon, I said. The sun was setting. The plane, the very northern end of the surf on the shoal, and the sun were all in one straight line."

She looked around suddenly at me. "I remember now, you asked me that, didn't you, Bill? Whether he could see surf from the raft. And I'd forgotten."

I nodded. It would make a difference, all right; but you still had to find the reef. It was hopeless.

Barclay lit a cigarette. "Okay. Now, what was the position?"

"Fifty miles north-north-east of Scorpion Reef."

He stared coldly. "You said westward last night."

"I'm sure I didn't," she replied.

"Make up your mind – fast."

"It's north-north-east."

"We'll see," he said crisply. "George, get that chart, the parallel rulers, and dividers."

Barfield brought them up and the two of them studied the chart. Shannon regarded them as if they were lice. Barclay's face was thoughtful. "North-north-east – "

I knew what he would find, and waited, tensely.

He picked the distance off and set the dividers along the line. Then he turned his head and stared bleakly at Shannon Macaulay.

"Come again?"

"You asked me what he told me," she said indifferently. "I have just repeated it, word for word. What else would you like me to do?"

"Tell the truth, for once."

"I am telling the truth."

He sighed. "The chartmaker was lying. The nearest sounding shown here is 45 fathoms." He paused and nodded to Barfield. "George."

I was too wild to be scared. "Listen, Barclay. This whole thing is going to come unzipped. If he hurts her, it's you I'm coming for, and you're going to have to use that gun to stop me. If you think you can find that reef without my help, go ahead."

It hung poised, ready to go either way. "Don't be a damned fool," I went on. "If she were going to lie, would she give you a stupid position like that? Maybe there is a shoal there, or somewhere within fifteen miles or so. All that area hasn't been sounded. Macaulay could have been off in his reckoning. The only thing to do is go there and see, and you'll never get there unless I take you. You name it. Now."

He saw I was right.

Barfield lounged on the seat with a cup of coffee in his hand. "The hero," he said. "We've got a real, live hero aboard, Joey."

*   *   *

The breeze held steady out of the northeast, day after day, and the miles ran behind us. I'd bought time for us, but I hadn't bought much, and every day's run was bringing us nearer the showdown. I knew what would happen when we got down there and couldn't find any shoal. Something had to happen before then; we had to get a break. But they didn't drop a stitch. When one was asleep the other was watching me, never letting me get too near. And there was always Shannon Macaulay. They had me tied, and they knew it. It was unique, a masterpiece in its own way; we were at sea in a 36-foot sloop, so all four of us had to be sitting right on top of the explosion if it came. I couldn't hide her or get her out of the way.

It was noon, the fourth day out of Sanport. I was working out our position on the chart when an idea began to nudge me. We wouldn't pass near enough to Scorpion Reef to sight it, so they had to take my word as to where we were. Barclay knew approximately, of course, because he checked the compass headings against each day's position, but he had to accept my figures for the distance run.

I was thinking. It might work.

Twenty or twenty-five miles beyond the point where Macaulay was supposed to have crashed lay the beginnings of the Northern Shelves. If there were a shoal or reef in a hundred miles it would be out there. The chances were a thousand to one that it was somewhere in that vast shallow area that he had actually gone into the drink, even though they were about a hundred billion to one against our ever finding where. So if I put us out there when they thought we were on the location she had given them –

We might find a shoal. And any shoal would do.

I set the little cross down 15 miles to the westward and a little north of our actual position and tore up my work sheet. Take ten miles out tomorrow noon and I'd have it made without exciting Barclay's suspicions. It was Wednesday. I told him we'd make it by Friday.

I didn't say anything to Shannon. The object of the whole thing was to get her off the boat, and if she knew why I wanted her off she wouldn't go. She'd have some foolish idea about not letting me face it alone, and I'd never convince her that alone was the only way I had a chance.

Barclay apparently suspected nothing as he checked positions with me the next day. In fact he seemed satisfied with the efforts I had been taking all that day. We kept looking for white water, listening for the sound of surf breaking; but no signs of shoal appeared.

Barclay had become more quiet, cold, and unapproachable as Friday wore on and we saw nothing.

Barfield's face was ugly as he watched Shannon now, and several times I saw him glance questioningly at Barclay. We were all in the cockpit. I had the tiller.

"Listen," I said harshly. "Both of you. Try to get it through your heads.

We're not looking for the corner of Third and Main. There are no street
signs out here. We're in the general area. But Macaulay could have been
out ten miles in his reckoning. My figures could be from two to five miles
out in any direction. Error adds up."

He was listening, his face expressionless.

I went on. I had to make them see. "When Macaulay crashed, there was
a heavy sea running. There's not much now but a light ground swell. There
could have been surf piled up that day high enough to see it five miles away,
and now you might think it was just a tide-rip. We've got to criss-cross the
whole area, back and forth. It may take two days, or even longer."

He looked coldly at me. "Don't take too long."

Dawn came, the sea was empty and blue as far as the eye could see.

Barclay took the glasses and stood up, scanning the horizon all the way
around. Then he said, "Make some coffee, George."

Barfield grunted and went below. In a few minutes Barclay followed
him. I could hear the low sound of their voices in the cabin. She sat across
from me in the cockpit, her face stamped with weariness. When she saw
me looking at her she tried to smile.

I turned and hurried back to her. "Go forward," I said. "Lie down on
deck, against the forward side of the cabin. Stay there. If anything happens
to me, you can raise the jib alone. Just the jib. Keep running before the
wind in a straight line and you'll hit the coast of Mexico or Texas – "

"No," she whispered fiercely.

I peeled her arms loose and pushed her. "*Hurry!*" She started to say
something more, looked at my face, and turned, running forward. She
stepped up from the cockpit and went along the starboard side of the
cabin, stumbling once and almost falling.

I had to hurry. They'd be coming up any minute. I slipped forward and
stood on the deck, looking down the hatch.

"*Surf!*" I yelled. "Surf, ho!"

Barclay came up fast, his head turning toward the direction of my arm.
I hit him hard and he went sprawling over the side. I was falling too, on
top of Barfield as he emerged from the hatch. He bulled his way up on
deck, crashing us both down on the deck. A big fist beat at my face, as
I groped for his throat. He got his gun out of his hip pocket. I chopped
his hand hard enough, and it slid out of his hand along the grating.

He hit me on the temple and my head slammed back against the planks.
He was coming to his knees, groping behind him for the gun. I tried to
push myself up, and then beyond him I saw her. She ran along the deck
and dropped into the cockpit. She picked up the gun and was swinging it
at his head. He should have fallen, but it had no more effect on him than a
dropped chocolate eclair. He heaved upward, lashing out behind him with
one big arm. She fell, and her head struck the coaming at the forward end
of the cockpit. I came to my feet and lunged at him and we fell over and

beyond her onto the edge of the deck just as the sloop rolled again and we slid over the side into the water.

I came out into sunlight and sparkling blue, and sobbed for air. Seconds went by, and I knew he wasn't coming up. He'd had the breath knocked out of him when we hit the deck, just before we slid overboard, and he'd drowned down there. I looked around again. There was no trace of Barclay.

I could hear the boat's engine behind me, fainter now, and I turned to see which way it was circling. I stared. It wasn't turning. It was two hundred yards away, going straight ahead for Yucatan with nobody at the helm. I didn't see her anywhere. She'd been knocked out when she fell. And I had lashed the tiller.

I reached down mechanically and started taking off my dungarees and slippers.

Even when you don't have anywhere to go, you keep swimming. I swam toward the boat, disappearing now, and toward the coast of Yucatan a hundred and twenty miles away. The sun was on my left. It climbed higher.

I didn't panic, but I had to be careful about letting the loneliness and immensity of it get hold of me or thinking too much about how near we had been to winning at last. I wondered if she had been killed, or badly hurt, and saw in a moment that wasn't safe either. I concentrated on swimming. One stroke, and then another stroke. Don't think. Don't think about anything.

It could have been an hour, or two hours. I looked off to the right and saw the mast. It was at least a mile away and wouldn't see me, but I gave a sob of relief that almost strangled me because it meant she was all right. She'd only been knocked out. She'd probably never find me, but she could make it.

But the time I'd spent showing Shannon navigational and boat-handling points paid off. She had no idea where I'd gone overboard, but she was cutting the whole area into a big grid, searching.

Each time the ground swell lifted me, I kicked myself as high as I could and waved. Those binoculars paid off. I could see the boat headed toward me, and I knew that Goddess had her ancestral Viking fates working for us at last.

19

We didn't have to do much talking about the way we felt. About all I could say for the next few days was "You Swede, you big, lovely, magnificent Swede." She seemed equally happy. I tried to brush aside the cloud that haunted her. Her last months with Macaulay; the strain of the chase had cut into her more deeply than I realized. I repeated the plans I had for changing the name of the boat and its port of registry; for cruising the small ports where we'd be safe from any pursuit for the eighty thousand dollars which would take care of us both for a long time. She smiled agreement each time, but her eyes gave her away. Several times she awoke at night shivering and I knew it wasn't the tropical breezes. Something continued to haunt her, to keep her from the full paradise that should have been ours.

Time stood still for us. I spent the next few days painting the name, *Freya*, and San Juan as our port of registry on the stern. My living Freya – she liked that better than Swede – helped. She was a natural at anything you taught her. She learned to use the aqualung and we spent hours at it, diving down to look at the myriad wonders of marine life. She became fascinated with it as if it were another world.

And then it happened. We were far off the Northern shelves working toward the Yucatan straits. The chart told me we were right on the hundred fathom curve. It was a very hot sunny day and Shannon suggested we go in for a swim. She was beautiful as she adjusted her mask and dived over the side. I fixed my mask and went under the hull to see if we'd begun to collect any marine growth. It was cool and pleasant, and I paused to watch the silvery flow of hair about her head as she swam beneath me.

A few minutes later I noticed a small shovel-nosed shark off to one side and below. I swam down to watch him. It was quite small and not dangerous. When I looked for Shannon she was gone. I swam to the surface but she was nowhere in sight. I began to be uneasy. But maybe she had gone back aboard for some reason. I was turning to look behind me again when a flash of silver caught the corners of my eyes at the edge of the mask. I froze with horror. She was at least a hundred feet below me, going straight down.

Why had she done it? It had been an accident. It must have been. She was deliriously happy with me. She had no reason for throwing her life away. The pressure must have twisted her sense of direction. She'd been confused, and I'd been too far away to help.

No! She'd known exactly what she was doing. There had been hints. She'd known the violence and the terror of being hunted and had said there's no escape. That's why she'd looked at me as if I were an innocent child when I ranted about those little ports. She knew we'd never get away with it.

Alone, I found myself sighting again for 23.50 north, 88.45 west, the spot where she'd gone down. Macaulay could be right. It could be possible to find a pinpoint in the Gulf. There was the exact spot! See, where that seagull is on that drift wood. Looking down into the water I could see a silvery shape.

It was beckoning up at me. I heard her voice say, "Come with me, we'll live in rapture."

Something heavy was on my shoulders. I felt straps across my chest. I was wearing the aqualung.

I screamed.

I can still close my eyes and see the whole thing – the blue, and that last, haunting flash of silver, gesturing as it died. It was beckoning. Toward the rapture. The rapture . . .

20

It was after 2 a.m. when the master of the *Joseph H. Hallock* closed the journal. The poor devil, he thought. The poor, tortured devil. Four o'clock – and we raised the sloop a little after five.

Changing the name of the sloop didn't alter the identity of any kind of seagoing craft. There were papers. And more papers. It was as futile as writing your own name on a borrowed passport. Manning should have known, too, that it took about ten pounds of paperwork and red tape to dock at any foreign port – including fishing villages. They all had port authorities, and they all demanded consular clearances and bills of health from the last port of call; registry certificate, customs lists, crew lists, and so on, ad infinitum, and in the case of pleasure craft they probably required passports and visas for everybody aboard. Manning should have known they didn't have a prayer of a chance.

He was in his bunk puzzling over it. Suddenly he sat upright. "I'll be damned," he said softly. "I'll just be damned. It would be perfect."

It was sunset again, two days later. The tanker was waddling, full-bellied, up the coast of-Florida just south of Fowey Rocks. She was well inshore from the main axis of the Stream, since they had made arrangements by radio to have a Coast Guard boat meet them off Miami and take the *Freya* off their hands. Or at least that was the master's excuse to Mr Davidson, the mate.

When you resolved the contradiction and acknowledged that Manning couldn't possibly have believed any of that moonlit dream about escape to the tropics in a boat, he mused, what did you have left? You had left the twin facts that Manning was a writer, and that he was trying to save himself and that girl he was so much in love with.

They had nowhere to go, the girl had said. Nowhere to go, that is, as long as they were being sought by a gang of criminals and also by the police. But if they weren't being actively sought by anyone, they could come back to their own country, where they would attract less attention than anywhere else on earth. And they would no longer be sought if everyone believed them dead.

But I don't know any of this, he thought. I'm only theorizing. I don't really want to know, absolutely and finally, because I'd be obligated to report it. They hadn't committed any real crime, unless it was a crime to defend oneself, and he hoped they got away with it.

Then he saw what he had been watching for, astern and slightly inshore from the *Freya*. It could be driftwood, or it could be a head, or two heads. He peered aft in the gathering twilight, and almost raised the glasses.

No, he thought reluctantly; if I *know* I have to report it. But nobody is interested in the unverified vaporings of a sentimental old man.

They would make it ashore without any trouble, with the lifebelts. And they probably had enough money to buy some clothes to replace their bathing suits. Not that they would be likely to attract any attention in Florida, however, if they went around in their bathing attire for years.

But they were drifting back rapidly. Would he have to lift the glasses to satisfy himself? The objects separated momentarily for an instant before they merged again as one. And one of them had been definitely lighter in color than the other. The master sighed.

"Bon voyage," he said softly. He turned and went into the chartroom with the glasses still swinging from his neck.

BLACK

Paul Cain

THE MAN SAID: "McCary."

"No." I shook my head and started to push past him, and he said: "McCary," again thickly, and then he crumpled into a heap on the wet sidewalk.

It was dark there, there wasn't anyone on the street – I could have walked away. I started to walk away and then the sucker instinct got the best of me and I went back and bent over him.

I shook him and said: "Come on, chump – get up out of the puddle."

A cab came around the corner and its headlights shone on me – and there I was, stooping over a drunk whom I'd never seen before, who thought my name was McCary. Any big-town driver would have pegged it for a stick-up, would have shoved off or sat still. That wasn't a big town – the cab slid alongside the curb and a fresh-faced kid stuck his face into the light from the meter and said: "Where to?"

I said: "No place." I ducked my head at the man on the sidewalk. "Maybe this one'll ride – he's paralyzed."

The kid clucked: "Tch, tch."

He opened the door and I stooped over and took hold of the drunk under his armpits and jerked him up and across the sidewalk and into the cab. He was heavy in a funny limp way. There was a hard bulge on his left side, under the arm.

I had an idea. I asked the kid: "Who's McCary?"

He looked self-consciously blank for a minute and then he said: "There's two – Luke and Ben. Luke's the old man – owns a lot of real estate. Ben runs a pool-hall."

"Let's go see Ben," I said. I got into the cab.

We went several blocks down the dark street and then I tapped on the glass and motioned to the kid to pull over to the curb. He stopped and slid the glass and I said: "Who's McCary?"

"I told you."

I said: "What about him?"

The kid made the kind of movement with his shoulders that would pass for a shrug in the sticks. "I told you – he runs a pool-hall."

I said: "Listen. This guy came up to me a few minutes ago and said 'McCary' – this guy is very dead."

The kid looked like he was going to jump out of the cab. His eyes were hanging out.

I waited.

The kid swallowed. He said: "Let's dump him."

I shook my head slightly and waited.

"Ben and the old man don't get along – they've been raising hell the last couple of weeks. This is the fourth." He jerked his head towards the corpse beside me.

"Know him?"

He shook his head and then – to be sure – took a flashlight out of the side-pocket and stuck it back through the opening and looked at the man's dead face. He shook his head again.

I said: "Let's go see Ben."

"You're crazy, Mister. If this is one of Ben's boys he'll tie you up to it, and if it ain't . . ."

"Let's go see Ben."

Ben McCary was a blond fat man, about forty – he smiled a great deal.

We sat in a little office above his pool-hall and he smiled heartily across all his face and said: "Well, sir – what can I do for you?"

"My name is Black. I came over from St Paul – got in about a half hour ago."

He nodded, still with the wide hearty smile; stared at me cordially out of his wide-set blue eyes.

I went on: "I heard there was a lot of noise over here and I thought I might make a connection – pick up some change."

McCary juggled his big facial muscles into something resembling innocence.

"I don't know just what you mean, Buddy," he said. "What's your best game?"

"What's yours?"

He grinned again. "Well," he said, "you can get plenty of action up in the front room."

I said: "Don't kid me, Mister McCary. I didn't come over here to play marbles."

He looked pleasantly blank.

"I used to work for Dickie Johnson down in K C," I went on.

"Who sent you to me?"

"Man named Lowry – that's the name on the label of his coat. He's dead."

McCary moved a little in his chair but didn't change his expression.

"I came in on the nine-fifty train," I went on, "and started walking uptown to a hotel. Lowry came up to me over on Dell Street and said 'McCary,' and fell down. He's outside in a cab – stiff."

McCary looked up at the ceiling and then down at the desk. He said: "Well, well" – and took a skinny little cigar out of a box in one of the desk-drawers and lighted it. He finally got around to looking at me again and said: "Well, well," again.

I didn't say anything.

After he'd got the cigar going, he turned another of his big smiles on and said: "How am I supposed to know you're on the level?"

I said: "I'll bite. What do *you* think?"

He laughed. "I like you," he said. "By – ! I like you."

I said I thought that was fine and, "Now let's try to do some business."

"Listen," he said. "Luke McCary has run this town for thirty years. He ain't my old man – he married my mother and insisted on my taking his name."

He puffed slowly at his cigar. "I guess I was a pretty ornery kid" – he smiled boyishly – "when I came home from school I got into a jam – you know – kid stuff. The old man kicked me out."

I lighted a cigarette and leaned back.

"I went down to South America for about ten years, and then I went to Europe. I came back here two years ago and everything was all right for a while and then the old man and I got to scrapping again."

I nodded.

"He'd had everything his own way too long. I opened this place about three months ago and took a lot of his gambling business away – a lot of the shipyard men and miners . . ."

McCary paused, sucked noisily at his cigar.

"Luke went clean off his nut," he went on. "He thought I was going to take it all away from him . . ." McCary brought his big fist down hard on the desk. "And by the – ! I *am*. Lowry's the third man of mine in two weeks. It's plenty in the open now."

I said: "How about Luke's side?"

"We got one of the – " he said. "A runner."

"It isn't entirely over the gambling concession?"

"Hell, no. That's all it was at first. All I wanted was to make a living. Now I've got two notch-joints at the other end of town. I've got a swell protection in with the law and I'm building up a liquor business that would knock your eye out."

I asked: "Is Luke in it by himself?"

McCary shook his head slowly. "He don't show anywhere. There's a fellah named Stokes runs the works for him – a young fellah. They been partners nearly eight years. It's all in Stokes' name . . ."

"What does Stokes look like?"

"Tall – about your build. Shiny black hair, and a couple of big gold teeth" – McCary tapped his upper front teeth with a fat finger – "here."

I said: "How much is he worth to you?"

McCary stood up. He leaned across the desk and grinned down at me and said: "Not a nickel." His eyes were wide and clear like a baby's. He said slowly: "The old man is worth twenty-five hundred smackers to *you.*"

I didn't say anything and McCary sat down and opened another drawer and took out a bottle of whiskey. He poured a couple of drinks.

"I think the best angle for you," he said, "is to go to Stokes and give him the same proposition you gave me. Nobody saw you come in here. It's the only way you can get near the old man."

I nodded. We drank.

"By – ! I like your style," he said. "I've been trying to get along with an outfit of yokels."

We smiled at one another. I was glad he said he liked me because I knew he didn't like me at all. I was one up on him, I didn't like him very well either.

Stokes sat on a corner of the big library-table, his long legs dangling.

He said: "You're airing Ben – how do we know you'll play ball with us?" His eyes were stony.

I looked at the old man. I said: "I don't like that fat – son of yours – and I never double-cross the best offer."

Luke McCary was a thin little man with a pinched red face, bushy white hair. He sat in a big armchair on the other side of the table, his head and neck and wild white hair sticking up out of the folds of a heavy blue bathrobe.

He looked at me sharply. He said: "I don't want any part of it."

"Then I'll have to act on the best offer."

Stokes grinned.

The old man stood up. He said: "Why – damn you and your guts . . ." He opened a humidor on the table and took out a small automatic. "I can shoot the buttons off your vest, young fella . . . I can shoot you for a yegg right now, and no one'll ever know the difference . . ."

I said: "*You'll* know the difference – for not having taken advantage of talent, when you had the chance."

He put the automatic back in the box and sat down and smiled gently at Stokes.

Stokes was looking at the floor. He said: "Five grand if you wipe out the whole outfit. Run 'em out of town, stick 'em in jail, poison 'em . . . Anything."

"Wouldn't you like a new railroad station too?"

They didn't say anything for a minute. They looked at me.

I went on: "No sale. I'll take care of Ben for that – but busting up the organization would mean sending for a few friends – would cost a hell of a lot more than five . . ."

The old man looked the least bit scared for a second – then he said: "Ben'll do."

"How about laying something on the line?"

Stokes said: "Don't be silly."

The old man cackled. "Well I never saw such guts," he said.

I said: "All right, gentlemen. Maybe I'll call you later."

Stokes went downstairs with me. He smiled in a strange way. "I never knew the old man to go for anything that looks as tricky as this. I guess it looks good because Ben thinks you're working for him."

I nodded. I said: "Uh huh – Ben's a swell guy. He'll probably blast me on sight."

"I don't think you'll find him at his joint."

I waited and Stokes leaned against the door, said: "There's a big outfit downstate that's been running twelve trucks a week through here from the Border. They've paid off for this division of the highway for years – to the old man. The last two convoys have been hi-jacked at Four-mile Creek, north of town – a couple drivers were killed . . ."

He paused, looked wise a minute, went on: "That was Ben. There was a convoy due through last night – they run in bunches of four, or six – it didn't show up. It's a cinch for tonight – and that's where Ben'll be."

I said: "That's fine. How do I get there?"

Stokes told me to follow the main highway north, and where to take the cutoff that crossed Four-mile. I thanked him and went out.

I walked down to a drugstore on the corner and called a cab. When it came, I got in and had the driver jockey around until he was parked in a spot where I could watch the front door of the McCary house.

After a while, Stokes came out and got into a roadster and snorted up past us and turned down the side street. I told the driver to follow him. I don't think the driver knew who it was. It didn't matter a hell of a lot anyway.

I got out and told the driver to wait and walked on down Dell Street, keeping close to the fence. It was raining pretty hard again. I passed the place where Lowry had come up to me, and I went on to the corner; and then went back the same way until I came to the narrow gate I had missed in the darkness.

It was more a door than a gate, set flush with the high fence. I finagled with the latch for a while and then pushed the gate open slowly and went into a yard. It was a big yard, full of old lumber and old box-car trucks – stuff like that. There was a long shed along one side, and a small two-story building on the far side.

I stumbled along as quietly as I could towards the building and then I went around the corner of a big pile of ties, and Stokes' roadster was sitting there very dark and quiet in the rain. I went past it and up to the building and along the wall until I saw the lighted window.

I had to rustle around quietly and find a box and stand on it to see through the little square window. The panes were dirty; the inside looked like a time-office. Stokes and Ben McCary and another man were there. They were arguing about something. McCary was walking around waving his arms; Stokes and the other man were sitting down. I couldn't hear a word they said. The rain was roaring on the tin-roof of the shed and all I could hear was a buzz of voices.

I didn't stay there very long. It didn't mean anything. I got down and put the box back and wandered around until I found McCary's car. Anyway, I guessed it was his car. It was a big touring-car and it was parked near the gate on the opposite side of the block from Dell Street, where Stokes had come in.

I got in and sat in the back seat. The side-curtains were drawn and it was nice to get out of the rain for a while.

In about ten minutes, the light went out and I could hear voices coming towards the car. I sat down on the floor. The three of them stood outside for a minute talking about "a call from Harry" – then Stokes and the other man went off towards Stokes' car, and McCary squeezed into the front seat and stepped on the starter.

I waited till we had burned through the gate and were halfway up the block, and then I put a gun against the back of McCary's neck. He straightened out in the seat and eased the brake on. I told him to go on to the old man's house.

We sat in the big room upstairs. The old man sat in the big armchair by the table, and Ben sat across from him. I was half lying down in another chair out of the circle of light and I had the gun on my lap.

The old man was fit to be tied. He was green with hate and he kept glaring at Ben out of his little red-rimmed eyes.

I said: "Well, gran'pa – if you'll make out that check now, we'll finish this business."

The old man swallowed.

"You can give me *your* twenty-five hundred in cash," I went on to Ben. "Then I'll put the chill on both of you – and everybody'll be happy."

They must have thought I meant it. Ben got rigid, and the old man cleared his throat and made a slow pass at the humidor.

I fiddled with the gun. I threw a pack of cigarettes on the table and said: "Smoke?"

The old man looked at the cigarettes and at the gun in my hand, and relaxed.

I said: "Still and all – it don't quite square with my weakness for efficiency, yet. Maybe you boys'll get together and make me an offer for Stokes. He's the star – he's been framing both of you."

I don't think Ben was very surprised – but the old man looked like he'd swallowed a mouse.

"He's been in with Ben on the truck heistings," I went on. "He's been waiting for a good spot to dump you – working on your connections."

The old man said: "That's a – damned lie."

"Suit yourself."

I went on to Ben: "He made the five-grand offer for your hide, in Luke's name, tonight – and he gave me the Four-mile steer . . ." I hesitated a moment. "Only you wouldn't try three in the same spot, would you?"

Ben finally got his smile working. He started to say something but I interrupted him:

"Stokes told me you rubbed the two boys on the trucks, too."

Ben's smile went out like a light. He said: "Stokes shot both those men himself – and there wasn't any need for it. They were lined up alongside the road . . ."

Something in the soft way he said it made it sound good.

I said: "He'll be around your place – no?"

"He went home."

Ben gave me the number and I called up, but there wasn't any answer.

We sat there without saying anything for several minutes, and then the door downstairs opened and closed and somebody came up.

I said to Ben: "What'll you bet?"

The door opened and Stokes came in. He had a long gray raincoat on and it made him look even taller and thinner than he was. He stood in the doorway looking mostly at the old man; then he came in and sat down on a corner of the table.

I said: "Now that the class is all here, you can start bidding."

The old man laughed deep in his throat. Stokes was watching me expressionlessly, and Ben sat smiling stupidly at his hands.

"I'm auctioning off the best little town in the state, gentlemen," I went on. "Best schools, sewage system, post-office . . . Best street-lighting, water supply . . ."

I was having a swell time.

The old man was staring malevolently at Stokes. "I'll give you twenty-five thousand dollars," he said to me, "to give me that pistol and get out of here."

If I'd thought there was any chance of collecting, I might have talked to him. Things happen that way sometimes.

I looked at my watch and put the gun down on the arm of the chair where it looked best and picked up the phone.

I asked Ben: "Where's the business going to be pulled off tonight?"

Ben wanted to be nice. He said: "A coffee joint about six miles north of town." He glanced at Stokes. "This – tried to swing it back to Four-mile when he thought you'd be there sniping for me."

"The boys are there now?"

He nodded. "The trucks have been stopping there to eat lately."

I asked the operator for long-distance, and asked for the Bristol Hotel in Talley, the first town north. The connection went right through. I asked for Mister Cobb.

When he answered, I told him about the coffee place, and that I wasn't sure about it; and told him he'd find the stuff that had been heisted in the sheds of the yard on Dell Street. I wasn't sure of that either, but I watched Ben and Stokes when I said it and it looked all right. Cobb told me that he'd gotten into Talley with the convoy about midnight and had been waiting for my call since then.

I hung up. "There'll be some swell fireworks out there," I said. "There's a sub-machine-gun on every truck – double crews. And it don't matter much," I went on to Ben, "how good your steer is. They'll be watching out all the way."

Stokes stood up.

I picked up the gun. "Don't move so far, Skinny," I said. "It makes me nervous."

He stood there staring at the gun. The water was running off his raincoat and it had formed into a little dark pool at his feet.

He said: "What the hell do you want?"

"I wanted you to know that one of the kids you shot up last week at Four-mile was my boss' brother. He went along for the ride."

I don't think Stokes could move. I think he tried to move sidewise or get his hand into his pocket, or something, but all he could do was take a deep breath. Then I shot him in the middle of the body where he shot the kid, and he sank down on the floor with his legs crossed under him, like a tailor.

The old man didn't get up. He sat a little deeper in his chair and stared at Stokes.

Ben moved very fast for a fat man. He was up and out the door like a bat out of hell. That was OK with me – he couldn't get to the coffee place before the trucks got there. I had the keys to his car, and it was too far anyway.

I got up and put the rod away and went over to the table and picked up my cigarettes. I looked down at the old man, said: "Things'll be a little quieter now, maybe. You'll get the dough for haulage through your territory, as usual. See that it gets through."

He didn't answer.

I started for the door and then there was a shot out in front of the house. I ran on down to the front door. It was open and Ben was flat on the threshold – had fallen smack on his face, half through the door.

I ducked back through the hall and tried a couple locked doors. When I came up through the hall again, the old man was on his knees beside Ben, and was rocking back and forth, moaning a little.

I went through another room and into the kitchen and on through, out the back door. I crossed the backyard and jumped a low fence and walked through another yard to a gate that led into an alley. I sloshed along through the mud until I came to a cross-street, and went on down to the corner that was diagonally across the block from the McCary house.

A cab came down the street and I waited until it was almost to the corner, stepped out in front of it. The driver swerved and stepped on the gas, but he had slowed enough to give me time to jump on the running-board.

I stuck my head in to the light from the meter. That turned out to be my best hunch of the evening because in another second, the driver would have opened up my chest with one of the dirtiest looking .45's I ever saw, at about two feet. It was the kid who had picked Lowry and me up. He hesitated just long enough when he saw who I was.

We nearly ran into a tree and I had time to reach in and knock that cannon out of his hand. He stepped on the brake, and reached for the gun, but I beat him to it by a hair and stuck it in my overcoat pocket and got in beside him.

I said: "Shame on you – almost crashing an old pal like me."

He sat tight in the seat and got a weak grin working and said: "Where to?"

"Just away."

We went on through the mud and rain, and turned into a slightly better lighted street.

I said: "How did you know Ben shot Lowry?"

The kid kept his head down, his eyes ahead. "Lowry and me have lived together for two years," he said. "He used to be in the hack racket too, till he got mixed up with McCary . . ."

"Lowry won a lot of jack in one of Ben's crap games a couple days ago, and Ben wanted him to kick back with it – said everybody that worked for him was automatically a shill, and couldn't play for keeps. But Lowry's been dropping every nickel he made in the same game, for months. That was okay with Ben. It was all right to lose, but you mustn't win."

I nodded, lighted a cigarette.

"Ben shot Lowry tonight at the joint on Dell Street. I know it was him because Lowry's been afraid of it – and that's why he said 'McCary.'"

"Did you know it was Lowry when you picked us up?"

"Not until I used the light. Then, when we got to Ben's I saw him get out of his car and go in just ahead of you – then I was sure. I took Lowry up to his pa's after you went in."

The kid drove me to the next town south. I forget the name. I got a break on a train – I only had to wait about ten minutes.

FINDERS KILLERS!

John D. MacDonald

1

WE WAITED FOR him to run, because that was the final proof of guilt that we needed. We had him bottled up in a Chicago apartment. Our boys drove the cabs, delivered the milk, cleaned the street in front and in general covered him like a big tent. I don't know exactly how we gave it away. But we did. We threw it to him.

You can say we were careless. That's in the same league with Monday morning quarterbacking. Our excuse was that we didn't know he was tipped. He walked into the apartment house and never came out again. Three hours later when we took the wire and tape off the fat woman across the hall from where he had lived, we learned how he'd used that cold, dark, drizzly evening to good advantage.

She was a tall woman, and fat. We knew he wore size 10B shoes. Hers were 9A. He tapped at her door. He hit her so hard that she still remembers hearing the tapping, but she can't remember opening the door. Figuring the rest was easy. He merely undressed and wrapped his own clothes around his middle, tying them in place. Then he got into her clothes. He took her raincape and a big floppy hat. Maybe he'd taken the precaution of shaving himself closely. Maybe not. It was a dark night.

He walked out. Aragon, holding the night glasses on the apartment door, didn't spot him. The boys in the cellar played back the recording of him going to bed. It was a sensitive pickup. I heard the shoes drop, the springs creak, the sleepy yawn.

And that was the way Torran walked out on us – walked out with two hundred and forty thousand dollars in brand new treasury notes in five-hundred dollar denominations – all in serial sequence, most of it still in the mint wrappers. In addition he had an estimated twenty-five thousand in smaller bills, all used stuff. He had a lot of the bonds, too. Negotiable stuff. Very hot. Even if they'd just dumped out the bank guards without the holes in the backs of their heads, the bonds would have been hot.

They had carried the guards across the Connecticut line before dumping them out. Torran and Holser. We knew that much. We didn't have to worry about Holser. Some kids on a picnic found Holser a hundred feet from the highway. The thigh had gone bad under the dirty bandage. There was a hole in the back of his head. The slug matched the ones taken from the two guards.

There is not the slightest point in going over the history of how we located Torran. It was dull work. It took seven months. Then we had him bottled. We still couldn't be certain that there wasn't a third party involved. So we watched him. I was the one who advised against moving in and grabbing him. "Wait a little," I said. "He'll either run some more, or he'll have company." Either way, I thought, we couldn't lose.

I'd been with it for seven months. By painstaking spade work I'd uncovered the initial lead that eventually led to him. I was a hero. So Torran slipped away. So I was a bum.

It took three days to prove we hadn't the faintest idea whether he'd left town, and if so, how, and in what direction.

Broughton called me in.

His eyebrows look like white caterpillars. He looks like a deacon in the neighborhood church. He's the Broughton who went into that New Orleans hotel room in '37. He expected one man to be in there. There was a slip. There were four of them. When it was over, Broughton was still standing up. The lead he was carrying didn't pull him down until he got back out into the hall. *That* Broughton!

"Sit down, Gandy," he said.

I sat. No excuses. They never go.

"Washington is disturbed, Gandy," he said.

"As well they might be, Mr Broughton."

"I've watched you carefully, Gandy. You've got a lot of presence. You speak well and you think clearly. But you're too ambitious. You expect too much, too fast."

"And?"

"And I could butter you up to keep you aboard. During your four years with us, you've done well. But now you're marked. You saw what the papers did to us. That was unfortunate. Now you're not Agent Gandy any more in Washington. You're Russ Gandy, the one who lost Torran."

"So I lost him. So I'll find him again."

"That's what I'm trying to tell you. You're being reassigned to duty with the School."

"Why are you telling me this?"

He looked at me and the blue eyes went hard and then softened. "I was pretty ambitious for a while, Gandy. Until the afternoon I had Barrows trapped and he walked away from it."

"I see," I said. I stood up. I was too mad to stay sitting. "Suppose I go find him anyway?"

"Not as an employee of the Bureau. A private citizen has no standing."

"Do I have your permission to dictate a resignation to your secretary?"

He shrugged. "Go ahead. Make it effective as of now."

With my hand on the doorknob I turned and said, "Thanks."

He looked as though he had already forgotten me. "Oh . . . that's all right, Gandy. Just remember that this talk was off the record."

"Of course."

After I dictated the resignation and signed it, I went and cleaned out my desk. In four years I'd cleaned out a lot of desks. This was different. There was no new desk waiting.

My file on Torran belonged to the Bureau. I flipped through it. I knew it by heart. I took out two pictures – not the best two – but good enough, folded them and stuffed them in my pocket. They'd been taken with a telephoto lens from the window across the way where Aragon was holed up.

I left the office without kissing anyone good-by. The check would be sent to my bank marked for deposit. Four hundred and twenty something. The last check.

I went back to the crummy room I'd rented and in which I'd spent only sleeping time. On four years of salary and expenses, when all you think about night and day is a job of work, you save dough. I looked at the bankbook. Twenty-nine hundred in the savings account. Four thousand in the checking account.

I'd left the little badge and the Bureau weapon and the identification card with Broughton. I sat on the bed and cried without making a sound. Like a kid. He'd been too right. I was ambitious. And they'd taken away my toys.

What the hell was Torran to me now? I took out the pictures. I looked at them. One was an enlargement of the face. Aragon had caught him just as he came out into the sunlight. Torran. A bad boy. No punk. Thirty-four, approximately. Eight of those thirty-four years had been spent in prison. Auburn, Atlanta, Ossining. Armed robbery. Extortion. Now it was a big one. Bank robbery, kidnaping and murder.

The joker was that he looked like a nice guy. Big mouth, slightly crooked nose. Laugh wrinkles around the eyes. The old prison pictures were no good because he'd been out for five years. In the picture he looked like he was on the verge of smiling. Or laughing – at me. How do you figure a guy like that? You can't blame society. Good family, good education. So he was just a wrongo. One of those guys who work twice as hard as anyone else while they try to make it the "easy" way.

Now he had made a big strike. But keeping it was a horse of a new shade.

I looked at the pictures and called him everything in the book. I went out and had a steak; then bought a bottle, brought it home and killed it. It came close to killing me. When I woke up after fifteen hours of sleep it was nine in the morning.

Torran's pictures were on the floor. I picked them up and cursed him some more. It was easier to hate him than to hate myself. Before the war I was an accountant. One year at a desk telling myself I'd get used to it sooner or later. Then five years of war to prove to me that I couldn't settle down. I took the exams and made the Bureau.

After four years it had begun to look to me as though pretty soon I'd be telling J. Edgar to move over and make room for new blood. I liked the chase and I liked to catch them. But you try to be too smart – you try to move too fast. Boom.

I wanted to catch Torran. I wanted to catch him so very bad I could taste it.

But what can one man do? Now the Bureau would be going after him twice as hard. Good sense would have said to drop it. I went in and looked at myself in the mirror. I didn't look so sensible. In fact, I thought I looked a little bit like some of the boys I'd caught during the last four years. Long hard face with heavy bones. Lids that cover maybe too much of the eyes at the outer corners. Big stubborn cleft chin. Hair that's mine, but looks as though it were made from the end of the tail of a handy horse. Beard stubble. I shaved it off. My hand shook. I stopped now and then to drink more water. I got so full of water I wondered when I'd start to make sloshing noises.

After three cups of coffee at the corner café, I could think again. What Broughton had said about private citizens stuck in my head.

My local contacts weren't too bad. By late afternoon it was fixed. In three days I'd have my license as a private investigator in the State of Illinois. License and a permit to carry a gun. So I got in the car and went to Boston. Once you start to do something, you can keep on even though you know it isn't smart.

I left Chicago on Monday at six p.m. I went through Toledo, Cleveland, Buffalo, Syracuse and Albany. I was in Boston at eight o'clock on Tuesday. I went to bed, got up at eight in the morning and located the house in Newton Center where May Marie Sipsol lived with her aunt. It was her bearer bonds that Torran had taken along with the cash. It was just her bad luck that her daddy died exactly when he did.

She was a blonde with a skin like milk in a blue glass – a trembly uncertain mouth, and eyes so close together they threatened to overlap. She wanted none of me. She was a timid eighteen. She spoke of the authorities and what they were doing and she said she couldn't pay me. I said I didn't want pay. I said I wanted a percentage on recovery. I said ten would be enough. The bonds totaled a ten thousand face. Eleven thousand for Russ.

We were alone in a room with Italian antique furniture. It smelled like dust. When I realized that she meant what she said, I took her by the shoulders and shook her until her eyes didn't focus. Her aunt came in and bellowed at me. I pushed the aunt out of the room and locked the door. May Marie whimpered. I shook her again and she wanted to kiss me. Her breath was bad.

Pretty soon she decided that this was a "great love" and that I was a very dramatic type and it was all pretty much like out of a Raymond Chandler movie. By the time the cops the aunt had called started beating on the door, I had our little contract all signed and tucked into the back of my wallet – the wallet with the little holes where the gold badge had been pinned.

She gave the cops and her aunt undiluted hell. She raged like an anemic tigress. I held my breath and kissed her again and left with my contract.

I was back to Chicago on Thursday afternoon. I picked up my documents, bought a .357 Magnum, phoned the office and found out from my only friend there that – in cautious doubletalk – Torran was still at large.

On Friday morning I got up and went to work. I went on the basis that he had left town. Assuming that, I knew he was too smart to use any common carrier. He had no car. So he had stolen a car. Most cars not stolen for repaint and resale are recovered. He wouldn't drive it too far. Not Torran. He'd want to get well out of town. An hour out, or maybe two. I went to headquarters and my pretty new documents gave me the in I needed. Torran had left the apartment house at eight o'clock on a Thursday evening. I copied down a list of the cars stolen after eight and before ten. I was informed that my ex-coworkers had been in. That was all right with me.

One, and the one I liked the best, I almost missed, because it wasn't reported until nearly midnight. The people had gone to a movie eight blocks from where we had Torran bottled up. Their car, a black Pontiac sedan, 1947 model, had been left in the parking lot near the theater. They'd gone into the theater at twenty after eight. That made sense. Torran was smart enough to pick a car that had just been parked, and he'd have had time to get there and watch the lot entrance. He wouldn't want a flashy car.

There was a blue check after the entry. I looked it up in the recovery register. Recovered in Beloit, Wisconsin, on Friday – reported to the Chicago police at one in the afternoon. They had informed the owner and he had said he'd go up and get it Saturday.

None of the others looked as promising.

Friday noon I was in Beloit. When I made inquiries about the car, the local cops gave me a bored look and said that it had already been checked by the Bureau.

After I smiled enough, they let me know the facts. It was on the main drag in a meter zone. It had been tagged for all night parking, then tagged again for overtime in a meter Friday morning. Then they checked against stolen car numbers and towed it in and told Chicago. The answer to my big question was disappointing. Were there any cars stolen from here Thursday night – any time between ten and two? Sorry, no. No missing persons – with car and all? Nope.

A sour lead, and I couldn't tell if I was right. I went back to Chicago and checked out of my room. I waited until night before leaving. Then I left from the parking lot street at eight-thirty. I was Torran, wearing woman's clothes. My feet hurt. I was in a stolen car. I wanted to shed the clothes.

I took Route 20 out through Elgin. I stayed well within the speed limits, as no doubt Torran had done. I pretended it was raining. I looked for a chance to change my clothes. I'd need some sort of shelter from the rain, or else have to do it in the car. The longer I kept my own clothes wrapped around me, the more wrinkled and conspicuous they'd get. The ideal spot would be one where I could change and also ditch the women's clothes.

That's a tough assignment on a rainy night in a heavily populated section. I didn't have much hope of it working out. He could have pulled off in any number of places after leaving Starks. At Rockford I turned right on Route 51. I crossed from South Beloit over into Beloit and parked as near as I could to where the car had been found. It was twenty-five after ten. Allow Torran ten minutes to change and he would have gotten in just before quarter to eleven at the latest.

I lit a cigarette and sat in the car for a few minutes trying to think. I went for a walk. Three blocks away was a bus station. Every night a southbound bus left for Rockford, La Salle, Bloomington, Decatur and Vandalia at eleven-fifteen. I liked that one. The hunted animal doubles back on its tracks.

I found the driver having coffee. I asked him if he'd taken the bus on that run the previous Thursday week. He took a tattered mimeographed schedule out of his inside pocket, studied it and said that he had. I asked him if he remembered any specific people on that trip and he gave me a look of complete disgust. "I drive one hell of a lot of buses," he said. I showed him the picture of Torran. It rang no bell.

He warmed up a bit for a five-dollar tip. I sat beside him with my coffee. "Now think back. Did *anything* happen that was unusual that night? It was raining. Remember? Anything at all that might have puzzled you?"

He started to shake his head slowly and then stopped shaking it. He looked into space for a moment. "Now wait a minute. I don't know if this is anything or not. I make my Bloomington stop. Below there, some place just outside Heyworth, a car goes by me doing maybe ninety. Up ahead it slows down to a creep and I got to pass it. Zoom, it goes by me again. Looks like a girl driving. She slows up again and I got to pass her. Then she scoots by again and I don't ever catch up to her again. The third time she goes by she leans on the horn like she was saying hello to somebody. You know – shave and a haircut, two bits."

"Could she have been looking for somebody on the bus?"

"That's what I was thinking."

"Anybody get off at Decatur?"

"Three or four, I think."

"Nothing funny about them, about any one of them?"

"Now, you know, I just remembered. One of them had a ticket to Vandalia, but she got off at Decatur."

"She?"

"Yeah. Big heavy woman with no baggage."

"And a big hat?"

"Damn if that isn't right! One hell of a big hat!"

I added another five to what he already had. I thanked him and went to the ticket office and got a timetable of that late run. It's roughly a hundred and forty miles from Beloit due south to Bloomington. Even with two stops the bus made it in under three hours, getting to Bloomington at ten after two in the morning.

I was in Bloomington at ten minutes of two. A bored man with gray pouches under his eyes lounged behind the ticket grille.

"Were you on a week ago Thursday at this time?"

He yawned. "I'm on every night, friend. In the daytime I try to sleep. The neighborhood is full of kids. I'm learning to hate children."

"Would you remember if someone, it might have been a girl, just missed the southbound bus from Beloit to Vandalia?"

"If you'd come around a year from now, friend, I'd still remember the lady. You don't see much of that material in bus stations. She came plunging in here five minutes after number seventy had pulled out."

"Nice?"

"About five eight. She stood right where you're standing. Hair like harvest wheat – with rain beads caught in it. Moon-pool eyes, pal, and a funny, tough, scratchy little voice, like a tired phonograph needle. She asked me if the bus had left and I said yes and away she went. It was like she pulled me along on a string. I went right to the door. She got into a big gray sedan and went away from here so fast that the tires yelped."

"What make?"

"Oh, the car? Who knows? Big and new. Cad, Buick, Packard. Take any car. Say, that's pretty good! Take any car."

"A dark-eyed blonde. Hair cut short?"

"Nope. Nice and long. The kind to run barefoot through."

"Age?"

"Twenty-two, three, four."

"Clothes?"

"Brother, I was too busy taking them off to take a look at them. Something green, I think. But it could have been blue."

At Decatur I found that I was too close to falling asleep at the wheel, so I checked in at a hotel. In the morning I bought a road atlas and took it into the sandwich shop with me to read while having breakfast. I looked at the map with the idea of trying to outguess them – rather to guess the way they would.

Obviously Torran had phoned from some place along his escape route and told the girl his plan. I had them spotted at Decatur in the rain in her car with Torran still in his disguise and with dawn not too many hours away. Either they were going to make a long run for it together, or she was going to take him to some hideout. If he had called from Beloit – which seemed the most probable, then I could draw a circle two hundred miles in radius around Bloomington and safely assume that she had roared over to Bloomington from some place within that circle.

It didn't look as though she could have made it from St Louis. If she had to get ready for a trip, Springfield might be a logical starting point. Yet, if it were Springfield, why not let Torran ride all the way to Decatur? If it were Peoria, she should have been in Bloomington in plenty of time. Galesburg seemed just about right. If she'd been in Chicago, then why hadn't he gone to see her before he began to suspect that he was being covered?

At any rate, Torran was going to be too smart to make any two-hundred mile run in a big car at that time of night. There are two many town cops who like to wake themselves up in the small hours by hauling down big cars on the road. Torran had gotten into Decatur by bus at just about three in the morning. He hadn't seen the blonde in a long time. He needed to change back to his own clothes. Everything pointed to their holing up close to Decatur. A tourist court was indicated. I was in for some routine legwork.

2

I hit twelve places before lunch. Each place I hit drained some of the confidence out of me. The second place after lunch was called the Sunset Rest Courts and it was three miles out of town on Route 36 heading east.

The woman was very brisk and friendly. "Yes, we had a girl and her mother register a week ago Thursday – I should say Friday morning at three-fifteen. The girl woke me up. We had a light burning that night because we had a vacancy. She said she had planned on driving all night but her mother was taken sick. Nothing serious."

"A blond girl?"

"Yes. Quite pretty. I showed her the vacant room and she seemed satisfied. Here's the register card."

I looked at it. Mrs Walter B. Richardson and Anne Richardson, of Moline. Make of car – Buick. License – Illinois 6c424. All in angular backhand script – finishing school script. I wrote down the license number, fairly certain that they had taken advantage of the dark night to put down the wrong number.

"Are you from the police? Is something wrong? We've never had any trouble here. We try to run a – "

"You're in no trouble. I'm just looking for someone. This won't even get on the records. Do you know which way they went?"

"Well, Mrs Richardson must have recovered in a terrific hurry. They left here a little after seven. They went out of here so fast that I actually dressed and went over to see if they'd taken anything from the room. I can see the road from my bed. They went up the highway, heading east, and then turned up there at the fork and went south on Route One Twenty-one."

"Did they have any reason to believe that you might have seen which way they went?"

"No. I'm a very light sleeper. I was about to get up anyway. As I say, I just happened to see them turn south."

"Could I take a look at the room?"

"If you want to. There've been quite a few people in it during the week."

"Then maybe there's no point in it. Who cleaned it after they left?"

"I did."

"Did you find anything of interest that was left behind?"

"N-n-no, not really."

"What did you find that puzzled you?"

"A razor blade in the bathroom waste-basket. Lots of women use razor blades, of course. But this one had stiff black stubble on it, and caked shaving cream of some sort. I just thought it seemed odd. No one was in there but the two women between the times I cleaned the bathroom."

I left and drove slowly down 121. It was definitely a secondary road. The shoulder was narrow and the brush was high in the shallow ditch. In the patches where the brush was thickest I went about eight miles an hour.

After about two miles I saw something in the brush. I got out and took a look. An old white rag caught on the base of some weeds. The second time I saw something, it was jackpot. A brown wool dress, ripped down the back and under the arms. Big shoes with the leather stiff from dampness, the stitches pulled by strain. Heavy stockings, a rain cape and a big floppy hat. The works had been rolled into a tight bundle and fastened with a woman's belt. After I was certain of what I had found, I bundled it back up and got ready to toss it farther into the brush. A truck went by, a farm truck, and the driver looked curiously at me. I locked the bundle in the back end of my car with my luggage.

I sat behind the wheel and studied the maps. Either the gray Buick was hot or it wasn't. If it was, I could be in trouble. If it wasn't, then the smartest thing for the two of them to do would be to make a lot of road time. I was willing to accept south as the direction. His first run had been to the north. South looked good.

But the south is pretty roomy. Again I had to try to think like Torran. Unless the girl had brought clothes for him, which wasn't likely, he'd be anxious to pick up a wardrobe. The best wardrobes come from the big cities. The big cities, more often than not, are inclined to have the most alert boys in the cop line. His picture would be widely plastered around. I sat and thought and scratched my head. I just didn't have enough. With Torran alone I could chance guessing his next move. You study a man's life long enough and you can detect the pattern of his thoughts. But Miss X added a new factor. I could guess his decisions but I could not guess either hers or their combined decisions.

So I went to Beloit for the second time. I arrived late Saturday night. Sunday morning I went to the phone company offices, presented my credentials, asked for information about any long distance calls which had been made from the bus station ten days ago. After some stalling, the chief operator on duty dug into the records and came up with three long distance calls made from the bus station between ten-thirty and eleven-fifteen. The one to Cleveland I didn't consider. Nor the one to Evansville, Indiana. The one I liked was made at five after eleven to a place called Britcher City, a town of fifteen thousand midway between Urbana and Danville on US 150 east and a bit south of Bloomington. The call was to anyone at Britcher City 3888.

I hadn't checked out of my hotel room. I found a place that would grease my car, change the oil. I took an hour nap and had a quick sandwich before leaving Beloit at noon. It was a hundred and ninety mile trip to Britcher City. I drove by the city limit sign at five minutes of four. I found a square red brick hotel called the Westan Arms and got a room. I used a pay phone in the lobby to call 3888.

I heard it ring three times at the other end and then a voice said, "Good afternoon. Westan Arms Hotel." I nearly dropped the receiver. "Sorry," I said, "wrong number." I hung up. Sometimes it happens that way.

I went to the desk. The gray-haired woman desk clerk said, "Yes, Mr Gandy?"

The boyish grin was the right one to use. "I've got a problem, ma'am."

"I hope we can help you."

"I believe a young lady left here recently. I don't know what name she was registered under. She may have checked out ten days ago. Blonde tall girl with dark eyes."

"Oh, her!" the woman said with surprising coldness. "Friend of yours?"

"It's very important to me to locate her."

"Well, we don't know much about her, to tell the truth, even though she did live here for two months. Her name is Marta Sharry. Is that the one?"

"I don't know. I'd have to see her handwriting to make certain. Would that be too much trouble?"

She shrugged and turned around to a file behind the counter. She hunted for three or four minutes, then pulled out a card. The angular backhand was familiar.

"That's her writing. Did she leave a forwarding address?"

"No, she didn't. I thought there was something funny about her. No mail and no phone calls, until that last one – all the time she was here. We wondered if she was hiding from somebody."

"Did she act as though she were hiding?"

"No. She used to take liquor to her room and drink it alone. She used to sleep every day until one or two in the afternoon. Along about five o'clock *he* would come for her and she'd go out with him."

It was time for the boyish grin again. "Who is he?"

She smiled a bit wryly. "Every city has its Joe Talley, I suppose. He runs something that is supposed to be a private club. I don't know why the police don't close it. Heaven knows all that goes on there. He'd bring her back here at three and four in the morning. We don't like that sort of guest, but she was quiet and she always paid her bills. I'll bet you Joe Talley knows where she went."

"Did she have a gray Buick?"

The elderly woman sniffed. "Not when she came here, she didn't. Very remarkable. Joe Talley blossoms out in a new car and suddenly she has his old one, with different plates."

"Where did she garage it?"

"Down at the corner. Landerson's Service."

I pushed the register card back to her. Miss Marta Sharry, New York City. Not much information there. "Where is Talley's place?"

"On Christian Street. Go down Main and turn left on Christian three blocks from here. It's eight blocks out on the left and it looks boarded up, but it isn't. There's an iron deer in the yard. You'll see the sign on the gate. The Talley Ho." She lowered her voice and looked around. "They *gamble* there," she said.

I thanked her with as much enthusiasm as I could manage. I went to the place where she'd kept the car. It was open. A pimply boy was on duty. Just remembering the blonde seemed to up his blood pressure. He had big wet eyes and they glowed.

I made like I was a friend of hers. The license *was* 6c424. That surprised me a bit.

Again I was shot with luck. He smirked and said, "I guess that fancy name, that Marta Sharry, was kind-of a stage name, huh?"

"Oh, she told you her right name?"

He had the decency to blush. "No. She had the registration in one of them little plastic things on the key chain. I took it out once because I wanted to see how old she was. The name on it was something like Anne Richards."

"Anne Richardson?"

"Yeah. That's it."

"Good thing Joe Talley didn't catch you spying on her, eh?"

He licked his lips. His eyes shifted away from me. "I wasn't doing nothing," he said sullenly.

"Did she come and get the car when she left town?"

"She phoned, and I drove it over to her. I helped load her bags in the back. She give me five bucks."

"She seem nervous?"

"No. Kind of excited. Joe Talley came along. He sat beside her in the front seat and I walked back here. I saw her come by ten minutes later and he wasn't with her then."

"What time was that?"

"Sometime before midnight."

From there I went to the Talley Ho. There didn't seem to be anyone around. It was a big three-story Victorian frame house, with a cupola, a bunch of scroll saw work and an iron deer standing next to a chipped bird bath in the shaggy lawn under the shade of big elms.

I went back to the hotel and slept until ten. When I went back to the Talley Ho I found the narrow side street lined with parked cars. There was a guard at the gate.

"This is a private club, mister."

"So I've heard. I'm a stranger in town. I thought maybe I could join."

"Maybe you can and maybe you can't. Write us a letter and we'll let you know."

"Couldn't I talk to the manager?"

"No. Sorry. I got my orders. Nobody gets in unless they got a card."

"That's a hell of a note. Miss Sharry wrote me and told me that Joe Talley would treat me right if I ever came through here."

He turned the flashlight on my face again. "You know her?"

"No. I just made up the name."

"No need to get fresh, stranger."

"Hell, I like standing out here. Don't you?"

"Wait a minute," he said. "Anybody comes along I'll be right back, tell 'em. What's your name?"

"Gandy. Russ Gandy."

He was gone five minutes. He came back with a taller man. At their request I came inside the gate. I stood while they put the flash on me again.

"What's your business, Gandy?"

"I'll talk to Talley, if you'll get him out here."

"He's out of town. I'm in charge."

"What's your name?"

"Brankis."

"Come over here a minute, Brankis. This is personal."

We went over by the deer. I tapped a cigarette on its cast iron muzzle and lit it. "It's like this, Brankis. I ran into you-know-who in Chicago. He told me he had Anne Richardson staked out here. At the Westan Arms. I phoned her couple weeks ago. She told me that a guy named Joe Talley is all right, and – "

"Anne Richardson? Who the hell is she?"

"Don't be cute, Brankis. She's Torran's girl." I purposely made it a little loud.

"Dammit, lower your voice!"

I laughed at him. "Then the name means something to you?"

"How do you figure with Torran?" he said in a half whisper. "Nobody's ever been hotter than he is. So why should he pop to you?"

"Maybe you can call me an associate, Brankis."

"What kind of a word is that? Associate, yet. Joe isn't going to like any link-up between him and Torran through that girl. She's all mouth."

"Like any lush. Now can I come in and play? I just want to kill some time."

"No, friend. Anybody coming in gets Joe's okay and I told you Joe is out of town."

"That's too bad. I got some merchandise for him."

"Merchandise? What kind of merchandise?"

"Brankis, you must be a real small wheel in this outfit. Annie knows more than you do. She told me Joe Talley is always in the market for this kind of merchandise."

It was too dark to see his face. I waited, hoping it would work. When he spoke he piled the words on too fast to cover up the period of silence. "Oh, that stuff."

"Yes, I got it down at the hotel. Want to come look it over and set a price?"

"Sure. I'll come take a look." He couldn't admit Joe had been leaving him out in the cold, and he had to see the merchandise to know just how far out he'd been left.

We went to the gate and he said, "George, I'll be back in a while. You have any problems, ask Mac what to do."

We went out and got in my car. I stopped for the first cross street and glanced at him, seeing his face for the first time, liking the youngness, the weakness, the loose viciousness of his mouth. I started up, took out my cigarettes and, as I offered him one, I managed to drop the whole pack at his feet. He bent over instinctively to pick them up. As he got into the right position I hit the brakes hard. His head dented the glove compartment door and he sighed once and flowed down onto the floor, like some thick, slow-running liquid.

I parked in shadows and looked him over. All he carried was a sap in black woven leather with a coil spring handle. I bent over him, folded his hat double to cushion the blow and hit him hard behind the ear, flush on the mastoid bone. I took his pulse. It was slow and steady.

I headed toward Danville, found a dirt road that turned left. The sign said the towns of Pilot and Collision were up that road. How does a town get to be called Collision?

The sky had cleared and the moon made a good light. The road was a little soft in spots. Farmhouse lights were off. The road made a right angle turn to the left and another to the right. When I saw a break in a fence, I got out and checked the ditch. It was shallow and dry. The pasture seemed firm enough. I put the car in low and drove across toward a dark clump of trees. I parked and hauled him out and used my tow rope to tie him to a tree. I wrapped him up so that all he could do would be roll his eyes and wag his tongue. He was limp, sagging in the rope. I sat and smoked and waited for him to come around.

After a long time he sighed. Then he groaned. I knew he could see my cigarette end, glowing in the darkness.

"Whassa marra?" he asked. "Whassa idea?"

I didn't answer him. He was silent for a long time. He said, "What do you want?" Panic crouched behind the level tone.

I watched him and let him sweat. To him, I was just a dark shadow sitting on the front fender of the car.

"What are you going to do to me?" he asked. His voice shook.

A farm dog howled at the moon far away. A sleepy rooster crowed in a half-hearted way. Down the line a diesel hooted at a crossing.

"It was all Joe's idea," he said. "I'm not in on it. He met her in the hotel. She got tight out at the place. She hinted about Torran. Just little hints. So Joe pried it all out of her. She told him how she was waiting for word from Torran when he got ready to make his run for it. She didn't know where or when Torran was going to run. She had five thousand he'd given her in Chicago right after the job, when they split up. She was to buy a car and get it registered under her own name." He stopped talking and waited for me to say something.

He started again, his voice pitched higher than before. "Joe started thinking about all that cash. All that money, and he worked the girl up to where she was thinking of crossing Torran, because Torran had been pretty rough with her. The more he thought about getting his hands on that dough, the better he liked the idea. He talked it over with me. The idea was to get Torran to run with the girl to right where Joe wanted him to run. It had to be done delicate because if Torran felt maybe the girl was steering him some special place, he'd smell a cross."

Again he waited and again I said nothing.

"What are you going to do to me? I'm telling you everything I know." It was half wail and half whine. "Joe fixed her up with the car and figured that because of the dough in serial sequence and the bearer bonds, Torran would want to get out of the country to where maybe he could buy a banana citizenship and get a better percentage than trying to fence the stuff here where it's too hot to touch. And if Joe got the dough here he'd be in the same trouble. Mexico has an easy border to cross, even with them looking for you. So Joe figured help him get into Mexico through the girl, and take it away from him down there.

"Joe goes to Mexico a lot because if you spend too much here, the tax boys get curious. He's got a house down there he rents by the year. In Cuernavaca. As soon as the girl got the word from Torran she told Joe and he flew down to set it up. If Torran goes to Canada or flies out of the country some other place, Joe is licked. The girl was supposed to get away from Torran for a couple minutes and wire me so I could phone Joe. The wire hasn't come yet."

I flipped a cigarette away, stood up, walked over to him. I said casually, "If I kill you, Brankis, you can't phone Joe and tell him about this, can you?"

"Now wait a minute!" he said in a voice like a woman's.

"Or maybe I'll tip Joe Talley that you opened up like a book."

"A deal, mister," he said breathlessly. "I keep my mouth shut and so do you. Honest."

"And I get word on that wire the minute you get it."

"Yeah. Sure!"

I untied him and slapped him around and took him back and left him. I went right to Western Union. A bored night man looked at my credentials without interest, sneered at a twenty-dollar bribe and told me the only ones to see telegrams were the persons to whom said telegrams were addressed. There was no time to arrange a tap on the Talley Ho phone. I added two more twenties. He ignored me. I added two more. One hundred dollars.

He yawned and picked up the money. "It was marked deliver," he said, "and I sent it out twenty minutes before you came in. It was from National

City, California, and it read: *Plan to take cruise to Acapulco starting tomorrow.*
It was signed *Betty*."

He pocketed my money and shuffled back and sat down and picked up
a magazine.

3

Thirty-one hours later I was sitting by a window on the port side of the
Mexico City–Acapulco plane as it lifted off the runway at seven in the
morning. There was a wad of traveler's checks in my pocket and a bad
taste in my mouth. I had wasted too much time getting the *turista* permit,
making travel connections.

We climbed through the sunlit air of the great plateau, lifted over the
brow of the mountains near Tres Cumbres and started the long, downhill
slant to Acapulco on the Pacific. It was hard to figure just how quickly
Torran and the girl would get there. My phone calls to California had
established that there was no scheduled cruise to Acapulco at the date the
wire had indicated.

Probably Torran had made arrangements to have a boat pick him off the
lower California coast and smuggle him down to Acapulco. The odds were
against his tarrying in Mexico long. Extradition was too simple. The same
method of travel would take him down the Central American coastline to
some country where an official would listen joyfully to the loud sound of
American dollars.

One thing I could be certain of. Joe Talley would be there. And I would
know Joe Talley. I'd memorized a recent picture of him – a beefy blond
with a rosebud mouth and slate eyes. I knew Torran's face as well as I
knew my own.

Traffic wasn't heavy as it was the off season for Acapulco, the summer-rate
season. The air was bumpy. A large family across the way was airsick, every
one of them. We flew to Cuernavaca, over the gay roofs of Taxco. Brown
slowly disappeared from the landscape below us and it began to turn to a
deep jungle green.

At nine o'clock we lifted for the last low range of hills and came down
to the coast. The Pacific was intensely blue, the surf line blazing white.
The hotels were perched on the cliffs that encircled the harbor. The wide
boulevard ran along the water's edge.

There are hunches. All kinds. This was one of those. I looked at the city
as we came in for the landing. I looked at it and I didn't feel anything and
then all of a sudden I felt confident and good. I felt that whatever was going
to happen, it would happen right down there.

We made a bumpy landing and as soon as we were down I knew why

Acapulco was not at the peak of its season. The heat was like when a barber wraps your face in a steaming towel. It was heat that bored a hole in you and let all the strength run out. It was heat that kept your eyes stinging from the sweat running into the corners.

I stood in the shadow of the wing as they untied the baggage and handed it down. I took my bag and walked across the runway, and it was so hot the soles of my feet began to burn. I took the sedan which had HOTEL DE LAS AMERICAS on the front of it, remembering that it had been recommended to me in Mexico City. No one else was going to that hotel. The airsick family piled into a shabbier sedan labeled HOTEL PAPAGAYO.

The hotel was something right out of the imagination of an assistant to a Hollywood producer. High on the cliff, with cabañas, shops, pools, outdoor cocktail lounges, outdoor dining room and dance floor. I registered, took a cabaña, took a shower and put on the Acapulco clothes I'd bought in Mexico City. Protective coloration. I wanted to look like an American tourist. The shirt had a pattern of tropical parrots. The shorts were lime yellow. The sandals had straps that hurt me across the instep. I topped it off with a white mesh cap with a ballplayer's bill, oval slanting sun glasses.

I told my troubles to the desk clerk. "I'm trying to find a friend here in town. I don't know what hotel he's at. How would I go about it?"

"An American, sir?"

"Yes."

He gave me a list of the six most likely hotels. The flaw was that Joe Talley might not be using his own name. But there was no real reason for him not to do so. His name would mean nothing to Torran. Torran was big time. Talley was a small town crook. And just before lunch I found him. He was at the Papagayo. It was one of those breaks you get. I was just getting out of the taxi in front of the place when I saw him coming across the road from the beach. He had a dark pretty girl with him. Both of them seemed a little unsteady on their feet. They passed right in front of the cab and went into the hotel grounds. Joe was speaking Spanish to the girl. She was giggling. I don't know how good the Spanish was. It sounded good and she seemed to be enjoying it. The black hair on the girl wasn't a dye job. Of that I was certain.

There were enough people around so that I could follow them into the grounds. I shoved money at the cab driver. I got such a wide grin I knew it was too much. I went in. The cabañas were on either side of long walks behind the hotel. Tropical foliage was lush around them. I kept them in sight. They turned into the last but one on the central walk and I saw Talley unlock the door.

I strolled around. I went by to the end of the walk, came back, and when I was sure I wasn't observed, I ducked into the thick brush beside their cabaña. The windows were open. Through the screen I heard the buzz of a fan, the clink of bottleneck on glass, the girl's thin giggle. They kept talking Spanish to each other. They stopped talking after a while. I didn't risk raising my eyes above the sill until I heard the roar of a shower. Then I looked in.

It was Talley who was taking the shower. I could see the girl. She had changed into a white dress. She went over to the bureau and started making up her face. I walked away from there. I had vaguely planned to have Talley lead me to Torran and Anne. If Joe Talley could take Torran, it was all to the good. If he couldn't, he'd knock Torran off balance long enough for me to take him. But Talley was playing. He was like a guy with nothing on his mind. It bothered me. He ought to be pretty well tightened up. Just the thought of coming up against Torran ought to keep him nibbling on his hands. Something had gone wrong in my guessing.

An hour later the girl came out of the cabaña alone. She had a big bright red purse slung over her shoulder. I tossed a mental coin and decided to stay with Joe Talley. So I intercepted her where I could keep Talley's cabaña in sight.

"Do you speak any English?" I asked her.

She gave me a long cold look, then wrinkled her nose in a very charming little smile. "A leedle."

"Can I buy you a drink?"

"Dreenk? No, *gracias*. Other time, maybee."

A nice old lady schoolteacher walked by, glanced at the girl and gave me a sour look. I tried to make a date with the girl, but she walked on.

I shrugged and found a bench where I could see Talley's cabaña. The long hours went by. I was hungry and thirsty and out of cigarettes. I cursed Talley, Torran, Anne Richardson, Mexico and the three hundred and seventy thousand dollars.

When Anne Richardson came by me, it caught me by surprise. I was waiting for Talley to come out. It shook me to see her and know that it could be the one. I went over the ticket agent's description. Hair like harvest wheat, he had said. Moon-pool eyes, whatever those are. The funny, tough, scratchy little voice would be the payoff.

I had to make a quick revision of all my guesses. It was like coming in on the third act, not knowing your lines or what has happened so far. I moved in behind her as she headed down the walk. She wore an aqua cotton two-piece dress with a bare midriff. She walked on high cork soles, and she was tall enough not to need them, and her walk was something to remember and speculate about and bring back to mind on long cold winter nights. A man like Torran should pick inconspicuous women. She was as noticeable as a feather bed in a phone booth.

She went to Joe Talley's cabaña, tried the door and went in. My play was to walk slowly by and see if I could duck into the shrubs again. This time they'd be speaking English, at least. But before I could get by, the door banged open and she came out again, blanched to the color of roquefort, sucking at the air through parted lips. I took a quick step back, caught her wrist and spun her around.

"Let go, let *go!*" she panted, fighting me. The voice was small, scratchy.

"Get back in there, Anne!" I said, pushing her toward the door. Her ankle turned because of the high cork soles and I caught her before she fell. My using her name took a lot of the scrap out of her. Her eyes were wide and hot as she looked at me. Moon-pool eyes, to that ticket agent, are the ones so dark that you can't see where the irises leaves off and the pupils begin.

"Who are you?"

I shoved her again, reached around her to the door and pushed it open, pulled her in. She turned her back to me and I spun her around and caught her hand just as she yanked the small automatic out of her white purse. I tore the gun out of her hand and it hurt her fingers and she yelled with the pain. But I heard it as though it came from a long distance.

I was too busy looking at Joe Talley. He was pretty messy. Through the open bathroom door I could see the top half of him. The shower was still on and turned too hot so that steam drifted around him. He lay on his back with his legs still in the shower and the big knife was stuck through his throat at an angle so that the tip of it came out under his ear.

The girl made a dive for the door and I caught her in time, whirled her back, picked her up bodily and threw her onto the bed. "Be good," I said. She lay there and stared at me. I opened her purse, took out cigarettes, lit one. I looked around the room. The search had been pretty complete. The bottle on the bureau. Two glasses had been used. The third was still clean, still upside down on the tray. I poured some of the defunct's bourbon, a liberal dose, took it over and pushed Anne's legs out of the way so I could sit on the bed.

"I could use some of that," she said in a wheedling tone.

"Tell me some things and maybe you'll get some."

"Why did you kill him, honey?" I knew she hadn't. I knew she didn't have time to do it. But she didn't know I knew.

Her eyes darkened curiously. "I'm asking you that, mister."

"I'm turning you in to the local cops. I think they have cells with dirt floors. I think the jailers will give me a vote of thanks for putting something like you in there. The bugs are bad, but they'll keep you entertained."

"You can't bluff me, mister. Who are you?"

"How did you get here so fast from National City? You and Torran."

"Who's Torran? Somebody I ought to know?"

"From way back," I said.

"Why did you kill Joe Talley, mister?"

I took another pull at the drink. Her eyes kept flicking to the glass and now and then she'd lick her underlip.

"We're going around in circles, Anne. I didn't kill him. And I know you didn't. But I do know who did. Interested?"

She sat up, pulled her knees up, hugged them. "Who?"

"I'll give you a little. You give me a little first."

She shut her eyes for a long three seconds. "We got here fast because there was a light plane staked out for us at Ensenada."

"A girl killed him. A Mexican girl wearing a white dress and carrying a big red purse. She was pretty. He brought her back here from the beach around noon. They both looked a little high."

Still hugging her knees, she said five or six words that she shouldn't have known. Her lips writhed like bloody worms as she said them.

I asked, "Where's Torran?"

Suddenly a thought seemed to strike her.

Her eyes went wide. She scrambled off the bed, took one hesitant step toward the door and then stood there. "Look, I just realized that maybe . . ."

"Go ahead and talk. Get it off your chest," I told her. "I know that you and Joe Talley planned to hijack Torran's take and you crossed Torran by sending the wire to Brankis. I know which bus Torran took dressed as a fat lady, and I know the place he tossed the getup out of the gray Buick, and I know how you honked at the bus."

It was meant to shake her. It did. Her face went white again. She sat down beside me on the bed.

"Who are you?"

"I'm just a guy interested in three hundred and seventy thousand dollars, sweet."

She ran her fingertips along the back of my hand. "If I could trust you, mister."

"How do you mean?"

"Wouldn't I be a damn fool if I steered you to that money and then you took it all?"

I nodded gravely. "You'd grab it all for yourself if you could, wouldn't you?"

She looked at me. "I need help. Joe was going to help. I'm afraid he talked to the wrong people. I'm afraid he was killed by somebody who wants the money."

"Where's Torran?"

"How can I trust you?"

"You can't. But I think you're on a spot where you're going to have to trust somebody."

She turned into my arms and caught her hand strongly at the back of my neck and kissed me. She could be considered an expert. The kiss was as smarting hot as the sauce that came with the one meal I had in Mexico City.

"It's nice," I said casually, "but it isn't worth three hundred and seventy thousand." I blocked the slap she threw at me and watched her as she went over to the bureau.

She picked up the bottle and tilted it high. Her throat worked convulsively for five long swallows. She lowered the bottle, said, "Haaaah", tilted it high again and took three more swallows. She wiped her wet mouth on the back of her hand, leaving a smear of deep red.

"I've got to tell you," she said, "because I've got to have help. Torran is sick. He got sick in National City, and he's been running a hell of a high fever. He's out of his head sometimes. That made it simple for me to contact Joe as soon as we landed. Joe made the arrangement for a house up the beach, a small place walled in and private. Torran's there. The bad thing was not knowing how to get the money away from him. It's all crammed into a huge money belt. Even sick like that, I couldn't risk it. And I'm not killing anybody, even for that amount of money.

"Joe has contacts. He got some sedative and handed it to me early this morning. I couldn't get it down Torran until noon.

"When he was out, I got the belt off him. I know it isn't safe to stay here. I can't get it out of Mexico without Joe's help. So I hid it in the house and came to get Joe and tell him. Now I'm afraid to go back there, because if Joe talked to the wrong people and there's another group after that money, they'll be at the house now. If you come back with me and help me get the money, and help me get it to El Salvador, I'll give you seventy thousand."

"Half, sweet."

"One hundred thousand. No more. Final offer." The liquor had gotten into her blood stream. Her lips looked swollen and she weaved slightly.

"Half, and be good, or I'll take it all."

She leered at me. "Maybe we could stick together, huh? Your money is my money?" She laughed. It looked funny to see her standing there laughing, because behind her I could see Joe Talley's hand, palm upward, the steam curling around it.

She turned toward the bottle. I got there first. She cursed me. She clawed at my face and I slapped her so hard her eyes went off focus. Then she turned sweet. "You gotta help me, honey," she said. "Gee, I don't know your name."

"Russ, sweet. Be good. Stand by the door. There's prints to get rid of. That heat is going to make time of death tough for them to determine."

I cleaned up and we left. A man was standing up the walk talking to a woman who stood in front of the neighboring cabaña. I turned back toward the door, waved, and said, "See you later, boy."

*   *   *

Her face and eyes were empty as we got into the cab. She gave the address "Ocho Calle Revocadera."

"You know the language?"

"Twenty words, Russ."

I held my hands low and took a look at the automatic. It was a toy. Twenty-five caliber. Curly designs etched into the steel. The clip was full. The cab took fifteen minutes to put us by the gate in the wall around the house. She sat in the cab and started to tremble. "I'm scared," she said in a low tone.

I held the door and she got out. I paid the driver and the cab went away from there. I looked at the gate. There was a chain for a padlock, but no padlock. I slipped the catch and pushed it open. The lawn was deep green, unkempt. Flowers straggled in wild confusion along the side of the pink stone house.

"What room is he in?"

She was shivering again. "In . . . in the back."

"Did you lock the place up?"

"Yes."

I took a look at the side door. The wood was splintered and pieces of the brass lock lay on the stone step. I pushed her to one side, kicked the door open and went in fast, whirling on balance, the way I had been taught. The hallway was empty, dim. I listened. The house was silent.

"Come in," I whispered. She came in obediently. She was chewing on her lip. The liquor was sweating its way out of her.

"Where did you hide it?" I whispered, my lips close to her ear.

"You'll take me with you, Russ?"

"Of course."

"Promise."

"I promise."

"Come on, then." She walked with extreme caution. I followed her. It was hard to walk silently on the gayly patterned tile floor. She peered into the next room and then walked in. Suspended from the ceiling was a huge fixture, like a fruit bowl. She pointed up at it. I picked up the antique Spanish chair from its position near the door and put it silently under the fixture. She put her hand on my shoulder and stepped up onto the chair, reached her hands up and around the edge of the fixture.

The flick of movement was off to the side. I turned, firing as I turned, my snapping shot drowned by the resounding smash of a heavier weapon. He stood gaunt in the doorway, wearing only pajama pants, his eyes glittering and feverish, black stubble on his face, his lips cracked and caked with white.

As the muzzle swung toward me, I saw the tiny holes appearing in his naked chest, all left of center. His left. The little automatic shot well. He tried to hold onto the doorway and steady the weapon. He trembled with effort but he could not stay the slow sagging of the muzzle. When he fired it, it was aimed at the tile. It smashed tile, whirred by my head and chunked into the wall behind me. His knees made a clocking sound on the tile and he folded awkwardly onto his face, getting one hand up but not far enough.

I turned toward Anne Richardson. Both her hands were clamped on the rim of the light fixture and her feet were still on the chair. But her knees sagged so that all her weight was on her hands, and on the fixture. It pulled free of the ceiling and she came down with it, hitting cruelly against the heavy arm of the chair, tumbling off onto the floor while the glass splashed into all corners of the room.

I knelt by her and turned her over gently and saw where the bullet had entered, just below the bare midriff, dead center, ranging upward. She gave me an odd little smile and said, "Tell . . . tell them I . . ." Then she chopped her heels at the floor so hard she broke the straps of both cork-soled shoes and they came off. She arched up a few inches and dropped back and died. I wondered what I was supposed to tell them.

I went to the front door and listened. There was no traffic in the road. The nearest beach house was four hundred yards away, and the sound of the surf was loud.

Torran was dead. That look of affability was gone in death. He looked weak, vicious, cruel. He looked like a punk, a dirty small time killer. I searched the house. The kitchen was small. The girl in the white dress lay with her head under the sink, face down, the big red purse under her stomach, her white dress high on the bare strong brown thighs. The slug had made an evil mess of the back of her head. Her companion, a dark man I had never seen before, was one eighth alive. At least he was breathing. His pulse had a flutter like the wings of a captive moth. He had two in the belly.

When Torran had regained the belt, he had put it where a sick person could be expected to put it. Under his pillow. I opened it. Each compartment was hard as a stone with money. It was crammed in so tightly the belt would have to be cut to get it out without tearing it.

I looked at it. All the money in the world. Fresh money, still in the mint wrappers. All the money in the world for all the things in the world. I sat on the bed that smelled of fever and sickness in the room with the drawn blinds and ran my fingertips back and forth across the visible edges of the stacks of bills. I thought of crazy but possible things.

It was done very, very neatly. It was done the way experts do it. A gardener was working in front of my cabaña at the Hotel de las Americas. Another man was coming down the path with a covered tray. I unlocked the door and went in. When I was three steps inside the room the gardener shoved the muzzle of the weapon through the screen of the side window. The waiter tossed napkin and tray aside, kept the light machine gun the napkin had covered. He held it centered on the small of my back. At the same instant the third man stepped out of my bathroom and covered me with a professional-looking revolver.

I raised my arms and stood there. With no accent at all the man in front of me said, "Sit down and hold onto your ankles."

I did as directed. They took the gun first. Then they took the money belt off me. They put the gun and the money belt on the bed. They seemed to be waiting for someone. I felt better. I had a lovely idea. "Police?" I asked. My voice sounded like something crawling up the side of a wall.

"But of course," the English-speaking one said.

We all waited. Broughton came in. The white caterpillar eyebrows showed no surprise, no elation. He looked like the deacon standing at the end of the pew waiting for the collection plate to be handed back.

"You saved us some trouble, Gandy," he said.

"Glad I could help."

"We didn't find Brankis until yesterday. We've gotten excellent cooperation from the Mexican authorities."

"Put that in your report, Broughton."

He nodded. "I will. You nearly made it, Gandy. One day later . . ."

"My hard luck, I suppose," I said. "Can I get up on my feet?"

He nodded. I got up. He showed expression for the first time. I was something low, dirty and evil. Something you'd find under a wet rock. Something he wanted to step on.

"We're taking you back," he said.

"Kind of you, sir."

I grinned at him. I gave him a big broad grin and he turned away from it. I was laughing inside. I was laughing so hard I hurt. Let him have his fun. Sooner or later he was going to find out about the wire I sent before returning to my cabaña – that wire to Washington Bureau Headquarters, giving the case code name, reporting recovery, requesting instructions.

You see, it looked like all the money in the world, but sometimes even that isn't enough.

MURDER'S MANDATE

W. T. Ballard

1 BLOND MENACE

SAM BOYD WAS sitting in Tony Foster's law office when Roger Bowman was ushered in. He made no effort to lift his big shoulders away from the leather chair back. A slight motion of the lawyer's hand told Boyd that Foster wanted him to remain.

Roger Bowman paused, staring at Boyd. Bowman was a thin man, in his middle fifties, with a tight-lipped mouth that was only partly screened by a close-clipped mustache.

"I want to speak to you alone," he said to Foster. "This is highly confidential." His tone was pointed.

"Boyd's my confidential man," said Foster. "Sit down."

For an instant it seemed to the watching Boyd that Bowman would refuse, then with a slight shrug to express his anger, he eased himself onto the edge of a chair.

Boyd appeared half asleep, but he was studying Bowman's face, thinking that here was a bad man to anger, and it seemed that Foster was angering him unnecessarily.

"You're the Norcross lawyer," Bowman said to Foster sharply. "I'm here to warn you."

"Warn me?" Foster made his voice surprised.

"Warn you," said Bowman, keeping his tone level with visible effort. "Norcross and I owned Western Chemical together and I bought his share in Nineteen-forty-two for seventy thousand dollars. In return he was to stay out of the business."

Foster nodded. "And I advised him not to sell. Your price wasn't enough, counting the good will after fifteen years of operation."

"That wasn't for you to say." Bowman sounded bitter. "Frank Norcross made the deal. He's dead, and now this daughter of his, with you as her lawyer, files suit, claiming that her father was not physically fit to transact business – that I took advantage of him."

Foster showed no feeling. "We've two doctors ready to so testify. Are you here to settle out of court?"

"Settle?"

Bowman lost control for an instant and rose from his chair. Sam Boyd rose also. That was one reason he was there – to see that visitors behaved.

Bowman looked at the still seated lawyer, at the standing Boyd.

"Hiding behind a strong-arm, huh?" He sounded contemptuous. "Well, here's something your strong-arm man can't help you with. Read this! You'll forgive me if I keep hold of it. I don't trust you, my friend."

He drew a piece of paper from his pocket, circled the desk and held it so that Foster could read.

"You should recognize Frank Norcross' signature. If you doubt it's his, we'll try a handwriting expert."

"What is this?" he asked.

A mocking note came back into Bowman's voice.

"Only a letter, signed by Frank Norcross, admitting that he had a secret agreement with the German Dye Trust in direct violation with the trading with the enemy act. I gave him the choice of signing this when I bought him out, or of being exposed. I should have exposed him, but we'd been partners for fifteen years, and he was an old man. I bought him out instead.

"I broke the German connection, I straightened out the business and made it pay, and I'm not going to have his daughter step in and grab the results of my hard work. Either you withdraw this recovery suit, or I'll publish this letter! I'll take it into court and explain why it was necessary for me to force Norcross out in the first place."

"Blackmail," Foster said softly. "You forced him to sell for peanuts, knowing that he wouldn't dare refuse, and now you are trying to blackmail us."

Bowman shrugged. "You can't anger me," he said, returning the letter to his pocket. "I just wanted you to know I had a little ace up my sleeve that you hadn't heard about."

Foster didn't answer. Instead he reached for the phone and put in a long distance call for Ann Norcross at Las Vegas, Nevada. It took five minutes for the call to be completed, and no one in the office spoke during the interval.

When the connection was made Foster said, tightly:

"Listen, Ann, this is very important. Roger Bowman is in my office. He has a letter that your father signed, a letter which states that your father had a working agreement with the German Dye Trust and that he maintained the connection even after we entered the war . . ." He listened a moment. "That's right, it's dynamite. We wouldn't have a chance if he tells the story in court and makes the jury believe it . . . No, I don't know what to do. It's up to you."

He was silent for a few minutes more, his hand over the phone's mouth-piece, listening to the girl at the other end of the wire. Then he turned to Bowman.

"She wants to see that letter, the original."

"Not a chance," Bowman told him. "Is she trying some of her humor? That letter doesn't get out of my hands. If she wants to see it, tell her to come here. I certainly won't take it to Vegas just to give her a look."

"But this is important to her," Foster said. "You can't blame her for wanting to see the original. A copy wouldn't mean anything. She'd want to check her father's signature."

"Tell her to come here."

Foster spoke into the phone, then turned back.

"She can't this week, and the case starts next Tuesday."

"That's her worry."

"Didn't either of you fellows ever hear of a photostat?" Sam Boyd said in a lazy voice.

They looked at each other. Foster seemed to be asking Bowman a silent question. Finally the man shrugged.

"Okay, but who will take it over there?"

"I will," said Sam Boyd. "There's a place in this building that will photograph your letter. Come on."

An hour later he had the photostat and his instructions. Bowman had tried to back out. Foster hadn't seemed anxious himself. The fight seemed to have gone out of the lawyer. He seemed ready to quit. That wasn't like him, and it worried Boyd.

Not until after his boss had gone for the evening did he remember that he had never seen Ann Norcross. It would be too bad if he gave the photostat to the wrong person.

There should be some way to identify her. He thought of one and went whistling to the files. Under "N" he found two files on the Norcrosses. There was a letter bearing the girl's signature on top. Carefully he studied it before closing the drawer.

Boyd took a plane for Las Vegas the next morning. Arriving there, he drove to the address that had been given him as Ann Norcross' home, asked for her, and was admitted.

The girl who came to the room in a few moments was blonde and cool-looking. The coolness impressed Boyd more than anything else about her. For outside it was hot. The desert sun had roasted him on the long drive from the airport, despite the fact that the calendar said spring.

"You're Mr Boyd?" she said. "You have a copy of the letter?"

"The photostat," he corrected her, drawing the envelope from his pocket. "You won't mind signing a receipt. It's for your own protection, Miss Norcross."

He produced the receipt and handed it to her. She hardly glanced at it. Turning to a small desk, she scrawled her name at the bottom of the paper.

Boyd accepted it, glanced at the signature, and a tiny frown was the only indication he gave of his surprise. Then he looked up.

"There's something wrong here," he said. "You're not Ann Norcross!"

The girl had been waiting, one hand extended, the other hidden by the edge of the desk.

"No," she said shortly. "I'm not Ann Norcross. But I want that photostat." She brought her other hand into sight, exposing the small gun which it held. "Shall we argue, or do I get it?"

He glanced from her face to the gun.

"I never argue with guns." He was being distantly polite as he passed the envelope across the desk.

Outside the house a car made noise in the driveway. The girl backed away, still holding the gun. She opened the envelope with her free hand, drew out the photostat and glanced at it for an instant. Then her lips curved in a smile.

"Very nice, Mr Boyd," she said. "There's a closet over there, on your right. Open the door. I'm going to lock you in. I trust you won't smother. But first – shall I take charge of this?"

She had stepped up behind him, poking the hard nose of her gun against his spine. With a deft movement she reached around and got the small bankers' special from under his arm. Then with an extra shove she hurried him to the closet and locked the door. He could hear the faint click her heels made on the red tile of the floor outside.

The closet was small and dark and close, and Sam Boyd was big. It was a tight squeeze for him even to turn around. The walls were thick and muffled sound, so he could hear nothing after the closing of the other door.

But, hearing that, he waited no longer. He put his shoulders against the rear wall and, using his left foot, proceeded to kick out one of the door panels. The wood split under the third kick and he managed to reach through the resulting hole, turn the key and unlock the door.

He pushed it open and stepped into the room. His small gun lay in the exact center of the desk. He picked it up, breaking it and noting that the cylinder was empty. Gaining the entrance in a dozen running steps, moving fast for a big man, he pulled the door open.

A yellow roadster was just turning from the long drive into the main road beyond. He had a glimpse of two people in the car and thought that one was the blonde, but could not be sure.

The cab which had brought him from the airport was still parked at the edge of the drive. The driver, hunched under the wheel was eyeing him thoughtfully.

Boyd watched the yellow car angrily for a moment, then turned and walked toward the cab.

"Did you see the driver of that roadster?" he asked.

"Yeah." The driver shifted slightly and squinted after the speeding car.

"Know him?"

"Yeah."

Sam Boyd lost patience. "Look, friend. I'm not playing guessing games. If you know the character, tell me who he is. If not, get out from under that wheel and let me punch your nose."

The driver took a look at Boyd, at the heavy shoulders, the lean waist, and the gray-blue eyes that glittered a little under the edge of the snap-brimmed hat. He grinned a trifle weakly.

"No offence, pardner. The driver's name is Bowman, Roger Bowman. He's some kind of big shot from Los Angeles. His outfit built a plant at Vegas a couple of years ago."

Not a muscle of Sam Boyd's face showed his surprise, and he wasted no time trying to guess why Roger Bowman should have given him the photostat yesterday and gone to the trouble of having the blonde steal it back today.

"This is the Norcross ranch, isn't it?"

The driver nodded.

"Know Ann Norcross when you see her?"

He got another nod.

"Was the blonde who left in Bowman's car Miss Norcross?"

The driver shook his head. Boyd decided that it hurt the man to talk.

"Any idea where Bowman hangs out when he's around Vegas?" he asked.

"Yeah. He rented the old Barber place, over on Mountain View Road."

"Supposing," said Boyd, opening the car's door, "you take me there. And don't kill yourself gossiping on the way over."

When Boyd finally reached the house on Mountain View Road, after a long drive, he saw that it was surprisingly large. It stood back in a grove of cottonwoods which marked the course of an underground river. Telling his driver to wait, he went up the path toward the porch. There was no sign of the yellow roadster, but there was a small coupé parked in the drive.

There was no response to his knock so he tried again, glancing at his watch. It was almost an hour since he had left the Norcross place, and Boyd had a suspicion that his driver had purposely taken him all over the desert before coming here.

Still no one appeared and Boyd walked back down the path to where the small coupé was parked. There was a California registration slip strapped to the steering post as he bent in, trying to read the name.

The car was registered to Ann Norcross.

Boyd swore under his breath. As a general thing, he liked trouble, for it made things more interesting. But there was something going on here that he didn't understand, and he did not like mystery.

He went back to the porch, conscious that his driver was watching him. The door was fastened and he went over to one of the windows, trying the screen.

He heard a call, and looked around. The driver had his head out of the cab.

"Hey, you can't do that!"

"Who says I can't?" Boyd said.

With the help of a knife he managed to work the screen loose. There was a fairly wide crack between the upper and lower sash, a crack which would admit his knife blade. He thrust it in, reached the catch and managed to turn it. Behind him, he heard the sound of a motor. He spun around, yelling, but it was no use. The cab was already in motion, and Boyd's yell merely seemed to increase its speed.

Boyd started to swear, then grinned wryly.

"Guess the jockey doesn't care for house-breaking," he muttered. "Well, there was four dollars on his meter. Let him try and collect."

Boyd turned back to the window. It went up easily, now that the catch was free. He stepped over the sill into a long room.

The Venetian blinds were three-quarters closed, making the place shadowed, but he could vaguely see the book-lined walls and the heavy furniture of a library.

He had pushed the blind aside to enter, and he reached backward now and tugged at the cord to flatten the blades. Light came through to show him something which he had not seen before. A man lay on his side on the floor near the hall door, his back toward Boyd.

2 IN CUSTODY

For an instant Sam Boyd did not move. Every nerve in his big body was alive, tense. The gun came out from under his arm as if by instinct to nestle so deeply in his big palm that its snub nose hardly showed beyond the curving edge of his big fingers.

Then he remembered that the blonde had removed the shells from the cylinder, and with a little grunt of self-disdain he shoved the gun back into place.

Carefully he moved forward as if fearing his soles would slip on the thick nap of the blue Chinese rug. His eyes were intent on the figure, watching for motion, for sign of life. There was none, and Sam Boyd understood why as he bent forward to give the body a closer inspection. There was a deep scalp wound from which blood had leaked down through the hair to the rug, so deep a wound that there could be no question but that the man was dead.

But Sam Boyd gave the wound only a passing glance, for his eyes had locked on the dead man's face. It was Roger Bowman, the man who had given him the photostat, and then sent the blonde to take it away, the man who had driven the yellow roadster away from the Norcross ranch only a little over an hour before.

Sam Boyd didn't like death and he liked murder less. There was something about murder that demanded action. It imposed a mandate upon the living, forcing them to take action, to do something.

Sam Boyd didn't want to do anything. He hadn't liked Roger Bowman and the man's death left him utterly unmoved, but there was Foster to be considered. Foster had given him a job to do, a photostat to deliver.

The photostat had no commercial value – or did it? Certainly it had had value to Roger Bowman, or rather the letter which it reproduced had had value.

And Ann Norcross. What about her? Where was she? Her coupé was parked in the driveway. Was she somewhere in this house?

Boyd turned, scowling, and pulled open the door into the hall. The whole business was a mess. The temptation was to get out of here, now, to get back to Los Angeles and forget the whole dreary business.

Boyd soon found Ann Norcross. Though he didn't know who the pretty girl with tape on her wrists and tape across her lips was until he freed her. All he knew was that some pretty girl had been bound and left sitting in the corner of the pantry.

Her reaction was hardly what he had expected. He had hardly freed her mouth when she said angrily:

"Perhaps you'll tell me the meaning of this?"

"I'd hoped that you could tell me," Boyd said. "You might start with your name."

She gave him a long, steady, questioning look. Her eyes were brown and large and level. There was no fear about her.

"I'm Ann Norcross," she said finally. "I suppose you aren't the man who tied me up?"

He shook his head and, somehow, she believed him.

"What happened?" he asked her.

"I came out to see Roger Bowman," she explained. "He phoned me this morning. When I knocked, the front door opened and I stepped in. It was dark in the hall, coming out of the light. I thought the man I saw was

Mr Bowman, but I couldn't be sure. Whoever it was grabbed me before I knew what was happening and held a cloth with some sweet smelling stuff over my face."

"Chloroform," Boyd guessed.

She ignored the interruption. "When I came to, I was bound, gagged, in that pantry. I don't know how long I'd been there. A long time, I guess."

Boyd nodded. Bowman had evidently lured the girl here to clear the way for his blonde to receive the photostat. But who had killed Bowman?

"Bowman's dead," he said, and told her who he was and what had happened.

She listened, her face not changing expression, even when he mentioned the photostat. But when he mentioned the blonde who had impersonated her, she spoke all right.

"That's Laura," she decided without hesitation.

"Laura?"

"Jack Dillon's girl. Laura Bingham, I've heard her name is, but she is known only as Laura – and she's the star of the show at the Horseshoe."

Boyd nodded slowly. He had heard of the Horseshoe, a night-club and gambling place, but he had never seen it. The place had opened since his last visit to Vegas.

"This doesn't help us," he said. "We – "

He stopped short as from without came the sound of several cars turning into the drive.

"Visitors!" he muttered.

He thought of the dead man in the library. This was going to be bad. Very, very bad. He took the girl's arm and hurried her across the kitchen to the porch beyond. Several khaki-clad men were coming up the walk and the one in front carried a heavy service gun.

"Hold it, you!" he ordered.

Sam Boyd held it, but the girl with him pushed forward.

"What's the matter, Al?" she asked.

The man with the gun stopped, staring at the girl.

"Why, Miss Norcross, what are you doing here?"

"It's a long story," she said. "But you – how did you happen to show up here?"

Sam Boyd already knew the answer for he had spotted his cab driver at the edge of the driveway. The uniformed man confirmed his guess.

"That lug," – he indicated to the cab driver – "came bursting into the office and said that somebody was crashing into the Bowman place." He looked at Sam Boyd. "Know this man?" he asked the girl.

She surprised Boyd by nodding. "He's a friend of mine," she said. "He works for my lawyer. He came over from Los Angeles to see me."

"But what's he doing here?" The khaki-clad man was still suspicious, although he had replaced his gun in its open holster.

"He came to find me," she said. "I've been held a prisoner here since before noon."

"A prisoner?" They all stared at her. "By Bowman?"

She shook her head. "I don't know, and we'll never find out from Roger Bowman. He's dead."

The policeman, a sergeant, looked at Sam Boyd with angry bafflement.

"I don't get it," he said. "This Roger Bowman was a big shot. Why, he owned that new plant out on the road to Boulder. Why should he want to tie Miss Norcross up, and how did you know she was here anyhow?"

Boyd shrugged. "I'm psychic."

The sergeant scratched his head, shoving his uniform cap back to expose a shock of thick black hair.

"The Chief is going to want a better story than that," he said. "Suppose you come down and tell him. You too, Miss Norcross."

"Do we ride with you?" Sam Boyd asked, elaborately polite, "or will we be allowed the luxury of this cab?"

"Take the cab," the sergeant told him. "One thing about this country. You aren't going far unless we want you to."

Sam Boyd, gazing at the wide expanse of sweeping desert agreed sadly. That was the trouble with this country. In early days, its remoteness had made it a perfect hiding place for outlaws. But times change. The very remoteness, the few main roads, made it a place from which escape was almost impossible. A phone call or a wire, and officers would be waiting along each of the main highways to pick you up.

He turned without a word and piloted the girl toward the waiting cab. The driver lounged beside his vehicle eyeing Boyd uncertainly.

"Hope you ain't mad about me going for the cops," he said tentatively. "But a man's gotta be careful, and when I see you prying at that window, I says, 'Herbert, this is no place for you.'"

"I should forget the four bucks I owe you," Boyd told him sourly, "but I won't. The police station, my man, and don't spare the horsepower . . ."

The Police Chief was small and old, and tired-looking. His white hair needed cutting. His mustaches drooped a little and had a brownish stain at the ends from contact with the cigar which he held clamped between his thin lips.

He listened without comment to the sergeant's report, then ignoring Boyd, looked at the girl.

"Well, Ann?"

The girl moved a little uneasily under the stare of his level blue eyes.

"That's about the way it is," she said. "This man" – she indicated the silent Boyd – "was sent down here with some papers for me. He didn't find me at my place so he went over to Bowman's."

"Why?" The chief's voice was soft, but the question had the effect of a pistol shot.

When the girl fumbled for words, Boyd picked it up. He was used to thinking on his feet, used to matching wits with some of the smartest lawyers on the Coast.

"Bowman was a former partner of Miss Norcross' father," he said easily. "I knew that. I'd also seen him drive away from the Norcross house with a girl in his car. I thought it might be Miss Norcross, so I had the taxi bring me over to Bowman's. The driver will bear me out."

"That doesn't explain why you should pry open a window." The Chief's voice was chilly.

"Doesn't it?" Sam Boyd sounded surprised. "Miss Norcross' coupé was parked in the drive. I figured that if she was with Bowman she would most certainly come back after her car. I wasn't going to sit down in the sun and wait – not when there was a nice comfortable house handy."

The Chief's voice was heavy with irony. "I suppose you always break into houses, merely to wait?"

"Why not?" said Boyd. "I knew Bowman wouldn't care."

"Maybe he did," said the Chief softly. "Maybe he met you inside the house, objected, and you killed him. He hadn't been dead long when my men got there."

They stared at each other. Sam Boyd's lips twisted a little.

"Maybe," he said. "I never argue with cops. If that's what you think, Chief, lock me up. But you'd better make it good because I don't think my boss will like the idea, and my boss is one of the best lawyers in the world."

Anger brought a dull flush up into the Chief's sallow cheeks.

"I don't like smart people either," he warned.

"And I don't like being accused of murder," Boyd said levelly.

"Then tell the truth!" The Chief had come out of his chair. "Tell the truth or maybe we'll pound it out of you!"

Boyd grinned. This was the kind of language he understood, the kind of people he was used to doing business with.

"I can save you trouble," he said softly. "Call up LA. Ask the boys down at Headquarters just how far you get, pounding information out of Sam Boyd. It's been tried, my friend. A lot of people have split knuckles from pounding against my hard head."

"Think pretty well of yourself." The Chief had dropped his voice. He settled back in the desk chair, his whole manner changing.

"No," said Boyd slowly. "Matter of fact, I don't. I'm probably something of a heel when you come right down to it, but calling me that is a privilege I reserve for my friends."

The Chief chuckled. "I almost like you," he said, "but that doesn't mean that I'm going to let you get away with murder. I don't think that either of you are telling the truth – at least, all the truth. I can't beat up Miss Norcross, and for the moment I'm willing to take your word that a beating wouldn't make you talk. You can go now, but don't leave town until I say the word."

Boyd's mouth twisted. "I'll bet I'd have a swell chance," he said bitterly. "Come on, Ann."

Silently the girl rose and followed him to the door. When they reached it the Chief's voice stopped them.

"When your conscience begins to hurt I'll always be here, ready to listen to your confession."

Boyd shut the door quietly. He didn't speak, all the way down the dirty hall, nor as he held the door for the girl to pass outside.

But as they walked toward the gaudy lights of Fremont he said softly:

"That old devil's smart. He knows that something is going on, and he's bound to find out sooner or later about that photostat. Have you mentioned it to anyone?"

She shook her head.

"When he does," Boyd went on, "he'll be sure you hired me to kill Bowman to keep him from showing that letter in court and exposing your dad. You didn't by any chance kill him at that, did you, chick?"

She turned, startled. "What are you saying? You saw me tied up."

He nodded. "What am I saying? But then, I'm a heel, as I told the Chief. I think of things like that. You might have had help, a friend who tied you after you bashed in Bowman's head."

"You're crazy!"

He nodded. "It helps, this is a crazy business. You didn't know about your father's tie-up with the Germans, did you? If you had, you'd never have started that suit to recover his share of the company."

"My father wasn't tied up with Germans!" He could tell by her tone that she was suddenly and deeply angry, although he could not see her face in the darkness. "My father was one of the most patriotic men who ever lived!"

Boyd sounded mocking. "I suppose he signed that letter I saw from patriotic motives."

"I don't know what he thought he was signing," she flashed. "You see, my father was so nearly blind that he could barely find his way around a room alone. Roger Bowman tricked him. We knew it then, although my father refused to believe it. Dad thought the company was in a bad way, due to the war. He sold out because he felt that his blindness made him a hindrance rather than a help."

Boyd whistled softly into the darkness. "A nice man, Bowman. I'm almost sorry I wasn't the one to slam in his head. A shame Foster didn't know this."

She nodded. "I told him, on the phone, yesterday. He was much surprised."

Boyd thought Foster was in for more surprises. He meant to wire him as soon as they got back to town.

3 DEAL FOR HALF A MILLION

The big horseshoe sign above the door glittered as if it were studded with real diamonds instead of light bulbs. Boyd took a look at it from the far side of Fremont before crossing the crowded street.

The town had grown since he had been there last. Two or three big stores gave it a really businesslike look in spite of the string of gambling clubs, saloons and restaurants.

The Horseshoe Club was something different. Vegas had had night-clubs before, mostly beyond the limits of the dusty town, but this was a night-club in the center of the city, a club patterned after the early concert saloons of Frontier days.

Boyd crossed the street and pushed open the door. To the right was a long bar, flanked by two roulette wheels and a crap layout, for even here gambling held sway. But it was not the main attraction. The room was filled with small tables, and at the end there was a stage.

A modern swing band filled one end of the platform and the leader acted as master of ceremonies for the show. It was strictly modern, and a burlesque was on the boards when Boyd walked in.

The place was crowded. Smoke made long heavy bluish layers beneath the ceiling. Hurrying waitresses kept the beer mugs on the crowded tables filled.

The noise of the place was almost deafening, but before Boyd had reached the bar, it died away to a mere murmur. Even the waitresses stilled the clinking of the glasses on the trays as the master of ceremonies stepped toward the center of the stage.

"All right, boys and girls! What do you want?"

"We want Laura!" It was a shout which shook the blue layers of tobacco smoke and threatened to lift the ceiling. "Give us Laura!"

"You've got her!"

The announcer spread his hands. The drums roared and a slide man went after a high note as the band swung into the "Trolley Song."

Laura appeared suddenly from the wings. She was riding on a child's toy street car, the bell clanging loudly. The customers took up the beat with the heavy glass beer mugs. The place was bedlam. Then all was still as the girl swung free of the toy and sang.

She could sing, and she could dance. Sam Boyd had seen a lot worse acts along the strip in Hollywood. The crowd loved it. They loved her, and let the world know it.

There must have been five hundred in the room. Workers, soldiers, tourists, all mixed up and yelling for the blonde who had stopped the show, the girl who had just danced off into the wings.

There was a door at the end of the bar which evidently led back stage. Sam Boyd set his glass on the bar and made toward it. Inside the door was a man. He was young, dark-haired. He sat on a tilted chair, his feet propped against the opposite wall so that his legs blocked the passage.

He looked up, saw Boyd in the curtained entrance and failed to smile.

"Wrong door, Mac. Beat it."

Boyd looked at him and decided he didn't like what he saw. He took a step forward.

The seated man tried to reach under his coat and get up at the same time. He could have been reaching for a match. Boyd had no way of knowing, and he wasn't one to take chances. His big hand shot out, caught the man's right foot before the fellow could lower it to the floor and heaved.

The man stopped reaching under his coat and clawed the air in a desperate effort to save his balance. He failed, landing against the dirty floor on the back of his neck.

Boyd knelt on his chest, found the gun which the man's groping fingers had failed to reach and transferred it to his own pocket. Then he rose, watching his victim climb slowly to his feet.

Most of the fight had disappeared from the dark-haired man, but he tried to bluster.

"Say, what are you trying to do?"

"I did it," said Boyd gently. "Next time a gentleman comes calling on a lady, don't play tough, chum. Someone might misunderstand. Someone might feed you your gun and make you like it. Now, where's Laura's room?"

The man hesitated and Boyd raised a big hand for a backward cuff.

"Remember, Cousin," he said.

The man remembered. "Orders are she ain't to be bothered," he said sullenly.

"I'm giving the orders." Boyd sounded like a patient man about at the end of his forbearance. "Where's the room?"

The man told him and Boyd pushed on down the passage with never a backward look.

He paused before the door of the girl's dressing room and his big knuckles beat out a steady tattoo.

"Come in, Jack." Her voice was not distinct.

Boyd opened the door. "It isn't Jack," he said, and stepped in, shutting the door behind him.

Laura had been standing with her back to the door, staring through the dark window. She turned now and there was no surprise, no expression of any kind on her face.

"Hi, Mac," she said. "I've been expecting you to show up."

"Have you?" said Sam Boyd. He was thinking she was one of the most beautiful women he had ever seen – beautiful and dangerous.

She nodded. "Sure, ever since I heard Roger Bowman got bumped. How come you didn't tell the cops about the little act I put on for you this afternoon?"

"Maybe I liked the color of your eyes."

She gave him a long, careful look.

"Sing another tune, mister. Little Laura's been at this racket a long spell now. You aren't the type to go soft for a dame."

"Maybe I thought they wouldn't believe me."

"Sure, and maybe you thought you'd get the little photostat back and that no one would find out your girl friend's dad had played a double game with the Nazis."

"You guess too well," he said.

Her laugh had the tinkly sound of breaking glass.

"Now you're getting smart. Play it straight with little Laura and we'll all live long and be healthy. How much is the little piece of shiny paper worth?"

Sam Boyd stuck one hand into his pocket. He drew forth some change – a quarter, two dimes and several pennies. He considered them carefully, then selected one of the dimes and extended it toward the girl. Her blue eyes glittered a little.

"Look, Mac. You think you're a rugged character, but you aren't rugged enough to play games with little Laura. I know my cards, Mac. I'm holding them in this and I'm going to cash in."

"Are you?" he said. "What would the cops do if I told them about the photostat, if I suggested that maybe you killed Bowman to get possession of it."

"That's silly," she said. "I didn't kill Roger Bowman. I rode home with him and he loaned me the car to come back to town."

"And you've got the photostat. It seems a little strange that Bowman would go to all the trouble he did to get it and then leave it with you."

She smirked. "That's what he did though. He was going to meet someone at the house and he didn't want to have it with him. He gave it to me for safe keeping."

Her words still didn't make sense and Sam Boyd said so.

"I think I'll tell the cops," he said. "It will be hard on Miss Norcross but better that the world find out about her father than that the cops stretch my neck for a killing I didn't do. Who did Bowman meet at that house? Do you know?"

"Sure," said the girl, and smiled thinly. "He met his murderer. All you've got to do is decide who that is."

"It isn't my business," Boyd said. "I'm going to spill to the cops."

He started to turn, but even as he did, the door behind him opened.

"You ain't going to tell the cops one thing," said a voice.

It was a high voice, a little shrill, but it matched its owner perfectly. He was a little man, barely five feet, yet so well-proportioned that he looked like a bantam fighting cock. Black hair, heavy beard, so that although he had shaved closely only a short time before his cheeks were blue black.

Once seen, no one ever forgot Jack Dillon, and Boyd had seen him any number of times. Dillon had played many small roles in pictures, had at one time led a band composed of men not much larger than he was, but Boyd had not associated him with the name of the Horseshoe's owner until Dillon came into the room.

"So, it's you?"

"It's me."

There was a full foot difference in their height. Dillon would almost have had to stand on a chair to reach Boyd's jaw, but nothing in the man's attitude showed that he was conscious of the difference in their size.

"I had a hunch it was you when Laura spoke about a Boyd," Dillon said. "You always managed to get yourself in trouble."

"Am I in trouble?" Sam Boyd managed to sound faintly surprised.

"Mister," said Dillon, "you never knew what trouble was until you came to this town. You're in to your neck now and unless you get some help, you'll be in over your ears."

"Help, from whom?"

"Me," said the little man, and expanded his chest until it seemed to gain a good two inches. "I got this town right where I want it. When I snap my fingers, it rolls over and says uncle."

Sam Boyd looked impressed. "You don't say! You mean that if you gave the word, the murder rap the cops are holding over my head would be fixed."

"Like that." The little man was certain of himself. He winked at the blonde when he thought Sam Boyd was not looking.

"Swell," Boyd said. "I always knew you were my pal. Just call that old Chief up and fix things, will you?"

"Not so fast."

Dillon drew a long, ivory cigarette holder from his breast pocket, fitted a smoke into its end and lit it carefully. The holder was so long that Boyd feared it might over-balance the little man who held it up at a cocky angle and surveyed Boyd through the smoke.

"You think we're dumb," he accused. "Oh, don't bother to deny it. I know how your mind works. But we aren't. We realize that the company Roger Bowman controlled is worth a great deal of money. It wasn't such a large company before the war, but now it's expanded so that it's one of the big three or four in the industry."

"So," said Boyd. He stole a glance toward the blonde, but her full attention was on the little man.

"So," said Dillon. "And Miss Norcross has a good chance of winning her case in court, of getting back what Bowman took from her father – if we don't tell what we know about that photostat."

"Fine," said Boyd. "But you're overlooking one thing, my miniature friend. What about the original letter?"

Dillon stopped him by raising both hands, small palms outward.

"We thought of that." He smiled. "Even now my men are taking steps to get it."

"You know where it is?"

Dillon gave him a thin-lipped smile. "Laura here was a friend of Mr Bowman's. He told her things which he told to few people. You see, we have things under control, very good control. All you have to do is to make your deal with us."

"And the deal is?"

"Half a million dollars," said the little man. In spite of his composure his tone quavered a little as he mentioned the sum. "A mere half million."

"Fine," said Boyd. "Do you want it in dollar bills?"

Dillon got mad. "You think you're humorous!" he yelled. "You think you don't need us, but you'll find out, you and that high and mighty Norcross dame! You'll come to us, both of you, crawling on your knees. I tell you, we got things arranged!"

"You wouldn't have had a hand in arranging Bowman's death, would you?" Boyd said softly. He was no longer smiling. "You wouldn't have figured this all out and then rubbed Bowman, just to put yourself in a trading position?"

"Why, you –" Dillon clawed at his coat. "I'll – "

Boyd reached out a big hand. He brushed the cigarette holder out of the way and seized Dillon's lapels, lifting the man until the small shoes were clear of the floor.

"Stop reaching. If you get that gun out, I'll make you eat it."

He turned suddenly, swung Dillon in a circle and let go of his hold so that the small man crashed into the blonde, just as she straightened from the dressing table, a gun in her hand. Both of them went down in a tangle of arms and legs. Boyd stooped and picked up both guns.

He made no effort to assist either of his victims to their feet.

"You two have the wrong slant." There was a trace of bitterness in his voice. "Maybe you can do business with Miss Norcross. You'll have to talk to her. But I don't enter into it, not at all."

He turned and walked out. The same guard was seated beside the entrance, his feet blocking the passage. When he saw Boyd coming he leaped up. Boyd half-expected trouble, but the guard made no effort to block his progress. After Boyd had passed he paused in the doorway, hesitated for an instant, then drew the man's gun from his pocket.

"Here," he said. "I didn't mean to keep this so long. You may need it later – need it bad – to put a bullet between my shoulders."

He thrust the gun into the startled man's hands and left the place.

4 LAURA SPRINGS A SURPRISE

Back at his hotel the clerk stopped Sam Boyd.

"There's a man waiting in your room, Mr Boyd," he said. "He seemed to think it was all right if he went up."

Boyd nodded and walked across the lobby toward the elevator.

The man awaiting him in his room was Lawyer Tony Foster, his employer. Foster was sitting in the easy chair in the corner of the room, his feet on the bed.

"I got a plane as soon as your wire came," he said. "I was lucky. I got here twenty minutes ago."

"You'd have been lucky if the plane had taken you the other way," Boyd grunted.

The lawyer became concerned. "As bad as that?"

"Worse," said Boyd, and slung his hat on the bed. "The cops can't make up their minds, but they have a sneaking hunch that I did for Bowman and that Miss Norcross hired me to do it. She's sweet."

"Who?" The lawyer seemed amused. "The case?"

"The girl," said Boyd. "She's living back in the Dark Ages when women were women and didn't carry welding torches, but nothing breaks her nerve. Even being tied up for hours in that closet didn't seem to faze her, but there's a lot of things I don't get. Why did Bowman give us that photostat and then take all the trouble to make certain Miss Norcross didn't see it?"

"Only Bowman could answer that."

"And he's dead. We've got other little playmates taking a hand in the game too."

The lawyer straightened with interest. "Who?"

Boyd told him about the blonde and Dillon.

"I don't know whether you remember the little runt or not," he added. "He was around LA up until a couple of months ago. He's a bad hombre for my money. If he saw a chance at a dishonest dollar, he wouldn't have hesitated to beat in Bowman's head."

Foster was interested. "Think he did it?"

"The best we've got so far," Boyd admitted. "He's got kind of a warped brain. Might have figured that with Roger Bowman out of the way, he could cut in on this Norcross deal. Even offered to sell me the photostat and the original letter."

Foster seemed startled. "You mean he has them both?"

"He's got the photostat," Boyd said, "and he claims that he has one of his men out picking up the letter." He took a restless turn on the room. "Tell me," he went on, "how much chance would the Norcross girl have of upsetting the sale, of getting back part of the company, without that letter?"

"Before Bowman died, I'd have said she had an excellent chance," Foster said. "Her father was in poor health at the time he signed that letter."

"And almost blind," Boyd cut in.

The lawyer nodded. "And almost blind," he repeated, showing no surprise at Boyd's knowledge. "Besides which, Bowman had Norcross out at his ranch at the time of the sale. Ann was in Florida, doing war work."

"And you? How come you weren't around to protect their interest?"

"I was in Washington," Foster explained. "I didn't know anything about the sale until months after it happened. By then, there wasn't any use in saying anything to Norcross. He was a sick man."

"The girl doesn't believe her father ever knew what was in the letter he signed," Boyd pointed out. "How blind was he at the time?"

Foster snapped his long fingers. "I never thought of that," he said. "Of course she's right. Let these people produce their photostat! Let them show the original of the letter if they can. We'll call Norcross' doctor, we'll laugh their letter out of court. The fight won't be as hard as it was before Bowman died. He didn't have any heirs."

"Oh, yes he did."

Both men had been so intent on the conversation that they had not been conscious that Boyd's door was not quite latched, that someone was standing outside it.

Boyd crossed the room in three strides and jerked the door wide. Laura was standing in the hall, her white dress covered with a short mink coat.

She looked more beautiful than ever, in fact as beautiful as any woman that Boyd had ever seen.

Foster's eyes widened as she came in. She might have been a queen, or a top-flight movie star, from the way she looked around casually.

"Who's this?" Foster said.

"This," Boyd said, "is Miss Laura Bingham – known better as simply Laura. Laura – Mr Foster, the Norcross attorney."

The girl inclined her sleek blonde head, looking at Foster's heavily lined face with interest.

"He's cute," she said.

Boyd would hardly have termed his boss cute. He could think of a number of adjectives which would have fitted the lawyer better, but Foster did not seem to mind. He grinned at the girl, but his eyes were cool and watchful, and not smiling.

"So, Roger Bowman left an heir," he said. "Would you mind telling us who?"

The girl did not smile. "Me," she said. "How do you like those apples, uncle? I'm his wife."

"His wife?"

Both stared at her. But if she was conscious of their stares, she gave no sign. There was a hand-bag under her arm. From it she extracted a folded paper which she handed to Foster.

He opened it wordlessly and, peering over his shoulder, Boyd saw that it was a marriage license. Subconsciously he noted the date. It had been issued that morning.

Boyd sensed Foster's surprise. It wasn't anything that the lawyer did, or said. He said nothing. He merely folded the paper carefully and passed it back to the girl. She seemed a little disappointed by his reaction. "Aren't you going to say anything?" she asked.

He shrugged. "What's there to say, as far as that license and the fake ceremony are concerned?"

"It wasn't fake!" she flared. "Roger had been after me to marry him for a long time."

"So you chose the day he died to say yes?" There was a tinge of sarcasm in Foster's voice.

She was sullen. "I didn't know this ape," – she indicated Boyd with a nod of her blonde head – "was going to bash Roger's brains out, but since that happened, I'm not going to let some little chick go into court and do me out of my rights. I am Roger's widow, and what was his is mine."

"That is for the courts to decide," said Foster. "Good night, please."

She bit her lower lip. It was evident that she had expected a much different reception.

"When you change your mind," she flashed, "I'll be out at Roger's – my ranch. You can come to me next time."

The door slammed and Boyd and Foster looked at each other.

"See what I mean?" said Boyd.

The lawyer nodded thoughtfully. "They move fast," he said, more to himself than Boyd. "Do you suppose she was really married to him?"

Boyd shrugged. "From what I've seen of this country, they could probably fake the license, get some snide justice of the peace to say that he married them, and make it stick."

The lawyer shrugged, glancing at his watch.

"I've got a date to meet Ann Norcross in the lobby in ten minutes," he said. "As far as I can see, there's no use us poking into the Bowman murder. It isn't our business."

Boyd's mouth was bitter. "It's not your business," he said as they moved toward the door, "but the Chief of Police is making it mine. He's trying to put me right in the middle and, for my money, he's making a good job of it, a very good job, indeed. . . ."

The airport was long, and windy, and deserted. Sam Boyd had taxied to the field and asked for the pilot who had flown the special plane in from Los Angeles an hour ago. The pilot was long and thin and bitter. He wasn't bitter at Boyd, merely at age which put him to piloting pleasure craft while other men flew fighters.

Boyd had not finished talking to the pilot when a shadow moved across from the operations building and joined him. The man was not in uniform, but he had no need to be.

"Your name Boyd?" he snapped.

Boyd's impulse was to tell him that the name was Knopke. That the K was silent, as in cat. He liked the name Knopke and had always meant to use it, some time. But this time didn't seem to be just right. This cop looked smart.

"Yes, I'm Boyd," he said, instead.

"And what would you be doing out here?"

Boyd spread his hands. "Trying to talk this gentleman into giving me a ride to LA. Anything wrong with that?"

"For you, yes." The cop found a tooth pick in his vest pocket and used it thoughtfully. "There's a little bit of murder you're concerned in. The Chief wouldn't like it if you went around taking plane rides before it's cleared up. Wouldn't you like to ride back to town with me?"

Boyd said that he wouldn't like to, but that he would.

"I'm an agreeable fellow," he added, as they reached the squad car and climbed in. "My friends all call me Sunshine. You wouldn't care to call me Sunshine, would you?"

The cop didn't answer. It was obvious that he considered his passenger a screwball and he was a little leery of screwballs.

Fremont Street was ablaze with lights as they drove along it, and Boyd glanced at his watch. It was after twelve. That was the one thing he liked about this town. It never went to bed.

He said good-by pleasantly to his driver before the hotel and was warned to keep out of trouble. Boyd nodded. He intended to do just that.

He walked into the hotel lobby, and he halted at sight of Ann

Norcross, huddled in one of the leather chairs. She rose and met his questioning look.

"I'm waiting for Mr Foster," she said. "And I'm beginning to worry."

Boyd showed his surprise. "I thought Foster was going to meet you here?"

"He did," she explained. "An hour and a half ago. He told me what had happened and we agreed that if this man Dillon would listen to a reasonable settlement, we'd better deal with him. Whether my father knew what he was signing when he put his name to that letter or not, it still would arouse suspicion with some people."

"So you're going to buy Dillon off?" Boyd was disappointed, and let the disappointment show in his voice. "If you have money to throw around – "

"Oh, but I haven't." The girl shook her head. "I hardly have a cent. All the money we had went for doctors, to try and save Dad."

"But it costs money to sue corporations."

"Mr Foster took care of that," she explained. "He took the case on a contingency basis. He gets half of everything we recover. But I'm worried. I'm afraid that Mr Dillon has done something to him."

"Let your Uncle Samuel worry about that," Boyd said. "You wait right here – or better still, go on home. I'll phone you when I find out anything."

"No," she told him. "I'm coming with you."

He started to argue, but Sam Boyd was used to reading people and one look at this girl's eyes told him that argument wouldn't do any good. Tiredly, he shrugged. It was bad enough to go up against the midget gunman without having a girl on his hands to worry about.

Boyd was not kidding himself. Dillon was tough, and he had a lot of men around the Horseshoe, men who would be as tough as he was, but facing them would be easier than handling this girl. Once and for all, Sam Boyd decided that he did not care for women.

When Boyd and Ann Norcross reached the Horseshoe, the place seemed to be doing more business than it had been earlier, if that were possible. It was so jammed that it was almost impossible for them to force their way through the press.

Boyd used his big shoulders and elbows and the girl hung on to the tails of his coat. He got a lot of dirty looks from people whom his elbows thrust out of the way, but he was too big for anyone to want to argue with him.

They gained the door leading behind scenes, to find the same guard barring the passage. He started to jump up, recognized Boyd, and took his feet out of the way.

"Okay, Mac, she's all yours."

"Where'll I find Dillon?" Boyd asked.

The guard shrugged. "In his office, I guess. It's on your right as you go back, but he's sore as a boil."

At the moment, Sam Boyd was a little sore himself. Like most even-tempered men, he was slow to anger, but this had been building up all day, ever since the blonde had locked him in the closet.

He went on, conscious that Ann still followed, still had hold of his coat tails.

They must have made a humorous picture but the guard did not smile. Evidently he'd had enough of Sam Boyd earlier.

It was not hard to find Dillon's office. They could hear the man's squeaky voice long before they reached the door. Dillon was bawling someone out and making an elegant job of it.

Boyd didn't knock. He twisted the knob, hoved the door wide, and was in the room before Dillon realized he was there.

A man faced the little gunman across the desk – a tall man in a dinner jacket. Evidently he was one of the employees and he'd done something to arouse Dillon's wrath. The little man was cursing him in three languages.

He stopped in the middle of a word as he saw Boyd and thrust one shaking finger toward him.

"Get out and stay out!" he ordered the detective.

"No," said Boyd, and the muscle along the side of his jaw corded a little. "Not until I've talked with you, Jackie boy. Not until you've told me a lot of things."

Dillon seemed to forget the man he'd been bawling out as he focussed his full anger on Boyd.

"Get out!" he repeated. "You've caused me nothing but trouble. I hope I go deaf before I ever hear your name mentioned again!"

"Me cause you trouble?" Boyd was surprised.

"Look," said Dillon. "I got a nice quiet, respectable business here. I'm minding my own affairs, staying out from behind the eight ball. I've got an entertainer, the best in the business, and a looker that doesn't have to give nothing to any movie star that ever lived. So what happens! She meets this Roger Bowman and he makes a play. Now she tells me they're hitched, and walks out. So where am I at? My customers are yelling for Laura, and there ain't no Laura."

"Was she really married to Bowman?"

"How the devil do I know?" The little man was practically beside himself with anger. "Does it make a difference whether she'd married the lug or whether she got one of her pals to fix her up with a fake license? I lose her, which is all that matters."

"You change quick," said Boyd. "The last time I saw you, you were backing up her game."

"That's your fault!" Dillon was savage. "You got tough. You let her see you weren't afraid of me, so she washed me out of the deal. She flashed the marriage license she'd been holding out. She said she didn't need me any more, and walked out."

"Did you tell Foster this?"

"Foster?" Dillon stared. "What's this Foster got to do with it?"

"Miss Norcross' attorney," Boyd said. "He came over to see you an hour or so ago."

"You're crazy!" Dillon told him with conviction. "I ain't seen any Fosters, or any other attorneys for that matter."

"But he did come over here." Ann Norcross spoke for the first time. "He told me he was coming to see you."

"He didn't," said Dillon, and Boyd couldn't tell whether the little man was lying or not. He stared at Dillon for a full minute, trying to decide. Then he said, "Grab your hat. You're coming for a ride with us."

"A ride?" snapped Dillon. "Who do you think you are?"

"You're coming," said Boyd, and brought the banker's special into sight. "Better have your friend here come too. He might stir up trouble if we left him behind." He indicated the silent man in the dinner jacket.

Dillon started to argue, but Boyd moved the gun suggestively.

"You know me, Jackie. It would give me the greatest of pleasure to shoot off a couple of fingers. Your customers are making so much racket out front that no one would ever know the difference."

Dillon wilted. "Okay, Sam, okay." All the fight seemed to have gone out of him. "This is one day they can tear out of the calendar and throw away. I hope I never see another day like it so long as I live."

"Got a car?"

The little man nodded. "Out back."

"Then come on."

"Where are we going?"

"Roger Bowman's ranch, and you might as well make it quick."

5 FINGER OF SUSPICION

A lot of lights were on in the rambling ranchhouse when Sam Boyd and his companions turned into the grounds, and a coupé was parked in the drive. As they pulled up behind it, Ann Norcross gave a little cry.

"Why, that's my car! I loaned it to Mr Foster."

Boyd didn't answer. He was too busy herding his charges into the wide porch and across to the front door. The door was not locked and, at Boyd's orders, Jack Dillon pushed it open.

"Call Laura," Boyd directed, moving his gun for emphasis.

The little man raised his squeaky voice. It echoed back to them through the house – the only answer. Boyd swore softly under his breath. He started to tell the little man to call again, but there was no need, for the squeaky voice once more filled the house, and now there was a note of urgent nervousness in it. Still there was no answer.

Ann Norcross pushed closer to Boyd as if she found comfort in his nearness.

"What's it mean?" she asked.

Again he didn't answer because he was not sure. Instead, he told Dillon:

"Go ahead. Let's have a look at the joint."

They had a look, and they found Laura in the same room that Roger Bowman's body had occupied earlier that afternoon. She was dead. Boyd judged that she hadn't been dead long, and she had died in the same manner that death had reached Bowman. Someone had hit her on the top of the head. Hit her hard.

Ann Norcross showed emotion that she had not shown that afternoon.

"I didn't know her," she said, "but she was beautiful. It was a shame for her to die!"

Sam Boyd had his own ideas about that. Laura had been beautiful, yes. But the old saying was running through his head – "Beauty is as beauty does," and Laura had used her beauty not wisely, but too well.

Dillon hadn't spoken since they had found the girl's body. He stood looking down at her, his small face chalk-white, his fists clenched.

"If I ever find out who did this – " He let the words choke off as if they caught in his throat. "Come on! Let's look around the house."

Boyd offered no objections. All he did was to manage to keep Dillon and the man in the dinner coat in front of him.

They searched the place, but it was not until they opened the door off the kitchen behind which Ann Norcross had been hidden that they found Foster.

There was tape over the attorney's lips, tape around his ankles and wrists, and a swelling blue bump on his forehead. He groaned weakly as they dragged him out into the light, and Dillon's man in the dinner jacket unfastened him and freed his mouth.

Dillon pounced on Foster like a striking snake.

"Who did it?" he demanded. "Who killed her, and tied you up?"

Foster shook his head as if to clear it.

"Is she dead – the blonde, I mean?" He struggled to his feet, stood swaying for a moment, his eyes settling on Dillon. "You ought to know," he said to the little man in a different voice. "You hit me on the head. You probably killed her after you tied me up and stuck me in the same cupboard you put Ann Norcross in this afternoon."

"I?" Dillon stared at him.

"You came in while we were arguing," said Foster. "I told you to keep out of it, and you hit me on the head."

"He's crazy!" Dillon appealed to Sam Boyd. "I haven't been out here all evening! I've got witnesses to prove I didn't leave the place."

"Then you've got a double." The lawyer felt his head tenderly. "A striking double. We'll let the police decide."

"Wait!" said Sam Boyd. "Wait a minute. Did you tell Foster about your being tied up in that cupboard, Ann?"

"Why no. I – "

"Then how'd you know, Foster?" demanded Boyd. "How'd you know she was tied up in that cupboard, unless you put her there yourself? How'd you know anything about it?"

Foster laughed, a twisted, nasty sound.

"Just who are you working for anyhow?"

"I thought I was working for you," Boyd said slowly. "But I didn't count on murder. Murder is something that has to be straightened out."

"Are you trying to say that I murdered that blonde? That's ridiculous! And naturally you have no proof. As for Bowman, I wasn't even here when he was killed. I didn't fly up from Los Angeles until evening."

"Yes, you did," said Boyd.

He felt weary, depressed. He had worked for this man for three years. He supposed he should feel some loyalty, some regret, but he didn't. He didn't seem to feel anything at all where Foster was concerned.

"You flew up early this morning just after I left LA," he accused. "You arranged for someone else to fly up this afternoon, in your name, just in case of a slip. I talked to the man who was supposed to have flown you this afternoon. He described his passenger, it wasn't you, nor anybody like you. And that business of knowing where Miss Norcross was tied up. You couldn't have known unless you had been here. I think you planned to kill Bowman. As for the blonde, she cut herself in and you had to get rid of her."

"But I was tied up – hit on the head!" protested Foster.

"That's an old stunt," Boyd said. "You were trapped here. You had Miss Norcross' car parked in the drive. You heard us coming and you couldn't get out. It was easy enough to stick the tape on your mouth and ankles. The way it was wrapped on your wrists wasn't so hot. You could have worked loose if you tried."

He was watching the lawyer as he spoke, but he didn't see the gun until it showed in Foster's hand. It was a little gun with two barrels – a museum piece called a sleeve gun.

"All right!" said Foster. "You asked for it. You had to be too smart and make this your business. The local cops would never have figured it out."

"You can't kill all of us with that pop-gun," Boyd told him.

"I can kill the first one who moves!" said Foster. "I hope it's you."

It wasn't. It was Jack Dillon. He had been standing off a little to the right. He took a step forward.

"You killed Laura," he said in his squeaky voice.

"Stand still, you fool!" There was panic in Foster's voice.

"No," said Dillon, and took another step.

The little gun spat. It was hardly an explosion. Even as it sounded, Sam Boyd was in motion. One hand pushed Ann Norcross out of the way. The other made a sweeping arc, driving for Foster's chin. His knuckles hit. The force of the blow drove Foster's head backward so hard that his neck almost snapped.

He went over as though Sam Boyd had used an ax.

Dillon was sitting on the floor, his small arms clasped around his stomach.

"Hurt?" Boyd asked. He was beginning to like this little tough.

"He killed Laura," said Dillon. He pulled the little double-barreled gun toward him with his foot and picked it up, staring at the curious mechanism. "To get shot with this!" He sounded disgusted. "Let's see if it works."

Before Boyd could stop him, he reversed the gun and put a bullet into Foster's stomach.

"I hope that hurts," he muttered, dropping the empty gun. "Hurts like the devil!"

He bent forward and kept bending until he was almost double. Boyd jumped toward him, grabbing his small shoulder, straightening the little man. He was dead.

Foster moaned and tried to move. He couldn't, and his eyes got scared.

"A doctor," he mumbled.

"A doctor isn't going to do you any good," Boyd told him, "although there'll be one on the way with the cops in a minute. Ann is calling them. He shot you in the middle, pal. Know what that means?"

Foster knew. It showed in his eyes.

"Might as well talk," said Boyd. "You won't feel like talking before long."

"Nothing to talk about," Foster was gasping a little. "You haven't got a thing on me."

Boyd shrugged. "You killed Dillon. We can all swear to that, and the little fellow didn't even have a gun. They'll execute you for that pal, if by some miracle you should recover from that stomach ache, so why not be right for once in your worthless life and admit that you were in with Bowman in an effort to rob Ann's father of his share of the company."

"But that doesn't make sense!" the girl protested.

"Sure it does," said Boyd. "He's a smart lawyer, too smart to let a deal like that pass unless he was in on it. Anyhow, I'm guessing that after the steal, Bowman didn't come through with a fair share. Right, Foster?"

The man's eyes were beginning to glaze with pain. He nodded weakly.

"The rat!"

"So," said Boyd, Foster gets the idea of putting the pressure on Bowman by getting you to sue to recover the company."

"He did talk me into it," Ann said. "I'd never have thought of it myself."

"Sure," said Boyd. "The suit was a good idea, but one thing Foster didn't know was that Bowman had played a cute trick. Taking advantage of your father's blindness Bowman got him to sign that letter. I was in the office when Bowman brought it in, and I'll vouch for Foster's surprise."

"Doctor!" the lawyer moaned.

"Look," said Boyd, "there's a doctor coming, but when the cops get here, they'll waste time, questioning you. Tell us now, and the sawbones can go right to work on you."

There was a little foam on Foster's lips. Boyd wiped it away.

"Am I right?"

The wounded man nodded. "Right," he whispered. "Norcross was a sick man. We told him that the expansion of the company was hindered by his condition. He was a trusting old soul. He took my word. I was to get half of his share in the company, but Bowman never paid off."

"So?"

"So I started this suit. Then Bowman produced the letter and we had it photostated. Last night we got together and made a deal. He'd settle with me and I'd advise Ann to take a small sum. Only we didn't want the photostat floating around. If the FBI ever heard of it, there would be an investigation and the whole business might come out."

"Well?"

"Bowman got his girl to pose as Ann Norcross and steal the photostat. He came back to the house here, but he didn't bring it with him. He let her keep it. That made me sore. He acted as if he didn't trust me."

"Tell it straight," said Boyd. "You mean that when Bowman came back, you thought he had the photostat and killed him. You meant to go ahead with the suit all the time. You didn't know until after you'd killed him that the photostat wasn't there. When you found it missing, you didn't know what to do, so you laid low until time to meet me, and then when the blonde stuck her little oar in you followed her out here and killed her. With her and Bowman dead, you had a fair chance to win the suit, and you'd get half."

"You suspected him from the first?" Ann asked soberly.

Boyd shrugged. "No one but Foster and Bowman knew I was bringing that photostat down here, and Bowman didn't know what time I'd arrive.

Yet he and his blonde were at your ranch, waiting, while you were tied up at Bowman's. It was all too pat unless Foster was in on the deal. Then Foster, being a smart lawyer, should have blocked the original sale. I can't say that I suspected him, but I was suspicious. That's why I went out to the airport to check up with the pilot."

"You're smart," she said. "I want you to handle the suit for me."

"You need a lawyer – not a roughneck."

"We'll get a lawyer." She nodded. "But I need someone to tell me what to do."

"I'd go to the FBI" he said. "I'd tell them about the letter, about your father's blindness. They'll investigate – don't worry. If they find out that your dad was not trading with the enemy, you're a cinch to win your suit."

"I said you were smart," she said.

Sam Boyd grinned. He knew that he wasn't so smart, but it was nice that Ann thought so.

"Here come the cops," he told her, as cars made noise in the driveway. "At least, chick, I'm smart enough to know that."

CIGARETTE GIRL
James M. Cain

I'D NEVER SO much as laid eyes on her before going in this place, the
Here's How, a night-club on Route 1, a few miles north of Washington,
on business that was 99 percent silly, but that I had to keep myself. It was
around 8 at night, with hardly anyone there, and I'd just taken a table,
ordered a drink, and started to unwrap a cigar, when a whiff of perfume
hit me, and she swept by with cigarettes. As to what she looked like, I had
only a rear view, but the taffeta skirt, crepe blouse, and silver earrings were
quiet, and the chassis was choice, call it fancy, a little smaller than medium.
So far, a cigarette girl, nothing to rate any cheers, but not bad either, for a
guy unattached who'd like an excuse to linger.

But then she made a pitch, or what I took for a pitch. Her middle-aged
customer was trying to tell her some joke, and taking so long about it the
proprietor got in the act. He was a big, blond, guy, with kind of a decent
face, but he went and whispered to her as though to hustle her up, for
some reason apparently. I couldn't quite figure it out. She didn't much
seem to like it, until her eye caught mine. She gave a little pout, a little
shrug, a little wink, and then just stood there, smiling.

Now I know this pitch and it's nice, because of course I smiled back,
and with that I was on the hook. A smile is nature's freeway: it has
lanes, and you can go any speed you like, except you can't go back.
Not that I wanted to, as I suddenly changed my mind about the
cigar I had in my hand, stuck it back in my pocket, and wigwagged
for cigarettes. She nodded, and when she came over said: "You stop
laughing at me."

"Who's laughing? Looking."

"Oh, of course. That's different."

I picked out a pack, put down my buck, and got the surprise of my life:

she gave me change. As she started to leave, I said "You forgot something, maybe?"

"That's not necessary."

"For all this I get, I should pay."

"All what, sir, for instance?"

"I told you: the beauty that fills my eye."

"The best things in life are free."

"On that basis, fair lady, some of them, here, are tops. Would you care to sit down?"

"Can't."

"Why not?"

"Not allowed. We got rules."

With that she went out toward the rear somewhere, and I noticed the proprietor again, just a short distance away, and realized he'd been edging in. I called him over and said: "What's the big idea? I was talking to her."

"Mister, she's paid to work."

"Yeah, she mentioned about rules, but now they got other things too. Four Freedoms, all kinds of stuff. Didn't anyone ever tell you?"

"I heard of it, yes."

"You're Mr *Here's How*?"

"Jack Conner, to my friends."

I took a V from my wallet, folded it, creased it, pushed it toward him. I said: "Jack, little note of introduction I generally carry around. I'd like you to ease these rules. She's cute, and I crave to buy her a drink."

He didn't see any money, and stood for a minute thinking. Then: "Mister, you're off on the wrong foot. In the first place, she's not a cigarette girl. Tonight, yes, when the other girl is off. But not regular, no. In the second place, she's not any chiselly-wink, that orders rye, drinks tea, takes the four bits you slip her, the four I charge for the drink – and is open to propositions. She's class. She's used to class – out West, with people that have it, and that brought her East when they came. In the third place she's a friend, and before I eased any rules I'd have to know more about you, a whole lot more, than this note tells me.

"Pleased to meet you and all that, but as to who you are, Mr Cameron, and what you are, I still don't know – "

"I'm a musician."

"Yeah? What instrument?"

"Any of them. Guitar, mainly."

Which brings me to what I was doing there. I do play the guitar, play it all day long, for the help I get from it, as it gives me certain chords, the big ones that people go for, and heads me off from some others, the fancy ones on the piano, that other musicians go for. I'm an arranger, based in Baltimore, and had driven down on a little tune detecting. The guy who takes most of my work, Art Lomak, the band leader, writes a few tunes himself, and had gone clean off his rocker about one he said had been stolen, or thefted as they call it. It was one he'd been playing a little, to try it and work out faults, with lyric and title to come, soon as the idea hit him. And then he rang me, with screams. It had already gone on the air, as 20 people had told him, from this same little honky-tonk, as part of a 10 o'clock spot on the Washington FM pick-up. He begged me to be here tonight, when the trio started their broadcast, pick up such dope as I could, and tomorrow give him the low-down.

That much was right on the beam, stuff that goes on every day, a routine I knew by heart. But his tune had angles, all of them slightly peculiar. One was, it had already been written, though it was never a hit and was almost forgotten, in the days when states were hot, under the title *Nevada*. Another was, it had been written even before that, by a gent named Giuseppe Verdi, as part of the *Sicilian Vespers*, under the title *O Tu Palermo*. Still another was, Art was really burned, and seemed to have no idea where the thing had come from. They just can't get it, those big schmalzburgers like him, that what leaks out of their head might, just once, have leaked in. But the twist, the reason I had to come, and couldn't just play it for laughs, was: Art could have been right. Maybe the lilt *was* from him, not from the original opera, or from the first theft, *Nevada*. It's a natural for a 3/4 beat, and that's how Art had been playing it. So if that's how they were doing it here, instead of with *Nevada*'s 4/4, which followed the Verdi signature, there might still be plenty of work for the lawyers Art had put on it, with screams, same like to me.

Silly, almost.

Spooky.

But maybe, just possibly, right.

So Jack, this boss character, by now had smelled something fishy, and suddenly took a powder, to the stand where the fiddlers were parked, as of course the boys weren't there yet, and came back with a Spanish guitar. I took it, thanked him, and tuned. To kind of work it around, in the direction of Art's little problem, and at the same time make like there was nothing at all to conceal, I said I'd come on account of his band, to catch it during the broadcast, as I'd heard it was pretty good. He didn't react, which left me nowhere, but I thought it well to get going.

I played him *Night and Day*, no Segovia job, but plenty good, for free. On "Day and Night", where it really opens up, I knew things to do, and talk suddenly stopped among the scattering of people that were in there. When I finished there was some little clapping, but still he didn't react, and I gave thought to mayhem. But then a buzzer sounded, and he took another powder, out toward the rear this time, where she had disappeared. I began a little beguine, but he was back. He bowed, picked up his B, bowed again, said: "Mr Cameron, the guitar did it. She heard you, and you're in."

"Will you set me up for two?"

"Hold on, there's a catch."

He said until midnight, when one of his men would take over, she was checking his orders. "That means she handles the money, and if she's not there, I could just as well close down. You're invited back with her, but she can't come out with you."

"Oh. Fine."

"Sir, you asked for it."

It wasn't quite the way I'd have picked to do it, but the main thing was the girl, and I followed him through the OUT door, the one his waiters were using, still with my Spanish guitar. But then, all of a sudden, I loved it, and felt even nearer to her.

This was the works of the joint, with a little office at one side, service bar on the other, range rear and centre, the crew in white all around, getting the late stuff ready. But high on a stool, off by herself, on a little railed-in platform where waiters would have to pass, she was waving at me, treating it all as a joke. She called down: "Isn't this a balcony scene for you? You have to play me some music!"

I rattled into it quickly, and when I told her it was *Romeo and Juliet*, she said it was just what she'd wanted. By then Jack had a stool he put next to hers, so I could sit beside her, back of her little desk. He introduced us, and it turned out her name was Stark. I climbed up and there we were, out in the middle of the air, and yet in a way private, as the crew played it funny, to the extent they played it at all, but mostly were too busy even to look. I put the guitar on the desk and kept on with the music. By the time I'd done some *Showboat* she was calling me Bill and to me she was Lydia. I remarked on her eyes, which were green, and showed up bright against her creamy skin and ashy blonde hair. She remarked on mine, which are light, watery blue, and I wished I was something besides tall, thin, and red-haired. But it was kind of cute when she gave a little pinch and nipped one of my freckles, on my hand back of the thumb.

Then Jack was back, with champagne iced in a bucket, which I hadn't ordered. When I remembered my drink, the one I *had* ordered, he said Scotch was no good, and this would be on him. I thanked him, but after he'd opened and poured, and I'd leaned the guitar in a corner and raised my glass to her, I said: "What's made him so friendly?"

"Oh, Jack's always friendly."

"Not to me. Oh, no."

"He may have thought I had it coming. Some little thing to cheer me. My last night in the place."

"You going away?"

"M'm-h'm."

"When?"

"Tonight."

"That's why you're off at 12?"

"Jack tell you that?"

"He told me quite a lot."

"Plane leaves at 1. Bag's gone already. It's at the airport, all checked and ready to be weighed."

She clinked her glass to mine, took a little sip, and drew a deep, trembly breath. As for me, I felt downright sick, just why I couldn't say, as it had all to be strictly allegro, with nobody taking it serious. It stuck in my throat a little when I said: "Well – happy landings. Is it permitted to ask which way that plane is taking you?"

"Home."

"And where's that?"

"It's – not important."

"The West, I know that much."

"What else did Jack tell you?"

I took it, improvised, and made up a little stuff, about her high-toned friends, her being a society brat, spoiled as usual, and the heavy dough she was used to – a light rib, as I thought. But it hadn't gone very far when I saw it was missing bad. When I cut it off, she took it. She said: "Some of that's true, in a way. I was – fortunate, we'll call it. But – you still have no idea, have you, Bill, what I really am?"

"I've been playing by ear."

"I wonder if you want to know?"

"If you don't want to, I'd rather you didn't say."

None of it was turning out quite as I wanted, and I guess maybe I showed it. She studied me a little and asked: "The silver I wear, that didn't tell you anything? Or my giving you change for your dollar? It didn't mean anything to you, that a girl would run a straight game?"

"She's not human."

"*It means she's a gambler.*"

And then: "Bill, does that shock you?"

"No, not at all."

"I'm not ashamed of it. Out home, it's legal. You know where that is now?"

"Oh! *Oh!*"

"Why oh? And *oh?*"

"Nothing. It's – Nevada, isn't it?"

"Something wrong with Nevada?"

"No! I just woke up, that's all."

I guess that's what I said, but whatever it was, she could hardly miss the upbeat in my voice. Because, of course, that wrapped it all up pretty, not only the tune, which the band would naturally play for her, but her too, and who she was. Society dame, to tell the truth, hadn't pleased me much, and maybe that was one reason my rib was slightly off key. But gambler I could go for, a little cold, a little dangerous, a little brave. When she was sure I had really bought it, we were close again, and after a nip on the freckle her fingers slid over my hand. She said play her *Smoke* – the smoke she had in her eyes. But I didn't, and we just sat there some little time.

And then, a little bit at a time, she began to spill it: "Bill, it was just plain cock-eyed. I worked in a club, the Paddock, in Reno, a regular institution. Tony Rocco – Rock – owned it, and was the squarest bookie ever – why he was a Senator, and civic, and everything. And I worked for him, running his wires, practically being his manager, with a beautiful salary, a bonus at Christmas, and everything. And then wham, it struck. This federal thing. This 10 percent tax on gross. And we were out of business. It just didn't make sense. Everything else was exempted. Wheels and boards and slots, whatever you could think of, but us. Us and the numbers racket, in Harlem and Florida and Washington."

"Take it easy."

"That's right, Bill. Thanks."

"Have some wine?"

". . . Rock, of course, was fixed. He had property, and for the building, where the Paddock was, he got $250,000 – or so I heard. But then came the tip on Maryland."

That crossed me up, and instead of switching her off, I asked her what she meant. She said: "That Maryland would legalize wheels."

"What do you smoke in Nevada?"

"Oh, I didn't believe it. And Rock didn't. But Mrs Rock went nuts about it. Oh well, she had a reason."

"Dark, handsome reason?"

"I don't want to talk about it, but that reason took the Rocks for a ride, for every cent they got for the place, and tried to take me too, for other things beside money. When they went off to Italy, they thought they had it fixed, he was to keep me at my salary, in case Maryland *would* legalize, and if not, to send me home, with severance pay, as it's called. And instead of that – "

"I'm listening."

"I've said too much."

"What's this guy to you?"

"Nothing! I never even saw him until the three of us stepped off the plane – with our hopes. In a way it seemed reasonable. Maryland has tracks, and they help with the taxes. Why not wheels?"

"And *who* is this guy?"

"I'd be ashamed to say, but I'll say this much: I won't be a kept floozy. I don't care who he thinks he is, or – "

She bit her lip, started to cry, and really shut up then. To switch off, I asked why she was working for Jack, and she said: "Why not? You can't go home in a barrel. But he's been swell to me."

Saying people were swell seemed to be what she liked, and she calmed down, letting her hand stay when I pressed it in both of mine. Then we were really close, and I meditated if we were close enough that I'd be warranted in laying it on the line, she should let that plane fly away, and not go to Nevada at all. But while I was working on that, business was picking up, with waiters stopping by to let her look at their trays, and I hadn't much chance to say it, whatever I wanted to say. Then, through the IN door, a waiter came through with a tray that had a wine bottle on it. A guy followed him in, a little noisy guy, who said the bottle was full and grabbed it off the tray. He had hardly gone out again, when Jack was in the door, watching him as he staggered back to the table. The waiter swore the bottle was empty, but all Jack did was nod.

Then Jack came over to her, took another little peep through the window in the OUT door, which was just under her balcony, and said: "Lydia, what did you make of him?"

"Why – he's drunk, that's all."

"You notice him, Mr Cameron?"

"No – except it crossed my mind he wasn't as tight as the act he was putting on."

"Just what crossed *my* mind! How could he get that drunk on a split of Napa red? What did he want back here?"

By now, the waiter had gone out on the floor and came back, saying the guy wanted his check. But as he started to shuffle it out of the bunch he had tucked in his vest, Jack stopped him and said: "He don't get any check – not till I give the word. Tell Joe I said stand by and see he don't get out. *Move!*"

The waiter had looked kind of blank, but hustled out as told, and then Jack looked at her. He said: "Lady, I'll be back. I'm taking a look around."

He went, and she drew another of her long, trembly breaths. I cut my eye around, but no one had noticed a thing, and yet it semed kind of funny they'd all be slicing bread, wiping glass, or fixing cocktail setups, with Jack mumbling it low out of the side of his mouth. I had a creepy feeling of things going on, and my mind took it a little, fitting it together, what she had said about the bag checked at the airport, the guy trying to make her, and most of all, the way Jack had acted, the second she showed with her cigarettes, shooing her off the floor, getting her out of sight. She kept staring through the window, at the drunk where he sat with his bottle, and seemed to ease when a captain I took to be Joe planted himself pretty solid in a spot that would block off a runout.

Then Jack was back, marching around, snapping his fingers, giving orders for the night. But as he pressed the back door, I noticed his hand touched the lock, as though putting the catch on. He started back to the floor, but stopped as he passed her desk, and shot it quick in a whisper: "He's out there, Lydia, parked in back. This drunk, like I thought, is a finger he sent in to stop you, but he won't be getting out for the airport, right now."

"Will you call me a cab, Jack?"

"Cab? I'm taking you."

He stepped near me and whispered: "Mr Cameron, I'm sorry, this little lady has to leave, for – "

"I know about that."

"She's in danger – "

"I've also caught on to that."

"From a no-good imitation goon that's been trying to get to her here, which is why I'm shipping her out. I hate to break this up, but if you'll ride with us, Mr Cameron – "

"I'll follow you down."

"That's right, you have your car. It's Friendship Airport just down the road."

He told her to get ready, while he was having his car brought up, and the boy who would take her place on the desk was changing his clothes. Step on it, he said, but wait until he came back. He went out on the floor and marched past the drunk without even turning his head. But she sat watching me. She said: "You're not coming, are you?"

"Friendship's a little cold."

"But not mine, Bill, no."

She got off her stool, stood near me and touched my hair. She said: "Ships that pass in the night pass so close, so close." And then: "I'm ashamed, Bill. I'd have to go for this reason. I wonder, for the first time gambling's really much good." She pulled the chain of the light, so we were half in the dark. Then she kissed me. She said: "God bless and keep you, Bill."

"And you, Lydia."

I felt her tears on my cheek, and then she pulled away and stepped to the little office, where she began putting a coat on and tying a scarf on her head. She looked so pretty it came to me I still hadn't given her the one little bouquet I'd been saving for the last. I picked up the guitar and started *Nevada*.

She wheeled, but what stared at me were eyes as hard as glass. I was so startled I stopped, but she kept right on staring. Outside a car door slammed, and she listened at the window beside her. Then at last she looked away, to peep through the Venetian blind. Jack popped in, wearing his coat and hat, and motioned her to hurry. But he caught something and said, low yet so I could hear him: "Lydia! What's the matter?"

She stalked over to me, with him following along, pointed her finger, and then didn't say it, but spat it: "He's the finger – that's what's the matter, that's all. He played *Nevada*, as though we hadn't had enough trouble with it already. And Vanny heard it. He hopped out of his car and he's under the window right now."

"Then OK, let's go."

I was a little too burned to make with the explanations, and took my time, parking the guitar, sliding off, and climbing down, to give them a chance to blow. But she still had something to say, and to me, not to him. She pushed her face up to mine, and mocking how I had spoken, yipped. "Oh! . . . *Oh!* OH!" Then she went, with Jack. Then I went, clumping after.

Then it broke wide open.

The drunk, who was supposed to sit there, conveniently boxed in, while she went slipping out, turned out more of a hog-calling type, and instead of playing his part, jumped up and yelled: "Vanny! *Vanny!* Here she comes! She's leaving! VANNY!"

He kept it up, while women screamed all over, then pulled a gun from his pocket, and let go at the ceiling, so it sounded like the field artillery. Jack jumped for him and hit the deck, as his feet shot from under him on the slippery wood of the dance floor. Joe swung, missed, swung again, and landed, so Mr Drunk went down. But when Joe scrambled for the gun, there came this voice through the smoke: "Hold it! As you were – and leave that gun alone."

Then hulking in came this short-necked, thick-shouldered thing, in Homburg hat, double-breasted coat, and white muffler, one hand in his pocket, the other giving an imitation of a movie gangster. He said keep still and nobody would get hurt, but "I won't stand for tricks." He helped Jack up, asked how he'd been. Jack said: "Young man, let me tell you something – "

"How you been? I asked."

"Fine, Mr Rocco."

"Any telling, Jack – I'll do it."

Then, to her: "Lydia, how've *you* been?"

"That doesn't concern you."

Then she burst out about what he had done to his mother, the gyp he'd handed his father, and his propositions to her, and I got it, at last, who this idiot was. He listened, but right in the middle of it, he waved his hand toward me and asked: "Who's this guy?"

"Vanny, I think you know."

"Guy, are you the boy friend?"

"If so I don't tell you".

I sounded tough, but my stomach didn't feel that way. They had it some more, and he connected me with the tune, and seemed to enjoy it a lot, that it had told him where to find her, on the broadcast and here now tonight. But he kept creeping closer, to where we were all lined up, with the drunk stretched on the floor, the gun under his hand, and I suddenly felt the prickle, that Vanny was really nuts, and in a minute meant to kill her. It also crossed my mind, that a guy who plays the guitar has a left hand made of steel, from squeezing down on the strings, and is a dead sure judge of distance, to the last eighth of an inch.

I grabbed for my chord and got it.

I choked down on his hand, the one he held in his pocket, while hell broke loose in the place, with women screaming, men running, and fists trying to help. I had the gun hand all right, but when I reached for the other he twisted, butted, and bit, and for that long I thought he'd get loose, and that I was a gone pigeon. The gun barked, and a piledriver hit my leg. I went down. Another gun spoke and he went down beside me. Then there was Jack, the drunk's gun in his hand, stepping in close, and firing again.

I blacked out.

I came to, and then she was there, a knife in her hand, ripping the cloth away from the outside of my leg, grabbing napkins, stanching blood, while somewhere ten miles off I could hear Jack's voice, as he yelled into a phone. On the floor right beside me was something under a tablecloth.

That went on for some time, with Joe calming things down and some people sliding out. The band came in, and I heard a boy ask for his guitar. Somebody brought it to him, and then, at last, came the screech of sirens, and she whispered some thanks to God.

Then, while the cops were catching up, with me, with Jack, and what was under the cloth, we both went kind of haywire, me laughing, she crying, and both in each other's arms. I said: "Lydia, Lydia, you're not taking that plane. They legalize things in Maryland, one thing specially, except that instead of wheels, they generally use a ring."

THE GETAWAY

Gil Brewer

VINCENTI LIT A fat joint, took a big toke, then glanced sideways at the wheelman of the silver Continental Mark IV. Vincenti was loose. He was always loose. He had a job to do and would be paid well. He was a heavy and he only worked to contract.

"Nervous?" the paunchy, red-faced driver asked. He wore medium blue with a plum maroon tie.

Vincenti did not answer. He took another deep toke and chewed on the acrid smoke. Tall, slim, impeccably groomed in pearl gray, with eyes like slate, he somehow resembled a statue.

The wheelman's name was Morganza. He was also the finger. His hair looked like a wet, blue-black cap, and there was something anxious in his pale eyes.

"I'd be nervous," he said.

"You are."

"I mean if I was you."

"I wouldn't doubt that."

Vincenti's voice was silken. It appealed to women, along with everything else about the man, and he enjoyed that fact.

They were on Franklin and mid-afternoon Tampa traffic moved glitteringly, sedately. Then Morganza made a sharp right and slowed the flash car. They drew to the curb.

Vincenti's practiced finger flicked the roach out the window. He was patient. He had to be.

"It's that loan company, across there. Acme," Morganza said. He coughed lightly and checked his wrist where gold gleamed. "Due — right now."

Vincenti watched the Acme Loan entrance. His nose was a blade and his chin held a deep cleft. He sighed and yearned for Vegas with some fresh broad. Well, it would come later, after he returned to LA.

The grass had given him a small lift.

Suddenly Morganza said, "Here it is, you."

Vincenti looked quickly towards the Acme Loan.

An enormous man in eye-shattering white, slow-moving, ponderous but with the provoking grace of an elephant, still young, shoved from the Acme entrance into the street. Another man, short, reed-like, gripping a tan straw hat, was with him. They stood there on the sidewalk. The short man gestured ubiquitously, while the big man grew like a tree.

Morganza opened his door and stepped out.

"Which the hell one?" Vincenti's voice was flat, like tepid tea.

"Biggie," Morganza jerked, and was gone, melting into the afternoon.

Vincenti lifted long legs and slid over beneath the wheel, planting his feet. He waited, watching the big man.

So, this was Nemo Lucelli, god of the Gulf Coast, with wormy fingers that fatted into Miami's guts, palpated Jacksonville, and saw to the Bahamas skim. Overlord of Florida crime, glutting on everything from prostitution and narcotics to illegal Florida gambling; twisting the coattails of governors, senators, and shipping magnates. It was reported authoritatively that his Mexican connection was the fatted calf itself. And anachronistic Murder Inc. was nothing to Lucelli's bloodbath.

The Big Nemo . . . but Vincenti hadn't figured him this big in girth.

The National Syndicate wanted Nemo wasted.

Vincenti knew he would be able to retire for maybe three years after this job, able to thoroughly feed his own ravening appetites. Women. Young girls.

He tightened his teeth, his slate-colored eyes checking every corner for *soldatos*, bodyguards, the lieutenants of Lucelli's regime. The Tampa hierarchy did not know Vincenti and would not make him. Morganza was from Chi, with *capo* Ringotti. Morganza would already be at Tampa International, a fly duck.

A quick-moving soldier opened a Caddy limousine door, and Lucelli lurched towards the shiny car, leaving the short fellow still gesticulant.

Vincenti knew that car would be slug-proof.

A door slammed. Vincenti saw the fat man in white lift a glass from a portable bar in the limo. Then the Caddy purred into traffic.

Vincenti knew it had to be obtuse.

Now was the word. Or as close to *now* as conditions would permit. Make the damn hit and get out.

Vincenti quickly lit a previously rolled joint, took a vigorous toke, and skunked after the Cad, holding his breath, experiencing a tingle in his solar plexus. This was the biggest hit he'd ever attained, and he was playing it to rule . . . the rule cooked up on the cross-country jet flight.

Hit – *now*. No maps. No clockwork. No shenanigans.

It had to be *hit now*, because Lucelli's fortress could be creepy, and there was the ever-gnawing probability that winds would blow news of this top-brass execution decision.

There was *always* a long tongue, no matter how the odds looked.

Vincenti toked the fat joint deeply, holding the narcotic smoke, the red ember sputtering. Ordinarily he spent days, sometimes weeks, on a hit – planning, scheming, checking every angle. Not this time. No time was this time.

He knew he had to be high. It was in and hit and run.

Desperation was beginning to drive him now.

He worked at desperation. He was a pro. His card was death and the deal was no shuffle, no cut.

They were approaching West Shore Boulevard, the limo blurringly smooth at a sixty clip.

Traffic was heavy.

The afternoon sighed, turned, and rolled over towards four o'clock. Black palm fronds fingered the yellow haze like cemetery hands.

Abruptly the limousine crawled into a circular drive rimmed with glistening poplars and silk oaks, slowed to gleam and glitter in the shadows of a portico fronting a small yellow-stone cottage – small by Lucelli's standards, Vincenti mused, firing another joint. Actually the cottage was a minor mansion.

Still . . . it didn't look like home ground, for some reason.

He tooled the outside lane slowly, turning to check. Sure enough, Lucelli was out of the limo and the big car was pulling away in the drive.

Vincenti checked the rearview mirror, holding his breath.

The Cad crept back onto the boulevard and increased speed.

Lucelli was alone back there at the yellow-stone cottage.

Vincenti wheeled the Continental to the right, down a curving red-brick street shaded with ancient water oaks.

He couldn't believe it! He couldn't!

The *now* was in solid.

Curtly, then, the professional took over. He sped down the block, turned fast right again, marking where the yellow-stone cottage would stand on the boulevard.

He parked at the curb, allowed his right hand to check the spring-holstered, silenced Luger beneath his left arm, then just sat there a moment.

The quiet-looking stone home to the right, behind fastidious dark green Florida poppy hedge, seemed uninhabited. Vincenti had the salesman's antennae about matters like that.

Anyway, it was *now* – not later.

He lit still another joint, left the car, and walked rapidly along the outside poppy hedge that bordered a blue-gravel drive. He glanced neither right nor left. He held smoke in his lungs and the afternoon was a cinema screen, flickering impossible paradise.

The large homes on either side were set distantly.

He approached a yellow-stone wall. The cottage where Lucelli had stopped took up, in grounds, obviously most of the block. The place with the hedges was a cheapie.

He flicked the roach away, touched the wall, and with a smooth leap elbowed the rim.

He clung there, taking it in – a kidney-shaped swimming pool under silk oaks, the water like green ice. Walls. Footpaths. Flowers in bloom. A mocking blue jay.

Glass doors open on glitter and shadow.

Nobody. No sound other than the blue jay.

Then . . . soft music. Bartok. Vincenti prided himself on a secret vice. Lucelli the Slaughterhouse, attending Bartok?

He sniffed – sniffed again. Musk. Incense. Lucelli. *Avanti*. Nemo Lucelli!

A white shape moved through velvet-red shadows inside the cottage.

Vincenti went up the wall, and down into a horseshoe flowerbed of yellow roses. He barely landed here before he was running lightly, silently, around the pool, past canvas deck chairs, luxuriously padded chaises, across a broad flagged patio with a half-finished drink on a redwood table, and over to the glass doors.

He could feel his heart astounding his chest. He was sweating now, as he let the Luger fit into his palm, and gripped the cool butt, fingering cold steel.

"Who is it?" The voice was fat, hoarse, and deep, from inside the cottage.

Vincenti whapped the Luger's sliding blue-steeled breech open with an oily click, and leaped between the glass doors.

Everything happened at once. The music. The jay screaming. Nemo Lucelli standing there like an elephant in a white terry-cloth robe, belted around the enormous girth, a fat, manicured hand with a square-cut diamond, holding a martini glass, a woman's voice:

"What is it – Nemo?"

Vincenti said, "Hello."

Nemo Lucelli backed through an alcove into a sprawling, shadowed living room with huge hassocks and a fireplace. He paused against a glass cocktail table, his mouth working around unspoken words.

"They said you broke word," Vincenti told Lucelli. "They said to waste you."

"Wait – " Lucelli said.

His drink spilled on the thick gold rug.

Vincenti emptied the Luger. It made gasping sounds. Crimson blossoms appeared across Lucelli's chest. He gave a tremendous leap backwards and crashed down on the glass-topped cocktail table, shattering the plate.

He was dead. His eyes were open.

The jay screamed. The music softly curtained the diminishing afternoon as Vincenti released the spent clip from the Luger and slapped a fresh one in its place.

"Nemo?"

The woman's voice again, up and to the left, coming near.

She burst into the room, saw the hulk covered by terry cloth amid the jagged shards of broken glass, the blood. She put one hand to her mouth and bit knuckle. Then she flung coppery red hair out of one eye and stared at Vincenti

"Hello and good-bye," Vincenti said.

He lifted the Luger.

"You fool!" the girl who was more than mere woman said. She whirled and spat on the bloody body of Nemo Lucelli. "I wanted him dead! Don't kill me – think, you fool!"

Vincenti frowned, staring at this girl.

She was beautiful, with long, flowing red hair. She wore a black swimsuit – a bikini – that was revealing enough to make a man hold his breath. Tall, she was, firm-breasted, long-thighed, with broad red lips, large blue eyes – a wish, a promise.

"Who are you?" Vincenti said.

"Not now – not here." She spoke rapidly. "There's no time. They're coming back, don't you see? Nemo sent them for some brandy." She paused, put both hands to her cheeks. "You kill me, you'll never get away – they'll know somebody else did this. I know what to do – let me do it. I hated him! I was bought and paid for. Everybody knows it. They'll think I did this. They know it's been coming. Don't you see – here – they're here now!"

She pointed towards a front window. Beyond the sound of the music was the sound of a car's wheels on gravel, and Vincenti saw gleams and glitters out there in the silky shade from the limo's paint job.

The girl snatched up a red robe from a chair.

"Where's your car, you idiot – hurry!"

Thinking how it had to be the weed, Vincenti grabbed her hand and turned running, dragging her – because truly it was good in this direction, too – this girl was his alibi.

If he made it.

"Where?" she gasped.

He said nothing, holstered the Luger, thinking how they would believe she had killed Lucelli. He grabbed the Luger from its holster again, thinking, You forgot, you fool! It's that damned Acapulco Gold.

He flung the Luger into the pool with a splash that shattered the icy green, and they ran through the flower beds to the yellow-stone wall.

"Hey!"

It was a shout from back in the cottage.

"It's them," the girl whispered, cringing against Vincenti.

Vincenti did not hesitate. He grasped her around the smooth, plump thighs and lifted her quickly to the top of the wall.

"Drop down," he said, scrambling after her.

There were shouts from inside the cottage.

Vincenti slipped over the wall just as somebody fired in his direction. Chips of shattered stone flew in the afternoon.

"Run for the street – my car," he told the girl, thrusting her ahead.

"They climbed the wall!" a man shouted from behind.

They made the Continental.

"Let me drive," the girl said. "There's only one place to go – my plane at the St Petersburg-Clearwater Airport. This area'll be crawling. It's our only chance."

"Get in," Vincenti told her. "I'm driving." He was also thinking fast. She was right. Word would go out. *Soldatos* would be everywhere, watching for her and whoever was with her. They would be at every entrance to the city, every highway would soon be covered. There was only the one chance: with her.

They were away fast, with the girl directing him on back routes. It was all Vincenti could do to hold the speed down, and there was a snarl of discouragement in his chest, but it began to lessen with each mile. This girl – this girl was something to consider – a beauty – and with quick brains, too.

Lucelli was dead. He would have plenty of money. This girl would have plenty, too – it was a fast deal and a good one.

Soon they were out of Tampa on the Courtney-Campbell Causeway, headed for Route 19. Vincenti began to relax a touch, but he did not let up on the accelerator. He knew anything could happen. Lucelli's web could reach out . . .

"What's your name?" he asked the girl, trying to think about more comforting things.

"Anette," she said.

"Okay, Anette. Looks as if we'll be together for a time. But where'll we go?" He hesitated, then took a shot at it. "I'm from LA."

"My money's in Vero Beach – that's where I live. I was just visiting Nemo at one of his castles, see? We'll fly my Cessna to Vero – agreed?"

"Then where?"

"There's only one where. Europe. We'll head for Miami, and fly to England first. It's the only way, and it can be damned thin. Nemo rules – ruled this state." She slid closer to Vincenti. "What's your name?"

He told her.

"But what's your first name?"

"Harry."

"Gee, I dig that – Harry."

He allowed himself to comfort her somewhat by placing one hand on her knee, while visions danced in his head.

Sugar plums, he thought. Sweet sugar plums.

Presently they reached the St Pete-Clearwater Airport. In less than fifteen minutes they were seated in Anette's four-seat Cessna; a beautiful ship, colored red, white, and yellow – sleek in the early twilight.

They came down the runway with Anette at the controls. She had asked him if he could fly.

"I leave that up to pilots."

"Vero, here we come," she said, and they were airborne.

Vincenti took his first clean breath of freedom. There was little chance of being caught now. He had done his job. Lucelli was dead. He would collect payment by cable in London. He had his passport with him. He was always ready for anything.

They winged above Tampa Bay. The waters, in the last of the sunlight, looked as if studded with diamonds. He saw the vast span of the Howard Frankland Bridge up ahead, cars like ants speeding along the whiteway.

He lit two joints and passed her one.

She smiled at him and took a big toke.

"Hey," he said suddenly. "You're going down – we're flying pretty damned low."

"Want to show you how pretty it can be. Then, after, we'll get to know each other. There's an automatic pilot, see? Nemo had it installed for me. I'm setting it now."

They were flying at tremendous speed towards the looming bridge span.

Vincenti did not want to show his tight fright to this girl. She was truly something.

She pushed the throttle up all the way, and turned to smile at him again.

"This grass is good stuff," she said.

He said, just to make words, "You didn't tell me your last name."

She stood up, stepped over, and slipped beside him. But she seemed somehow stiff and sober.

"Well, honey," she said. "My last name's Lucelli." She looked straight into his eyes and ruffled the back of his hair. "I'm Nemo Lucelli's daughter. You see, now? And you're one of us. You know how it is, avenging a death in the family." Excitement was in her eyes. "That's how it is, honey – Harry Vincenti!"

He stared at her as the words registered. Fear stabbed him. He hurled her aside. She sprawled to the deck.

"Lucelli," he heard himself say.

Tears rushed into the girl's eyes. "I *loved* my father. But you wouldn't dig that, you pig!" She screamed it. "He was a great, kind man. I loved him. You killed him. I'll die for him!"

He struck her across the mouth, then whirled to look through the windshield. The bridge loomed dead ahead. He dove for the controls.

The plane smashed into the bridge and exploded with a shattering roar of flame.

Harry Vincenti crashed headlong through the windshield. He arced through the air like a limber rag doll and sprawled sliding in a bloody path in the far second lane of traffic.

He was dead before the big semi ran over him, but it didn't really matter.

PREVIEW OF MURDER

Robert Leslie Bellem

1 DATE WITH A RECLUSE

IT WAS A cheap, frowsy hotel in a cheap shoddy neighborhood a good distance south of Hollywood Boulevard. It was standing like a tired harridan on the east side of the street so that the setting sun in the west painted its shabby brick façade the color of old blood that nobody wanted any more.

Over the entrance faded gilt lettering said "Chaple Arms," which could have been a misspelling of "Chapel" or might be the proprietor's name. The cars parked along the curb in front were old, worn-out models in need of polish they would never get, with dented fenders and recap tires any self-respecting junk dealer would have sneered at.

Drifting past in second gear, I watched a mangy alley cat in the doorway, licking its chops and working on a bird it had killed. That was the only visible movement, the only sign of life. It was just as much a sign of death, if you thought about it from the bird's viewpoint: only the bird was beyond caring. The Chaple Arms didn't seem to care, either. It was that kind of hotel. One more stain on the steps couldn't possibly matter.

The voice on the phone that afternoon hadn't matched any of this. Asking me to come here at six sharp, it had sounded austere and dignified, with culture and education back of it. And money. It had sounded like a lot of money.

In the private detective business you develop a sort of extra sense which reacts to subtle nuances like that. So I was disappointed when I copped a glimpse of the Chaple Arms. It wasn't a place where money lived. Maybe it had been, once, a long time ago. Could be. But now it was a fleabag.

I looked at my strap-watch. Five of six. I drove my jaloppy to the next corner and made a U-turn, wheeled back and found a berth almost directly across the street from the tawdry brick building. At three of six I ankled past the alley cat, noticed that the bird was all gone except a few wing feathers, and barged into a dingy lobby that smelled as unclean as it looked.

The linoleum on the floor was worn through in spots by the feet of trudging years, showing that it had been laid on an original installation of white tiles. There were two overstuffed chairs against the righthand wall, as wrinkled and sagging as the bags under a sick man's eyes, and on the left there was a short, stained marble-top counter with a desk clerk behind it, pigeonholing folded circulars into a rectangular wooden tier of square open-front letterboxes.

His black alpaca coat was shiny with age, freckled with small gray flakes the exact shade of his hair. His back was toward me and he didn't look around when I spoke to him.

So I spoke again, louder. "Hey, you with the dandruff on your shoulders," I said.

He kept right on stuffing circulars into pigeon-holes. Then I lamped two little twisted black wires running down along his collar, and I leaned over the counter and nudged him on the spine with my forefinger. Leaning over the counter made me feel pretty sure no laundry would ever be able to take the grease stains from the front of my clothes. Touching the clerk with my finger made me feel as if I would never wash my hands clean again, no matter how much soap and water I used.

He jumped slightly and turned around, and the little twisted wires ran from a button in his ear to a black plastic box hooked heavily to his breast pocket. He had a face like crinkled parchment and eyes as sadly apologetic as a cocker spaniel's. He jiggled something on the plastic box, a switch that clicked audibly.

"Wear a hearing aid," he said in a powdery voice. "Generally keep it turned off to save the batteries. You scared me a rifle, poking me like that."

"Sorry, old-timer," I said. "Although I should think you'd be used to it if you keep your back to the customers all the time."

"Got me a little mirror on the wall." He jerked a thumb. "Usually watch it so's nobody sneaks up on me, but I guess I kind of forgot this time. Preoccupied." He let a small sigh dribble past lips as loose as dangling rubber bands. "Something I could do for you?"

"I want to see a guy that lives here – name of Fullerton. Joseph T. Fullerton."

"Nobody sees Joseph T. Fullerton, mister. Nobody ain't seen Joseph T. Fullerton in nine, ten years to my knowledge. Not even the maids which brush up his rooms. You prolly think I'm kidding you, but I ain't."

"I've got an appointment," I said.

For all that meant to him he might as well have had his hearing aid switched off. "For six o'clock," I added. "It's six now, even up."

"No offense, mister, but I just plain don't believe you."

"About it being six o'clock?"

"About you having no appointment to see Mr Fullerton. Like I said, nobody sees him. Nobody at all. He don't allow it."

"I'm Nick Ransom," I said patiently, and took a card out of my wallet to prove it. I put the card on the counter. "Somebody calling himself Joseph T. Fullerton phoned me at my office this afternoon and asked me to be here at six sharp. Maybe it was a rib, but that voice didn't sound like a practical joker's. You might give Fullerton a jingle and check on it. That is, if there really is a Joseph T. Fullerton registered here."

"Orders is never to disturb him under no circumstances." With mild curiosity he read my card, his rubber-band lips moving as he spelled out the words. "Nick Ransom. Confidential Investigations. That's be kind of a cop, wouldn't it?"

"Private."

He made with another dribbling sigh.

"Nothing like this ain't never happened before since I been working here." He moved to a small old-fashioned switchboard and peered at it, picked up a fragment of pale blue paper that had scribbling on it. "Well, I be danged. Day man must of left this for me and I never seen it when I come on duty at five. Says somebody named Nick Ransom is to be tooken straight up to Mr Fullerton."

"Yeah," I said. I set fire to a gasper.

He shook his head wearily. More dandruff snowed down on the alpaca coat's shoulders.

"Reason I never noticed it, they ain't been no calls go through the board since I come on shift. Danged day man shouldn't of left it tucked behind the keys that way. He ought to of told me."

"So now you know," I said. "And it's two minutes past six. I don't like to keep a client waiting."

"Course not. Dumb me, making you stand around."

He hit a tap-bell under the counter. It had a clean, tinkly sound that broke across the lobby and lost itself, discouraged, against musty velour draperies on the opposite wall. There followed a whirring hiccuppy noise from somewhere in the rear, and an antique elevator creaked jerkily down an open grillwork shaft. Its wrought iron gate slid open, rattling on worn grooves, and a kid in his early twenties stepped out smartly.

"Pete," the clerk said, "show this here gent up to Three-seventeen."

Pete's glimmers widened. He was a tall punk, not quite up to my six feet plus but slender and lithe and broad of shoulder in a nondescript uniform a size too small for his build. He probably had inherited it from a whole series of predecessors, but he wore it with a nice jauntiness that certainly didn't belong in a joint like the Chaple Arms.

He had wavy brown hair and even white teeth, and an uncompromising jaw that went well with the humorous up-quirk at the corners of his lips.

"Maybe I'd better borrow that ear gadget of yours," he said, and grinned. "I'd have sworn you said Three-seventeen."

"I did say Three-seventeen," the clerk told him.

"But that's – "

"Fullerton's, yeh. And Fullerton don't never have no callers. He does now."

"Right-o," Pete said. "This way, sir."

He led me toward the elevator.

Just as I was stepping into the cage, the clerk at the counter lifted his powdery voice.

"Hey, mister." He beckoned me, and I went back to him. "You wouldn't want to spare me one of them cigarettes of yours, I don't suppose?" he said. "Not that I'm awful partial to cigarettes. Cigars is my preference, only I'm a mite strapped this week, and – "

I dug a four-bit piece out of my jeans, gave it to him. "Buy yourself a perfecto."

"Criminity. Fifty cents! Biggest tip I taken in for more'n a year. Thanks." He leaned forward. "Confidential, mister, the real reason I called you back, I wondered would you do me a little favor."

"Such as?"

"If you *do* get to see Joseph T. Fullerton, I'd sure love to hear what he really looks like. Ain't never seen him myself, and I got a bump of curiosity a mile high."

"I'll give you a verbal portrait," I said, and went over to the elevator again.

The good-looking Pete clanged the door shut and pulled a rope, and the cage moved upward in little jerky bumps, like hiccups. Midway between the first and second floors I dredged out another half-dollar and spun it around my thumb.

"Speaking of Fullerton," I said.

"Were we speaking of Mr Fullerton, sir?"

The punk quirked a smile at me.

"Discreet bellhops in a trap like this," I said. I put away the four-bit piece and started toying with a folded dollar bill. "Been working here long, son?"

"Four years. Putting myself through college. USC." He eyed the folded buck as we creaked past the second-floor landing. "You were asking about Fullerton?"

"Uh-huh. He's a recluse, I gather."

"A mild word for it. Nobody ever sees him. When the maids tidy up he hides in a sort of closet he's got rigged as a tuckaway. The help take him his meals. I get his supper from a place around the corner and leave it in his living room."

"But you've never met him?"

"I've talked to him through his hideaway door, is all. Third floor, sir." He clanged the cage open and pointed. "Three-seventeen is just past that turn in the corridor." Then, when I handed him the dollar: "Thanks, sir. Want to know something?"

"That was my last loose buck, Buster."

He grinned. "This is for free." The grin got turned off like a spigot. "I don't think you're going to like visiting Mr Fullerton. It's a spooky experience until you get used to it. Lots of luck, sir."

2 TALK WITH A CORPSE.

I walked along the hallway with the elevator's ancient hesitant creaks dwindling down behind me. Presently I came to a door and bunted it with my knuckles, then stepped aside, just in case Joseph T. Fullerton happened to be the kind of hermit with homicidal eccentricities such as shooting guns through thin wooden paneling.

"Nick Ransom out here!" I said loudly. "By appointment."

"You're five minutes late."

There was something vaguely familiar in this voice, a texture my subconscious mind picked up and fingered and tried to recognize. It was a voice of the same general timbre and intonation as that of the guy who had phoned me, yet different and somehow more natural, as if, over the wire, he had disguised his delivery just a little so it wouldn't strike a responsive echo in my memory.

Now, though, he didn't seem to care if I caught hep. It bothered me because I couldn't place it, and for some reason I couldn't savvy I felt a shiver crawling down my back, the way you do when you dream something not too pleasant at night.

"Come in," it said. "It's unlocked for you."

I grasped the knob and it turned in my hand. I pushed on the portal but nothing happened; it didn't give.

"Opens outward. I forgot to tell you. Special arrangement of mine. Pull."

Whoever he was, he was no stranger to me. I combed through my mental card index file but the thing eluded me, like trying to pin down a shadow. I pulled, and the door swung smoothly on oiled hinges. I barged into a room that had nobody in it but me, and the empty room spoke my name.

It said, "Hello, Nick. I understand you've quit the stunting racket and gone into private detective work," in the voice of a man I had known a long time ago; a man buried and gone these past fourteen years or more. The empty room said, "It's good to see you again, Nick," and the voice belonged to a dead man.

I could remember, and see and hear it all now, those years ago – and I knew.

I was standing on the sidelines of a movie set, out of camera range, watching two guys who were going to be blasted to bits the next minute – not make-believe blasted for a spool of film, but actually and horribly blown apart like chopped meat. That was fourteen years ago, but the fourteen years faded and vanished like a lap dissolve shot so that time was telescoped and the past merged into the present, the present became the past.

I was on a cavernous sound stage at Paragon Pix seeing a sequence in rehearsal, a sequence destined never to be played because in another sixty seconds the leading man would be a corpse. He would be the late lamented Ronald Barclay, as handsome a ham as ever starred in the flickering tintypes.

Barclay was tall and swarthy, with the brand of boudoir eyes that made matrons swoon and their daughters crave to leave home. He had dark wavy hair with touches of frost at the temples which he refused to let the makeup department do anything about, and he was built like a Roman gladiator. In private life he carried a baseball bat to beat off the women who tried to surrender their all at his shrine.

I watched him there on the set, rehearsing a brief piece of business for a closeup, a bit of action which I myself would duplicate later in a long shot. That long shot was where the peril would be, and since Paragon Pix couldn't afford to risk Barclay's million-dollar good looks, I was the stunt expert they had hired to double for him in the hazard scene.

Not that I considered it especially hazardous. According to the scenario he was to pick up a cigarette box from a table and open it, whereupon a bomb which the villain had planted in the box would blow up like a cannon cracker. Of course the explosion wouldn't show in the closeup. The director would cut out the scene just as Barclay lifted the gadget.

Then I would step in and replace him while the camera was moved some distance away. I would lift the lid of the box, and a small charge of flashlight powder would ignite in such a way that I couldn't get burned if I remembered to be careful and hold my hands in the right position.

The special effects department would subsequently doctor the footage, intensify the size of the flame-flash, and a loud boom would be dubbed onto the sound track. Meanwhile, the initial closeup had to be timed out with Barclay himself going through the motions.

I watched as a prop man walked on-stage and placed the cigarette box in position. I saw Barclay reach for it ahead of schedule as if idly curious to inspect it. There came a thunderous roar that shook the set. *Ker-blaaam!*

With my ears ringing and my glimmers smarting, half-blinded, I plunged forward from the sidelines, hearing behind me the shouts of the director and his camera crew, the screams of the script girl, the stunned oaths of carpenters and grips and juicers milling around in momentary panic. I reached the crumpled, unconscious forms of Ronald Barclay and the property man who had been standing too close to him when the blast went off. I bent down and beat out the flames that were charring their ripped and red-stained clothes.

Five minutes later I helped load both men into the ambulance that came wailing onto the lot from a nearby hospital. I couldn't help thinking that the ambulance might have been toting my own gory fragments instead of theirs if the bomb had waited until my turn had come to handle it.

Barclay kicked the bucket before the internes could hoist him onto an operating table. His subsequent funeral was a nine-day wonder even for Hollywood, where nine-day wonders seldom last more than a day and a half.

The prop man wasn't so lucky. He lived. Permanently maimed, he survived his injuries and eventually dropped out of the news, out of sight. Nobody cared; nobody bothered to fasten official blame on him for accidentally loading the mock bomb with dynamite instead of harmless flashlight powder.

Besides, he had paid for his blunder. It cost him two legs and an arm. You don't prosecute a basket case who can't fight back. You just let him fade into oblivion.

Fourteen years . . .

In my mind those years slowly stretched out into proper perspective, resumed their long endless shape of days and weeks and months. I snapped back to the present, and I was no longer a stunt expert on that cavernous Paragon sound stage. I was now a private dick in the drab living room of a fleabag called the Chaple Arms. I was here by the request of a telephone voice and listening to that same disembodied voice coming from nowhere; hearing it and remembering it, remembering that the last time I'd heard it was just before a property cigarette box exploded.

But it wasn't the voice of the bomb crippled prop man, who had lived. It was the voice of Ronald Barclay, the handsome star, who had died.

It was a trick, natch. It had to be a trick. Some dizzy jerk with a perverted sense of humor was needling me, giving me a bad time. I glowered around the room at the cheap window curtains, the shabby-genteel mission furniture, the threadbare carpet and dingy walls.

A heavy-set bozo glowered back at me from over near a corner – a tall, scowling character in tweeds, with a truculent glint in his peepers. He was my own reflection in a full-length mirror set into a closet door. Nobody else was around.

"Now just one condemned minute," I snarled. "I can go along with a gag as well as the next slob. But – "

"It's no gag, Nick," Ronald Barclay's voice said. "And you needn't be so jittery I'm behind the mirror. It's one of those new-fangled two-way glasses. I can see out through it, but all you can see is yourself." There was a brief chuckle, not entirely mirthful. "I'm talking through a hole in the wall. You can't find it, though, because it's covered with wallpaper."

"That's where you usually find vermin in a drop like this," I said. "Behind the wall-paper. And quit explaining your dime-store hocuspocus magic act in Ronald Barclay's voice. Barclay was sort of a friend of mine in the old days, as friendly as a star ever gets with a mere stunt man, and he's dead. I don't like it. Stop imitating him."

"I can't stop, because I'm not imitating him, and because I'm not dead. I'm alive and I'm Ronald Barclay." Bitterness was in that. "Have a drink, Nick. I left a bottle of Scotch on that table behind you. Vat 69. That's your brand, as I recall."

Sure it was my brand. I picked up the bottle and let some of its mellow lightning slide down my throat. I needed it. My nerves were jumpy.

"Everybody in Hollywood knows the kind of Scotch I prefer," I growled. "That proves nothing."

"Do you remember the time I went on a brannigan and you took me to your apartment and kept me there three days to sober me up for a new picture I was starting?"

I stiffened. I had never told a living soul about that crazy episode. Nobody else knew it except Barclay himself, unless he had blabbed it to some third party before he died.

I was getting confused. Dead men can't talk from behind mirrors. I took another swig from the bottle and exhaled the aroma around a test question.

"What kind of pajamas did I loan you to wear? What color?"

"You didn't. Your spare pajamas were all in the laundry. You borrowed a nightgown from a girl in the next apartment. It was a cerise chiffon."

I strangled. "You *are* Barclay! Come out of hiding. I want to look at you."

"Nobody looks at me, Nick. Not even you. Nobody's looked at me since I moved in here after the hospital released me. Nobody ever will."

"But – but – "

"It was really the prop man who died, Nick. His name was Tom Fullerton, in case you've forgotten. He died, and I lived. A little piece of me lived. No legs. One arm. Half a face." There was a catch in the voice, almost like a sob. Then it steadied. "I was a vain man, Nick, remember? When I found out I was going to live and look like a butchered frog, I couldn't take it. Not as Ronald Barclay I couldn't."

I stared at the mirror. All I saw was my own optics bulging like oysters being squeezed from two fists.

"Women had worshipped me," Barclay's voice said. "Now if they saw me it would be with horror and loathing. I didn't want that. I didn't want sympathy. I wanted to die, but the doctors wouldn't let me die, curse them. So I cooked up a scheme."

"I get it," I said thickly. "You arranged to have the property man, Joe Fullerton, buried in your name. And you took his. It was a trade, a switch. You couldn't stand being a maimed Ronald Barclay, but a crippled Fullerton you could adjust to. You bribed the right people, and – good glory, it's fantastic!"

"On the contrary, it was fairly simple. Fullerton had no family; neither had I. Who'd know the difference? I didn't have to bribe anybody. Fullerton was blasted beyond recognition. So was I. Even the fingerprints of my one remaining hand had been destroyed. No fingerprints. No teeth in my mouth for dental chart comparisons. No mouth, period – until the plastic surgeons built me something I could use for a mouth, such as it is."

"You mean you just kept insisting you were Fullerton and the hospital staff believed you?"

"Yes. Luckily the real Fullerton had an accident policy – twenty thousand dollars for the loss of two limbs, forty for the loss of three. I collected the forty thousand and moved to the Chaple Arms. I've been here ever since."

"Come on out," I said earnestly. "I want to see you."

"Nobody sees me, Nick. How often must I say it?"

"So you're in a wheel-chair," I said. "Which is why your door opens outward, so you can get away in case of fire. So you're a no-legged guy with a missing arm and a face that would give dames the screaming meemies. But I'm no dame; I'm a friend of yours. I want to see you. I can take it."

"No." His voice sharpened. "And don't come any closer to this closet. It wouldn't do you any good. There's no knob on the outside. And if you smash the glass I'll kill you. I've got one good hand and it's holding a gun, and I'd kill anybody who looked at me. I'm not fooling, Nick. Don't force me to do something I wouldn't want to do!"

3 DEAD MAN'S DIARY

Ronald Barclay sounded sincere and a little hysterical, and maybe a touch demented along with it. Only a loony guy would do what he had done, live the way he had been living. And if he really had a roscoe he was as dangerous as sparks in a gunpowder factory.

I backed off, gave the Vat 69 another fast belt.

"Okay," I said, "so you don't want to be looked it. And for fourteen years you've pretended to be deceased. That much I'll buy. As an amateur psychologist I might even understand it. But why did you ask me to come here? And after keeping your secret all these years, why let me in on it now?"

"Because I trust you. And I need a favor."

"What favor?"

"I want you to be my decoy."

"I don't get that," I said.

He said through the hole in the wall: "Decoy. Lure. Bait."

"I still don't get it."

"I'm asking you to entice a certain person here to my rooms. I don't care what pretext you use. That I leave up to your judgment. Just so you fetch him here and leave him."

"So it's a him, not a her," I said. "Maybe if I stick around long enough I'll learn even more. Don't let me hurry you, pal. I have the evening free."

"You have a sarcastic tongue, too. You always had. Don't rush me, Nick. Let me tell it my way. This man I want brought here to me . . . What's the matter with you?"

"Nothing. Go ahead. I'm listening."

"Why have you got your head cocked to one side like that?"

"I told you I was listening." I was, too. Not only to Ronald Barclay's voice, but to something else that might have been only my imagination. "Go on with your story. You've got a reason for wanting a certain character lured here. What's the reason and who is the guy?"

"He's the man who murdered me," Barclay said, and at the same instant I whipped out the .32 automatic I always pack in an armpit rig, hurled my tonnage across the room.

I didn't plunge toward the mirrored closet. I catapulted at the door to the outer corridor. If there's anything that broils me to a crisp it's an eavesdropper. And I'd already had enough weirdness and mystification for one afternoon.

The trick door gave me trouble because I forgot it opened outward. I grasped the knob, twisted it, pulled, and almost dislocated my wrist with the sudden yank. Then I remembered to push.

I pushed. I bounced over the threshold into the musty hallway with its dead, rancid smells, and there was nobody in sight. There was nothing except gloomy, thickening shadows as dusk gathered. I might as well have peered up and down the passages of an abandoned morgue. The silence was a thing you could practically pick up and rub in your fingers.

I went back into the room and pulled the door shut after me. I had the jitters. I had the kind of shakes you get from talking to an invisible dead man who was alive enough and crazy enough to belong in a padded cell.

I needed another snort of the crazy man's Scotch but I didn't take it because my brain felt too fuzzy as it was. Next thing I knew I would be having delirium tremens. Maybe I already had delirium tremens.

I should have stayed out there in the hall while I had the chance. I should have copped a fast scram. I should have gone home where I could try to forget I'd ever been in a joint called Chaple Arms. But no, I had to barge on back into the room.

Barclay's voice came through the wallpaper-covered speaking hole. It sounded grim.

"You took your life in your hands pulling that caper, Nick. For a minute I thought you were trying to get at me. I almost shot you through this mirror. What was the idea? What spooked you?"

"I realize the risk now," I said sourly. "But I thought I'd heard somebody outside stealing an earful." I holstered my heater. "Evidently I was haywire. And for pipe's sake quit yacking at me about shooting through the mirror. You're giving me a complex." I made a resentful mouth at the looking glass. "If you want me to leave, say the word. I'll go quietly; I'd be glad to. I'm getting so I don't like it here, if I ever did."

"I apologize, Nick. I'm sorry. And I don't want you to leave. Not just yet."

I did want to leave, but I didn't say so.

"And another thing," was what I said. "Just before I dived at the door you spouted a line of dizzy dialogue about the man who murdered you. Let's stop making with that kind of double talk. Nobody murdered you, because you're still alive. Taking your word for it, of course. Consequently – "

"Alive! You can't call anyone in my condition alive."

"All I know about your condition is what you've told me. Have you shown yourself? No."

"I don't intend to," he said harshly. "As for the murder part, call it a maimed man's sardonic figure of speech. In my own estimation I'm worse than dead, but skip it. There *was* a man who got killed, though, remember? A prop man. Joseph T. Fullerton, whose name I stole. How do you classify that?"

"An accident."

"Wrong. It was murder. Premeditated murder, as cold and calculated as slaughtering cattle in a packing house." He hesitated a second. "Nick, on that picture with the explosion sequence, do you recall the director?"

"Sure," I said. "Emil Heinrich. A kraut. He's big stuff now. He climbed slow, but he climbed high. Head man of Paragon Pix. He's come a long way. What about him?"

"He'd just been married a short while to an extra girl named Marian Lodge. Pretty, but not a brain in her head."

"He'd still married to her," I said. "And she's still pretty. And she still hasn't got a brain in her head. So what?"

"Heinrich thought I was on the make for her."

"Were you?"

"My home-wrecking was strictly on the screen. You know that. I never looked at her sidewise, but Heinrich had notions. He actually accused me, once. I laughed at him." The voice went brittle, metallic. "I laughed at him. Heaven help me."

"Make your point," I said.

The short hairs were beginning to prickle at the nape of my neck and I felt that shiver going down my spine, crawling inch by inch like a bad dream.

There was a rustling noise behind the wallpaper. "Yesterday I was getting ready to discard an old trunk, Nick. A trunk that belonged to Joe Fullerton, part of his stuff that was moved here with me when I took his name, assumed his identity. I'd rummaged through it before, thrown away the things of his I didn't need, then I'd used it to store junk of my own. But yesterday I decided to get rid of it. I emptied it out."

"And?"

"I discovered a false bottom compartment I'd never noticed before. It had a book in it, a diary. Fullerton's private diary. I wouldn't know why a man would want to keep a thing like that. Diaries are for women, I always thought. But Fullerton had one. Made daily entries – up to the day before he was killed."

"All right, build it up. Make me wait for the punch line."

"This is serious, Nick, not funny. I'm going to read you part of the last page Fullerton wrote. Listen. 'Twice yesterday I found Heinrich messing around my props. He didn't see me watching him, but I saw things I'm going to take up with the union if this keeps up. What right has a kraut director got to butt in on the property department? If he thinks I'm not capable of measuring a load of flashlight powder in a cigarette box let him take it up with the producer. Let him tell the brass hats in the front office. Next time I catch him poking around that prop bomb I'm going to raise a mess, job or no job. Up to now I've kept my mouth shut, but he better lay off. I don't like outsiders fooling with my private can of flash powder, either'."

I said in a choked voice, "Is that all?"

"Isn't it enough, Nick? After fourteen years I know what really happened! Heinrich was jealous of me. He tampered with the cigarette box bomb. In spite of Fullerton's watchfulness and suspicions he succeeded in fixing it to go off prematurely, when I picked it up. And he substituted something powerful for the harmless flash powder that was supposed to be in it."

"Now wait. You're just guessing. You're not sure he did that."

"All right, so I'm guessing. Theorizing. But it adds."

He couldn't convince me.

"Not necessarily," I said. "Maybe I was the one he was after. Maybe he had a grudge against me, for some reason I can't figure. After all, I was the stunt man who was scheduled to let the thing explode in my hands."

"Originally, that's true. Unknown to you, though, Heinrich altered the script just a little. An important little. When we started rehearsing the scene he rearranged the action so that you wouldn't be first to handle the cigarette box. He directed me to pick it up and pry open the lid for that closeup. He told me it was a dummy box; harmless. And certainly I had no reason to disbelieve him.

"He said he would then cut the scene, let you double for me in the following long shot, and go on with the action from there. He was smooth, Nick. He sold it to me and I never suspected what was coming. You know how it worked out. I picked up the real bomb and it went bang. And all these years I thought it was a mischance, an accident – until I found the prop man's diary. Then I knew Heinrich had planned to kill me."

I dredged out a gasper, set fire to it. The smoke burned my gullet like acid, like the fumes of blasting powder, like the hot sting that had scorched my nostrils fourteen years ago on a Paragon sound stage when I had beat out the flames charring the crimson-stained clothing of two crumpled shapes who once had been husky, healthy men.

"You can't make it stick, pal," I said. "Not on the diary of a guy dead and buried all this time."

"There's no statute of limitations on homicide, Nick."

"All right, give it to the cops and see what happens. They'd slip you the big nix. Insufficient proof, for one thing. All you can offer is unsupported surmise. And Emil Heinrich is a powerful hombre these days. A bozo in his position packs weight." I put my coffin nail in an ash-tray, snubbed it out, and had a swig from the Scotch bottle. "You'd wind up before a rigged lunacy commission. They'll say you're off your rocker. Fourteen years of hiding your ugliness from the world drove you out of your mind."

"Do you think that?"

I hedged. "Never mind what I think. The main point is, you could wind up in a room with soft walls."

"Not while I've got one hand to hold a gun."

"Back at that again," I said.

"And anyhow, I don't plan to go to the police. I want Heinrich here. I want a private showdown with him."

"Oh-oh," I said. "No, thanks. Include me out. I'm no assassin. I'm not even an assistant assassin. If you're looking for homicide help, get another boy."

His voice went smooth, persuasive. "Don't let my gun talk put wrong ideas in your head. I'm not going to kill him. He's worth a lot more to me alive. Alive and successful and prosperous. Do you think forty thousand dollars can last forever? Most of the money I got from Joe Fullerton's insurance policy has been spent. And I'm too settled here to relish the idea of being moved to an almshouse. I don't want charity, and I refuse to be a public charge. I simply want to talk to Heinrich."

"Blackmail, eh? A shakedown."

"That's a little crude. I want to sell him the Fullerton diary for enough cash to see me through the rest of my life. Is that unfair?"

4 KILL AND VANISH

Such guff as this I didn't swallow. It was too transparent, too obvious. Barclay had bumpery on his mind and I wanted no part of that. By the same token you can't come right out and say no to a potential madman with a gat in his clutch. It was a situation calling for finesse.

I lied diplomatically.

"Hmmm-m-m," I said. "Just a financial transaction, huh? That's different." I moved casily toward the door.

"Where are you going?" he asked uneasily.

"To do what you asked. To arrange to lure Heinrich here."

"You're really going to help me?"

"Anything for a pal," I said, and pushed the portal open.

It resisted me. Something was against it, outside in the hall. Something with weight that didn't want to yield.

I shoved with all my hundred and ninety pounds of heft, suddenly and explosively. From the mirrored closet behind me came a displeased oath. Barclay must have thought I was taking a runout on him.

And I was. Or anyhow that had been my intention until I smacked the corridor door wide open and knocked somebody sprawling on the hallway's thin-worn carpet. Then I changed my mind, because I had finally nailed my eavesdropper.

He was the deaf desk clerk, with the parchment face, from downstairs. The door batted him all the way across the passage and he fetched up against the opposite wall, huddled, flopping, a bag of bones in a black alpaca coat. I grabbed him, dragged him back and pulled him into the room.

It was pretty dark now, but not too dark for me to see a wheel-chair rolling toward me. The mirrored closet gaped wide, and the fragment of man who used to be Ronald Barclay was out of his hiding place. Maybe my unexpected maneuver with the door had brought him forth because of curiosity. Or maybe he'd had an idea of pursuing me, guessing that I was going to scram and leave him in the lurch.

He might even have figured a double-cross and decided to gun me in the back. I don't know and I never found out. I didn't have time to ask him.

I only knew that in the gloom of night-fall he didn't look so hideous. Sitting in the wheel-chair, he had a blanket over his lap so you couldn't actually tell that his legs were missing. Without the lights turned on, his face could have passed for a face for it was a pale blur above a white shirt even paler and blurrier.

One sleeve was empty, pinned to the chest. The other had an arm in it which ended in a stubby hand, the hand being busy propelling the chair by its wheel-rim. That was swell. As long as it was busy it couldn't do anything about the nickel-plated .38 revolver resting on the blanketed lap.

That's what I thought.

The pale blur of face spouted harsh curses. "You tricked me!" he raved. "You tricked me out of the closet so you could look at me."

"Stow it." I was leaning over the desk clerk. "This lad was listening, and – "

The sky came down and hit me on the noggin. All the stars in the heavens fell with the sky and danced in my optics, and all at once I was pitching down a long black tunnel that gulped me like a raw oyster. My head came off and floated away. It wasn't a head, it was a balloon, and somebody had cut the string. It drifted on a rising current, and the current became a whirlpool of pain filled with India ink.

Blooey. I didn't even feel the floor when it bounced me . . .

There was one dim light in the room, and two eyes fastened on me. I didn't like them. They were too wide open, too glassy. Eyes are supposed to blink once in a while. These didn't. They regarded me with the cold impassive speculation of a fish three days on ice. Expressionless. Unsympathetic.

The devil with them. I wanted sympathy. My skull throbbed like an ulcer in a movie producer's stomach. I was an ill man. I was a sick dick and I didn't like being stared at.

Ronald Barclay hadn't liked it either. I reflected dourly. And when he didn't like a thing he was a man who resented it the hard way. For a one-armed guy he certainly packed a wallop. It takes a hefty bash to put me down for the count, but he had what it takes. I decided I was lucky he had only whammed me with a .38. If it had been a .45 it would probably have finished me.

As it was, I had a lump on top of my conk the size of second base and I was lying on the floor, sniffing the dust of the thin carpet and looking into a pair of cold- cod-fish glims belonging to somebody sprawled a couple of feet fierninst me. I didn't mind the character being so close, but that steady mackerel focus gave me the fantods.

I got more than the fantods when it slowly dawned on me that the bozo wasn't breathing.

He had a vacant, expressionless face as wrinkled as parchment, as colorless as wax candles. There was a wired button in one ear and a switched-off plastic box hanging from his alpaca coat, but he wasn't using the equipment as a hearing aid. He was the desk clerk, and he was defunct. He couldn't be anything else, the way his left temple was crushed in.

I whispered something silently.

The fog cleared out of my brain and I tabbed a wheel-chair beyond the clerk's lifeless husk. The last time I'd seen that wheel-chair it had contained Ronald Barclay. Now it contained nobody. It was just an empty wheel-chair.

I sat up and waited for nausea to hit me the way it does when you've got a minor concussion and move too fast. My head vibrated like strings on a hockshop banjo and my stomach churned.

As soon as it stopped churning I lurched to my feet. Astonishingly, I didn't fall down again. For a guy with a cracked plate, this was a major accomplishment. I felt well enough to hip a quick dram from that fifth of Vat 69 on the table, and then I felt even better. I dug inside my coat, unshipped my roscoe and was back in business. I prowled the apartment.

First I looked in the closet behind the trick mirror. It was a big roomy space, dark as the inside of a rubber boot until I used the beam of my pencil flash. Barclay wasn't there. When I moved to the bedroom he wasn't in there, either. I drew another blank in the bathroom – no Barclay. Par for the course. But in a padlocked alcove between bedroom and bath I stumbled onto all the clues a snoop would ever need.

The padlock was duck soup for the pick I carry on my keyring, and the alcove was actually a miniature workshop. It had a wooden bench with precision lathes, motors, tools, strips and bars and hunks of metal that looked like aluminium or duralumin. It had an assortment of chromium steel coil springs, leather straps and the oddest looking hinges and pivots I'd ever gandered.

The corners of the alcove were piled with contraptions too beautifully fashioned to be called junk, but too outlandish to be called anything else. Some of the things had ball-and-socket couplings with mechanical latching devices. Others were whittled of wood and padded with leather to turn a harness-and-saddlemaker green with envy. It was a museum collection, a handicraft exhibit meriting booth space at an exposition. It had probably cost Ronald Barclay ten or twelve solitary and laborious years out of his life, and it was worth maybe seven dollars for scrap.

I heard footfalls.

I whirled, skulked silently back to the living room in time to hear a doorknob click and see it turn. I brought up my cannon and snicked off the safety.

The door swung outward and a tall, wide-shouldered punk ankled into the room – a punk with brown hair in crisp waves and an uncompromising chin as substantial as a granite cornerstone. He had a stethoscope clasped around his neck and dangling down onto his manly chest, but he was no doctor. Doctors don't wear second-hand bellhop uniforms a size too small for them.

"Hi, Pete," I said, and drew a bead on him. I was proud of myself for remembering that Pete was what the desk clerk had called him. "Freeze, please."

He didn't jump all the way out of his brogans, but he gave it the old college try. He goggled at my gat, backed against a wall and froze as instructed.

"Hey!" he strangled.

I kept him covered. "Just a formality, Pete. I'm a little nervous. For all I knew it might have been Frankenstein's monster coming in. It might have been Jack the Ripper. It could have been anybody, but it turns out to be a combination bellhop and elevator jockey wearing a stethoscope. The stethoscope confuses me. Let's hear about it."

"You – you're alive!"

"Yeah." I gestured to the desk clerk crumpled on the floor in a motionless lump. "But he's not. Explain the stethoscope, please. Talk it up."

Pete regarded me with bewilderment. "I thought you were dead. When I found you a minute ago, you looked like it."

"Ah. So you've been in here before."

"Certainly. That's why I rushed out to get my stethoscope. To try you for heartbeats. You didn't seem to have a pulse."

"Don't tell me you're a sawbones in your spare time?"

"I'm studying to be one." He was as dignified as only a young guy who takes himself seriously can be. "I'm in my final semester of pre-med. Winthrop is the name, Peter Warren Winthrop." His rugged jaw firmed and his kisser showed no good-humored quirk at the corners. "Just because I wear this monkey suit and accepted a dollar tip from you, don't get wrong ideas."

"I get many wrong ideas," I said.

5 MURDER ON THE MAKE

Putting away my rod, I flashed Pete a fast swivel at my private badge. It didn't seem to be much of a surprise to him.

"Okay, son," I said. "You were in here a moment ago. Why?"

"I was looking for old Duffy," Pete said.

"Him?" I flicked a glance at the deceased bozo.

Pete nodded. "He wasn't at his desk and the switchboard had a buzz. I thought perhaps he'd slipped upstairs without calling for the elevator, so I ran my car up here to Three, the top, and started scouting the halls. Duffy had a bit of listening at doors occasionally. Wood makes a good sound conductor when you put a hearing aid microphone against the panels. So I noticed this particular door open and looked in."

"You saw what?"

"You and Duffy were on the floor. He was dead. I wasn't sure about you, so I went for my stethoscope."

"That's all?"

"Yes, sir. Except the wheel-chair, of course."

"Nobody was in it when you first looked?"

"Nobody." He frowned. "I assume it's Mr Fullerton's chair. But if so, where's Fullerton?"

"That's what I'm wondering," I said. "And his name isn't Fullerton; it's Barclay. Not that it matters to you. What does matter is, he's gone. He was here, but he isn't here now. You didn't tab anybody going down the stairs?"

"I did not. Although the stairway is nowhere near my elevator, so that doesn't spell anything." He frowned again. "But if Fullerton, or Barclay or whatever his name is – if he uses a wheel-chair he must be crippled. That's an assumption on my part, of course, for I never laid eyes on him. But presuming he *is* a cripple – "

"He's one-armed and legless."

"You mean you saw him?"

"Unfortunately, yes."

"Then if he's like you say, how could he get out of his wheel-chair and go down two flights of steps?" Pete's peepers narrowed and suspicion slid into them. Suspicion of me. "And who murdered Duffy?"

"The answer is in an alcove between the bedroom and bath," I said. "Barclay experimented in prosthetics. He dabbled at inventing artificial limbs. That's why I asked if you saw anybody scramming. He must have had a set of gams he could get around on."

"I – see."

"You didn't think I croaked Duffy and abolished Barclay down the drainpipes and clouted myself unconscious, did you? You needn't answer that. I can guess how you figured it, only you figured it wrong. Now where's a phone?"

He pointed to a hand-set on a stand. "But you can't go through the switchboard because Duffy isn't there to give you a line."

"Poor old guy," I said. "He probably never got to spend that four bits for a perfecto. But at least he satisfied his curiosity about what the lodger in Three-seventeen looked like. He saw him. And the price he paid was much too high."

I shooed Pete out into the hall, followed him, shut the door behind us.

"Let's go, chum," I said. "I've got dialing to do and connections to make. There's a maniac killer on the loose and he's thirsting for revenge, gunning for a movie mogul. This is a thing for the cops."

It was for the cops, all right, but the cops wouldn't have it. That cost them another bump-off before the night ended.

And it came near installing me in a coffin. Sometimes when my sleep is restless I can still feel those fingers closing like metal bands around my throat. Those are the nights I get up and drink myself very, very drunk . . .

My coupe could do eighty with a tail wind. On a downgrade it might even nudge ninety. I held it to fifty, though, because the last thing I wanted was a ticket for speeding. Not that the ticket would bother me, but you don't like to be delayed by motorbike bulls when you're trying to reach a guy and warn him he's a ripe target for a madman's bullet.

I whammed west on Sunset to Highland, north on Highland past Hollywood Boulevard and aimed for the hills above that. The multi-colored lights of Los Angeles spread out behind and below me like a vast carpet of glowing embers, infernal, patterned in blotchy angles and lines that merged and dimmed against the far infinity of horizon and night.

Ahead, the convoluted hills rose darkly to a star-flecked sky, with here and there a pinprick twinkle on a knoll or cliffside, as if the crests had stretched far up and seized some of the stars to wear for diamonds. Lights in the windows of hilltop houses always look that way from a distance, and in Hollywood it's considered swanky indeed to live in a district hilltop house.

That was why Emil Heinrich lived in one. Heinrich was big stuff.

I tooled my crate along a curving roadway and climbed. What I had to do was a cop job, but the cops wouldn't handle it. They were a pack of dopes, particularly my old friend Ole Brunvig of the Homicide Squad. In my mind's ear I could still hear the echo of Brunvig's grainy, dyspeptic voice when I called him up from the lobby of the Chaple Arms.

"Nick Ransom, yeah," I said. "There's been a kill. A desk clerk, name of Duffy, made the mistake of looking at Ronald Barclay, and Barclay extinguished him. Now Barclay's on the prowl to pull another bump."

"He – what?"

I repeated it. "Barclay croaked this clerk named Duffy and now he's out gunning for – "

"Stop kidding me. How can the clerk be out gunning for somebody if he's croaked?"

"Not the clerk!" I yelped. "He's defunct. It's Barclay who's on the loose, getting ready to kill again. The name he's been using is Joseph T. Fullerton, but he's really Ronald Barclay." This sounded a little complex, but I let it go. "You remember Barclay. He used to be the hottest ham in the Paragon roster."

"Oh. That Barclay. For a moment you had me puzzled." Sudden peevishness sprouted through the sarcasm. "Sure I remember Ronald Barclay. He died fourteen years ago. Killed by an explosion on a sound stage. So now his ghost is horsing around Hollywood and you want him pinched for murder, hey?"

"Yes, but he's not a ghost. He's alive, and he's got a roscoe and he's on the prowl for the guy who put him in his grave."

"Now cut that out!" Brunvig blew his lid. "If he's alive, nobody put him in his grave. If he was in his grave, he isn't alive. Lay off the drunken comedy."

"It's not comedy and I'm sober," I said hotly. "Barclay is not dead. He never was. His funeral was phony. The explosion cost him both legs and an arm, but it didn't really kill him. I'm telling you he knocked me senseless a little while ago and bumped a hotel clerk named Duffy and then walked out while I was too unconscious to stop him."

"Oho. He walked out." Brunvig's voice rose to a shrill scream of rage, through which you could hear the gnashing of teeth. "He walked out. He's got no legs, but he walked out. All right, Sherlock, that tears it. I've had enough."

"Listen," I said. "You don't understand!"

"I understand plenty. You're intoxicated. You're fried up to the scalp. Okay, you've had your fun with me. Now go to bed and sleep it off before I get sore and jerk your license." Violently he hung up in my ear.

You couldn't blame him too much. Try to convince anybody that a screen star dead fourteen years is actually alive. Try to make a skeptical cop believe there's a legless, one-armed bozo walking around packing murder in his pocket, hunting the party whose bomb had blasted him to a living death. You had to see it, as I'd seen it, to know it was true. Otherwise it sounded as screwy as an opium smoker's dream.

So I got nowhere with Brunvig. I rang him back and he refused to talk to me. He wouldn't even take the call.

That dumped it spang in my lap, which was what I deserved. It was my own fault. I should have made a getaway from Barclay's suite when I'd had the chance, should have tipped the law to come slap a strait jacket on him when I first realized he was dangerously insane.

Instead, I'd turned my back on him so he could bash me. Worse, I'd dragged a poor old deaf yuck into the room and got him conked to his ancestors. I felt almost as guilty as if I'd killed Duffy myself.

Any way you looked at it, Barclay was now my personal responsibility. It was up to me to track him down, collar him before he slew any more citizens. Finding him shouldn't be too difficult, I concluded. He had an obsession, a fixed idea. He craved vengeance on Emil Heinrich, therefore he would make a bee-line for Heinrich's opulent igloo in the Hollywoodland hills, probably by taxi. This called for a chase sequence, yoicks and tally-ho in a thundering hurry.

Not that I cared about Heinrich. If he had actually gimmicked the cigarette-box bomb fourteen years ago it was high time retribution caught up with him. It had to be legal retribution, though, and not meted out by a maniac with a penchant for murdering innocent bystanders. I didn't want any more dead guys like Duffy weighing on my conscience.

So I left Peter Warren Winthrop, bellhop, elevator jockey and medical student holding down the fort at the Chaple Arms. I posted him in the frowsy, unclean lobby and ordered him to keep phoning Homicide until he persuaded them to send a tech squad and a meat basket for Duffy's remainders.

"Stay with it, son, and don't take no for an answer," I said.

Then I blipped out to my bucket and lit a shuck for high ground.

Now, ten minutes later, I twisted my tiller, scooted around a series of curves that slanted upward in tilted coils like rope a careless giant had tossed away. And presently I came to my destination.

Heinrich had a layout in keeping with his lofty position as head cheese of a major studio. It was a cubistic stucco affair on three different levels, as if the architect had melted it and let it drip down the face of the hill until it congealed there in an unsymmetrical jumble of gray blocks.

An abrupt driveway angled to a parking area in front of the garage, which might have held ten Cadillacs if you squeezed them in with a shoe-horn. From this terraced plateau, monolithic steps led up to the next level. You didn't really need an alpenstock to make the climb.

At the top of the steps there was a flat expanse, part patio, part lawn, part flag-stones, part garden and part swimming pool. Lake Michigan was bigger than the swimming pool. Skirting it, you came to the house itself, its main entrance recessed in a sort of embrasure. By that time you were ready for artificial respiration.

I thumbed the bell-push, waited for my pulse to get back down out of the stratosphere. By and by the chrome-plated door opened and a stuffed shirt in butler's livery inspected me with the cordial sunny warmth of December in Siberia.

"Yes, sir?" He let the words slide past his sinuses, like a repressed whinny.

"Mr Heinrich," I said, and briefly flashed my badge.

"The master is not at home, sir. And if I may say so, sir, I find your approach to be most crude in its subterfuge."

"Hah?"

"The badge, sir. A special, I believe. Not a genuine police shield at all." He leered at me. "You are not the only imposter who has tried to obtain an interview on false credentials. Most of them pretend to be gas meter readers, telephone repairmen and termite inspectors. I give you credit for more originality," he added grudgingly. "But the fact remains that actors, musicians and scenario writers seeking employment with Paragon must see Mr Heinrich at the studio, not at his residence. Good night, sir."

6 BODY ON THE LAM

As that butler said "good night" he started to close the door in my face, very politely, very properly. And very firmly.

I leaned against its velvety chromium surface, just as politely and twice as firmly. I'm a patient guy, but I was fed up with people giving me the brushoff. I reached around the edge of the portal, harvested a fistful of the butler's livery and hauled him up close to me. I thrust my kisser two inches from his, so he could smell the Scotch on my breath.

"Pal," I said, "I'm coming in. If you insist on it I'll trudge the length of you like a welcome mat, but I'm coming in. I've got to talk to Heinrich and I've got to have permission to prowl the property. Do you take me to your boss right now or shall we wrestle for it?"

"He – he's not home!" he squawked, flapping like a hen laying a square egg. "Let go of me!"

I shook him a little, just enough to make his tonsils rattle.

"Don't lie to me, baby. There's a killer loose. He's looking for your employer and he's toting a thirty-eight for a divining rod. Take me to Heinrich. Pronto."

"He's out. There's no-nobody home except Mrs Heinrich and myself. The rest of the household staff have the evening off. You let g-go of me or I'll call the p-police!"

"I wish you would," I said grimly. "Maybe they'll listen to you. They wouldn't to me."

Still holding him, I shoved him backward into a reception hall that needed only a layer of turf to make it a polo field.

"But first take me to Mrs Heinrich," I said. "That's assuming you were levelling about her hubby not being home." I kicked the door shut behind me, listened for the click that satisfied me the latch had snapped. "Meanwhile, don't let anybody else in. Except the cops, of course. I wasn't fooling about a killer being loose."

He flapped some more. "You c-can't – "

"Don't be tiresome," I said. "I'll even let you announce me to the lady. Nick Ransom is the handle. Maybe she'll remember me from the days when she was an extra named Marian Lodge and I was a stunt man around the lots."

"But – but Mrs Heinrich doesn't like to be disturbed during her star bath."

"Star bath?"

"Like a sun bath, only at night. Something about the cosmic rays. She read it in a book."

I took this in stride. The night was so full of whacky events I was growing calloused to it. And Marian always had a bird-brain.

"We'll disturb her anyhow," I said. "Get going."

Muttering, he led me along the reception hall to a corridor, and along that to a stairway, and up this to a level which seemed to project outward into empty space. Actually it was a glassed-in-solarium with the domed roof rolled open; a basking room built out over the cliffside with no visible means of support, ending on a sheer drop down into the next precinct.

The butler cleared his throat apologetically, spoke my name and scuttled away with his coat tails dipping lint. He never did phone Headquarters, the heel. He was all bluff and no hole card.

I stood there trying to adjust my eyes to the dark. There was movement on something that might be a chaise longue. You couldn't quite tell in the blackness. The movement was white, though. Fascinatingly white. And a drawling she-male voice said:

"Nick Ransom, of all people. This *is* a surprise. Imagine, after all these years. And just as rugged as ever."

I went toward her, wondering how she could spot my ruggedness in a room as dark as the bottom of the La-Brea tar pits. Presently my glimmers got their second wind and there was just enough starlight to show me the shapely outlines of a jane on a daybed. Just to make sure, I lit a match on my thumbnail.

Then I said: "Yipe!" and my flabbergasted exclamation blew out the flame.

The doll was Marian Lodge, all right; Marian Heinrich, now. Brunette, statuesque, relaxed, and utterly uninhibited.

She laughed. "Shocked, Nick? That's out of character."

"Yeah, but I wasn't expecting – "

"To get the full benefit of star bath rays you must have them flow over you like sea foam. All over you. Over all of you. Come sit by me, darling."

"No," I said firmly, "I'll talk from here. It's serious, and I want to keep my mind on it."

"Silly boy." Silk whispered intimately and a zipper whe-eeked. "Now you can be serious. Come kiss me hello."

I sidled closer, cautiously.

"That was years ago. Before you got married. Speaking of husbands – "

"Let's not." She sat up, snared my fingers, tugged me down on the cushions. "Husbands bore me. Especially mine."

"Where is he tonight?"

"Out chasing, I suppose. As usual. Don't worry, he won't bother us. He never gets home until late. Kiss me."

I could be as persistent as she was. "Any way of getting hold of him by phone?"

"Heaven forbid." She hauled at my wrist. "I'm so glad you came to see me, Nick. Like old times."

Old times, my elbow. I'd been on two mild parties with her and she wanted to build it up to a feature production. In technicolor. What she was doing with my captured hand would have made a wooden Indian throw away his cigars. I was no wooden Indian, though. I was a private eye hunting a homicidal madman. "Cut it out, tutz," I said. "I want to ask you something."

"The answer is yes. Now kiss me."

"Remember Ronald Barclay?"

"Do I! Mmm-mmm. I adored that man. Kiss me."

By main strength, I got my fingers away from her. "Did he ever make a pass at you?"

"No." She sighed regretfully. "Darn it."

"But your husband was jealous of him, wasn't he?"

"I wish you'd stop reminding me of my husband at a time like this. For all I care he can drop dead."

This startled me. It made two people who yearned for Heinrich to pass away. Heinrich was not a popular guy.

"You might be surprised if he did die, hon," I said. "Tonight. With a hole in the head. A bullet-hole, that is."

She snagged my other hand and was reckless with it. Her sultry breath danced along my cheek. She was driving me crazy.

"Silly. You don't have to shoot him," she murmured. "I won't even tell him you were here."

"I didn't say *I'd* shoot him!" I choked. "I meant . . . Hey, cut it out. Quit it."

Star glow dropped little glints in her sleek black hair and her lips were a dark flutter of challenge and demand. But whatever I was going to do about it never got done, because just then a voice full of adenoids whinnied at us from the solarium entrance.

A butler is handy to have around, sometimes.

"I beg pardon," the butler said. "There's a person at the door who insists upon seeing Mr Ransom."

I leaped up to my feet. In the same motion I unholstered my fowling piece. If this was Ronald Barclay trying to trick me out where he could use me for a clay pigeon, slugs were going to fly through the blue California night.

"Describe him," I said.

"He's rather young, sir. And tall. He gave his name as Peter Warren Winthrop, and when I refused to admit him he asked me to convey a message to you. Something to the effect, sir, that Duffy has disappeared."

I made a record getting downstairs to see Peter Warren Winthrop. He had plenty to say and not much breath to say it with.

"It's the truth, Ransom, so help me," Pete Winthrop said. His athletic shoulders twitched under a gabardine topcoat and he sounded like a guy who has experienced a profound shock, like encountering a herd of polka-dotted zebras. "I know it's hard to believe. I could scarcely believe it myself. But it's true."

We were outdoors, pacing the patio flagstones. Behind us, Heinrich's cubistic wigwam was buttoned up tighter than a bald man's scalp, and I'd warned the butler to keep it that way when I ankled out to parley with the Chaple Arms bellhop. Keeping step with him now, and holding to the thick shadows, I had my gat in my grasp and my peepers peeled for possible peril.

"How'd you discover it, son?" I said.

"I – I had put through another call to your friend Brunvig at Homicide Headquarters, but as soon as I mentioned your name to him and said I was phoning to report the same murder you had told him about, he slammed up on me. Then I got an idea."

"Yeah?"

He nodded, and told me about it. "I decided I would go out and try to find any kind of policeman – you know, a motorcycle officer or radio prowl car cop, maybe even a flatfoot pounding a beat. Anybody with a badge and a little authority. But first I wanted to make sure none of the tenants up on three would wander into Three-seventeen and see Duffy's corpse and throw the whole house into a panic. I couldn't remember whether we had left the door of the suite open or closed, locked or unlocked."

"So you went up there."

"Yes. And he was gone. Duffy, I mean. Vanished. Not a trace of him. Do you realize what that means? It means that Fullerton, or Barclay as you called him – it means he was there in the hotel all the time. Hiding some place. Hiding while you and I went down and started phoning from the lobby." The punk shivered visibly in his topcoat. "You'd gone away and left me there with a killer. And he had moved Duffy's body as soon as the coast was clear."

"Moved it where?"

"How should I know? Not in any of the broom closets or linen pantries. I looked. I was scared, but I looked anyhow. But I didn't try any of the rooms. We've got a full house, everything occupied. I couldn't very well start knocking on doors, asking guests to let me in so I could search for a dead man. I didn't know *what* to do. Then I figured I'd better come here and tell you about it. I figured you might have some angles."

"All I ran into was curves," I said dourly.

I was thinking of Marian Heinrich and her star bath. She would do no more star bathing tonight. Thick, sinister clouds were drifting in from Santa Monica, sullen and ominous, wrapping up the stars in black cotton batting. You couldn't see the surrounding hills, you couldn't even see the flagstones you were walking on. All you could see was a mental image of something maniacal and monstrous, something on artificial legs stalking you through a darkness as thick as oatmeal cooked in a vat of dye.

"He was clever," Pete Winthrop said. "Nobody can prove he murdered Duffy if Duffy's corpse can't be found. The cops will never believe your story, now. Which gives him a clear field to ambush Heinrich."

"Not while we do sentry duty," I said.

"We?"

"Beat it if you're yellow," I growled. "I'll do what has to be done."

"I didn't mean it that way," he said apologetically. "I was just flattered to think you wanted me." Impressed. Boyish. A punk with a chance to assist a private dick and overwhelmed by it. And a little uncertain, too. "Mightn't it be a good idea to phone the law again and try to persuade them to send somebody to help us stand guard?"

7 FINGERS OF GUILT

We had paced all the way back to the front door by that time, Peter and I. And as if in answer to his suggestion, the portal opened not more than half an inch.

"Mr Ransom, sir," came through the opening in a shaky whinny.

"Close that door and keep it locked!" I rasped.

"Y-yes, sir," the butler said. "But I thought you should be informed that I fear I delayed too long in attempting to call the police as you originally suggested. Our line seems to be dead, sir." The door swung shut and the latch clicked.

"Golly!" Pete Winthrop made a gulping noise in his gullet. "A dead phone. A cut wire. Barclay's here – on the grounds!"

I gave him a shove. "Scatter. Stay up here on the patio level. Keep moving. I'll patrol down along the driveway and garage. That way I'll be set in case he tries to dry-gulch Heinrich coming home in his car. I don't suppose you've got a heater?"

"Heater?"

"Gun."

"No."

"Barclay has, so watch out. Don't jump him if you see him."

"What *shall* I do?"

"Yell for me and duck for cover. Don't let him get you in the open."

We separated, and I went catfooting down the long monolithic stairway. There was one thing in our favor – the rear of the estate was walled in by a precipitous hill, barricading it against approach or escape. You couldn't get in that way unless you used a block and tackle or descended by parachute. You couldn't get out without a helicopter.

This made my strategy valid. The lower-level driveway was the only entrance, and the only exit. And the house itself was practically impregnable when its doors and windows were locked. Clenching my cannon, I was ready for the payoff.

Silence pressed down around me. With the coming of the clouds, even the hillside crickets had quit being chirpy. I kept listening for anything that might sound like the metallic clank of artificial legs in motion, the scrape of soles on cement paving.

Away back in the recesses of my think-tank something bothered me, something that refused to be dragged out so I could inspect it. It was an evasive wisp, a fragment that played hide-and-seek with my subconscious. I felt the same way about it that I'd felt when I had first heard an empty room speak my name with Ronald Barclay's voice. Haunted, uncomfortable.

I had a curious sensation that Barclay didn't exist, that he never had existed; that everything had been a figment of my imagination. But the throbbing lump on top of my noggin contradicted any such nonsense.

Barclay had been real enough. Figments of the imagination don't slug you to dreamland, and they don't croak poor old deaf guys like Duffy. And I had glimpsed the maimed ham with my own optics. I had lamped him in his wheel-chair, definitely legless under the lap blanket, definitely one-armed, with a shirt sleeve pinned up emptily.

"Ransom!"

The shout came hoarsely from above, and then I heard a series of scuffling sounds, the violent rustling of underbrush. I leaped for the steps, took them three at a time, catapulted across lawn and patio toward those continuing noises.

Hard by the tiled area bordering the swimming pool there was a row of clumped hydrangea bushes. I couldn't see them stirring, but I heard them.

Flying blind, I plunged forward – and overshot the mark.

Something reached out, tripped me. As I stumbled, a heavy and panting burden landed on my back with an impact that drove me down on all fours like a bear. I didn't lose my roscoe, but for all the good it did me I might as well have pitched it into the pool. The hand that held it was pressed knuckle-deep in loam and I couldn't raise it, couldn't even move it.

Weight crushed me, flattened me, and then fingers clamped around my throat from behind. They were hot, inexorable fingers as relentless as steel springs.

They throttled me, pressing against my jugular and carotid artery, collapsing my gullet and robbing my bellows of air. I bucked and arched my spine and sunfished like a rodeo bronc, but all I threw was snake-eyes. I didn't throw my rider.

Then I didn't throw anything. I got thrown. I was propelled headlong into the swimming pool and I sank like an anchor.

They say a drowning gee sees his whole life pass by him in a series of flashback montage memories. Not me. I just saw the scenes of the past few hours. Plummeting downward in cold water, I reviewed everything that had happened.

My head stopped throbbing and my mind sharpened like a razor on a hone. I saw the cat eating a bird on the steps of the Chaple Arms. I saw Ronald Barclay's hotel suite, the trick mirror in the closet door, the little padlocked alcove workship where he had dabbled in prosthetics. I saw the defunct Duffy lying with his temple crushed in, a button fastened in one ear and wires running down to a switched-off hearing gadget he would never need again.

I saw a legless figure in a rolling wheel-chair, a one-armed form with a vague blur of face and a gat in his lap, and the voice of a guy I'd once considered my friend. I had the memory of a kraut director named Heinrich who had climbed to the top of the cinema heap, slowly but implacably, until he was chief poo-bah of a major studio.

And I saw a voluptuous and uninhibited quail, feather-brained, black of hair and gorgeously white of skin, lolling in a darkened solarium taking a star bath, letting her lovely contours soak up cosmic rays while she expressed a fervent wish that her hubby would drop dead.

I hit bottom. And, as I hit, I found all the answers. A fine time to be finding answers, when you're drowning at the bottom of a swimming pool.

On the other hand, when you're a murderer and you've strangled a guy and dumped him in the deep six, you'll likely stand by to see if he floats to the surface again. That's so you can shoot him, bludgeon him or shove him under to make certain he dies – if he's not already dead. Naturally, if he's dead he'll stay beneath the water and you needn't worry about him any more.

I stayed under water.

I wasn't deceased. I wasn't even unconscious. But I knew if I came up for air I would be a goner. The instant my conk popped out it would be a bull's-eye, either for a bullet or a fractured skull if I happened to be within reaching distance of the pool's edge. I realized this even while my lungs were bursting and every muscle struggled to impel me off the bottom.

I fought it. I reverted to my stunting days when I could stay immersed as long as the scenario demanded. I held my breath, got my feet planted solidly on the slippery tile floor of the immense pool and slowly started walking. Very slowly, so I couldn't create surface ripples. And keeping my mental fingers crossed, hoping I was headed in the right direction.

My soles detected a slant – downward.

I reversed myself. My ears were pounding now, and my chest was full of molten metal that seared and burned like a blast furnace. But I had learned which way the pool's bottom tilted, and I was heading for the shallow end. All I needed was another minute.

Too bad Emil Heinrich was such a big shot at Paragon Pix. Too bad he had so much dough. If he had been less wealthy his swimming pool would be smaller. I could reach the shallow part sooner. But no, Heinrich had to be in the top chips. Try that on your philosophy. A guy earned too much geet, and because of it people died.

I couldn't hold my breath any longer.

I let some of it out and it streamed up over my head like an immense balloon. Like a drifting blister. Like bubble gum. It popped and broke on the surface. I could hear it.

Okay, killer. You happy now? You know what that air-bubble spells. You've murdered me. That was the last of my air. Now you can go away. I'm on the bottom and I'm croaked.

Oh, yeah? That's what you think.

The pool's floor slanted more abruptly. I kept walking. I got my cigarette holder out of my inside coat pocket. It was a plastic cigarette holder with silver filigree. A client had given it to me one time, by way of showing gratitude. I never use it, except when I'm trying to impress other clients. Cigarette holders are an affectation. I like to inhale my poison straight.

Nice cigarette holder. Not as long as a symphony conductor's baton, but long enough. A hollow tube, slightly flared at one end; a mouthpiece on the other.

Shallow water now. Still deep enough to cover me, but shallow. Careful now. Keep at least six inches of water over your head, Ransom, old boy. Don't break the surface.

I stuck the holder in my mouth and poked its opposite end out of the pool. I blew through it, cleared it.

Then I breathed through it. I breathed air. Wonderful element, air. Puts oxygen in your blood and hair on your chest. I breathed air through the plastic tube, and nobody knew it. Nobody could see me. To all intents and purposes I was a cadaver at the bottom of the water. For a cadaver I was feeling pretty spry.

I kept breathing, not moving. No telling how long it would be before I dared take a chance and scramble out onto dry land. I couldn't tell who was watching, any more than the watcher could tell I was alive. I breathed, and waited. I waited and breathed.

Nobody lives forever. I walked and broke water and found the hand rails of a ladder and got my feet on the rungs, hauled myself to the bordering tiles. No gunshots. No swat on the steeple. Nothing but darkness and the squishing of my shoes and the splashy *drip-drip-drip* from my ruined tweeds.

That, and distant bitter dialogue, and a motor idling lazily on the driveway down below.

The motor had a rich hollow chuckle from its exhaust, like an Indian tomtom in a rain barrel. It sounded healthy and powerful and expensive. It sounded like five miles to the gallon, provided the driver did a lot of coasting.

The masculine voices sounded sore.

I skittered to the steep concrete escarpment the Heinrich menage used for an outdoor stairway and probed my way down through a night that was just as dark as it had ever been. On the parking area this side of the driveway there was something that could have been a Cadillac, a Packard, a Lincoln or a streamlined Diesel locomotive.

Its rear end was pointing inward, twin tail-lights and amber back-up lights glowing like a Christmas tree. Apparently the guy at the wheel had come up the drive and then jockeyed the massive heap around so he could back into the garage and be ready for a fast straight-ahead takeoff in the morning.

His head lamps made the driveway and parking level as bright as a movie set under sun arcs, but he wasn't at his tiller now. He had got out and walked around to open the garage doors, and I recognized him in the red-and-amber glow of his stern lights. He was Emil Heinrich, short, dumpy, potbellied, with a face like a full moon. His wife had said he wouldn't be home until late, but he had fooled her.

He was talking in a thick, guttural monotone to somebody who lurked in the shadows at the sedan's far side.

"Zo. You want me to bay you one hundred thousandt tollars for dis diary. The diary of a dead man, agguzing me of murter. You zay you vill turn me ofer to the law if I revuze. Pah! Id iss ridiculous. I vill gif you one thousandt tollars cash, vich I habben to haf in mein bocket for small change. One thousandt, for your nuisanz walue." He spat. "Take id or leaf id."

"I'll take it as first payment."

I knew that voice. How well I knew that voice! Resonant. Determined. I didn't have to gander its owner, hidden around the far side of the sedan. Hearing it was enough.

Heinrich reached into a coat pocket as if to bring forth the promised lettuce. He made a mistake. A bad mistake. He dragged a roscoe out instead.

Flame lanced out around the sneezing *ka-chow!* of gunfire. It wasn't Heinrich's gun that fired, though. He never got around to it. He lurched, took three mincing steps backward, crossed his ankles awkwardly and twisted as he fell. After he fell he didn't even move.

8 LAST KILL, LAST CHASE

Catapulting down the remaining steps, I was unable to draw a bead on the killer because the chuckle-purring sedan was in the way. I had my own heater ready, but I couldn't use it. A car door slammed. The chuckle-purr snarled into a roar. Rear tires spun, screeched, got traction. The sedan made like jet propulsion going down the driveway.

I snapped a cap at where I thought its gas tank ought to be. Nothing happened. My rod had been too long under water. The cartridge must have been just slightly defective, enough to let the powder get soaked.

I swore, ejected it, jacked another shell into the firing chamber and tried again. But by that time the getaway crate had careened onto the road and was gone. The gat jumped in my fist and my slug went *pee-yowp!* against the opposite cliff. Clean miss.

Then I wasted time. I bent down in the darkness, inspected Heinrich's porky poundage. His wife had got her wish. She was a widow now. Scratch one studio executive. A tunnel that only a .38 could make was drilled all the way through his chest. No matter how important you are in Hollywood, a .38 slug in your heart brings you down to size.

The nickel-plated revolver on Ronald Barclay's legless lap had been .38 caliber. That was the final clue.

I lunged to my coupé where I'd parked it over to one side of the garage apron. Unfortunately, I'd left it headed inward. Now I had to get it started, get it horsed around in the opposite direction. That wasted more time. I finally made it and went thundering down the driveway, around the bend into the road. Then I widened out, fed my clattering cylinders all the coal they would take. I made knots. I bored a hole in the night that the night would never repair.

Down out of the hills, a siren cut loose behind me and a red spotlight stabbed my rear-view mirror.

I pulled over. A prowl car drew abreast. I bounced out, rushed to the cop chariot and yodeled:

"Boys, you've got a passenger!" I flashed my badge, piled into the police buggy. "Let's go! And get me Lieutenant Ole Brunvig on your two-way short wave. Brunvig of Homicide. This is murder."

The cops bought it. I must have sounded plenty sincere. They believed me. The one sitting alongside the driver cut in his transmitter, talked to his hand mike. Presently Brunvig's voice rasped in the cowl speaker.

I snaked the hand mike away from the cop and made with the words. Terse words that boiled out of me like Mount Vesuvius in eruption. After a while the loud-speaker snapped back at me. I had a date with Brunvig at the Chaple Arms.

The prowl car picked up velocity. The guy at the wheel was good. He sent only three pedestrians scampering up palm trees. He took only the first skin of red paint off a passing Pacific Electric bus. He should have been a barber. He could shave you with his front fender and never leave a whisker.

Ole Brunvig's official bucket was just pulling up in front of the Chaple Arms as we screamed to a halt behind him. Up ahead, a sedan was parked – a new, stream-lined monster that didn't belong to this neighborhood at all. It made the rest of the heaps on the street look like scrap iron. And the sedan was Emil Heinrich's.

I leaped to the sidewalk, grabbed Ole's arm and yanked him into the flea-bag hotel's dingy lobby without missing a stride. There was nobody holding down the greasy, marble-topped desk. I ducked around back of it, found a chart for the rectangular tier of wooden letter boxes.

"One-thirty-nine!" I yeeped. "Ground floor. Come on!"

Brunvig hadn't had a chance to say anything. He still didn't. He just unlimbered his cannon and kept pace with me around a rear hallway to the door I wanted. I pointed at the keyhole.

"Okay," he grunted. "If I get busted back to harness for this, I'll reach down your throat and yank you inside out." Then, expertly, he shot the lock to splinters.

I hit the portal a mighty lick and went sailing into a small, cheerless room.

"This is all of it, punk," I said to Peter Warren Winthrop. "You're through. You're through being a bellhop, elevator operator and medical student. And you're through killing people."

He straightened up from a Gladstone bag he had been hastily packing. "What?"

"Playing stupid will buy you nothing," I said. "The giveaway was when you throttled me, dunked me in the pool. Up until then I hadn't suspected you. My attention was all on Ronald Barclay. I'd sensed something haywire about the Barclay theory, but I couldn't nail it down. Then you choked me, hurled me to a watery grave – at which juncture the finger pointed straight at you. A lot of fingers. Ten of them, to be exact."

"What the devil are you talking about?"

"I'm talking about two hands closing around my throat. One set of fingers pressing my carotid artery, and the other set digging into my jugular vein on the opposite side of my neck. Then I knew it couldn't be Barclay who had jumped me, because he was a one-armed guy. And the fingers strangling me were real. Human. Alive. Hot. Not one real hand and one artificial. Both hands were genuine. That eliminated Barclay."

"This is all Greek to me," he said.

I sneered at him. "It was to me, too, until I savvied the clue of the ten fingers. Then everything else clicked into place. I remembered pushing Barclay's living room door open, and encountering resistance – the pressure of somebody leaning against it outside in the hall. I remembered giving it a shove, and bouncing poor old Duffy across the corridor so that he landed like a sack of bones.

"At the time I thought he'd been eavesdropping. But eavesdroppers don't lean against doors when you catch them at it. They turn and run for cover."

"So what?"

"So the next time I saw Duffy he was deceased of a cracked superstructure. And his hearing aid was switched off, which didn't spell anything to me at the time. It did later, though, when I began adding things up. With his ear gadget turned off to save the batteries, he couldn't have been listening at the door."

The punk shifted uneasily. "I don't get what you're driving at. It sounds like a lot of hogwash."

"Yeah?" I said. "Well, how about this? You followed me up to Heinrich's

igloo in the Hollywoodland hills, ostensibly to inform me that Duffy's corpse
had vanished. But I hadn't told you I was going to the Heinrich stash. I never
mentioned Heinrich's name to you. And you couldn't have heard me say it
when I phoned Lieutenant Brunvig at Headquarters, because Brunvig cut
me off before I brought Heinrich into the conversation. Yet you trailed
me, found me. How?"

"Why, I – I – that is, I – "

"*You* were the eavesdropper," I said. "Not Duffy. You, Peter Warren
Winthrop. That accounts for the stethoscope. A stethoscope is a handy
listening device. Plug it in your ears and put the diaphragm end against a
wall or a door and you can hear whatever is being said inside a room. Know
what I think? I think you listened to everything Ronald Barclay told me.
You found out who he was. And what he had on Emil Heinrich – which was
plenty, from a blackmailer's viewpoint. You probably wondered how you
could make use of the information to line your own pockets. And while
you listened, Duffy came upstairs and caught you with your stethoscope
to the door."

He turned a little pallid around the fringes. I had him winging now.

"Poor old Duffy," I said. "He saw you eavesdropping, and you slugged
him to keep him from raising a row. Maybe you didn't mean to kill him –
I wouldn't know about that. But you did kill him. You crushed his temple.
Then you took a powder, leaving his body propped against the door. That
was the pressure I felt when I shoved it open. The resistance was Duffy's
dead weight. When I bounced him across the hall he was already defunct,
although I didn't suspect it. And in the gloom and dusk I didn't notice
the depression in his skull."

"Now see here – "

"Having murdered one guy, you were in up to your ears." I ignored his
attempted interruption. "And you saw a chance for a fortune in shakedown
dough. You pranced into the room as I dragged Duffy over the threshold.
Ronald Barclay wheeled his chair out of the closet at the same instant. I
thought he was the one who slugged me senseless, but now I know it must
have been you.

"You bashed me. Then you croaked Barclay. He was a defenseless cripple
and you cooled him, pilfered his thirty-eight and the diary. You toted his
remainders out of the room to make it look as if he'd left under his own
steam."

The punk made a raucous sound.

"Sheepdip," he said.

"Sure, sheepdip," I said. "I swallowed it. Because I found an alcove
where he'd experimented in making artificial legs, I actually believed he
had walked out. I was a fool. I should have realized that was impossible. He
dabbled in prosthetics, yes; but everything he made was junk. Useless.

"So anyhow you came back, perhaps thinking you'd killed me as well as Duffy and Barclay. I surprised you by being alive and on my feet, with a gun aimed at you. I'll give you credit – you played it smart. I had the drop on you, and you made the best of a bad situation. Later you got a nice break when the cops refused to come to the hotel. That forced me to lone-wolf it out to Heinrich's tepee. It left you alone, gave you time to arrange new plans."

"Such as?" he blustered.

"Such as moving Duffy's corpse, hiding it where you had already hidden Barclay's," I said. "I doubt you ever made a telephone call to Police Headquarters."

Ole Brunvig growled: "Right. He didn't."

"Okay," I said to the punk. "With your two victims stashed out of sight, you trailed me from inside. You also cut their phone line. Then, when we separated, you faked a fracas on the upper level, drew me in and thought you bumped me. Now you had a free hand to intercept Heinrich when he came home. You could demand a hundred grand blackmail for a diary that might convict him of a kill fourteen years ago."

I paused. "The fact that Heinrich offered to buy it makes me think that he *did* gimmick the bomb that croaked a prop man and maimed Barclay. I'm not too sorry you knocked him off. If that had been the only murder you pulled tonight I'd be inclined to say the devil with it. But you cooled Duffy and Barclay, and they didn't deserve it."

"Can you prove any of this?"

"I can try," I said, and ankled to a closet on my left, yanked it open.

Two stiffs fell out. One of them wore a hearing aid. Duffy. The other had one arm and no legs. Barclay.

Winthrop's hand went into the Gladstone he had been packing. It came up with a nickel plated .38 fowling piece, the rod he had stolen from Ronald Barclay when he glommed the Fullerton diary.

Long before he could trigger the gat, though, Ole Brunvig cut loose with his service revolver. There were two sharp thunderclap barks, spaced so closely together they sounded almost like one. Winthrop yowled like a banshee and slammed against the wall with ketchup spurting from both shoulders.

Brunvig showed his teeth. "Now he knows what it's like to be maimed. Look at that bag, Sherlock, and see if you can find the diary."

I found it. And Peter Warren Winthrop took his shattered shoulders to the gas chamber the following month.

Sometimes I wonder if Marian Heinrich still indulges in star baths. One of these nights I'm going up in the hills to see.

FOREVER AFTER

Jim Thompson

IT WAS A few minutes before five o'clock when Ardis Clinton unlocked the rear door of her apartment, and admitted her lover. He was a cow-eyed young man with a wild mass of curly black hair. He worked as a dishwasher at Joe's Diner, which was directly across the alley.

They embraced passionately. Her body pressed against the meat cleaver, concealed inside his shirt, and Ardis shivered with delicious anticipation. Very soon now, it would all be over. That stupid ox, her husband, would be dead. He and his stupid cracks – all the dullness and boredom would be gone forever. And with the twenty thousand insurance money, ten thousand dollars double-indemnity . . .

"We're going to be so happy, Tony," she whispered. "You'll have your own place, a real swank little restaurant with what they call one of those intimate bars. And you'll just manage it, just kind of saunter around in a dress suit, and – "

"And we'll live happily ever after," Tony said. "Just me and you, baby, walking down life's highway together."

Ardis let out a gasp. She shoved him away from her, glaring up into his handsome empty face. "Don't!" she snapped. "Don't say things like that! I've told you and told you not to do it, and if I have to tell you again. I'll – !"

"But what'd I say?" he protested. "I didn't say nothin'."

"Well . . ." She got control of herself, forcing a smile. "Never mind, darling. You haven't had any opportunities and we've never really had a chance to know each other, so – so never mind. Things will be different after we're married." She patted his cheek, kissed him again. "You got away from the diner, all right? No one saw you leave?"

"Huh-uh. I already took the stuff up to the steam-table for Joe, and the waitress was up front too, y'know, filling the sugar bowls and the salt and pepper shakers like she always does just before dinner. And – "

"Good. Now, suppose someone comes back to the kitchen and finds out you're not there. What's your story going to be?"

"Well . . . I was out in the alley dumping some garbage. I mean – " he corrected himself hastily, "maybe I was. Or maybe I was down in the basement, getting some supplies. Or maybe I was in the john – the lavatory, I mean – or – "

"Fine," Ardis said approvingly. "You don't say where you were, so they can't prove you weren't there. You just don't remember where you were, understand, darling? You might have been any number of places."

Tony nodded. Looking over her shoulder into the bedroom, he frowned worriedly. "Why'd you do that now, honey? I know this has got to look like a robbery. But tearin' up the room now, before he gets here – "

"There won't be time afterwards. Don't worry, Tony. I'll keep the door closed."

"But he might open it and look in. And if he sees all them dresser drawers dumped around, and – "

"He won't. He won't look into the bedroom. I know exactly what he'll do, exactly what he'll say, the same things that he's always done and said ever since we've been married. All the stupid, maddening, dull, tiresome – !" She broke off abruptly, conscious that her voice was rising. "Well, forget it," she said, forcing another smile. "He won't give us any trouble."

"Whatever you say," Tony nodded docilely. "If you say so, that's the way it is, Ardis."

"But there'll be trouble – from the cops. I know I've already warned you about it, darling. But it'll be pretty bad, worse than anything you've ever gone through. They won't have any proof, but they're bound to be suspicious, and if you ever start talking, admitting anything – "

"I won't. They won't get anything out of me."

"You're sure? They'll try to trick you. They'll probably tell you that I've confessed. They may even slap you around. So if you're not absolutely sure . . ."

"They won't get anything out of me," he repeated stolidly. "I won't talk."

And studying him, Ardis knew that he wouldn't.

She led the way down the hall to the bathroom. He parted the shower curtains, and stepped into the tub. Drawing a pair of gloves from his pocket, he pulled them onto his hands. Awkwardly, he fumbled the meat cleaver from beneath his shirt.

"Ardis. Uh – look, honey."

"Yes?"

"Do I have to hit you? Couldn't I just maybe give you a little shove, or – "

"No, darling," she said gently. "You have to hit me. This is supposed to be a robbery. If you killed my husband without doing anything to me, well, you know how it would look."

"But I never hit no woman – any woman – before. I might hit you too hard, and – "

"Tony!"

"Well, all right," he said sullenly. "I don't like it, but all right."

Ardis murmured soothing endearments. Then, brushing his lips quickly with her own, she returned to the living room. It was a quarter after five, exactly five minutes – but *exactly* – until her husband, Bill, would come home. Closing the bedroom door, she lay down on the lounge. He negligee fell open, and she left it that way, grinning meanly as she studied the curving length of her thighs.

Give the dope a treat for a change, she thought. Let him get one last good look before he gets his.

Her expression changed. Wearily, resentfully, she pulled the material of the negligee over her legs. Because, of course, Bill would never notice. She could wear a ring in her nose, paint a bull's eye around her navel, and he'd never notice.

If he had ever noticed, just once paid her a pretty compliment . . .

If he had ever done anything different, ever said or done anything different at all – even the teensiest little bit . . .

But he hadn't. Maybe he couldn't. So what else could she do but what she was doing? She could get a divorce, sure, but that was all she'd get. No money; nothing with which to build a new life. Nothing to make up for those fifteen years of slowly being driven mad.

It's his own fault, she thought bitterly. I can't take any more. If I had to put up with him for just one more night, even one more hour . . . !

She heard heavy footsteps in the hallway. Then, a key turned in the doorlatch, and Bill came in. He was a master machinist, a solidly built man of about forty-five. The old-fashioned gold-rimmed glasses on his pudgy nose gave him a look of owlish solemnity.

"Well," he said, setting down his lunch bucket. "Another day, another dollar."

Ardis grimaced. He plodded across to the lounge, stooped, and gave her a half-hearted peck on the cheek.

"Long time no see," he said. "What we havin' for supper?"

Ardis gritted her teeth. It shouldn't matter, now; in a few minutes it would all be over. Yet somehow it *did* matter. He was as maddening to her as he had ever been.

"Bill . . ." She managed a seductive smile, slowly drawing the negligee apart. "How do I look, Bill?"

"Okay," he yawned. "Got a little hole in your drawers, though. What'd you say we was havin' for supper?"

"Slop," she said. "Garbage. Trash salad with dirt dressing."

"Sounds good. We got any hot water?"

Ardis sucked in her breath. She let it out again in a kind of infuriated moan. "Of course, we've got hot water! Don't we always have? Well, don't we? Why do you have to ask every night?"

"So what's to get excited about?" he shrugged. "Well, guess I'll go splash the chassis."

He plodded off down the hall. Ardis heard the bathroom door open, and close. She got up, stood waiting by the telephone. The door banged open again, and Tony came racing up the hall.

He had washed off the cleaver. While he hastily tucked it back inside his shirt, Ardis dialed the operator. "Help," she cried weakly. "Help . . . police . . . murder!"

She let the receiver drop to the floor, spoke to Tony in a whisper. "He's dead? You're sure of it?"

"Yeah, yeah, sure I'm sure. What do you think?"

"All right. Now, there's just one more thing . . ."

"I can't, Ardis. I don't want to. I – "

"Hit me," she commanded, and thrust out her chin. "Tony, I said to hit me!"

He hit her. A thousand stars blazed through her brain, and disappeared. And she crumpled silently to the floor.

. . . When she regained consciousness, she was lying on the lounge. A heavy-set man, a detective obviously, was seated at her side, and a white-jacketed young man with a stethoscope draped around his neck hovered nearby.

She had never felt better in her life. Even the lower part of her face, where Tony had smashed her, was surprisingly free of pain. Still, because it was what she should do, she moaned softly; spoke in a weak, hazy voice.

"Where am I?" she said. "What happened?"

"Lieutenant Powers," the detective said. "Suppose you tell me what happened, Mrs Clinton."

"I . . . I don't remember. I mean, well, my husband had just come home, and gone back to the bathroom. And there was a knock on the door, and I supposed it was the paper-boy or someone like that. So – "

"You opened the door and he rushed in and slugged you, right? Then what happened?"

"Well, then he rushed into the bedroom and started searching it. Yanking out the dresser drawers, and – "

"What was he searching for, Mrs Clinton? You don't have any considerable amount of money around do you? Or any jewelry aside from what you're wearing? And it wasn't your husband's payday, was it?"

"Well, no. But – "

"Yes?"

"I don't know. Maybe he was crazy. All I know is what he did."

"I see. He must have made quite a racket, seems to me. How come your husband didn't hear it?"

"He couldn't have. He had the shower running, and – "

She caught herself, fear constricting her throat. Lieutenant Powers grinned grimly.

"Missed a bet, huh, Mrs Clinton?"

"I – I don't know what you're – "

"Come off of it! The bathtub's dry as an oven. The shower was never turned on, and you know why it wasn't. Because there was a guy standing inside of it."

"B-but – but I don't know anything. I was unconscious, and – "

"Then, how do you know what happened? How do you know this guy went into the bedroom and started tearing it apart? And how did you make that telephone call?"

"Well, I . . . I wasn't completely unconscious. I sort of knew what was going on without really – "

"Now, you listen to me," he said harshly. "You made that fake call of yours – yes, I said *fake* – to the operator at twenty-three minutes after five. There happened to be a prowl car right here in the neighborhood, so two minutes later, at five-twenty-five, there were cops here in your apartment. You were unconscious then, more than an hour ago. You've been unconscious until just now."

Ardis' brain whirled. Then, it cleared suddenly, and a great calm came over her.

"I don't see quite what you're hinting at, lieutenant. If you're saying that I was confused, mixed up – that I must have dreamed or imagined some of the things I told you – I'll admit it."

"You know what I'm saying! I'm saying that no guy could have got in and out of this place, and done what this one did, in any two minutes!"

"Then the telephone operator must have been mistaken about the time," Ardis said brightly. "I don't know how else to explain it."

Powers grunted. He said he could give her a better explanation – and he gave it to her. The right one. Ardis listened to it placidly, murmuring polite objections.

"That's ridiculous, lieutenant. Regardless of any gossip you may have heard, I don't know this, uh, Tony person. And I most certainly did not plot with him or anyone else to kill my husband. Why – "

"He says you did. We got a signed confession from him."

"Have you?" But of course they didn't have. They might have found out about Tony, but he would never have talked. "That hardly proves anything, does it?"

"Now, you listen to me, Mrs Clinton! Maybe you think that – "

"How is my husband, anyway? I do hope he wasn't seriously hurt."

"How *is* he?" the lieutenant snarled. "How would he be after gettin' worked over with – " He broke off, his eyes flickering. "As a matter of fact," he said heavily, "he's going to be all right. He was pretty badly injured, but he was able to give us a statement and – "

"I'm so glad. But why are you questioning me, then?" It was another trick. Bill had to be dead. "If he gave you a statement, then you must know that everything happened just like I said."

She waited, looked at him quizzically. Powers scowled, his stern face wrinkling with exasperation.

"All right," he said, at last. "All right, Mrs Clinton. Your husband is dead. We don't have any statement from him, and we don't have any confession from Tony."

"Yes?"

"But we know that you're guilty, and you know that you are. And you'd better get it off your conscience while you still can."

"While I still can?"

"Doc" – Powers jerked his head at the doctor. At the man, that is, who appeared to be a doctor. "Lay it on the line, doc. Tell her that her boy friend hit her a little too hard."

The man came forward hesitantly. He said, "I'm sorry, Mrs Clinton. You have a – uh – you've sustained a very serious injury."

"Have I?" Ardis smiled. "I feel fine."

"I don't think," the doctor said judiciously, "that that's quite true. What you mean is that you don't feel anything at all. You couldn't. You see, with an injury such as yours – "

"Get out," Ardis said. "Both of you get out."

"Please, Mrs Clinton. Believe me, this isn't a trick. I haven't wanted to alarm you, but – "

"And you haven't," she said. "You haven't scared me even a little bit, mister. Now, clear out!"

She closed her eyes, kept them closed firmly. When, at last, she re-opened them, Powers and the doctor – if he really had been a doctor – were gone. And the room was in darkness.

She lay smiling to herself, congratulating herself. In the corridor outside, she heard heavy footsteps approaching; and she tensed for a moment. Then, remembering, she relaxed again.

Not Bill, of course. She was through with that jerk forever. He'd driven her half out of her mind, got her to the point where she couldn't have taken another minute of him if her life depended on it. But now . . .

The footsteps stopped in front of her door. A key turned in the lock, the door opened and closed.

There was a clatter of a lunchpail being set down; then a familiar voice – maddeningly familiar words:

"Well. Another day, another dollar."

Ardis' mouth tightened; it twisted slowly, in a malicious grin. So they hadn't given up yet! They were pulling this one last trick. Well, let them; she'd play along with the gag.

The man plodded across the room, stooped, and gave her a half-hearted peck on the cheek. "Long time no see," he said. "What we havin' for supper?"

"Bill . . ." Ardis said. "How do I look, Bill?"

"Okay. Got your lipstick smeared, though. What'd you say we was having for supper?"

"Stewed owls! Now, look, mister. I don't know who you – "

"Sounds good. We got any hot water?"

"Of course, we've got hot water! Don't we always have? Why do you always have to ask if – if – "

She couldn't go through with it. Even as a gag – even someone who merely sounded and acted like he did – it was too much to bear.

"Y-you get out of here!" she quavered. "I don't have to stand for this! I *c-can't* stand it! I did it for fifteen years, and – "

"So what's to get excited about?" he said. "Well, guess I'll go splash the chassis."

"Stop it! *STOP IT!*" Her screams filled the room . . . silent screams ripping through silence. "He's – you're dead! I know you are! You're dead, and I don't have to put up with you for another minute. And – and – !"

"Wouldn't take no bets on that if I was you," he said mildly. "Not with a broken neck like yours."

He trudged off toward the bathroom, wherever the bathroom is in Eternity.

THE BLOODY TIDE
Day Keene

1 OUT OF THE JUG

MORNING WAS SLOW in coming. I'd waited for it a long time. Three years the man said. And three years I had done without any nonsense about parole or executive clemency.

I was washed and dressed and waiting when the rising siren blew. As McKenny, the screw on our tier, clomped down the steel catwalk to pull the master switch, he paused in front of my cell and grinned:

"This is the day, eh, Charlie?"

The lump in my throat was so big all I could do was nod.

Breakfast wasn't much better. The pock marks in the plaster of the mess hall bothered me. I knew them for what they were. If it hadn't been for Swede, I could be dead instead of going out this morning. I could be with Mickey and Saltz. I could be down in solitary with the other ring-leaders of the riot. I could even be with Swede.

The thought cost me my appetite. When we finally filed out of the mess hall a front-of-the-prison guard asked if my name was Charlie White. When I said it was, he led the way to a small room in the administration building. The clothes I'd signed for the day before were hanging on a wire hanger.

"When you're dressed," he said, "turn the things you're wearing now over to the supply clerk. Then go straight down the hall to the warden's office." He laughed. "That is, unless you want to keep your denim as a souvenir."

I said, "No, thank you. I don't want any souvenirs. All I want of this is a faint recollection."

"Then stay out of trouble," he told me.

The warden had my dossier on his desk. He looked from it to me and said, "I'd planned to talk to you, White. You're several cuts above the average man we get here and I don't want to see you back. But right now you're so filled with self-pity and feeling so pushed around that nothing I could say would do a bit of good."

He laid a typed receipt, a sealed envelope, a small sheaf of bills, and some silver on the corner of his desk. "So if you'll sign a receipt for the one hundred and twenty-six dollars and fifty cents that is credited to your account, I'll keep my mouth shut and let someone else do the talking."

That would probably be Father Reilly. The priest had given me the only news I'd had of Beth. I knew she was clerking in a store in Palmetto City. I knew she knew about Zo. But if Beth had filed suit for divorce, I hadn't been served with the papers.

"Good-by and good luck, White," the warden concluded the interview.

I started to crack, "Thanks for nothing," but something stopped me. Perhaps it was the fact I had plenty for which to thank him. The warden had leaned over backwards to see that the attempted break hadn't earned me any bad time.

The same guard took me in tow again. But we weren't headed for the chaplain's office. It was the first time I had been in a death house. I didn't like it.

Swede was sitting on the edge of a desk in a small windowless conference room. He looked much the same as he always had except his tan was gone, the lines in his face were deeper, and his eyes seemed even bluer.

The guard said I had ten minutes, and closed and locked the door. The lump in my throat grew still larger. Ten minutes wasn't long enough to even start thanking the old man for what he'd done for me. I'd have been in the attempted break up to my eyes if Swede hadn't landed a hard right on my jaw that had belted me back on my cot unconscious.

When I'd come to again, Mickey and Saltz were dead, and Swede had picked up the big tab for caving in a guard's head.

"*Stay out of this, kid,*" he'd warned me, "*You only got six months to go. I got life and ninety-nine years.*"

Swede sucked hard at his cigarette as if with time running out on him he wanted to enjoy every puff to the maximum. "Ten minutes," he said, "isn't long. So let me do the talking, kid. Would you say I was a Holy Joe?"

The lump in my throat let go and I laughed nervously.

"Then keep that in mind," Swede said. "You and me are a lot alike, Charlie. We both like the water. We've both made a good living on and out of it. But were we content with that? No." He gestured with his cigarette.

"That's why I asked the warden if I could talk to you. A man does a lot of thinking when he gets in one of these quick-fry joints. And it all boils down to this: A man hauls in the fish he baits for and at the depth at which he fishes."

He lighted a cigarette from the butt of the one he was smoking. "In the old days it was different. A man had to depend on himself and there was a lot of wide open space for him to do it in. But times have changed. After years of sailing by guess, society has set out certain buoys and markers." He asked if I had a silver dollar. There was one in the silver the warden had given me. Swede traced the lettering on the head side with a finger. "*E Pluribus Unum*. Know what that means, Charlie?"

I said, "Something about one for all or all for one."

Swede shook his head. "No. It means *one out of many*. And that's you and me, Charlie. And the screw who brought you here. And the warden. And the guy who's going to fry me tonight. We're all just one out of many. And you've got to swim with the school and keep its rules or – Well, look what's happened to me. Look what happened to you when you tried to sail on your own.

"As rackets go, you had a good one. But let's add up the score. On the debit side it cost you your wife, your boat, and got you three years in the can. On the profit side you had a dozen roaring good drunks in *Habana*, a fancy dame, and the false knowledge that you were smarter than your fellow fishing-boat captains. There were no lulls in your business. You brought in a good load every time. Okay. How much dough have you got?"

I told him. "One hundred and twenty-six dollars and fifty cents."

Swede hooted. "For three years of your time. There are guys netting mullet out of Naples, and Palmetto City for that matter, who are making that much in one night. But netting mullet is hard work. So is fishing the grouper banks. And you and me had to be wise guys. You hear from your wife yet?"

I said I had not.

"Well," Swede admitted. "I don't know why you should. A man can starve a dame. He can cuss her. He can beat her every night and twice on Sunday and she'll still think he's her personal Marshall plan in a silver champagne bucket. But only if she knows she's the only woman in his life."

He went on before I could speak.

"But are you willing to admit you made a mistake and cut bait or fish? No. You're so rotten filled with self-pity and hate, it's a shame." He snuffed out his cigarette. "I know how you feel, Charlie. I've got a temper, too. That's one of the reasons I'm here." He read my mind. "But don't do it. Killing your former partner because he ran out on you when the law stepped in, will only bring you back here. And I mean *here*."

Swede lighted a third cigarette. "Look. When you came back from that mess over there in '45 or '46 you'd been living in a bloody tide for four years. Life meant nothing. A thousand lives meant nothing. We had a similar red tide in the Gulf while you were gone. Fish died by the tens of millions. The shores and tide flats were heaped so high with dead fish they stunk. Everyone swore things would never be the same again.

"But they are. The water gradually cleared and the fish began to spawn again. Nature is building back. And that's what you've got to do, Charlie. Forget this. You're in clean water again. If you're smart, you'll stay there. Get a job fishing on shares. Swab out a charter boat if you have to. Then when you get something to offer her, find your wife. Get down on your knees if you have to and beg her to forgive you and come home."

I said that sounded like good advice.

Swede looked at me a long minute, then snuffed out his cigarette. "But you aren't going to take a damn word of it. Okay, kid. It's your funeral."

The guard opened the door. "That's it."

"I've been wasting my time," Swede told him. He walked out of the room without offering to shake hands. "I won't bother to say good-bye. It's just *auf Wiedersehen*, Charlie. I'll try to save a quart and a blonde for you down there."

I walked back through the yard with the guard and out the front door of the prison. It was the same sun on the outside of the wall but it was brighter somehow. It almost blinded me. I stood on the steps for a moment looking at the cars in the parking lot and flipping a mental coin.

If Beth was waiting for me, I'd follow Swede's advice. If she wasn't, I was off to the races. I'd identify, locate, and kill *Señor Peso* if I had to call for the quart and the blonde that Swede had promised to save.

Señor Peso was obviously a *nom de plume* and a cover. It sounded like a gag. The prosecutor had made much of that fact at my trial. But it was the only name I had.

Swede lost. Beth wasn't waiting – but Zo was. I walked over to the yellow jeepster she was driving and her voice reached out and caressed me.

"Hello, honey. Am I glad to see you." Zo lifted her lips to be kissed. "I've been waiting out here since daybreak."

Her lips were clinging. Her fingers dug into my back. After three years in a cell, it was like kissing a jet plane. I said:

"You shouldn't kiss strange men like that. You won't go to heaven."

She wrinkled her nose at me. "Who wants to go to heaven? And since when are you a stranger?" She slid over on the seat. "Get in, honey. You drive."

I said, "What? Without a driver's license? You want me to break the law?"

She thought that was very funny. "Okay. I'll drive." When I still didn't get into the jeepster, she fished in her purse for the Havana bank pass book that had been in her possession when the law had swooped down on me. "And don't jump to false conclusions. No one let you down. The big shot couldn't show up at your trial. It would have jeopardized the whole set-up." She handed me the pass book.

I had lied to Swede. I wasn't broke. I was filthy. And I was still important to the gang. Every month I had spent in a cell, someone, *Señor Peso* presumably, had deposited one thousand dollars to my account. The last figure showed $36,124.00.

Zo asked, "Feel better?"

The Devil came up behind me and pushed. *To hell with Beth. To hell with everything*, I thought. *To hell with trying to kill Señor Peso. In his way the guy had played square with me. Why should I try to goose into his grave an egg who laid so many golden pesos?*

I got into the jeepster and Zo pulled out of the parking lot and headed south on Florida 16 into Starke. I asked her where we were headed. She said:

"Over to the West Coast. I've engaged a double cabin on a little cove just above Dead Man's Bay. But we won't be there long. One of the boys will put in with a converted Tarpon Springs sponge boat in the next few days and take us on to Havana and Shrimp Cay. That all right with you?"

Her head was bare. She was wearing a strapless sun dress that made her shoulders look like they were made of rich cream. Heat and palm trees, the slap of blue waves, and Zo. It sounded good to me.

"Yeah. Sure. That's fine," I told her.

She pulled to the side of the road and handed me an opened bottle of rum. Then, the same devil who was pushing me lighting twin candles in her eyes, she kissed me, hard. "Okay. Until then. You drink and dream, I'll drive . . ."

It was afternoon when we reached the cabin. We'd stopped twice to eat. Once in Gainesville and once in Cross City. I'd also picked up another bottle of rum. After being away from it so long, it hit me almost as hard as Zo's kisses.

The cabin, when we reached it, was a pleasant blur in a stand of slash pine on an isolated section of the shore. A rutted sand road led back to it. As nearly as I could tell, the nearest house was a mile away. The gulf looked the same as it always had, blue and endless and inviting.

It gave me an idea. If I wanted to stay with the party, I had to get some coffee in and some water on me. I told Zo, "I'm going to dunk the body. Put some coffee on, will you, babe?"

She laughed. "You're out of training, honey. But go ahead. You do just that. I figured you might want to swim and you'll find some trunks in the bedroom closet."

She got busy at the stove and I staggered on into the bedroom. Zo had told me we'd be alone, but as I closed the bedroom door I could have sworn I heard someone say:

"You got him, eh?"

I opened the door and asked her, "Who was that?"

At the time it didn't seem important. I closed the door again and tried to hang up my coat but I was so high I hung it upside down and an envelope fell out and skittered across the floor. I recognized it as the envelope the warden had given me along with my discharge papers and what money I had coming. Sitting on the bed I tore it open, and two tens and a five dollar bill fell out. Forcing my eyes to focus, I read:

> Sweetheart,
>   I'd be there when you get out if I could possibly manage it but I have to hang on to my job. So, as a substitute, in case you are broke, I am enclosing my last week's salary for train fare. I love you and I'm waiting.
>   We'll start all over.
>
>   Beth

It was the type of letter Beth would write. Beth loved me and she was waiting. And here I was all mixed up with Zo again. I was still so long that Zo called:

"What's the matter? You aren't sick, are you, honey?"

I told her the truth. "Yeah. Plenty." I got a grip on the rum and tried to do some straight thinking. With Beth out of my life forever, nothing would ever be right again. The money and excitement and Zo were poor substitutes for what I really wanted. Beth was my wife. She was my life. I loved her.

I fished my coat from the door and staggered back into the living room. "So I'm a heel," I told Zo. "I'm sorry. But you and I are washed up as of now. I'm going back to Palmetto City and my wife."

She wanted to know if I was kidding.

I said I was never more serious.

She wasn't so pretty now. Her black eyes narrowing to slits, she spat, "You're either drunk or crazy. How much can you make commercial fishing or running a charter boat?"

I said, "Even so. I'm going back to Palmetto City and Beth and get a job and open the old house and raise five or six red-headed kids and be disgustingly honest."

Her eyes opening wide, she screamed, "No. Don't!"

I thought she was screaming at me. She wasn't. The blow came from one side and behind me. I turned in time to see a blur of white face through the fog of pain that was reaching up to engulf me. Then the leaded butt of a gaff hook used as a club landed a second time, and I floated out into space on a red tide.

Just as I passed the last buoy marking the channel of consciousness I thought I heard the flat slap of a pistol. Then a black roller swept me under.

2 SPROUTING WINGS

The tarpon was huge, two hundred pounds or more, the largest I'd ever hooked. He broke water a dozen times while I was playing him. I was bathed in sweat. My arms and shoulders felt like they had been pounded with a mallet by the time I got him within ten feet of the boat. Then he really went crazy.

With a series of high-powered jolts like the current they were going to shoot into Swede, he lashed into a flurry of frenzy that almost tore the rod out of my hands. I eased the star drag too late. He didn't want any part of where he was and streaked off into the blue, snapping the wire leader as if it had been string.

I looked over the edge of the cruiser to see what had frightened him. A twenty-foot shark looked back. I was still trying to figure out who had tied the shark under my boat, when he tried to climb into the cockpit with me and I beat at him frantically with my fists.

It was the sharpness of the pain that knifed the fog away. With the first of returning consciousness I lay, gasping, looking up into the dark, thinking what a screwy dream it had been.

The tied shark was an old gag. All of the guides on the waterfront had used it at one time or another to give their charter passengers a thrill. A six-foot shark tied under a cruiser could make a two-pound trout fight like a fifty-pound blue marlin.

Then, one by one the shattered pieces of reality began to fall into place like the curlicues of a gigantic jigsaw puzzle.

I was lying on the floor of the cabin on the shore of Dead Man's Bay. I'd just read the letter from Beth and told Zo I was going back to my wife when an unidentified party, presumably male, had popped out of nowhere and beaten me half to death with the loaded butt of a gaff hook.

It didn't make sense to me. I had no illusions about Zo. She'd never sprout any wings. I hadn't asked her how she'd lived during the three years I'd been in prison. It hadn't mattered. A jealous boy friend was the obvious answer. But why in the name of time should he pop up and try to beat in my brains when I'd just announced I was going back to my wife?

Then I thought of the voice I'd heard when I'd gone into the bedroom.

"*You got him, eh?*"

Zo had denied there was a voice. But there obviously had been. In the light of what had happened, it began to look like she had contracted to deliver me to the cabin on Dead Man's Bay like so much beef.

On the other hand, she had screamed, "*No. Don't!*" just prior to the first blow.

I gave up trying to think and got to my feet. The interior of the cabin was as black as a fish wholesaler's heart. I tried to find the light switch and, failing, struck a match instead.

According to the alarm clock on the mantel I had been out for hours. It only lacked a few minutes of midnight. The rum bottle was standing on the table. I rinsed my mouth with a drink. Then, striking another match, I walked on into the bedroom – and wished I hadn't.

Zo was lying on the bed, her eyes wide open and staring at the ceiling. But they weren't seeing anything. I struck another match and looked closer. She was cold. The flat slap of a pistol I had heard had been meant for her. She had been dead as long as I had been unconscious.

I lighted a third match and looked around the room. The sense of unreality persisted. A chair had been tipped just so. A shattered rum bottle lay by the side of the bed. Another had drained out its contents on the rug.

Catching sight of a dark object in her hand, I bent over the bed and looked at it. It was the leaded gaff hook with which I had been slugged.

I walked out into the other room and found my coat. The pistol with which she had been killed was in my right-hand coat pocket.

I could see the scene as described by the papers. A recently released con and his moll had rented the cabin to celebrate his release. A drunken brawl had ensued and during it I had killed her.

There was a metallic "pong" as the alarm clock on the mantel passed the hour. A hundred and some odd miles away, in Raiford, Swede was taking the big jump. He knew all the answers now.

"*Here. And I mean right here,*" he had told me.

Swede had been right about a lot of things. If only I'd listened to him. If only I'd opened the letter from Beth before I had met Zo.

The match burned down and burned my fingers. I didn't feel it. This was murder and I was tagged. I walked out the door and stood on the screened-in porch. The night was black but filled with stars. The tide was out and the sweet-sour smell of the tide flats filled the air. I'd never wanted so much to live or felt I had so much to live for. I thought of what I'd told Zo.

"*Even so. I'm going back to Palmetto City and Beth and get a job and open the old house and raise five or six red-headed kids and be disgustingly honest.*"

That was a laugh. The only place I was going was back to Raiford. A half-dozen guards had seen me get into the jeepster. The waitresses at both Gainesville and Cross City would testify that they had seen us together and I had been drinking heavily.

The jeepster was still in front of the cabin. The smart thing for me to do would be to drive to the nearest phone and call the state patrol and get it over. No one would believe my story. I couldn't describe the guy I'd seen. He was as vague as my testimony concerning *Señor Peso.*

The big veins in my temple began to pound. *Señor Peso.* The guy was beginning to haunt me. If it hadn't been for him, I'd still be operating the

Beth II out of Bill's Boat Basin as a deep-sea charter cruiser. It had been his voice on the phone the time I'd been behind in my payments that had started off all of the fireworks.

"*This is Señor Peso, Captain White. How would you like to make a quick five thousand dollars?*"

How would I like to drop a mullet net around ten ton of pompano? All I had to do for the money was meet the *Andros Ancropolis*, a converted sponge boat, eighty miles out in the gulf and bring in a few small waterproof packages that fit easily in my bait well. I didn't know what was in them. I was afraid to ask. I needed that five thousand bad.

That had been the beginning. A trip to Veracruz had followed. Then one to Pinar del Rio. Then one to Havana where I'd met Zo. After that I was in so deep it hadn't mattered. I met who I was ordered to meet, took what I was ordered to get, and brought it back to various points ranging from drops in the Ten Thousand Islands as far north at Palmetto City with a few trips up the bay to Tampa.

I only made one restriction. I refused to run wet-backs. I hadn't spent three years of my life in the navy fighting for the so-called American way of life only to turn around and smuggle in for pay the very guys who were trying to destroy it.

After the one proposition along that line, *Señor Peso* hadn't mentioned the subject again. All of the Coast Guard boys knew me. The older officers had known my father. I never had any trouble getting clearance papers. No one ever stopped me. Until that last time.

Then only my good service record, a purple heart, all the cash I had in the bank, the confiscation of my new boat, and me pleading guilty to assault with a deadly weapon during the fracas that followed the boarding, had saved me from a long Federal rap. That trip, my bait well had been filthy with forty grand worth of Swiss watches and French perfumes on which no duty had been paid.

But I still hadn't ever met *Señor Peso*. All my instructions had come by phone. My money came in the mail, in cash. And once the law had laid its arm on me, he had run out on me cold. When the prosecution had asked me for whom I was running the stuff, all I could offer was a mythical *Señor Peso*. It was a wonder I hadn't gotten life.

Not that it mattered now. Zo was dead and I was tagged. And if he hadn't come forward before, I couldn't expect *Señor Peso* to come out in the open now. Staring up at the stars, I remembered the dead girl's words at the prison.

"*And don't jump to false conclusions. No one let you down. The big shot couldn't show up at your trial. It would have jeopardized the whole set-up.*"

It sounded logical. He'd made good to the tune of $36,000.00. Zo with her talk of Havana and a converted sponger putting in had obviously been under instructions that – if they had been carried out – would have proven profitable to me. No. I couldn't blame *Señor Peso* for this. This was a personal affair between the dead girl and myself and the man who had killed her.

The night was cool. I put on my coat and lighted a cigarette just as a pair of headlights turned off the highway a quarter of a mile away and bounced down the rutted sand road toward the cabin. I kicked the screen door open and walked out and stood with my hand on the butt of the gun in my pocket, in the shadow of a big slash pine fifty feet from the wooden porch.

The car was blue and white, a state patrol car, with two uniformed troopers in it. They skirted the yellow jeepster and parked in front of the porch.

Getting out, one of them said, "It looks quiet enough to me. Probably a false alarm."

"Probably," his partner agreed. He flicked the car's searchlight around among the trees, missing me by inches. Then he pointed it at the shoreline. "Lonely sort of place, though." He was a bit impatient with his partner. "Well, go ahead. Bang on the door. Wake 'em up and ask 'em if anyone screamed."

His partner banged the screen door. "State Police."

When no one answered, he opened the screen and walked in, sweeping a path before him with his flashlight. A moment later I heard him whistle. Then the lights in the bedroom came on and he shouted to his partner:

"Hey. Come in here, Jim. That fisherman who called the barracks wasn't whoofing. Some dame was screaming all right. But she isn't screaming now. She's dead."

So much was clear. The man who had killed Zo had waited as long as he could hoping her body would be discovered. When it wasn't, he'd called the State Patrol. He really wanted to pin this thing on me and he didn't want me to get too far away before the law stepped in.

I hoped the trooper would leave his keys in the car. He didn't. Sliding out from behind the wheel, he clipped his keys on his belt before drawing his gun and striding into the cabin.

I inched over toward the jeepster. A few minutes before I'd been considering calling the State Patrol and turning myself in. Now I was damned if I would. I didn't want to go back to Raiford. I didn't want to die. At least not without seeing Beth and telling her I was sorry.

The ignition key was still in the jeep. Keeping it between me and the cabin, I walked the length of the patrol car, raised the hood as quietly as I could and yanked out a handful of wires. Then I walked back and climbed in the jeepster, crossed my fingers and kicked it over. Over the roar of the motor, I heard one of the troopers say:

"What the hell?"

Then I'd spun the jeepster in a sharp U turn that threw up a screen of sand and was bouncing down the rutted road with both troopers shouting after me and spraying the back of the car and the windshield with lead.

I made the highway without being hit and into a little town on the north bank of a river. I had, at the most, a five or ten minute start. I'd put the patrol car temporarily out of action, but their two-way radio was still working. It would only be a matter of minutes before road blocks would be set up and every law-enforcement officer in Dixie, Bronson, Alachua, Marion and Citrus counties would be alerted for a killer driving a new yellow jeepster.

A tired-looking tourist driving a mud-splattered '48 with Iowa license plates was just pulling out of the town's only filling station as I passed it. I drove on to the edge of town and the bridge across the river. There was a small gap between the black-and-white guard rail and the bridge.

Pointing the jeepster at the gap, I rammed down the gas and hopped out. It hit the gap dead center and disappeared with a splintering of wood and a screech of metal. A moment later there was a great splash. The '48 behind me braked to a stop and the tourist stuck his head out the window.

"Holy smoke," he said. "What happened, fellow? Did your car go out of control?"

"No," I told him. "I did." I opened the door on the far side, climbed in beside him, and rammed the nose of the gun that had killed Zo in his ribs. "Look," I said, "I have a date with a road block where this road joins US 19. That is, unless I get there first. How fast will this crate go?"

He looked at the gun in his ribs and swallowed hard. "Well," he admitted, "I've had it up to ninety. And my foot wasn't all the way to the floor."

I said, "Then put it there. As of now."

3 CLOSE CALL

It could be the law would figure out I was in Palmetto City. If it did, it wasn't my fault. I'd left a trail only a snake with Saint Vitus dance could follow. I hadn't doubled back once but I'd done a lot of twisting and changing of means of transportation. I'd kissed the Iowa tourist goodby at Inglis after giving him the impression I had a boat waiting for me in Withlacoochee Bay. From there I'd picked up a ride on a fruit truck as far as Dunnellon and US 41. I'd taken a bus from there to Tampa and spent most of the day buying new clothes piecemeal.

When I'd finished buying slacks and a sport coat and a loud gabardine shirt and washing the blood from the back of my head, I looked a lot more like a northern tourist than I did a local boy who'd spent most of his life on the water.

The Tampa papers were filled with the thing. The headline on the evening paper read:

EX-CONVICT MURDERS SWEETHEART

The story was about as I expected. The way the law figured it, Zo
and I had staged a drunken party to celebrate my release. During it,
we had quarreled and I killed her. I was, variously reported, seen north
near Tallahassee, boarding a forty-foot sloop in Withlacoochee Bay, and
hopping a south-bound freight at Dunnellon.

But the law was merely confused, not stupid. Once they sifted out the
false reports, the net would begin to tighten. And Beth was in Palmetto
City. The chances were there was a stake-out right now on the house in
which she was living.

I'd taken a plane from Tampa to Palmetto City. But I didn't dare take
a cab from the airport to the return address she had given on her letter.
I had been born in the town. I'd lived there most of my life. I knew all
the cab drivers. All of them knew me. I also knew the law. Ken Gilly, a
kid with whom I had gone to school, was now a lieutenant in charge of
the detective bureau.

Getting out of the airport as fast as I could without attracting attention,
I strolled past the dark ball park and out to the mole in the bay where,
night or day, there were always a dozen or so northern tourists fishing. It
was dark on the mole and as good a place to kill time as any.

My plans were all tentative. I wanted to talk to Beth. I wanted to tell her
I was sorry things turned out as they had for us. Then I wanted to talk to
one or two of the boys who still berthed their fishing cruisers at Bill's Boat
Basin. One of them, Matt Heely, owed me plenty. And I was willing to
call it square for a free trip to Shrimp Cay.

It was too late for me to turn honest now. Once there I'd attempt to
contact *Señor Peso* through channels and see what he had in mind when he
had sent Zo to re-establish contact with me. If he decided I was too hot to
be of any use to him, there was still the thirty-six grand in my Havana bank
account. And a man had to be pretty stupid if he couldn't have one hell of
a time drinking himself to death on thirty-six thousand dollars anywhere
south of the Tropic of Cancer.

The tide was in. The moon was right. You could have caught fish with
dough-balls and a bent pin. At one o'clock I interrupted the excited shoe
clerk from Chicago who was pulling in pig-fish, about the size of the ones I
usually used as bait for snook, and who was teaching me how to fish, telling
him that while it all was very interesting I thought I would turn in.

The return address on Beth's letter was less than a mile from the mole.
It proved to be a small white frame garage apartment on a palm tree and
bougainvillea-tangled alley on the south-east side of town, not far from the
store in which she was clerking. It was a hell of a place for the wife of a man
who'd made the money I'd made to live in. Shame heated the collar of my
sport shirt. Swede had been right about the bloody tide, too. I must have
been out of my mind to treat Beth the way I had.

Of course she could be living in the big old house on the island across the deep water channel from the mainland. But she couldn't live there and work in town. The only way it could be reached was by boat. Unless she had rented the old place to bring in a little additional income, the chances were that nothing but snakes and raccoons and rabbits and field mice had lived on the island for three years.

There was no police car in front or in the alley. Keeping close to the wall, I climbed the stairs and rapped lightly on the door. Either Beth wasn't asleep or she was sleeping lightly. Almost immediately she asked, "Yes? Who is it?"

I took a deep breath and told her. "Charlie."

A moment of silence followed. Then slippered feet scuffed across the floor and only a screen door separated us. A single beam of moonlight, flooding in through a hole in the vine that almost covered the porch, spotlighted her white face. I'd forgotten she was so pretty. Even with her cheeks stained with tears and dark lines under her eyes, she was beautiful. And one time she had loved me and I had thrown her away for a mess of Zo.

Pressing her nose against the screen she said, "You shouldn't have come here, Charlie. The police were here not two hours ago and I promised Ken Gilly I'd call him if you did contact me."

I said, "Then you know?"

She brushed a lock of red hair away from her forehead. "Yes. I know. It was in the papers."

I got it off my chest with a rush. "I didn't do it, Beth. I didn't kill her. And I didn't open your letter, I didn't realize what it was, until after I'd reached the cabin. When I did read it, I told Zo I was coming back to Palmetto and you. And that was when it happened. Someone slugged me and shot Zo."

She said, "And you expect me to believe that?"

I asked, "Have I ever lied to you, Beth?"

She thought a moment. "No. That's one thing you've never done." She unhooked the screen. "Come in. Come in before one of the neighbors sees you."

Inside the room I tried to take her in my arms but she pushed me away.

"No. I want time to think. This may change things for both of us. What do you intend to do now, Charlie?"

I told her.

Beth said, "In other words, if you can evade the law and get out of the country, you're going right back in the same old racket. You're going to work for this *Señor Peso* again."

I asked her what else I could do.

She told me. "Be a man. If you didn't kill that girl there must be some way we can prove it."

I asked her, "How?"

She shook her head. She was standing so close to me that one of her curls brushed my face. It was all I could do to keep from digging both of my hands in her hair and pulling her to me. "I don't know," she admitted. Then, woman-like, she persisted, "But there must be some way. Perhaps, Mr Clifton could help us."

He was the guy she worked for. I'd never liked him. Few of the local people did, even if they did trade in his store. A cocky little Yankee, he'd come to Palmetto City twenty years before and built an idea into the biggest business in town. He wouldn't be undersold. If a fellow merchant ran a loss leader costing from two cent, Clifton would lose five to get the business. And he had.

From a two-by-four dry-goods store he'd branched out into a block square four story high merchandise carnival, handling everything from apples to zithers. If you couldn't buy it at Clifton's, it wasn't for sale.

I asked, "Why should he help us?"

Beth was frank about it. "Mr Clifton's in love with me. He's asked me to marry him. He even offered to buy the old house out on the island so I'd have some money and wouldn't have to work while I made up my mind whether or not to divorce you."

I said, "Oh, yeah?"

Beth put me back in my place. "*You* should get sore."

The strain was beginning to get me. I sat down on the edge of the bed and buried my head in my hands. "Okay, honey," I admitted. "I'm sorry. I haven't got a beef. Not with the way I've loused up our lives."

She sat down on the bed beside me. "Kiss me, Charlie."

I said that after the way I'd treated her I shouldn't think she'd want me to. Her lips inches from mine, she repeated, "I asked you to kiss me, Charlie."

I took her face in my hands and kissed her. But it wasn't the way I kissed Zo. It was more like I'd kissed her in front of the alter after the Reverend Paul had finished marrying us and the world was going to be our oyster. She was something sweet and beautiful and fragile. She was good. She was something that had been missing out of my life for a long time.

When I lifted my face, her eyes were shining in the dark and patting my cheek with one hand she kissed me back of her own accord. "It's going to be all right, honey," she told me. "I don't know how we'll do it. But we will *make* it right."

A car purred to a stop in the alley. Heavy feet began to climb the stairs. A moment later there was a light knock on the door.

Standing up in front of me, Beth asked, "Yes?"

"It's Ken again, Beth," Gilly told her. "I'm sorry to disturb you but I thought you ought to know. Charlie's been traced to a men's store in Tampa where he bought a complete new outfit. We're setting up roadblocks on the causeway and all roads leading into Palmetto City."

"Oh," Beth said. "Oh."

Ken sounded tired. "I wish the guy hadn't headed back this way. Heaven knows I don't want to make the pinch. Charlie's my friend. But what can I do?"

Beth suggested. "Maybe he didn't do it, Ken. Maybe he didn't kill that girl."

Lieutenant Gilly was skeptical. "Yeah. Maybe. And maybe some day filet of grunt will sell for as much as snapper fingers. Well, Tampa only being sixty miles away, I thought I'd let you know. You want me to post a guard in the alley?"

Beth's fingers tightened on mine. "No. I don't think that will be necessary, Ken. Even if Charlie should come here I don't think he'd hurt me."

"No," Gilly agreed. "Well, it's just as well. I can use every man I have on the road blocks. But if he should slip through and come here, you let me know now, Beth."

He clumped on back down the stairs. A moment later the police cruiser purred off into the night. I could feel the cold sweat start on my cheeks. The boys were beginning to haul in the net – and I was in it. It wouldn't be long now.

Beth sat back on the bed, all business. "No one ever comes in here but me, and I was going to suggest you stay here until after I'd talked to Mr Clifton. Now that's out. When you don't show up at the blocks, they're going to know you got through and someone is bound to suggest the police search this apartment. There's only one logical place for you to stay."

I asked her where that was.

She said, "Out at the house. You know it and the island better than anyone else. An army couldn't find you there if you didn't want them to. Now, tell me the whole thing from the minute you were released from prison yesterday morning."

I gave her a play by play description. But I still didn't like the Clifton angle and said so. "You say the guy loves you. You say he's asked you to divorce me and marry him. Well, what's his reaction going to be when you tell him I'm in town? He's going to reach for his phone and call the cops. The guy is a bargain hunter. And it's a lot cheaper for him to turn me in to be burned than it is for him to pay for a divorce."

Beth said I wasn't doing Mr Clifton justice. He was really a very fine and a very honorable man. She shook her curls in my face. "Besides I'm not going to tell him you're in town. You have to admit he is smart?"

I said I did.

Beth continued. "All I am going to tell him is that I don't think you killed that girl and ask his advice on how to go about hiring a private detective to prove it."

It didn't sound too bad. The guy was smart. And Beth was right about the island. I could hide out on it indefinitely. "Well, okay," I agreed. "But how are you going to contact me?"

She said she would find some way to do so without making Ken Gilly suspicious. "After all, it's our house. I have a right to go out there anytime I want to. Maybe I want to put it in shape to be sold."

I asked her when she'd been out there last.

She said, "Not since shortly after your trial. For a long time I didn't care what happened to it. Now, if we can straighten out this mess you're in, we're going back there to live."

I got up to go while the going was good and Beth walked to the door with me. "I love you, Charlie."

I said that went double. I felt some better. I felt a lot better. But we still had a long row to hoe. I didn't see how anyone could possibly prove I hadn't killed Zo.

I wanted to stay. I knew Beth wanted me to. But Ken Gilly was nobody's fool. When I didn't show at the road blocks he'd know I had slipped into town before they had been established and would put a stake-out on Beth's apartment without telling her anything about it.

Beth kissed me at the screen door. "I'll be out – soon. With good news to report."

Keeping close to the wall and out of the moonlight, I tiptoed sideways down the stairs to the alley and made my way towards the nearest street. I'd gone perhaps twenty yards from the foot of the stairs when the big guy stepped out from behind the bole of a pineapple palm.

"You there," he stopped me. "What's your name? And what are you doing prowling an alley at two o'clock in the morning?"

My first thought was, *Ken left a stake-out after all.*

I thought fast: I didn't know the man. He was obviously new to the force, at least since I'd been sent to Raiford. If he took me in, I was dead. I still had the murder gun in my pocket. They'd burn me like they'd burned Swede. My only chance was to bluff and run.

"Why, my name is Olson," I lied. I tried to feint him off guard by making him look where I was pointing. "I live in that house back there, officer. And I'm on my way downtown to try to locate an all-night drug store."

"Oh," he said. "I see."

There was a glint of silver in the moonlight. I thought at first he was throwing a gun on me. Then his arm reversed itself and started up in a familiar arc and I knew what he had in his hand. Backing a step, I let it rip air where my belly had been.

Then, stepping in before he could recover his balance, I smashed a hard right to his jaw that smacked him off his feet and his head into an empty garbage can with sufficient force to make it ring like a bell-buoy.

He was out, cold. Striking a match I leaned over him. I still didn't know him. But whoever he was I doubted if he was an officer of the law. If he was, he was the first cop I'd ever seen who carried a six-inch fish knife.

Then the light in the window of the apartment just over my head came on and some old dame asked nervously:

"What was that? Who's that out there in the alley?"

I said, "Me-arrh."

"Oh," she said. "Bad kitty."

Then I tiptoed out of there fast before she stopped to think that kitty cats didn't strike matches.

4 DEAD MAN'S BAY

The water was warm but the air was cold. The tide had changed and was going out. The pull of it was terrific. It had been three years since I'd done any swimming. I thought when I reached mid-channel that the tide was going to sweep me out into the gulf. As it was, I lost one of my shoes off the length of plank on which I had piled my clothes and which I was pushing ahead of me.

It would have been much easier to steal a boat. But I knew how most bait-camp men were. They hated to lose a boat almost as badly as a wife. A good boat cost two hundred dollars. You could get married for five. And I didn't want to direct any attention to the island.

The knife man worried me. Who was he? How had he known I would be coming down that alley? Why had he tried to kill me? He wasn't the man who had killed Zo. That much I knew. It hadn't been his voice that had said, "*You got him, eh?*" Nor was he the man who had slugged me with the butt of the gaff hook. He was a much larger man whose muscles strained the shoulders of his coat. If he had swung the gaff, it would have caved in my head.

As the low-lying trees grew to their proper place in the night sky, I felt for bottom and found it. The storms of the last three years hadn't changed the coast line of the island, not on the lee side at least. The deep water extended to within a few feet of the shore. I waded up on to the sand and slapped and tramped myself dry and warm before I put on my clothes.

Now, I was really home. My rotting nets, unused since before I had gone into the Service, still hung on their long drying racks. A half-dozen hulks and stove-in row-boats lay buried in the sand, including the bare ribs of the fifty-foot bottom that had been my father's boat. I was glad the old man was dead. I was the first of our family to do time and the disgrace would have broken his heart.

Dressed, I turned for a last look at the mainland. It was a good mile and a half across the channel. I couldn't see the running lights of any boats. My passage, so far as I knew, had been unobserved.

I padded, barefoot, up the weed-overgrown path toward the house, hoping I didn't step on a snake. The path was a jungle of vines. I wiggled my way through them, being careful not to disturb them any more than I had to. I didn't know how long I would have to stay on the island. And when both his road blocks and stake-out failed, Gil would undoubtedly make a perfunctory search of the home place.

Then I thought of something both Beth and I had forgotten – food. Unless there were some canned goods in the pantry, food was going to be a problem. But I'd face that when I came to it. As long as I knew I was going to live, I could live on fish and rabbits if I had to.

The house itself was set well back from the shore in a clearing that we had farmed from time to time. Now the ground was sour and overrun with saw palmetto. Even in the waning moonlight I could see the fifteen-foot wide porch across the front was sagging badly in spots, supported only by the thick-trunked red and purple bougainvillea and flame vine that had been old before I was born.

I picked an orange from a tree and tried to suck it but the grove was as sour as the garden. I wondered why Clifton had offered to buy the place from Beth. Probably out of pity or in the hope of buttering her up so she would say yes to his proposal. The old place was out of the world. I mean that literally.

No one but a typical cracker fishing family or a pair of kids as much in love as Beth and I had been would want to live in such a place. And the rest of the island was as bad. It was still as wild as it had been when the wreckers had been a power in Key West and Billy Bowlegs had terrorized gulf shipping.

I walked up the stairs to the porch. Coiled in a pool of moonlight, a ten-button rattlesnake watched me from the shredded canvas of a once-expensive chaise longue I had given Beth when we'd first been married.

I opened the door and went in. The big front room smelled old and musty. By striking a match I found a lamp with some oil in it and lit it. Even as old and decrepit as it was, after three years in a six by eight cell, the house looked good to me. At least here I could breathe. There were some canned goods in the pantry but not much, enough perhaps for three or four meals.

The more I thought about Beth asking Mr Clifton to suggest a good private detective to prove I hadn't killed Zo, the screwier it sounded. If the guy was really in love with her, he wasn't going to cut off his prospects by sweeping the legal sand spurs out of her husband's path to her side.

When she contacted me, I'd suggest she try to arrange passage for us both and meet me somewhere down in the Caribbean. I was pretty certain that Matt Heely would run us down, for a fresh piece of change, if not for the money he owed me. Matt was as bad as I'd been. He made good money but he threw it away with both fists and was always in financial hot water when it came time to pay his insurance or the installments on his boat.

Crossing the kitchen floor, I plowed up a pine splinter with my big toe that made me see stars for a minute. The quarter-inch callouses on my feet were gone. I'd have to have shoes of some kind. Then I thought of the old pair of sneakers I'd discarded just before making my final trip down to Shrimp Cay for the load with which I'd been caught. They should be up in the attic somewhere. Beth was as bad as a magpie. She never threw anything away on the theory that some time she might find a use for it. And this was one of the times.

Holding the lamp in one hand, I padded up the back stairs to the second floor and stopped in front of the door of the bedroom that Beth and I had used. I hadn't had it on the first floor but here I had an eerie feeling that I was being watched. I opened the door and held the lamp high.

It was the same with the three other bedrooms on the floor. They were all as Beth had left them when she'd left the island, stripped to the bare mattress with the bedding folded neatly and piled at the foot of each bed. It was my nerves, nothing more. I started to light a cigarette as I climbed the stairs to the attic, then decided to conserve my supply. Cigarettes were another thing that Beth and I had forgotten.

The old house had been built by my grandfather when both labor and lumber were cheap. Rumpus rooms hadn't been thought of, but he'd finished the attic as a ballroom so he and his friends could dance when a party of boats had come out from the mainland or a rare passenger vessel, New Orleans or Havana bound, had dropped anchor in the deep channel.

The finished section was thirty by forty feet, paneled in rare woods, with two large dormer windows on each side and two more windows at each end. But it had been a long time since it had been used as a ballroom. The windows had been boarded up and covered with cobwebs for years. Even when I had been a small boy, the attic had become a family catch-all.

I pushed open the heavy door and walked in and a sudden gust of wind blew out the flame of my lamp. Cursing the wind, I walked a few more feet. Then setting the lamp on the bare floor I lifted the hot glass chimney, struck a match and applied it to the wick.

I wasn't alone in the attic. Sitting in built-in bunks against the wall were perhaps a dozen men, their eyes as flat and expressionless as those of the coiled rattlesnake I had seen on the chaise longue. I'd seen their faces before.

At least I'd seen similar faces in the stews of Marseille, Port Said, Sevastopol, Hamburg, and two dozen other war-torn ports. They were the faces of wanted men. Men wanted in their own countries for treason and murder and fabulous thefts. Men willing to pay a stiff price to escape the noose, the guillotine, the firing squad, and the garrote.

I straightened. "What the hell?"

A thin-faced man with a heavy accent said, "Someone make out that light."

It was the only word spoken. Another man snatched the lamp from me and extinguished it. I reached for the gun that had killed Zo and remembered it was in the pocket of my coat. And I'd left my coat in the kitchen.

Then the first of a dozen fists found me and beat me to my knees with the deadly precision of men who have nothing left to lose. I fought back to my feet and the ring of fists hemming me in gave way for a moment as I tried to pound my way to the door. Then a foot thudded into me. As I went screaming to the floor, still other feet found my head, my chin.

The huge tarpon was back on my line. Only this time, like a fool, I'd allowed the line to become entangled with my ankles and he'd pulled me over the side of the cruiser and was heading, seemingly, for the bottom of the gulf out in fifty fathoms.

I was cold. I was wet. I was strangling. I was sinking through endless fathoms of black water, towed by the huge fish. It was strange what a man would dream.

Then an alarm bell rang in my head. I wasn't dreaming. I was drowning. It wasn't a fish pulling me down. It was a weight. I fumbled at the cord. Then I managed to open my knife and cut it.

The swift descent ended abruptly and I shot surfaceward. Just as my lungs were about to burst I broke water. I gasped a mouthful of air and sunk again, but just under the surface this time.

When my head broke water again, I turned on my back and floated. Perhaps five hundred feet away the running lights of a boat were circling and I could hear the faint throb of an underwater exhaust. I lay with my cheek to the water watching the lights. As they came toward me again I turned on my belly, ready to dive.

Then from the wheel of the boat, Matt Heely said, "Like a stone. Poor Charlie." He sounded sad.

The boat passed to port. Its stern lights grew small, then disappeared, and I was alone in the night. I tried to raise myself in the water and was partially successful. There were no short lights in sight. That meant I was a long way out in the gulf.

I turned on my back again and floated until my breathing was normal. Then I tried to find shore again and had better luck this time. Almost parallel with the water I could see a faint pinprick of light that didn't look like a waning star. I swam toward it slowly, floating frequently to rest, hoping it was the light on Quarantine Key.

*   *   *

I had to reach shore. I meant to. I had the whole set-up now. I knew who had killed Zo. I knew why she had been sent to meet me. I knew why thirty-six thousand dollars had been credited to my account. I not only knew who had killed her, but why. More, I knew what the men were doing in the attic of the old home place and how they had gotten there.

The sky grew blacker, then faded into a dead gray. All of the stars disappeared. A light on-shore wind sprang up and whipped up a froth of white caps. I swam on doggedly. The gray turned to a dirty mauve and then to a bright crimson before breaking into day. I found a drifting mossy, old plank and used it to rest on.

It had been Quarantine Light I had seen. I passed to starboard of it on an incoming tide, unobserved. The same thing happened with the Coast Guard plane making its routine morning flight. I was just another speck in an endless carpet of water.

Then the water turned a pale green and I knew I was on the outer bar. I waded a few hundred yards, then sat neck-deep on the edge of blue water for perhaps half an hour before striking out again to cover the last half mile.

I came ashore a few hundred yards above the former luxury hotel on the beach that the government had bought and turned first into a rehabilitation center and then into a veteran's hospital. An early-rising former GI hunting for shells along the beach looked at me curiously, then decided I was a fellow patient.

"Out for an early morning swim, eh?"

I said that was right and asked him if he had a cigarette. He had and gave me one. I sucked the smoke into my lungs gratefully. Nothing had ever tasted quite so good except the cigarette I had smoked after I'd finished my part of the demolition work on Saipan.

It was perhaps six o'clock. There was no one but myself and the former GI on the beach. That much was fortunate. The law was still looking for me. And all I had on was a pair of shorts. I'd kicked off my pants and ripped off my shirt perhaps fives miles out.

My new friend looked at my battered face and grinned, and I knew what he was thinking. As soon as they get a little dough together, a lot of the boys out at the hospital swarm into town and raise hell in an attempt to forget that they will never be the men that they once were. I touched my face. It was tender to the touch but the long immersion in salt water had cauterized the cuts. And if it looked like the rest of my body, it was a sight in technicolor.

His grin widened. "Kinda pitched one, eh?"

I said, "That's right. And am I going to get hell. You don't know where I can borrow some clothes, do you, buddy, just long enough to sneak by the desk?"

That was right up his alley. He'd held up a few bars himself. "Why not cop a suit from the old ward-room?" he asked. He nodded at an open ground-floor door. "You know. In where the orderlies hang up their civies when they change into whites."

I patted him on the back. "Thanks. That's an idea, fellow."

There was a clatter of dishes in the kitchen as the help brought up breakfast, but I was alone in the locker-room. I picked out a white sport shirt and a gray gabardine suit and a pair of two-toned sport shoes that didn't fit too badly. A broad-brimmed panama hat that I could pull down over my eyes and so hide most of my face completed the ensemble. The name of the guy who owned the clothes was Phillips. His hospital pass was in a glassine case in the outer breast pocket of the coat. Making a mental note to reimburse him for the loan if I lived through the fireworks I intended to touch off, I walked down a long corridor and out the front door of the hospital.

A sleepy guard barely glanced at the pass.

"A long night, eh, fellow?" he yawned.

I agreed it had been a long night.

5 SENOR PESO

Clifton's was always crowded, from eight o'clock in the morning until midnight. It was around ten when I got there. According to the headlines of the paper on the news rack next to the cigarette counter, I was still driving the cops nuts.

I hadn't attempted to crash the road blocks set up on either side of Tampa. I hadn't been seen in Palmetto City. The general public had been alerted to watch for me. I was known to be armed, and dangerous. I was described as pale, six feet tall, weighing in the neighborhood of two hundred pounds and wearing blue slacks, a checked sport coat, and white shoes. I was probably bareheaded as I was never known to wear a hat.

I turned the pages of the paper. Swede was on page four, in a one-column two-inch box. All it said about him was that Swen (Swede) Olson, former fishing guide and convicted murderer, had been executed at midnight for killing a prison guard during an abortive attempted break. Swede's troubles were over. I though of what he'd told me in the death house.

A man hauls in the fish he baits for and at the level at which he fishes.

If that wasn't good logic, I'd eat it.

The snip back of the cigarette counter asked if I wanted to buy the paper or rent it. I laid twenty-seven cents of Phillips' change on the counter.

"Tut, tut. What if Mr Clifton should hear you? Remember the customer is always right. But just to show you my heart is in the right place I'll take the paper and a deck of cigs."

She slammed the cigarettes on the counter. My picture was on the front page of the paper next to a picture of Beth. She'd looked straight into my face but hadn't recognized me.

I cracked the cellophane wrapper, then tapped the picture of Beth. "Now could I have some information. Where can I find this girl? I was told she worked at the cigarette counter."

The snip snapped, "She did. But right now you'll probably find her in Mr Clifton's office." She patted her blonde hair. "Not that I can see what he sees in her."

I walked back through an aisle lined with tables cluttered with merchandise to the elevator and asked to be taken to the fourth floor. No one, including the elevator operator, gave me a second look.

The office was large and modern. Behind a half-glass partition I could hear a man, presumably Clifton, saying, "But, my dear girl, I'd like to help you. You know that. But I can't see what good hiring a private detective would do. I've been talking to Lieutenant Gilly since you first mentioned the matter this morning and he says there isn't a doubt but what White killed that girl in the cabin on Dead Man's Bay."

Beth stuck to her guns. "I don't believe it."

I opened the door and walked in.

A dapper little man, perhaps five feet four, with wide-spread intelligent eyes, a high forehead and hair so black it looked like it had been dyed, Clifton waved me out of the office. "I'm sorry, sir," he said. "But whatever it is, I'm too busy to see you right now. Please come back later."

I closed the door and leaned against it.

Beth recognized me and dug a fist into her mouth to keep from screaming. "Charlie," she said finally. "What are you doing here?"

I drew a chair up to the desk and sat down. "Well, it got a little hot out on the island. In fact, quite a few things have happened since I saw you last night. And as you said maybe Mr Clifton would help us, I thought I'd come and see what he could do."

The little guy looked at me like I was something obnoxious. "Nothing. I can do absolutely nothing," he said. "As I was just telling Beth – " he corrected himself – "Mrs White, Lieutenant Gilly says there is no doubt about your guilt and I can't afford to be involved in such a sordid matter."

Beth said, "What do you mean, 'things got a little hot out on the island'?"

I lighted a cigarette and told the story just as it had happened. When I had finished, Clifton said:

"But that's preposterous. Who were these men in your attic?"

I said I imagined they were wet-backs that Señor Peso had paid Matt Heely or one of the other boys working for him to smuggle in from Cuba or Mexico.

"The old house," I pointed out, "is ideally situated. A boat can bring them in. A boat can distribute them along the coast in the guise of tourists and the law never be the wiser unless one of them should be picked up accidentally. Even then, I imagine by the time they leave the house they're well equipped with fake papers. As I see it, they're just another item of profit with *Señor Peso*."

Clifton made a gesture of distaste. "That name." He lighted a cigarette and smoked it in short, quick puffs. "And you say at the end of the attack that this Matt Heely took you out into the gulf in his fishing cruiser, weighted your ankles and dropped you in?"

I said that was correct.

Now he was openly skeptical. "I don't believe it. Even if you had managed to cut the cord you couldn't have swam that far."

Beth said, "That wasn't far for Charlie. He was on a water demolition team during the war. You know. One of the boys with goggles and rubber flippers who swam in the night before the first assault wave hit a beach and blew up all the obstacles they could."

Clifton eyed me with fresh respect. "I don't know what to think or what to say," he said finally. "Just what is it you want of me, White?"

I said, "You have a cruiser down at the yacht basin. I want you and Beth to come out to the island with me and check my story. In other words I want a friend in court before I turn myself in. A responsible business man who can back at least a portion of my story."

He thought a moment. "You think this Matt Heely could be *Señor Peso*?"

I said, "Matt could be. He's smart enough." I snuffed out my cigarette. "If I'm right it was *Señor Peso* who killed Zo and pinned her death onto me. It was *Señor Peso* who hired a knife man to wait outside Beth's apartment last night. It was *Señor Peso* who ordered me dropped in the gulf."

He protested, "But why?"

I said that would probably come out when we found out who he was. He sat silent a long moment drumming with his fingers on his desk. Then Beth turned her smile on him and said:

"Please."

She really had the guy wrapped around her little finger. He was so nuts about her it oozed out all of his pores.

"Well, all right," he said finally. "But let's have an understanding, White. If we do go out to the island and find nothing in the old house to substantiate your fantastic story, you will turn yourself in to Lieutenant Gilly as soon as we return to the mainland and allow the law to take its course. Is that understood?"

I said it was.

He said, "Then you go ahead to the yacht basin. Mrs White and I will follow."

I passed a half-a-dozen cops on my way down to the basin. One or two of them glanced at me casually but none of them attempted to stop me.

His boat was a thirty-eight footer, double cabin, with a flying bridge. He knew how to handle it, too. If he hadn't been a successful merchandiser, he'd have made a good fishing boat captain. What's more he knew the bottom of the channel like the lines in his well-kept hand. Easing the nose of the cruiser in between the rotting pilings of what once had been a pier, he made it possible for Beth to step ashore without even getting her feet wet. I helped him tie up to a piling, then followed him ashore.

Seen in broad daylight the old house looked better than it had in the moonlight. There was nothing wrong with it or the path or the clearing that a few dollars and elbow grease wouldn't make right again.

The first place I went was the kitchen. But the coat I'd left on a chair was gone, and with it the gun that had killed Zo.

Clifton was impatient. "Well, let's get on with it," he said. "Let's see this fabulous attic."

As I led the way up the stairs, he asked if I was armed. When I said I wasn't he said:

"Then it's a good thing that I brought a gun with me." He was openly skeptical. "Heaven knows I wouldn't want to face an attic filled with wet-back desperadoes without a gun."

I paused on the second floor for a deep breath, then walked up the attic stairs and threw the heavy door open. The floor was thick with dust. There were no built-in bunks against the wall. The walls were lined solidly with the antique furniture that various Whites had discarded over a period of a hundred years.

Beth began to cry.

Clifton was silent a moment. Then drawing his gun, he motioned me back down stairs to the second floor. "I was afraid it would be like this," he admitted. "But what in the name of time did you hope to gain by telling us such a fantastic story?"

I asked him why the gun.

"You're not mentally right," he said. "You can't be."

I lighted a cigarette and leaned against the jamb of one of the closed bedroom doors. "That can be," I admitted. "Heaven knows I've made a mess of my life. But tell me this, *Señor Peso*. Did you ever see a Florida attic that had been closed up for three years that wasn't covered with cobwebs?"

His voice shrill, he asked, "What was that you just called me?"

I said, "Answer my question. No. You never did. You could get the men who were in here last night out of the attic and onto the mainland. You could rip out the bunks and move the old furniture back. You could cover the floor with dust. But you couldn't replace the cobwebs. That's something only a spider can do."

He wet his lips with the tip of his tongue. "You're crazy. You're out of your mind."

I said, "We'll leave that up to the law. And while the law is at it, I want them to check your whereabouts at the time that Zo was killed. I doubt you have an alibi. You can't have. Because you were the guy who shot her and dusted me with a gaff hook."

His voice grew even shriller. "And just why should I do such a thing? What was my motive?"

I nodded at Beth. "My wife. She was the one thing you couldn't get at a bargain. You couldn't buy her. But you could buy me. That's why you sent Zo to meet me. That's why you deposited the thirty-six grand to my account. That's why you had Zo steam me up about heading straight for Cuba and Shrimp Cay. That's why you were at the cabin, to make certain she had me in tow.

"And everything went just fine until I read Beth's letter and told Zo it was no dice, that I was heading back to Palmetto City and Beth. It was you to whom Zo cried out just before you shot her. Shot her because you saw another way to accomplish your purpose. With me back in a cell at Raiford waiting to be burned for murder, I couldn't very well return to Beth. And, in time, you knew you'd get what you wanted."

He laughed. "A jury would howl at that story."

I said, "Okay. Let's test it. Let's go back to the mainland. I'll tell my story and you tell yours."

He shook his head. "No. I'm afraid we can't do that. I'm a prominent man in Palmetto City and my business enemies would be certain to try to make capital of this."

I said, "You mean you're afraid that the Feds might look at your invoices and begin to wonder where you're getting some of your goods that you're able to sell for less than your fellow merchants pay for it wholesale. Hell. It's been right in front of my nose all the time. No one but you could be *Señor Peso*."

The little man sighed. Then looking at Beth he said, "I'm sorry."

"Sorry for what?" she asked him.

He said, "That I can't allow such a scurrilous story as this to be bruited about. I'm very sorry, my dear. I'd hoped to make you very happy. But now – " He thumbed the safety of his gun.

I said, "It won't wash, Clifton. One dame on a gun is enough. Besides, just how do you intend to explain our bodies?"

His eyes overly-bright, he said, "That's simple. I'll tell the police the fantastic story you told me. Then I'll tell them when I called you a liar, you saw that you were trapped and shot your wife and committed suicide."

It was still as death in the old second-floor hallway. A chorus of dust particles were dancing in the sunlight streaming in the front window. Clifton lifted the gun in his hand and the door of the bedroom behind me opened and Ken Gilly stepped out in the hall saying:

"I wouldn't, Mr Clifton. With all your dough, you've got a much better chance hiring a high-priced lawyer." Ken cocked the big gun in his own hand. "Of course if you insist."

Around us the doors of the other bedrooms opened. There was an officer in each one, one of them a police stenographer who was still scrawling curlicues on his pad.

Clifton wasn't a fool. He dropped his gun. "You win," he said looking at me. "You're smarter than I gave you credit for being." He looked at Ken. "Well, let's get back to the mainland so I can contact my lawyers." His smile was thin. "But you haven't a damn thing on me but some foolish conversation."

Putting his gun away, Ken rubbed thoughtfully at the knuckles he had bruised beating at least a portion of the truth out of Matt Heely after I had gone to him with my story, directly from the hospital.

"Oh, I don't know," he said slowly. "A little of this, a little of that. A guy talks here. A guy talks there. And the first thing you know, it builds into a conviction." He waved his hand at the stairs. "Take Mr Clifton away, boys. We're going to give him a bargain, board and lodging free for nothing."

When they had gone, Ken turned to me, offered me his hand.

"Welcome, Charlie." He brushed my nose with the tip of one finger. "But keep that clean now, fellow. Hear me?"

I said I did and intended to.

Then he was gone and Beth and I were alone and she was in my arms.

"I love you, love you so, Charlie," she whispered.

Swede had been right about a lot of things. He'd told me:

"A man can starve a dame. He can cuss her. He can beat her every night and twice on Sunday and she'll still think he's her personal Marshall plan in a silver champagne bucket. But only if she knows she's the only woman in his life."

I hadn't known how really big a lump in the throat could be. All I could say was her name. But that was all right with Beth. She understood. The bloody tide was over for both of us. There was nothing ahead but clear sailing in clean water.

She lifted her face to mine. "Hey, you, Mister Man. Remember me? How's about a kiss?"

And that was all right with me, too.

DEATH COMES
GIFT-WRAPPED
William P. McGivern

SERGEANT BURT MORAN was a tall man with hard flat features and eyes that were cold and dull, like those of a snake. He was that comparatively rare thing among cops, a man equally hated by crooks and by his fellow officers. Operators on both sides of the law forgot their differences and came to agreement on one point at least: that Moran was a heel by any or all standards.

Moran was a bully who shook down petty crooks for a few bucks whenever he got the chance. But he left the big boys alone. He lacked the imagination to serve them and, consequently, he never got in on the important payoff. There would have been some dignity in being a big grafter, but Moran grubbed for his few extra dollars the hard way, the cheap way, the way that earned him nothing else but contempt.

There was a streak of savage brutality in him that caused the underworld to mingle their contempt with a certain fear. Moran had killed six men in the line of duty, three of whom were unarmed at the time, and another who had died after Moran had worked him over with a sap for fourteen hours. The story of the men he'd killed wasn't told because a corpse is an unsatisfactory witness. Moran knew this. He knew all about killing.

Now, at two o'clock in the morning, in the cheap room of a cheap hotel, Moran was going to learn about murder. He had to commit a murder because of something new in his life, something that he had always sneered at in the lives of other men.

Moran was in love. And he had learned that love, like anything else, costs money.

He stood just inside the doorway of the room and watched the scrawny, thin-faced man who was staring at him from the bed. The man was Dinny Nelson, a small-time bookie who, Moran knew, carried all his assets in a hip wallet.

Dinny brushed a hand over his sleep-dulled features and said, "What's the pitch, Moran? You got no right busting in here."

Moran drew his gun and leveled it at Dinny. He knew what would happen with crystal clarity, not only to Dinny and the portions of his body hit by the heavy slugs, but after that, to Dinny's corpse, to the police department and to himself, Moran. It was an old story to him. He had killed six men in the line of duty and he knew the way everything worked. No one would doubt his story.

Dinny saw his fate in Moran's face. He began to beg in a cracked voice. "No, no, you can't," he said. "There's no reason to kill me – I ain't done nothing. Don't."

Moran fired three shots and they were very loud in the small, thin-walled room. Dinny's body jack-knifed with the impact of the slugs, rolled from the bed to the floor. He didn't live long. Moran watched expressionlessly as Dinny's limbs twisted spasmodically, then became rigid and still. Underneath Dinny's body the roses in the faded pattern of the rug bloomed again, bright and scarlet.

There was two thousand, three hundred and thirty dollars in Dinny's wallet. Moran left thirty. The money made a comfortable bulge against his leg as he sauntered to the phone . . .

While the coroner did his work and two lab technicians went over the room, Moran told his story to Lieutenant Bill Pickerton, his immediate superior at Homicide.

"Tonight I seen him taking bets in the lobby," Moran said. "This was eleven. I started across to him but he seen me and ducked into the bar and then out to the street. So I drifted away. Around two I came back, came right up here to his room. I told him to get dressed but the fool went for me. I had to shoot him."

Lieutenant Pickerton rubbed his long jaw. "This stinks worse than your usual stuff, Moran. You could have handled him with your fists. He doesn't have a gun."

Moran shrugged. "Why should I risk getting beat over the head with a chair or something?"

Pickerton looked at him with active dislike. "Okay, turn in a written report tomorrow morning. The old man won't like this, you know."

"To hell with the old man," Moran said. "He wants us to bring 'em in with a butterfly net, I suppose."

"All right," Pickerton said. He paid no more attention to Moran, but studied the body and the room with alert, careful eyes.

Downstairs, Moran hailed a cab and gave the driver the address of the

Diamond Club. He stared out the window at the dark streets of the Loop, his impassive face hiding the mirth inside him.

When Moran had realized that a night club singer couldn't be impressed by a cop's salary, he had looked around in his dull, unimaginative fashion for a way to get some money. Nothing had occurred to him for quite a while. Then the idea came, the idea that a cop could literally get away with murder.

After he got that much, the rest was easy. He had picked Dinny because he wasn't big-time, but big enough as far as money went. Now it was all over and he had the money. There would be a routine investigation of course, but there was no one to come forward with Dinny's version of what had happened. Therefore, the department would have to accept Moran's story. They might raise hell with him, threaten him some, but that didn't matter.

Moran's hand touched the unfamiliar bulge of money in his pocket and a rare smile touched the corner of his mouth. It didn't matter at all.

He paid off the driver in front of the Diamond Club on Randolph Street and walked past the headwaiter with a familiar smile. The headwaiter smiled cordially, for Moran's visits to the club had been frequent over the past two months, dating from the time Cherry Angela had joined the show.

Moran found a corner table and watched the girl singing at the mike. This was Cherry Angela. The blue spot molded her silver evening dress to her slim, pliant body, revealing all the curving outlines. She wore her platinum hair loose, falling in soft waves to her shoulders, and her eyes and features were mocking as she sang an old, old story about a man and a woman.

Moran forgot everything watching the girl. And there was an expression of sullen hunger on his face.

She came to his table after the number and sat down with lithe grace. "Hi, copper," she said, and her voice was amused. "Like my song?"

"I liked it," Moran said.

Her lean face was mocking. "I should do a black-flip from sheer happiness, I suppose. Would a beer strain your budget?"

"Go ahead," Moran said, flushing. "I've spent plenty on you, baby."

"You tired of it?" she said lightly.

Moran put his hands under the table so she wouldn't see their trembling. She was in his blood like nothing else had ever been in his life. But he got nothing from her but mockery, or sarcasm that shriveled him up inside.

He knew that she let him hang around for laughs, enjoying the spectacle of a forty-year-old flatfoot behaving like an adolescent before her charms. For just a second then he wanted to tell her what he had done tonight, and about the money in his pocket. He wanted to see her expression change, wanted to see respect for him in her eyes.

But he resisted that impulse. Fools bragged. And got caught. Moran wasn't getting caught.

Some day he'd have her where he wanted. Helpless, crawling. That was what he wanted. It was a strange kind of love that had driven Moran to murder.

He took her home that night but she left him at the doorway of her apartment. Sometimes, if he'd spent a lot of money, she let him come up for a nightcap, but tonight she was tired.

Leaving her, Moran walked the five miles to his own apartment, hoping to tire himself out so that he could sleep without tormenting himself with visions of what she might be doing, or who she might be with.

But once in bed, he knew the walk hadn't helped. He was wide awake and strangely nervous. After half an hour of tossing he sat up and snapped on the bed lamp. It was five-thirty in the morning, and he had a report to make on the murder in about four hours. He needed sleep, he needed to be rested when he told his story, and thinking about that made sleep impossible.

He picked the evening paper from the floor, glanced over the news. There was a murder on page one, not his, but somebody else's. He thought about his murder then and realized with a slight shock of fear that it had been on his mind all the time. It was the thing keeping him from sleep. Not Cherry Angela.

He frowned and stared out the window at the gray dawn. What was his trouble? This killing tonight was just like the others. And they hadn't bothered him. There must be a difference somewhere, he decided. It came to him after a while. The others had been killings. This one was murder. And the difference was that murder made you think.

Moran lay back in the bed, but he didn't go to sleep. He kept thinking.

At ten after eleven Moran had finished his report. He read it over twice, frowning with concentration, then took it down to Lieutenant Bill Pickerton's office.

There was someone with Pickerton, a young man with mild eyes and neatly combed hair. He was sitting beside Pickerton's desk, and the two men were talking baseball.

Pickerton nodded to Moran, said, "This is Don Linton from the commissioner's office, Moran."

Moran shook hands with Linton and put his report before Pickerton. Pickerton handed it to Linton. Linton said, "Excuse me," put on rimless glasses and bent his head to the report.

Moran lit a cigarette and dropped the match in Pickerton's ashtray. He guessed that Linton was here to look into the Dinny Nelson killing. His eyes were hot from his sleepless night and he was irritable.

"Is that all you want?" he asked Pickerton.

Linton answered. He said, "No. I've got a few questions. Have a chair, Sergeant."

Pickerton remained silent.

Moran sat down, trying to control the heavy pounding of his heart. They had nothing on him. It was his word, the word of a cop, and it was the only word they'd get.

"Okay, this seems clear," Linton said. He put his glasses away, studied Moran directly. "I'm from the commissioner's office, Moran. The commissioner wants me to ascertain that the shooting of Dinny Nelson was justified. Let's start with this. You're a homicide sergeant, assigned to roving duty in the Loop. Why did you make it your business to go to Nelson's room to arrest him on a gambling charge?"

Moran was ready for that one. He explained that he'd seen Dinny taking bets in the hotel lobby, that it seemed a pretty flagrant violation, so he'd decided to pick him up, even though it wasn't his beat.

Moran's voice was steady as he talked. All of this was true. He *had* seen Dinny taking a bet, had tried to pick him up, and Dinny had given him the slip. On that ground Moran felt confident.

"Okay," Linton said casually. "Now according to our information Dinny Nelson usually carried a sizeable amount of cash with him. But there was just thirty dollars on his body after you shot him. Got any ideas about that, Sergeant?"

"No," Moran said.

There was silence. Pickerton and Linton exchanged a glance. Then Linton put his fingertips together precisely and looked at Moran. "Did you leave the hotel room at any time after the shooting? I mean did you step out and leave the body alone?"

"No," Moran said. He wondered what Linton was getting at.

"You see, there was a bellhop on the floor at the time. He had brought some aspirin up to a woman. He has a record for theft and it occurred to us that if you left the room for any length of time, he might have slipped in, stolen the money and left before you returned."

"I didn't leave the room," Moran said. He felt scared. They might be telling the truth, but he doubted it. They were setting a trap, leaving an opening for him to dive into. A man guilty and scared would grab any out. Moran wet his lips and kept quiet. Crooks who got caught got scared. They started lying, blundered, and hung themselves talking. That wouldn't happen to him. They had his story.

Linton asked him then why he hadn't subdued Dinny with his fists. That was better. That was the sort of stuff he expected. Half an hour later Linton said he had enough, and Moran walked to the door. He was sweating. He was glad to get out. Linton might look like a law student, but his mind was sharp, strong like a trap.

As he reached the door, Linton said, "By the way, you know Cherry Angela, don't you?"

Moran's hand froze on the knob. He turned and his body was stiff and tense. "Yeah," he said. His voice wasn't steady.

Linton looked pleasantly interested, that was all. "I've heard her sing," he said. "And I heard you were a friend of hers." He said nothing else, volunteered no other information, but continued to watch Moran with a polite expression.

Moran stood uncertainly for a moment, then nodded quickly to the two men and went out to the elevators. Waiting for a car, he wondered how Linton knew he was a friend of Cherry's. They must already have done some checking into his activities. Moran lit a cigarette and wasn't surprised to notice that his fingers were trembling . . .

That day was hell. He couldn't sleep, and food tasted like sawdust. Also, he kept thinking, turning everything over in his mind a thousand times. That made him tense and jumpy.

That night Moran went to the Diamond Club for Cherry's early show. When he walked through the archway he saw her sitting at a corner table with a man. There was a champagne bottle beside them in an ice bucket and they were talking very seriously. Moran felt a bitter anger and unconsciously his hands balled into fists.

He started toward their table, moving deliberately. This is the time for a show-down, he thought. I'll chase that punk out of here and have it out with her.

Then he recognized the young man with her, and the shock of that recognition sent a cold tremor through his body.

It was Linton, the investigator from the commissioner's office.

Moran's face felt hot and stiff. He turned clumsily, hoping they hadn't seen him, and went back across the room, forcing himself to walk casually.

But splintered thoughts were flicking into his mind with frightening intensity. What was Linton doing here? What was Cherry telling him? More important, what was Linton asking her?

Ignoring the headwaiter's puzzled smile, Moran hurried out of the club. He walked a block quickly before his heart stopped hammering and he was able to think. He knew he had behaved foolishly. He should have gone to her table, said hello and sat down. Any change in his normal routine would look suspicious now.

Lighting a cigarette, he realized that he must see Cherry tonight, find out what Linton had been after. He retraced his steps until he came to a doorway about fifty feet from the entrance of the Diamond Club. There he stopped and prepared to wait. For he had to be sure that Linton was gone before going in to see Cherry.

It was a long wait.

The last show ended, noisy customers streamed out, but still Linton had not appeared. Moran's throat was dry from too many cigarettes, and his eyes burned from lack of sleep. But he waited, a deep shadow in the doorway.

Then Linton appeared and Moran cursed bitterly under his breath. For Cherry was with him, bundled up in furs and chattering so that her voice carried along the street to him.

The doorman went out in the street to hail them a cab. There were plenty of cabs out and that was a break. Linton and Cherry climbed into one, and Moran hurried down the block from the club and caught the next cruiser. He told the driver to follow Linton's cab and it led them to Cherry's apartment.

Moran ordered his driver to stop half a block away. He watched while Cherry and Linton got out and went into her building. But their cab waited and in a few seconds Linton appeared again and drove away.

Moran let out a relieved sigh. He paid off his cab and walked slowly along the darkened street until he came abreast of Cherry's entrance. For a second he hesitated, wetting his lower lip uncertainly. It was stupid for him to barge in on Cherry now. It would look as if he were afraid, guilty.

But he felt he had to know what Linton had wanted. That was the only way he could release the tight, aching feeling in his stomach. He made up his mind and turned into her entrance.

She opened the door in answer to his knock, her eyes widening with surprise. "Well, it's a small world," she said. "I just left one of your buddies."

"I know," Moran said, and stepped inside. She had changed into a green robe and as she turned he saw the flash of her legs, slim, smooth and bare. But they didn't distract him now.

"What did he want?" he said watching her closely.

"The copper?" She shrugged and went to a table for a cigarette. "What does any copper want? Information."

He walked to her side and suddenly all the twisted feeling he had for her crystalized to hatred. She was so cool, so bored and indifferent, while he was ready to crack in pieces from the pressure inside him.

Raising his thick hand he struck the cigarette from her mouth with brutal force. She staggered, face whitening with shock and anger. But he caught her shoulders and jerked her close to him.

"Now," he said, in a low hard voice. "You talk, baby. What did that guy want?"

"You're hurting me," she said, breathing angrily. "He wanted to know about you. Now let me go."

"What did you tell him?" he asked hoarsely.

She turned from him and sat down on the couch. "I didn't tell him anything," she said, rubbing her bruised shoulders. "Now you can get the hell out of here. No guy pushes me around, Moran."

"Forget that," Moran said. "I didn't mean to get rough. But I'm in a jam, baby. I had to shoot a guy last night and the old women in the commissioner's office are on my tail. They're trying to frame me, and that's why that guy Linton was snooping around you."

Cherry's lean face was interested. She said, "Did you kill the guy, Moran?"

"I shot him. He went for me and I shot him, that's all."

"Oh," she said. She smiled. "You wouldn't do anything original, I guess. Nothing that might put an extra buck in your pocket."

"I get along on my pay," Moran said.

"And your friends have to, too," she said. "That's why you haven't got any, I suppose."

"I didn't get anything out of shooting the guy," Moran said. That was smart. Not talking, not bragging. Guys talked to dames, then the dames talked. That wasn't for Moran.

Cherry grinned ruefully and leaned back against the fat pillows on the couch. There was one light in the room, a lamp on an end table that caught lights in her loose blonde hair and accentuated the soft curves of her body. Yawning, she put her legs onto the couch. The green robe parted revealing her slim calves in the soft light. She didn't seem to notice.

She was smiling, but there was a hard light in her eyes. "Tell me, Moran," she said, "how does it feel to kill a man?"

Moran swallowed heavily. He couldn't wrench his eyes from her long bare legs, or stop the sudden drumming in his temples.

When he spoke, his voice was dry. "It's like anything else you do, like smoking a cigarette or buying a paper, that's all."

She sighed. "You're such a clod, Moran. You're like a big heap of dough that's turning sour."

He came closer to her. "I could be different with you," he said. "You drive me crazy, baby."

She laughed with real amusement. "In the Casanova role you're a riot."

"Damn you," he said hoarsely.

She laughed again and sat up, putting her feet on the floor. "Let's break this up," she said. "You're a jerk and always will be, Moran. I might have liked you a little if you were smart, or if you had a spare buck to spend on a girl, but as you stand you're hopeless. So beat it, will you? And stop hanging around the club."

"Now wait," Moran said. His anger broke, melted away. "You don't mean that. I'll go, but let me see you again."

Her voice was hard. "No. You're all through. Beat it."

Moran stood beside her, reached for her hand. "What would you think if I was smart, if I did have a little dough?"

"I don't want to play twenty questions," she said coldly.

"This is no gag," he said. When he saw interest in her face, he slid on the couch beside her and began speaking rapidly, the words spilling out in a rush. "I got a little dough," he said. "I got it from Dinny Nelson last night. He was the guy I shot. I blew him out like a candle, then took his bundle. It's all yours, baby, for anything you want. But we got to play it quiet until I get a clean bill from the commissioner's office. You see that, don't you?"

"Are you on the stuff?" she said. "Is this story coming out of a pipe?"

"No, no it's on the level," he said. "I did it for you, baby. I shot hell out of him and got the dough. And I'm in the clear."

"Let's see the dough," she said skeptically.

He took the roll from his pocket. He had kept it on him because there was no safer place. Now he spread it in her lap and watched her face. She fingered the money gently and gradually a little smile pulled at her lips. "I might change my ideas about you," she said at last.

"Sure you will," Moran said eagerly. "I'm okay, baby. You'll see."

"I kind of want to find out," she said, grinning at him. "Want to excuse baby a minute?"

He watched her as she walked to the bedroom door. Something tightened in him as he saw the way her shoulders tapered gracefully to her slender waist, and the way her hips moved under the silken robe. She turned at the doorway and winked at him, and he saw the gleam of her long legs before she disappeared.

It was worth it, Moran thought exultantly. He felt happy for the first time since the murder. This was going to make it all right, and the tight ache inside him melted away and he knew it was gone for good.

He lit a cigarette and leaned back against the cushions, closing his eyes. Linton could go to hell, and so could Pickerton. They had nothing on him, now or ever.

He opened his eyes when he heard the click of the doorknob. Straightening up, he crushed out a cigarette and got to his feet, a grin on his face.

The bedroom swung open and Moran's heart lurched sickeningly.

Lieutenant Pickerton walked into the room, a gun in his hand. The gun was pointed at Moran's stomach.

"You're all through," he said.

Moran stood still, the grin pasted on his face, his mind frozen in the paralysis of panic. He tried to speak but no words came out, and the noise he made was like the grunt of an animal.

There was the sound of a key in the front door and then Linton came in, gun in hand.

He glanced at Pickerton. "You get it all?"

"The works," Pickerton nodded.

Linton came to Moran's side, deftly slipped the gun from his shoulder holster. "You're under arrest for the murder of Dinny Nelson," he said formally. "Anything you say may be used against you. As you know," he added dryly.

"Yeah, I know," Moran said numbly. Linton's words, the old familiar words, released him from paralysis.

Cherry appeared in the bedroom doorway, stepped around Pickerton and entered the room. She picked up a cigarette and smiled. Her fingers moved to the mark on her cheek where he had struck her.

Then she looked at Moran. "They wanted me to get you to talk," she said. "I wasn't going to, because I'm no informer. I might have warned you that Pickerton was hiding in the bedroom, but after you hit me, I had to pay you back."

"That was just one of the stupid things you did," Pickerton said. He shook his head disgustedly. "What made you think you were smart enough to get away with murder? Your speed is the little stuff, Moran."

Moran wet his lips. "What did I do wrong?" he asked. He didn't know what was happening to him but he felt weak and drained.

Pickerton glanced at Linton. "You tell him," he said.

"We had nothing on you," Linton said, "except your bad record, and the fact that Dinny's money had been taken. But you acted from the start in a suspicious manner. During our first talk you were nervous, sweating. Later you came to the Diamond Club, but when you saw me with Cherry, you turned and got out. We saw you, of course.

"Pickerton came here to Cherry's apartment because we knew you'd come here. A smart man wouldn't have. I took Cherry home, drove off. You immediately barged into the building and I came back and followed you up here."

He glanced at Cherry, then back at Moran. "You were too nervous to be subtle with her, or to go easy. You pushed her around and that did what we hadn't been able to do, convinced her to help us. She played you like a sucker. You spilled everything to her, which is the thing only a fool would have done. Fortunately for us, Moran, you're a fool." His face became curious. "A cop should have known better. Didn't you stop to think at all?"

"I was thinking about the murder," Moran said slowly. "It was on my mind. That left no room for any thinking about the smart thing to do."

Pickerton took his arm and started him toward the door.

Linton walked over and shook hands with Cherry. "Thanks for the help," he said. He hesitated, then smiled. "I'd like to see you some time when I'm off duty."

Cherry pulled the robe tight around her slim waist. "Any old time – just any old time."

Linton grinned. "I'll call you."

He took Moran's other arm and the three men went out the door.

Moran walked like a dead man.

THE GIRL BEHIND THE HEDGE

Mickey Spillane

THE STOCKY MAN handed his coat and hat to the attendant and went through the foyer to the main lounge of the club. He stood in the doorway for a scant second, but in that time his eyes had seen all that was to be seen; the chess game beside the windows, the foursome at cards and the lone man at the rear of the room sipping a drink.

He crossed between the tables, nodding briefly to the card players, and went directly to the back of the room. The other man looked up from his drink with a smile. "Afternoon, inspector. Sit down. Drink?"

"Hello, Dunc. Same as you're drinking."

Almost languidly, the fellow made a motion with his hand. The waiter nodded and left. The inspector settled himself in his chair with a sigh. He was a big man, heavy without being given to fat. Only his high shoes proclaimed him for what he was. When he looked at Chester Duncan he grimaced inwardly, envying him his poise and manner, yet not willing to trade him for anything.

Here, he thought smugly, *is a man who should have everything yet has nothing. True, he has money and position, but the finest of all things, a family life, was denied him.* And with a brood of five in all stages of growth at home, the inspector felt that he had achieved his purpose in life.

The drink came and the inspector took his, sipping it gratefully. When he put it down he said, "I came to thank you for that, er . . . tip. You know, that was the first time I've ever played the market."

"Glad to do it," Duncan said. His hands played with the glass, rolling it around in his palms. He eyebrows shot up suddenly, as though he was amused at something. "I suppose you heard all the ugly rumors."

A flush reddened the inspector's face. "In an offhand way, yes. Some of them were downright ugly." He sipped his drink again and tapped a cigarette on the side table. "You know," he said. "If Walter Harrison's death hadn't been so definitely a suicide, you might be standing an investigation right now."

Duncan smiled slowly. "Come now, inspector. The market didn't budge until after his death, you know."

"True enough. But rumor has it that you engineered it in some manner." He paused long enough to study Duncan's face. "Tell me, did you?"

"Why should I incriminate myself?"

"It's over and done with. Harrison leaped to his death from the window of a hotel room. The door was locked and there was no possible way anyone could have gotten in that room to give him a push. No, we're quite satisfied that it was suicide, and everybody that ever came in contact with Harrison agrees that he did the world a favor when he died. However, there's still some speculation about you having a hand in things."

"Tell me, Inspector, do you really think I had the courage or the brains to oppose a man like Harrison, and force him to kill himself?"

The inspector frowned, then nodded. "As a matter of fact, yes. You *did* profit by his death."

"So did *you*," Duncan laughed.

"Ummmm."

"Though it's nothing to be ashamed about," Duncan added. "When Harrison died the financial world naturally expected that the stocks he financed were no good and tried to unload. It so happened that I was one of the few who knew they were as good as gold and bought while I could. And, of course, I passed the word on to my friends. Somebody had might as well profit by the death of a . . . a rat."

Through the haze of the smoke Inspector Early saw his face tighten around the mouth. He scowled again, leaning forward in his chair. "Duncan, we've been friends quite a while. I'm just cop enough to be curious and I'm thinking that our late Walter Harrison was cursing you just before he died."

Duncan twirled his glass around. "I've no doubt of it," he said. His eyes met the inspector's. "Would you really like to hear about it?"

"Not if it means your confessing to murder. If that has to happen I'd much rather you spoke directly to the DA."

"Oh, it's nothing like that at all. No, not a bit, Inspector. No matter how hard they tried, they couldn't do a thing that would impair either my honor or reputation. You see, Walter Harrison went to his death through his own greediness."

The inspector settled back in his chair. The waiter came with drinks to replace the empties and the two men toasted each other silently.

"Some of this you probably know already, Inspector," Duncan said . . .

"Nevertheless, I'll start at the beginning and tell you everything that happened. Walter Harrison and I met in law school. We were both young and not too studious. We had one thing in common and only one. Both of us were the products of wealthy parents who tried their best to spoil their children. Since we were the only ones who could afford certain – er – pleasures, we naturally gravitated to each other, though when I think back, even at that time, there was little true friendship involved.

It so happened that I had a flair for my studies whereas Walter didn't give a damn. At examination time, I had to carry him. It seemed like a big joke at the time, but actually I was doing all the work while he was having his fling around town. Nor was I the only one he imposed upon in such a way. Many students, impressed with having his friendship, gladly took over his papers. Walter could charm the devil himself if he had to.

And quite often he had to. Many's the time he's talked his way out of spending a week end in jail for some minor offense – and I've even seen him twist the dean around his little finger, so to speak. Oh, but I remained his loyal friend. I shared everything I had with him, including my women, and even thought it amusing when I went out on a date and met him, only to have him take my girl home.

In the last year of school the crash came. It meant little to me because my father had seen it coming and got out with his fortune increased. Walter's father tried to stick it out and went under. He was one of the ones who killed himself that day.

Walter was quite stricken, of course. He was in a blue funk and got stinking drunk. We had quite a talk and he was for quitting school at once, but I talked him into accepting the money from me and graduating. Come to think of it, he never did pay me back that money. However, it really doesn't matter.

After we left school I went into business with my father and took over the firm when he died. It was that same month that Walter showed up. He stopped in for a visit, and wound up with a position, though at no time did he deceive me as to the real intent of his visit. He got what he came after and in a way it was a good thing for me. Walter was a shrewd businessman.

His rise in the financial world was slightly less than meteoric. He was much too astute to remain in anyone's employ for long, and with the Street talking about Harrison, the Boy Wonder of Wall Street, in every other breath, it was inevitable that he open up his own office. In a sense, we became competitors after that, but always friends.

Pardon me, Inspector, let's say that I was his friend, he never was mine. His ruthlessness was appalling at times, but even then he managed to charm his victims into accepting their lot with a smile. I for one know that he managed the market to make himself a cool million on a deal that left me gasping. More than once he almost cut the bottom out of my business, yet he was always in with a grin and a big hello the next day as if it had been only a tennis match he had won.

If you've followed his rise then you're familiar with the social side of his life. Walter cut quite a swath for himself. Twice, he was almost killed by irate husbands, and if he had been, no jury on earth would have convicted his murderer. There was the time a young girl killed herself rather than let her parents know that she had been having an affair with Walter and had been trapped. He was very generous about it. He offered her money to travel, her choice of doctors and anything she wanted . . . except his name for her child. No, he wasn't ready to give his name away then. That came a few weeks later.

I was engaged to be married at the time. Adrianne was a girl I had loved from the moment I saw her and there aren't words enough to tell how happy I was when she said she'd marry me. We spent most of our waking hours poring over plans for the future. We even selected a site for our house out on the Island and began construction. We were timing the wedding to coincide with the completion of the house and if ever I was a man living in a dream world, it was then. My happiness was complete, as was Adrianne's, or so I thought. Fortune seemed to favor me with more than one smile at the time. For some reason my own career took a sudden spurt and whatever I touched turned to gold, and in no time the Street had taken to following me rather than Walter Harrison. Without realizing it, I turned several deals that had him on his knees, though I doubt if many ever realized it. Walter would never give up the amazing front he affected.

At this point Duncan paused to study his glass, his eyes narrowing. Inspector Early remained motionless, waiting for him to go on.

"Walter came to see me," Duncan said. "It was a day I shall never forget. I had a dinner engagement with Adrianne and invited him along. Now I know that what he did was done out of sheer spite, nothing else. At first I believed that it was my fault, or hers, never giving Walter a thought . . .

Forgive me if I pass over the details lightly, Inspector. They aren't very pleasant to recall. I had to sit there and watch Adrianne captivated by this charming rat to the point where I was merely a decoration in the chair opposite her. I had to see him join us day after day, night after night, then hear the rumors that they were seeing each other without me, then discover for myself that she was in love with him.

Yes, it was quite an experience. I had the idea of killing them both, then killing myself. When I saw that that could never solve the problem I gave it up.

Adrianne came to me one night. She sat and told me how much she hated to hurt me, but she had fallen in love with Walter Harrison and wanted to marry him. What else was there to do? Naturally, I acted the part of a good loser and called off the engagement. They didn't wait long. A week later they were married and I was the laughing stock of the Street.

Perhaps time might have cured everything if things hadn't turned out the way they did. It wasn't very long afterwards that I learned of a break in their marriage. Word came that Adrianne had changed and I knew for a fact that Walter was far from being true to her.

You see, now I realized the truth. Walter never loved her. He never loved anybody but himself. He married Adrianne because he wanted to hurt me more than anything else in the world. He hated me because I had something he lacked . . . happiness. It was something he searched after desperately himself and always found just out of reach.

In December of that year Adrianne took sick. She wasted away for a month and died. In the final moments she called for me, asking me to forgive her; this much I learned from a servant of hers. Walter, by the way, was enjoying himself at a party when she died. He came home for the funeral and took off immediately for a sojourn in Florida with some attractive showgirl.

God, how I hated that man! I used to dream of killing him! Do you know, if ever my mind drifted from the work I was doing I always pictured myself standing over his corpse with a knife in my hand, laughing my head off.

Every so often I would get word of Walter's various escapades, and they seemed to follow a definite pattern. I made it my business to learn more about him and before long I realized that Walter was almost frenzied in his search to find a woman he could really love. Since he was a fabulously wealthy man he was always suspicious of a woman wanting him more than his wealth, and this very suspicion always was the thing that drove a woman away from him.

It may seem strange to you, but regardless of my attitude, I saw him quite regularly. And equally strange, he never realized that I hated him so. He realized, of course, that he was far from popular in any quarter, but he never suspected me of anything else save a stupid idea of friendship. But having learned my lesson the hard way, he never got the chance to impose upon me again, though he never really had need to.

It was a curious thing, the solution I saw to my problem. It had been there all the time, I was aware of it being there, yet using the circumstances never occurred to me until the day I was sitting on my veranda reading a memo from my office manager. The note stated that Walter had pulled another coup in the market and had the Street rocking on its heels. It was one of those times when any variation in Wall Street reflected the economy of the country, and what he did was undermine the entire economic structure of the United States. It was with the greatest effort that we got back to normal without toppling, but in doing so a lot of places had to close up. Walter Harrison, however, had doubled the wealth he could never hope to spend, anyway.

As I said, I was sitting there reading the note when I saw her behind the window in the house across the way. The sun was streaming in, reflecting the gold in her hair, making a picture of beauty so exquisite as to be unbelievable. A servant came and brought her a tray, and as she sat down to lunch I lost sight of her behind the hedges and the thought came to me of how simple it would all be.

I met Walter for lunch the next day. He was quite exuberant over his latest adventure, treating it like a joke.

I said, "Say, you've never been out to my place on the Island, have you?"

He laughed, and I noticed a little guilt in his eyes. "To tell you the truth," he said, "I would have dropped in if you hadn't built the place for Adrianne. After all . . ."

"Don't be ridiculous, Walter. What's done is done. Look, until things get back to normal, how about staying with me a few days. You need a rest after your little deal."

"Fine, Duncan, fine! Anytime you say."

"All right, I'll pick you up tonight."

We had quite a ride out, stopping at a few places for drinks and hashing over the old days at school. At any other time I might have laughed, but all those reminiscences had taken on an unpleasant air. When we reached the house I had a few friends in to meet the fabulous Walter Harrison, left him accepting their plaudits and went to bed.

We had breakfast on the veranda. Walter ate with relish, breathing deeply of the sea air with animal-like pleasure. At exactly nine o'clock the sunlight flashed off the windows of the house behind mine as the servant threw them open to the morning breeze.

Then she was there. I waved and she waved back. Walter's head turned to look and I heard his breath catch in his throat. She was lovely, her hair a golden cascade that tumbled around her shoulders. Her blouse was a radiant white that enhanced the swell of her breasts, a gleaming contrast to the smooth tanned flesh of her shoulders.

Walter looked like a man in a dream. "Lord, she's lovely!" he said. "Who is she, Dunc?"

I sipped my coffee. "A neighbor," I said lightly.

"Do you . . . do you think I could get to meet her?"

"Perhaps. She's quite young and just a little bit shy and it would be better to have her see me with you a few times before introductions are in order."

He sounded hoarse. His face had taken on an avid, hungry look. "Anything you say, but I have to meet her." He turned around with a grin. "By golly, I'll stay here until I do, too!"

We laughed over that and went back to our cigarettes, but every so often I caught him glancing back toward the hedge with that desperate expression creasing his face.

Being familiar with her schedule, I knew that we wouldn't see her again that day, but Walter knew nothing of this. He tried to keep away from the subject, yet it persisted in coming back. Finally he said, "Incidentally, just who is she?"

"Her name is Evelyn Vaughn. Comes from quite a well-to-do-family."

"She here alone?"

"No, besides the servants she has a nurse and a doctor in attendance. She hasn't been quite well."

"Hell, she looks the picture of health."

"Oh, she is now," I agreed. I walked over and turned on the television and we watched the fights. For the sixth time a call came in for Walter, but his reply was the same. He wasn't going back to New York. I felt the anticipation in his voice, knowing why he was staying, and had to concentrate on the screen to keep from smiling.

Evelyn was there the next day and the next. Walter had taken to waving when I did and when she waved back his face seemed to light up until it looked almost boyish. The sun had tanned him nicely and he pranced around like a colt, especially when she could see him. He pestered me with questions and received evasive answers. Somehow he got the idea that his importance warranted a visit from the house across the way. When I told him that to Evelyn neither wealth nor position meant a thing he looked at me sharply to see if I was telling the truth. To have become what he was he had to be a good reader of faces and he knew that it *was* the truth beyond the shadow of a doubt.

So I sat there day after day watching Walter Harrison fall helplessly in love with a woman he hadn't met yet. He fell in love with the way she waved until each movement of her hand seemed to be for him alone. He fell in love with the luxuriant beauty of her body, letting his eyes follow her as she walked to the water from the house, aching to be close to her. She would turn sometimes and see us watching, and wave.

At night he would stand by the window not hearing what I said because he was watching her windows, hoping for just one glimpse of her, and often I would hear him repeating her name slowly, letting it roll off his tongue like a precious thing.

It couldn't go on that way. I knew it and he knew it. She had just come up from the beach and the water glistened on her skin. She laughed at something the woman said who was with her and shook her head back so that her hair flowed down her back.

Walter shouted and waved and she laughed again, waving back. The wind brought her voice to him and Walter stood there, his breath hot in my face. "Look here, Duncan, I'm going over and meet her. I can't stand this waiting. Good Lord, what does a guy have to go through to meet a woman?"

"You've never had any trouble before, have you?"

"Never like this!" he said. "Usually they're dropping at my feet.

I haven't changed, have I? There's nothing repulsive about me, is there?"

I wanted to tell the truth, but I laughed instead. "You're the same as ever. It wouldn't surprise me if she was dying to meet you, too. I can tell you this . . . she's never been outside as much as since you've been here."

His eyes lit up boyishly. "Really, Dunc. Do you think so?"

"I think so. I can assure you of this, too. If she does seem to like you it's certainly for yourself alone."

As crudely as the barb was placed, it went home. Walter never so much as glanced at me. He was lost in thought for a long time, then: "I'm going over there now, Duncan. I'm crazy about that girl. By God, I'll marry her if it's the last thing I do."

"Don't spoil it, Walter. Tomorrow, I promise you. I'll go over with you."

His eagerness was pathetic. I don't think he slept a wink that night. Long before breakfast he was waiting for me on the veranda. We ate in silence, each minute an eternity for him. He turned repeatedly to look over the hedge and I caught a flash of worry when she didn't appear.

Tight little lines had appeared at the corner of his eyes and he said, "Where is she, Dunc? She should be there by now, shouldn't she?"

"I don't know," I said. "It does seem strange. Just a moment." I rang the bell on the table and my housekeeper came to the door. "Have you seen the Vaughns, Martha?" I asked her.

She nodded sagely. "Oh, yes, sir. They left very early this morning to go back to the city."

Walter turned to me. "Hell!"

"Well, she'll be back," I assured him.

"Damn it, Dunc, that isn't the point!" He stood up and threw his napkin on the seat. "Can't you realize that I'm in love with the girl? I can't wait for her to get back!"

His face flushed with frustration. There was no anger, only the crazy hunger for the woman. I held back my smile. It happened. It happened the way I planned for it to happen. Walter Harrison had fallen so deeply in love, so truly in love that he couldn't control himself. I might have felt sorry for him at that moment if I hadn't asked him, "Walter, as I told you, I know very little about her. Supposing she is already married."

He answered my question with a nasty grimace. "Then she'll get a divorce if I have to break the guy in pieces. I'll break anything that stands in my way, Duncan. I'm going to have her if it's the last thing I do!"

He stalked off to his room. Later I heard the car roar down the road. I let myself laugh then.

I went back to New York and was there a week when my contacts told me of Walter's fruitless search. He used every means at his disposal, but he couldn't locate the girl. I gave him seven days, exactly seven days. You see, that seventh day was the anniversary of the date I introduced him to Adrianne. I'll never forget it. Wherever Walter is now, neither will he.

When I called him I was amazed at the change in his voice. He sounded weak and lost. We exchanged the usual formalities; then I said, "Walter, have you found Evelyn yet?"

He took a long time to answer. "No, she's disappeared completely."

"Oh, I wouldn't say that," I said.

He didn't get it at first. It was almost too much to hope for. "You . . . mean you know where she is?"

"Exactly."

"Where? Please, Dunc . . . where is she?" In a split second he became a vital being again. He was bursting with life and energy, demanding that I tell him.

I laughed and told him to let me get a word in and I would. The silence was ominous then. "She's not very far from here, Walter, in a small hotel right off Fifth Avenue." I gave him the address and had hardly finished when I heard his phone slam against the desk. He was in such a hurry he hadn't bothered to hang up . . .

Duncan stopped and drained his glass, then stared at it remorsefully. The Inspector coughed lightly to attract his attention, his curiosity prompting him to speak. "He found her?" he asked eagerly.

"Oh yes, he found her. He burst right in over all protests, expecting to sweep her off her feet."

This time the Inspector fidgeted nervously. "Well, go on."

Duncan motioned for the waiter and lifted a fresh glass in a toast. The Inspector did the same. Duncan smiled gently. "When she saw him she laughed and waved. Walter Harrison died an hour later . . . from a window in the same hotel."

It was too much for the Inspector. He leaned forward in his chair, his forehead knotted in a frown. "But what happened? Who was she? Damn it, Duncan . . ."

Duncan took a deep breath, then gulped the drink down.

"Evelyn Vaughn was a hopeless imbecile," he said.

"She had the beauty of a goddess and the mentality of a two-year-old. They kept her well tended and dressed so she wouldn't be an object of curiosity. But the only habit she ever learned was to wave bye-bye . . ."

ENTER SCARFACE

Armitage Trail

TONY GUARINO, DESTINED to be the greatest of all America's notorious gang leaders, was eighteen when he committed his first serious crime. And the cause, as is so often the case, was a woman.

But what a woman! Standing there in the dark alley that gave access to the street from the sheet-iron stage door of the cheap burlesque house, Tony could visualize her easily. A tall, stately blonde with golden hair, and a pink and white complexion and long, graceful white legs. From the audience he had watched those legs many times while she danced her way through the performance and they never failed to give him a tingly thrill that left him rather breathless.

The stage door opened suddenly, letting a square of yellow light out on the throng of dark, overdressed men and older boys waiting, like so many wolves, for their night's prey. Then the door slammed shut with a dull clang, plunging the alley into darkness again, and a girl swished rapidly through the crowd, seemingly oblivious of the hands that reached out to detain her and of the raucous voices that brazenly offered invitations.

It was she! Nobody but Vyvyan Lovejoy used that particular heavy, sensuous perfume. Tony plunged after her, toward the lights and noise that indicated the street.

She paused at the sidewalk, a lithe, slender figure, overdressed in a vivid green ensemble suit with a skirt that was both too short and too tight, and glittering with much imitation jewelry. People with a proper perspective would have recognized her for the false and dangerous beacon of allure that she was, but to Tony she was marvelous, something to worship and possess.

He moved up beside her and took off his cap. That was one of the things he had learned from the movies, the only social tutor he had ever had.

"Good evening, Miss Lovejoy."

She turned on him the face he thought so lovely. He couldn't see that its complexion was as false as her jewelry; couldn't see the ravages of dissipation that lay beneath the paint and powder; didn't notice the hard cruel lines about the garish mouth, nor the ruthless greed in the painted, rather large nose. As she surveyed him, contempt came into her hardened bold face and her greenish eyes took on a strange glitter.

"You!" she said. "Again."

"No – yet." Tony laughed at what he thought a brilliant witticism. "And I'm goin' to keep on bein' here every night till you gimme a date."

The girl laughed, a short, sharp, mirthless sound that was more like a grunt.

"Can y'imagine the nerve o' th' punk?" she demanded, as though addressing an audience, but her cold green eyes bored straight into Tony's defiant black ones. "Just a mere child without even a car and tryin' to date *me* up. Say, kid, do you know who my boy friend is?"

"No, and I don't care," retorted Tony with the passion-inspired recklessness of the Latin. "But I'm goin' to be."

"Well, it's Al Spingola."

Something inside of Tony suddenly went cold. Al Spingola was one of the city's important gang leaders, a ruthless man with a big income, a lot of hoodlums who were loyal to him because they feared him and he paid them well, and a quick trigger finger himself. A dangerous man!

"Aw, I bet he ain't so hot," answered Tony stubbornly.

"Well, maybe not," conceded Vyvyan, "but at least he can give a girl somp'm more substantial than kisses. . . Whenever you get a flock o' dough, kid, an' a big car, why come around and then maybe I'll talk to you."

She laughed again and stepped out to the curb as a big shiny limousine drew up with a rush and stopped. Tony started after her. Then he paused as he recognized the man at the wheel of that car. It was Al Spingola! A heavy-set, swarthy man with hard, reckless dark eyes and a cruel mouth with thick, brutal lips, handsomely dressed in gray and with an enormous diamond glittering in his tie. As everyone knew, the most important part of his dress lay snugly against his hip, a snub-nosed blue steel revolver seldom seen, but when it was, sure to be heard and felt by somebody. Tony realized that for him to say another word to Vyvyan then would be certain death. Not at the moment, of course, because that place was too public. But within a few days his body would be found in an alley somewhere.

Spingola glanced at Tony as the girl climbed into the car. And the boy felt cold and nervous until the expensive machine purred away at high speed. Spingola, like others of his ilk, always drove at high speed, thereby lessening his availability as a target.

Tony watched the car race away, then he put on his cap and lighted a cigarette. Walking around the corner to a poolroom which was his main hang-out, he sat down in one of the high chairs to think out this thing that was his first adult problem. Usually his mind, even though uneducated, was alert and precise, its processes rapid and sound. But now it was dulled by the gnawing, overpowering hunger of his first great passion. Of course he had had any number of affairs with the neighborhood girls; no boy as good-looking as he could help that. But somehow they hadn't satisfied him. He wanted something bigger, more mature than the shallow, entirely physical emotion that these girls offered. He was shockingly old for his age, as is almost every boy from such an environment. He looked twenty-five with his wise eyes, cynical mouth and well-developed beard that left a heavy pattern on his swarthy cheeks. And he possessed more actual knowledge of mankind and its vagaries than most men acquire in a lifetime. You could have set him down flat broke in any city in the world and he wouldn't have missed a meal. Nor would he have needed to steal; stealing was the way of people without brains. He held a contempt for thieves; particularly those of the petty larceny variety.

"Say!" whispered a surly voice in his ear.

Tony looked up into a rat face topped by a dirty, rumpled checked cap.

"Well?" he said coldly.

"Some of us are goin' out and knock over some gas stations," answered the other boy hoarsely. "Want to come along?"

"No."

"It'll be an even split all round."

"*No*, I said. I ain't riskin' a pinch for a coupla bucks."

"Aw, there'll be more'n that, Tony. All them places got fifty, sixty bucks layin' around. An' there'll only be about four of us."

"*Screw!*" snarled Tony. "Before I paste you one."

The other boy hurried away, muttering to himself. To the other boys who loafed around this poolroom, Tony was a puzzle. They never became intimate with him the way they did with each other. Somehow it just never occurred to them to do so. They realized the difference; so did he. But neither of them knew the reason. A psychologist would have explained it by saying that Tony had a "mental percentage" on the others, that it was the difference between a man destined for leadership and men destined to run in the pack.

Most of the boys in the neighborhood made illegal forays nightly. Never in their own ward, of course, because that would have alienated the alderman. Whereas when they made raids only in outside wards, their own alderman – in case they were arrested – would come down to the station, tell what fine reputations they had in their neighborhood, and help get them out. Then on election day, each hoodlum not only voted fifteen or twenty times, but hordes of them swept through the ward and threatened everybody with dire reprisals if the alderman were not re-elected by a handsome majority. And the people, realizing the truth of these threats, re-elected the alderman, even though they knew he was a grand old thug.

Tony always refused to join these nightly expeditions for ill-gotten gains. "Petty larceny stuff," as he contemptuously referred to their depredations, did not interest him. He wanted to be a "big shot," a leader, perhaps a politician. He had a hunger for command, for power, for wealth. And he meant to have it all. In the meantime, though he had no job that anybody knew of and although he refused to fall in with the criminal ways of his neighbors, he dressed better than they and seemed to have all the money he needed. Many of the boys wondered about that, but inasmuch as he chose to volunteer nothing, it was likely to remain a mystery for, in that neighborhood, one did not inquire into the source of income of even an intimate friend. And Tony had no intimate friends.

There was a sudden commotion at the front door of the poolroom and several burly men came in. Some of the people already present tried to escape by the back door, only to be confronted and driven back in by other burly men coming in there. Detectives, of course, going to look over the crowd.

Knowing that they had nothing on him, Tony watched with faint amusement and a large sense of virtue while the dicks went through the poorly lighted, smoke-filled room, tapping hips, asking questions, occasionally bestowing a hard, backhand slap on the ugly mouth of some hoodlum who tried to talk back. As he had expected, they made no move to molest him.

"This kid's all right," said a man he recognized as Lieutenant Grady from the neighborhood station. "He's Ben Guarino's brother."

"That don't mean anything," retorted a burly, cold-eyed man whose hard-boiled demeanor identified him as from headquarters.

"Does to Tony!" snapped Grady. "We've never heard of him bein' outside the law yet, either in this ward or any other."

"Thanks, Lieutenant!" smiled Tony. "Can't I buy a cigar for you and the boys?"

They all laughed at that. Not a man of them but what was old enough to be his father, yet he called them "boys" and they liked it. With all the poise and self-possession of a judge on his own bench, Tony led the crowd of officers to the front of the poolroom and purchased cigars for them all. Then they exchanged cheery "Good nights" with him and departed. Already Tony had learned the manifold advantage of having a good "rep" with the cops. Also he knew the great power that came from having people in one's debt, even for such little things as cigars. Tony seldom accepted a favor from anyone, but if he did, he always tried to return one twice as big, thus removing his moral debt to them and making them indebted to him. He had the mind and soul of a master politician.

Tony suddenly realized that the stuffy, smoke-filled atmosphere of the poolroom had given him a headache, and decided to go home. Except for occasional oases like the poolroom, the neighborhood was a desert of gloom and deserted frowsiness. Street lights were infrequent and those that existed were of the old-fashioned, sputtering type that, like some people, made a lot of noise but accomplished little. It hadn't rained that night, yet there was an unhealthy dampness about. The dingy old buildings, with their ground-floor windows boarded up like blind eyes, seemed to hover malevolently over the narrow, dirty streets. One street that served as a push-cart market by day was littered with boxes and papers and heaps of reeking refuse. An occasional figure, either hunting or hunted, skulked along. Infrequently, a car raced past, awakening echoes that could be heard for blocks through the quiet streets. Over all hung a brooding stir of everpresent menace, an indefinable something that made sensitive strangers to the neighborhood suddenly look back over their shoulders for no good reason.

This was the setting of gangland, its spawning place, its lair and one of its principal hunting grounds. It was also Tony's neighborhood, the only environment he had ever known. But he could not see that a great scheme of circumstances, a web much too intricate for him to understand, had gradually been shaping his destiny since the day of his birth, that it was as difficult for him to keep from being a gangster as it was for a Crown Prince to keep from becoming King.

Tony reached the little grocery store that his parents owned, and above which the family lived, passed to the door beyond, inserted his key and clattered up the dirty, uncarpeted steps. A light was on in the dining room, which also served as the parlor. Seated in an old rocker which had been patched with wire, sat Ben Guarino reading the paper, his blue uniformed legs and heavy, square-toed black shoes resting on the dirty red and white checked tablecloth. His revolver, resting in its holster, hung suspended by the cartridge belt from the back of another rickety chair upon which rested his uniform coat and cap.

As Tony came in, Ben looked up. He was a stocky chap in the middle twenties with a brutal mouth and jaw and defiant dark eyes that usually held a baleful glitter. For a number of reasons, all of which he kept to himself, Tony felt that his brother was going to be a big success as a policeman. To Tony, the only difference between a policeman and a gangster was a badge. They both came from the same sort of neighborhoods, had about the same education and ideas, usually knew each other before and after their paths diverged, and always got along well together if the gangsters had enough money.

"Where you been so late?" demanded Ben truculently.

"What the hell's it to you?" retorted Tony, then remembering the favor he was going to ask, became peaceable. "I didn't mean to be cross, Ben. But I got a nasty headache."

"Down to that O'Hara joint again, I s'pose?"

"Well, a fellow's got to have some place to go in the evening. And the only other place is some dance hall with a lot o' them cheap, silly broads."

"Gettin' choosy about your women, now, eh?"

"Yes."

"Well, that's right," answered Ben with a grin. "There's nothin'll take a man to the top – or to the bottom – faster than a high-toned woman eggin' him on." Suddenly his feet struck the floor and he leaned forward, his eyes boring straight into those of his brother. "Say, what's this I hear about you deliverin' packages for Smoky Joe?"

"Well?"

"Didn't you know there was dope in them packages?"

"No, I didn't. But now that I do, it's goin' to cost him more."

"You let that stuff alone."

"Oh, all right. I s'pose some cop belly-ached to you about it. Well, he can have that little graft, if he wants it. I got other things I can do."

"Yes, I guess you have," agreed Ben drily, "from all I hear. So you been a lookout down at Mike Rafferty's gamblin' joint, too?"

"Yes. And why not? That's a decent way of makin' a few bucks. Would you rather have me out pullin' stick-ups like the rest of the guys in the neighborhood?"

"Of course not." He leaned forward and spoke seriously. "Don't ever get in no serious trouble, Tony; it would ruin me at headquarters."

"I won't. Don't worry about me. You got enough to do to watch your own step."

"What do you mean?"

"Nothin'," answered Tony casually with a smile, enjoying the sudden fear that had come into his brother's face. "That's just a friendly tip from a fellow that knows more than you think he does."

"Who?" demanded Ben hoarsely.

"Me." Tony grinned again and flipped his cigarette ashes on the bare floor. "Say, Ben, can I have your car tomorrow night?"

"No. I'm usin' it myself. That's my night off."

"How about the next night?"

"No. You'd prob'ly get in trouble with it. Kids and cars don't go together."

"All right. I'll have one o' my own pretty soon and I'm goin' to get it as easy as you got that one."

With which parting shot, Tony went in to bed, slamming the door shut behind him. How a fellow making a hundred and fifty a month could acquire honestly a car that cost nearly three thousand dollars was too much for Tony. But then all policemen had big cars, and captains had strings of apartment buildings and sent their children to European finishing schools.

The strange quiet that momentarily descended over the Guarino household at this time of night was balm to Tony. It was the only period of the twenty-four hours that he could spend at home without feeling that he was about to go crazy. The rest of the time it was noise . . . noise . . . noise. . . . He wondered if other people's homes were as uninviting and repellent; all those he had ever seen were.

He undressed quickly and climbed into the grimy bed which he and Ben shared. He wanted to sleep before Ben came in so that they couldn't argue any more. But his mind was racing and it kept swinging around to Vyvyan Lovejoy. Even to think about her made him alternately hot and cold all over and left him trembling with anticipation. He *would* have her; nobody could stop him – not even Al Spingola.

The fact that the woman he wanted belonged to another made not the slightest difference to Tony. All life was a battle and the strongest man got the gravy. Anyway, she had said she would talk to him if he had a car and some money. Well, he'd get 'em both, and be back at that stage door tomorrow night.

A CANDLE FOR
THE BAG LADY

Lawrence Block

HE WAS A thin young man in a blue pinstripe suit. His shirt was white with a button-down collar. His glasses had oval lenses in brown tortoiseshell frames. His hair was a dark brown, short but not severely so, neatly combed, parted on the right. I saw him come in and watched him ask a question at the bar. Billie was working afternoons that week. I watched as he nodded at the young man, then swung his sleepy eyes over in my direction. I lowered my own eyes and looked at a cup of coffee laced with bourbon while the fellow walked over to my table.

"Matthew Scudder?" I looked up at him, nodded. "I'm Aaron Creighton. I looked for you at your hotel. The fellow on the desk told me I might find you here."

Here was Armstrong's, a Ninth Avenue saloon around the corner from my Fifty-seventh Street hotel. The lunch crowd was gone except for a couple of stragglers in front whose voices were starting to thicken with alcohol. The streets outside were full of May sunshine. The winter had been cold and deep and long. I couldn't recall a more welcome spring.

"I called you a couple times last week, Mr Scudder. I guess you didn't get my messages."

I'd gotten two of them and ignored them, not knowing who he was or what he wanted and unwilling to spend a dime for the answer. But I went along with the fiction. "It's a cheap hotel," I said. "They're not always too good about messages."

"I can imagine. Uh. Is there someplace we can talk?"

"How about right here?"

He looked around. I don't suppose he was used to conducting his business in bars but he evidently decided it would be all right to make an exception. He set his briefcase on the floor and seated himself across the table from me. Angela, the new day-shift waitress, hurried over to get his order. He glanced at my cup and said he'd have coffee, too.

"I'm an attorney," he said. My first thought was that he didn't look like a lawyer, but then I realized he probably dealt with civil cases. My experience as a cop had given me a lot of experience with criminal lawyers. The breed ran to several types, none of them his.

I waited for him to tell me why he wanted to hire me. But he crossed me up.

"I'm handling an estate," he said, and paused, and gave what seemed a calculated if well-intentioned smile. "It's my pleasant duty to tell you you've come into a small legacy, Mr Scudder."

"Someone's left me money?"

"Twelve hundred dollars."

Who could have died? I'd lost touch long since with any of my relatives. My parents went years ago and we'd never been close with the rest of the family.

I said, "Who – ?"

"Mary Alice Redfield."

I repeated the name aloud. It was not entirely unfamiliar but I had no idea who Mary Alice Redfield might be. I looked at Aaron Creighton. I couldn't make out his eyes behind the glasses but there was a smile's ghost on his thin lips, as if my reaction was not unexpected.

"She's dead?"

"Almost three months ago."

"I didn't know her."

"She knew you. You probably knew her, Mr Scudder. Perhaps you didn't know her by name." His smile deepened. Angela had brought his coffee. He stirred milk and sugar into it, took a careful sip, nodded his approval. "Miss Redfield was murdered." He said this as if he'd had practice uttering a phrase which did not come naturally to him. "She was killed quite brutally in late February for no apparent reason, another innocent victim of street crime."

"She lived in New York?"

"Oh, yes. In this neighborhood."

"And she was killed around here?"

"On West Fifty-fifth Street between Ninth and Tenth avenues. Her body was found in an alleyway. She'd been stabbed repeatedly and strangled with the scarf she had been wearing."

Late February. Mary Alice Redfield. West Fifty-fifth between Ninth and Tenth. Murder most foul. Stabbed and strangled, a dead woman in an alleyway. I usually kept track of murders, perhaps out of a vestige of professionalism, perhaps because I couldn't cease to be fascinated by

man's inhumanity to man. Mary Alice Redfield had willed me twelve hundred dollars. And someone had knifed and strangled her, and –
"Oh, Jesus," I said. "The shopping bag lady."
Aaron Creighton nodded.

New York is full of them. East Side, West Side, each neighborhood has its own supply of bag women. Some of them are alcoholic but most of them have gone mad without any help from drink. They walk the streets, huddle on stoops or in doorways. They find sermons in stones and treasures in trashcans. They talk to themselves, to passersby, to God. Sometimes they mumble. Now and then they shriek.

They carry things around with them, the bag women. The shopping bags supply their generic name and their chief common denominator. Most of them seem to be paranoid, and their madness convinces them that their possessions are very valuable, that their enemies covet them. So their shopping bags are never out of their sight.

There used to be a colony of these ladies who lived in Grand Central Station. They would sit up all night in the waiting room, taking turns waddling off to the lavatory from time to time. They rarely talked to each other but some herd instinct made them comfortable with one another. But they were not comfortable enough to trust their precious bags to one another's safekeeping, and each sad crazy lady always toted her shopping bags to and from the ladies' room.

Mary Alice Redfield had been a shopping bag lady. I don't know when she set up shop in the neighborhood. I'd been living in the same hotel ever since I resigned from the NYPD and separated from my wife and sons, and that was getting to be quite a few years now. Had Miss Redfield been on the scene that long ago? I couldn't remember her first appearance. Like so many of the neighborhood fixtures, she had been part of the scenery. Had her death not been violent and abrupt I might never have noticed she was gone.

I'd never known her name. But she had evidently known mine, and had felt something for me that prompted her to leave money to me. How had she come to have money to leave?

She'd had a business of sorts. She would sit on a wooden soft drink case, surrounded by three or four shopping bags, and she would sell newspapers. There's an all-night newsstand at the corner of Fifty-seventh and Eighth, and she would buy a few dozen papers there, carry them a block west to the corner of Ninth and set up shop in a doorway. She sold the papers at retail, though I suppose some people tipped her a few cents. I could remember a few occasions when I'd bought a paper and waved away change from a dollar bill. Bread upon the waters, perhaps, if that was what had moved her to leave me the money.

I closed my eyes, brought her image into focus. A thickset woman, stocky rather than fat. Five-three or -four. Dressed usually in shapeless clothing, colorless gray and black garments, layers of clothing that varied with the season. I remembered that she would sometimes wear a hat, an old straw affair with paper and plastic flowers poked into it. And I remembered her eyes, large guileless blue eyes that were many years younger than the rest of her.

Mary Alice Redfield.

"Family money," Aaron Creighton was saying. "She wasn't wealthy but she had come from a family that was comfortably fixed. A bank in Baltimore handled her funds. That's where she was from originally, Baltimore, though she'd lived in New York for as long as anyone can remember. The bank sent her a check every month. Not very much, a couple of hundred dollars, but she hardly spent anything. She paid her rent – "

"I thought she lived on the street."

"No, she had a furnished room a few doors down the street from where she was killed. She lived in another rooming house on Tenth Avenue before that but moved when the building was sold. That was six or seven years ago and she lived on Fifty-fifth Street from then until her death. Her room cost her eighty dollars a month. She spent a few dollars on food. I don't know what she did with the rest. The only money in her room was a coffee can full of pennies. I've been checking the banks and there's no record of a savings account. I suppose she may have spent it or lost it or given it away. She wasn't very firmly grounded in reality."

"No, I don't suppose she was."

He sipped at his coffee. "She probably belonged in an institution," he said. "At least that's what people would say, but she got along in the outside world, she functioned well enough. I don't know if she kept herself clean and I don't know anything about how her mind worked but I think she must have been happier than she would have been in an institution. Don't you think?"

"Probably."

"Of course she wasn't safe, not as it turned out, but anybody can get killed on the streets of New York." He frowned briefly, caught up in a private thought. Then he said, "She came to our office ten years ago. That was before my time." He told me the name of his firm, a string of Anglo-Saxon surnames. "She wanted to draw a will. The original will was a very simple document leaving everything to her sister. Then over the years she would come in from time to time to add codicils leaving specific sums to various persons. She had made a total of thirty-two bequests by the time she died. One was for twenty dollars – that was to a man named John Johnson whom we haven't been able to locate. The remainder all ranged from five hundred to two thousand dollars." He smiled. "I've been given the task of running down the heirs."

"When did she put me into her will?"

"Two years ago in April."

I tried to think what I might have done for her then, how I might have brushed her life with mine. Nothing.

"Of course the will could be contested, Mr Scudder. It would be easy to challenge Miss Redfield's competence and any relative could almost certainly get it set aside. But no one wishes to challenge it. The total amount involved is slightly in excess of a quarter of a million dollars – "

"That much."

"Yes. Miss Redfield received substantially less than the income which her holdings drew over the years, so the principal kept growing during her lifetime. Now the specific bequests she made total thirty-eight thousand dollars, give or take a few hundred, and the residue goes to Miss Redfield's sister. The sister – her name is Mrs Palmer – is a widow with grown children. She's hospitalized with cancer and heart trouble and I believe diabetic complications and she hasn't long to live. Her children would like to see the estate settled before their mother dies and they have enough local prominence to hurry the will through probate. So I'm authorized to tender checks for the full amount of the specific bequests on the condition that the legatees sign quitclaims acknowledging that this payment discharges in full the estate's indebtedness to them."

There was more legalese of less importance. Then he gave me papers to sign and the whole procedure ended with a check on the table. It was payable to me and in the amount of twelve hundred dollars and no cents.

I told Creighton I'd pay for his coffee.

I had time to buy myself another drink and still get to my bank before the windows closed. I put a little of Mary Alice Redfield's legacy in my savings account, took some in cash, and sent a money order to Anita and my sons. I stopped at my hotel to check for messages. There weren't any. I had a drink at McGovern's and crossed the street to have another at Polly's Cage. It wasn't five o'clock yet but the bar was doing good business already.

It turned into a funny night. I had dinner at the Greek place and read the *Post*, spent a little time at Joey Farrell's on Fifty-eighth Street, then wound up getting to Armstrong's around ten-thirty or thereabouts. I spent part of the evening alone at my usual table and part of it in conversation at the bar. I made a point of stretching my drinks, mixing my bourbon with coffee, making a cup last a while, taking a glass of plain water from time to time.

But that never really works. If you're going to get drunk you'll manage it somehow. The obstacles I placed in my path just kept me up later. By two-thirty I'd done what I had set out to do. I'd made my load and I could go home and sleep it off.

I woke around ten with less of a hangover than I'd earned and no memory of anything after I'd left Armstrong's. I was in my own bed in my own hotel room. And my clothes were hung neatly in the closet, always a good sign on a morning after. So I must have been in fairly good shape. But a certain amount of time was lost to memory, blacked out, gone.

When that first started happening I tended to worry about it. But it's the sort of thing you can get used to.

It was the money, the twelve hundred bucks. I couldn't understand the money. I had done nothing to deserve it. It had been left to me by a poor little rich woman whose name I'd not even known.

It had never occurred to me to refuse the dough. Very early in my career as a cop I'd learned an important precept. When someone put money in your hand you closed your fingers around it and put it in your pocket. I learned that lesson well and never had cause to regret its application. I didn't walk around with my hand out and I never took drug or homicide money but I certainly grabbed all the clean graft that came my way and a certain amount that wouldn't have stood a white glove inspection. If Mary Alice thought I merited twelve hundred dollars, who was I to argue?

Ah, but it didn't quite work that way. Because somehow the money gnawed at me.

After breakfast I went to St Paul's but there was a service going on, a priest saying Mass, so I didn't stay. I walked down to St Benedict the Moor's on Fifty-third Street and sat for a few minutes in a pew at the rear. I go to churches to try to think, and I gave it a shot but my mind didn't know where to go.

I slipped six twenties into the poor box. I tithe. It's a habit I got into after I left the department and I still don't know why I do it. God knows. Or maybe He's as mystified as I am. This time, though, there was a certain balance in the act. Mary Alice Redfield had given me twelve hundred dollars for no reason I could comprehend. I was passing on a ten percent commission to the church for no better reason.

I stopped on the way out and lit a couple of candles for various people who weren't alive anymore. One of them was for the bag lady. I didn't see how it could do her any good, but I couldn't imagine how it could harm her, either.

I had read some press coverage of the killing when it happened. I generally keep up with crime stories. Part of me evidently never stopped being a policeman. Now I went down to the Forty-second Street library to refresh my memory.

The *Times* had run a pair of brief back-page items, the first a report of the killing of an unidentified female derelict, the second a follow-up giving her name and age. She'd been forty-seven, I learned. This surprised me, and then I realized that any specific number would have come as a surprise.

Bums and bag ladies are ageless. Mary Alice Redfield could have been thirty or sixty or anywhere in between.

The *News* had run a more extended article than the *Times*, enumerating the stab wounds – twenty-six of them – and described the scarf wound about her throat – blue and white, a designer print, but tattered at its edges and evidently somebody's castoff. It was this article that I remembered having read.

But the *Post* had really played the story. It had appeared shortly after the new owner took over the paper and the editors were going all out for human interest, which always translates out as sex and violence. The brutal killing of a woman touches both of those bases, and this had the added kick that she was a character. If they'd ever learned she was an heiress it would have been page three material, but even without that knowledge they did all right by her.

The first story they ran was straight news reporting, albeit embellished with reports on the blood, the clothes she was wearing, the litter in the alley where she was found and all that sort of thing. The next day a reporter pushed the pathos button and tapped out a story featuring capsule interviews with people in the neighborhood. Only a few of them were identified by name and I came away with the feeling that he'd made up some peachy quotes and attributed them to unnamed nonexistent hangers-on. As a sidebar to that story, another reporter speculated on the possibility of a whole string of bag lady murders, a speculation which happily had turned out to be off the mark. The clown had presumably gone around the West Side asking shopping bag ladies if they were afraid of being the killer's next victim. I hope he faked the piece and let the ladies alone.

And that was about it. When the killer failed to strike again the newspapers hung up on the story. Good news is no news.

I walked back from the library. It was fine weather. The winds had blown all the crap out of the sky and there was nothing but blue overhead. The air actually had some air in it for a change. I walked west on Forty-second Street and north on Broadway, and I started noticing the number of street people, the drunks and the crazies and the unclassifiable derelicts. By the time I got within a few blocks of Fifty-seventh Street I was recognizing a large percentage of them. Each mini-neighborhood has its own human flotsam and jetsam and they're a lot more noticeable come spring-time. Winter sends some of them south and others to shelter, and there's a certain percentage who die of exposure, but when the sun warms the pavement it brings most of them out again.

When I stopped for a paper at the corner of Eighth Avenue I got the bag lady into the conversation. The newsie clucked his tongue and shook his head. "The damnedest thing. Just the damnedest thing."

"Murder never makes much sense."

"The hell with murder. You know what she did? You know Eddie, works for me midnight to eight? Guy with the one droopy eyelid? Now he wasn't the guy used to sell her the stack of papers. Matter of fact that was usually me. She'd come by during the late morning or early afternoon and she'd take fifteen or twenty papers and pay me for 'em, and then she'd sit on her crate down the next corner and she'd sell as many as she could, and then she'd bring 'em back and I'd give her a refund on what she didn't sell."

"What did she pay for them?"

"Full price. And that's what she sold 'em for. The hell, I can't discount on papers. You know the margin we got. I'm not even supposed to take 'em back, but what difference does it make? It gave the poor woman something to do is my theory. She was important, she was a businesswoman. Sits there charging a quarter for something she just paid a quarter for, it's no way to get rich, but you know something? She had money. Lived like a pig but she had money."

"So I understand."

"She left Eddie seven-twenty. You believe that? Seven hundred and twenty dollars, she willed it to him, there was this lawyer come around two, three weeks ago with a check. Eddie Halloran. Pay to the order of. You believe that? She never had dealings with him. I sold her the papers, I bought 'em back from her. Not that I'm complaining, not that I want the woman's money, but I ask you this: Why Eddie? He don't know her. He can't believe she knows his name, Eddie Halloran. Why'd she leave it to him? He tells this lawyer, he says maybe she's got some other Eddie Halloran in mind. It's a common Irish name and the neighborhood's full of the Irish. I'm thinking to myself, Eddie, schmuck, take the money and shut up, but it's him all right because it says in the will. Eddie Halloran the newsdealer is what it says. So that's him, right? But why Eddie?"

Why me? "Maybe she liked the way he smiled."

"Yeah, maybe. Or the way he combed his hair. Listen, it's money in his pocket. I worried he'd go on a toot, drink it up, but he says money's no temptation. He says he's always got the price of a drink in his jeans and there's a bar on every block but he can walk right past 'em, so why worry about a few hundred dollars? You know something? That crazy woman, I'll tell you something, I miss her. She'd come, crazy hat on her head, spacy look in her eyes, she'd buy her stack of papers and waddle off all businesslike, then she'd bring the leftovers and cash 'em in, and I'd make a joke about her when she was out of earshot, but I miss her."

"I know what you mean."

"She never hurt nobody," he said. "She never hurt a soul."

"Mary Alice Redfield. Yeah, the multiple stabbing and strangulation." He shifted a cud-sized wad of gum from one side of his mouth to the other, pushed a lock of hair off his forehead and yawned. "What have you got, some new information?"

"Nothing. I wanted to find out what you had."

"Yeah, right."

He worked on the chewing gum. He was a patrolman named Andersen who worked out of the Eighteenth. Another cop, a detective named Guzik, had learned that Andersen had caught the Redfield case and had taken the trouble to introduce the two of us. I hadn't known Andersen when I was on the force. He was younger than I, but then most people are nowadays.

He said, "Thing is, Scudder, we more or less put that one out of the way. It's in an open file. You know how it works. If we get new information, fine, but in the meantime I don't sit up nights thinking about it."

"I just wanted to see what you had."

"Well, I'm kind of tight for time, if you know what I mean. My own personal time, I set a certain store by my own time."

"I can understand that."

"You probably got some relative of the deceased for a client. Wants to find out who'd do such a terrible thing to poor old Cousin Mary. Naturally you're interested because it's a chance to make a buck and a man's gotta make a living. Whether a man's a cop or a civilian he's gotta make a buck, right?"

Uh-huh. I seem to remember that we were subtler in my day, but perhaps that's just age talking. I thought of telling him that I didn't have a client but why should he believe me? He didn't know me. If there was nothing in it for him, why should he bother?

So I said, "You know, we're just a couple weeks away from Memorial Day."

"Yeah, I'll buy a poppy from a Legionnaire. So what else is new?"

"Memorial Day's when women start wearing white shoes and men put straw hats on their heads. You got a new hat for the summer season, Andersen? Because you could use one."

"A man can always use a new hat," he said.

A hat is cop talk for twenty-five dollars. By the time I left the precinct house Andersen had two tens and a five of Mary Alice Redfield's bequest to me and I had all the data that had turned up to date.

I think Andersen won that one. I now knew that the murder weapon had been a kitchen knife with a blade approximately seven and a half inches long. That one of the stab wounds had found the heart and had probably caused death instantaneously. That it was impossible to determine whether strangulation had taken place before or after death. That *should* have been possible to determine – maybe the medical examiner hadn't wasted too much time checking her out, or maybe he had been reluctant to commit himself. She'd been dead a few hours when they found her – the estimate was that she'd died around midnight and the body wasn't reported until half-past five. That wouldn't have ripened her all that much, not in winter weather, but most likely her personal hygiene was nothing to boast about, and she was just a shopping bag lady and you couldn't bring her back to life, so why knock yourself out running tests on her malodorous corpse?

I learned a few other things. The landlady's name. The name of the off-duty bartender, heading home after a nightcap at the neighborhood after-hours joint, who'd happened on the body and who had been drunk enough or sober enough to take the trouble to report it. And I learned the sort of negative facts that turn up in a police report when the case is headed for an open file – the handful of nonleads that led nowhere, the witnesses who had nothing to contribute, the routine matters routinely handled. They hadn't knocked themselves out, Andersen and his partner, but would I have handled it any differently? Why knock yourself out chasing a murderer you didn't stand much chance of catching?

In the theater, SRO is good news. It means a sellout performance, standing room only. But once you get out of the theater district it means single room occupancy, and the designation is invariably applied to a hotel or apartment house which has seen better days.

Mary Alice Redfield's home for the last six or seven years of her life had started out as an old Rent Law tenement, built around the turn of the century, six stories tall, faced in red-brown brick, with four apartments to the floor. Now all of those little apartments had been carved into single rooms as if they were election districts gerrymandered by a maniac. There was a communal bathroom on each floor and you didn't need a map to find it.

The manager was a Mrs Larkin. Her blue eyes had lost most of their color and half her hair had gone from black to gray but she was still pert. If she's reincarnated as a bird she'll be a house wren.

She said, "Oh, poor Mary. We're none of us safe, are we, with the streets full of monsters? I was born in this neighborhood and I'll die in it, but please God that'll be of natural causes. Poor Mary. There's some said she should have been locked up, but Jesus, she got along. She lived her life. And she had her check coming in every month and paid her rent on time. She had her own money, you know. She wasn't living off the public like some I could name but won't."

"I know."

"Do you want to see her room? I rented it twice since then. The first one was a young man and he didn't stay. He looked all right but when he left me I was just as glad. He said he was a sailor off a ship and when he left he said he'd got on with another ship and was on his way to Hong Kong or some such place, but I've had no end of sailors and he didn't walk like a sailor so I don't know what he was after doing. Then I could have rented it twelve times but didn't because I won't rent to colored or Spanish. I've nothing against them but I won't have them in the house.

The owner says to me, Mrs Larkin he says, my instructions are to rent to anybody regardless of race or creed or color, but if you was to use your own judgment I wouldn't have to know about it. In other words he don't want them either but he's after covering himself."

"I suppose he has to."

"Oh, with all the laws, but I've had no trouble." She laid a forefinger alongside her nose. It's a gesture you don't see too much these days. "Then I rented poor Mary's room two weeks ago to a very nice woman, a widow. She likes her beer, she does, but why shouldn't she have it? I keep my eye on her and she's making no trouble, and if she wants an old jar now and then whose business is it but her own?" She fixed her blue-gray eyes on me. "You like your drink," she said.

"Is it on my breath?"

"No, but I can see it in your face. Larkin liked his drink and there's some say it killed him but he liked it and a man has a right to live what life he wants. And he was never a hard man when he drank, never cursed or fought or beat a woman as some I could name but won't. Mrs Shepard's out now. That's the one took poor Mary's room, and I'll show it to you if you want."

So I saw the room. It was kept neat.

"She keeps it tidier than poor Mary," Mrs Larkin said. "Now Mary wasn't dirty, you understand, but she had all her belongings. Her shopping bags and other things that she kept in her room. She made a mare's nest of the place, and all the years she lived here, you see, it wasn't tidy. I would keep her bed made but she didn't want me touching her things and so I let it be cluttered as she wanted it. She paid her rent on time and made no trouble otherwise. She had money, you know."

"Yes, I know."

"She left some to a woman on the fourth floor. A much younger woman, she'd only moved here three months before Mary was killed, and if she exchanged a word with Mary I couldn't swear to it, but Mary left her almost a thousand dollars. Now Mrs Klein across the hall lived here since before Mary ever moved in and the two old things always had a good word for each other, and all Mrs Klein has is the welfare and she could have made good use of a couple of dollars, but Mary left her money instead to Miss Strom." She raised her eyebrows to show bewilderment. "Now Mrs Klein said nothing, and I don't even know if she's had the thought that Mary might have mentioned her in her will, but Miss Strom said she didn't know what to make of it. She just couldn't understand it at all, and what I told her was you can't figure out a woman like poor Mary who never had both her feet on the pavement. Troubled as she was, daft as she was, who's to say what she might have had on her mind?"

"Could I see Miss Strom?"

"That would be for her to say, but she's not home from work yet. She works part-time in the afternoons. She's a close one, not that she hasn't the right to be, and she's never said what it is that she does. But she's a decent sort. This is a decent house."

"I'm sure it is."

"It's single rooms and they don't cost much so you know you're not at the Ritz Hotel, but there's decent people here and I keep it as clean as a person can. When there's not but one toilet on the floor it's a struggle. But it's decent."

"Yes."

"Poor Mary. Why'd anyone kill her? Was it sex, do you know? Not that you could imagine anyone wanting her, the old thing, but try to figure out a madman and you'll go mad your own self. Was she molested?"

"No."

"Just killed, then. Oh, God save us all. I gave her a home for almost seven years. Which it was no more than my job to do, not making it out to be charity on my part. But I had her here all that time and of course I never knew her, you couldn't get to know a poor old soul like that, but I got used to her. Do you know what I mean?"

"I think so."

"I got used to having her about. I might say Hello and Good morning and Isn't it a nice day and not get a look in reply, but even on those days she was someone familiar to say something to. And she's gone now and we're all of us older, aren't we?"

"We are."

"The poor old thing. How could anyone do it, will you tell me that? How could anyone murder her?"

I don't think she expected an answer. Just as well. I didn't have one.

After dinner I returned for a few minutes of conversation with Genevieve Strom. She had no idea why Miss Redfield had left her the money. She'd received $880 and she was glad to get it because she could use it, but the whole thing puzzled her. "I hardly knew her," she said more than once. "I keep thinking I ought to do something special with the money, but what?"

I made the bars that night but drinking didn't have the urgency it had possessed the night before. I was able to keep it in proportion and to know that I'd wake up the next morning with my memory intact. In the course of things I dropped over to the newsstand a little past midnight and talked with Eddie Halloran. He was looking good and I said as much. I remembered him when he'd gone to work for Sid three years ago. He'd been drawn then, and shaky, and his eyes always moved off to the side of whatever he was looking at. Now there was confidence in his stance and he looked years younger. It hadn't all come back to him and maybe some of it was lost forever. I guess the booze had him pretty good before he kicked it once and for all.

We talked about the bag lady. He said, "Know what I think it is? Somebody's sweeping the streets."

"I don't follow you."

"A cleanup campaign. Few years back, Matt, there was this gang of kids found a new way to amuse theirselves. Pick up a can of gasoline, find some bum down on the Bowery, pour the gas on him and throw a lit match at him. You remember?"

"Yeah, I remember."

"Those kids thought they were patriots. Thought they deserved a medal. They were cleaning up the neighborhood, getting drunken bums off the streets. You know, Matt, people don't like to look at a derelict. That building up the block, the Towers? There's this grating there where the heating system's vented. You remember how the guys would sleep there in the winter. It was warm, it was comfortable, it was free, and two or three guys would be there every night catching some Z's and getting warm. Remember?"

"Uh-huh. Then they fenced it."

"Right. Because the tenants complained. It didn't hurt them any, it was just the local bums sleeping it off, but the tenants pay a lot of rent and they don't like to look at bums on their way in or out of their building. The bums were outside and not bothering anybody but it was the sight of them, you know, so the owners went to the expense of putting up cyclone fencing around where they used to sleep. It looks ugly as hell and all it does is keep the bums out but that's all it's supposed to do."

"That's human beings for you."

He nodded, then turned aside to sell somebody a *Daily News* and a *Racing Form*. Then he said, "I don't know what it is exactly. *I* was a bum, Matt. I got pretty far down. You probably don't know how far. I got as far as the Bowery. I panhandled, I slept in my clothes on a bench or in a doorway. You look at men like that and you think they're just waiting to die, and they are, but some of them come back. And you can't tell for sure who's gonna come back and who's not. Somebody coulda poured gas on me, set me on fire. Sweet Jesus."

"The shopping bag lady – "

"You'll look at a bum and you'll say to yourself, 'Maybe I could get like that and I don't wanta think about it.' Or you'll look at somebody like the shopping bag lady and say, 'I could go nutsy like her so get her out of my sight.' And you get people who think like Nazis. You know, take all the cripples and the lunatics and the retarded kids and all and give 'em an injection and Goodbye, Charlie."

"You think that's what happened to her?"

"What else?"

"But whoever did it stopped at one, Eddie."

He frowned. "Don't make sense," he said. "Unless he did the one job and the next day he got run down by a Ninth Avenue bus, and it couldn't happen to a nicer guy. Or he got scared. All that blood and it was more than he figured on. Or he left town. Could be anything like that."

"Could be."

"There's no other reason, is there? She musta been killed because she was a bag lady, right?"

"I don't know."

"Well, Jesus Christ, Matt. What other reason would anybody have for killing her?"

The law firm where Aaron Creighton worked had offices on the seventh floor of the Flatiron Building. In addition to the four partners, eleven other lawyers had their names painted on the frosted glass door. Aaron Creighton's came second from the bottom. Well, he was young.

He was also surprised to see me, and when I told him what I wanted he said it was irregular.

"Matter of public record, isn't it?"

"Well, yes," he said. "That means you can find the information. It doesn't mean we're obliged to furnish it to you."

For an instant I thought I was back at the Eighteenth Precinct and a cop was trying to hustle me for the price of a new hat. But Creighton's reservations were ethical. I wanted a list of Mary Alice Redfield's beneficiaries, including the amounts they'd received and the dates they'd been added to her will. He wasn't sure where his duty lay.

"I'd like to be helpful," he said. "Perhaps you could tell me just what your interest is."

"I'm not sure."

"I beg your pardon?"

"I don't know why I'm playing with this one. I used to be a cop, Mr Creighton. Now I'm a sort of unofficial detective. I don't carry a license but I do things for people and I wind up making enough that way to keep a roof overhead."

His eyes were wary. I guess he was trying to guess how I intended to earn myself a fee out of this.

"I got twelve hundred dollars out of the blue. It was left to me by a woman I didn't really know and who didn't really know me. I can't seem to slough off the feeling that I got the money for a reason. That I've been paid in advance."

"Paid for what?"

"To try and find out who killed her."

"Oh," he said. "*Oh.*"

"I don't want to get the heirs together to challenge the will, if that was what was bothering you. And I can't quite make myself suspect that one of her beneficiaries killed her for the money she was leaving him. For one thing, she doesn't seem to have told people they were named in her will. She never said anything to me or to the two people I've spoken with thus far. For another, it wasn't the sort of murder that gets committed for gain. It was deliberately brutal."

"Then why do you want to know who the other beneficiaries are?"

"I don't know. Part of it's cop training. When you've got any specific leads, any hard facts, you run them down before you cast a wider net. That's only part of it. I suppose I want to get more of a sense of the woman. That's probably all I can realistically hope to get, anyway. I don't stand much chance of tracking her killer."

"The police don't seem to have gotten very far."

I nodded. "I don't think they tried too hard. And I don't think they knew she had an estate. I talked to one of the cops on the case and if he had known that he'd have mentioned it to me. There was nothing in her file. My guess is they waited for her killer to run a string of murders so they'd have something more concrete to work with. It's the kind of senseless crime that usually gets repeated." I closed my eyes for a moment, reaching for an errant thought. "But he didn't repeat," I said. "So they put it on a back burner and then they took it off the stove altogether."

"I don't know much about police work. I've been involved largely with estates and trusts." He tried a smile. "Most of my clients die of natural causes. Murder's an exception."

"It generally is. I'll probably never find him. I certainly don't expect to find him. Just killing her and moving on, hell, and it was all those months ago. He could have been a sailor off a ship, got tanked up and went nuts and he's in Macao or Port-au-Prince by now. No witnesses and no clues and no suspects and the trail's three months cold by now, and it's a fair bet the killer doesn't remember what he did. So many murders take place in blackout, you know."

"Blackout?" He frowned. "You don't mean in the dark?"

"Alcoholic blackout. The prisons are full of men who got drunk and shot their wives or their best friends. Now they're serving twenty-to-life for something they don't remember. No recollection at all."

The idea unsettled him, and he looked especially young now. "That's frightening," he said. "Really terrifying."

"Yes."

"I originally gave some thought to criminal law. My Uncle Jack talked me out of it. He said you either starve or you spend your time helping professional criminals beat the system. He said that was the only way you made good money out of a criminal practice and what you wound up doing was unpleasant and basically immoral. Of course there are a couple of superstar criminal lawyers, the hotshots everybody knows, but the other ninety-nine percent fit what Uncle Jack said."

"I would think so, yes."

"I guess I made the right decision." He took his glasses off, inspected them, decided they were clean, put them back on again. "Sometimes I'm not so sure," he said. "Sometimes I wonder. I'll get that list for you. I should probably check with someone to make sure it's all right but I'm not going to bother. You know lawyers. If you ask them whether it's all right to do something they'll automatically say no. Because inaction is always safer than action and they can't get in trouble for giving you bad advice if they tell you to sit on your hands and do nothing. I'm going overboard. Most of the time I like what I do and I'm proud of my profession. This'll take me a few minutes. Do you want some coffee in the meantime?"

His girl brought me a cup, black, no sugar. No bourbon, either. By the time I was done with the coffee he had the list ready.

"If there's anything else I can do – "

I told him I'd let him know. He walked out to the elevator with me, waited for the cage to come wheezing up, shook my hand. I watched him turn and head back to his office and I had the feeling he'd have preferred to come along with me. In a day or so he'd change his mind, but right now he didn't seem too crazy about his job.

The next week was a curious one. I worked my way through the list Aaron Creighton had given me, knowing what I was doing was essentially purposeless but compulsive about doing it all the same.

There were thirty-two names on the list. I checked off my own and Eddie Halloran and Genevieve Strom. I put additional check marks next to six people who lived outside of New York. Then I had a go at the remaining twenty-three names. Creighton had done most of the spadework for me, finding addresses to match most of the names. He'd included the date each of the thirty-two codicils had been drawn, and that enabled me to attack the list in reverse chronological order, starting with those persons who'd been made beneficiaries most recently. If this was a method, there was madness to it; it was based on the notion that a person added recently to the will would be more likely to commit homicide for gain, and I'd already decided this wasn't that kind of a killing to begin with.

Well, it gave me something to do. And it led to some interesting conversations. If the people Mary Alice Redfield had chosen to remember ran to any type, my mind wasn't subtle enough to discern it. They ranged in age, in ethnic background, in gender and sexual orientation, in economic status. Most of them were as mystified as Eddie and Genevieve and I about the bag lady's largesse, but once in a while I'd encounter someone who attributed it to some act of kindness he'd performed, and there was a young man named Jerry Forgash who was in no doubt whatsoever. He was some form of Jesus freak and he'd given poor Mary a couple of tracts and a Get Smart – Get Saved button, presumably a twin to the one he wore on the breast pocket of his chambray shirt. I suppose she put his gifts in one of her shopping bags.

"I told her Jesus loved her," he said, "and I suppose it won her soul for Christ. So of course she was grateful. Cast your bread upon the waters, Mr Scudder, Brother Matthew. You know there was a disciple of Christ named Matthew."

"I know."

He told me Jesus loved me and that I should get smart and get saved. I managed not to get a button but I had to take a couple of tracts from him. I didn't have a shopping bag so I stuck them in my pocket, and a couple of nights later I read them before I went to bed. They didn't win my soul for Christ but you never know.

I didn't run the whole list. People were hard to find and I wasn't in any big rush to find them. It wasn't that kind of a case. It wasn't a case at all, really, merely an obsession, and there was surely no need to race the clock. Or the calendar. If anything, I was probably reluctant to finish up the names on the list. Once I ran out of them I'd have to find some other way to approach the woman's murder and I was damned if I knew where to start.

While I was doing all this, an odd thing happened. The word got around that I was investigating the woman's death, and the whole neighborhood became very much aware of Mary Alice Redfield. People began to seek me out. Ostensibly they had information to give me or theories to advance, but neither the information nor the theories ever seemed to amount to anything substantial, and I came to see that they were merely there as a prelude to conversation. Someone would start off by saying he'd seen Mary selling the *Post* the afternoon before she was killed, and that would serve as the opening wedge of a discussion of the bag woman, or bag women in general, or various qualities of the neighborhood, or violence in American life, or whatever.

A lot of people started off talking about the bag lady and wound up talking about themselves. I guess most conversations work out that way.

A nurse from Roosevelt said she never saw a shopping bag lady without hearing an inner voice say *There but for the grace of God.* And she was not the only woman who confessed she worried about ending up that way. I guess it's a specter that haunts women who live alone, just as the vision of the Bowery derelict clouds the peripheral vision of hard-drinking men.

Genevieve Strom turned up at Armstrong's one night. We talked briefly about the bag lady. Two nights later she came back again and we took turns spending our inheritances on rounds of drinks. The drinks hit her with some force and a little past midnight she decided it was time to go. I said I'd see her home. At the corner of Fifty-seventh Street she stopped in her tracks and said, "No men in the room. That's one of Mrs Larkin's rules."

"Old-fashioned, isn't she?"

"She runs a daycent establishment." Her mock-Irish accent was heavier than the landlady's. Her eyes, hard to read in the lamplight, raised to meet mine. "Take me someplace."

I took her to my hotel, a less decent establishment than Mrs Larkin's. We did each other little good but no harm, and it beat being alone.

Another night I ran into Barry Mosedale at Polly's Cage. He told me there was a singer at Kid Gloves who was doing a number about the bag lady. "I can find out how you can reach him," he offered.

"Is he there now?"

He nodded and checked his watch. "He goes on in fifteen minutes. But you don't want to go there, do you?"

"Why not?"

"Hardly your sort of crowd, Matt."

"Cops go anywhere."

"Indeed they do, and they're welcome wherever they go, aren't they? Just let me drink this and I'll accompany you, if that's all right. You need someone to lend you immoral support."

Kid Gloves is a gay bar on Fifty-sixth west of Ninth. The decor is just a little aggressively gay lib. There's a small raised stage, a scattering of tables, a piano, a loud jukebox. Barry Mosedale and I stood at the bar. I'd been there before and knew better than to order their coffee. I had straight bourbon. Barry had his on ice with a splash of soda.

Halfway through the drink Gordon Lurie was introduced. He wore tight jeans and a flowered shirt, sat on stage on a folding chair, sang ballads he'd written himself with his own guitar for accompaniment. I don't know if he was any good or not. It sounded to me as though all the songs had the same melody, but that may just have been a similarity of style. I don't have much of an ear.

After a song about a summer romance in Amsterdam, Gordon Lurie announced that the next number was dedicated to the memory of Mary Alice Redfield. Then he sang.

> *She's a shopping bag lady who lives on*
> *the sidewalks of Broadway*
> *Wearing all of her clothes and her years*
> *on her back*
> *Toting dead dreams in an old paper sack*
> *Searching the trashcans for something she*
> *lost here on Broadway –*
> *Shopping bag lady . . .*
>
> *You'd never know but she once was an*
> *actress on Broadway*

Speaking the words that they stuffed in
her head
Reciting the lines of the life that she led
Thrilling her fans and her friends and her
lovers on Broadway –
Shopping bag lady . . .

There are demons who lurk in the corner
of minds and of Broadway
And after the omens and portents and
signs
Came the day she forgot to remember her
lines
Put her life on a leash and took it out
walking on Broadway –
Shopping bag lady . . .

There were a couple more verses and the shopping bag lady in the song wound up murdered in a doorway, dying in defense of the "tattered old treasures she mined in the trashcans of Broadway." The song went over well and got a bigger hand than any of the ones that had preceded it.

I asked Barry who Gordon Lurie was.

"You know very nearly as much as I," he said. "He started here Tuesday. I find him whelming, personally. Neither overwhelming nor underwhelming but somewhere in the middle."

"Mary Alice never spent much time on Broadway. I never saw her more than a block from Ninth Avenue."

"Poetic license, I'm sure. The song would lack a certain something if you substituted Ninth Avenue for Broadway. As it stands it sounds a little like 'Rhinestone Cowboy.'"

"Lurie live around here?"

"I don't know where he lives. I have the feeling he's Canadian. So many people are nowadays. It used to be that no one was Canadian and now simply everybody is. I'm sure it must be a virus."

We listened to the rest of Gordon Lurie's act. Then Barry leaned forward and chatted with the bartender to find out how I could get backstage. I found my way to what passed for a dressing room at Kid Gloves. It must have been a ladies' lavatory in a prior incarnation.

I went in there thinking I'd made a breakthrough, that Lurie had killed her and now he was dealing with his guilt by singing about her. I don't think I really believed this but it supplied me with direction and momentum.

I told him my name and that I was interested in his act. He wanted to know if I was from a record company. "Am I on the threshold of a great opportunity? Am I about to become an overnight success after years of travail?"

We got out of the tiny room and left the club through a side door. Three doors down the block we sat in a cramped booth at a coffee shop. He ordered a Greek salad and we both had coffee.

I told him I was interested in his song about the bag lady.

He brightened. "Oh, do you like it? Personally I think it's the best thing I've written. I just wrote it a couple of days ago. I opened next door Tuesday night. I got to New York three weeks ago and I had a two-week booking in the West Village. A place called David's Table. Do you know it?"

"I don't think so."

"Another stop on the K-Y circuit. Either there aren't any straight people in New York or they don't go to nightclubs. But I was there two weeks, and then I opened at Kid Gloves, and afterward I was sitting and drinking with some people and somebody was talking about the shopping bag lady and I had had enough Amaretto to be maudlin on the subject. I woke up Wednesday morning with a splitting headache and the first verse of the song buzzing in my splitting head, and I sat up immediately and wrote it down, and as I was writing one verse the next would come bubbling to the surface, and before I knew it I had all six verses." He took a cigarette, then paused in the act of lighting it to fix his eyes on me. "You told me your name," he said, "but I don't remember it."

"Matthew Scudder."

"Yes. You're the person investigating her murder."

"I'm not sure that's the right word. I've been talking to people, seeing what I can come up with. Did you know her before she was killed?"

He shook his head. "I was never even in this neighborhood before. *Oh.* I'm not a suspect, am I? Because I haven't been in New York since the fall. I haven't bothered to figure out where I was when she was killed but I was in California at Christmas-time and I'd gotten as far east as Chicago in early March, so I do have a fairly solid alibi."

"I never really suspected you. I think I just wanted to hear your song." I sipped some coffee. "Where did you get the facts of her life? Was she an actress?"

"I don't think so. Was she? It wasn't really *about* her, you know. It was inspired by her story but I didn't know her and I never knew anything about her. The past few days I've been paying a lot of attention to bag ladies, though. And other street people."

"I know what you mean."

"Are there more of them in New York or is it just that they're so much more visible here? In California everybody drives, you don't see people on the street. I'm from Canada, rural Ontario, and the first city I ever spent much time in was Toronto, and there are crazy people on the streets there but it's nothing like New York. Does the city drive them crazy or does it just tend to draw crazy people?"

"I don't know."

"Maybe they're not crazy. Maybe they just hear a different drummer. I wonder who killed her."

"We'll probably never know."

"What I really wonder is *why* she was killed. In my song I made up some reason. That somebody wanted what was in her bags. I think it works as a song that way but I don't think there's much chance that it happened like that. Why would anyone kill the poor thing?"

"I don't know."

"They say she left people money. People she hardly knew. Is that the truth?" I nodded. "And she left me a song. I don't even feel that I wrote it. I woke up with it. I never set eyes on her and she touched my life. That's strange, isn't it?"

Everything was strange. The strangest part of all was the way it ended.

It was a Monday night. The Mets were at Shea and I'd taken my sons to a game. The Dodgers were in for a three-game series which they eventually swept as they'd been sweeping everything lately. The boys and I got to watch them knock Jon Matlack out of the box and go on to shell his several replacements. The final count was something like 13–4. We stayed in our seats until the last out. Then I saw them home and caught a train back to the city.

So it was past midnight when I reached Armstrong's. Trina brought me a large double and a mug of coffee without being asked. I knocked back half of the bourbon and was dumping the rest into my coffee when she told me somebody'd been looking for me earlier. "He was in three times in the past two hours," she said. "A wiry guy, high forehead, bushy eyebrows, sort of a bulldog jaw. I guess the word for it is underslung."

"Perfectly good word."

"I said you'd probably get here sooner or later."

"I always do. Sooner or later."

"Uh-huh. You okay, Matt?"

"The Mets lost a close one."

"I heard it was thirteen to four."

"That's close for them these days. Did he say what it was about?"

He hadn't, but within the half hour he came in again and I was there to be found. I recognized him from Trina's description as soon as he came through the door. He looked faintly familiar but he was nobody I knew. I suppose I'd seen him around the neighborhood.

Evidently he knew me by sight because he found his way to my table without asking directions and took a chair without being invited to sit. He didn't say anything for a while and neither did I. I had a fresh bourbon and coffee in front of me and I took a sip and looked him over.

He was under thirty. His cheeks were hollow and the flesh of his face was stretched over his skull like leather that had shrunk upon drying.

He wore a forest green work shirt and a pair of khaki pants. He needed a shave.

Finally he pointed at my cup and asked me what I was drinking. When I told him he said all he drank was beer.

"They have beer here," I said.

"Maybe I'll have what you're drinking." He turned in his chair and waved for Trina. When she came over he said he'd have bourbon and coffee, the same as I was having. He didn't say anything more until she brought the drink. Then, after he had spent quite some time stirring it, he took a sip. "Well," he said, "that's not so bad. That's okay."

"Glad you like it."

"I don't know if I'd order it again, but at least now I know what it's like."

"That's something."

"I seen you around. Matt Scudder. Used to be a cop, private eye now, blah blah blah. Right?"

"Close enough."

"My name's Floyd. I never liked it but I'm stuck with it, right? I could change it but who'm I kidding? Right?"

"If you say so."

"If I don't somebody else will. Floyd Karp, that's the full name. I didn't tell you my last name, did I? That's it, Floyd Karp."

"Okay."

"Okay, okay, okay." He pursed his lips, blew out air in a silent whistle. "What do we do now, Matt? Huh? That's what I want to know."

"I'm not sure what you mean, Floyd."

"Oh, you know what I'm getting at, driving at, getting at. You know, don't you?"

By this time I suppose I did.

"I killed that old lady. Took her life, stabbed her with my knife." He flashed the saddest smile. "Steee-rangled her with her skeeee-arf. Hoist her with her own whatchacallit, petard. What's a petard, Matt?"

"I don't know, Floyd. Why'd you kill her?"

He looked at me, he looked at his coffee, he looked at me again.

He said, "Had to."

"Why?"

"Same as the bourbon and coffee. Had to *see*. Had to taste it and find out what it was like." His eyes met mine. His were very large, hollow, empty. I fancied I could see right through them to the blackness at the back of his skull. "I couldn't get my mind away from murder," he said. His voice was more sober now, the mocking playful quality gone from it. "I tried. I just couldn't do it. It was on my mind all the time and I was afraid of what I might do. I couldn't function, I couldn't think, I just saw blood and death all the time. I was afraid to close my eyes for fear of what I might see. I

would just stay up, days it seemed, and then I'd be tired enough to pass
out the minute I closed my eyes. I stopped eating. I used to be fairly heavy
and the weight just fell off of me."

"When did all this happen, Floyd?"

"I don't know. All winter. And I thought if I went and did it once I
would know if I was a man or a monster or what. And I got this knife,
and I went out a couple nights but lost my nerve, and then one night –
I don't want to talk about that part of it now."

"All right."

"I almost couldn't do it, but I couldn't *not* do it, and then I was doing
it and it went on forever. It was *horrible*."

"Why didn't you stop?"

"I don't know. I think I was afraid to stop. That doesn't make any sense,
does it? I just don't know. It was all crazy, insane, like being in a movie and
being in the audience at the same time. Watching myself."

"No one saw you do it?"

"No. I threw the knife down a sewer. I went home. I put all my clothes
in the incinerator, the ones I was wearing. I kept throwing up. All that
night I would throw up even when my stomach was empty. Dry heaves,
Department of Dry Heaves. And then I guess I fell asleep, I don't know
when or how but I did, and the next day I woke up and thought I dreamed
it. But of course I didn't."

"No."

"And what I did think was that it was over. I did it and I knew I'd never
want to do it again. It was something crazy that happened and I could
forget about it. And I thought that was what happened."

"That you managed to forget about it?"

A nod. "But I guess I didn't. And now everybody's talking about her.
Mary Alice Redfield, I killed her without knowing her name. Nobody knew
her name and now everybody knows it and it's all back in my mind. And
I heard you were looking for me, and I guess, I guess . . ." He frowned,
chasing a thought around in his mind like a dog trying to capture his
tail. Then he gave it up and looked at me. "So here I am," he said. "So
here I am."

"Yes."

"Now what happens?"

"I think you'd better tell the police about it, Floyd."

"Why?"

"I suppose for the same reason you told me."

He thought about it. After a long time he nodded. "All right," he said.
"I can accept that. I'd never kill anybody again. I know that. But – you're
right. I have to tell them. I don't know who to see or what to say or, hell,
I just – "

"I'll go with you if you want."

"Yeah. I want you to."

"I'll have a drink and then we'll go. You want another?"

"No. I'm not much of a drinker."

I had it without the coffee this time. After Trina brought it I asked him how he'd picked his victim. Why the bag lady?

He started to cry. No sobs, just tears spilling from his deep-set eyes. After a while he wiped them on his sleeve.

"Because she didn't count," he said. "That's what I thought. She was nobody. Who cared if she died? Who'd miss her?" He closed his eyes tight. "Everybody misses her," he said. "Everybody."

So I took him in. I don't know what they'll do with him. It's not my problem.

It wasn't really a case and I didn't really solve it. As far as I can see I didn't do anything. It was the talk that drove Floyd Karp from cover, and no doubt I helped some of the talk get started, but some of it would have gotten around without me. All those legacies of Mary Alice Redfield's had made her a nine-day wonder in the neighborhood. It was one of those legacies that got me involved.

Maybe she caught her own killer. Maybe he caught himself, as everyone does. Maybe no man's an island and maybe everybody is.

All I know is I lit a candle for the woman, and I suspect I'm not the only one who did.

BLACK PUDDING

David Goodis

THEY SPOTTED HIM on Race Street between Ninth and Tenth. It was Chinatown in the tenderloin of Philadelphia and he stood gazing into the window of the Wong Ho restaurant and wishing he had the cash to buy himself some egg-foo-yung. The menu in the window priced egg-foo-yung at eighty cents an order and he had exactly thirty-one cents in his pocket. He shrugged and started to turn away from the window and just then he heard them coming.

It was their footsteps that told him who they were. There was the squeaky sound of Oscar's brand-new shoes. And the clumping noise of Coley's heavy feet. It was nine years since he'd heard their footsteps but he remembered that Oscar had a weakness for new shoes and Coley always walked heavily.

He faced them. They were smiling at him, their features somewhat greenish under the green neon glow that drifted through after-midnight blackness. He saw the weasel eyes and buzzard nose of little Oscar. He transferred his gaze to the thick lips and puffed-out cheeks of tall, obese Coley.

"Hello, Ken." It was Oscar's purring voice, Oscar's lips scarcely moving.

"Hello," he said to both of them. He blinked a few times. Now the shock was coming. He could feel the waves of shock surging towards him.

"We been looking for you," Coley said. He flipped his thick thumb over his shoulder to indicate the black Olds 88 parked across the street. "We've driven that car clear across the country."

Ken blinked again. The shock had hit him and now it was past and he was blinking from worry. He knew why they'd been looking for him and he was very worried.

He said quietly, "How'd you know I was in Philly?"

"Grapevine," Oscar said. "It's strictly coast-to-coast. It starts from San Quentin and we get tipped off in Los Angeles. It's a letter telling the Boss you been paroled. That's three weeks ago. Then we get letters from Denver and Omaha and a wire from Chicago. And then a phone call from Detroit. We wait to see how far east you'll travel. Finally we get the call from Philly, and the man tells us you're on the bum around Skid Row."

Ken shrugged. He tried to sound casual as he said, "Three thousand miles is a long trip. You must have been anxious to see me."

Oscar nodded. "Very anxious." He sort of floated closer to Ken. And Coley also moved in. It was slow and quiet and it didn't seem like menace but they were crowding him and finally they had him backed up against the restaurant window.

He said to himself, *They've got you, they've found you and they've got you and you're finished.*

He shrugged again. "You can't do it here."

"Can't we?" Oscar purred.

"It's a crowded street," Ken said. He turned his head to look at the lazy parade of tenderloin citizens on both sides of the street. He saw the bums and the beggars, the winos and the ginheads, the yellow faces of middle-aged opium smokers and the grey faces of two-bit scufflers and hustlers.

"Don't look at them," Oscar said. "They can't help you. Even if they could, they wouldn't."

Ken's smile was sad and resigned. "You're so right," he said. His shoulders drooped and his head went down and he saw Oscar reaching into a jacket pocket and taking out the silver-handled tool that had a button on it to release a five-inch blade. He knew there would be no further talk, only action, and it would happen within the next split-second.

In that tiny fraction of time, some gears clanged to shift from low to high in Ken's brain. His senses and reflexes, dulled from nine years in prison, were suddenly keen and acutely technical and there was no emotion on his face as he moved. He moved very fast, his arms crossing to shape an X, the left hand flat and rigid and banging against Oscar's wrist, the right hand a fist that caught Coley in the mouth. It sent the two of them staggering backward and gave him the space he wanted and he darted through the gap, sprinting east on Race Street toward Ninth.

As he turned the corner to head north on Ninth, he glanced backward and saw them getting into the Olds. He took a deep breath and continued running up Ninth. He ran straight ahead for approximately fifteen yards and then turned again to make a dash down a narrow alley. In the middle of the alley he hopped a fence, ran across a back-yard, hopped another fence, then a few more backyards with more fence-hopping, and then the opened window of a tenement cellar. He lunged at the window, went in head-first,

groped for a handhold, couldn't find any, and plunged through eight feet
of blackness on to a pile of empty boxes and tin cans. He landed on his side,
his thigh taking most of the impact, so that it didn't hurt too much. He rolled
over and hit the floor and lay there flat on his belly. From a few feet away a
pair of green eyes stared at him and he stared back, and then he grinned
as though to say, *Don't be afraid, pussy, stay here and keep me company, it's
a tough life and an evil world and us alleycats got to stick together.*

But the cat wasn't trusting any living soul. He let out a soft meow and
scampered away. Ken sighed and his grin faded and he felt the pressure
of the blackness and the quiet and the loneliness. His mind reached slowly
for the road going backward nine years . . .

It was Los Angeles, and they were a small outfit operating from a first-floor
apartment near Figueroa and Jefferson. Their business was armed robbery
and their work-area included Beverly Hills and Bel-Air and the wealthy
residential districts of Pasadena. They concentrated on expensive jewelry
and wouldn't touch any job that offered less than a ten-grand haul.

There were five of them, Ken and Oscar and Coley and Ken's wife and
the Boss. The name of the Boss was Riker and he was very kind to Ken until
the possession of Ken's wife became a need and then a craving and finally
an obsession. It showed in Riker's eyes whenever he looked at her. She was
a platinum blonde dazzler, a former burlesque dancer named Hilda. She'd
been married to Ken for seven months when Riker reached the point where
he couldn't stand it any longer and during a job in Bel-air he banged Ken's
skull with the butt end of a revolver. When the police arrived, Ken was
unconscious on the floor and later in the hospital they asked him questions
but he wouldn't answer. In the courtroom he sat with his head bandaged
and they asked him more questions and he wouldn't answer. They gave
him five-to-twenty and during his first month in San Quentin he learned
from his lawyer that Hilda had obtained a Reno divorce and was married
to Riker. He went more or less insane and couldn't be handled and they
put him in solitary.

Later they had him in the infirmary, chained to the bed, and they tried
some psychology. They told him he'd regain his emotional health if he'd talk
and name some names. He laughed at them. Whenever they coaxed him to
talk, he laughed in their faces and presently they'd shrug and walk away.

His first few years in Quentin were spent either in solitary or the infirmary,
or under special guard. Then, gradually, he quieted down. He became very
quiet and in the laundry-room he worked very hard and was extremely
co-operative. During the fifth year he was up for parole and they asked
him about the Bel-Air job and he replied quite reasonably that he couldn't
remember, he was afraid to remember, he wanted to forget all about it and
arrange a new life for himself. They told him he'd talk or he'd do the limit.
He said he was sorry but he couldn't give them the information they wanted.

He explained that he was trying to get straight with himself and be clean inside and he wouldn't feel clean if he earned his freedom that way.

So then it was nine years and they were convinced he'd finally paid his debt to the people of California. They gave him a suit of clothes and a ten-dollar bill and told him he was a free man.

In a Sacramento hash-house he worked as a dishwasher just long enough to earn the bus-fare for a trip across the country. He was thinking in terms of the town where he'd been born and raised, telling himself he'd made a wrong start in Philadelphia and the thing to do was go back there and start again and make it right this time, really legitimate. The parole board okayed the job he'd been promised. That was a healthy thought and it made the bus-trip very enjoyable. But the nicest thing about the bus was its fast engine that took him away from California, far away from certain faces he didn't want to see.

Yet now, as he rested on the floor of the tenement cellar, he could see the faces again. The faces were worried and frightened and he saw them in his brain and heard their trembling voices. He heard Riker saying, "They've released him from Quentin. We'll have to do something." And Hilda saying, "What can we do?" And Riker replying, "We'll get him before he gets us."

He sat up, colliding with an empty tin can that rolled across the floor and made a clatter. For some moments there was quiet and then he heard a shuffling sound and a voice saying, "Who's there?"

It was a female voice, sort of a cracked whisper. It had a touch of asthma in it, some alcohol, and something else that had no connection with health or happiness.

Ken didn't say anything. He hoped she'd go away. Maybe she'd figure it was a rat that had knocked over the tin can and she wouldn't bother to investigate.

But he heard the shuffling footsteps approaching through the blackness. He focused directly ahead and saw the silhouette coming towards him. She was on the slender side, neatly constructed. It was a very interesting silhouette. Her height was approximately five-five and he estimated her weight in the neighborhood of one-ten. He sat up straighter. He was very anxious to get a look at her face.

She came closer and there was the scratchy sound of a match against a matchbox. The match flared and he saw her face. She had medium-brown eyes that matched the color of her hair, and her nose and lips were nicely sculptured, somewhat delicate but blending prettily with the shape of her head. He told himself she was a very pretty girl. But just then he saw the scar.

It was a wide jagged scar that started high on her forehead and crawled down the side of her face and ended less than an inch above her upper lip. The color of it was a livid purple with lateral streaks of pink and white. It was a terrible scar, really hideous.

She saw that he was wincing, but it didn't seem to bother her. The lit match stayed lit and she was sizing him up. She saw a man of medium height and weight, about thirty-six years old, with yellow hair that needed cutting, a face that needed shaving, and sad lonely grey eyes that needed someone's smile.

She tried to smile for him. But only one side of her mouth could manage it. On the other side the scar was like a hook that pulled at her flesh and caused a grimace that was more anguish than physical shame. Such a pretty girl. And so young. She couldn't be more than twenty-five. Well, some people had all the luck. All the rotten luck.

The match was burned halfway down when she reached into the pocket of a tattered dress and took out a candle. She went through the process of lighting the candle and melting the base of it. The softened wax adhered to the cement floor of the cellar and she sat down facing him and said quietly, "All right, let's have it. What's the pitch?"

He pointed backward to the opened window to indicate the November night. He said, "It's chilly out there. I came in to get warm."

She leaned forward just a little to peer at his eyes. Then, shaking her head slowly, she murmured, "No sale."

He shrugged. He didn't say anything.

"Come on," she urged gently. "Let's try it again."

"All right." He grinned at her. And then it came out easily. "I'm hiding."

"From the Law?"

"No," he said. "From trouble."

He started to tell her about it. He couldn't understand why he was telling her. It didn't make sense that he should be spilling the story to someone he'd just met in a dark cellar, someone out of nowhere. But she was company and he needed company. He went on telling her.

It took more than an hour. He was providing all the details of events stretched across nine years. The candlelight showed her sitting there, not moving, her eyes riveted to his face as he spoke in low tones. Sometimes there were pauses, some of them long, some very long, but she never interrupted, she waited patiently while he groped for the words to make the meaning clear.

Finally he said, " – It's a cinch they won't stop, they'll get me sooner or later."

"If they find you," she said.

"They'll find me."

"Not here."

He stared at the flickering candle. "They'll spend money to get information. There's more than one big mouth in this neighborhood. And the biggest mouths of all belong to the landlords."

"There's no landlord here," she told him. "There's no tenants except me and you."

"Nobody upstairs?"

"Only mice and rats and roaches. It's a condemned house and City Hall calls it a firetrap and from the first floor up the windows are boarded. You can't get up because there's no stairs. One of these days the City'll tear down this dump but I'll worry about that when it happens."

He looked at her. "You live here in the cellar?"

She nodded. "It's a good place to play solitaire."

He smiled and murmured. "Some people like to be alone."

"I don't like it," she said. Then, with a shrug, she pointed to the scar on her face. "What man would live with me?"

He stopped smiling. He didn't say anything.

She said, "It's a long drop when you're tossed out of a third-story window. Most folks are lucky and they land on their feet. I came down head first, cracked my collar-bone and got a fractured skull, and split my face wide open."

He took a closer look at the livid scar. For some moments he was quiet and then he frowned thoughtfully and said, "Maybe it won't be there for long. It's not as deep as I thought it was. If you had it treated – "

"No," she said. "The hell with it."

"You wouldn't need much cash," he urged quietly. "You could go to a clinic. They're doing fancy tricks with plastic surgery these days."

"Yeah, I know." Her voice was toneless. She wasn't looking at him. "The point is, I want the scar to stay there. It keeps me away from men. I've had too many problems with men and now, whenever they see my face, they turn their heads the other way. And that's fine with me. That's just how I want it."

He frowned again. This time it was a deeper frown and it wasn't just thoughtful. He said, "Who threw you out of the window?"

"My husband." She laughed without sound. "My wonderful husband."

"Where is he now."

"In the cemetery," she said. She shrugged again, and her tone was matter-of-fact. "It happened while I was in hospital. I think he got to the point where he couldn't stand to live with himself. Or maybe he just did it for kicks, I don't know. Anyway, he got hold of a razor and cut his own throat. When they found him, he was very, very dead."

"Well, that's one way of ending a marriage."

Again she uttered the soundless laugh. "It was a fine marriage while it lasted. I was drunk most of the time. I had to get drunk to take what he dished out. He had some weird notions about wedding vows."

"He wasn't faithful to you?"

"Oh! It wasn't that. No. He went out of his way to throw me into the company of other men. At first I thought it was odd, but then I found that it was deliberate, calculated. He expected me to compromise myself and then he'd demand money and if I didn't co-operate he'd beat me. It was a hell of a thing to happen to anyone with any decent ideals. I don't like blackmail – even now. But then it was mental torture to me. So I got it in the neck either way. I used to have bad dreams about it, and I mean bad. I still have them sometimes, so then I need sweet dreams, and that's when I reach for the pipe."

"The pipe?"

"Opium," she said. She said it with fondness and affection. "Opium." There was tenderness in her eyes. "That's my new husband."

He nodded understandingly.

She said, "I get it from a Chinaman on Ninth Street. He's a user himself and he's more than eighty years old and still in there pitching, so I guess with O it's like anything else, it's all a matter of how you use it." Her voice dropped off just a little and her eyes were dull and sort of dismal as she added, "I wish I didn't need so much of it. It takes most of my weekly salary."

"What kind of work you do?"

"I scrub floors," she said. "In night-clubs and dance-halls. All day long I scrub the floors to make them clean and shiny for the night-time customers. Some nights I sit here and think of the pretty girls dancing on them polished floors. The pretty girls with flowers in their hair and no scars on their faces –" She broke it off abruptly, her hand making a brushing gesture as though to disparage the self-pity. She stood up and said, "I gotta go out to do some shopping. You wanna wait here till I come back?"

Without waiting for his answer, she moved across the cellar toward a battered door leading to the backyard. As she opened the door, she turned and looked at him. "Make yourself comfortable," she said. "There's a mattress in the next room. It ain't the Ritz Carlton exactly, but it's better than nothing."

He was asking himself whether he should stay there.

He heard her saying, "Incidentally, my name is Tillie."

She stood there waiting.

"Kenneth," he said. "Kenneth Rockland."

But that wasn't what she was waiting for. Several moments passed, and then somehow he knew what she wanted him to say.

He said, "I'll be here when you come back."

"Good." The candlelight showed her crooked grin, a grimace on the scarred face. But what he saw was a gentle smile. It seemed to drift toward him like a soothing caress. And then he heard her saying. "Maybe I'll come back with some news. You told me it was two men. There's a chance I can check on them if you'll tell me what they look like."

He shook his head. "You better stay out of it. You might get hurt."

"Nothing can hurt me," she said. She pointed her finger at the wreckage of her face. Her tone was almost pleading as she said, "Come on, tell me what they look like."

He shrugged. He gave a brief description of Oscar and Coley. And the Olds 88.

"Check," Tillie said. "I don't have 20–20 but I'll keep them open and see what's happening."

She turned and walked out and the door closed. Ken lifted himself from the floor and picked up the candle. He walked across the cement floor and the candle showed him a small space off to one side, a former coal-bin arranged with a mattress against the wall, a splintered chair and a splintered bureau and a table stacked with books. There was a candleholder on the table and he set the candle on it and then he had a look at the books.

It was an odd mixture of literature. There were books dealing with idyllic romance, strictly from fluttering hearts and soft moonlight and violins. And there were books that probed much deeper, explaining the scientific side of sex. There was one book in particular that looked as though she'd been concentrating on it. The pages were considerably thumbed and she'd used a pencil to underline certain paragraphs. It was clear that she was faced with the hell of a personal problem she was trying to solve intelligently and couldn't.

He shook his head slowly. He thought, *It's a damn shame . . .*

And then, for some unaccountable reason, he thought of Hilda. She flowed into his mind with a rustling of silk that sheathed the exquisite contours of her slender torso and legs. Her platinum blonde hair was glimmering and her long-lashed green eyes were beckoning to say, Come on, take my hand and we'll go down Memory Lane.

He shut his eyes tightly. He wondered why he was thinking about her. A long time ago he'd managed to get her out of his mind and he couldn't understand what had brought her back again. He begged himself to get rid of the thought, it was a white-hot memory that disturbed him profoundly. Without sound he said, *Goddamn her.*

And suddenly he realised why he was thinking of Hilda. It was like a curtain lifted to reveal the hidden channels of his brain. He was comparing Hilda's physical perfection with the scarred face of Tillie. His eyes were open and he gazed down at the mattress on the floor and for a moment he saw Hilda on the mattress. She smiled teasingly and then she shook her head and said, *Nothing doing.* So then she vanished and in the next moment it was Tillie on the mattress but somehow he didn't feel bitter or disappointed; he had the feeling that the perfection was all on Tillie's side.

He took off his shoes and lowered himself to the mattress. He yawned a few times and then he fell asleep.

*   *   *

A voice said, "Kenneth – "

He was instantly awake. He looked up and saw Tillie. He smiled at her and said, "What time is it?"

"Half-past five." She had a paper bag in her hand and she was taking things out of the bag and putting them on the table. There was some dried fish and a package of tea leaves and some cold fried noodles. She reached deeper into the bag and took out a bottle containing colorless liquid.

"Rice wine," she said. She set the bottle on the table. Then again she reached into the bag and her hand came out holding a cardboard box.

"Opium?" he murmured.

She nodded. "I got some cigarettes, too." She took a pack of Luckies from her pocket, opened the pack and extended it to him.

He sat up and put a cigarette in his mouth and used the candle to light it. He said, "You going to smoke the opium?"

"No, I'll smoke what you're smoking."

He put another cigarette in his mouth and lit it and handed it to her.

She took a few drags and then she said quietly, "I didn't want to wake you up, but I thought you'd want to hear the news."

He blinked a few times. "What news?"

"I saw them," she said.

He blinked again. "Where?"

"On Tenth Street." She took more smoke into her mouth and let it come out of her nose. "It was a couple hours ago, after I come out of the Chinaman's."

He sat up straighter. "You been watching them for two hours?"

"Watching them? I been with them. They took me for a ride."

He stared at her. His mouth was open but no sound came out.

Tillie grinned. "They didn't know I was in the car."

He took a deep breath. "How'd you manage it?"

She shrugged. "It was easy. I saw them sitting in the car and then they got out and I followed them. They were taking a stroll around the block and peeping into alleys and finally I heard the little one saying they might as well powder and come back tomorrow. The big one said they should keep on searching the neighborhood. They got into an argument and I had a feeling the little one would win. So I walked back to the car. The door was open and I climbed in the back and got flat on the floor. About five minutes later they're up front and the car starts and we're riding."

His eyes were narrow. "Where?"

"Downtown," she said. "It wasn't much of a ride. It only took a few minutes. They parked in front of a house on Spruce near Eleventh. I watched them go in. Then I got out of the car – "

"And walked back here?"

"Not right away," she said. "First I cased the house."

Silly Tillie, he thought. *If they'd seen her they'd have dragged her in and killed her.*

She said, "It's one of them little old-fashioned houses. There's a vacant lot on one side and on the other side there's an alley. I went down the alley and came up on the back porch and peeped through the window. They were in the kitchen, the four of them."

He made no sound, but his lips shaped the word. "Four?" And then, with sound, "Who were the other two?"

"A man and a woman."

He stiffened. He tried to get up from the mattress and couldn't move. His eyes aimed past Tillie as he said tightly, "Describe them."

"The man was about five-ten and sort of beefy. I figure about two hundred. He looked about forty or so. Had a suntan and wore expensive clothes. Brown wavy hair and brown eyes and – "

"That's Riker," he murmured. He managed to lift himself from the mattress. His voice was a whisper as he said, "Now let's have the woman."

"She was something," Tillie said. "She was really something."

"Blonde?" And with both hands he made a gesture begging Tillie to speed the reply.

"Platinum blonde," Tillie said. "With the kind of a face that makes men turn round and stretch their necks to look at. That kind of a face, and a shape that goes along with it. She was wearing – "

"Pearls," he said. "She always had a weakness for pearls."

Tillie didn't say anything.

He moved past Tillie. He stood facing the dark wall of the cellar and seeing the yellow-black play of candlelight and shadow on the cracked plaster. "Hilda," he said. "Hilda."

It was quiet for some moments. He told himself it was wintertime and he wondered if he was sweating.

Then very slowly he turned and looked at Tillie. She was sitting on the edge of the mattress and drinking from the bottle of rice-wine. She took it in short, measured gulps, taking it down slowly to get the full effect of it. When the bottle was half-empty she raised her head and grinned at him and said, "Have some?"

He nodded. She handed him the bottle and he drank. The Chinese wine was mostly fire and it burned all the way going down and when it hit his belly it was electric hot. But the climate it sent to his brain was cool and mild and the mildness showed in his eyes. His voice was quiet and relaxed as he said, "I thought Oscar and Coley made the trip alone. It didn't figure that Riker and Hilda would come with them. But now it adds. I can see the way it adds."

"It's a long ride from Los Angeles," Tillie said.

"They didn't mind. They enjoyed the ride."

"The scenery?"

"No," he said. "They weren't looking at the scenery. They were thinking of the setup here in Philly. With Oscar putting the blade in me and then the funeral and Riker seeing me in the coffin and telling himself his worries were over."

"And Hilda?"

"The same," he said. "She's been worried just as much as Riker. Maybe more."

Tillie nodded slowly. "From the story you told me, she's got more reason to worry."

He laughed lightly. He liked the sound of it and went on with it. He said, through the easy laughter, "They really don't need to worry. They're making it a big thing and it's nothing at all. I forgot all about them a long time ago. But they couldn't forget about me."

Tillie had her head inclined and she seemed to be studying the sound of his laughter. Some moments passed and then she said quietly, "You don't like black pudding?"

He didn't get the drift of that. He stopped laughing and his eyes were asking what she meant.

"There's an old saying," she said. "Revenge is black pudding."

He laughed again.

"Don't pull away from it," Tillie said. "Just listen to it. Let it hit you and sink in. Revenge is black pudding."

He went on laughing, shaking his head and saying, "I'm not in the market."

"You sure?"

"Positive," he said. Then, with a grin, "Only pudding I like is vanilla."

"The black tastes better," Tillie said. "I've had some, and I know. I had it when they told me he had done away with himself."

He winced slightly. He saw Tillie getting up from the mattress and moving towards him. He heard her saying, "That black pudding has a wonderful flavor. You ought to try a spoonful."

"No," he said. "No, Tillie."

She came closer. She spoke very slowly and there was a slight hissing in her voice. "They put you in prison for nine years. They cheated you and robbed you and tortured you."

"That's all past," he said. "That's from yesterday."

"It's from now." She stood very close to him. "They're itching to hit you again and see you dead. They won't stop until you're dead. That puts a poison label on them. And there's only one way to deal with poison. Get rid of it."

"No," he said. "I'll let it stay the way it is."

"You can't," Tillie said. "It's a choice you have to make. Either you'll drink bitter poison or you'll taste that sweet black pudding."

He grinned again. "There's a third choice."

"Like what?"

"This." And he pointed to the bottle of rice-wine. "I like the taste of this. Let's stay with it until it's empty."

"That won't solve the problem," Tillie said.

"The hell with the problem." His grin was wide. It was very wide and he didn't realise that it was forced.

"You fool," Tillie said.

He had the bottle raised and he was taking a drink.

"You poor fool," she said. Then she shrugged and turned away from him and lowered herself to the mattress.

The forced grin stayed on his face as he went on drinking. Now he was drinking slowly because the rice-wine dulled the action in his brain and he had difficulty lifting the bottle to his mouth. Gradually he became aware of a change taking place in the air of the cellar; it was thicker, sort of smokey. His eyes tried to focus and there was too much wine in him and he couldn't see straight. But then the smoke came up in front of his eyes and into his eyes. He looked down and saw the white clay pipe in Tillie's hand. She was sitting on the mattress with her legs crossed, Buddha-like, puffing at the opium, taking it in very slowly, the smoke coming out past the corners of her lips.

The grin faded from his face. And somehow the alcohol-mist was drifting away from his brain. He thought, *She smokes it because she's been kicked around.* But there was no pity in his eyes, just the level look of clear thinking. He said to himself, *There's only two kinds of people in this world, the ones who get kicked around and the ones who do the kicking.*

He lowered the bottle to the table. He turned and took a few steps going away and then heard Tillie saying, "Moving out?"

"No," he said. "Just taking a walk."

"Where?"

"Spruce Street," he said.

"Good," she said. "I'll go with you."

He shook his head. He faced her and saw that she'd put the pipe aside. She was getting up from the mattress. He went on shaking his head and saying, "It can't be played that way. I gotta do this alone."

She moved toward him. "Maybe it's good-bye."

"If it is," he said, "there's only one way to say it."

His eyes told her to come closer. He put his arms around her and held her with a tenderness and a feeling of not wanting to let her go. He kissed her. He knew she felt the meaning of the kiss, she was returning it and as her breath went into him it was sweet and pure and somehow like nectar.

Then, very gently, she pulled away from him. She said, "Go now. It's still dark outside. It'll be another hour before the sun comes up."

He grinned. It was a soft grin that wasn't forced. "This job won't take more than an hour," he said. "Whichever way it goes, it'll be a matter of minutes. Either I'll get them or they'll get me."

He turned away and walked across the cellar toward the splintered door. Tillie stood there watching him as he opened the door and went out.

It was less than three minutes later and they had him. He was walking south on Ninth, between Race Street and Arch, and the black Olds 88 was cruising on Arch and he didn't see them but they saw him, with Oscar grinning at Coley and saying, "There's our boy."

Oscar drove the car past the intersection and parked it on the north side of the Arch about twenty feet away from the corner. They got out and walked toward the corner and stayed close to the brick wall of the corner building. They listened to the approaching footsteps and grinned at each other and a few moments later he arrived on the corner and they grabbed him.

He felt Coley's thick arm wrapped tight around his throat, pulling his head back. He saw the glimmer of the five-inch blade in Oscar's hand. He told himself to think fast and he thought very fast and managed to say, "You'll be the losers. I made a connection."

Oscar hesitated. He blinked puzzledly. "What connection?"

He smiled at Oscar. Then he waited for Coley to loosen the armhold on his throat. Coley loosened it, then lowered it to his chest, using both arms to clamp him and prevent him from moving.

He made no attempt to move. He went on smiling at Oscar, and saying, "An important connection. It's important enough to louse you up."

"Prove it," Oscar said.

"You're traced." He narrowed the smile just a little. "If anything happens to me, they know where to get you."

"He's faking," Coley said. Then urgently, "Go on, Oscar, give him the knife."

"Not yet," Oscar murmured. He was studying Ken's eyes and his own eyes were somewhat worried. He said to Ken, "Who did the tracing?"

"I'll tell that to Riker."

Oscar laughed without sound. "Riker's in Los Angeles."

"No he isn't," Ken said. "He's here in Philly."

Oscar stopped laughing. The worry deepened in his eyes. He stared past Ken, focusing on Coley.

"He's here with Hilda," Ken said.

"It's just a guess," Coley said. "It's gotta be a guess." He tightened his bear-hug on Ken. "Do it, Oscar Don't let him stall you. Put the knife in him."

Oscar looked at Ken and said, "You making this a quiz game?"

Ken shrugged. "It's more like stud poker."

"Maybe," Oscar admitted. "But you're not the dealer."

Ken shrugged again. He didn't say anything.

Oscar said, "You're not the dealer and all you can do is hope for the right card."

"I got it already," Ken said. "It fills an inside straight."

Oscar bit the edge of his lip. "All right, I'll take a look." He had the knife aiming at Ken's chest, and then he raised it and moved in closer and the tip of the blade was touching Ken's neck. "Let's see your hole-card, sonny. All you gotta do is name the street and the house."

"Spruce Street," Ken said. "Near Eleventh."

Oscar's face became pale. Again he was staring at Coley.

Ken said, "It's an old house, detached. On one side there's a vacant lot and on the other side there's an alley."

It was quiet for some moments and then Oscar was talking aloud to himself, saying, "He knows, he really knows."

"What's the move?" Coley asked.

He sounded somewhat unhappy.

"We gotta think," Oscar said.

"This makes it complicated and we gotta think it through very careful."

Coley muttered a four-letter word. He said, "We ain't getting paid to do our own thinking. Riker gave us orders to find him and bump him."

"We can't bump him now," Oscar said. "Not under these conditions. The way it stacks up, it's Riker's play. We'll have to take him to Riker."

"Riker won't like that," Coley said.

Oscar didn't reply. Again he was biting his lip and it went on that way for some moments and then he made a gesture toward the parked car. He told Coley to take the wheel and he'd sit in the back with Rockland. As he opened the rear door he had the blade touching Ken's side, gently urging Ken to get in first. Coley was up front behind the wheel and then Oscar and Ken occupied the rear seat and the knife in Oscar's hand was aimed at Ken's abdomen.

The engine started and the Olds 88 moved east on Arch and went past Eighth and turned south on Seventh. There was no talk in the car as they passed Market and Chestnut and Walnut. They had a red light on Locust but Coley ignored it and went through at forty-five.

"Slow down," Oscar said.

Coley was hunched low over the wheel and the speedometer went up to fifty and Oscar yelled, "For Pete's sake, slow down. You wanna be stopped by a red car?"

"There's one now," Ken said, and he pointed toward the side window that showed only the front of a grocery store. But Oscar thought it might really be a side-street with a police car approaching, and the thought was in his brain for a tiny fraction of a second. In that segment of time he turned his head to have a look. Ken's hand moved automatically to grab Oscar's wrist and twist hard. The knife fell away from Oscar's fingers and Ken's other hand caught it. Oscar let out a screech and Ken put the knife in Oscar's breast just over his heart. The car was skidding to a stop as Ken stabbed Oscar to finish him. Coley was screaming curses and trying to hurl himself sideways and backwards toward the rear seat and Ken showed him the knife and it didn't stop him. Ken ducked as Coley came vaulting over the top of the front seat, the knife slashing upward to catch Coley as he came on. It buried itself deep enough into his breast to reach the heart and left Coley collapsed with his legs still over the front seat and his body sprawling across the lifeless form of Oscar in the back.

"I'm dying," Coley gurgled. "I'm – " That was his final sound. His eyes opened very wide and his head snapped sideways and he was through for this night and all nights.

Ken opened the rear door and got out. He had the knife in his pocket as he walked with medium-fast stride going south on Seventh to Spruce. Then he turned west on Spruce and walked just a bit faster. Every now and then he glanced backward to see if there were any red cars but all he saw was the empty street and some alley cats mooching around under the street lamps.

In the blackness above the roof-tops the bright yellow face of the City Hall clock showed ten minutes past six. He estimated the sky would be dark for another half-hour. It wasn't much time, but it was time enough for what he intended to do. He told himself he wouldn't enjoy the action, and yet somehow his mind was suffused with a kind of anticipatory satisfaction. It looked like Tillie had been right about that black pudding.

He quickened his pace just a little, crossed Eighth Street and Ninth, and walked faster as he passed Tenth. There were no lit windows on Spruce Street but as he neared Eleventh the moonlight blended with the glow of a street lamp and showed him the vacant lot. He gazed across the empty space to the wall of the old-fashioned house.

Then he was on the vacant lot and moving slowly and quietly toward the rear of the house. He worked his way to the sagging steps of the back porch, saw a light in the kitchen window, climbed two steps and three and four and peering through the window and seeing Hilda.

She was alone in the kitchen, sitting at a white-topped table and smoking a cigarette. There was a cup and saucer on the table, the saucer littered with coffee-stained cigarette butts. As he watched, she got up from the table and went to the stove to lift a percolator off the fire and pour another cup of coffee.

She moved with a slow weaving of her shoulders and a flow of her hips that was more drifting than walking. He thought, *She still has it, that certain way of moving around, using that body like a long-stemmed lily in a quiet breeze. That's what got you the first time you laid eyes on her. The way she moves. And one time very long ago you said to her, "To set me on fire, all you have to do is walk across a room." You couldn't believe you were actually married to that hothouse-prize, that platinum blonde hair like melted eighteen-karat, that face, she still has it, that body, she still has it. It's been nine years, and she still has it.*

She was wearing bottle-green velvet that set off the pale green of her eyes. The dress was cut low, went in tight around her very narrow waist and stayed tight going down all the way past her knees. She featured pearls around her throat and in her ears and on her wrists. He thought, *You gave her pearls for her birthday and Christmas and you wanted to give her more for the first wedding anniversary. But they don't sell pearls in San Quentin. All they sell is plans for getting out. Like lessons in how to crawl through a pipe, or how to conceal certain tools, or how to disguise the voice. The lessons never paid off, but maybe now's the time to use what you learned. Let's try Coley's voice.*

His knuckles rapped the kitchen door, and his mouth opened to let out Coley's thick, low-pitched voice saying, "It's me and Oscar."

He stood there counting off the seconds. It was four seconds and then the door opened. It opened wide and Hilda's mouth opened wider. Then she had her hand to her mouth and she was stepping backward.

"Hello, Hilda." He came into the kitchen and closed the door behind him.

She took another backward step. She shook her head and spoke through the trembling fingers that pressed against her lips. "It isn't – "

"Yes," he said. "It is."

Her hand fell away from her mouth. The moment was too much for her and it seemed she was going to collapse. But somehow she managed to stay on her feet. Then her eyes were shut tightly and she went on shaking her head.

"Look at me," he said. "Take a good look."

She opened her eyes. She looked him up and down and up again. Then, very slowly, she summoned air into her lungs and he knew she was going to let out a scream. His hands moved fast to his coat pocket and he took out Oscar's knife and said quietly, "No noise, Hilda."

She stared at the knife. The air went out of her without sound. Her arms were limp at her sides. She spoke in a half-whisper, talking to herself. "I don't believe it. Just can't believe it – "

"Why not?" His tone was mild. "It figures, doesn't it? You came to Philly to look for me. And here I am."

For some moments she stayed limp. Then, gradually, her shoulders straightened. She seemed to be getting a grip on herself. Her eyes narrowed just a little, as she went on looking at the silver-handled switch-blade in his hand. She said, "That's Oscar's knife – ?"

He nodded.

"Where is Oscar?" she asked. "Where's Coley?"

"They're dead." He pressed the button on the handle and the blade flicked out. He said, "It's a damn shame. They wouldn't be dead if they'd let me alone."

Hilda didn't say anything. She gave a little shrug, as though to indicate there was nothing she could say. He told himself it didn't make sense to wait any longer and the thing to do was put the knife in her heart. He wondered if the knife was sharp enough to cut through ice.

He took a forward step, then stopped. He wondered what was holding him back. Maybe he was waiting for her to break, to fall on her knees and beg for mercy.

But she didn't kneel and she didn't plead. Her voice was matter-of-fact as she said, "I'm wondering if we can make a deal."

It caught him off balance. He frowned slightly. "What kind of deal?"

"Fair trade," she said. "You give me a break and I'll give you Riker."

He changed the frown to a dim smile. "I've got him anyway. It's a cinch he's upstairs sound asleep."

"That's fifty percent right," she said. "He's a very light sleeper. Especially lately, since he heard you were out of Quentin."

He widened the smile. "In Quentin I learned to walk on tiptoe. There won't be any noise."

"There's always noise when you break down a door."

The frown came back. "You playing it shrewd?"

"I'm playing it straight," she said. "He keeps the door locked. Another thing he keeps is a .38 under his pillow."

He slanted his head just a little. "You expect me to buy that?"

"You don't have to buy it. I'm giving it to you."

He began to see what she was getting at. He said, "All right, thanks for the freebee. Now tell me what you're selling."

"A key," she said. "The key to his room. He has one and I have one. I'll sell you mine at bargain rates. All I want is your promise."

He didn't say anything.

She shrugged and said, "It's a gamble on both sides. I'll take a chance that you'll keep your word and let me stay alive. You'll be betting even-money that I'm telling the truth."

He smiled again. He saw she was looking past him, at the kitchen door. He said, "So the deal is, you give me the key to his room and I let you walk out that door."

"That's it." She was gazing hungrily at the door. Her lips scarcely moved as she murmured, "Fair enough?"

"No," he said. "It needs a tighter contract."

Her face was expressionless. She held her breath.

He let her hold it for awhile, and then he said, "Let's do it so there's no gamble. You get the key and I'll follow you upstairs. I'll be right in back of you when you walk into the room. I'll have the blade touching your spine."

She blinked a few times.

"Well?" he said.

She reached into a flap of the bottle-green velvet and took out a door-key. Then she turned slowly and started out of the kitchen. He moved in close behind her and followed the platinum blonde hair and elegant torso going through the small dining-room and the parlor and toward the dimly-lit stairway. He came up at her side as they climbed the stairs, the knife-blade scarcely an inch away from the shimmering velvet that covered her ribs.

They reached the top of the stairs and she pointed to the door of the front bedroom. He let the blade touch the velvet and his voice was a whisper saying, "Slow and quiet. Very quiet."

Then again he moved behind her. They walked slowly toward the bedroom door. The blade kissed the velvet and it told her to use the key with a minimum of sound. She put the key in the lock and there was no sound as she turned the key. There was only a slight clicking sound as the lock opened. Then no sound while she opened the door.

They entered the room and he saw Riker in the bed. He saw the brown wavy hair and there was some grey in it along the temples. In the suntanned face there were wrinkles and lines of dissipation and other lines that told of too much worry. Riker's eyes were shut tightly and it was the kind of slumber that rests the limbs but not the brain.

Ken thought, *He's aged a lot in nine years; it used to be mostly muscle and now it's mostly fat.*

Riker was curled up, his knees close to his paunch. He had his shoes off but otherwise he was fully dressed. He wore a silk shirt and a hand-painted necktie, his jacket was dark grey cashmere and his slacks were pale grey high-grade flannel. He had on a pair of argyle socks that must have set him back at least twenty dollars. On the wrist of his left hand there was a platinum watch to match the large star-emerald he wore on his little finger. On the third finger of his left hand he had a three-karat diamond. Ken was looking at the expensive clothes and the jewelry and thinking, *He travels first-class, he really rides the gravy train.*

It was a bitter thought and it bit deeper into Ken's brain. He said to himself, *Nine years ago this man of distinction beat you up and left you for dead. You've had nine years in Quentin and he's had the sunshine, the peaches-and-cream, the uninterrupted and desirable company of the extra-lovely Mrs Riker while you lived alone in a cell –*

He looked at the extra-lovely Mrs Riker. She stood motionless at the side of the bed and he stood beside her with the switchblade aiming at her velvet-sheathed flesh. She was looking at the blade and waiting for him to aim it at Riker, to put it in the sleeping man and send it in deep.

But that wasn't the play. He smiled dimly to let her know he had something else in mind.

Riker's left hand dangled over the side of the bed and his right hand rested on the pillow. Ken kept the knife aimed at Hilda as he reached toward the pillow and then under the pillow. His fingers touched metal. It was the barrel of a revolver and he got a two-finger hold on it and eased it out from under the pillow. The butt came into his palm and his middle finger went through the trigger-guard and nestled against the back of the guard, not touching the trigger.

He closed the switchblade and put it in his pocket. He stepped back and away from the bed and said, "Now you can wake up your husband."

She was staring at the muzzle of the .38. It wasn't aiming at anything in particular.

"Wake him up," Ken murmured. "I want him to see his gun in my hand. I want him to know how I got it."

Hilda gasped and it became a sob and then a wail and it was a hook of sound that awakened Riker. At first he was looking at Hilda. Then he saw Ken and he sat up very slowly, as though he was something made of stone and ropes were pulling him up. His eyes were riveted to Ken's face and he hadn't yet noticed the .38. His hand crept down along the side of the pillow and then under the pillow.

There was no noise in the room as Riker's hand groped for the gun. Some moments passed and then there was sweat on Riker's forehead and under his lip and he went on searching for the gun and suddenly he seemed to realise it wasn't there. He focused on the weapon in Ken's hand and his body began to quiver. His lips scarcely moved as he said, "The gun – the gun –"

"It's yours," Ken said. "Mind if I borrow it?"

Riker went on staring at the revolver. Then very slowly his head turned and he was staring at Hilda. "You," he said. "You gave it to him."

"Not exactly," Ken said. "All she did was tell me where it was."

Riker shut his eyes very tightly as though he was tied to a rack and it was pulling him apart.

Hilda's face was expressionless. She was looking at Ken and saying, "You promised to let me walk out – "

"I'm not stopping you," he said. Then, with a shrug and a dim smile, "I'm not stopping anyone from doing what they want to do." And he slipped the gun into his pocket.

Hilda started for the door. Riker was up from the bed and lunging at her, grabbing her wrist and hurling her across the room. Then Riker lunged again and his hands reached for her throat as she tried to get up from the floor. Hilda began to make gurgling sounds but the noise was drowned in the torrent of insane screaming that came from Riker's lips. Riker choked her until she died. And even then he stayed where he was and went on screaming at her.

Ken stood there, watching it happen. His mind absorbed and recorded every detail of the scene. He thought, *Well, they wanted each other, and now they got each other.*

He walked out of the room and down the hall and down the stairs. As he went out of the house he could still hear the screaming. On Spruce, walking toward Eleventh, he glanced back and saw a crowd gathering outside the house and then he heard the sound of approaching sirens. He waited there and saw the police-cars stopping in front of the house, the policemen rushing in with drawn guns. Some moments later he heard the shots and he knew that the screaming man was trying to make a getaway. There was more shooting and suddenly there was no sound at all. He knew they'd be carrying two corpses out of the house.

He turned away from what was happening back there, walked along the curb toward the sewer-hole on the corner, took Riker's gun from his pocket and threw it into the sewer. In the instant that he did it, there was a warm sweet taste in his mouth. He smiled, knowing what it was. Again he could hear Tillie saying, "Revenge is black pudding."

Tillie, he thought. And the smile stayed on his face as he walked north on Eleventh. He was remembering the feeling he'd had when he'd kissed her. It was the feeling of wanting to take her out of that dark cellar, away from the loneliness and the opium. To carry her upward toward the world where they had such things as clinics, with plastic specialists who repaired scarred faces.

The feeling hit him again and he walked faster.

A MATTER OF PRINCIPAL

Max Allan Collins

IT HAD BEEN a long time since I'd had any trouble sleeping. Probably Vietnam, and that was gunfire that kept me awake. I've never been an insomniac. You might think killing people for a living would give you restless nights. Truth is, those that go into that business simply aren't the kind who are bothered by it much.

I was no exception. I hadn't gone into retirement because my conscience was bothering me. I retired because the man I got my contracts through got killed – well, actually I killed him, but that's another story – and I had enough money put away to live comfortably without working, so I did.

The A-frame cottage on Paradise Lake was secluded enough for privacy, but close enough to nearby Lake Geneva to put me in contact with human beings, if I was so inclined, which I rarely was, with the exception of getting laid now and then. I'm human.

There was also a restaurant nearby, called Wilma's Welcome Inn, a rambling two-story affair that included a gas station, modest hotel accommodations and a convenience store. I'd been toying with the idea of buying the place, which had been slipping since the death of Wilma; I'd been getting a little bored lately and needed something to do. Before I started putting people to sleep, I worked in a garage as a mechanic, so the gas station angle appealed to me.

Anyway, boredom had started to itch at me, and for the past few nights I'd had trouble sleeping. I sat up all night watching satellite TV and reading paperback westerns; then I'd drag around the next day, maybe drifting to sleep in the afternoon just long enough to fuck up my sleep cycle again that night.

It was getting irritating.

At about three-thirty in the morning on the fourth night of this shit,

I decided eating might do the trick. Fill my gut with junk food and the blood could rush down from my head and warm my belly and I'd get the fuck sleepy, finally. I hadn't tried this before because I'd been getting a trifle paunchy, since I quit working, and since winter kicked in.

In the summer I'd swim in the lake everyday and get exercise and keep the spare tire off. But in the winter I'd just let my beard go and belt-size, too. Winters made me fat and lazy and, now, fucking sleepless.

The cupboard was bare so I threw on my thermal jacket and headed over to the Welcome Inn. At this time of night the convenience store was the only thing open, that and one self-serve gas pump.

The clerk was a heavy-set brunette named Cindy from nearby Twin Lakes. She was maybe twenty years old and a little surly, but she worked all night, so who could blame her.

"Mr Ryan," she said, flatly, as I came in, the bell over the door jingling.

"Cindy," I said, with a nod, and began prowling the place, three narrow aisles parallel to the front of the building. None of the snacks appealed to me – chips and crackers and Twinkies and other preservative-packed delights – and the frozen food case ran mostly to ice-cream sandwiches and popsicles. In this weather, that was a joke.

I was giving a box of Chef Boyardee lasagna an intent once-over, like it was a car I was considering buying, when the bell over the door jingled again. I glanced up and saw a heavy-set man – heavy-set enough to make Cindy look svelte – with a pockmarked face and black-rimmed glasses that fogged up as he stepped in.

He wore an expensive topcoat – tan, a camel's hair number you could make payments on for a year and still owe – and his shoes had a bright black city shine, barely flecked with ice and snow. His name was Harry Something, and he was from Chicago. I knew him, in another life.

I turned my back. If he saw me, I'd have to kill him, and I was bored, but not that bored.

Predictably, Harry Something went straight for the potato chips; he also rustled around the area where cookies were shelved. I risked a glimpse and saw him, not two minutes after he entered, with his arms full of junk food, heading for the front counter.

"Excuse me, miss," Harry Something said, depositing his groceries before Cindy. His voice was nasal and high-pitched; a funny, childish voice for a man his size. "Could you direct me to the sanitary napkins?"

"You mean Kotex?"

"Whatever."

"The toiletries is just over there."

Now this was curious, and I'll tell you why. I had met Harry Something around ten years before, when I was doing a job for the Outfit boys. I was never a mob guy, mind you, strictly a freelancer, but their money was as good as anybody's. What that job was isn't important, but Harry and his partner Louis were the locals who had fucked up, making my outsider's presence necessary. Harry and Louis had not been friendly toward me. They had threatened me, in fact. They had beaten the hell out of me in my hotel room, when the job was over, for making them look bad.

I had never taken any sort of revenge out on them. I occasionally do take revenge, but at my convenience, and when a score strikes me as worth settling. Harry and Louis had really just pushed me around a little, bloodied my nose, tried to earn back a little self-respect. So I didn't hold a grudge. Not a major grudge. Fuck it.

As to why Harry Something purchasing Kotex in the middle of the night at some backwoods convenience store was curious, well, Harry and Louis were gay. They were queens of crime. Mob muscle who worked as a pair, and played as a pair.

I don't mean to be critical. To each his own. I'd rather cut my dick off than insert it in any orifice of a repulsive fat slob like Harry Something. But that's just me.

And me, I'm naturally curious. I'm not nosy, not even inquisitive. But when a faggot buys Kotex, I have to wonder why.

"Excuse me," Harry Something said, brushing by me.

He hadn't seen my face – he might not recognize me, in any case. Ten years and a beard and twenty pounds later, I wasn't as easy to peg as Harry was, who had changed goddamn little.

Harry, having stocked up on cookies and chips and Kotex, was now buying milk and packaged macaroni and cheese and provisions in general. He was shopping. Stocking up.

And now I knew what he was up to.

I nodded to surly Cindy, who bid me goodbye by flickering her eyelids in casual contempt, and went out to my car, a blue sporty Mazda I'd purchased recently. I wished I'd had the four-wheel drive, or anything less conspicuous, but I didn't. I sat in the car, scooched down low; I did not turn on the engine. I just sat in the cold car in the cold night and waited.

Harry Something came out with two armloads of groceries – Kotex included, I presumed – and he put them in the front seat of a brown rental Ford. Louis was not waiting for him. Harry was alone.

Which further confirmed my suspicions.

I waited for him to pull out onto the road, waited for him to take the road's curve, then started up my Mazda and glided out after him. He had turned left, toward Twin Lakes and Lake Geneva. That made sense, only I figured he wouldn't wind up either place. I figured he'd be out in the boonies somewhere.

I knew what Harry was up to. I knew he wasn't exactly here to ski. That lardass couldn't stand up on a pair of skis. And he wasn't here to go ice-fishing, either. A city boy like Harry Something had no business in a touristy area like this, in the off-season – unless Harry was hiding out, holing up somewhere.

This would be the perfect area for that.

Only Harry didn't use Kotex.

He turned off on a side road, into a heavily wooded area that wound back toward Paradise Lake. Good. That was very good.

I went on by. I drove a mile, turned into a farmhouse gravel drive and headed back without lights. I slowed as I reached the mouth of the side road, and could see Harry's tail lights wink off.

I knew the cabin at the end of that road. There was only one, and its owner only used it during the summer; Harry was either a renter, or a squatter.

I glided on by and went back home. I left the Mazda next to the deck and walked up the steps and into my A-frame. The nine millimeter was in the nightstand drawer. The gun hadn't been shot in months – Christ, maybe over a year. But I cleaned and oiled it regularly. It would do fine.

So would my black turtle-neck, black jeans, black leather bomber jacket, and this black moonless night. I slipped a .38 revolver in the bomber jacket right side pocket, and clipped a hunting knife to my belt. The knife was razor sharp with a sword point; I sent for it out of the back of one of those dumb-ass ninja magazines – which are worthless except for mail-ordering weapons.

I walked along the edge of the lake, my running shoes crunching the brittle ground, layered as it was with snow and ice and leaves. The only light came from a gentle scattering of stars, a handful of diamonds flung on black velvet; the frozen lake was a dark presence that you could sense but not really see. The surrounding trees were even darker. The occasional cabin or cottage or house I passed was empty. I was one of only a handful of residents on Paradise Lake who lived year-round.

But the lights were on in one cabin. Not many lights, but lights. And its chimney was trailing smoke.

The cabin was small, a traditional log cabin like Abe Lincoln and syrup, only with a satellite dish. Probably two bedrooms, a living room, kitchenette and a can or two. Only one car – the brown rental Ford.

My footsteps were lighter now; I was staying on the balls of my feet and the crunching under them was faint. I approached with caution and gun in hand and peeked in a window on the right front side.

Harry Something was sitting on the couch, eating barbecue potato chips, giving himself an orange-mustache in the process. His feet were up on a coffee table. More food and a sawed-off double-barrel shotgun were on the couch next to him. He wore a colorful Hawaiian shirt; he looked like Don Ho puked on him, actually.

Hovering nervously nearby, was Louis, a small, skinny, bald ferret of a man, who wore jeans and a black shirt and a white tie. I couldn't tell whether he was trying for trendy or gangster, and frankly didn't give a shit, either way.

Physically, all the two men had in common was pockmarks and a desire for the other's ugly body.

And neither one of them seemed to need a sanitary napkin, though a towelette would've come in handy for Harry Something. Jesus.

I huddled beneath the window, wondering what I was doing here. Boredom. Curiosity. I shrugged. Time to look in another window or two.

Because they clearly had a captive. That's what they were doing in the boonies. That's why they were stocking up on supplies at a convenience store in the middle of night and nowhere. That's why they were in the market for Kotex. That's what I'd instinctively, immediately known back at the Welcome Inn.

And in a back window, I saw her. She was naked on a bed in the rustic room, naked but for white panties. She was sitting on the edge of the bed and she was crying, a black-haired, creamy-fleshed beauty in her early twenties.

Obviously, Harry and Louis had nothing sexual in mind for this girl; the reason for her nudity was to help prevent her fleeing. The bed was heavy with blankets, and she'd obviously been keeping under the covers, but right now she was sitting and crying. That time of the month.

I stood in the dark in my dark clothes with a gun in my hand and my back to the log cabin and smiled. When I'd come out into the night, armed like this, it wasn't to effect a rescue. Whatever else they were, Harry and Louis were dangerous men. If I was going to spend my sleepless night satisfying my curiosity and assuaging my boredom by poking into their business, I had to be ready to pay for my thrills.

But the thing was, I recognized this young woman. Like Harry, I spent a lot of hours during cold nights like this with my eyes frozen to a TV screen. And that's where I'd seen her: on the tube.

Not an actress, no – an heiress. The daughter of a Chicago media magnate whose name you'd recognize, a guy who inherited money and wheeled-and-dealed his way into more, including one of the satellite super-stations I'd been wasting my eyes on lately. The Windy City's answer to Ted Turner, right down to boating and womanizing.

His daughter was a little wild, frequently seen in the company of rock stars (she had a tattoo of a star – not Mick Jagger, a five-pointed *star* star – on her white left breast, which I could see from the window) and was a Betty Ford clinic drop-out. Nonetheless, she was said to be the apple of her daddy's eye, even if that apple was a tad wormy.

So Harry and Louis had put the snatch on the snatch; fair enough. Question was, was it their own idea, or something the Outfit put them up to?

I sat in the cold and dark and decided, finally, that it just didn't matter who or what was behind it. My options were to go home, and forget about it, and try (probably without any luck) to get some sleep; or to rescue this somewhat soiled damsel in distress.

What the hell. I had nothing better to do.

I went to the front door and knocked.

No answer.

Shit, I knew somebody was home, so I knocked again.

Louis cracked open the door and peered out and said, "What is it?" and I shot him in the eye.

There was the harsh, shrill sound of a scream – not Louis, who hadn't had time for that, but the girl in the next room, scared shitless at hearing a gunshot, one would suppose.

I paid no attention to her and pushed the door open – there was no night latch or anything – and stepped over Louis, and pointed the nine millimeter at Harry, whose orange-ringed mouth was frozen open and whose bag of barbecue potato chips dropped to the floor, much as Louis had.

"Don't, Harry," I said.

I could see in Harry's tiny dark eyes behind his thick black-rimmed glasses that he was thinking about the sawed-off shotgun on the couch next to him.

"Who the fuck . . ."

I walked slowly across the rustic living room toward the couch; in the background, an old colorized movie was playing on their captive's daddy's super-station. I plucked the shotgun off the couch with my left hand and tucked it under my arm.

"Hi, Harry," I said. "Been a while."

His orange-ringed mouth slowly began to work and his eyes began to blink and he said, "Quarry?"

That was the name he'd known me by.

"Taking the girl your idea, or are you still working for the boys?"

"We . . . we retired, couple years ago. God. You killed Louis. Louis. You killed Louis . . ."

"Right. What were you going to put the girl's body in?"

"Huh?"

"She's obviously seen you. You were obviously going to kill her, once you got the money. So. What was the plan?"

Harry wiped off his orange barbecue ring. "Got a roll of plastic in the closet. Gonna roll her up in it and dump her in one of the gravel pits around here."

"I see. Do that number with the plastic right now, for Louis, why don't you? Okay?"

Tears were rolling down Harry's stubbly pockmarked cheeks. I didn't know whether he was crying for Louis or himself or the pair of them, and I wasn't interested enough to ask.

"Okay," he said thickly.

I watched him roll his partner up in the sheet of plastic, using duct tape to secure the package; he sobbed as he did it, but he did it. He got blood on his Hawaiian shirt; it didn't particularly show, though.

"Now I want you to clean up the mess. Go on. You'll find what you need in the kitchen."

Dutifully, Harry shuffled over, got a pan of warm water and some rags, and got on his knees and cleaned up the brains and blood. He wasn't crying anymore. He moved slow but steady, a fat zombie in a colorful shirt.

"Stick the rags in the end of Louis' plastic home, would you? Thank you."

Harry did that, then the big man lumbered to his feet, hands in the air, and said, "Now me, huh?"

"I might let you go, Harry. I got nothing against you."

"Not . . . not how I remember it."

I laughed. "You girls leaned on me once. You think I'd kill a person over something that trivial? What kind of guy do you think I am, Harry?"

Harry had sense enough not to answer.

"Come with me," I said, and with the nine millimeter's nose to Harry's temple, I walked him to the door of the bedroom.

"Open it," I said.

He did.

We went in, Harry first.

The girl was under the covers, holding the blankets and sheets up around her in a combination of illogical modesty and legitimate fear.

Her expression melted into one of confusion mingled with the beginnings of hope and relief, when she saw me.

"I've already taken care of the skinny one," I said. "Now Harry and me are going for a walk. You stay here. I'm going to get you back to your father."

Her confusion didn't leave, but she began to smile, wide, like a kid Christmas morning seeing her gifts. Her gift to me was dropping the blankets and sheets to her waist.

"Remember," I said. "Stay right there."

I walked Harry out, pulling the bedroom door shut behind me.

"Where are her clothes?"

He nodded to a closet. Same one he'd gotten the plastic out of.

"Good," I said. "Now let's go for a walk. Just you and me and Louis."

"Loo . . . Louis?"

"Better give Louis a hand, Harry."

Harry held the plastic-wrapped corpse in his arms like a B-movie monster carrying a starlet. The plastic was spattered with blood, but on the inside. Harry looked like he was going to cry again.

I still had the sawed-off shotgun under my arm, so it was awkward, getting the front door open, but I managed.

"Out on the lake," I said.

Harry looked at me, his eyes behind the glasses wary, glancing from me to his plastic-wrapped burden and back again.

"We're going to bury Louis at sea," I said.

"Huh?"

"Just walk, Harry. Okay? Just walk."

He walked. I followed behind, nine millimeter in one hand, sawed-off in the other. Harry in his Hawaiian shirt was an oddly comic sight, but I was too busy to be amused. Our feet crunched slightly on the ice. No danger of falling in. Frozen solid. Kids ice-skated out here. But not right now.

We walked a long way. We said not a word, until I halted him about mid-way. The black starry sky was our only witness.

"Put him down, Harry," I said. The nine millimeter was in my waistband; the shotgun was pointed right at him.

He set his cargo gently down. He stood looking gloomily down at the plastic shroud, like a bear contemplating its own foot caught in a trap.

I blasted both barrels of the shotgun; they blew the quiet night apart and echoed across the frozen lake and rattled the world.

Harry looked at me, stunned.

"What the fuck . . .?"

"Now unroll Louis and toss him in," I said, standing near the gaping hole in the ice. "I'm afraid that plastic might float."

Horrified, the big man did as he was told. Louis slipped down the hole in the ice and into watery nothingness like a turd down the crapper.

"Slick," I said, admiringly.

"Oh Jesus," he said.

"Now you," I said.

"What?"

I had the nine millimeter out again.

"Jump in," I said. "Water's fine."

"Fuck you!"

I went over quickly and pushed the big son of a bitch in. He was flailing, splashing icy water up on me, as I put six bullets in his head, which came apart in pieces, like a rotten melon.

And then he was gone.

Nothing left but the hole in the ice, the water within it making some frothy reddish waves that would die down soon enough.

I gathered the weapons and the plastic and, folding the plastic sheet as I walked, went back to the cabin.

This was reckless, I knew. I shouldn't be killing people who lived on the same goddamn lake I did. But it was winter, and the bodies wouldn't turn up for a long time, if ever, and the Outfit had used this part of the world to dump its corpses since Capone was just a mean street kid. Very little chance any of this would come back at me.

Nonetheless, I had taken a risk or two. I ought to get something out of it, other than killing a sleepless night.

I got the girl's clothes and went in and gave them to her. A heavy-metal t-shirt and designer jeans and Reeboks.

"Did you kill those men?" she said, breathlessly, her eyes dark and glittering. She had her clothes in her lap.

"That's not important. Get dressed."

"You're wonderful. You're goddamn fucking wonderful."

"I know," I said. "Everybody says the same thing. Get dressed."

She got dressed. I watched her. She was a beautiful piece of ass, no question. The way she was looking at me made it clear she was grateful.

"What can I do for you?" she said, hands on her hips.

"Nothing," I said. "You're on the rag."

That made her laugh. "Other ports in a storm."

"Maybe later," I said, and smiled. She looked like AIDs-bait to me. I could be reckless, but not that reckless.

I put her in my car. I hadn't decided yet whether or not to dump the brown rental Ford. Probably would. I could worry about that later. Right now, I needed to get her to a motel.

She slept in the car. I envied her, and nudged her awake when we reached the motel just inside the Illinois state line.

I'd already checked in. I ushered her in to the shabby little room, its floor space all but taken up by two twin beds, and she sat on the bed and yawned.

"What now?" she said. "You want your reward?"

"Actually, yes," I said, sitting next to her. "What's your father's number?"

"Hey, there's time for that later . . ."

"First things first," I said, and she wrote the number out on the pad by the phone.

I heard the ring, and a male voice said, "Hello?"

I gave her the receiver. "Make sure it's your father, and tell him you're all right."

"Daddy?" she said. She smiled, then she made a face. "I'm fine, I'm fine . . . the man you sent . . . what?"

She covered the receiver, eyes confused again. "He says he didn't send anybody."

I took the phone. "Good evening, sir. I have your daughter. As you can hear, she's just fine. Get together one-hundred-thousand dollars in unmarked, nonsequential tens, twenties and fifties, and wait for the next call."

I hung up.

She looked at me with wide eyes and wide-open mouth.

"I'm not going to kill you," I said. "I'm just turning a buck."

"You bastard!"

I put the duct tape over her mouth, taped her wrists behind her and taped her ankles too, and went over and curled up on the other bed, nine millimeter in my waistband.

And slept like a baby.

CITIZEN'S ARREST

Charles Willeford

IT WAS FAIRLY late in the afternoon when I stopped at Gwynn's Department Store on my way home to look at some new fishing tackle. Gwynn's is the best store in the entire city; there are three full floors of everything imaginable. So I always took my time shopping at Gwynn's; a man who's interested in the outdoors can spend several hours in there just looking around.

My back was to the man at the counter – the thief, I should say – because I was looking at the shotguns in the rack behind the locked glass doors. He must have seen me, of course, but he didn't know, I suppose, that I could see his reflection in the glass doors as he stood at the next counter. There was no clerk in the immediate vicinity; there were just the two of us in this part of the store on the ground floor. Casually, as I watched him in the polished glass, he snatched the heavy lighter off the counter and slipped it into the deep right-hand pocket of his green gabardine raincoat.

I was pretty well shocked by this action. As a kid, I had pilfered a few things from ten-cent stores – pencils and nickel key-rings, and once a twenty-five-cent "diamond" ring – but this was the first time in my life I had ever seen anybody deliberately *steal* something. And it was an expensive table lighter: $75 not counting tax. Only a minute or two before I had examined the lighter myself, thinking how masculine it would look on the desk in my office or on the coffee table in a bachelor's apartment. Of course, as a married man, I couldn't afford to pay that much money just for a cigarette lighter, but it was a beautiful piece of work, a "conversation piece," as they say in the magazine ads. It was a chromium-plated knight in armor about six inches tall. When you flipped up the visor on the helmet a butane flame flared inside the empty head, and there was your light. There had been a display of these lighters in shining armor on the gift counter, and now, as the big man sauntered toward the elevators, there was one less.

If I'd had time to think things over I am inclined to believe now that I would have ignored the theft. As I've always said, it was none of my business, and nobody wants to get involved in a situation that is bound to be unpleasant, but at that particular moment a young clerk appeared out of nowhere and asked me if I needed any help. I shook my head, and pointed my chin in the general direction of the elevators.

"Do you see that man over there in the green raincoat? I just saw him take one of those knight table lighters off the counter and put it into his pocket."

"Do you mean he stole it?" he asked, in a kind of stage whisper.

"No." I shook my head again. "I didn't say that. All I said was that he put the lighter into his pocket and then walked over to the elevators."

The big man entered the elevator, together with a teenaged boy who badly needed a haircut, and the operator clanged the door closed.

The clerk, who couldn't have been more than twenty-two or three, cleared his throat. "I'm afraid, sir, that this sort of thing is a little out of my province. Would you mind talking to our floor manager, Mr Levine?"

I shrugged in reply, but there was a sinking sensation in my stomach all the same. By mentioning the theft I had committed myself, and now I knew that I had to go through with it no matter how unpleasant it turned out to be.

The clerk soon returned with Mr Levine, a squat bald man in his early forties. He wore a plastic name tag and a red carnation on the left lapel of his black silk suitcoat.

I briefly explained the theft to Mr Levine. He pursed his lips, listened attentively, and then checked out my story by going over to the glass case of shotguns to prove to himself that the gift counter was reflected perfectly in the polished surface.

"Would you be willing, Mr – ?"

"Goranovsky."

"Would you be willing, Mr Goranovsky, to appear in court as a witness to this shoplifting? Providing, of course, that such is the case."

"What do you mean, if such is the case? I told you I saw him take it. All you have to do is search him, and if you find the lighter in his raincoat – in the right hand pocket – the case is cut and dried."

"Not exactly, sir. It isn't quite that simple." He turned to the clerk, whose eyes were bright with excitement, and lowered his voice. "Call Mr Sileo, and ask him to join us here."

The clerk left, and Mr Levine steepled his fingers. "Mr Sileo is our security officer," he explained. "I don't want you to think that we don't appreciate your reporting this matter, Mr Goranovsky, because we do, but Gwynn's can't afford to make a false accusation. As you said, there was no clerk in the vicinity at the time, and it's quite possible that the gentleman might have gone off to search for one."

I snorted in disgust. "Sure, and if he can't find one on the second floor, maybe he'll find one on the third."

"It's possible," he said seriously, ignoring my tone of voice. "Legally, you see, no theft is involved unless he actually leaves the store without paying for the item. He can still pay for the lighter, or put it back on the counter before he leaves."

"Sure, I see. Why not forget the whole thing? I'm sorry I brought the matter up."

"No, please. I merely wanted to explain the technical points. We'll need your cooperation, and it's Mr Gwynn's policy to prosecute shoplifters; but you can't make charges without an airtight case and a reliable witness. If we arrest him within the store, all the man has to say is that he was looking for a clerk, and there isn't anything we can do about it. He very well may be looking for a clerk. If such is the case, we could very easily lose the goodwill of a valuable customer."

"I understand; I'm a businessman myself. In fact, I hope I'm wrong. But if I'm not, you can count on me to appear in court, Mr Levine. I've gone this far."

We were joined by Mr Sileo. He was slight, dark, and businesslike. He looked more like a bank executive than a detective, and I had a hunch that he had an important job of some kind with Gwynn's, that he merely doubled as a security officer. In a businesslike manner, he quickly and quietly took charge of the situation.

I was directed to stand by the elevators and to point out the thief when he came down. Mr Levine was stationed in the center aisle, and Mr Sileo took up his post by the Main Street entrance. If, by chance, the shoplifter turned right after leaving the elevator – toward the side exit to 37th Street – Mr Levine could follow him out, and Mr Sileo could dart out the main door and circle around the corner to meet the man outside on 37th Street. Mr Sileo explained the plan so smoothly, I supposed it was some kind of standing procedure they had used effectively before. The eager young clerk, much to his disgust, was sent back to work by Mr Levine, but he wasn't needed.

To my surprise, when I looked at my watch, only ten minutes had passed since I reported the theft. The next ten minutes were much longer as I waited by the elevators for the man in the green raincoat to reappear. He didn't look at me as he got off, and I pointed him out by holding my arm above my head, as Mr Sileo had directed, and then trailed the man down the wide corridor at a safe distance. I wondered if he had a gun, and at this alarming thought I dropped back a little farther, letting Mr Levine get well ahead of me. Mr Sileo, who had picked up my signal, went out the front door as soon as it became apparent that the man was going to use the Main Street exit. I could see Mr Sileo through the glass door as he stood on the front sidewalk; he was pretending to fumble a cigarette out of his pack. A moment later, just about the time I reluctantly reached the Main Street doorway myself, Mr Levine and Mr Sileo were escorting the big man back inside the store.

I couldn't understand the man's attitude; he was smiling. He had a huge nose, crisscrossed with prominent blood veins, and he had a large mouth, too, which probably looked bigger than it was because of several missing teeth.

The four of us moved silently down the right side aisle a short distance to avoid blocking the doorway. For a strained moment nobody said anything.

"I'm sorry, sir," Mr Sileo said flatly, but pleasantly, "but this gentleman claims that you took a desk lighter off the counter and put it into your pocket without paying for it."

I resented the offhand way Mr Sileo had shifted all of the responsibility onto me. The big man shrugged and, if anything, his genial smile widened, but his bluish white eyes weren't smiling as he looked at me. They were as cold and hard as glass marbles.

"Is that right?" He chuckled deep in his throat. "Is this the lighter you mean?" He took the chrome-plated knight out of his raincoat pocket.

"Yes," I said grimly, "that's the one."

He unbuttoned his raincoat and, after transferring the lighter to his left hand, dug into his pants pocket with his right.

"This," he said, handing a slip of paper to Mr Sileo, "is my receipt for it."

Mr Sileo examined the receipt and then passed it to Mr Levine. The floor manager shot me a coldly furious look and returned the slip of paper to the man. The thief reached into his inside jacket pocket for his checkbook. "If you like," he said, "you can look at the checkstub, as well."

Mr Sileo shook his head, and held his hands back to avoid taking the checkbook. "No, sir, that's quite all right, sir," he said apologetically.

Mr Levine made some effusive apologies for the store which I thought, under the circumstances, were uncalled for – but the big man cut him off in the middle of a long sentence.

"No harm done," he said good-naturedly, "none at all. In your place, I'd have checked, too. In all probability," he qualified his remark.

"It was my mistake," I said, finally. "I'm sorry you were inconvenienced." And then, when neither Mr Levine nor Mr Sileo said anything to me, and the big man just stood there – grinning – I turned on my heel and left the store, resolving, then and there, never to spend another dime in Gwynn's as long as I lived.

There had been no mistake. I had seen the man take the lighter, and there had been no clerks anywhere near us at the time. I stood beside my car at the curb, filled with frustration as I ran things all over again in my mind. A trick of some kind had been pulled on the three of us, but how the man had worked it was beyond my comprehension. I opened the door on the sidewalk side and slid across the seat. As I fastened my seat belt, a meaty hand opened the door and the big man in the green raincoat grinned in at me. He held out the shining knight for my inspection.

"Want to buy a nice table lighter, buddy?" he said, chuckling deep in his throat. I can let you have it without any tax."

I swallowed twice before I replied. "I knew you stole the lighter, but how did you get the receipt?"

"Will you buy the lighter if I tell you?"

"No, damn you; I wouldn't give you ten cents for it!"

"Okay, Mr Do-Gooder," he said cheerfully, "I'll tell you anyway. This morning there were several lighters on the counter, and I bought one of them at ten a.m. After stashing the first one in a safe place, I came back late this afternoon and got this one free. Unfortunately, you happened to see me pick it up. The receipt I got this morning, however, served me very well for the second. The store stays open until nine-thirty tonight, and I had planned to come back after dinner and get another one. So long as I took them one at a time, one receipt is as good as three, if you get my meaning. So the way I figure it, you ought to buy this one from me because I can't come back tonight for my third lighter. You cost me some money, fella."

"I've got a good mind to go back in and tell Mr Sileo how you worked it."

"Really? Come on, then. I'll go in with you."

"Get the hell out of here!"

He chuckled, slammed the door, and walked away.

My fingers trembled as I lit a cigarette. There was no mistaking my reaction now – I was no longer frustrated, I was angry. If the man had been my size – or smaller – I would have chased after him and knocked out the remainder of his front teeth. I also considered, for a short moment, the idea of telling Mr Levine how he had been cheated. All they had to do was to inventory their remaining lighters (there couldn't be too many of them in stock, an expensive item like that) and they would soon find out that they were one short. But after the cold way they had treated me, I didn't feel like telling them anything.

A policeman's head appeared at the car window. "Is this your car, sir?"

"Of course."

"Will you get out, please, and join me on the sidewalk?" He walked around the front of the car and I unfastened my seat belt and slid back across the seat; I was more than a little puzzled.

"Take a look," he said, pointing at the curb when I joined him on the sidewalk. "You're parked well into the red zone."

"That isn't true," I said indignantly. "Only the front bumper's in the zone; my wheels are well behind the red paint. There's supposed to be a little leeway, a limit of tolerance, and I'm not blocking the red zone in any way – "

"Don't argue with me, sir," he said wearily, taking a pad of tickets out of his hip pocket. "Ordinarily, I'd merely tell you to repark or move on, but this time I'm giving you a ticket. A good citizen in a green raincoat reported your violation to me at the corner just now, and he was a gentleman who had every right to be sore. He said he told you that you were parked in the red zone – just as a favor – and you told him to go to hell. Now, sir, what is your name?"

SLEEPING DOG

Ross Macdonald

THE DAY AFTER her dog disappeared, Fay Hooper called me early. Her normal voice was like waltzing violins, but this morning the violins were out of tune. She sounded as though she'd been crying.

"Otto's gone." Otto was her one-year-old German shepherd. "He jumped the fence yesterday afternoon and ran away. Or else he was kidnapped — dognapped, I suppose is the right word to use."

"What makes you think that?"

"You know Otto, Mr Archer – how loyal he was. He wouldn't deliberately stay away from me overnight, not under his own power. There must be thieves involved." She caught her breath. "I realize searching for stolen dogs isn't your métier. But you *are* a detective, and I thought, since we knew each other . . ." She allowed her voice to suggest, ever so chastely, that we might get to know each other better.

I liked the woman, I liked the dog, I liked the breed. I was taking my own German shepherd pup to obedience school, which is where I met Fay Hooper. Otto and she were the handsomest and most expensive members of the class.

"How do I get to your place?"

She lived in the hills north of Malibu, she said, on the far side of the county line. If she wasn't home when I got there, her husband would be.

On my way out, I stopped at the dog school in Pacific Palisades to talk to the man who ran it, Fernando Rambeau. The kennels behind the house burst into clamor when I knocked on the front door. Rambeau boarded dogs as well as trained them.

A dark-haired girl looked out and informed me that her husband was feeding the animals. "Maybe I can help," she added doubtfully, and then she let me into a small living room.

I told her about the missing dog. "It would help if you called the vets and animal shelters and gave them a description," I said.

"We've already been doing that. Mrs Hooper was on the phone to Fernando last night." She sounded vaguely resentful. "I'll get him."

Setting her face against the continuing noise, she went out the back door. Rambeau came in with her, wiping his hands on a rag. He was a square-shouldered Canadian with a curly black beard that failed to conceal his youth. Over the beard, his intense, dark eyes peered at me warily, like an animal's sensing trouble.

Rambeau handled dogs as if he loved them. He wasn't quite so patient with human beings. His current class was only in its third week, but he was already having dropouts. The man was loaded with explosive feeling, and it was close to the surface now.

"I'm sorry about Mrs Hooper and her dog. They were my best pupils. He was, anyway. But I can't drop everything and spend the next week looking for him."

"Nobody expects that. I take it you've had no luck with your contacts."

"I don't have such good contacts. Marie and I, we just moved down here last year, from British Columbia."

"That was a mistake," his wife said from the doorway.

Rambeau pretended not to hear her. "Anyway, I know nothing about dog thieves." With both hands, he pushed the possibility away from him. "If I hear any word of the dog, I'll let you know, naturally. I've got nothing against Mrs Hooper."

His wife gave him a quick look. It was one of those revealing looks that said, among other things, that she loved him but didn't know if he loved her, and she was worried about him. She caught me watching her and lowered her eyes. Then she burst out, "Do you think somebody killed the dog?"

"I have no reason to think so."

"Some people shoot dogs, don't they?"

"Not around here," Rambeau said. "Maybe back in the bush someplace." He turned to me with a sweeping explanatory gesture. "These things make her nervous and she gets wild ideas. You know Marie is a country girl – "

"I am not. I was born in Chilliwack." Flinging a bitter look at him, she left the room.

"Was Otto shot?" I asked Rambeau.

"Not that I know of. Listen, Mr Archer, you're a good customer, but I can't stand here talking all day. I've got twenty dogs to feed."

They were still barking when I drove up the coast highway out of hearing. It was nearly forty miles to the Hoopers' mailbox, and another mile up a blacktop lane that climbed the side of a canyon to the gate. On both sides of the heavy wire gate, which had a new combination padlock on it, a hurricane fence, eight feet high and topped with barbed wire, extended out of sight. Otto would have to be quite a jumper to clear it. So would I.

The house beyond the gate was low and massive, made of fieldstone and steel and glass. I honked at it and waited. A man in blue bathing trunks came out of the house with a shotgun. The sun glinted on its twin barrels and on the man's bald head and round brown, burnished belly. He walked quite slowly, a short, heavy man in his sixties, scuffing along in huarachas. The flabby brown shell of fat on him jiggled lugubriously.

When he approached the gate, I could see the stiff gray pallor under his tan, like stone showing under varnish. He was sick or afraid, or both. His mouth was profoundly discouraged.

"What do you want?" he said over the shotgun.

"Mrs Hooper asked me to help find her dog. My name is Lew Archer."

He was not impressed. "My wife isn't here, and I'm busy. I happen to be following soybean futures rather closely."

"Look here, I've come quite a distance to lend a hand. I met Mrs Hooper at dog school and – "

Hooper uttered a short, savage laugh. "That hardly constitutes an introduction to either of us. You'd better be on your way right now."

"I think I'll wait for your wife."

"I think you won't." He raised the shotgun and let me look into its close-set, hollow round eyes. "This is my property all the way down to the road, and you're trespassing. That means I can shoot you if I have to."

"What sense would that make? I came out here to help you."

"You can't help me." He looked at me through the wire gate with a kind of pathetic arrogance, like a lion that had grown old in captivity. "Go away."

I drove back down to the road and waited for Fay Hooper. The sun slid up the sky. The inside of my car turned ovenhot. I went for a walk down the canyon. The brown September grass crunched under my feet. Away up on the far side of the canyon, an earthmover that looked like a crazy red insect was cutting the ridge to pieces.

A very fast black car came up the canyon and stopped abruptly beside me. A gaunt man in a wrinkled brown suit climbed out, with his hand on his holster, told me that he was Sheriff Carlson, and asked me what I was doing there. I told him.

He pushed back his wide cream-colored hat and scratched at his hairline. The pale eyes in his sun-fired face were like clouded glass inserts in a brick wall.

"I'm surprised Mr Hooper takes that attitude. Mrs Hooper just came to see me in the courthouse. But I can't take you up there with me if Mr Hooper says no."

"Why not?"

"He owns most of the county and holds the mortgage on the rest of it. Besides," he added with careful logic, "Mr Hooper is a friend of mine."

"Then you better get him a keeper."

The sheriff glanced around uneasily, as if the Hoopers' mailbox might be bugged. "I'm surprised he has a gun, let alone threatening you with it. He must be upset about the dog."

"He didn't seem to care about the dog."

"He does, though. *She* cares, so *he* cares," Carson said.

"What did she have to tell you?"

"She can talk to you herself. She should be along any minute. She told me that she was going to follow me out of town." He drove his black car up the lane. A few minutes later, Fay Hooper stopped her Mercedes at the mailbox. She must have seen the impatience on my face. She got out and came toward me in a little run, making noises of dismayed regret.

Fay was in her late thirties and fading slightly, as if a light frost had touched her pale gold head, but she was still a beautiful woman. She turned the gentle force of her charm on me.

"I'm dreadfully sorry," she said. "Have I kept you waiting long?"

"Your husband did. He ran me off with a shotgun."

Her gloved hand lighted on my arm, and stayed. She had an electric touch, even through layers of cloth.

"That's terrible. I had no idea that Allan still had a gun."

Her mouth was blue behind her lipstick, as if the information had chilled her to the marrow. She took me up the hill in the Mercedes. The gate was standing open, but she didn't drive in right away.

"I might as well be perfectly frank," she said without looking at me. "Ever since Otto disappeared yesterday, there's been a nagging question in my mind. What you've just told me raises the question again. I was in town all day yesterday so that Otto was alone here with Allan when – when it happened." The values her voice gave to the two names made it sound as if Allan were the dog and Otto the husband.

"When what happened, Mrs Hooper?" I wanted to know.

Her voice sank lower. "I can't help suspecting that Allan shot him. He's never liked any of my dogs. The only dogs he appreciates are hunting dogs – and he was particularly jealous of Otto. Besides, when I got back from town, Allan was getting the ground ready to plant some roses. He's never enjoyed gardening, particularly in the heat. We have professionals to do our work. And this really isn't the time of year to put in a bed of roses."

"You think your husband was planting a dog?" I asked.

"If he was, I have to know." She turned toward me, and the leather seat squeaked softly under her movement. "Find out for me, Mr Archer. If Allan killed my beautiful big old boy, I couldn't stay with him."

"Something you said implied that Allan used to have a gun or guns, but gave them up. Is that right?"

"He had a small arsenal when I married him. He was an infantry officer in the war and a big-game hunter in peacetime. But he swore off hunting years ago."

"Why?"

"I don't really know. We came home from a hunting trip in British Columbia one fall and Allan sold all his guns. He never said a word about it to me but it was the fall after the war ended, and I always thought that it must have had something to do with the war."

"Have you been married so long?"

"Thank you for that question." She produced a rueful smile. "I met Allan during the war, the year I came out, and I knew I'd met my fate. He was a very powerful person."

"And a very wealthy one."

She gave me a flashing haughty look and stepped so hard on the accelerator that she almost ran into the sheriff's car parked in front of the house. We walked around to the back, past a freeform swimming pool that looked inviting, into a walled garden. A few Greek statues stood around in elegant disrepair. Bees murmured like distant bombers among the flowers.

The bed where Allan Hooper had been digging was about five feet long and three feet wide, and it reminded me of graves.

"Get me a spade," I said.

"Are you going to dig him up?"

"You're pretty sure he's in there, aren't you, Mrs Hooper?"

"I guess I am."

From a lath house at the end of the garden, she fetched a square-edged spade. I asked her to stick around.

I took off my jacket and hung it on a marble torso where it didn't look too bad. It was easy digging in the newly worked soil. In a few minutes, I was two feet below the surface, and the ground was still soft and penetrable.

The edge of my spade struck something soft but not so penetrable. Fay Hooper heard the peculiar dull sound it made. She made a dull sound of her own. I scooped away more earth. Dog fur sprouted like stiff black grass at the bottom of the grave.

Fay got down on her knees and began to dig with her lacquered fingernails. Once she cried out in a loud harsh voice, "Dirty murderer!"

Her husband must have heard her. He came out of the house and looked over the stone wall. His head seemed poised on top of the wall, hairless and bodiless, like Humpty Dumpty. He had that look on his face, of not being able to be put together again.

"I didn't kill your dog, Fay. Honest to God, I didn't."

She didn't hear him. She was talking to Otto. "Poor boy, poor boy," she said. "Poor, beautiful boy."

Sheriff Carlson came into the garden. He reached down into the grave and freed the dog's head from the earth. His large hands moved gently on the great wedge of the skull.

Fay knelt beside him in torn and dirty stockings. "What are you doing?"

Carlson held up a red-tipped finger. "Your dog was shot through the head, Mrs Hooper, but it's no shotgun wound. Looks to me more like a deer rifle."

"I don't even own a rifle," Hooper said over the wall. "I haven't owned one for nearly twenty years. Anyway, I wouldn't shoot your dog."

Fay scrambled to her feet. She looked ready to climb the wall. "Then why did you bury him?"

His mouth opened and closed.

"Why did you buy a shotgun without telling me?"

"For protection."

"Against my dog?"

Hooper shook his head. He edged along the wall and came in tentatively through the gate. He had on slacks and a short-sleeved yellow jersey that somehow emphasized his shortness and his fatness and his age.

"Mr Hooper had some threatening calls," the sheriff said. "Somebody got hold of his unlisted number. He was just telling me about it now."

"Why didn't you tell me, Allan?"

"I didn't want to alarm you. You weren't the one they were after, anyway. I bought a shotgun and kept it in my study."

"Do you know who they are?"

"No. I make enemies in the course of business, especially the farming operations. Some crackpot shot your dog, gunning for me. I heard a shot and found him dead in the driveway."

"But how could you bury him without telling me?"

Hooper spread his hands in front of him. "I wasn't thinking too well. I felt guilty, I suppose, because whoever got him was after me. And I didn't want you to see him dead. I guess I wanted to break it to you gently."

"This is gently?"

"It's not the way I planned it. I thought if I had a chance to get you another pup – "

"No one will ever take Otto's place."

Allan Hooper stood and looked at her wistfully across the open grave, as if he would have liked to take Otto's place. After a while, the two of them went into the house.

Carlson and I finished digging Otto up and carried him out to the sheriff's car. His inert blackness filled the trunk from side to side.

"What are you going to do with him, Sheriff?" I asked.

"Get a vet I know to recover the slug in him. Then if we nab the sniper, we can use ballistics to convict him."

"You're taking this just as seriously as a real murder, aren't you?" I observed.

"They want me to," he said with a respectful look toward the house.

Mrs Hooper came out carrying a white leather suitcase which she deposited in the back seat of her Mercedes.

"Are you going someplace?" I asked her.

"Yes. I am." She didn't say where.

Her husband, who was watching her from the doorway, didn't speak. The Mercedes went away. He closed the door. Both of them had looked sick.

"She doesn't seem to believe he didn't do it. Do you, Sheriff?"

Carlson jabbed me with his forefinger. "Mr Hooper is no liar. If you want to get along with me, get that through your head. I've known Mr Hooper for over twenty years – served under him in the war – and I never heard him twist the truth."

"I'll have to take your word for it. What about those threatening phone calls? Did he report them to you before today?"

"No."

"What was said on the phone?"

"He didn't tell me."

"Does Hooper have any idea who shot the dog?"

"Well, he did say he saw a man slinking around outside the fence. He didn't get close enough to the guy to give me a good description, but he did make out that he had a black beard."

"There's a dog trainer in Pacific Palisades named Rambeau, who fits the description. Mrs Hooper has been taking Otto to his school."

"Rambeau?" Carlson said with interest.

"Fernando Rambeau. He seemed pretty upset when I talked to him this morning."

"What did he say?"

"A good deal less than he knows, I think. I'll talk to him again."

Rambeau was not at home. My repeated knocking was answered only by the barking of the dogs. I retreated up the highway to a drive-in where I ate a torpedo sandwich. When I was on my second cup of coffee, Marie Rambeau drove by in a pickup truck. I followed her home.

"Where's Fernando?" I asked.

"I don't know. I've been out looking for him."

"Is he in a bad way?"

"I don't know how you mean."

"Emotionally upset."

"He has been ever since that woman came into the class."

"Mrs Hooper?"

Her head bobbed slightly.

"Are they having an affair?"

"They better not be." Her small red mouth looked quite implacable.

"He was out with her night before last. I heard him make the date. He was gone all night, and when he came home, he was on one of his black drunks and he wouldn't go to bed. He sat in the kitchen and drank himself glassy-eyed." She got out of the pickup facing me. "Is shooting a dog a very serious crime?"

"It is to me, but not to the law. It's not like shooting a human being."

"It would be to Fernando. He loves dogs the way other people love human beings. That included Otto."

"But he shot him."

Her head drooped. I could see the straight white part dividing her black hair. "I'm afraid he did. He's got a crazy streak, and it comes out in him when he drinks. You should have heard him in the kitchen yesterday morning. He was moaning and groaning about his brother."

"His brother?"

"Fernando had an older brother, George, who died back in Canada after the war. Fernando was just a kid when it happened and it was a big loss to him. His parents were dead, too, and they put him in a foster home in Chilliwack. He still has nightmares about it."

"What did his brother die of?"

"He never told me exactly, but I think he was shot in some kind of hunting accident. George was a guide and packer in the Fraser River Valley below Mount Robson. That's where Fernando comes from, the Mount Robson country. He won't go back on account of what happened to his brother."

"What did he say about his brother yesterday?" I asked.

"That he was going to get his revenge for George. I got so scared I couldn't listen to him. I went out and fed the dogs. When I came back in, Fernando was loading his deer rifle. I asked him what he was planning to do, but he walked right out and drove away."

"May I see the rifle?"

"It isn't in the house. I looked for it after he left today. He must have taken it with him again. I'm so afraid that he'll kill somebody."

"What's he driving?"

"Our car. It's an old blue Meteor sedan."

Keeping an eye out for it, I drove up the highway to the Hoopers' canyon. Everything there was very peaceful. Too peaceful. Just inside the locked gate, Allan Hooper was lying face down on his shotgun. I could see small ants in single file trekking across the crown of his bald head.

I got a hammer out of the trunk of my car and used it to break the padlock. I lifted his head. His skin was hot in the sun, as if death had fallen on him like a fever. But he had been shot neatly between the eyes. There was no exit wound; the bullet was still in his head. Now the ants were crawling on my hands.

I found my way into the Hoopers' study, turned off the stuttering teletype, and sat down under an elk head to telephone the courthouse. Carlson was in his office.

"I have bad news, Sheriff. Allan Hooper's been shot."

I heard him draw in his breath quickly. "Is he dead?"

"Extremely dead. You better put out a general alarm for Rambeau."

Carlson said with gloomy satisfaction, "I already have him."

"You have him?"

"That's correct. I picked him up in the Hoopers' canyon and brought him in just a few minutes ago." Carlson's voice sank to a mournful mumble. "I picked him up a little too late, I guess."

"Did Rambeau do any talking?"

"He hasn't had a chance to yet. When I stopped his car, he piled out and threatened me with a rifle. I clobbered him one good."

I went outside to wait for Carlson and his men. A very pale afternoon moon hung like a ghost in the sky. For some reason, it made me think of Fay. She ought to be here. It occurred to me that possibly she had been.

I went and looked at Hooper's body again. He had nothing to tell me. He lay as if he had fallen from a height, perhaps all the way from the moon.

They came in a black county wagon and took him away. I followed them inland to the county seat, which rose like a dusty island in a dark green lake of orange groves. We parked in the courthouse parking lot, and the sheriff and I went inside.

Rambeau was under guard in a second-floor room with barred windows. Carlson said it was used for interrogation. There was nothing in the room but an old deal table and some wooden chairs. Rambeau sat hunched forward on one of them, his hands hanging limp between his knees. Part of his head had been shaved and plastered with bandages.

"I had to cool him with my gun butt," Carlson said. "You're lucky I didn't shoot you – you know that, Fernando?"

Rambeau made no response. His black eyes were set and dull.

"Had his rifle been fired?"

"Yeah. Chet Scott is working on it now. Chet's my identification lieutenant and he's a bear on ballistics." The sheriff turned back to Rambeau. "You might as well give us a full confession, boy. If you shot Mr Hooper and his dog, we can link the bullets to your gun. You know that."

Rambeau didn't speak or move.

"What did you have against Mr Hooper?" Carlson said.

No answer. Rambeau's mouth was set like a trap in the thicket of his beard.

"Your older brother," I said to him, "was killed in a hunting accident in British Columbia. Was Hooper at the other end of the gun that killed George?"

Rambeau didn't answer me, but Carlson's head came up. "Where did you get that, Archer?"

"From a couple of things I was told. According to Rambeau's wife, he was talking yesterday about revenge for his brother's death. According to Fay Hooper, her husband swore off guns when he came back from a certain hunting trip after the war. Would you know if that trip was to British Columbia?"

"Yeah. Mr Hooper took me and the wife with him."

"Whose wife?"

"Both our wives."

"To the Mount Robson area?"

"That's correct. We went up after elk."

"And did he shoot somebody accidentally?" I wanted to know.

"Not that I know of. I wasn't with him all the time, understand. He often went out alone, or with Mrs Hooper," Carlson replied.

"Did he use a packer named George Rambeau?"

"I wouldn't know. Ask Fernando here."

I asked Fernando. He didn't speak or move. Only his eyes had changed. They were wet and glistening-black, visible parts of a grief that filled his head like a dark underground river.

The questioning went on and produced nothing. It was night when I went outside. The moon was slipping down behind the dark hills. I took a room in a hotel and checked in with my answering service in Hollywood. About an hour before, Fay Hooper had called me from a Las Vegas hotel. When I tried to return the call, she wasn't in her room and didn't respond to paging. I left a message for her to come home, that her husband was dead.

Next, I called R.C.M.P. headquarters in Vancouver to ask some questions about George Rambeau. The answers came over the line in clipped Canadian tones. George and his dog had disappeared from his cabin below Red Pass in the fall of 1945. Their bodies hadn't been recovered until the following May, and by that time they consisted of parts of the two skeletons. These included George Rambeau's skull, which had been pierced in the right front and left rear quadrants by a heavy-caliber bullet. The bullet had not been recovered. Who fired it, or when or why, had never been determined. The dog, a husky, had also been shot through the head.

I walked over to the courthouse to pass the word to Carlson. He was in the basement shooting gallery with Lieutenant Scott, who was firing test rounds from Fernando Rambeau's .30/30 repeater.

I gave them the official account of the accident. "But since George Rambeau's dog was shot, too, it probably wasn't an accident," I said.

"I see what you mean," Carlson said. "It's going to be rough, spreading all this stuff out in court about Mr Hooper. We have to nail it down, though."

I went back to my hotel and to bed, but the process of nailing down the case against Rambeau continued through the night. By morning, Lieutenant

Scott had detailed comparisons set up between the test-fired slugs and the ones dug out of Hooper and the dog. I looked at his evidence through a comparison microscope. It left no doubt in my mind that the slugs that killed Allan Hooper and the dog Otto had come from Rambeau's gun.

But Rambeau still wouldn't talk, even to phone his wife or ask for a lawyer.

"We'll take you out to the scene of the crime," Carlson said. "I've cracked tougher nuts than you, boy."

We rode in the back seat of his car with Fernando handcuffed between us. Lieutenant Scott did the driving. Rambeau groaned and pulled against his handcuffs. He was very close to the breaking point, I thought.

It came a few minutes later when the car turned up the lane past the Hoopers' mailbox. He burst into sudden fierce tears as if a pressure gauge in his head had broken. It was strange to see a bearded man crying like a boy, and whimpering, "I don't want to go up there."

"Because you shot him?" Carlson said.

"I shot the dog. I confess I shot the dog," Rambeau said.

"And the man?"

"No!" he cried. "I never killed a man. Mr Hooper was the one who did. He followed my brother out in the woods and shot him."

"If you knew that," I said, "why didn't you tell the Mounties years ago?"

"I didn't know it then. I was seven years old. How would I understand? When Mrs Hooper came to our cabin to be with my brother, how would I know it was a serious thing? Or when Mr Hooper asked me if she had been there? I didn't know he was her husband. I thought he was her father checking up. I knew I shouldn't have told him – I could see it in his face the minute after – but I didn't understand the situation till the other night, when I talked to Mrs Hooper."

"Did she know that her husband had shot George?"

"She didn't even know George had been killed. They never went back to the Fraser River after 1945. But when we put our facts together, we agreed he must have done it. I came out here next morning to get even. The dog came out to the gate. It wasn't real to me – I was drinking most of the night – it wasn't real to me until the dog went down. I shot him. Mr Hooper shot my dog. But when he came out of the house himself, I couldn't pull the trigger. I yelled at him and ran away."

"What did you yell?" I said.

"The same thing I told him on the telephone: 'Remember Mount Robson.'"

A yellow cab, which looked out of place in the canyon, came over the ridge above us. Lieutenant Scott waved it to a stop. The driver said he'd just brought Mrs Hooper home from the airport and wanted to know if that constituted a felony. Scott waved him on.

"I wonder what she was doing at the airport," Carlson said.

"Coming home from Vegas. She tried to call me from there last night. I forgot to tell you."

"You don't forget important things like that," Carlson said.

"I suppose I wanted her to come home under her own power."

"In case she shot her husband?"

"More or less."

"She didn't. Fernando shot him, didn't you, boy?"

"I shot the dog. I am innocent of the man." He turned to me: "Tell her that. Tell her I am sorry about the dog. I came out here to surrender the gun and tell her yesterday. I don't trust myself with guns."

"With darn good reason," Carlson said. "We know you shot Mr Hooper. Ballistic evidence doesn't lie."

Rambeau screeched in his ear, "You're a liar! You're all liars!"

Carlson swung his open hand against the side of Rambeau's face. "Don't call me names, little man."

Lieutenant Scott spoke without taking his eyes from the road. "I wouldn't hit him, Chief. You wouldn't want to damage our case."

Carlson subsided, and we drove on up to the house. Carlson went in without knocking. The guard at the door discouraged me from following him.

I could hear Fay's voice on the other side of the door, too low to be understood. Carlson said something to her.

"Get out! Get out of my house, you killer!" Fay cried out sharply.

Carlson didn't come out. I went in instead. One of his arms was wrapped around her body; the other hand was covering her mouth. I got his Adam's apple in the crook of my left arm, pulled him away from her, and threw him over my left hip. He went down clanking and got up holding his revolver.

He should have shot me right away. But he gave Fay Hooper time to save my life.

She stepped in front of me. "Shoot me, Mr Carlson. You might as well. You shot the one man I ever cared for."

"Your husband shot George Rambeau, if that's who you mean. I ought to know. I was there." Carlson scowled down at his gun, and replaced it in his holster.

Lieutenant Scott was watching him from the doorway.

"You were there?" I said to Carlson. "Yesterday you told me Hooper was alone when he shot Rambeau."

"He was. When I said I was there, I meant in the general neighborhood."

"Don't believe him," Fay said. "He fired the gun that killed George, and it was no accident. The two of them hunted George down in the woods. My husband planned to shoot him himself, but George's dog came at him and he had to dispose of it. By that time, George had drawn a bead on Allan.

Mr Carlson shot him. It was hardly a coincidence that the next spring Allan financed his campaign for sheriff."

"She's making it up," Carlson said. "She wasn't within ten miles of the place."

"But you were, Mr Carlson, and so was Allan. He told me the whole story yesterday, after we found Otto. Once that happened, he knew that everything was bound to come out. I already suspected him, of course, after I talked to Fernando. Allan filled in the details himself. He thought, since he hadn't killed George personally, I would be able to forgive him. But I couldn't. I left him and flew to Nevada, intending to divorce him. I've been intending to for twenty years."

Carlson said: "Are you sure you didn't shoot him before you left?"

"How could she have?" I said. "Ballistics don't lie, and the ballistic evidence says he was shot with Fernando's rifle. Nobody had access to it but Fernando and you. You stopped him on the road and knocked him out, took his rifle and used it to kill Hooper. You killed him for the same reason that Hooper buried the dog – to keep the past buried. You thought Hooper was the only witness to the murder of George Rambeau. But by that time, Mrs Hooper knew about it, too."

"It wasn't murder. It was self-defense, just like in the war. Anyway, you'll never hang it on me."

"We don't have to. We'll hang Hooper on you. How about it, Lieutenant?"

Scott nodded grimly, not looking at his chief. I relieved Carlson of his gun. He winced, as if I were amputating part of his body. He offered no resistance when Scott took him out to the car.

I stayed behind for a final word with Fay. "Fernando asked me to tell you he's sorry for shooting your dog."

"We're both sorry." She stood with her eyes down, as if the past was swirling visibly around her feet. "I'll talk to Fernando later. Much later."

"There's one coincidence that bothers me. How did you happen to take your dog to his school?"

"I happened to see his sign, and Fernando Rambeau isn't a common name. I couldn't resist going there. I had to know what had happened to George. I think perhaps Fernando came to California for the same reason."

"Now you both know," I said.

THE WENCH IS DEAD

Fredric Brown

1

A FUZZ IS a fuzz is a fuzz when you awaken from a wino jag. God, I'd drunk three pints of muscatel that I know of and maybe more, maybe lots more, because that's when I drew a blank, that's when research stopped. I rolled over on the cot so I could look out through the dirty pane of the window at the clock in the hockshop across the way.

Ten o'clock said the clock.

Get up, Howard Perry, I told myself. Get up, you B.A.S. for bastard, rise and greet the day. Hit the floor and get moving if you want to keep that job, that all-important job that keeps you drinking and sometimes eating and sometimes sleeping with Billie the Kid when she hasn't got a sucker on the hook. That's your life, you B.A.S., you bastard. That's your life for a while. This is it, this is the McCoy, this is the way a wino meets the not-so-newborn day. You're learning, man.

Pull on a sock, another sock, pants, shirt, shoes, get the hell to Burke's and wash a dish, wash a thousand dishes for six bits an hour and a meal or two a day when you want it.

God, I thought, did I really have the habit? Nuts, not in three months. Not when you've been a normal drinker all your life. Not when, much as you've always enjoyed drinking, it's always been in moderation and you've always been able to handle the stuff. This was just temporary.

And I had only a few weeks to go. In a few weeks I'd be back in Chicago, back at my desk in my father's investment company, back wearing white shirts, and B.A.S. would stand for Bachelor of Arts in Sociology. That was a laugh right now, that degree. Three months ago it had meant something – but that was in Chicago, and this was LA, and now all it meant was bastard. That's all it had meant ever since I started drifting.

It's funny, the way those things can happen. You've got a good family and a good education, and then suddenly, for no reason you can define, you start drifting. You lose interest in your family and your job, and one day you find yourself headed for the Coast.

You sit down one day and ask yourself how it happened. But you can't answer. There are a thousand little answers, sure, but there's no *big* answer. It's easier to worry about where the next bottle of sweet wine is coming from.

And that's when you realize your own personal B.A.S. stands for bastard.

With me, LA had been the end of the line. I'd seen the *Dishwasher Wanted* sign in Burke's window, and suddenly I'd known what I had to do. At pearl-diver's wages, it would take a long time to get up the bus fare back to Chicago and family and respectability, but that was beside the point. The point was that after a hundred thousand dirty dishes there'd *be* a bus ticket to Chicago.

But it had been hard to remember the ticket and forget the dishes. Wine is cheap, but they're not giving it away. Since I'd started pearl-diving I'd had grub and six bits an hour for seven hours a day. Enough to drink on and to pay for this dirty, crumby little crackerbox of a room.

So here I was, still thinking about the bus ticket, and still on my uppers on East Fifth Street, LA. Main Street used to be the tenderloin street of Los Angeles and I'd headed for it when I jumped off the freight, but I'd found that the worst district, the real skid row, was now on Fifth Street in the few blocks east of Main. The worse the district, the cheaper the living, and that's what I'd been looking for.

Sure, by Fifth Street standards, I was being a pantywaist to hold down a steady job like that, but sleeping in doorways was a little too rugged and I'd found out quickly that panhandling wasn't for me. I lacked the knack.

I dipped water from the cracked basin and rubbed it on my face, and the feel of the stubble told me I could get by one more day without shaving. Or anyway I could wait till evening so the shave would be fresh in case I'd be sleeping with Billie.

Cold water helped a little but I still felt like hell. There were empty wine bottles in the corner and I checked to make sure they were completely empty, and they were. So were my pockets, except, thank God, for tobacco and cigarette papers. I rolled myself a cigarette and lighted it.

But I needed a drink to start the day.

What does a wino do when he wakes up broke (and how often does he wake otherwise?) and needs a drink? Well, I'd found several answers to that. The easiest one, right now, would be to hit Billie for a drink if she was awake yet, and alone.

I crossed the street to the building where Billie had a room. A somewhat newer building, a hell of a lot nicer room, but then she paid a hell of a lot more for it.

I rapped on her door softly, a little code knock we had. If she wasn't awake she wouldn't hear it and if she wasn't alone she wouldn't answer it.

But she called out, "It's not locked; come on in," and she said "Hi, Professor," as I closed the door behind me. "Professor" she called me, occasionally and banteringly. It was my way of talking, I guess. I'd tried at first to use poor diction, bad grammar, to fit in with the place, but I'd given it up as too tough a job. Besides, I'd learned Fifth Street already had quite a bit of good grammar. Some of its denizens had been newspapermen once, some had written poetry; one I knew was a defrocked clergyman.

I said, "Hi, Billie the Kid."

"Just woke up, Howie. What time is it?"

"A little after ten," I told her. "Is there a drink around?"

"Jeez, only ten? Oh well, I had seven hours. Guy came here when Mike closed at two, but he didn't stay long."

She sat up in bed and stretched, the covers falling away from her naked body. Beautiful breasts she had, size and shape of half grape-fruits and firm. Nice arms and shoulders, and a lovely face. Hair black and sleek in a page-boy bob that fell into place as she shook her head. Twenty-five, she told me once; and I believed her, but she could have passed for several years less than that, even, now without make up and her eyes still a little puffy from sleep. Certainly it didn't show that she'd spent three years as a B-girl, part-time hustler, heavy drinker. Before that she'd been married to a man who'd worked for a manufacturing jeweler; he'd suddenly left for parts unknown with a considerable portion of his employer's stock, leaving Billie in a jam and with a mess of debts.

Wilhelmina Kidder, Billie the Kid, my Billie. Any man's Billie if he flashed a roll, but oddly I'd found that I could love her a little and not let that bother me. Maybe because it had been that way when I'd first met her over a month ago; I'd come to love her knowing what she was, so why should it bother me? What she saw in me I don't know, and didn't care.

"About that drink," I said.

She laughed and threw down the covers, got out of bed and walked past me naked to the closet to get a robe. I wanted to reach for her but I didn't; I'd learned by now that Billie the Kid was never amorous early in the morning and resented any passes made before noon.

She shrugged into a quilted robe and padded barefoot over to the little refrigerator behind the screen that hid a tiny kitchenette. She opened the door and said, "God damn it."

"God damn what?" I wanted to know. "Out of liquor?"

She held up over the screen a Hiram Walker bottle with only half an inch of ready-mixed Manhattan in it. Almost the only thing Billie ever drank, Manhattans.

"As near out as matters. Honey, would you run upstairs and see if Mame's got some? She usually has."

Mame is a big blonde who works behind the bar at Mike Karas' joint, The Best Chance, where Billie works as B-girl. A tough number, Mame. I said, "If she's asleep she'll murder me for waking her. What's wrong with the store?"

"She's up by now. She was off early last night. And if you get it at the store it won't be on ice. Wait, I'll phone her, though, so if she *is* asleep it'll be me that wakes her and not you."

She made the call and then nodded. "Okay, honey. She's got a full bottle she'll lend me. Scram."

I scrammed, from the second floor rear to the third floor front. Mame's door was open; she was out in the hallway paying off a milkman and waiting for him to receipt the bill. She said, "Go on in. Take a load off." I went inside the room and sat down in the chair that was built to match Mame, overstuffed. I ran my fingers around under the edge of the cushion; one of Mame's men friends might have sat there with change in his pocket. It's surprising how much change you can pick up just by trying any overstuffed chairs or sofas you sit on. No change this time, but I came up with a fountain pen, a cheap dime-store-looking one. Mame had just closed the door and I held it up. "In the chair. Yours, Mame?"

"Nope. Keep it, Howie, I got a pen."

"Maybe one of your friends'll miss it," I said. It was too cheap a pen to sell or hock so I might as well be honest about it.

"Nope, I know who lost it. Seen it in his pocket last night. It was Jesus, and the hell with him."

"Mame, you sound sacrilegious."

She laughed. "Hay-*soos*, then. Jesus Gonzales. A Mex. But when he told me that was his handle I called him Jesus. And Jesus was *he* like a cat on a hot stove!" She walked around me over to her refrigerator but her voice kept on. "Told me not to turn on the lights when he come in and went over to watch out the front window for a while like he was watching for the heat. Looks out my side window too, one with the fire escape. Pulls down all the shades before he says okay, turn on the lights." The refrigerator door closed and she came back with a bottle.

"Was he a hot one," she said. "Just got his coat off – he threw it on that chair, when there's a knock. Grabs his coat again and goes out my side window down the fire escape." She laughed again. "Was that a flip? It was only Dixie from the next room knocking, to bum cigarettes. So if I ever see Jesus again it's no dice, guy as jumpy as that. Keep his pen. Want a drink here?"

"If you'll have one with me."

"I don't drink, Howie. Just keep stuff around for friends and callers. Tell Billie to give me another bottle like this back. I got a friend likes Manhattans, like her."

When I got back to Billie's room, she'd put on a costume instead of the robe, but it wasn't much of a costume. A skimpy Bikini bathing suit. She pirouetted in it. "Like it, Howie? Just bought it yesterday."

"Nice," I said, "but I like you better without it."

"Pour us drinks, huh? For me, just a quickie."

"Speaking of quickies," I said.

She picked up a dress and started to pull it over her head. "If you're thinking that way, Professor, I'll hide the family treasures. Say, that's a good line; I'm getting to talk like you do sometimes."

I poured us drinks and we sat down with them. She'd stepped into sandals and was dressed. I said, "You've got lots of good lines, Billie the Kid. But correct me – was that lingerie instead of a bathing suit, or am I out of date on fashions?"

"I'm going to the beach today, Howie, for a sun-soak. Won't go near the water so why not just wear the suit under and save changing? Say, why don't you take a day off and come along?"

"Broke. The one thing to be said for Burke as an employer is that he pays every day. Otherwise there'd be some dry, dry evenings."

"What you make there? A fin, maybe. I'll lend you a fin."

"That way lies madness," I said. "Drinks I'll take from you, or more important things than drinks. But taking money would make me – " I stopped and wondered just what taking money from Billie would make me, just how consistent I was being. After all, I could always send it back to her from Chicago. What kept me from taking it, then? A gal named Honor, I guess. Corny as it sounds, I said it lightly. "I could not love thee, dear, so much, loved I not Honor more."

"You're a funny guy, Howie. I don't understand you."

Suddenly I wanted to change the subject. "Billie, how come Mame doesn't drink?"

"Don't you know hypes don't like to drink?"

"Sure, but I didn't spot Mame for one."

"Hype with a big H for heroin, Howie. Doesn't show it much, though. I'll give you that."

"I haven't known enough junkies to be any judge," I said. "The only one I know for sure is the cook at Burke's."

"Don't ever try it, Howie. It's bad stuff. I joy-popped once just to see what it was like, but never again. Too easy to get to like it. And Howie, it can make things rough."

I said, "I hear your words of wisdom and shall stick to drink. Speaking of which – " I poured myself another.

2

I got to the restaurant – it's on Main a block from Fifth – at a quarter after eleven, only fifteen minutes late. Burke was at the stove – he does his own cooking until noon, when Ramon comes on – and turned to glare at me but didn't say anything.

Still feeling good from the drinks, I dived into my dishwashing.

The good feeling was mostly gone, though, by noon, when Ramon came on. He had a fresh bandage on his forehead; I wondered if there was a new knife wound under it. He already had two knife scars, old ones, on his cheek and on his chin. He looked mean, too, and I decided to stay out of his way. Ramon's got a nasty temper when he needs a jolt, and it was pretty obvious that he needed one. He looked like a man with a kingsize monkey, and he was. I'd often wondered how he fed it. Cooks draw good money compared to other restaurant help, but even a cook doesn't get enough to support a five or six cap a day habit, not at a joint like Burke's anyway. Ramon was tall for a Mexican, but he was thin and his face looked gaunt. It's an ugly face except when he grins and his teeth flash white. But he wouldn't be grinning this afternoon, not if he needed a jolt.

Burke went front to work the register and help at the counter for the noon rush, and Ramon took over at the stove. We worked in silence until the rush was over, about two o'clock.

He came over to me then. He was sniffling and his eyes were running. He said, "Howie, you do me a favor. I'm burning, Howie, I need a fix, quick. I got to sneak out, fifteen minutes."

"Okay, I'll try to watch things. What's working?"

"Two hamburg steak dinners on. Done one side, five more minutes other side. You know what else to put on."

"Sure, and if Burke comes back I'll tell him you're in the can. But you'd better hurry."

He rushed out, not even bothering to take off his apron or chef's hat. I timed five minutes on the clock and then I took up the steaks, added the trimmings and put them on the ledge, standing at an angle back of the window so Burke couldn't see that it was I and not Ramon who was putting them there. A few minutes later the waitress put in a call for stuffed peppers, a pair; they were already cooked and I didn't have any trouble dishing them.

Ramon came back before anything else happened. He looked like a different man – he would be for as long as the fix lasted. His teeth flashed. "Million thanks, Howie." He handed me a flat pint bottle of muscatel. "For you, my friend."

"Ramon," I said, "you are a gentleman and a scholar." He went back to his stove and started scraping it. I bent down out of sight to open the bottle. I took a good long drink and then hid it back out of sight under one of the tubs.

Two-thirty, and my half-hour lunch break. Only I wasn't hungry. I took another drink of the muskie and put it back. I could have killed it but the rest of the afternoon would go better if I rationed it and made it last until near quitting time.

I wandered over to the alley entrance, rolling a cigarette. A beautiful bright day out; it would have been wonderful to be at the beach with Billie the Kid.

Only Billie the Kid wasn't at the beach; she was coming toward me from the mouth of the alley. She was still wearing the dress she'd pulled on over the bathing suit but she wasn't at the beach. She was walking toward me, looking worried, looking frightened.

I walked to meet her. She grabbed my arm, tightly. "Howie. Howie, did you kill Mame?"

"Did I – *what?*"

Her eyes were big, looking up at me. "Howie, if you did, I don't care. I'll help you, give you money to get away. But – "

"Whoa," I said, "Whoa, Billie. I didn't kill Mame. I didn't even rape her. She was okay when I left. What happened? Or are you dreaming this up?"

"She's dead, Howie, murdered. And about the time you were there. They found her a little after noon and say she'd been dead somewhere around two hours. Let's go have a drink and I'll tell you what all happened."

"All right," I said. "I've got most of my lunch time left. Only I haven't been paid yet – "

"Come on, hurry." As we walked out of the alley she took a bill from her purse and stuffed it into my pocket. We took the nearest ginmill and ordered drinks at a booth at the back where we weren't near enough anyone to be heard. The bill she'd put in my pocket was a sawbuck. When the waitress brought our drinks and the change I shoved it toward Billie. She shook her head and pushed it back. "Keep it and owe me ten, Howie. You might need it in case – well, just in case." I said, "Okay, Billie, but I'll pay this back." I would, too, but it probably wouldn't be until I mailed it to her from Chicago and it would probably surprise the hell out of her to get it.

I said, "Now tell me, but quit looking so worried. I'm as innocent as new-fallen snow – and I don't mean cocaine. Let me reconstruct my end first, and then tell yours. I got to work at eleven-twenty. Walked straight there from your place, so it would have been ten after when I left you. And – let's see, from the other end, it was ten o'clock when I woke up, wouldn't have been over ten or fifteen minutes before I knocked on your door, another few minutes before I got to Mame's and I was up there only a few minutes. Say I saw her last around twenty after ten, and she was okay then. Over."

"Huh? Over what?"

"I mean, you take it. From when I left you, about ten minutes after eleven."

"Oh. Well, I straightened the room, did a couple things, and left, it must have been a little after twelve on account of the noon whistles had blown just a few minutes ago. I was going to the beach. I was going to walk over to the terminal and catch the Santa Monica bus, go to Ocean Park. Only first I stopped in the drugstore right on the corner for a cup of coffee. I was there maybe ten-fifteen minutes letting it cool enough to drink and drinking it. While I was there I heard a cop car stop near but I didn't think anything of it; they're always picking up drunks and all.

"But while I was there too I remembered I'd forgot to bring my sun glasses and sun-tan oil, so I went back to get them.

"Minute I got inside the cops were waiting and they asked if I lived there and then started asking questions, did I know Mame and when I saw her last and all."

"Did you tell them you'd talked to her on the phone?"

"Course not, Howie. I'm not a dope. I knew by then something had happened to her and if I told them about that call and what it was about, it would have brought you in and put you on the spot. I didn't even tell them you were with me, let alone going up to Mame's. I kept you out of it.

"They're really questioning everybody, Howie. They didn't pull me in but they kept me in *my* own room questioning me till just fifteen minutes ago. See, they really worked on me because I admitted I knew Mame – I had to admit that 'cause we work at the same place and they'd have found that out.

"And of course they knew she was a hype, her arms and all; they're checking everybody's arms and thank God mine are okay. They asked me mostly about where we worked, Mike's. I think they figure Mike Karas is a dealer, what with Mame working for him."

"Is he, Billie?"

"I don't know, honey. He's in some racket, but it isn't dope."

I said, "Well, I don't see what either of us has to worry about. It's not our – My God, I just remembered something."

"What, Howie?"

"A guy saw me going in her room, a milkman. Mame was in the hall paying him off when I went up. She told me to go on in and I did, right past him."

"Jesus, Howie, did she call you by name when she told you to go on in? If they get a name, even a first name, and you living right across the street – "

I thought hard. "Pretty sure she didn't, Billie. She told me to go in and take a load off, but I'm pretty sure she didn't add a Howie to it. Anyway, they may never find the milkman was there. He isn't likely to stick his neck out by coming to them. How was she killed, Billie?"

"Somebody said a shiv, but I don't know for sure."

"Who found her and how come?"

"I don't know. They were asking me questions, not me asking them. That part'll be in the papers, though."

"All right," I said. "Let's let it go till this evening, then. How's about this evening, Billie, are you going to The Best Chance anyway?"

"I *got* to, tonight, after that. If I don't show up, they'll want to know why and where I was and everything. And listen, don't you come around either, after hours tonight or in the morning. You stay away from that building, Howie. If they find that milkman they might even have him staked out watching for you. Don't even walk *past*. You better even stay off that block, go in and out the back way to your own room. And we better not even see each other till the heat's off or till we know what the score is."

I sighed.

I was ten minutes late reporting back and Burke glared at me again but still didn't say anything. I guess I was still relatively dependable for a dishwasher, but I was learning.

I made the rest of the wine last me till Baldy, the evening shift dishwasher, showed up to relieve me. Burke paid me off for the day then, and I was rich again.

3

Someone was shaking me, shaking me hard. I woke to fuzz and fog and Billie the Kid was peering through it at me, looking really scared, more scared than when she'd asked me yesterday if I'd killed Mame.

"Howie, wake up." I was in my own little shoe-box of a room, Billie standing by my cot bending over me. I wasn't covered, but the extent of my undressing had been to kick off my shoes.

"Howie, listen, you're in trouble, honey. You got to get out of here, back way like I come in. Hurry."

I sat up and wanted to know the time.

"Only nine, Howie. But hurry. Here. This will help you." She screwed off the top of a half pint bottle of whisky. "Drink some quick. Help you wake up."

I took a drink and the whisky burned rawly down my throat. For a moment I thought it was going to make me sick to my stomach, but then it decided to stay down and it did clear my head a little. Not much, but a little.

"What's wrong, Billie?"

"Put on your shoes. I'll tell you, but not here."

Luckily my shoes were loafers and I could step into them. I went to the basin of water, rubbed some on my face. While I washed and dried and ran a comb through my hair Billie was going through the dresser; a towel on the bed, everything I owned piled on it. It didn't make much of a bundle.

She handed it to me and then was pulling me out into the hallway, me and everything I owned. Apparently I wasn't coming back here, or Billie didn't think I was.

Out into the alley, through to Sixth Street and over Sixth to Main, south on Main. A restaurant with booths, mostly empty. The waitress came over and I ordered coffee, black. Billie ordered ham and eggs and toast and when the waitress left she leaned across the table. "I didn't want to argue with her in front of you, Howie, but that food I ordered is for you; you're going to eat it all. You got to be sober."

I groaned, but knew it would be easier to eat than to argue with a Billie the Kid as vehement as this one.

"What is it, Billie? What's up?"

"Did you read the papers last night?"

I shook my head. I hadn't read any papers up to about nine o'clock and after that I didn't remember what I'd done or hadn't. But I wouldn't have read any papers. That reminded me to look in my pockets to see what money I had left, if any. No change, but thank God there were some crumpled bills. A five and two ones, when I pulled them out and looked under cover of the table. I'd had a little over nine out of the ten Billie had given me to buy us a drink with, a little under five I'd got from Burke. That made fourteen and I'd spent seven of it somehow – and God knows how since I couldn't possibly have drunk that much muskie or even that much whisky at Fifth Street prices. But at least I hadn't been rolled, so it could have been worse.

"They got that milkman, Howie," Billie was saying. "Right off. He'd given Mame a receipt and she'd dropped it on that little table by the door so they knew he'd been there and they found him and he says he'll know you if he sees you. He described you too. You thinking straight by now, Howie?"

"Sure I'm thinking straight. What if they *do* find me? Damn it, I didn't kill her. Didn't have any reason to. They can't do any more than question me."

"Howie, haven't you ever been in trouble with cops? Not on anything serious, I guess, or you wouldn't talk like that. That milkman would put you right on the scene at close to the right time and that's all they'd want. They got nobody else to work on.

"Sure they'll question you. With fists and rubber hoses they'll question you. They'll beat the hell out of you for days on end, tie you in a chair with five hundred watts in your eyes and slap you every time you close them. Sure they'll question you. They'll question you till you wish you *had* killed Mame so you could tell 'em and get it over with and get some sleep. Howie, cops are tough, mean bastards when they're trying to pin down a murder rap. This is a murder rap, Howie."

I smiled a little without meaning to. Not because what she'd been saying was funny, but because I was thinking of the headlines if they did beat the truth out of me, or if I had to tell all to beat the rap. *Chicago Scion in Heroin Murder Case.* Chicago papers please copy.

I saw the hurt look on Billie's face and straightened mine. "Sorry," I said. "I was laughing at something else. Go on."

But the waitress was coming and Billie waited till she'd left. She shoved the ham and eggs and toast in front of me. "Eat," she said. I ate.

"And that isn't all, Howie. They'll frame you on some other charge to hold you. Howie, they might even frame you on the murder rap itself if they don't find who else did it. They could do it easy, just take a few little things from her room – it had been searched – and claim you had 'em on you or they were in your room. How'd you prove they weren't? And what'd your word be against a cop's? They could put you in the little room and gas you, Howie. And there's something else, too."

"Something worse that *that*?"

"I don't mean that. I mean what they'd do to me, Howie. And that'd be for *sure*. A perjury rap, a nice long one. See, I signed a statement after they questioned me, and that'd make it perjury for me if you tell 'em the truth about why you went up to see Mame. And what else could you tell them?"

I put down my knife and fork and stared at her. I hadn't been *really* worried about the things she'd been telling me. Innocent men, I'd been telling myself, aren't framed by the cops on murder charges. Not if they're willing to tell the truth down the line. They might give me a bad time, I thought, but they wouldn't hold me long if I leveled with them. But if Billie had signed a statement, then telling them the truth was out. Billie was on the wrong side of the law already; they *would* take advantage of perjury to put her away, maybe for several years.

I said, "I'm sorry, Billie. I didn't realize I'd have to involve you if I had to tell them the truth."

"Eat, Howie. Eat all that grub. Don't worry about me; I just mentioned it. You're in worse trouble than *I* am. But I'm glad you're talking straight; you sound really awake now. Now you go on eating and I'll tell you what you've got to do.

"First, this milkman's description. Height, weight and age fairly close but not exact on any, and anyway you can't change that. But you got to change clothes, buy new ones, because Jesus, the guy got your clothes perfect. Blue denim shirt cut off above elbows, tan work pants, brown loafers. Now first thing when you leave here, buy different clothes, see?"

"All right," I said. "How else did he describe me?"

"Well, he thought you had blond hair and it's a little darker than that, not much. Said you needed a shave – you need one worse now – and said you looked like a Fifth Street bum, a wino maybe. That's all, except he's sure he could identify you if he ever saw you again. And that's bad, Howie."

"It is," I said.

"Howie, do you want to blow town? I can lend you – well, I'm a little low right now and on account of Karas' place being watched so close I won't be able to pick up any extra money for a while, but I can lend you fifty if you want to blow town. Do you?"

"No, Billie," I said. "I don't want to blow town. Not unless you want to go with me."

God, what had made me *say that?* What had I meant by it? What business had I taking Billie away from the district she knew, the place where she could make a living – if I couldn't – putting her further in a jam for disappearing when she was more or less a witness in a murder case? And when I wanted to be back in Chicago, back working for my father and being respectable, within a few weeks anyway.

What had I meant? I couldn't take Billie back with me, much as I liked – maybe loved – her. Billie the Kid as the wife of a respectable investment man? It wouldn't work, for either of us. But if I hadn't meant that, what the hell *had* I meant?

But Billie was shaking her head. "Howie, it wouldn't work. Not for us, not right now. If you could quit drinking, straighten out. But I know – I know you can't. It isn't your fault and – oh, honey, let's not talk about that now. Anyway, I'm *glad* you don't want to lam because – well, because I *am*. But listen – "

"Yes, Billie?"

"You've got to change the way you look – just a little. Buy a different colored shirt, see? And different pants, shoes instead of loafers. Get a haircut – you need one anyway so get a short one. Then get a hotel room – off Fifth Street. Main is okay if you stay away from Fifth. And shave – you had a stubble when that milkman saw you. How much money you got left?"

"Seven," I said. "But that ought to do it. I don't need *new* clothes; I can swap with uncle."

"You'll need more than that. Here." It was a twenty.

"Thanks, Billie. I owe you thirty." Owe her thirty? Hell, how much did I owe Billie the Kid already, outside of money, things money can't buy? I said, "And how'll we get in touch with one another? You say I shouldn't come to your place. Will you come to mine, tonight?"

"I – I guess they won't be suspicious if I take a night off, Howie, as long as it wasn't that first night. Right after the – after what happened to Mame. All right, Howie. You know a place called The Shoebox on Main up across from the court house?"

"I know where it is."

"I'll meet you there tonight at eight. And – and stay in your room, wherever you take one, till then. And – and try to stay sober, Howie."

4

It shouldn't be hard, I thought, to stay sober when you're scared. And I was scared, now.

I stayed on Main Street, away from Fifth, and I did the things Billie had suggested. I bought a tan work shirt, and changed it right in the store where I bought it for the blue one I'd been wearing. I stopped in the barber school place for a fourbit haircut and, while I was at it, a two-bit shave. I had one idea Billie hadn't thought of; I spent a buck on a used hat. I hadn't been wearing one and a hat makes a man look different. At a shoe repair shop that handled used shoes I traded in my loafers and a dollar fifty for a pair of used shoes. I decided not to worry about the trousers; their color wasn't distinctive.

I bought newspapers; I wanted to read for myself everything Billie had told me about the murder, and there might be other details she hadn't mentioned. Some wine too, but just a pint to sip on. I was going to stay sober, but it would be a long boring day waiting for my eight o'clock date with Billie the Kid.

I registered double at a little walk-up hotel on Market Street around the corner from Main, less than a block from the place of my evening date. She'd be coming with me, of course, since we wouldn't dare go to her place, and I didn't want there to be even a chance of trouble in bringing her back with me. Not that trouble would be likely in a place like that but I didn't want even the minor trouble of having to change the registration from single to double if the clerk saw us coming in, not for fifty cents difference in the price of the room.

I sipped at the wine slowly and read the papers. The *Mirror* gave it the best coverage, with pictures. A picture of Mame that must have been found in her room and that had been taken at least ten years ago – she looked to be in her late teens or early twenties – a flashlight shot of the interior of her room, but taken after her body had been removed, and an exterior of The Best Chance, where she'd worked. But, even from the *Mirror*, I didn't learn anything Billie hadn't told me, except Mame's full name and just how and when the body had been discovered. The time had been 12:05, just about the time Billie was leaving from her room on the floor below. The owner of the building had dropped around, with tools, to fix a dripping faucet Mame (Miss Mamie Gaynor, 29) had complained about the day before. When he'd knocked long enough to decide she wasn't home he'd let himself in with his duplicate key. The milkman's story and the description he'd given of me was exactly as Billie had given them.

I paced up and down the little room, walked the worn and shabby carpet, wondering. Was there – short of the sheer accident of my running into that milkman – any danger of my being picked up just from that description? No, surely not. It was accurate as far as it went, but it was too vague, could fit too many men in this district, for anyone to think of me in connection with it. And now, with a change of clothes, a shave, wearing a hat outdoors, I doubted if the milkman would recognize me. I couldn't remember his face; why would he remember mine? And there was no tie-in otherwise, except through Billie. Nobody but Billie knew that I'd even met Mame. The only two times I'd ever seen her had been in Billie's place when she'd dropped in while I was there, once for only a few minutes, once for an hour or so. And one other time I'd been up to her room, that time to borrow cigarettes for Billie; it had been very late, after stores and bars were closed.

The fact that I'd disappeared from my room in that block? That would mean nothing. Tomorrow a week's rent was due; the landlord would come to collect it, find me and my few possessions gone, and rent it again. He'd think nothing of it. Why should he?

No, now that I'd taken the few precautions Billie had suggested, I was safe enough as long as I stayed away from her building.

Why was I hiding here now, then?

The wine was gone and I wanted more. But I knew what shape I'd be in by eight o'clock if I kept on drinking it, starting at this hour of the morning.

But I'd go nuts if I stayed here, doing nothing. I picked up the papers, read the funny sheets, a few other things. Back in the middle of one of them a headline over a short item caught my eye, I don't know for what reason. *Victim in Alley Slaying Identified.*

Maybe my eye had first caught the name down in the body of the story, Jesus Gonzales. And Mame's jittery guest of the night before her death had been named Jesus Gonzales.

I read the story. Yesterday morning at dawn the body of a man had been found in an areaway off Winston Street near San Pedro Street. He had been killed with a blunt instrument, probably a blackjack. As he had been robbed of everything he was carrying, no identification had been made at first. Now he had been identified as Jesus Gonzales, 41, of Mexico City, DF. He had arrived in Los Angeles the day before on the SS Guadalajara, out of Tokyo. His passport, which had been left in his room at the Berengia Hotel, and other papers left with it, showed that he had been in the Orient on a buying trip for a Mexico City art object importing firm in which he was a partner, and that he was stopping in Los Angeles for a brief vacation on his return trip.

Mame's Jesus Gonzales? It certainly looked that way. The place and time fitted; less than two blocks from her room. So did the time, the morning after he'd been frightened by that knock at the door and had left unceremoniously via the fire escape.

But why would he have hooked up with Mame? The Berengia is a swank hotel, only people with well-lined pockets stay there. Mame was no prize; at the Berengia he could have done better through his own bellhop.

Or could it be a factor that Mame was a junkie and, stopping in at The Best Chance, he'd recognized her as one and picked her for that reason? He could have been a hype himself, in need of a jolt and in a city where he had no contacts, or – and this seemed even more likely because of his just having landed from Tokyo – he'd smuggled some dope in with him and was looking for a dealer to sell it. The simplest and safest way to find a dealer would be through an addict.

It was just a wild guess, of course, but it wasn't too wild to be possible. And damn it, Mame's Jesus Gonzales *had* acted suspiciously and he *had* been afraid of something. Maybe he'd thought somebody was following him, following him and Mame home from The Best Chance. If he was the same Jesus Gonzales who'd just been killed and robbed only two blocks from her place, then he'd been dead right in being careful. He'd made his mistake in assuming that the knocker on Mame's door was the man who'd followed him and in going down the fire escape. Maybe his *Nemesis* had still been outside the building, probably watching from across the street, and had seen him leave. And on Winston Street *Nemesis* had caught up with him.

Nice going, B.A.S., old boy, I thought. You're doing fine. It isn't every skid-row pearl-diver who can reconstruct a crime out of nothing. Sheer genius, B.A.S., sheer genius.

But it was something to pass the time, a lot better than staring at the wall and wishing I'd never left Chicago. Better than brooding.

All right, suppose it figured so far – then how did Mame's death tie in with it? I didn't see how. I made myself pace and concentrate, trying to work out an answer.

I felt sure Mame had been telling me the truth about Gonzales as far as she knew it, or else she would have had no reason for mentioning it at all. Whatever his ulterior motive in picking her up, whether to buy dope or to find a contact for selling it, he hadn't yet leveled with Mame before that knock came. Otherwise she wouldn't have told it casually, as she had, as something amusing.

But the killer wouldn't have known that. He couldn't have known that Mame was not an accomplice. If what he was looking for hadn't been on the person of the man he'd killed he could have figured that it had already changed hands. Why hadn't he gone back to Mame's the same night? I didn't know, but there could have been a reason. Perhaps he had and she'd gone out, locking the door and the fire escape window. Or maybe by that time she had other company; if he had knocked she might have opened the door on the chain – and I remembered now that there was a chain on her door – and told him so. I couldn't ask Mame now what she'd done the rest of the night after her jittery caller had left.

But if Gonzales was a stranger in town, just off the boat, how would the killer have known he had brought in heroin? – or opium or cocaine; it could have been any drug worth smuggling. And the killer must have known *something*; if it had been just a robbery kill, for whatever money Gonzales was carrying, then he wouldn't have gone back and killed Mame, searched her room. He'd have done that only if he'd known something about Gonzales that made him think Mame was his accomplice.

I killed a few more minutes worrying about that and I had the answer. Maybe not *the* answer, but at least an answer that made sense. Maybe I was just mildly cockeyed, but this off-the-cuff figuring I'd been doing *did* seem to be getting somewhere.

It was possible, I reasoned, that Mame hadn't been the first person through whom Gonzales had tried to make a contact. He could have approached another junkie on the same deal, but one who refused to tell him her contact. Her? It didn't have to be a woman, but Mame had been a woman and that made me think he'd been working that way. Say that he'd wandered around B-joints until he spotted a B-girl as an addict; he could get her in a booth and try to get information from her. She could have stalled him or turned him down. Stalled him, most likely, making a phone call or two to see if she could get hold of a dealer for him, but tipping off her boy friend instead. Killing time enough for her boy friend to be ready outside, then telling Gonzales she couldn't make a contact for him.

And if any of that had sounded suspicious to Gonzales he would have been more careful the second try, with Mame. He'd get her to her room on the obvious pretext, make sure they were alone and hadn't been followed before he opened up. Only, between The Best Chance and Mame's room, he must have discovered that they were being followed.

Sure, it all fitted. But what good did it do me?

Sure, it was logical. It made a complete and perfect picture, but it was all guesswork, nothing to go to the cops with. Even if they believed me eventually and could verify my guesses in the long run, I'd be getting myself and Billie the Kid into plenty of trouble in the short run. And like as not enough bad publicity – my relations with Billie would surely come out, and Billie's occupation – to have my father's clients in Chicago decide I wasn't fit to handle their business.

Well, was I? Worry about the fact that you want a drink so damned bad, I told myself, that soon you're going to weaken and go down and get another bottle. Well, why not? As long as I rationed it to myself so I would be drinking just enough to hold my own and not get drunk, not until after eight o'clock anyway . . .

What time was it? It seemed like I'd been in that damned room six or eight hours, but I'd checked in at around eleven and the sun was shining straight down in the dirty area-way my window opened on. Could it be only noon? I went out to the desk and past it, looking at the kitchen-type electric clock on the wall over it as I went by. It was a quarter after twelve.

I decided to walk a while before I went back to the room with a bottle, kill some time first. God, the time I had to kill before eight o'clock. I walked around the court house and over to Spring Street. I'd be safe there.

Hell, I'd be safe anywhere, I thought. Except maybe right in that one block of Fifth Street, just on the chance the police did have the milkman staked out in or near that building. And with different clothes, wearing a hat, he probably wouldn't recognize me anyway. Billie the Kid had panicked, and had panicked me. I didn't have anything to worry about. Oh, moving out of that block, changing out of the clothes I'd been wearing, those things had been sensible. But I didn't have to quit my job at Burke's – if it was still open to me. Burke's was safe for me. Nobody at Burke's knew where I'd lived and nobody in the building I'd lived in knew where I worked.

I thought, why not go to Burke's? He'd have the sign out in the window, now that I was an hour and a half late, but if nobody had taken the job, I could give him a story why I was so late and get it back. I'd gotten pretty good at washing dishes; I was probably the best dishwasher he'd ever had and I'd been steadier than the average one. Sure, I could go back there unless he'd managed to hire a new one already.

And otherwise, what? I'd either have to look for a new job of the same kind or keep on taking money from Billie for however long I stayed here. And taking money from Billie, except in emergency, was out. That gal named Honor back in Chicago was getting to be a pretty dim memory, but I still had some self-respect.

I cut back to Main Street and headed for Burke's. The back way, so I could see if anyone was working yet in my place, and maybe ask Ramon what the score was before I saw Burke.

From the alley doorway I could see my spot was empty, dishes piling high. Ramon was busy at the stove. He turned as I walked up to him, and his teeth flashed white in that grin. He said, "Howie! Thank God you're here. No dishwasher, everybody's going nuts."

The bandage was gone from his forehead. Under where it had been were four long scratches, downward, about an inch apart.

I stared at the scratches and thought about Ramon and his monkey and Mame and *her* monkey, and all of a sudden I had a crazy hunch. I thought about how a monkey like Ramon's could make a man do anything to get a fix. I moistened my lips. Ramon's monkey might claw the hell out of his guts, but it hadn't put those four scratches on his face. Not directly.

I didn't say it, I'd have had more sense; my mouth said it. "Mame had sharp fingernails, huh?"

5

Death can be a sudden thing. Only luck or accident kept me from dying suddenly in the next second or two. I'd never seen a face change as suddenly as Ramon's did. And before I could move, his hand had hold of the front of my shirt and his other hand had reached behind him and come up with and raised a cleaver. To step back as it started down would have put me in even better position for it to hit, so I did the only thing possible; I stepped in and pushed him backward and he stumbled and fell. I'd jerked my head but the cleaver went too wild even to scrape my shoulders. And there was a thunking sound as Ramon's head hit a sharp corner of the big stove. Yes, death can be a sudden thing.

I breathed hard a second and then – well, I don't know why I cared whether he was alive or not, but I bent forward and reached inside his shirt, held my hand over where his heart should be beating. It wasn't.

From the other side of the window Burke's voice sang out, "Two burgers, with."

I got out of there fast. Nobody had seen me there, nobody was *going* to see me there. I got out of the alley without being seen, that I knew of, and back to Main Street. I walked three blocks before I stopped into a tavern for the drink I really needed *now*. Not wine, whisky. Wine's an anodyne but it dulls the mind. Whisky sharpens it, at least temporarily. I ordered whisky, a double, straight.

I took half of it in one swallow and got over the worst of it. I sipped the rest slowly, and thought.

Damn it, Howie, I told myself, you've *got* to think.

I thought, and there was only one answer. I was in over my head now. If the police got me I was sunk. B.A.S. or not, I'd have a hell of a time convincing them I hadn't committed two murders – maybe three; if they'd tied in Jesus Gonzales, they'd pin that on me, too.

Sure, *I* knew what had really happened, but what proof did I have? Mame was dead; she wouldn't tell again what she'd told me about her little episode with Jesus. Ramon was dead; he wouldn't back up my otherwise unsupported word that I'd killed him accidentally in defending myself.

Out of this while I had a whole skin, that was the only answer. Back in Chicago, back to respectability, back to my right name – Howard Perry, B.A.S., not Howard Perry, bastard, wino, suspected soon of being a psychopathic killer. Back to Chicago, and not by freight. Too easy to get arrested that way, vagged, and maybe by that time flyers would be out with my description. Too risky.

So was waiting till eight o'clock when it was only one o'clock now. I'd have to risk getting in touch with Billie the Kid sooner. I couldn't go to her place, but I could phone. Surely they wouldn't have all the phones in that building tapped.

Just the same I was careful when I got her number. "Billie," I said, "this is the Professor." That nickname wouldn't mean anything to anybody else.

I heard her draw in her breath sharply. She must have realized I wouldn't risk calling her unless something important had come up. But she made her voice calm when she answered, "Yes, Professor?"

"Something has come up," I said. "I'm afraid I won't be able to make our eight o'clock date. Is there any chance that you can meet me now instead – same place?"

"Sure, soon as I can get there."

Click of the receiver. She'd be there. Billie the Kid, my Billie. She'd be there, and she'd make sure first that no one was following her. She'd bring money, knowing that I'd decided I had to lam after all. Money that she'd get back, damn it, if it was the last thing I ever did. Whatever money she'd lend me now, plus the other two sums and enough over to cover every drink and every cigarette I'd bummed from her. But not for the love and the trust she'd given me; you can't pay for that in money. In my case, I couldn't ever pay for it, period. The nearest I could come would be by being honest with her, leveling down the line. That much she had coming. More than that she had coming but more than that I couldn't give her.

The Shoebox is a shoebox-sized place. Not good for talking, but that didn't matter because we weren't going to talk there.

She got there fifteen minutes after I did; I was on my second drink. I ordered a Manhattan when I saw her coming in the door.

"Hello, Billie," I said.

Hello, Billie. Goodbye, Billie. This is the end for us, today. It's got to be the end. I knew she'd understand when I told her, when I told her everything.

"Howie, are you in – "

"In funds?" I cut her off. "Sure, just ordered you a drink." I dropped my voice, but not far enough to make it conspicuous. "Not here, Billie. Let's drink our drink and then I've got a room around the corner. I registered double so it'll be safe for us to go there and talk a while."

The bartender had mixed her Manhattan and was pouring it. I ordered a refill on my whisky-high. Why not? It was going to be my last drink for a long while. The wagon from here on in, even after I got back to Chicago for at least a few weeks, until I was sure the stuff couldn't get me, until I was sure I could do normal occasional social drinking without letting it start me off.

We drank our drinks and went out. Out into the sun, the warm sunny afternoon. Just before we got to the corner, Billie stopped me. "Just a minute, Howie."

She ducked into a store, a liquor store, before I could stop her. I waited. She came out with a wrapped bottle and a cardboard carton. "The ready-mixed wasn't on ice, Howie, but it's all right. I bought some ice cubes too. Are there two glasses in the room?"

I nodded; we went on. There were two glasses in the room. The wagon not yet. But it wouldn't have been right not to have a last drink or two, a stirrup cup or two, with Billie the Kid.

She took charge of the two tumblers, the drinks. Poured the drinks over ice cubes, stirred them around a while and then fished the ice cubes out when the drinks were chilled.

While I talked. While I told her about Chicago, about me in Chicago, about my family and the investment company. She handed me my drink then. She said quietly, "Go on, Howie."

I went on. I told her what Mame had told me about her guest Jesus the night before she was killed. I told her of the death of Jesus Gonzales as I'd read it in the *Mirror*. I added the two up for her.

She made us another drink while I told her about Ramon, about what had happened, about how I'd just killed him.

"Ramon," she said. "He has knife scars, Howie?" I nodded. She said, "Knife scars, a hype, a chef. I didn't know his name, but I know who his woman was, a red-headed junkie named Bess, I think it's Bess, in a place just down the block from Karas' joint. It's what happened, Howie, just like you guessed it. It must have been." She sipped her drink. "Yes, Howie, you'd better go back to Chicago, right away. It could be bad trouble for you if you don't. I brought money. Sixty. It's all I have except a little to last me till I can get more. Here."

A little roll of bills, she tucked into my shirt pocket.

"Billie," I said. "I wish – "

"Don't say it, honey. I know you can't. Take me with you, I mean. I wouldn't fit, not with the people you know there. And I'd be bad for you."

"I'd be bad for you, Billie. I'd be a square, a wet blanket. I'll have to be to get back in that rut, to hold down – " I didn't want to think about it. I said, "Billie, I'm going to send you what I owe you. Can I count on your being at the same address for another week or so?"

She sighed. "I guess so, Howie. But I'll give you my sister's name and address, what I use for a permanent address, in case you ever – in case you might not be able to send the money right away."

"I'll write it down," I said. I tore a corner off the paper the bottle had been wrapped in, looked around for something to write with; I remembered the fountain pen I'd stuck in my trousers pocket at Mame's. It was still there.

I screwed off the cap. Something glittered, falling to the carpet, a lot of somethings. Shiny little somethings that looked like diamonds. Billie gasped. Then she was scrabbling on the floor, picking them up. I stared at the pen, the hollow pen without even a point, in my hand. Hollow and empty now. But there was still something in the cap, which I'd been holding so it hadn't spilled. I emptied the cap out into my hand. Bigger diamonds, six of them, big and deep and beautifully cut.

My guess had been wrong. It hadn't been heroin Gonzales had been smuggling. Diamonds. And when he'd found himself followed to Mame's, he'd stashed them there for safety. The pen hadn't fallen from his coat pocket; he'd hidden it there deliberately.

They were in two piles on the table, Billie's hands trembling a little as she handled them one at a time. "Matched," she said reverently. "My husband taught me stones, Howie. Those six big ones – over five carats each, cut for depth, not shallow, and they're blue-white and I'll bet they're flawless, all of them, because they're matched. And the fifteen smaller ones – they're matched too, and they're almost three carats apiece. You know what Karas would give us for them, Howie?"

"Karas?"

"Fifteen grand, Howie, at least. Maybe more. These aren't ordinary; they're something special. Sure, Karas – I didn't tell you everything, because it didn't matter then, when I said I thought maybe he had some racket – not dope. He handles stones, only stones. Gonzales might have heard of him, might have been trying to contact him through Mame."

I thought about fifteen thousand dollars, and I thought about going back to Chicago. Billie said, "Mexico, Howie. In Mexico we can live like kings – like a king and queen – for five years for that much."

And stop drinking, straighten out? Billie said, "Howie, shall I take these to Karas right now so we can leave quick?" She was flushed, breathing hard, staring at me pleadingly.

"Yes," I said. She kissed me, hard, and gathered them up.

At the doorway, hand on the knob. "Howie, were you kidding when you said you were in love with a girl named Honor in Chicago? I mean, is there a real girl named that, or did you just mean – ?"

"I was kidding, Billie the Kid."

The door closed.

Her heels clicked down the wooden hall. I poured myself a drink, a long one, and didn't bother to chill it with ice cubes. Yes, I'd known a girl named Honor in Chicago, once, but – . . . *but that was in another country, and besides, the wench is dead.*

I drank my drink and waited.

Twenty minutes later, I heard Billie's returning footsteps in the hall.

SO DARK FOR APRIL

Howard Browne

1

WHEN I GOT through telling the sergeant at Central Homicide about it, he said to sit tight and not touch anything, that somebody would be right over. I told him I wouldn't even breathe any more than was absolutely necessary and put back the receiver and went into the reception room to take another look at the body.

He was at the far end of the couch, slumped in a sitting position, with his chin on his chest and an arm hanging down. A wick of iron-gray hair made a curve against the waxen skin of a high forehead, his half-open eyes showed far too much white, and a trickle of dark blood had traced a crooked line below one corner of a slack-lipped mouth. His coat hung open, letting me see a circular red stain under the pocket of a soiled white shirt. From the center of the stain protruded the brown bone handle of a switch-blade knife.

I moved over to lean against the window frame and light a cigarette. It was one of those foggy wet mornings we get early in April, with a chill wind off the lake and the sky as dull as a deodorant commercial. Umbrellas blossomed along the walks eight floors below and long lines of cars slithered past with a hooded look.

I stood there breathing smoke and staring at the dead man. He was nobody I had ever seen before. He wore a handsomely tailored suit coat of gray flannel, dirty brown gabardine slacks spattered with green paint and an oil stain across one knee, and brown bench-made shoes. His shirt was open at the throat, showing a fringe of dark hair, and he wasn't wearing a tie.

The rummage-sale air of those slacks bothered me. This was no Skid

Row fugitive. His nails had that cared-for look, his face, even in death, held a vague air of respectability, and they didn't trim hair that way at barber college.

I bent down and turned back the left side of his coat. The edge of a black wallet showed in the inner pocket. That was where I stopped. This was cop business. Let the boys who were paid for it paw the corpse.

A black satin label winked up at me. I put my eyes close enough to read the stitched letters in it. A C G – in a kind of Old English script. The letters seemed too big to be simply a personal monogram, but then there's no accounting for tastes.

I let the lapel drop back to the way I had found it. The dead man didn't seem to care either way. Something glistened palely between the frayed cuffs and the tops of the custom-made shoes. I said, "Huh?" out loud and bent down to make sure.

No mistake. It made no sense but there it was. The pale white shine was naked flesh.

The dead man wasn't wearing socks.

2

Detective Sergeant Lund said, "Right smack-dab through the old ticker. He never even had time to clear his throat. Not this guy."

His curiously soft voice held a kind of grim respect. He straightened up and backed away a couple of steps and took off his hat and shook rain water from it onto the carpet and stared thoughtfully at me out of gun-metal eyes.

I moved a shoulder and said nothing. At the wicker table across the room the two plainclothes men were unshipping tape measures and flash-bulbs and fingerprint kits. Rain tapped the glass behind me with icy fingers.

"Your turn, Pine," Lund said in the same soft voice.

"He was like that when I came in," I said promptly. I looked at my strapwatch. "Exactly thirty-two minutes ago."

"How'd he get in here?"

"I usually leave the reception room unlocked, in case I have a client and the client cares to wait."

One corner of his mouth moved up faintly. "Somebody sure wanted this guy to wait, hey?"

I shrugged. He took a turn along the room and back again, hands deep in the pockets of his topcoat. Abruptly he said. "It says on your door you're a private dick. This a client?"

"No. I never saw him before."

"What's his name?"

"I don't know."

"No identification on him?"

"I didn't look. The sergeant at Central said not to."

He seemed mildly astonished. "A man dies in your office and you don't even show a little healthy curiosity? Don't be afraid of me, Pine. I haven't chewed off anybody's arm in over a week."

"I obey the law," I said mildly.

"Well, well," he said. He grinned suddenly, and after a moment I grinned back. Mine was no phonier than his. He snapped a thumb lightly against the point of his narrow chin a time or two while thinking a secret thought, then turned back to the body.

He went through the pockets with the deft delicacy of a professional dip. The blood, the knife handle, the sightless eyes meant about half as much to him as last week's laundry. When he straightened again there was a small neat pile of personal effects on one of the couch pillows and the dead man's pockets were as empty as his eyes.

The wallet was on top. Lund speared it, flipped it open. The transparent identification panels were empty, as was the bill compartment. Shoved into the latter, however, were three or four cards. Lund looked them over slowly and carefully, his thick brows drawn into a lazy V above his long, pointed nose.

"Credit cards on a couple Loop hotels," he said, almost to himself. "Plus one of these identification cards you get with a wallet. According to what it says here, this guy is Franklin Andrus, 5861 Winthrop Avenue. One business card. It calls him a sales representative for the Reliable Amusement Machine Corporation, Dayton, Ohio. No telephone shown and nobody listed to notify. Any of this mean anything to you, Mr Pine?"

"Sorry."

"Uh-huh. You ain't playing this too close, are you?"

"I'm not even in the game," I said.

"Initials in his coat don't agree with the name on these here cards. That must mean something, hey?"

I stared at the bridge of his nose. "His coat and somebody else's cards. Or his cards and somebody else's coat. Or neither. Or both."

His mouth hardened. "You trying to kid me, mister?"

"I guess that would be pretty hard to do, Sergeant."

He turned on his heel and went through the communicating door to my inner office, still carrying the wallet. He didn't bother to shut it, and through the opening I could see him reach for the phone without sitting down and dial a number with quick hard stabs of a forefinger. What he said when he got his party was too low-voiced for me to catch.

Two minutes later, he was back. He scooped up the stuff from the couch and said, "Let's talk, hey? Let's us try out that nice private office of yours."

I followed him in and drew up the Venetian blind and opened the window a crack to let out the smell of yesterday's cigarettes. On the outer ledge four pigeons were organizing a bombing raid. Lund shoved the phone and ashtray aside, dumped his collection on the desk pad and snapped on the lamp. I sat down behind the desk and watched him pull up the customer's chair across from me.

I got out my cigarettes. He took one, sniffed at it for no reason I knew of and struck a match for us both. He leaned back and hooked an arm over the chair back and put his dull gray eyes on me.

"Nice and cozy," he said. "All the comforts. Too bad they're not all like this."

"I could turn on the radio," I said. "Maybe get a little dance music."

He grunted with mild amusement. All the narrow-eyed suspicion had been tucked out of sight. He drew on his cigarette and blew a long blue plume of smoke at the ceiling. Another minute and he'd have his shoes off.

He let his gaze drift about the dingy office, taking in the Varga calendar, the filing cases, the worn tan linoleum. He said, "The place could stand a little paint, hey?"

"You drumming up business for your day off?" I asked.

That got another grunt out of him. "You sound kind of on the excited side, Pine. Don't be like that. You wouldn't be the first private boy got a customer shot out from under him, so to speak."

I felt my face burn. "He's not a customer. I told you that."

"I guess you did, at that," he said calmly. "It don't mean I have to believe it. Client getting pushed right in your own office don't look so good, hey? What the newshounds call a bad press."

I bit down on my teeth. "You just having fun, Sergeant, or does all this lead somewhere?"

"Why, we're just talking," he said mildly. "Just killing time, you might say, until the coroner shows up. That and looking over the rest of what the guy had on him."

He stuck out an untidy finger and poked at the pile. Besides the wallet, there were several small square transparent envelopes, some loose change, a pocket comb, and a small pair of gold tweezers.

He brought his eyes up to stare coldly at me, his mellow mood gone as quickly as it had arrived. He said harshly, "Let's lay off the clowning around, mister. You were working for him. I want to know doing what."

"I wouldn't bother to lie to you," I said. "I never saw the guy before in my life, I never talked to him on the phone, or got a letter from him. Period."

His sneer was a foot wide. "Jesus, you must think I'm green!"

"I'm not doing any thinking," I said.

"I hope to tell you, you aren't. Listen, I can book you, brother!"

"For what?"

"Obstructing justice, resisting an officer, indecent exposure. What the hell do you care? I'm saying I can book you!"

I didn't say anything. Some of the angry color faded slowly from his high cheeks. Finally he sighed heavily and picked up the necktie and gave it a savage jerk between his square hands and threw it down again.

"Nuts," he said pettishly. "I don't want to fight with you. I'm trying to do a job. All I want is a little cooperation. This guy just don't walk in here blind. You're a private dick, or so your door says. Your job is people in trouble. I say it's too damn big a coincidence him picking your office to get knocked off in. Go on, tell me I'm wrong."

"I'm not saying you're wrong," I said. "I'm saying what I've already said. He's a stranger to me. He could have come in here to get out of the wet or to sell me a slot machine or to just sit down and rest his arches. I admit he might have come here to hire me. It has happened, although not often enough. Maybe somebody didn't want him spilling any touchy secrets to me, and fixed him so he couldn't."

"But you never saw him before?"

"You're beginning to get the idea," I said.

"Go ahead," he said bitterly. "Crack wise. Get out the office bottle and toss off three inches of Scotch without a chaser and spit in my eye. That's the way you private eyes do it on TV eight times a night."

"I don't have an office bottle," I said.

The sound of the reception room door opening and closing cut off what Lund was about to say. A short plump man went past the half-open door of the inner office, carrying a black bag. Lund got up without a word and went out there, leaving me where I sat.

Some time passed. Quite a lot of time. The murmur of voices from the next room went on and on. Flash bulbs made soundless explosions of light and a small vacuum cleaner whirred. I stayed where I was and burned a lot of tobacco and crossed my legs and dangled my foot and listened to the April rain and thought my thoughts.

Thoughts about a man who might still be alive if I hadn't slept an hour later than usual. A man with mismatched clothing and no socks and an empty wallet. A man who would want to go on living, even in an age when living was complicated and not very rewarding. A man who had managed for fifty-odd years to hang on to the only life he'd ever be given to live before a switch-blade knife and a strong hand combined to pinch it off.

I went on sitting. The rain went on falling. It was so dark for April.

After a while the corridor door opened to let in two men in white coats. They carried a long wicker basket between them. They passed my door without looking in. There was more indistinct murmuring, then a young voice said, "Easy with them legs, Eddie," and the basket was taken out again. It was harder to carry the second time.

Sergeant Lund walked in, his face expressionless. He sat down heavily and lighted a cigarette and waved out the match and continued to hold it. He said, "Andrus died between eight-thirty and ten. The elevator man don't recall bringing him up. What time did you get here?"

"Ten-thirty, about. Few minutes either way."

"You wouldn't happen to own a switch-blade knife, hey?"

"With a brown bone handle?" I said.

He bent the used match and dropped it in the general vicinity of the ashtray. "Seven-inch blade," he muttered. "Like a goddam bayonet." He put the cigarette in a corner of his mouth and left it there. "This is a real cute killing, Pine. You notice how Andrus was dressed?"

"No socks," I said.

"That isn't the half of it, brother. New coat, old pants, fancy shoes. No hat and no topcoat. In weather like this? What's the sense?"

I spread my hands. "By me, Sergeant."

"You sure you wasn't work – "

"Don't say it!" I shouted.

The phone rang. A voice like a buzz-saw asked for Lund. He grunted into the mouthpiece, listened stolidly for nearly a full minute, then said, "Yeah," twice and passed back the receiver. I replaced it and watched him drag himself out of the chair, his expression a study in angry frustration.

"I had Rogers Park send a squad over to that Winthrop Avenue address," he growled. "Not only they don't find no trace of a Franklin Andrus; they don't even find the address! An empty lot, by God! All right. Hell with it. The lab boys will turn up something. Laundry marks, cuff dust, clothing labels. It'll take 'em a day or two, but I can wait. The old routine takes time but it always works."

"Almost always," I said absently.

He glowered down across the desk at me. "One thing I hope, mister. I hope you been holding out on me and I find it out. That's going to be jake with me."

He gathered up the dead man's possessions and stalked out. A little later one of the plainclothes men slipped in with his kit and took my fingerprints. He was nice about it, explaining they were only for elimination purposes.

3

By one o'clock I was back from having a sandwich and coffee at the corner drugstore. The reception room was empty, with only a couple of used flash bulbs, some smudges of fingerprint powder here and there and the smell of cheap cigars and damp cloth to remind me of my morning visitors. Without the dead man on it, the couch seemed larger than usual. There were no bloodstains. I looked to make sure.

I walked slowly into the other room and shucked off my trench coat.

From the adjoining office came the faint whine of a dentist's drill. A damp
breeze crawled in at the window and rattled the cords on the blind. Cars
hooted in the street below. Sounds that made the silence around me even
more silent. And the rain went on and on.

I sat down behind the desk and emptied the ashtray into the waste-basket
and wiped off the glass top. I put away the cloth and got out a cigarette and
sat there turning it, unlighted, between a thumb and forefinger.

He had been a nice-looking man. Fifty-five at the most. A man with a
problem on his mind. Let's say he wakes up this morning and decides to take
his problem to a private detective. So he gets out the classified book and looks
under the right heading. There aren't many, not even for a town the size of
Chicago. The big agencies he passes up, maybe because he figures he'll
have to go through a handful of henna-haired secretaries before reaching
the right guy. Then, not too far down the column, he comes across the
name Paul Pine. A nice short name. Anybody can pronounce it.

So he takes a cab or a bus and comes on down. He hasn't driven a car;
no car keys and no license on him. The waiting room is unlocked but no
alert gimlet-eyed private detective around. The detective is home in bed,
like a man with a working wife. So this nice-looking man with a problem
sits down to wait . . . and somebody walks in and sticks a quarter-pound
of steel in him.

That was it. That explained everything. Everything but what his problem
was and why he wasn't wearing socks and why his wallet was empty and
why his identification showed an address that didn't exist.

I got up and took a couple of turns around the room. This was no skin
off my shins. The boys from Homicide would have it all wrapped up in
a day or so. The old routine Lund had called it. I didn't owe that nice
old man a thing. He hadn't paid me a dime. No connection between
us at all.

Except that he had come to me for help and got a mouthful of blood
instead.

I sat down again and tried the phone book. No Franklin Andrus listed.
No local branch of the Reliable Amusement Machine Corp. I shoved the
book away and began to think about the articles that had come out of the
dead man's pockets. Gold tweezers, a pocket comb, five small transparent
envelopes, seventy-three cents in change, a dark blue necktie. There had
been a department store label on the tie – Marshall Field. I knew that
because I had looked while Lund was out of the room. But Field's has
more neckties than Pabst has bottles. No help there.

Is that all, Pine, I thought to myself. End of the line? You mean you're
licked? A nice, clean-necked, broad-shouldered, late-sleeping detective
like you?

I walked the floor some more. I went over to the window and leaned
my forehead against its coolness. My breath misted the glass and I wrote

my name in the mist with the end of my finger. That didn't seem to help any. I went on thinking.

Maybe what *hadn't* come out of his pockets was important. No keys, for instance. Not even to his apartment. Maybe he lived in a hotel. Not even cigarettes or a book of matches. Maybe he didn't smoke. Not even a handkerchief. Maybe he didn't have a cold.

I sat down again. There had been initials in his coat. A C G. No periods and stitched professionally in fancy letters against a square of black satin. Rather large, as I recalled. Too bad I hadn't looked inside the pocket for the tailor's label. Unless . . .

This time I used the classified book. T – for Tailors – Men's. I ran through the columns to the G's. There it was, bright and shining and filled with promise. A. Cullinham Grandfils, Custom Tailor. On Michigan Avenue, in the 600 block. Right in the center of the town's swankiest shopping district.

I closed the window, climbed into my trench coat and hat and locked up. The smell of dime cigars still hung heavy in the outer office. Even the hall seemed full of it.

4

It was made to look like a Greek temple, if you didn't look too close. It had a white limestone front and a narrow doorway with a circular hunk of stained glass above that. Off to one side was a single display window about the size of a visiting card. Behind the glass was a slanting pedestal covered with black velvet and on the velvet a small square of gray cloth that looked as though it might be of cheviot. Nothing else. No price tags, no suits, no firm name spelled out in severely stylized letters.

And probably no bargain basement.

I heaved back the heavy glass door and walked into a large room with soft dusty rose walls, a vaulted ceiling, moss green carpeting, and indirect lighting like a benediction. Scattered tastefully about were upholstered chairs and couches, blond in the wood and square in the lines. A few chrome ashstands, an end table or two, and at the far end a blond desk and a man sitting behind it.

The man stood up as I came in. He floated down the room toward me, a tall slender number in a cut-away coat, striped trousers and a gates-ajar collar. He looked like a high-class undertaker. He had a high reedy voice that said:

"Good afternoon, sir. May I be of service?"

"Are you the high priest?" I said.

His mouth fell open. "I beg your pardon?"

"Maybe I'm in the wrong place," I said. "I'm looking for the tailor shop. No name outside but the number checks."

His backbone got even stiffer although I hadn't thought that possible. "This," he said in a strangled voice, "is A. Cullinham Grandfils. Are you interested in a garment?"

"A what?"

"A garment."

"You mean a suit?"

"Ah – yes, sir."

"I've got a suit," I said. I unbuttoned my coat and showed it to him. All he did was look pained.

"What I came by for," I said, "was to get the address of a customer of yours. I'm not sure but I think his name's Andrus – Franklin Andrus."

He folded his arms and brought up a hand and turned his wrist delicately and rested his chin between his thumb and forefinger. "I'm afraid not. No. Sorry."

"You don't know the name?"

"I'm not referring to the name. What I am attempting to convey to you is that we do not give out information on our people."

I said, "Oh," and went on staring at him. He looked like the type you can bend easy. I dug out the old deputy sheriff's star I carried for emergencies like this and showed it to him, keeping the lettering covered with the ball of my thumb. He jerked down his arms and backed away as though I'd pulled a gun on him.

"This is official," I said in a tough-cop voice. "I'm not here to horse around. Do you cooperate or do we slap you with a subpoena?"

"You'll have to discuss the matter with Mr Grandfils," he squeaked. "I simply am not – I have no authority to – You'll just have to – "

"Then trot him out, Curly. I don't have all day."

"Mr Grandfils is in his office. Come this way, please."

We went along the room and through a glass door at the far end and along a short hall to another door: a solid panel of limed oak with the words A. Cullinham Grandfils, Private, on it in raised silver letters. The door was knocked on and a muffled voice came through and I was inside.

A little round man was perched in an enormous leather chair behind an acre of teakwood and glass. His head was as bald as a collection plate on Monday morning. A pair of heavy horn-rimmed glasses straddled a button nose above a tiny mouth and a chin like a ping-pong ball. He blinked owlishly at me and said, "What is it, Marvin?" in a voice so deep I jumped.

"This – ah – gentleman is the police, Mr Grandfils. He has demanded information I simply haven't the right to – "

"That will be all, Marvin."

I didn't even hear him leave.

"I can't stand that two-bit diplomat," the little man said. "He makes the bottom of my foot itch."

I didn't say anything.

"Unfortunately he happens to be useful," he went on. "The women gush at him and he gushes back. Good for business."

"I thought you only sold men's suits," I said.

"Who do you think picks them out? Take off that coat and sit down. I don't know your name."

I told him my name and got rid of the trench coat and hat and drew up a teakwood chair trimmed in silver and sat on it. He made a quarter-turn in the big chair and his glasses flashed at me in the soft light.

"Police, eh?" he said suddenly. "Well, you've got the build for it. Where did you get that ridiculous suit?"

"This ridiculous suit set me back sixty-five bucks," I said.

"It looks it. What are you after, sir?"

"The address of one of your customers."

"I see. Why should I give it to you?"

"He was murdered. The address on his identification was incorrect."

"Murdered!" His mouth dropped open, causing the glasses to slip down on his nose. "Good heavens! One of my people?"

"He was wearing one of your coats," I said.

He passed a tremulous hand across the top of his head. All it smoothed down was scalp. "What was his name?"

"Andrus. Franklin Andrus."

He shook his head immediately. "No, Mr Pine. None of my people has that name. You have made a mistake."

"The coat fitted him," I said doggedly. "He belonged in it. I might have the name wrong but not the coat. It was his coat."

He picked a silver paper-knife from the silver trimmed tan desk blotter and rapped it lightly over and over against the knuckles of his left hand. "Perhaps you're right," he said. "My coats are made to fit. Describe this man to me."

I gave the description, right down to the kidney-shaped freckle on the lobe of the left ear. Grandfils heard me out, thought over at length what I'd said, then shook his head slowly.

"In a general way," he said, "I know of a dozen men like that who come to me. The minor touches you've given me are things I never noticed about any of them. I'm not a trained observer and you are. Isn't there something else you can tell me about him? Something you've perhaps inadvertently overlooked?"

It hardly seemed likely but I thought back anyway. I said, "The rest of his clothing was a little unusual. That might mean something to you."

"Try me."

I described the clothing. By the time I was down to where the dead man hadn't been wearing socks, Grandfils had lost interest. He said coldly, "The man was obviously some tramp. None of my people would be seen on the street in such condition. The coat was stolen and the man deserved what happened to him. Frayed slacks! Heavens!"

I said, "Not much in his pockets, but I might as well tell you that too. A dark blue necktie with a Marshall Field label, a pair of gold-plated tweezers, several transparent envelopes about the size of a postage stamp, a pocket comb and some change . . ."

My voice began to run down. A. Cullinham Grandfils had his mouth open again, but this time there was the light of recognition in his eyes. He said crisply, "The coat was a gray flannel, Mr Pine?"

"Yeah?"

"Carlton weave?"

"Hunh?"

"Never mind. You wouldn't know that. Quite new?"

"I thought so."

He bent across the desk to move a key on an intercom. "Harry," he snapped into the box. "That gray flannel lounge suit we made for Amos Spain. Was it sent out?"

"A week already," the box said promptly. "Maybe ten days, even. You want I should check exactly?"

"Never mind." Grandfils flipped back the key and leaned into the leather chair and went on tapping his knuckles with the knife. "Those tweezers and envelopes did it, sir. He's an enthusiastic stamp collector. Less than a month ago I saw him sitting in the outer room lifting stamps delicately with those tweezers and putting them in such envelopes while waiting for a fitting."

"Amos Spain is his name?"

"It is."

"He fits the description I gave?"

"Physically, exactly. But not the frayed slacks and dirty shirt. Amos Spain wouldn't be found dead in such clothes."

"You want to bet?"

". . . Oh. Of course. I simply can't understand it!"

"How about an address on Spain, Mr Grandfils?"

He dug a silver-trimmed leather notebook out of a desk drawer and looked inside. "8789 South Shore Drive. Apartment 3C. It doesn't show a telephone, although I'm confident he has one."

"Married?"

He dropped the book back in the drawer and closed it with his foot. "We don't inquire into the private lives of our people, Mr Pine. It seems to me Mrs Spain is dead, although I may be wrong. I do know Amos Spain is reasonably wealthy and, I think, retired."

I took down the address and got up and put on my coat and said, "Thanks for your help, Mr Grandfils." He nodded and I opened the door. As I started out, he said:

"You really should do something about your suits, Mr Pine."

I looked back at him sitting there like one of those old Michelin tire ads. "How much," I said, "would you charge me for one?"

"I think we could do something quite nice for you at three hundred."

"For that price," I said, "I would expect two pairs of pants."

His chin began to bob and he made a sound like roosters fighting. He was laughing. I closed the door in the middle of it and went on down the hall.

5

The address on South Shore Drive was a long low yellow-brick apartment building of three floors and an English basement. A few cars were parked along a wide sweep of concrete running past the several entrances, and I angled the Plymouth into an open spot almost directly across from 8789.

The rain got in a few licks at me before I could reach the door. Inside was a small neat foyer, complete with bright brass mail boxes and an inner door. The card on the box for 3C showed the name Amos Spain.

I pressed the right button and after a longish moment a woman's voice came down the tube. "Yes?"

That jarred me a little. I hadn't actually expected an answer. I said, "Mrs Spain?"

"This is Mrs Monroe," the voice said. "Mr Spain's daughter. Are you from the post office?"

"Afraid not. I'm an officer, Mrs Monroe. Want to talk to you."

"An officer? Why, I don't believe . . . What about?"

"Not from down here, Mrs Monroe. Ring the buzzer."

"I'll do no such thing! How do I know you're a policeman? For all I know you could be a – a – "

"On a day like this? Don't be silly."

There was some silence and then the lock began to stutter. I went through and on up carpeted steps to the third floor. Halfway along a wide cheerful hallway was a partially open door and a woman in a flowered housecoat looking out at me.

She was under thirty but not very far under. She had wicked eyes. Her hair was reddish brown and there was a lot of it. Her skin was flawless, her cheekbones high, her mouth an insolent curve. She was long and slender in the legs, small in the waist, high in the breasts. She was dynamite.

I was being stared at in a coolly impersonal way. "A policeman you said. I'm fascinated. What is it you want?"

I said, "Do I get invited in or do we entertain the neighbors?"

Her eyes wavered and she bit her lip. She started to look back over her shoulder, thought better of it, then said, "Oh, very well. If you'll be brief."

She stepped back and I followed her across a tiny reception hall and on into an immense living room, with a dinette at one end and the open door to a kitchen beyond that. The living room was paneled, with beautiful leather chairs, a chesterfield, lamps with drum shades, a loaded pipe rack, a Governor Winthrop secretary, a fireplace with a gas log. Not neat, not even overly clean, but the right place for a man who puts comfort ahead of everything else.

I dropped my coat on a hassock and sat down on one of the leather chairs. Her lips hardened. "Don't get too comfortable," she said icily. "I was about to leave when you rang."

"It's a little chilly out for a housecoat," I said.

Her jaw hardened. "Just who do you think you are, busting in here and making smart remarks? You say you're a cop. As far as manners go, I believe it. Now I think I'd like to see some real proof."

I shrugged. "No proof, Mrs Monroe. I said officer, not policeman. A private detective can be called an officer without stretching too far."

"Private – " Her teeth snapped shut and she swallowed almost convulsively. Her face seemed a little pale now but I could have imagined that. "What do you want?" she almost whispered.

"Where's Amos Spain?" I said.

"My . . . father?"

"Uh-huh."

". . . I don't know. He went out early this morning."

"He say where?"

"No." Whatever had shocked her was passing. "Tom and I were still sleeping when he went out."

"Tom?"

"My husband."

"Where's he?"

"Still asleep. We got in late. Why do you want to know where my father is?"

I said, "I think it would be a good idea if you sat down, Mrs Monroe. I'm afraid I've brought some bad news."

She didn't move. Her eyes went on watching me. They were a little wild now and not at all wicked. She wet her lips and said, "I haven't the slightest idea what you're talking about. Bad news about what?"

"About your father. He's dead, Mrs Monroe. Murdered."

"I don't believe it," she said quickly. Almost too quickly.

"He's been identified. Not much chance for a mistake."

She turned away abruptly and walked stiffly over to a lamp table and took a cigarette from a green cloisonné box. Her hand holding the match wavered noticeably but nothing showed in her face. She blew out a long streamer of smoke and came back and perched carelessly on an arm of the couch across from me. The housecoat slipped open slightly, letting me see most of the inner curve of a freshly powdered thigh. I managed to keep from chewing a hole in the rug.

"There's been some mistake, Mr Pine. Dad never had an enemy in the world. What do you suggest I do?"

I thought back to be sure. Then I was sure. I said, "The body's probably at the morgue by this time and already autopsied. Might be a good idea to send your husband over. Save you from a pretty unpleasant job."

"Of course. I'll wake him right away and tell him about it. You've been very kind. I'm sorry if I was rude."

She hit me with a smile that jarred my back teeth and stood up to let me know the interview was over and I could run along home now and dream about her thigh.

I slid off the chair and picked up my hat and coat. While putting them on I moved over to the row of windows and looked down into the courtyard. Nobody in sight. Not in this weather. Rain blurred the glass and formed widening puddles in thin brown grass that was beginning to turn green.

I turned and said, "I'll be running along, Mrs Monroe," and took four quick steps and reached for the bedroom door.

There was nothing wrong with her reflexes, I'll say that for her. A silken rustle and the flash of flowered cloth and she was standing between me and the door. We stood there like that, breathing at each other, our faces inches apart. She was lovely and she smelled good and the housecoat was cut plenty low.

And her face was as hard as four anvils.

"I must have made a mistake," I said. "I was looking for the hall door."

"Only two doors," she said between her teeth. "Two doors in the entire apartment. Not counting the bathroom. One that lets you out and one to the bedroom. And you picked the wrong one. Go on. Get out of here before I forget you're not a cop."

On my way out I left the inner door downstairs unlocked. In case.

6

The rain went on and on. I sat there listening to it and wondering if Noah had felt this way along about the thirty-ninth day. Smoke from my fourth cigarette eddied and swirled in the damp air through the no-draft vent.

The Plymouth was still parked across from 8789, and I was in it, knowing suddenly who had killed Amos Spain and why Spain had been wearing what he wore and why he wasn't wearing what he hadn't worn. It was knowledge built piece by piece on what I had seen and heard from the moment I walked in and found the body on the couch. It was the kind of knowledge you can get a conviction with – if you have that one key piece.

The key piece was what I didn't have.

Now and then a car came into the wide driveway and stopped at one of the entrances to let somebody out or to pick somebody up. None of them was for the rat hole to which I was glued. A delivery truck dropped off a dinette set a couple of doors down and I couldn't have cared less.

I lighted another cigarette and crossed my legs the other way and thought about hunting up a telephone and calling Lund and telling him to come out and get the knife artist and sweat that key piece out in the open. Only I didn't want it that way. This was one I wanted to wrap up myself. It had been my office and my couch and almost my client, and I was the one the cops had tromped on. Not that the tromping had amounted to much. But even a small amount of police displeasure is not what you list under assets.

Another twenty minutes floated by. They would still be up there in that apartment wearing a path in the rug. Waiting, sweating blood, hanging on desperately, risking the chance that I had known more than I let on and was already out yelling for the cops.

I would have loved to know what they were waiting for.

When the break did come I almost missed it. An ancient Ford with a pleated front fender wheezed into the curb. A hatless young man in a rained-on gray uniform got out to look at the number over the entrance to 8789. He had a damp-looking cigarette pasted to one corner of his mouth and a white envelope in his left hand. The local postoffice dropping off a piece of registered mail.

And then I remembered Mrs Monroe's first question.

I slapped open the glove compartment and got out my gun and shoved it under the band of my trousers while I was reaching for the door. I crossed the roadway at a gallop and barged into the foyer just as the messenger took a not too clean thumb off the button for 3C. I made a point of getting out my keys to keep him from thinking Willie Sutton was loose again.

He never even knew I was in town. He said, "Postoffice; registered letter," into the tube and the buzzer was clattering before he had the last word out. He went through and on up the steps without a backward glance.

The door was off the latch, the way I had left it earlier. By the time the door to 3C opened, I was a few feet away staring vaguely at the closed door to 3B and trying to look like somebody's cousin from Medicine Hat. The uniformed man said, "Amos Spain?" and a deeper voice said, "I'm Mr Spain," and a signature was written and a long envelope changed hands.

Before the door could close I was over there. I said, "It's me again."

He was a narrow-chested number with a long sallow face, beady eyes, a thin nose that leaned slightly to starboard, and a chin that had given up the struggle. Hair like black moss covered a narrow head. This would be Tom Monroe, the husband.

Terror and anger and indecision were having a field day with his expression. His long neck jerked and his sagging jaw wobbled. He clutched the edge of the door, wanting to slam it but not quite daring to. The silence weighed a ton.

All this was lost on the messenger. He took back his pencil and went off down the hall, his only worry the number of hours until payday. I leaned a hand against the thin chest in front of me and pushed hard enough to get us both into the room. I shut the door with my heel, said, "I'll take that," and yanked the letter out of his paralyzed fingers. It had scaling wax along the flap and enough stamps pasted on the front to pay the national debt.

Across the room the girl in the flowered housecoat was reaching a hand under a couch pillow. I took several long steps and stiff-armed the small of her back and she sat down hard on the floor. I put my empty hand under the pillow and found a snub-nosed Smith & Wesson ·32, all chambers filled and dark red nail polish on the sight. I held it loosely along my leg and said, "Well, here we are," in a sprightly voice.

Monroe hadn't moved. He stared at me sullenly, fear still flickering in his small nervous eyes. The girl climbed painfully to her feet, not looking at either of us, and dropped down on the edge of a leather chair and put her face in her hands.

The man's restless eyes darted from me to the girl and back to me again. A pale tongue dabbed furtively at lips so narrow they hardly existed. He said hoarsely, "Just what the hell's the bright idea busting in here and grabbing what don't belong to you?"

I flapped the envelope loosely next to my ear. "You mean this? Not yours either, buster."

"It belongs to my father-in-law. I simply signed for it."

"Oh, knock it off," I said wearily. "You went way out of your league on this caper, Tom. You should have known murder isn't for grifters with simple minds."

A sound that was half wail, half sob filtered through the girl's fingers. The man said absently, "Shut up, Cora." His eyes skittered over my face. "Murder? Who's talking about murder? You the one who shoved in here a while ago and told Cora about Amos Spain?"

"I wasn't telling her a thing," I said. "She knew it long before. You told her."

"You might like to try proving that," he said.

"You bet," I said. I put the gun on the couch arm and looked at the envelope. Yesterday's postmark, mailed from New York City. Addressed in a spidery handwriting, with the return address reading: *B. Jones, General Delivery, Radio City Station, New York, NY*. I ripped open the flap and shook out the contents. A plain sheet of bond paper wrapped around three odd-looking stamps. One was circular with a pale rose background and black letters. The other two were square, one orange and one blue, with the same crude reproduction of Queen Victoria on both. All three wouldn't have carried a postcard across the street.

Monroe was staring at the stamps and chewing his lip. He looked physically ill. The girl was watching me now, her fingers picking at the edge of the housecoat, her face white and drawn and filled with silent fury.

I said, "It would almost have to be stamps. I should have guessed as much two hours ago. How much are they worth?"

"How would I know?" Monroe said sulkily. "They weren't sent to me. I never saw them before."

I slid the stamps back into the envelope and put the envelope in my pocket. "You'd know, brother. If you'd kept a better eye on Amos Spain you might even have gotten away with the whole thing."

"You've got nothing on us. Why don't you just shove off?"

"I've got everything on you," I said. "Not that I deserve any credit. The Army mule could have done the job. I can give you the State Attorney's case right now."

I picked up the gun and swung it lightly between a thumb and finger and sat on the couch arm. Rain beat against the windows in a muted murmur. From the kitchen came the lurch and whine of the refrigerator motor.

"Somebody named B. Jones," I said, "gets hold of some rare stamps. Illegally. Jones knows there are collectors around who will buy stolen stamps. Amos Spain is such a collector. A deal is made by phone or letter and the stamps are mailed to Spain. In some way you two find out about it. After the stamps are in the mail, perhaps. No point in trying to get them away from Uncle Sam; but there's another way. So the two of you show up here early this morning and force your way in on old Amos, who is still in bed. You tie him up a little, let's say, and gag him, leave him on the bed and come out here in the living room to wait for the postman with the stamps.

"But Amos isn't giving up. He gets loose, dresses and goes down the fire escape. He can't be sure when you're going to open the door and look in on him, so he puts on just enough clothes to keep from being pinched for indecent exposure. That's why he wasn't wearing socks, and why his clothes were mismatched.

"But by the time he's going down the fire escape, you look in. No Amos, and the window is open. You look out, spot him running away without topcoat or hat, and out you go after him. Tackling him on the street wouldn't do at all; your only hope is to nail him in some lonely spot and knock him off. How does it sound so far, neighbor?"

"Like a lot of words," Monroe growled.

"Words," I said, "are man's best friend. They get you fed, married, buried. Shall I tell you some more about words?"

"Go to hell."

I put down the gun and lit a cigarette and smiled. "Like I told you," I said, "you've got a simple mind. But I was telling you a story. I wouldn't want to stop now, so let's get back to Amos. You see, Amos had a big problem at this stage of the game. He couldn't go to the boys in blue and tell them about you and Cora, here. Doing that could bring out the business about the stamps and get him nailed for receiving stolen property. He had to get the two of you thrown out of his apartment before the envelope showed up.

"How to do it? Hire a strong-arm boy who won't ask questions. Where do you find a strong-arm boy on a moment's notice? The phone book's got half a column of them. Private detectives. Not the big agencies; they might ask too many questions. But one of the smaller outfits might need the business bad enough to do it Amos's way. At least it's worth trying.

"So Amos gets my address out of the phone book, the nearest one to him, and comes up to hire me. He has no idea you're following him which means he's not too careful about keeping out in the open where nothing can happen to him. He comes up to my office and I'm not in yet. He sits down to wait. You walk in and leave a switch knife in him. But that's only part of your job. You've got to fix it so there'll be a delay in identifying him – enough of a delay, at least to keep the cops away from here until the mailman comes and goes. Lifting his papers may slow things down, but you want more than that. Being a crook, you make a habit of carrying around phony identification cards. You substitute these for his own, lift whatever cash Amos had on him, slip out quick and come back here. Right so far?"

The fear had gone out of Monroe's eyes and there was the first faint sign of a smirk to his thin bloodless lips. He said airily, "If this is your idea of a way to kill a rainy afternoon, don't let me stop you. Mind if I sit down?"

"I don't care if you fall down," I said. "There's a little more and then we can all sit around and discuss the election until the cops arrive. A little more, like Cora knowing my name the first time I was here this afternoon. I hadn't told her my name, you see; just that I was a private dick. But to Cora there was only one private detective – the one whose office you'd killed Amos Spain in."

Behind me a quiet voice said, "Raise your hands."

I froze. Cora Monroe's .32 was on the couch arm, no more than six inches from my hand. I could have grabbed for it – and I could get buried for grabbing. I didn't grab.

A slender stoop-shouldered man in his early forties came padding on stocking feet in front of me. He had bushy graying hair, a long intelligent face and a capable-looking hand containing a nickel-plated Banker's Special revolver. The quiet voice belonged to him and he used it again, saying, "I won't tell you again. Put up your hands."

I put them up.

He went on pointing the gun at me while knocking the .32 off the couch with a single sweep of his other hand. It bounced along the carpet and hit the wall. He said gently, "I'll take those stamps."

"You will indeed," I said. My tongue felt as stiff as Murphy, the night he fell off the streetcar. "I guess I should have looked in the bedroom after all. I guess I thought two people should be able to lift three little stamps."

"The stamps, Mr Pine." The voice wasn't as gentle this time.

"Sure," I said. I put my hand in my coat and took out the envelope. I did it nice and slow, showing him I was eager to please. I held it out as he reached for it and I slammed my shoe down on his stocking foot with every pound I could spare.

He screamed like a woman and the gun went off. Behind me a lamp base came apart. I threw a punch, hard, and the gray-haired man threw his hands one way and the gun the other and melted into the rug without a sound.

Monroe was crouched near the side wall, the girl's .32 in his hand and madness in his eyes. While he was still bringing up the gun I jerked the Police Special from under the band of my trousers and fired.

He took a week to fall down. He put his hands together high on his chest and coughed a broken cough and took three wavering steps before he hit the floor with his face and died.

Cora Monroe hadn't moved from the leather chair. She sat stiff as an ice floe off Greenland, her face blank with shock, her nails sunk in her palms. I felt a little sorry for her. I bent down and picked the envelope off the floor and shoved it deep into a side pocket. I said, "How much were they worth, Cora?"

Only the rain answered.

I found the telephone and said what had to be said. Then I came back and sat down to wait.

It was ten minutes before I heard the first wail of distant sirens.

WE ARE ALL DEAD

Bruno Fischer

1

THE CAPER WENT off without a hitch except that Wally Garden got plugged.

There were five of us. My idea had been that three would be enough, figuring the less there were the bigger the cut for each. But Oscar Trotter made the decisions.

Looking at Oscar, you might take him for a college professor – one of those lean, rangy characters with amused, intelligent eyes behind horn-rimmed glasses. He sounded like one, too, when he didn't feel like sounding like somebody else. Maybe he'd been one once, among all the other things he'd ever been.

But there was no question of what he was now. He could give the toughest hood the jitters by smiling at him a certain way, and he could organize and carry out a caper better than any man I knew.

He spent a couple of weeks casing this job and then said five men would be needed, no more and no less. So there were four of us going in soon after the payroll arrived on a Friday afternoon. The fifth, Wally Garden, was cruising outside in a stolen heap.

Wally was far and away the youngest of us, around twenty-three, and he wasn't a regular. I didn't know where Oscar had picked him up; somebody had recommended him, he'd said. It must have been somebody Oscar had a lot of confidence in because Oscar was a mighty careful guy. Wally was supposed to be very good with a car, but I think what made Oscar pick him was that he was moon-faced and clear-eyed and looked like he was always helping old ladies across streets.

Protective coloration, Oscar called it. Have one appearance during the job and another while making the getaway.

So there was the kid, and Oscar Trotter who could pass for a professor, and Georgie Ross who had a wife and two children and made like a respectable citizen except for a few days a year, and Tiny who was an old-time Chicago gorilla but could have been your kindly gray-haired Uncle Tim.

As for me, I'd been around a long, long time in thirty-four years of living. I'd almost been a lawyer, once. I'd almost married a decent woman, once. I'd almost . . .

Never mind. I was thirty-four years old and had all my features in the right places, and whenever Oscar Trotter had a job I was there at his side.

Wally Garden's part was to swipe a car early in the afternoon and pick us up on a country road and drop us off at the factory and drive slowly for five hundred feet and make a U-turn and drive slowly back. He picked out a nice car – a shiny big Buick.

The factory manufactured plastic pipe. It was in New Jersey, on the outskirts of Coast City where real estate was cheap. The office of the large, low, sprawling plant was in a wing off by itself. From that wing a side door opened directly out to a two-lane blacktop road that had little traffic. There was an armed guard who arrived with the payroll and stayed until it was distributed, but he was an old man who was given that job because he couldn't work at anything else.

Oscar decided it would be a cinch. And it was.

We were in and out in seventy seconds – five seconds under the schedule Oscar had worked out. We barged in wearing caps and T-shirts and denim work pants, and we had Halloween masks on our faces and guns in our hands. Tiny had the guard's gun before the sluggish old man knew what was up. Seven or eight others were in the office, men and women, but they were too scared to cause trouble. Which was just as well. We weren't after hurting anybody if we could help it. We were after dough, and there it was on a long table in an adjoining room, in several hundred little yellow envelopes.

Seventy seconds – and we were coming out through the side door with two satchels holding the payroll, pulling off our masks and sticking away our guns before we stepped into the open air, then striding to the Buick Wally Garden was rolling over to us.

Some hero in the office got hold of a gun and started to fire it.

The newspapers next day said it was a bookkeeper who had it in his desk. One thing was sure – he didn't know a lot about how to use it. He stood at a window and let fly wildly.

None of the slugs came near us. Anyway, not at the four of us out in the open he was firing at. But he got Wally who was still a good twenty feet away. Got him through the car window as if he'd been an innocent bystander.

The car jerked as his foot slipped off the throttle and it stalled and stopped after rolling a few more feet. Through the windshield we saw Wally slump over the wheel.

Oscar yelled something to me, but I knew what to do. Sometimes I could think for myself. I ran around to the left front door.

The shooting had stopped. No more bullets, I supposed.

Wally turned a pale, agonized face to me as I yanked open the car door. "I'm hit," he moaned.

"Shove over," I said.

He remained bowed over the wheel. I pushed him. Oscar got into the car through the opposite door and pulled him. Groaning, Wally slid along the seat. Georgie and Tiny were piling into the back seat with the satchels. There was plenty of screaming now in the office, but nobody was coming out, not even the hero. I took Wally's place and got the stalled engine started and away we went.

Sagging between Oscar and me on the front seat, Wally started to cough, shaking all over.

"Where's it hurt, son?" Oscar asked gently.

Wally pushed his face against Oscar's shoulder, the way a frightened child would against his mother's bosom.

He gasped, "I feel . . . it stabs . . . my insides . . . bleeding."

He was the only one of us wearing a jacket. Oscar unbuttoned it and pulled it back. I glanced sideways and saw blood soaking a jagged splotch on the right side of his shirt. It looked bad.

Nobody said anything.

2

Tiny sat twisted around on the back seat watching through the rear window. It wasn't what was behind us we had to worry about as much as what was ahead. Pretty soon there would be roadblocks.

We traveled three and two-tenths miles on that road, according to plan. Then I swung the Buick left, off blacktop and onto an oiled country road running through fields and woods.

It was a bright spring afternoon, the kind of day on which you took deep breaths and felt it was good to be alive. Beside me Wally Garden started to claw at his right side. Oscar had to hold his hand to keep him from making the wound worse than it was.

Again I made a left turn. This time there was no road to turn onto but only an open field. Wally screamed between clenched teeth as the rough ground jounced the car.

Beyond the field were woods – big stuff, mostly, oaks and maples, with a fringe of high shrubs. Two cars, a Ford and a Nash, were where we'd left them this morning behind the shrubs. I rolled the hot car, the Buick, quite a way in among the trees.

It was dim in there, and cool and quiet. Wally's eyes were closed; he'd stopped squirming in agony. He would have toppled over if Oscar hadn't been holding him.

"Passed out?" I asked.

"Uh-huh," Oscar said.

Getting out of the car, he eased Wally's head and shoulder down on the seat. Wally lay on his side twitching and moaning and unconscious.

The Buick was going to be left right here – after, of course, we'd wiped off all our prints. The way we planned it, we'd hang around for two-three hours before starting back to New York in the two other cars. Until then we had plenty of time on our hands. We used some of it to make a quick count of the loot in the two satchels.

When Oscar Trotter had cased the job, he'd estimated that the take would be between forty and fifty grand. Actually it was around twenty-two grand.

What the hell! After a while you get to be part realist and part cynic, if the two aren't the same thing in this rotten racket. Nothing is ever as good as you plan or hope or dream. You're doing all right if you get fifty percent, and don't lose your life or freedom while doing it.

Every now and then I'd leave the others to go over for a look at Wally. The third time I did his eyes were open.

"How d'you feel, kid?"

He had trouble speaking. He managed to let me know he was thirsty.

There wasn't any water, but Georgie had a pint of rye. Wally, lying cramped on that car seat, gulped and coughed and gulped and pushed the bottle away. I thought it probably did him more harm than good.

"I'm burning up," he moaned.

I felt his brow. He sure was.

I went over to where Oscar and Georgie and Tiny were changing their clothes beside the Nash. This would be an important part of our protective coloration – completely different and respectable clothes.

The alarm was out for five men in a Buick, at least four of whom had been seen wearing caps and T-shirts and denim pants. I felt kind of sorry for anybody within a hundred miles who would be in T-shirts and denim pants. But we wouldn't be. We'd be wearing conservative business suits and shirts and neckties, and we'd be driving two in a Ford Georgie owned legally and three in a Nash Oscar owned legally, and why would any cop at a roadblock or toll gate waste time on such honest-looking citizens?

Except that in one of the cars there would be a wounded man. This was one contingency Oscar hadn't foreseen.

I said to Tiny who was standing in his underwear, "Give me a hand with the kid. He'll be more comfortable on the ground."

Oscar stopped buttoning a freshly laundered white shirt. "Leave him where he is."

"For how long?" I said.

There was a silence. I'd put our plight into words. This was as good a time as any to face it.

Oscar tossed me a smile. About the worst thing he did was smile. It was twisted and almost never mirthful.

"Until," he said, "somebody blunders into these woods and finds him." He tucked his shirt-tail into his pants and added hopefully, "It might take days."

Wally was nobody to me. But I said, "We can't do that."

"Have you a better idea, Johnny?" Oscar said.

"You're the big brain," I said.

"Very well then." Oscar, standing among us tall and slightly stooped, took off his horn-rimmed glasses. "Gentlemen, let us consider the situation."

This was his professorial manner. He could put it on like a coat, and when he did you knew he was either going to show how bright he was or pull something dirty.

"The odds are highly favorable," he drawled, "that before midnight we four will be out of New Jersey and in New York and each safe and snug at home. But not if we're burdened by a wounded and probably dying man. We'll never make it. If by chance we do make it, what do we do with him? At the least he needs a doctor. A doctor finds the bullet wound and calls in the police. Perhaps Wally wouldn't talk. Perhaps he will. He may be delirious and not know he's talking." Oscar's smile broadened. "There's no question, gentlemen, that we'd deserve to have our heads chopped off if we stuck our necks out so far."

Tiny said uneasily, "Yeah, but we can't just leave him here to die."

"Certainly not." Oscar's eyeglasses swung gently from his fingers. "He might die too slowly or scream and attract a passing car. There is, I'm afraid, only one alternative."

All right, but why did he have to say it in that mocking, lecturing manner, and why did he have to keep smiling all the time?

Georgie was down on one knee lacing his shoes so he wouldn't have to look at anybody. Tiny was scratching his hairy chest unhappily. I was a little sick to my stomach. And Oscar Trotter smiled.

"Tiny, your knife, please," Oscar drawled. "A gun would be too noisy."

Tiny dug his switchblade knife out of a pair of pants draped over the hood of the Nash. Oscar took it from him and moved to the Buick as if taking a stroll through the woods.

I turned away. I couldn't stop him, and if I could I wouldn't have. I'd seen that kid only twice in my life before today, the first time less than a week ago. I didn't know a thing about him except his name. He was

nobody at all to me. But I turned away and my hands shook as I set fire
to a cigarette.

Then Oscar was coming back.

"Well, Johnny," he taunted me, "from the first you wanted less men to
cut in on the loot, didn't you?"

I had an impulse to take a swing at him. But of course I didn't.

3

Much of the next three days I watched Stella jiggle about Oscar's apartment.
She was a bit on the buxom side, but in a cozy-looking, cuddly-looking way.
She went in for sheer, tight sweaters and little else, and she had what to jiggle
with. She belonged to Oscar.

I didn't know what the dames saw in him. He was no longer young and
you couldn't call him handsome by a long shot, but he always had a woman
around who had both youth and looks. Like Stella, who was merely the
current one. She was also a fine cook.

I was staying with them in Oscar's two-bedroom apartment on Riverside
Drive. I'd come down from Boston for that New Jersey caper, and afterward
there was nothing to take me back to Boston. Oscar was letting me use the
spare room while I was making up my mind whether to stay in New York
or push on to wherever the spirit moved me.

On that third day Oscar and I went up to the Polo Grounds to take in
a ball game. When Stella heard us at the door, she came out to meet us
in the foyer.

"There's a friend of yours in the living room," she told Oscar. "A
Mr Brant. He's been waiting over an hour."

I stepped to the end of the foyer and looked into the living room. The
meaty man sitting on the sofa and sucking a pipe was definitely no friend
of Oscar's. Or of mine. He was Bill Brant, a city detective attached to the
DA's office, which meant he was a kind of free-wheeling copper.

Oscar touched my arm. "I expected this. Merely the MO. I'll do the
talking." He turned to Stella. "Go do your work in the kitchen."

"I haven't any. Dinner's cooking."

"Go find something to do in the kitchen," he snapped.

She flounced away, wiggling almost as much as she jiggled. But the thing
is that she obeyed.

Oscar trained his women right. She was used to being sent out of the
room or sometimes clear out of the apartment when business was being
discussed. She was no innocent, of course, but in his book the less any
woman knew the better. It might be all right to trust Stella today, but
who knew what the situation would be tomorrow? So she went into the
kitchen and we went into the living room.

"Well, what d'you know!" Bill Brant beamed at me. "Johnny Worth too! Another piece fits into the picture. I guess you came to town for the Jersey stickup."

"I did?" I said and went over to the portable bar for a drink. I didn't offer the cop any.

"What's this about New Jersey?" Oscar was asking.

"We're cooperating with the police over there. You're a local resident. So was Wallace Garden who was found dead in the Buick."

"You misunderstood my question." Oscar was using his mocking drawl. "I'm not interested in the jurisdictional problems of the police. I'm simply curious as to the reason for your visit."

"Come off it," Brant said. "That payroll stickup has all your earmarks."

I helped myself to another drink. I hadn't been very much worried, but now I felt better. That, as Oscar had guessed, was all they seemed to have – the MO, the modus operandi, the well-planned, perfectly timed and executed armed robbery that cops identified with Oscar.

"Earmarks!" Oscar snorted. "Do they arrest citizens for that these days?"

"No, but it helps us look in the right direction." Brant sucked on his pipe. "That killing too. It's like you not to leave loose ends, even if it means sticking a knife into one of your own boys." He twisted his head around to me. "Or did he have you do the dirty work, Johnny?"

That was one thing about Oscar, I thought – he did his own dirty work. Maybe because he enjoyed it.

Aloud I said, "What the hell are you talking about?"

Brant sighed. What had he expected, that we'd up and confess all as soon as he told us he had a suspicion? We knew as well as he did that he didn't even have enough to take us to headquarters and sweat us, and likely never would have. But he was paid to try, and he hung around another ten minutes, trying. That got him nothing, not even a drink.

After he was gone, Stella came in from the kitchen and said dinner would be ready soon.

4

Another day passed and another. I was on edge, restless. I took walks along the Drive, I dropped in on friends, I went to the movies. Then I'd come back to Oscar's apartment and there would be Stella jiggling.

Understand me. I didn't particularly hanker for her – certainly not enough to risk fooling around with anything of Oscar Trotter's. Besides, I doubted that she would play. She seemed to like me, but strictly as her husband's friend. She was completely devoted to him.

No, it was just that any juicy dame within constant eyesight made my restlessness so much harder to take.

We were playing Scrabble on the cardtable, Oscar and Stella and I, when the doorbell rang.

It was evening, around eight-thirty. Oscar, of course, was way ahead; he was unbeatable at any game that required brains. Stella was way behind. I was in the middle, where I usually found myself in everything. As it was Stella's turn to play, I went to answer the doorbell.

A girl stood in the hall – a fairhaired, blue-eyed girl in a simple gray dress and a crazy little gray hat.

"Mr Trotter?" she said.

"You're right, I'm not," I said. "He's inside."

Without being invited in, she stepped over the threshold and closed the door behind her. "Please tell him Mrs Garden would like to see him."

"Sure." I started to turn and stopped. "Garden?" I said. "Any relative of – "

I caught myself. In my racket you became cautious about naming certain names under certain circumstances, especially when you weren't supposed to know them. There were all kinds of traps.

Gravely she said, "I was Wally's wife." She put her head back. "You must be Johnny. Wally told me about you."

I gawked at her. Standing primly and trimly in the foyer, she made me think of golden fields and cool streams and the dreams of youth.

I said, "Wait here," and went into the living room. Stella was scowling at the Scrabble board and Oscar was telling her irritably to do something or pass. I beckoned to him. He rose from the cardtable and came over to me.

"Wally's wife is in the foyer," I said.

Oscar took off his eyeglasses, a sign that he was disturbed. "He never mentioned a wife to me."

"To me either. He wasn't much of a talker."

"What does she want?"

"Seems to me," I said, "our worry is what does she know. If Wally – "

And then she was in the living room. Having waited maybe thirty seconds in the foyer, she wasn't waiting any longer. She headed straight for Oscar.

"You must be Mr Trotter," she said. "I'm Abby Garden."

Abby, I thought – exactly the name for a lovely girl of twenty, if she was that old.

Oscar put his glasses back on to stare at her. He seemed as startled as I'd been that such a dish could have been the moon-faced kid's wife. But he didn't say anything to her. In fact, his nod was rather curt. Then he looked across the room at Stella.

Stella was twisted around on her chair, giving Abby Garden that feminine once-over which in a moment took in age, weight, figure, clothes, make-up. Stella didn't look enthusiastic. Which was natural enough, considering that whatever she had the other girl had better.

"Baby," Oscar said to Stella, "take a walk to Broadway and buy a pack of cigarettes."

There were cigarettes all over the apartment. At another time he might have given her the order in one word, "Blow!" but this evening he was being polite about it in front of a guest. It amounted to the same thing. Stella undulated up the length of the room, and on the way her eyes never left the girl. No doubt she didn't care for being chased out for her. But she left, all right.

Me, whenever I told a dame to do anything, she either kicked up a fuss or ignored me. What did Oscar have?

I fixed drinks for the three of us. Abby wanted a rye highball without too much gingerale. Her hand brushed mine as she took the glass from me. That was sheer accident, but all the same my fingers tingled.

"Now then, Mrs Garden," Oscar said. His long legs stretched from the armchair in which he lounged. "What's your business with me?"

She rolled her glass between her palms. "Wally told me his share would come to thousands of dollars."

"And who," he said, "might Wally be?"

"Please, Mr Trotter." Abby leaned forward. "We can be open and aboveboard. Wally had no secrets from me. I didn't like it when he told me he was going in on that – that robbery. He'd already done one stretch. Six months for stealing cars. Before I met him." She bit her lower lip. "I tried to stop him, but he wouldn't listen to me."

Oscar looked utterly disgusted. He had no use for a man who blabbered to anybody, including his wife. Wally may very well have endangered us all.

"So?" Oscar said.

"Oh, you needn't worry I told the police. They asked me, of course. They questioned me for hours after they found poor Wally. But I told them I knew nothing about any holdup or who was in it." She gave him a piece of a small smile. "You see, I didn't want to get into trouble. After all, if I'd known beforehand, I was a kind of accessory, wasn't I?"

"So?" Oscar said again.

"There was one detective especially – a fat man named Brant. He kept asking me if I knew you." She looked Oscar straight in the eye. "He said you killed Wally."

"Now why would I do any such thing?"

"Brant said Wally was wounded during the getaway and then you or one of the others killed him with a knife to get him out of the way."

"My dear," Oscar said, more in sorrow than in anger, "can it be possible you fell for that line?"

"Is it a line? That's what I want to know."

Oscar sighed. "I see you're not familiar with police tricks. This is a particularly shabby one. Don't you see they made up this story to induce you to talk?"

"Then he wasn't killed with a knife?"

"No, my dear. The bullet killed him. He died in my arms. Wasn't that so, Johnny?"

"Yes," I said.

5

That word was my first contribution to the conversation, and my last for another while. Nursing a Scotch-on-the-rocks, I sat on the hassock near Abby's legs. They were beautifully turned legs. I looked up at her face. She was drinking her highball, and over the rim of the glass her wide blue eyes were fixed with rapt attention on Oscar, who was, now, being a salesman.

He was as good at that as at anything else. His honeyed voice was hypnotic, telling her how he'd loved Wally like a son, how he would have given his right arm to have saved him after that dastardly bookkeeper had plugged him, how the conniving, heartless coppers were out to make her hate him and thus betray him with that fantastic yarn that he, Oscar Trotter, would either have harmed or permitted anybody else to have harmed a hair of one of his own men.

He was good, and on top of that she apparently wasn't too bright. He sold her and she bought.

"Wally always warned me not to trust a cop." She split a very warm smile between both of us. "You look like such nice men. So much nicer than that fat detective."

Oscar purred, "Then I take it we're friends, Abby?"

"Oh, yes." She put her highball glass down on the coffee table. "And in a way we're partners, aren't we? When will I get my share?"

Suddenly there was frost in the room. The cheekbones ridged Oscar's lean face.

"What share?" he said softly.

"Why, Wally's share. He earned it, didn't he?" She was completely relaxed; she was free and easy and charming. "I read in the papers that there were twenty-two thousand dollars. One-fifth of that – "

"Young lady," Oscar cut in, "are you trying to blackmail me?"

"Not at all. I simply ask for what I'm entitled to. If money is owed to a man who dies, it goes to his wife."

She said that wide-eyed and innocent-faced, her earnest manner holding no hint of threat – merely a young and probably destitute widow wanting to clean up financial matters after her husband's untimely demise.

Huh! A few minutes ago I'd thought she wasn't so bright. Now I changed my mind.

I spoke up. "She's got something there, Oscar."

"You keep out of this."

"Not this time," I said. "I suggest we each give her five hundred bucks."

Oscar pushed his fingers under his glasses to rub his eyes. Then he nodded. He had no choice. We'd be in a bad way if she were to chirp to the cops.

"How much will that come to?" Abby asked me.

"Two grand. Wally wouldn't have gotten a fifth anyway. He was only the driver. Believe me, we're being more than fair."

"I'm sure you are," she said, and gave me a smile.

This was why I'd jumped in to negotiate – to get some such smile out of her, a smile of sheer joyous gratitude. A man has already gone quite a distance with a dame who thinks she's beholden to him for money. And with this one I was after going on and on and maybe never stopping.

"Just a minute," Oscar said.

Abby and I shifted our attention from each other to him.

"Prove you're Wally's wife," he said.

"But I am."

Oscar looked stern. "I know every switch on every con game. We don't even know Wally had a wife. If he did, we don't know you were the one. Prove it."

"Why, of course," she said. "I have my marriage license and other things at home. If you want me to bring – "

"I've a better idea," I said. I wasn't one to pass up any chance when I was on the make. I got off the hassock so quickly I almost spilled what was left in my glass. "I'll go with you right now and look over whatever you have."

"That's so good of you," she said so sweetly that my heart did a complete flip.

Oscar nodded and closed his eyes. When we left, he appeared to have fallen asleep in the armchair.

6

According to the marriage license, they'd been married seven months ago by the county clerk here in New York.

I sat in the only decent chair in the place. Nearby a train rumbled on the Third Avenue El. She didn't quite live in a slum, but the difference wasn't great. There wasn't much to this room, and there was less to the bedroom and kitchen and bathroom. They were all undersized and falling apart.

Wally's cut of the loot would have meant a lot to him and her, if he'd lived through it.

I handed the marriage license back to Abby. She fed me other stuff out of the shoebox on her lap – snapshots of her and Wally, his discharge papers from the army, the deposit book of a joint savings account containing less than fifty dollars, a letter from her mother from somewhere in Iowa complaining because she'd gone and married a man named Wallace Garden whom none of the family had met.

"Good enough," I said.

"How soon will I get the money?"

"Soon as I collect it from the others. Maybe tomorrow."

"Two thousand dollars," she reminded me.

"That's right," I said.

Abby put the lid on the shoebox and carried it into the bedroom. She didn't jiggle and wiggle like Stella. Her tight, slender figure in that trim gray dress seemed to flow when in motion.

I wanted her as I hadn't wanted anybody or anything in a very long time.

Take it easy, I warned myself while waiting for her to return. I could mark myself lousy in her book by rushing. All right, she'd been married to that round-faced kid, who'd been what he'd been, meaning no better than I, and she hadn't acted particularly upset over his death. But I didn't yet know what made her tick. I only knew that she looked like moonlight and roses and that it would be wise to handle her accordingly. She was already grateful to me. She'd be a lot more grateful when I brought her the two grand. Then would be time enough to take the next step – a big step or small step, depending on how she responded.

So I was a perfect little gentleman that evening. She put up a pot of coffee and we sat opposite each other at the table and she was as pleasant to talk to as to look at. She spoke of her folks' farm in Iowa and I spoke of my folks' farm in Indiana.

When I was leaving, she went to the door with me and put her hand in mine. And she said, "I'll see you soon, Johnny."

"Do you want to see me or the money?"

"Both," she said and squeezed my hand holding hers.

I walked on a cloud clear across town and then a couple of miles uptown to Oscar's apartment. I hadn't as much as kissed her good-night, or tried to, but what of that? My hand still tingled from the feel of hers.

I laughed at myself. Johnny Worth, the cynical hard guy, acting like a love-sick schoolboy! But I laughed at myself happily.

Oscar and Stella were in bed when I let myself in. Oscar heard me and came out of his bedroom in a bath-robe.

"She was Wally's wife all right," I told him. "Tomorrow I'll go collect the dough from Georgie and Tiny."

"You seem anxious," he said with an amused twist to his mouth.

I shrugged. "We promised her."

"I can read you like a book, Johnny." He nudged my ribs with his elbow. "Make much headway with her?"

I shrugged again.

"I guess not if you're back so early," Oscar said, leering amiably. "I can't imagine what she saw in that punk Wally. She has class. Well, good hunting."

"Good-night," I said and went into my room.

7

Next afternoon I set forth to make the collection for Abby. Oscar had given me his five hundred in the morning, and of course I had my own, so that left Georgie and Tiny to go.

Georgie Ross lived out in Queens, in a neat frame house with a patch of lawn in front. His wife and two teen-aged daughters hadn't any notion of how he picked up extra money to support them. His regular job, as a traveling salesman in housewares, didn't keep him very busy or bring in much income. He had time on a weekday afternoon to be mowing his lawn.

He stopped mowing when he saw me come up the street. He stood middle-aged and pot-bellied.

"For God's sake," he complained when I reached him, "you know better than to come here."

"Relax. You can say I'm a bill collector."

"Just don't come around, that's all I ask. What d'you want?"

"To collect a bill. Five C's for Wally Garden's widow."

His eyes bugged out. "You're kidding," he said. Meaning, if I knew him, not about the widow but about the money.

I told him I wasn't kidding and I told him about Abby's visit last evening.

"Listen," Georgie said, taking out a handkerchief and wiping his suddenly sweaty face, "I'm not shelling out that kind of dough for anybody's wife. I have my own family to think of. My God, do you know what my two girls cost me? Just their clothes! And my oldest, Dinah, is starting college next year. Is that expensive! I got to hang onto every penny."

"Some of those pennies were supposed to have gone to Wally."

"It's his tough luck he wasn't around to collect." He leaned against the handle of the mower. "I tell you this: we give her two grand now, she thinks she has us over a barrel and keeps coming back for more. Oscar ought to handle her different."

"How?"

"Well, he handled her husband," Georgie said.

That was a quiet, genteel street, and he fitted into it, by looking at him, the way anybody else in sight did. He resumed mowing his lawn.

I tagged after him. "Use your head, Georgie."

"You don't get one damn penny out of me."

I knew I was licked. I'd ask Oscar to try. He could persuade him if anybody could. I left Georgie plodding stolidly behind the mower.

Tiny was harder to find. He was like me, without anywhere to stay put. He was paying rent on a mangy room he'd sublet downtown, but he only slept in it. I made the rounds of the neighboring ginmills. What with lingering in this place and that and shooting the breeze with guys I knew, I didn't come across Tiny until after nine o'clock.

He was sitting wide-shouldered and gray-haired at the bar, drinking beer. He was always drinking beer.

He said, "Gee, am I glad to see you." Picking up his glass, he slid off the stool and we went to an isolated table. "I've been trying to get Oscar on the phone," he said, "but he ain't in. Stella says she don't know where he went." He glanced around. "Johnny, there's been a city dick asking me questions this afternoon. A fat guy."

"Brant?"

"Yeah, that's the name. He's got it, Johnny. He knows who was in on it and what happened to Wally and all."

I thought of Abby.

"Go on," I said.

"Remember last Wednesday when the five of us went over the route in Oscar's car? It was hot and when we came back through the Holland Tunnel from Jersey we stopped for beer on Tenth Avenue. Remember?"

"I remember."

"Somebody that knew us saw the five of us sitting in that booth together."

I let out my breath. Not Abby.

"Who was it?" I asked.

"Search me. This Brant, he wasn't telling. Some goddamn stoolie. He knew four of us – me and you, Oscar and Georgie. The one break is he hadn't never seen Wally before. Brant is one cagy cookie, but I wasn't born yesterday. I figure they showed the stoolie Wally's picture, but he wasn't sure. If he'd been sure, they'd be piling on us."

"That's right," I said. "The cops can't make any move officially unless they can link us to Wally. I saw Georgie this afternoon and he didn't mention being questioned."

"He's been by now, I guess. The way I figure, this stoolie didn't spill till today." Tiny took a slug of beer and wiped his mouth with the back of his hand. "But I don't get it, Johnny. A stoolie sees four of us and a strange guy in a beer joint. What makes this Brant so all-fired smart he can tell from that Wally was the strange guy and we was the ones did the job way over in Jersey a couple days later?"

"Because Oscar is too good."

"Come again?"

"The caper bore the marks of genius," I said, "and Oscar is a genius. Then Brant drops into Oscar's apartment a few days ago and finds me staying there, so he's got two of us tagged. Then he learns we two plus you and Georgie were drinking beer with a fifth guy who could've been Wally Garden, and he's got us all."

"The hell he has! All he's got is thoughts running in his head. He needs evidence. How'll he get it if we sit tight?"

"He won't," I said.

This was a good time to tell him about Abby. I told him.

When I finished, Tiny complained, "What's the matter with Oscar these days? First he lets us all be seen together in a beer joint – "

"I don't remember any of us objected. In fact, I remember it was your idea we stop off."

"Sure, but Oscar should know better. He's supposed to have the brains. Then he don't know the kid had a wife and would blab every damn thing to her. Where'd he pick up Wally, anyway?"

"He never told me," I said. "But there's the widow and we promised her two grand. I want five C's from you."

Tiny thought about it, and he came up with what, I had to concede, was a good question. "You said you saw Georgie this afternoon. Did he shell out?"

"Not yet."

"Expect him to?"

"Sure."

"Bet he don't?"

"Look, Oscar will get it out of him. I'm asking you."

Tiny said cheerfully. "Tell you what I'll do, Johnny. When Georgie shells out, I'll shell out."

And he looked mighty pleased with himself. He had confidence in Georgie's passion for hanging onto a buck.

8

So after chasing around for hours I had only the thousand I'd started out with. Well, that wasn't hay and the evening was young. I could bring the thousand to Abby and tell her it was part payment. She would be grateful. She would thank me. One thing could lead to another – and perhaps tonight would be the night, the beginning.

I took a hack to her place.

Through her door I heard music going full blast. I knocked. No answer, which wasn't surprising considering all the row a hot dance band was making. I knocked louder. Same result. I turned the knob and found the door unlocked.

Abby wasn't in the living room. The bedroom and the bathroom doors were both closed. The band music, coming from a tiny table radio, stopped and a disc jockey's voice drooled. In the comparative quiet I heard a shower running in the bathroom. I sat down to wait for her to come out.

The music started up again. It was too raucous; my mood was for sweet stuff. I reached over the table to turn off the radio, and my hand brushed a pair of horn-rimmed eyeglasses. She hadn't worn them when I'd seen her, but women were vain about such things. Probably only reading glasses.

She'd stopped showering. Now with the radio off, there was no sound in the apartment. Suddenly it occurred to me that I ought to let her know she had a visitor. Thinking she was alone, she might come trotting out without anything on. I wouldn't mind, but she might, and I was still on the perfect little gentleman technique.

I went to the bathroom door and said, "Abby."

"I'll be right out."

I hadn't time to wonder why she hadn't sounded surprised to hear a man in her apartment and why at the least she hadn't asked who I was. The explanation came almost at once – from the bedroom.

"What did you say, baby?" a man called.

"I'll be right out," she repeated.

Then it was quiet again except for the thumping of my heart.

I knew that man's voice. If there was any doubt about it, there were those eyeglasses on the table. A minute ago I'd given them hardly a glance because I hadn't any reason then to take a good look to see if they were a woman's style and size. They seemed massive now, with a thick, dark frame.

The bathroom doorknob was turning. I moved away from there until the table stopped me, and Abby came out. She was wearing a skimpy towel held around her middle and not another thing.

Her body was very beautiful. But it was a bitter thing for me to see now.

She took two or three steps into the room, flowing with that wonderful grace of hers, before she realized that the man standing by the table wasn't the one who had just spoken to her from the bedroom – wasn't the one for whom she didn't at all mind coming out like this. It was only I – I who had been dreaming dreams. Her free hand yanked up and across her breasts in that age-old gesture of women, and rage blazed in her blue eyes.

"You have a nerve!" She said harshly.

Again he heard her in the bedroom and again he thought she was speaking to him. He called, "What?" and the bedroom door opened, and he said, "With this door closed I can't hear a – " and he saw me.

Oscar Trotter was without jacket and shirt, as well as without his glasses.

I had to say something. I muttered, "The radio was so loud you didn't hear me knock. I came in." I watched Abby sidling along the wall toward the bedroom, clinging to that towel and keeping her arm pressed in front of her, making a show of modesty before me, the intruder, the third man. "I didn't expect she was having this kind of company," I added.

He shrugged.

A door slammed viciously. She had ducked into the bedroom where her clothes would be. He picked up his glasses from the table and put them on.

There was nothing to keep me here. I started to leave.

"Just a minute, Johnny. I trust you're not sore."

I turned. "What do you expect me to be?"

"After all, you had no prior claim on her." Oscar smiled smugly. "We both saw her at the same time."

He stood lean and slightly stooped and considerably older than I, and dully I wondered why everything came so easily to him – even this.

"Next time," I said, "remember to lock the door."

"I didn't especially plan this. I asked her out to dinner. My intention was chiefly business. Chiefly, I say, for I must confess she had – ah – impressed me last night."

This was his high-hat manner, the great man talking down to a lesser being. Some day, I thought wearily, I'd beat him up and then he'd kill me, unless I killed him first.

"You understand," he was drawling, "that I was far from convinced that our problem with her would be solved by giving her two thousand dollars. I had to learn more about her. After dinner we came up here for a drink." That smug smile again. "One thing led to another. You know how it is."

I knew how it was – how I'd hoped it would be with me. And I knew that he had never for one single moment made the mistake of acting the little gentleman with her.

I had forgotten about the money in my pocket. I took it out and dropped it on the table.

"Georgie and Tiny weren't keen about contributing," I told him. "There's just this thousand. You've earned the right to worry about the balance."

"I doubt that it will be necessary to give her anything now. You see, I'll be paying all her bills. She's moving in with me."

"How nice," I said between my teeth. "I'll be out of there as soon as I pack my bags."

His head was bent over the money. "Take your time," he said as he counted it into two piles. "I still have to tell Stella. Any time tomorrow will do." He pushed one pile across the table. "Here's yours."

So I had my five hundred bucks back, and that was all I had. Before I was quite out of the apartment, Oscar, in his eagerness, was already going into the bedroom where Abby was.

I went out quietly.

9

That night I slept in a hotel. I stayed in bed most of the morning, smoking cigarettes and looking up at the ceiling. Then I shaved and dressed and had lunch and went to Oscar's apartment for my clothes.

I found Stella all packed and about to leave. She was alone in the apartment. I could guess where Oscar was.

"Hello, Johnny," she said. "I'm leaving for good."

She wasn't as upset as I'd expected. She was sitting in the living room with her legs crossed and taking a final drink of Oscar's liquor.

"I know," I said. "When's she moving in?"

"Tonight, I guess." She looked into her glass. "You know, the minute she walked into this room the other night I had a feeling. Something in the way Oscar looked at her."

"I'm sorry," I said.

She shrugged. "I'm not sure I am. He was too damn bossy."

I went into the guest bedroom and packed my two bags. When I came out, Stella was still there.

"Johnny," she said, "have you any plans?"

"No."

"I called up a woman I know. She owns a rooming house off Columbus Avenue. She says she has a nice furnished apartment to let on the second floor, with kitchenette and bath. She says the room is large and airy and nicely furnished. A young married couple just moved out."

"Are you taking it?"

"I think I will." She uncrossed her knees and pulled her skirt over them. "Two people can be very comfortable."

I looked at her sitting there rather primly with eyes lowered – a placid, cozy, cuddly woman with a bosom made for a man to rest his weary head on. She wasn't Abby, but Abby was a ruined dream, and Stella was real.

"You and me?" I murmured.

"If you want to, Johnny."

I picked up my bags. "Well, why not?" I said.

10

Stella was very nice. We weren't in love with each other, but we liked each other and got along, which was more than could be said of a lot of couples living together.

We weren't settled a week in the rooming house near Columbus Avenue when Oscar phoned. Stella answered and spoke to him. I dipped the newspaper I was reading and listened to her say we'd be glad to come over for a drink that evening.

I said, "Wait a minute."

She waved me silent and told Oscar we'd be there by nine. When she hung up, she dropped on my lap, cuddling the way only she could.

"Honey, I want to go just to show I don't care for him any more and am not jealous of that Abby. You're sweeter than he ever was. Why shouldn't we all still be friends?"

"All right," I said.

Oscar answered the doorbell when we got there. Heartily he shook Stella's hand and then mine and said Abby was in the kitchen and would be out in a minute. Stella went into the kitchen to give Abby a hand and Oscar, with a hand on my shoulder, took me into the living room.

Georgie and Tiny were there. Georgie hadn't brought his wife, of course; he kept her strictly away from this kind of social circle. They were drinking cocktails, even Tiny who was mostly a beer man.

"Looks like a caper reunion," I commented dryly. "Except that there's one missing. Though I guess we could consider that his widow represents him."

There was an uncomfortable silence. Then Oscar said pleasantly, "Here, sour-puss, maybe this will cheer you up," and thrust a cocktail at me.

I took it and sipped.

Then Abby came in, bearing a plate of chopped liver in one hand and a plate of crackers in the other. She had a warm smile for me – the impersonal greeting of a gracious hostess. Stella came behind her with potato chips and pretzels, and all of a sudden Stella's jiggling irritated me no end.

Abby hadn't changed. There was no reason why I had expected she would. She still made me think of golden fields and cool streams, as she had the first time I'd laid eyes on her.

I refilled my glass from the cocktail shaker and walked to a window and looked out at the Hudson River sparkling under the sinking sun.

"Now that was the way to handle her," Georgie said. He had come up beside me; he was stuffing into his mouth a cracker smeared with liver. "Better than paying her off. Not only saves us dough. This way we're sure of her."

"That's not why he did it."

"Guess not. Who needs a reason to want a looker like that in his bed?

But the result's the same. And you got yourself Stella, so everybody's happy."

Everybody was happy and everybody was gay and got gayer as the whiskey flowed. But I wasn't happy and the more I drank the less gay I acted. Long ago I'd learned that there was nowhere a man could be lonelier than at a party. I'd known it would be a mistake to come, and it was.

Suddenly Georgie's face turned green and he made a dash for the bathroom. Oscar sneered that he'd never been able to hold his liquor and Tiny grumbled that the only drink fit for humans was beer and I pulled Stella aside and told her I wanted to go home.

She was not only willing; she was anxious. "Fact is, I don't feel so good," she said. "I need air."

We said our good-byes except to Georgie whom we could hear having a bad time in the bathroom. An empty hack approached when we reached the sidewalk and I whistled. In the hack, she clung to me, shivering, and complained, "My throat's burning like I swallowed fire. My God, his whiskey wasn't that bad!"

"You must be coming down with a cold," I said.

She wobbled when we got out of the hack and she held her throat. I had to half-carry her up the steps of the brownstone house and into our room. As I turned from her to switch on the light, she moaned, "Johnny!" and she was doubled over, clutching at her stomach.

For the next hour I had my hands full with her. She seemed to be having quite an attack of indigestion. I undressed her and put her to bed and piled blankets on her because she couldn't stop shivering. I found baking soda in the kitchen and fed her a spoonful and made tea for her. The cramps tapered off and so did the burning in her throat.

"Something I ate," she said as she lay huddled under the blankets. "But what? We didn't have anything for dinner that could hurt us. How do you feel, honey?"

"Fine."

"I don't understand it. That Abby didn't serve anything to speak of. Nothing but some chopped liver and – " She paused. "Honey, did you have the liver?"

"No. I can't stand the stuff."

"Then it was the liver. Something wrong with it. Call up Oscar and see if the others are all right."

I dialed his number. Oscar answered after the bell had rung for some time. His voice sounded weak.

"How are you over there?" I asked.

"Terrible. All four of us sick as dogs. And you?"

"I'm all right, but Stella has indigestion. We figure it was the chopped liver because that was the one thing she ate that I didn't."

"Could be," Oscar said. "Georgie seems to be in the worst shape; he's sleeping it off in the spare room. Tiny left a short time ago. Abby's in bed, and that's where I'll be in another minute. What bothers me most is a burning in my throat."

"Stella complained of the same thing. First I ever heard of indigestion making your throat burn."

"All I know," Oscar said, "is that whatever it is I have plenty of company in my misery. Abby is calling me."

He hung up.

I told Stella what he'd said. "The liver," she murmured and turned on her side.

That was at around one o'clock. At three-thirty a bell jarred me awake. I slipped out of bed and staggered across the room to the phone.

"I need you at once," Oscar said over the wire.

"Do you feel worse?"

"About the same. But Georgie has become a problem."

"Is he that bad?"

"Uh-huh. He went and died on my hands. I need your help, Johnny."

11

Georgie lay face-down on the bed in the guest room. He was fully dressed except for his shoes.

"Tiny took him in here before he left," Oscar told me. "After that I didn't hear a sound out of Georgie. I assumed he was asleep. Probably he went into a coma and slipped off without waking. When I touched him half an hour ago, he was already cold."

Oscar's face was the color of old putty. He could hardly stand without clinging to the dresser. Abby hadn't come out of the other bedroom.

I said, "Died of a bellyache? And so quickly?"

"I agree it must have been the chopped liver, which would make it ptomaine poisoning. But only Georgie ate enough of the liver to kill him. Abby says she remembers he gorged himself on it." Oscar held his head. "One thing's sure – he mustn't be found here. Brant is enough trouble already."

"This is plainly an accidental death."

"Even so, the police will use it as an excuse to get as tough as they like with us. We can't afford that, Johnny, so soon after the Coast City job. Best to get the body out."

I looked him over. He didn't seem in much better condition than the man on the bed.

"I can't do it alone," I said.

He dug his teeth into his lower lip and then fought to draw in his breath. "I'll help you."

But most of it had to fall on me. I fished car keys out of Georgie's pocket and went looking for his Ford. I found it a block and a half up Riverside Drive and drove it around to the service entrance of the apartment building. At that late hour it was possible to park near where you wanted to.

Oscar was waiting for me on the living room sofa. He roused himself and together we got that inanimate weight that had been pot-bellied Georgie Ross down the three flights of fire stairs and, like a couple of men supporting a drunk, walked it between us out of the building and across the terribly open stretch of sidewalk and shoved it into the Ford. For all we could tell, nobody was around to see us.

That was about as far as Oscar could make it. He was practically out on his feet. I told him to go back upstairs and I got behind the wheel and drove off with Georgie slumped beside me like a man asleep.

On a street of dark warehouses over on the east side, I pulled the car over to the curb and got out and walked away.

Stella was up when I let myself in. She asked me if I'd gone to Oscar's.

"I was worried about them," I told her. "Tiny and Georgie left. Oscar and Abby are about in your shape. How're you?"

"Better, though my stomach is very queazy."

I lay in bed wondering what the odds were on chopped liver becoming contaminated and if a burning throat could possibly be a symptom of ptomaine poisoning. I watched daylight trickle into the room and listened to the sounds of traffic building up in the street, and I was scared the way one is in a nightmare, without quite knowing of what.

Eventually I slept. It was past noon when I woke and Stella was bustling about in the kitchen. She was pretty much recovered.

Toward evening I went out for a newspaper. When I returned, Brant was coming down the stoop. Being a cop, he wouldn't have had trouble finding out where I'd moved too.

"Nice arrangement," he commented. "You shack up with Oscar's woman and Oscar with Wally Garden's widow. This way nobody gets left out in the cold."

"You running a gossip column now?" I growled.

"If I were, I'd print an item like this: How come Johnny Worth's pals are getting themselves murdered one by one?"

I held onto myself. All I did was raise an eyebrow. "I don't get it."

"Haven't you heard? George Ross was found dead this morning in his car parked near the East River Drive."

He had already spoken to Stella, but I didn't have to worry that she'd told him about last night's party and who'd been there. She wouldn't tell a cop anything about anything.

I said, "That's too bad. Heart attack?"

"Arsenic."

I wasn't startled. Maybe, after all, it was no surprise to me. Arsenic, it seemed, was a poison that made your throat burn.

I lit a cigarette. Brant watched my hands. They were steady. I blew smoke at him. "Suicide, I suppose."

"Why suicide?"

"It goes with poison."

"Why would he want to die?"

"I hardly knew the guy," I said.

"You've been seeing him. You were in a beer joint with him a week ago Wednesday."

"Was I? Come to think of it, I dropped in for a beer and there were some guys I knew and I joined them."

Brant took his pipe out of his fat face. "Two days later you and he were both in on that Coast City stickup."

"Who says?"

A cop who was merely following a hunch didn't bother me. We sparred with words, and at the end he sauntered off by himself. He hadn't anything. He couldn't even be sure that Georgie hadn't been a suicide.

But I knew, didn't I? I knew who had murdered him and had tried to murder all of us.

12

Oscar didn't say hello to me. He opened the door of his apartment and just stood there holding onto the doorknob, and his eyes were sick and dull behind his glasses. Though it was after six o'clock, he was still in his pajamas. His robe was tied sloppily, hanging crooked and twisted on his long, lean body. He needed a shave. He looked, to put it mildly, like hell.

I stepped into the foyer and moved on past him into the living room. He shambled after me.

I said, "I suppose Brant came to see you before he did me."

"Yes."

"So you know what killed Georgie."

He nodded tiredly.

"Abby still in bed?" I asked.

"I made her dress and go to a doctor when I learned it was arsenic. Don't want him coming here, not with the cops snooping. Whatever he gives her for it, I'll take too."

"Better not," I said. "Likely she'll mix more arsenic with it."

Oscar took off his eyeglasses. "Explain that, Johnny."

"I don't have to. You know as well as I do why she put arsenic in the chopped liver."

He stood swinging his glasses and saying nothing. He was not the man

I had known up until the time I had left the party last night, and it was not so much because he was ill. It was as if a fire had burned out in him.

"Boy, did she sucker you!" I said. "Me too, I admit. But it was mostly our own fault. We knew she didn't fall for your line that you hadn't killed Wally. We kidded ourselves she'd be willing to forgive and forget if we paid her off. We wanted to believe that because we wanted her. Both of us did. Well, you got her. Or the other way around – she got you. She got you to bring her to live here where she could get all of us together and feed us arsenic."

"No," he mumbled. He looked up. "She ate the liver too. She's been sick all night and all day. She's still in a bad way even though she managed to get out of bed and dressed."

"Huh! She had to put on an act."

"No, I can tell. And she wouldn't poison me. Look what she'd give up – this nice home, plenty of money. Why? For a stupid revenge? No. And she's fond of me. Loves me, I'm sure. Always affectionate. A wonderful girl. Never knew anybody like her. So beautiful and warm."

He was babbling. He was sick with something worse than poison, or with a different kind of poison. It was the sickness of sex or love or whatever you cared to call it, and it had clouded that brain that always before had known all the answers.

"Try to think," I said. "Somebody put arsenic in the chopped liver. Who but Abby would have reason?"

"Somebody else." That old twisted smile, which was not really a smile at all, appeared on his thin lips. "You, for instance," he said softly.

"Me?"

"You," he repeated. "You hate my guts for having gotten Abby. You hate her for being mine instead of yours."

I said, "Does it make sense that I'd want to kill Georgie and Tiny and Stella also?"

"There was a guy put a time bomb on an airplane and blew a lot of people to hell because he wanted to murder his wife who was on the plane. Last night was your first chance to get at Abby and me – and what did you care what happened to the others?"

"My God, you're so crazy over her you'd rather believe anything but the truth."

"The truth?" he said and kept smiling that mirthless smile. "The truth is you're the only one didn't eat the liver." He put on his glasses. "Now get out before I kill you."

"Are you sure she'll let you live that long?"

"Get out!"

I left. There was no use arguing with a mind in that state, and with Oscar it could be mighty dangerous besides.

The usual wind was sweeping up Riverside Drive. I stood on the sidewalk and thought of going home to eat and then I thought of Tiny. What had happened to him since he had left Oscar's apartment last night and had dragged himself to his lonely little room? At the least I ought to look in on him.

I walked over to Broadway and took the subway downtown. I climbed two flights of narrow, smelly stairs in a tenement and pushed in an unlocked door. There was just that one crummy room and the narrow bed against the wall and Tiny lying in it on his back with a knife sticking out of his throat.

13

I must have expected something like this, which was why I'd come. There had been four of us involved in the killing of Wally Garden. Now only two of us were left.

I touched him. He wasn't long dead; rigor mortis had not yet begun to set in. She had left her apartment on the excuse that she was going to a doctor and had come here instead.

There was no sign of a struggle. Tiny wouldn't have suspected anything. Lying here sick and alone, he'd been glad to see her – to see anybody who would minister to him, but especially the boss' lovely lady. She had bent over him to ask how he felt, and he must have been smiling up at that clean fresh young face when she had pushed the knife into his throat, and then she had quickly stepped back to avoid the spurting blood.

That was a switchblade knife, probably Tiny's own, the knife Oscar had borrowed from him to kill Wally Garden. Which would make it grim justice, if you cared for that kind of justice when you also were slated to be on the receiving end.

I got out of there.

When I was in the street, I saw Brant. He was making the rounds of Georgie's pals and he was up to Tiny. It was twilight and I managed to step into a doorway before he could spot me. He turned into the tenement I had just left.

I went into a ginmill for the drink I needed and had many drinks. But I didn't get drunk. When I left a couple of hours later, my head was clear and the fear was still jittering in the pit of my stomach.

I'd never been much afraid of anybody, not even of Oscar, but I was afraid of Abby.

It was her life or ours. I had to convince Oscar of that. Likely he would see the light now that Tiny had been murdered too, because who but Abby had motive? If he refused to strangle her, I would, and be glad to do it, squeezing that lilywhite throat until the clear blue eyes bulged and the sweet face contorted.

I got out of a hack on Riverside Drive. The wind was still there. I huddled against it a moment and then went up to the apartment.

Abby answered the door. She wore a sleazy housecoat hugging that slender body of hers. She looked limp and haggard and upset.

"Johnny," she said, touching my arm, "I'm glad you're here. The police took Oscar away."

"That so?" I stepped into the apartment.

She closed the door and tagged after me. "They wouldn't tell why they took him away. Was it because of Georgie?"

"No. I guess they're going to ask him how Tiny got a knife in his throat."

Abby clutched her bosom – the kind of gesture an actress would make, and she was acting. "It couldn't have been Oscar. He wasn't out of the house."

"But you were, weren't you?" I grinned at her. "You got only one of us with the arsenic, so you're using other methods, other weapons. Have you anything special planned for my death?"

She backed away from me. "You're drunk. You don't know what you're saying."

"You blame all four of us for Wally's death. You're out to make us pay for it."

"Listen, Johnny!" She put out a hand to ward me off. "I didn't care very much for Wally. When I married him, yes, but after a while he bored me. He was such a kid. He didn't tell me a thing about the holdup. Not a word. All I found out about it was from the police, when they questioned me later. I heard your name and Oscar's from that detective, Brant. So I tried to make some money on it. That's all I was after – a little money."

"You didn't take the money. Instead you worked it so Oscar would bring you to live with him where you could get at all of us."

"I like Oscar. Honest."

"Don't you mind sleeping with the man who killed your husband?"

She tossed her blonde hair. "I don't believe he did. He's so sweet. So kind."

I hit her. I pushed my fist into her lying face. She'd meant death for Georgie and Tiny, and she would mean death for me unless I stopped her.

She bounced off a chair and fell to the floor and blood trickled from her mouth. I hadn't come to hit her but to strangle her. But something beside fear possessed me. Maybe, heaven help me, I was still jealous of Oscar. I swooped down on her and grabbed her by her housecoat and yanked her up to her feet. The housecoat came open. I shook her and her breasts bobbed crazily and I slapped her face until blood poured from her nose as well as her mouth.

Suddenly I let go of her. She sank to the floor, holding her bloody face and moaning. At no time had she screamed. Even while I was beating her, she'd had enough self-possession not to want to bring neighbors in on us. She started to sob.

I'd come to do more to her, to stop her once and for all. But I didn't. I couldn't. I looked down at her sobbing at my feet, lying there slim and fair-haired, battered and bleeding, feminine and forlorn, and there was nothing but emptiness left in me.

After all, hadn't we killed her husband? Not only Oscar, but Georgie and Tiny and I as well were in a community of guilt.

I turned and walked out of the apartment. I kept walking to the brownstone house, and there in the room Stella and I shared a couple of plainclothes men were waiting for me.

14

They grabbed me, and Stella rose from a chair and flung herself at me.

"Honey, are you in trouble?"

I said dully, "Not much with the cops," and went with them.

For the rest of that night they sweated me in the station house. No doubt they had Oscar there too, but we didn't see each other. They kept us apart.

Sometimes Brant was there, sucking his pipe as he watched the regular cops give me the business. There was no more fooling around. They still had questions about Wally and about Georgie, but mostly they wanted to know about the murder of my pal Tiny.

Once, exhausted by their nagging, I sneered at them like a defiant low-grade mug, "You'll never get us."

Brant stepped forward and took his pipe out of his mouth. "Maybe we won't get you," he said gently, "but somebody else is doing it. Three of you already."

After that I stopped sneering. I stopped saying anything. And by morning they let me go.

Before I left, I asked a question. I was told Oscar had been released a couple of hours before.

I made my way home and Stella was waiting and I reached for her.

But there was no rest for my weariness against her cuddly body. She told me Oscar had been here looking for me with a gun.

"When was this?"

"Half an hour ago," she said. "He looked like a wild man. I'd never seen him like that. He was waving a gun. He said you'd beaten up Abby and he was going to kill you. Honey, did you really beat her up?"

I had taken my jacket off. I put it on.

Stella watched me wide-eyed. "If you're running away, take me with you."

"I'm not running," I said.

"But you can't stay. He said he'd be back."

"Did he?" I said hollowly.

I got my gun from where I'd stached it and checked the magazine and stuck the gun into my jacket pocket.

She ran to me. "What are you going to do? What's going on? Why don't you tell me anything?"

I said, "I don't want to die," and pushed her away from me.

I went only as far as the top of the stoop and waited there, leaning against the side of the doorway. I could watch both directions of the cheerful sun-washed street, and it wasn't long before Oscar appeared.

He looked worse than he had yesterday afternoon. His unshaven face was like a skeleton head. There was a scarecrow limpness about his lean body. All that seemed to keep him going was his urge to kill me.

Maybe if I were living with Abby, had her to love and to hold, I wouldn't give a damn what suspicions I had about her and what facts there were to back them up. I'd deny anything but my need for her body, and I'd be gunning for whoever had marred that lovely face.

I knew there was no use talking to him. I had seen Oscar Trotter in action before, and I knew there was only one thing that would stop him.

I walked down the steps with my right hand in my pocket. Oscar had both hands in his pockets. He didn't check his stride. He said, "Johnny, I – "

I wasn't listening to him. I was watching his right hand. When it came out of his pocket, so did mine. I shot him.

15

And now we are all dead.

There were five of us on that caper. Four are in their graves. I still have the breath of life in me, but the difference between me and the other four is only a matter of two days, when I will be burned in the chair.

It was a short trial. A dozen witnesses had seen me stand in the morning sunlight and shoot down Oscar Trotter. I couldn't even plead self-defense because he'd had no gun on him. And telling the truth as I knew it wouldn't have changed anything. The day after the trial began the jury found me guilty.

I sent for Stella. I didn't expect her to come, but she did. Yesterday afternoon she was brought here to the death house to see me.

She didn't jiggle. Something had happened to her – to her figure, to her face. Something seemed to have eaten away at her.

"Congratulations," I said.

Stella's voice had changed too. It was terribly tired. "Then you've guessed," she said.

"I've had plenty of time to think about it. Oscar didn't have a gun on him. I know now what he was about to do when he took his hand out of his pocket. He was going to offer me his hand. He had started to say, 'Johnny, I made a mistake.' Something like that. Because he still had a brain. When he'd learned that Tiny had been knifed in bed, he'd realized I'd been right about Abby. But the irony is that I hadn't been right. I'd been dead wrong."

"Yes, Johnny, you were wrong," she said listlessly.

"At the end you got yourself two birds with one stone. You told me a lie about Oscar gunning for me, and it turned out the way you hoped. I killed him and the state will kill me. I've had plenty of time to think back – how that night at Oscar's, as soon as we arrived you hurried into the kitchen to give Abby a hand. Why so friendly so quickly with Abby who'd taken your man from you? I saw why. You'd gone into the kitchen to put arsenic in the chopped liver."

"You can't prove it, Johnny," she whispered.

"No. And it wouldn't save me. Well, I had my answer why you were so eager to take up with me the minute Oscar was through with you. You had to hang around his circle of friends, and you had to bide your time to work the killings so you wouldn't be suspected. You succeeded perfectly, Stella. One thing took me a long time to understand, and that was why."

"Wally," she said.

I nodded. "It had to be. If you'd hated Oscar for throwing you over for Abby, you mightn't have cared if you killed the others at that party as long as you got those two. But there was Tiny's death – cold, deliberate, personal murder. The motive was the same as I'd thought was Abby's. The same master plan – those who'd been in on Wally's death must die. And so it had to be you and Wally."

Stella moved closer to me. Her pretty face was taut with intensity.

"I loved him," she said. "That wife of his, that Abby – she was a no-good louse. First time I ever saw her was when she came up to the apartment to see Oscar, but I knew all about her. From Wally. That marriage was a joke. You wouldn't believe this – you were crazy over her yourself, like Oscar was – but she was after anything wore pants. That was all she gave a damn for, except maybe money."

"I believe you," I said. "You must have been the one who persuaded Oscar to take Wally in on the caper."

"We fell for each other, Wally and I. One of those screwy, romantic pickups on a bus. We saw each other a few times and then planned to go away together. But we hadn't a cent. I knew Oscar was planning a big job. He thought he kept me from knowing anything that was going on. But I knew. Always. And I was smarter. I got a guy who owed me a favor to bring Oscar and Wally together. Oscar took him in on it." Her mouth went bitter. "How I hated the rackets! I wanted to get out of them. I hated Oscar. We had it all figured. We'd take Wally's cut, the few thousand dollars, and go out west and live straight and clean. A little house somewhere and a decent job and children." Her head drooped. "And Oscar killed him."

"He might have died anyway from the bullet wound."

"But not to give him at least a chance!" Stella hung onto her handbag with both hands. "You know why I came when you sent for me? To gloat. To tell you the truth if you didn't know it already and laugh in your face."

But she didn't laugh. She didn't gloat. She looked as sick and tired of it all as I was. She looked as if, like me, she no longer gave a damn about anything.

"It doesn't give you much satisfaction, does it?" I said. "It doesn't bring Wally back. It doesn't make it easy to live with yourself."

She swayed. "Oh, God! So much death and emptiness. And I can't sleep, Johnny. I've had my revenge, but I can't sleep."

"Why don't you try arsenic?" I said softly.

She looked at me. Her mouth started to work, but she didn't say anything. Then she was gone.

That was yesterday. Today Bill Brant visited me and told me that Stella had taken poison and was dead.

"Arsenic?" I said.

"Yeah. The same way Georgie Ross died. What can you tell me about it?"

"Nothing, copper," I said.

So that makes five of us dead, and very soon now I will join them, and we will all be dead. Except Abby, and she was never part of the picture. Wasn't she?

Stella was kidding herself by thinking she'd killed Oscar and me. Georgie and Tiny and finally herself, yes, but not us.

I needn't have been so quick with my gun on the street outside the brownstone house. I could have waited another moment to make sure that it was actually his life or mine.

Now, writing this in my cell in the death house, I can face up to the truth. I had shot him down in the clear bright morning because he had Abby.

DEATH IS A VAMPIRE

Robert Bloch

1 Won't You Walk into My Parlor?

THE GATE HANDLE was rusty. I didn't want to touch it. But that was the only way of getting in, unless I wanted to climb the high walls and leave part of my trousers on the iron spikes studding the top.

I grabbed the handle, pushed the gate open and walked down the flagstone path to the house.

If I were a botanist, I'd have been interested in the weeds growing along that path. As it was, they were only something to stumble over. I ignored them and stared at the mansion ahead.

The Petroff house was not quite as big as a castle and not quite as old as Noah's Ark. It looked like the kind of a place the Phantom of the Opera would pick for a summer home.

As far as I was concerned, it was something to donate to the next scrap drive.

But that was none of my business. My business was to sneak inside and wangle old Petroff into giving me an interview about his art treasures. The Sunday supplement needed a feature yarn.

I walked up to the big porch, climbed the stairs, and jangled the old-fashioned door pull. Nothing happened, so I did it again. Same result. It looked as though the Butler's Union had pulled its man off this job.

Just for fun I edged over and turned the door-knob. As I did, I noticed a garland hanging down from the metal projection. It was a wreath of smelly leaves. Not a funeral wreath – just leaves.

That was none of my business, either. I was interested in whether or not the door was unlocked.

It was. So I walked in.

Why not? When Lenehan gave me the assignment, he told me it was a tough one. He had talked to old Petroff over the phone, and Petroff had refused to meet the press or drool over his art treasures.

I expected to be met at the door by a bouncer with a shotgun. But this was easy, and I took advantage of it. It wasn't polite, but newspaper reporting isn't a polite occupation.

The door swung shut behind me, and I stood in a long hallway. It was hard to see anything specific in the afternoon twilight, but I got a musty whiff of stale air, mothballs, and just plain age and decay.

It made me cough. I coughed louder, hoping to rouse my host.

No results. I started down the hallway, still coughing from time to time. An open door led into a deserted library. I ignored it, passed a staircase, walked on.

Behind the stairs was another door. I halted there, for a faint light gleamed from underneath it. I groped for the handle and coughed again. Once more the cough was genuine – for hanging on the door-knob was another garland of those leaves.

Inside here the smell was terrific. Like a Bohemian picnic. Suddenly I recognized the odor. Garlic.

According to the stories going around, old Petroff was a bit of a screwball. But it couldn't be that he had turned the house into a delicatessen.

There was only one way to find out. I opened the door and walked into the parlor where the lamp burned.

It was quiet inside – quiet enough to hear a pin drop. In fact, you could tell which end hit the floor first: the head or the point.

But a pin had not hit the floor in this room. Petroff had.

He looked like his photo, all right. He was tall, thin, with black hair, curled and gray at the temples. A beaked nose and thick lips dominated his face.

He lay there on the floor, his nose pointing up at the ceiling. I got to his side in a hurry, and the floor creaked as I bent over him.

It didn't matter. The noise wouldn't bother him. Nothing would ever bother Igor Petroff again.

His hand was icy. His face was paper-white. I looked around for a mirror but didn't spot any. I pulled my cigarette case out and put it against his lips. The shiny metal clouded slightly. He was still breathing, at any rate.

Probably he'd had a stroke. I lifted his head and stared into his bloodless face. His collar was open. I felt for a pulse in his neck, then took my hand away, quick.

I stared down at his throat, stared down and saw the two tiny punctures in his neck, shook my head and stared again.

They looked like the marks of human teeth!

There was no use asking if there was a doctor in the house. I got up and dashed out into the hall to get to the phone. I got to it. I jiggled the receiver for nearly a minute before I noticed the dangling cord trailing on the floor. Whoever had bitten Petroff had also bitten through the cord.

That was enough for me. I made the two miles back to town in about ten minutes and five hundred gasps. I still had a gasp left in me when I ran into Sheriff Luther Shea's office at Centerville and knocked his feet off the desk.

"Accident out at the Petroff place!" I wheezed. "Get a doctor, quick!"

Sheriff Luther Shea was a fat little bald-headed man who seemed to enjoy keeping his feet on the desk. He put them right back up and scowled at me over his Number Elevens.

"What'sa big idea of bustin' in here? Who are you, anyhow?"

I faced my genial quiz-master without a thought of winning the sixty-four-dollar question.

"Can't you hear?" I yelled. "Call a doctor! Mr Petroff has been injured."

"Ain't no doctor in this town," he told me. "Now state your business, fella."

I stated it, but loud. He perked up his ears a little when I told him about Petroff, but he didn't take his feet off the desk until I flashed my press badge. That did it.

"No sense trying to find a doctor – nearest one's back in LA," he decided. "I'm pretty handy at first-aid. I'll get the car and we'll go out and pick him up."

Sheriff Shea banged the office door behind him, and I grabbed a phone. I got hold of Calloway right away and he promised to send the ambulance out to Centerville. Somehow, after having had a good look at Petroff, I didn't have much confidence in Sheriff Shea's "first-aid."

Then I put through a call to the paper.

Lenehan growled at me, and I barked right back.

"Somebody bit his throat? Say, Kirby – you drunk?"

I breathed into the phone. "Smell that," I said. "I'm cold sober. I found him lying on the floor with two holes in his neck. I'm still not sure he wasn't dead."

"Well, find out. Keep on this story and give me all you've got. We can hold three hours for the morning edition. Looks like murder, you say?"

"I didn't say a blamed thing about murder!" I yelled.

"Come on, quit stalling!" Lenehan yelled back. "What's your angle on this?"

I lowered my voice to a whisper. "Confidentially," I said, "my theory is that old Petroff bit himself in the throat just for the publicity."

Lenehan apparently didn't believe me, because he launched off into a discussion of my ancestry that was cut short when Sheriff Shea appeared in the doorway. He wore a rancher's black Stetson and a shoulder holster. On him it didn't look good.

"Come on, fella," he said, and I hung up.

His rattletrap Chevvy didn't deserve a C card, but we made time down Centerville's single street and chugged out along the highway.

"From the LA papers, huh?" he grunted. "Whatcha doing up at Petroff's?"

"My editor gave me an assignment to write a feature story about the art treasures of the Irene Colby Petroff estate. Do you know anything about them?"

"Don't know nothing, fella. When old man Colby was alive, he and the missus would come into town and do a little trading once in a while. Then he died and she married this foreign gigolo, Petroff, and that's the last we seen of them in town. Then she died, and since then the place has gone to pot. This business don't surprise me none. Hear some mighty funny gossip about what goes on out at Petroff's place. All fenced off and locked up tighter'n a drum. Ask me, he's hiding something."

"I got in without any trouble."

"What about the guards? What about the dogs? What about the locks on the gate?" I sat up. "No guards, no dogs, no locks," I told him. "Just Petroff. Petroff lying there on the floor with the holes in his throat."

We rounded a bend in the highway and approached the walls of the Petroff estate. The setting sun gleamed on the jagged spikes surmounting the walls. And it gleamed on something else.

"Who's that?" I yelled, grabbing Sheriff Shea's arm.

"Don't do that!" he grunted. "Nearly made me go off the road."

"Look!" I shouted. "There's a man climbing up the wall."

Sheriff Shea glanced across the road and saw the figure at the top of the wall. The car ground to a halt and we went into action. Shea tugged at his shoulder holster.

"Stop or I'll shoot!" he bawled.

The man on the wall considered the proposition and rejected it. He turned and jumped. It was a ten-foot drop but he landed catlike and was scuttling across the road by the time we reached the base of the wall.

"After him!" Shea grunted.

The man ran along the other side of the road, making for a clump of trees ahead. I dashed along behind. The fugitive reached the grove a few steps ahead of me and I decided on a little football practice.

It was a rather ragged flying tackle, but it brought him down. We rolled over and over, and on the second roll he got on top. He didn't waste time. I felt powerful fingers dig into my throat. I tore at his wrists. He growled and twisted his neck. I felt his mouth graze my cheek. He was trying to bite me.

I got his hands loose and aimed a punch at his chin, but he ducked and pressed his thumbs in my eyes. That hurt. I aimed another punch, but that wasn't good either. By this time he had those hands around my neck again, and things began to turn red. The red turned black. I heard him growling and snarling deep in his throat, and his fingers squeezed and squeezed.

This was no time for Queensbury rules. I kicked him in the tummy. With a grunt of appreciation he slumped back, clutching his solar plexus.

2 They Fly by Night

Sheriff Shea arrived, wheezing, and together we collared our prisoner and dragged him to his feet.

He was not pretty. He wore one of those one-piece overall outfits, and between the spikes on the wall and the tussle, he'd managed to destroy its integrity. Patches of his skin showed through, advertising the need of a bath. His yellow hair was matted and hung down over his eyes, which was just as well. They were as blue as a baby-doll's – and just as vacant. His lips hung slackly, and he was drooling. A prominent goitre completed the ensemble.

"Why, it's Tommy!" said the Sheriff. "He's a little touched," he whispered, "but harmless."

He didn't have to tell me the kid was touched. That I could easily believe. But the "harmless" part I doubted. I rubbed my aching eyes and neck while Shea patted Tommy on the back.

"What were you doing on the wall, Tommy?" he asked.

Tommy lifted a sullen face. "I was looking at the bats."

"What bats?"

"The bats that fly at twilight. They fly out of the windows and you can hear them squeaking at each other."

I glanced at Sheriff Shea. He shrugged.

"Ain't no bats around here except the ones in Tommy's belfry."

I took over. "What else were you looking at, Tommy?" I inquired.

He turned away. "I don't like you. You tried to hurt me. Maybe you're one of them! One of the bad people."

"Bad people?"

"Yes. They come here at night. Sometimes they come as men, wearing black cloaks. Sometimes they fly – that's when they're bats. They only come at night, because they sleep in the daytime."

Tommy was in full cry, now. I didn't try to stop him.

"I know all about it," he whispered. "They don't suspect me, and they'd kill me if they thought I knew. Well, I do know. I know why Petroff doesn't have any mirrors on the walls. I heard Charlie Owens, the butcher, tell about the liver he sends out every day – the raw liver, pounds of it. I know what flies by night."

"That's enough," said Sheriff Shea. "Whatever you know, you can tell us inside."

"Inside? You aren't going in there, are you? You can't take me in there! I won't let you! You want to give me to him. You'll let him kill me!"

Again, Shea cut him off. Grasping his arm, he guided the half-wit across the road. I followed. We made straight for the gate.

Shea halted. "Push it open," I said.

"It's locked."

I looked. A shiny new padlock hung from the rusty handle.

"It was open half an hour ago," I said.

"He always keeps it locked," Shea told me. "Usually has a man out here, too – a guard. And dogs in the kennels back of the house." He eyed me suspiciously. "You sure you were up here, Mr Kirby?"

"Listen," I advised him. "I was up here a little over half an hour ago. The gate was open. I went in and found Petroff on the floor. He had two holes in his throat and I'm not sure whether he was still breathing or not. I'll give you every explanation you want later, but let's go inside, quick. He may be dead."

Shea shrugged. He stood back and drew his revolver. The shot resounded, the lock shattered. I held Tommy tightly and pushed him through the gateway.

After that I took the lead. Up the steps, through the door, down the hall. It was slow going in the gathering twilight. We stumbled along toward the room behind the staircase.

"Here," I said. "Here's where I found him." I opened the door. The light was still on. I pointed to the floor. "Here," I said.

"Yeah?" grunted Shea. "Where is he?"

The room was empty. The rug was on the floor, but Petroff was not. I stared, and the room began to whirl. I took a deep breath and inhaled fresh air.

It was coming from the open French windows at the end of the room.

Of course! The windows were open. I had made some kind of a mistake. Petroff had been breathing. He had fainted, or something. After I left he recovered, went for a stroll on the porch beyond the open windows, and locked his gate. The holes in his throat. Maybe he'd cut himself while shaving.

I was a fool. A glance at Sheriff Shea confirmed the suspicion. He grinned at me.

But Tommy was not grinning.

"You were here before," he murmured. "You saw him lying here with holes in his throat."

"I – I made a mistake," I mumbled.

"No. When you were here it was still daylight. Now it's dusk. When you were here he was still asleep. But he comes alive at night."

"What do you mean? Who comes alive at night?"

"The vampire," he whispered. "He comes alive. And at night he flies. Look!"

Tommy screamed. His finger stabbed at the dusk beyond the opened windows.

We stared out into the night and saw the black shadow of a bat skimming off into the darkness, a mocking squeak rising from its throat.

In just a little while there was the devil of a lot of activity. The ambulance I had sent for finally arrived, and Shea had to stall them off with a trumped-up excuse about a fainting fit. Then Shea wanted to play detective and go over the place. Personally, I think he was dying to case the joint merely to collect some gossip.

I won't bother remembering the bawling-out he handed me. I had to take it, too. After all, my story sounded pretty phony now.

Tommy was the only one who believed me. And his support was not much help. A half-wit's comments on vampires don't make good testimony.

While Shea handled the ambulance men, Tommy kept talking.

"Look at the garlic wreaths on the doors," he said. "He must have been trying to keep them out. They can't bear garlic."

"Neither can I," I answered. "And I'm no vampire."

"Look at the books," Tommy exclaimed. "Magic."

I stepped over to the built-in bookshelves. This time Tommy really had something. There were rows of blackbound volumes; musty, crumbling treatises in Latin and German. I read the titles. It was indeed a library of demonology. Where there's smoke there's fire.

But what did that prove? Occultism isn't a rare hobby on the Coast. I knew half a hundred crackpots who belonged to "secret cults," and down Laguna way there was a whole colony of them.

Still, I ran my eyes and fingers along the rows. One of the books on the lower shelf protruded a bit more than was necessary. It offended my sense of neatness. As I reached in to push it back, a card slipped out from between yellowed pages. I palmed it, turned around just as Sheriff Shea reentered the room.

"Come on," he sighed. "Let's get out of here."

Driving back to town, with Tommy wedged between us on the front seat, Shea gave me another going over.

"I don't understand all this monkey business," he declared. "I don't know what you were doing in that house in the first place. Least I can do is hold you on suspicion of illegal entry. As for Tommy here, he's liable to get booked on the same charges. I'm gonna see his folks about this. But what I want to know is – where's Petroff?"

"I shot him." I grinned. "But the bats flew off with his body."

"Never mind that," Shea snapped. "You smart-aleck reporters aren't tampering with the law down here. I'd like to get the DA in on this, but there's nothing to go on, yet. Maybe after I hold you on suspicion a few days you'll be ready to talk. I want to know how you cut those telephone wires, too."

"Now listen," I said. "I've got work to do. I'm willing to play ball on this thing and help straighten matters out. If Igor Petroff has disappeared and I'm the last man who saw him alive – or dead – that's important to me, too. The paper'll want the story. But I'm down here on an assignment. I've got to move around."

"No, you don't. Case I didn't mention it, you're under arrest right now, Mr Kirby."

"That," I sighed, "is all I want to know."

I eased the car door open gently and swiftly. We were going thirty, but I took my chances. I jumped and hit the road.

Shea swore. He brought the rattling Chevvy to a halt, but by that time I was running along the ditch on the other side of the road. It was good and dark.

Shea bawled and waved his revolver, but he couldn't spot me. Then he turned the car around and zoomed back up the road. I went into the field, kept going. In a few minutes the road was far behind me, and I headed across to the other side of the field and another dirt road running parallel.

Here I found the truck that took me back to LA. I hopped off downtown, found a drug store, and called Lenehan at the office.

"Where in thunder are you?" he greeted me. "Just had this hick sheriff on the wire. He's bawling you're a fugitive from justice. And what's all this business about a disappearing body? Give."

I gave. "Hold the yarn," I pleaded. "I've got a new angle."

"Hold it?" yelled Lenehan. "I'm tearing it up! You and your disappearing Dracula! Petroff was drunk on the floor when you found him and you were drunk on your feet. He had the decency to wander off and sober up, but you're still drunk!"

I hung up.

Then I fished around in my pocket and pulled out the card I had snatched from the book in Petroff's library.

It was nicely engraved:

HAMMOND KING
Attorney at Law

I turned it over. A man's heavy scrawl spidered across the back read:

You may be interested in this volume on vampirism.
H. K.

The plot was thickening. Hammond King? I knew the name. A downtown boy. Wealthy attorney. What was the connection?

I called Maizie at the office.

"Hammond King," I said. "Check the morgue."

She got me the dope. I listened until she came to an item announcing that Hammond King was attorney for the Irene Colby Petroff estate. I stopped her and hung up.

It was eight o'clock. Not likely that Hammond King would still be at his office, but it was a chance worth taking. The phone book got me the number and I deposited my third nickel.

The phone rang for a long time. Perhaps he was going over a tort or something. Then a deep voice came over the wire.

"Hammond King speaking."

"Mr King – this is Dave Kirby, of the Leader. I'd like to come over there and talk to you."

"Sorry young man. If you'll phone my office tomorrow for a more definite appointment – "

"I thought we might have a little chat about vampires."

"Oh."

That stopped him.

"I'll be right over," I said. "So long."

He didn't answer. I whistled my way out of the phone booth, ordered a ham sandwich and a malted milk, disposed of same, and took a cab downtown.

The night elevator brought me to Hammond King's office. The door was open and I walked into one of those lavish layouts so typical of wealthy attorneys and impecunious booking agents.

I ignored the outer office and made for the big door marked "Private."

King was examining a bottle of Scotch with phony nonchalance.

My nonchalance was just as phony as I examined him.

He was a short, stocky man of about fifty-five. Gray hair and mustache to match. His eyes slanted behind unusually thick bifocals. He wore an expensive gray suit, and I admired his taste in ties. He looked like a hundred other guys, but he sent books on vampirism to his friends. You never know these days.

"Mr Kirby?" he inquired, getting up and extending his hand. "To what do I owe this pleasure?"

"I told you over the phone," I said. "I'd like to have a little chat with you about vampires."

"Oh."

The phony nonchalance faded away and the hand dropped to his side.

"I'd rather have talked to Mr Petroff about it," I continued. "Matter of fact, I dropped in on him this afternoon. But he wasn't there. That is, he was there, and then he wasn't. You know how vampires get restless about twilight."

"What do you mean?"

"You know what I mean, King," I said. "I just thought I'd warn you. In case anybody tries to bite you in the throat, it's your old client, Igor Petroff."

"How'd you know he was my client?"

"I know a lot of things," I told him, wishing it were true. "And what I don't know you'd better tell me, but fast. Unless, of course, you want it splashed all over the front page of the Leader."

"Let's be reasonable," Hammond King pleaded. "I'll be glad to help you all I can. Anything involving my client – "

The phone rang. King reached for the receiver, then drew his hand back.

"Pardon me, please," he said.

He got up and went into the outer office and shut the door.

3 The Bat's Kiss

I would have given my left arm to know who King was talking to. But I didn't have to give my left arm. All I needed to do was reach out with it and gently pick up the receiver. Call it eavesdropping, if you wish. You do a lot of things in this business.

"Mr King?" a girl's voice came over the wire. "This is Lorna Colby. I'm at the Eastmore Hotel, Room Nine-nineteen . . . No, Igor sent for me. He wanted to talk about a settlement on the will."

"Have you seen Petroff?" Hammond King barked into the phone at this end.

"No, not yet."

"Well, I'll be around in the morning, at ten. We've got to work fast, you understand? Something's happening that I don't like."

"What is it?" asked Lorna Colby.

"I can't talk now. See you tomorrow. Good night."

He hung up. I hung up. It was my turn to look at the Scotch bottle as he came in.

"Where were we?" he asked.

"You were just going to spill the beans," I said.

Hammond King smiled. "Was I? Lucky for me I got called away. I'm afraid I can't talk this matter over with you just at present. That call was from a client in Pasadena. I've got to take the train tonight."

I rose. One of his desk drawers was half opened. I reached in and scooped up a handful of garlic leaves.

"You had these left over from decorating the Petroff house, I presume," I told him. "Too bad you didn't think to put these on the French windows."

I slipped the garlic wreath into his hand and left the room. He stood there with his mouth open, giving a poor imitation of a stuffed moose.

I rode downstairs and walked around the corner and across the block to the Eastmore Hotel. I didn't bother to send my name up, but rode in person to the ninth floor. Nine-nineteen was down the hall to my left. I found the room and knocked on Lorna Colby's door.

There was no answer – except a sudden, ear-shattering scream.

I jerked the door-knob. The door opened on a tableau of frozen horror.

A blonde girl lay slumped on the bed. Crouching above her was a shadowy figure out of a nightmare. Its head was bending toward her neck. I saw lean, outstretched fingers claw down, saw the mouth descend – then the shadow straightened, turned, swooped across the room and out through the open window.

Lorna Colby lay there, clutching her throat and staring in wide-eyed terror. I stared, too. For the intruder had been Igor Petroff.

When I reached the window, the fire-escape outside was empty. Perhaps it had never held a figure. Perhaps I'd have done better to look for something flying in the sky.

I turned back to the bed. Lorna Colby was sitting up. There was still fear in her hazel eyes as she looked at me.

"Who are you?" she demanded.

I introduced myself. "Dave Kirby, of the Leader. You're Lorna Colby, of course?"

She nodded. "Yes. But how did you know? And what made you come here?"

"Hammond King sent me," I lied.

It was the right hunch.

"Then maybe you can tell me," she said, "what's wrong with my uncle? He sent me a wire to come down and talk about the estate. I waited to hear from him tonight. I was getting sleepy and lay down on the bed. When I opened my eyes again, he was in the room."

"Petroff?"

"Yes. You recognized him, too?"

I nodded.

"He must have come through the window some way. He just crouched over me, staring, and there was something wrong with his face. It was so white, but his eyes glared, and I couldn't look away. Then I felt his hands come down toward my neck, and I screamed, and then – "

I shook her, not gently. It was fun, but this was no time for amusement.

"Stop it!" I snapped. "Relax."

She cried a little. Then she sat up and fished around for her make-up. I took the opportunity to study her more closely.

Lorna Colby was tall, blonde, and about twenty-two. She had a good face and a better figure. All in all, the kind of a girl worth whistling after.

That noise like a ton of bricks was me, falling. She didn't notice it. After a while she patted her hair back and smiled.

"Your uncle is – ill," I said. "That's what Hammond King asked me to tell you. We're trying to keep things quiet until we can take him away for a rest."

"You mean he's crazy?"

I shrugged.

"I've always thought so," Lorna declared. "Even when Aunt Irene was alive, I knew there was something wrong with him. He led her an awful life."

She halted, bit her lower lip, and continued.

"After she died, he got worse. He kept dogs at the house, guarding it. He wanted to guard her tomb, he said. I haven't seen him now for almost a year. Nobody has seen him since the day she died. She had a heart attack, you know. He buried her in the private vaults on the estate. He wouldn't even let me see her or come to the funeral.

"I knew he hated me, and it came as a surprise when I got his wire yesterday, asking me to come down from Frisco to talk about the will. That didn't make sense, either. After all, Aunt Irene left him the whole estate, even though he can't touch the money for a year."

Something clicked into place. I decided to follow it up.

"By the way, who was your aunt's physician?" I asked.

"Dr Kelring."

"I'd like to talk to him," I told her. "It's important."

"You think he might know what's wrong with Uncle Igor?"

"That's right." I nodded. "He must know."

I looked him up in the book. Dr Roger Kelring. I called his downtown office, not hoping for much of anything. Still, this gang seemed to work late. Hammond King was on the job, and Igor Petroff was a regular night-owl. Or was he? "They fly by night."

The phone gave off that irritating sound known as a busy signal. That was enough for me.

"Come on, Miss Colby," I said. "We're going over to Dr Kelring's office."

"But you didn't talk to him," she objected.

"Busy signal," I explained. "On second thought, I'd just as soon not say anything to him in advance."

"What do you mean? Do you think he's mixed up in all this?"

"Definitely," I assured her. "I wouldn't be a bit surprised if your uncle was up there with him now."

Lorna put on her coat and we went downstairs. In the lobby, she halted indecisively.

"Wait a minute, Mr Kirby. Aren't we going to report seeing Uncle Igor in my room? After all, if he's sick somebody should be looking after him. He may be – "

"Dangerous? Perhaps. But let's not start something we can't finish. It's my hunch that he's over at Dr Kelring's office. Don't ask me why, but I've got reasons. Besides, you don't want to get mixed up in a lot of cross-questioning, do you?"

She agreed. I was relieved. What could I do if we called some Law? Tell them that a suspected vampire was running around attacking girls in hotel rooms?

Besides, I didn't think Igor Petroff was "running around." He might be flying around. Or he might be working according to a plan. Dr Kelring would know the plan.

We took a cab to Kelring's office, in a building off Pershing Square.

"What's the doctor like?" I asked Lorna.

"He's a rich woman's doctor," she told me. "You know – smooth, quiet, genial. He's about fifty, I guess. Bald-headed, with a little goatee. I only saw him once, at Aunt Irene's, a few months before she died. He was pleasant, but I didn't like him."

Lorna's voice betrayed her inner tension. I understood. It's not every night that a girl is attacked by a vampire, even if he's a member of the family.

Partly for that reason and partly for personal pleasure, I held her arm as we took the elevator up to Kelring's office. A light burned behind the outer door. I opened it and stepped in. I had no gun, but if there was anything doing, I counted on the surprise element.

There was one.

Seated at the desk in the reception room was a man of about fifty, bald-headed, and wearing a small goatee. His hand rested on the telephone as though he were going to pick it up and make another call.

But Dr Kelring would never make another call. He sat there staring off into space, and when I touched his shoulder his neck wobbled off at an angle so that his goatee almost touched the spot between his shoulder-blades. Roger Kelring was quite, was definitely, was unmistakably dead.

I was patting Lorna's shoulder and making with the reassurement when the phone rang. Its sharp note cut the air, and I jumped. For a moment I stared at Dr Kelring, wondering why his dead hand didn't lift the receiver and hold it to his ear.

Then I got around the desk, fast, and pried his cold fingers from the receiver.

"Lorna," I said, "how did – he – talk?"

"You mean Dr Kelring?" She shuddered.

"Yes."

"Oh, I don't remember . . . Yes, I think I do. He had a soft voice. Very soft."

"Good."

I whipped out my handkerchief and covered the mouthpiece. Just a hunch.

"Hello," I said lifting the receiver.

"Hello. That you, Kelring?"

I jumped as I recognized the voice. Hammond King!

"What is it?" I said, softly.

"Kelring, I must talk to you." He sounded frightened. Too frightened to analyze my voice.

"Go ahead. What's on your mind?"

"Did you ever read 'The Fall of the House of Usher'?"

"What?"

"You know what I'm talking about, Kelring. She's alive out there. I know it!"

"Who's alive?"

"Mrs Petroff. Don't stall me, Kelring. I'm desperate."

"What makes you think so, man?"

"It happened two months ago. I was out there at the house with Petroff, arguing about the will. You know he's been trying to get me to turn over the estate before the time stipulated. I won't bother with details, but I heard a noise. A woman's voice, coming from behind the wall. It came from the private staircase behind the bookshelves – the one leading down to the family burial vaults in the hillside."

"Get to the point, King," I said.

"He tried to hold me off, but I made him take me down there. I don't know how to tell you this – but beyond the iron grille entrance, in the vaults, I caught a glimpse of Irene Colby Petroff. Alive."

"But I pronounced her dead of heart failure," I said, remembering what I'd been told.

"She was alive, I tell you! She ran into one of the passages, but I recognized her face. I tried to get Petroff to open the grille and go in, but he dragged me back upstairs. Then he told me the story."

"What story?"

"You know, all right, Kelring. That's why I didn't call before. I wanted to investigate on my own. Now I need your help."

"Better tell me all you know, then."

"I know that she's a – vampire."

I held my breath. King didn't wait for any comment.

"Petroff broke down and confessed. Said he knew it and you knew it. She'd been mixed up in some kind of Black Magic cult in Europe when he met her. And when she died, she didn't really die. She lived on, after sundown, as a vampire."

"Preposterous!"

"I wasn't sure myself, then. I wanted to call in the police. But Petroff pleaded with me. Said he had the guard and the dogs and kept people away. He had her locked up down there, fed her raw liver. Because you were trying to work on a cure. He asked for a little more time. And he explained it all. Gave me books on demonology to read. I didn't know what to believe, but I promised to wait. Then, three nights ago, he called and told me that she had tried to attack him. He asked me to come out this afternoon and talk things over.

"I went out there about four today. Maybe I was a fool, but I took some garlic with me. The books say garlic wards them off. When I arrived, I found Petroff lying on the floor. There were two holes in his throat – the marks of a vampire's teeth. So he has become a vampire now!

"I got frightened and ran. I knew he had sent for his niece, Lorna Colby. I wanted to talk to her before I did anything. Then, tonight, a young man called on me. Said he was from the newspapers. He knows something, too.

"Kelring, I've made up my mind to act. I won't call the police. I – I can't. They'd laugh at me. But there's a monster loose tonight, and I can't stand waiting any longer. I'm going out to the Petroff place now."

"Wait!" I said.

His voice was shrill as he replied. "Do you know what I've been doing, Kelring? I've been sitting here molding silver bullets. Silver bullets for my gun. And I'm leaving now. I'm going out there to get him!"

"Don't be a fool!" I yelled, in my natural voice.

But he had hung up.

"Come on," I snapped at Lorna. "I'll call the police and report on Kelring now. But we're getting out before they come."

"Where are we going?"

"To Petroff's house," I answered.

She nodded. I moved around the table. As I did, I saw something on the floor. It was a spectacle-case. I picked it up, turned it over. It was an expensive case, with an engraved name. The silver signature read:

Hammond King

4 Vampire's Teeth

As the cab driver grumbled about the long haul, I told Lorna what I thought was wise.

I was too groggy to think clearly. Lenehan thought I was drunk, I'd jumped arrest, I'd eavesdropped, and impersonated, and messed up a murder. And it looked like an even busier day tomorrow unless I could straighten this tangle out tonight.

That's my only excuse, I guess. I was a punch-drunk fool to take Lorna to that house, with only a crazy hunch to guide us, and armed with nothing but my suspicions.

But I did it. We rolled up to the black, forbidding portals of the Petroff place. We walked up the porch of the Petroff mansion and the cab waited in the driveway. I didn't see Hammond King's car, and I was glad we had arrived first.

He was wrong, I thought. Petroff was not here. And if he wasn't, we could find that staircase, take a look into the vault, and see for ourselves whether Irene Colby Petroff walked or slept forever.

Never mind the details. The garlic odor choked us in the creaky hall. It flooded the parlor as I lit the lamp, tapped bookcases, and found the button that opened a section of the wall. Lorna shivered at my side. The setup looked like something out of "The Cat and the Canary."

I kept listening for sounds. All quiet on the Western Front. With the light streaming from the parlor behind us, we took the secret staircase in stride. Down below was another panel in the wall. I switched on the light and walked down a long corridor. It was damp. King had said the private vaults of the family were out under the hillside.

We rounded a turn and came to the iron grille barring the hall. A perpetual light burned behind it. I tried the door. It was open. It squeaked as I pushed.

The squeak was drowned in a scream.

I turned.

Something black scuttled around the corner of the passageway. Something swooped down on Lorna, engulfed her in a sable cloud. I saw glaring eyes, red lips – Igor Petroff was here!

I made a dive for him. Petroff didn't dodge. He stood there, and as I came on, his arm lashed out. The blow caught me off balance and as I wavered, his hand moved out. Something flashed down, and then I fell.

There was a blurred impression of movement, screaming, and scuffling. Petroff had dragged Lorna through the grille, down into the vaults.

I lurched to my feet as another figure raced around the bend. More blamed traffic down here, I thought, dazedly.

It was Hammond King.

He didn't see me. He stared, glassy-eyed, as he ran past into the gloom of the corridor beyond. He was carrying a gun. Silver bullets!

I dashed after him. As we took another flight of stairs, I gazed over his shoulder at the family vaults beyond.

Lorna stood in a corner, crouching against a wall. The cloaked figure of Igor Petroff glided towards her, and I thought of Dracula, and of childhood terrors, and of nightmares men still whisper about.

Hammond King didn't think. He began pumping shots from his gun, firing in maniac fury.

Petroff turned, across the room. And then, he smiled. He didn't fall down. He smiled. He smiled, and started to run toward Hammond King with his arms extended, and Hammond King gave a little choking gurgle and fell down.

I didn't fall. As Petroff advanced, I ran to meet him. This time I was not off-balance. I let him have one right on the point of his white chin. He grunted, but his arms swept up and then I felt the cold embrace as he clawed at me. I hammered into his ribs, but he was hard, rigid. Rigor mortis is like that, I thought madly.

He smelled of dampness and mold and ancient earth. His arms were strong and he was squeezing me. I dropped to the floor and he began to reach for my throat. He chuckled, then, deep in his throat, an animal growl. A growl of hunger, the growl of a carnivore that scents blood.

He had me by the neck, and I reached out with one hand and scrabbled frantically against the floor until I felt the cold steel of the gun Hammond King had dropped.

Petroff wrenched my arm back, trying to tear the gun from my fingers. I wanted to fight him off, but his other hand was at my neck, squeezing. I felt myself falling back, and I pulled my arm free and brought the gun-butt up against his head, once, twice, three times.

Igor Petroff wobbled like a rundown mechanical doll and dropped with a dull thud.

I got up and slapped Lorna's face. She came out of her trance, crying. Then I went over to Hammond King and slapped him around. Just a one-man rescue squad.

"Go upstairs, you two," I said. "The cab-driver's waiting outside. Tell him to go into Centerville and bring back Sheriff Shea. I'll meet you in a moment."

They left.

I went through the vault until I came to what I wanted to find. When I was quite finished with my inspection I went back upstairs.

Lorna and Hammond King were waiting in the parlor. She had fixed her hair again, and he looked well enough to smoke a cigarette.

"The police should be here in five minutes," King said.

"Good."

"Perhaps I'd better look outside," he suggested. "I'm expecting Dr Kelring."

"Kelring isn't coming," I said, gently. "He's dead."

"But I talked to him over the phone."

I told him who he'd talked to. And then I decided to tell him a few other things.

"You should have gone to the police the night you saw Mrs Petroff here," I said. "Then all this wouldn't have happened."

"But I saw her. She was alive."

"Right. But she wasn't a vampire. Too bad you believed that crazy story Petroff concocted. When you stumbled onto her existence, he had to think of something and the vampire story just popped out. After you half-swallowed it, he planned the rest. He had to convince you completely, and he was good at planning."

"What do you mean?"

"It all started, I think, when Petroff and Dr Kelring decided to fake Mrs Petroff's death. They were in on it together, to split the inheritance. They didn't have the nerve to kill her outright but drugged her, held a private funeral, and faked the death certificate. Then Petroff kept her a prisoner down here in the vaults. That's why he had dogs and a guard. She was alive until about three days ago."

"How do you know?"

"I just found her body in the vault," I explained. "And I've seen her living quarters – a room beyond. She's dead now, all right, and I'd say she died of starvation."

"I don't understand," Lorna sighed.

"Simple. When her fake death was accepted, Petroff and Dr Kelring were all set to divide the spoils. But there were no spoils – not for a year, according to the terms of her will. They hadn't counted on that. So Petroff was trying to get King, here, to advance money against the inheritance.

"King, being a smart attorney, would do no such thing. But after he saw Mrs Petroff alive and heard this vampire line, he began to weaken. Petroff took advantage of it, showing him books on demonology, and telling wild stories about secret cults."

Hammond King nodded miserably. "He was wearing me down," he admitted. "But I wouldn't release any money. I couldn't, legally."

I took over again. "Then, three days ago, Mrs Petroff actually died. Perhaps he deliberately starved her, perhaps not. In any event, she was dead, and his extortion plot and fake death was now actually murder. He wanted that money at once, needed it desperately.

"So he phoned you, King, and asked you to come out today, planning to show himself lying on the floor as the victim of a vampire attack. He had it figured that you'd be too shocked to call the police at once. Then, after dark, he would call upon you as a supposed vampire, threaten you with his bite, and get you to advance personal funds against the estate."

King was looking bewildered.

"But I'd never do that," he protested. "He must have been mad!"

"He was – and desperate, too." I grinned. "Here's where I come into the story. Dave Kirby, the Boy Reporter. I got here today just after you left in the afternoon. I blundered in before Petroff could escape, so he lay there on the floor, hoping to fool me. When I left for the sheriff, he took a powder.

"Now the jig was up, but Petroff decided to carry the plan through. If he worked fast, he might still succeed. He'd called Lorna, asked her to come to town. He had only one idea – to appear before her as a supposed vampire and thus further bolster his story when he saw King and demanded money. This he was doing as I arrived at Lorna's room. He fled, and undertook his next step in the plan – the murder of Dr Kelring."

"But why would he murder Kelring?" King asked.

I shrugged. "There were several reasons. The first is the one that led me to the scene. You remember, I came out to the house for an interview on the Petroff estate art treasures, an interview Petroff had already refused to grant."

"Yes?"

"There was a reason for my coming and a reason for his refusal. You see, my editor had a tip that several valuable vases recognized as part of the Petroff collection had been offered for sale at private auction. Get it?

"Petroff was already raising money by illegally disposing of art treasures belonging to the estate. Kelring must have just discovered this and demanded his cut. Otherwise, he would squeal about the fake death certificate. So Petroff had to kill him. Just as an added touch, he left a little souvenir after strangling him in his office."

I handed King his spectacle case.

"You nearly had credit for that piece of work," I said. "I'm sure he would have threatened to turn you in had you refused him money when he demanded it this evening. So it's lucky I had you on the phone and can support an alibi."

King blinked.

"After killing Dr Kelring he scooted out here to wait for you. He knew you'd be out to check up. He hadn't counted on Lorna and me arriving, but when we showed up first, he was ready. After that you dashed in, made your bang-bang with the silver bullets, and passed out. You aren't a good shot, King. Those bullets are in the walls, not in his body. But it wouldn't have mattered much. He wore a bullet-proof vest under the cloak. Felt it when I tackled him."

Lorna looked at me.

"You tackled him," she whispered. "That was wonderful. Even if he might be a vampire, you took the chance."

"But he wasn't a vampire. I knew that."

"Didn't you find him with holes in his throat?"

"Right. But he made them himself. Shallow cuts with a paper-knife, no doubt. You see, a vampire's bite will drain all blood. And there was no blood. I know something about superstitions myself, Lorna."

Sirens punctuated my sentence. The law was arriving in full force.

Suddenly I was very tired and very contented. Lenehan would get a story after all. And I'd get some sleep.

Lorna kissed me.

"What's that for?" I asked.

"For being brave. I don't care what you say, he might have been a vampire."

"Not a chance." I grinned. "I knew that from the beginning. When I looked at him on the floor this afternoon, his mouth was open. That was the tip-off."

"What do you mean?"

"He couldn't be a vampire because he couldn't bite anyone. After all, darling, who ever heard of a big, bad vampire with false teeth?"

DIVIDE AND CONQUER

Jack Ritchie

CHARLEY PHONED FOR me at around eleven and I walked the block and a half to the Green Dollar. The blackjack tables were going all right and the one-arms were taking heavy play, but I thought that something would have to be done for the faro games.

The Green Dollar is the one I started with, but now I've got two more places up the street. When I'm not around, I've got Charley running things.

He was sitting at the desk and looking worried when I opened the office door.

"We got trouble, Tommy," he said.

I lowered myself into a chair and lit up a king-size cigarette. "Don't we always have something on hand to annoy us?" I said.

"This is something different." Charley swiveled his chair to face me. "Maybe we got nothing to worry about and maybe it's big."

I bent the match and flipped it into an ash tray. "Somebody moving in?"

"Looks like it," Charley said. "A big gorilla was here sticking a finger in my chest. He let me know that he and his associates would appreciate a five hundred dollar weekly donation regular every week."

"You should have had him tossed out," I said.

Charley snorted at my suggestion. "I'm a cautious married man with two growing children. I didn't know how many friends he had and I wasn't anxious to find out."

"Anybody we know?"

"From the sound of him, I'd say mid-west. He couldn't be from around here. He thought I owned the joint."

"Think he might really be working alone?"

"Not completely, at any rate. I got the buzz that a runty little character is working the other side of the street. The big boy should get to the Four Deuces pretty soon."

I blew smoke into the air and rested my feet on a hassock. "Did he mention any names?"

"Said I could call him Mugger and that's as far as it went."

Charley took a cigar from the desk humidor and bit off the tip.

"Is anybody kicking in?" I asked.

"The way I get it, these boys just started." Charley lit the cigar. "Everybody's stalling and waiting to see what you're going to do about it."

Charley's eyes met mine. "I'm worried, Tommy," he said. "Gambling's legal in this state and pretty clean. I'd hate to see it spoiled."

The Four Deuces is the biggest and newest of my places. It's part nightclub and I run a floor show to keep the people entertained when they're not gambling.

The food costs me money and I break even on the liquor, but that's the way it always is in a place like mine. It's the big room with the machines, the dice, and the cards that makes it all worth while.

When I walked into my office, I found Juanita Reyes with her sandaled feet on my desk and making herself at home with a Manhattan.

She has a nightclub act with feathers and a lot of confidence and right now she was wearing her costume. It consisted of a little here and not so much there, and she had left her feathers in the dressing room.

She waggled a few fingers at me and smiled. "I knew you would come back," she said. "I'm irresistible."

Juanita took her feet off the polished desk and stretched herself lazily for my benefit. "How do you like my new costume? Just feel the material. It's the best."

"Why don't you take it off," I said. "It's a stifling hot night."

She fluffed her Mexican black hair. "It must be dreadfully warm for you, too." Juanita had long slender legs and softly curved thighs. She took a deep breath that put considerable strain on her black net brassiere and held the pose.

"Well," I said, grinning. "What I see seems all right."

She was reaching up behind her for the fasteners when the damn buzzer on my desk sounded.

I clicked on the switch and got the voice of Sid, the chief houseman.

"Something big out here is panting to see you. I smell trouble. You want to see him or do I form a posse and have him thrown out?"

"Send him in," I said. "But stick around in case I scream for help." I looked at Juanita. "You can toddle along. If you stay you'll just distract me."

"No," she said. "I want to watch. But impatiently."

The guy who came in was under six feet, but he carried the weight for somebody a good foot taller. You could blame heredity for his face, but you'd have a better case if you considered what a dozen barroom brawls could do.

He lifted a bushy eyebrow when he saw Juanita and she gave him a slow wink and a twitch of the hips. He stopped in his tracks and stared at her.

Standing at my desk, I snapped my fingers a couple of times. "I'm over here," I said.

He regarded me with acute distaste, but decided he might as well get down to business. "You the guy, Tommy Harrigan what owns dis joint?"

"Dat's me," I said. "And dat's me doll. Don't lay no finger on her."

He scowled at me. "Gettin' immediate to duh point, from now on you pay me five hunnert clams every week. Dis is for me bein' tender to you and not violunt. If you get what I mean."

"I bet he can scratch his knees without bending down," I said. "Juanita, will you see if the cook has any bananas."

"Personally," Juanita said, "I think he's kind of cute."

Mugger's cauliflower ears were reddening. "Dat wise lip makes it six hunnert a week."

"Is there anything else you might want, Bonzo," I asked. "I'll admit your case stumps me. I'm just used to feeding people."

He came toward me, his big ham fist beginning its swing. "Seven hunnert," he growled. "And dis is your receipt in advance."

I stepped away from the punch and picked up a piece of petrified wood I use for a paperweight. After I slipped under his second swing, I let him have the stone with a wallop to his jaw.

His eyes glazed and he dropped without argument to the rug.

Juanita watched his peaceful breathing. "Do you think that was quite fair?" she asked.

"Sure it was fair," I said indignantly as I hefted the paperweight. "This thing isn't heavier than two pounds. He still had a weight advantage of over forty."

Juanita lit a cigarette. "There's something wrong with your logic, but at the moment it escapes me."

I bent down beside Mugger and went through his pockets. Along with the usual things, he had a .45 automatic and a key to room 424 at the Holder Hotel. His wallet told me that his real name was Quincy Elwood Dowd.

"He's got seventeen dollars," I said, grinning up at Juanita. "He could really show you a good time."

"Ha!" she said, shrugging her shoulders. "Money isn't everything."

I unstrapped Mugger's holster and transferred it to my person.

"Why don't you call the police," Juanita said. "It would be so much simpler."

Sid stuck his head through the doorway just then and I had him get a couple of porters to carry Mugger out into the alley.

When I had on my hat and was ready to leave, Juanita put her hand on my shoulder. "Be careful," she said. "You don't know what you'll be missing if you should get killed now."

"Talk, talk." I said, brushing a strand of hair from her forehead. "I'll bet you're a virgin."

Some embarrassment touched her cheeks. "What a nasty thing to say about a modern girl."

At the Holder Hotel I went directly to Freddie, the desk clerk. "You got a big jerk registered here? Dowd is the name."

"Yeah," Freddie said, eyeing the bulge in my coat. "What for you packing a gun?"

"Was he alone?"

"He's got a single," Freddie said. "But he seemed to be traveling with a dame and a small guy." He spun the register around to show me. "They got three next to each other. 423, 424, and 425."

Dowd had number 424. Number 423 was registered in the name of a Miss Mavis Frawley and 425 to a Jim Beaker.

"The dame draws a whistle out of you," Freddie said. "Everything stacked right, but strictly out of stone. Doll face, but not a smile in a carload."

I drummed my fingers on the desk while I thought. "Freddie," I said. "Can you get me a clear empty medicine bottle? And fill it full of water, will you?"

"Okay," he said. "But I won't sleep tonight if you don't give me a glimmer of what's going on."

The smile I gave him was fond and affectionate. "It's too horrible for your young ears."

The man who opened the door to room 425 was a little squirt, but sharp. He had on a blue pin stripe shirt with button-down collar and a nifty blond hair-line moustache.

I smiled gently as I put the heel of my hand on his nose and shoved hard.

"Hey!" he yelled as he went staggering back on his heels. "What's the big idea?"

I let the front of my sport coat dangle open so he got a look at the gun.

"You a cop, or something?" he asked suspiciously.

"Do I look like a cop, Shorty?" I gave him a casual swipe with my open palm.

"Hey!" he yelled again. "Cut that out! Just who do you think you are, slappin' a innocent citizen around?"

"I'm practically nobody," I said, regarding him with a quiet smile. "But I represent the *Syndicate*."

"The Syndicate?" he squeaked. "What Syndicate?"

I shook my head sadly at his stupidity. "*The* Syndicate," I said. "And I'm from the Enforcement and Retaliation Division." I fixed him with a gimlet eye. "I've been briefed by the big boys that three of you Easterners are thinking of setting up business here."

He cringed when I lifted my hand to scratch my ear. "Just talk," he said nervously. "I kin listen without you getting free with the hands."

Beaker sweated while I studied him long and carefully. "Yes," I said finally. "You're the spitting image of Hoppy Nolan. Same type. Same build."

Beaker licked his lips. "Who's Hoppy Nolan?"

"Hoppy *was* a small time hood from Philly," I said. "He tried to buck the Syndicate about a year ago." I took off my Panama and held it over my heart for a few solemn seconds. "He got run over by an automobile."

Beaker's Adam's apple was traveling up and down.

"It was a tragedy and never should have happened," I said. "But the bottoms of Hoppy's feet were burned pretty bad and he wasn't so nimble."

I gave him a friendly shark grin and teetered a few inches toward him. "But how thoughtless of me," I said. "I forgot to introduce myself." I extended a hand. "The moniker is Matches O'Tool."

His head ducked between his shoulders and he stepped back. "You got me wrong, mister," he said quickly. "I was just passing through this burg. This minute I was packing to catch my train."

I got out a cigarette and after I lit it I allowed the match to burn almost to my fingertips before I blew it out. Beaker watched the small flame with horrified fascination.

"I'll be back in about an hour," I said. "You'll be on the train by then though, won't you?"

"Even," he said emphatically, "if there's no train."

The door of 423 was opened only part way by Mavis Frawley. Mavis had flaming red hair, green eyes, and the warmth of a bowl of ice cubes.

"Get that damn foot out of the door," she said, "or I'll scream for the cops."

"Go right ahead," I advised her, shoving my way in. "But you look to me like the type that doesn't do much screaming."

She watched me with smouldering eyes. "I charge a thousand bucks a minute," she said. "If you got less than that, see some of the girls down the hall."

"How unkind," I said. "Do I look like that kind of a man?"

Mavis walked over to a small table and put her hand on the phone. "Do I have to get someone to throw you out, or do you get what I'm hinting at?"

I smiled at her amiably. "Before you could get the operator I could toss you out of that window."

"You go to hell!"

"No need for animosity," I said. "I'm prepared to be friendly . . . this time."

Her eyes crackled with hate. "What do you want?"

"I wish it were you, baby," I said. "But this is business." I ground out my cigarette in the ash tray. "The name is Splasher O'Tool," I said. "The boss tells me that you've got a couple of monkeys trying to set up a stand in this town."

Mavis took her hand away from the phone. "The boss?"

"The boss," I said. "This town is sewed up tight and right. We can be downright unfriendly to competition."

"Why don't you try telling that to my 'boys', as you call them?"

"They've been informed," I said. I met and held her eyes. "Beaker got the idea right away, but Dowd is a little damaged."

For the first time she seemed uncertain, but she said, "You're not scaring me!"

"Of course not," I said.

We studied each other for awhile and she was becoming uneasy.

"Did I ever tell you about Myra Lawson?" I asked.

Mavis said nothing.

"Well," I said, cheerfully, "Myra used to deal blackjack at one of our places. Her take wasn't what it should have been and so we watched her until we found out why.

"She's still around, but she washes dishes for her meals now and doesn't go out in daylight," I said. "The acid, you know."

The little medicine bottle was now in my hand and I held it up. "Looks just like water, doesn't it?"

Her face got white and I gave her time to think.

Finally she asked, "How much time do I have to get out?"

"One hour," I said, as I rose and went leisurely to the door.

"I'll take it," she said bitterly. "But only because I can't operate without the boys."

Downstairs at the desk, Freddie beckoned to me. "Got a phone call from Sid. He says to call him right away."

In the phone booth I dialed the Four Deuces and asked for Sid.

"That baboon you laid out," Sid said, "left here fifteen minutes ago. On a hunch I had one of the porters tail him."

"And he's waiting for me?"

"Right. He ambled away but circled back. He's in the alley now with a piece of pipe. Should I call the cops?"

"No," I said. "I'm on a winning streak. I think I can handle it."

I walked back to the Four Deuces, but turned into the Bar & Grill that was on the other side of the alley. I went all the way through and into the back yard.

Peeking over the wood fence, I could make out Mugger in the shadows next to the rear exit. Evidently he was hoping that I'd step out for a breath of air.

Taking out the gun and reversing it, I tip-toed up behind him. Mugger had his attention glued to the door and so I had no trouble giving him a swipe behind the ear.

He sighed wearily and caved in, but before he could fall I got under him and slung him over my shoulder. He made a heavy load and I staggered as I carried him into the office and put him on the couch.

I put a glass and a bottle of whiskey next to him and waited. Mugger slept for ten minutes before painful consciousness returned. He groaned and grunted before opening his blood-shot eyes.

He directed a bleary glance at me. "Was dat you again?" he asked.

"Face it," I said. "I'm too damn tough for you."

Mugger kept his eyes closed. "Don't be so proud. You ain't touched me wid flesh and blood yet. What was it dis time? A gat?"

He forced open an eye to glare at me, but the whiskey bottle interrupted him. Aching every inch of the way, he managed to drag himself up to a sitting position and pour four fingers of the stuff.

Mugger drank deep and wiped his mouth with a sleeve. He stared moodily at the floor. "I feel ruint," he said.

"Don't take it so hard," I said. "Your friends didn't do any better and they're leaving town."

Mugger polished off the rest of the glass and tilted the bottle for a refill. "I knew it wouldn't work, but it's still discouragin'." He winced as he touched his head. "I'm gettin' too old for dis rough stuff."

He tasted the liquor again and examined the office and its furniture. "You get all dis splendor honest?"

"More or less," I said. "Brains had something to do with it."

"Don't rub it in," he said, brooding. "Well," he had a note of sadness in his voice. "I guess I better be leavin'. You ain't got a sawbuck or two for train fare? I'm near busted."

I considered his dejection for awhile. "The cops interested in you in any way?" I asked.

"Unless you're thinkin' of makin' a complaint, I'm pure as the driven snow right now," he said. "I just got out of the government boarding school and ain't had much time for bein' bad."

"You're getting gray hair, Mugger," I said. "Ever thought of trying legitimate? Like wearing a tux and a carnation and acting like a bouncer. Pays ninety-five a week."

"You serious?" Mugger's eyes rested on my face.

"But no pawing around Juanita," I said. "She's my claim."

"You're takin' the joy outta it," he said. "But I accept. The tear in my eye is hand-lickin' gratitude." He picked up his battered hat. "Only I need a day or two vacation. My head hurts."

When he left, I removed my coat and tie and stretched out on the couch. I thought, this divide and conquer business sometimes works. I closed my eyes.

I opened them when Juanita came in wearing a smile and an outfit that wasn't much more than the ribbons and bows holding it together.

She snapped the lock on the door and went around dimming the lights. "You look tired," she said.

"Had a hard day at the shop," I said.

She sat down beside me. "I've got a sparkle in my eyes," she said. "What are you thinking of?"

I reached for one of the bows.

She smiled and relaxed against me . . .

A REAL NICE GUY

William F. Nolan

Warm sun.

A summer afternoon.

The sniper emerged from the roof door, walking easily, carrying a custom-leather guncase.

Opened the case.

Assembled the weapon.

Loaded it.

Sighted the street below.

Adjusted the focus.

Waited.

There was no hurry.

No hurry at all.

He was famous, yet no one knew his name. There were portraits of him printed in dozens of newspapers and magazines; he'd even made the cover of *Time*. But no one had really seen his face. The portraits were composites, drawn by frustrated police artists, based on the few misleading descriptions given by witnesses who claimed to have seen him leaving a building or jumping from a roof, or driving from the target area in a stolen automobile. But no two descriptions matched.

One witness described a chunky man of average height with a dark beard and cap. Another described a thin, extremely tall man with a bushy head of hair and a thick moustache. A third description pegged him as balding, paunchy and wearing heavy hornrims. On *Time*'s cover, a large bloodsoaked question mark replaced his features – above the words WHO IS HE?

Reporters had given him many names: "The Phantom Sniper" . . . "The Deadly Ghost" . . . "The Silent Slayer" . . . and his personal favorite, "The

Master of Whispering Death." This was often shortened to "Deathmaster," but he liked the full title; it was fresh and poetic – and *accurate*.

He *was* a master. He never missed a target, never wasted a shot. He was cool and nerveless and smooth, and totally without conscience. And death indeed whispered from his silenced weapon: a dry snap of the trigger, a muffled pop, and the target dropped as though struck down by the fist of God.

They were *always* targets, never people. Men, women, children. Young, middle-aged, old. Strong ones. Weak ones. Healthy or crippled. Black or white. Rich or poor. Targets – all of them.

He considered himself a successful sharpshooter, demonstrating his unique skill in a world teeming with three billion moving targets placed there for his amusement. Day and night, city by city, state by state, they were always there, ready for his gun, for the sudden whispering death from its barrel. An endless supply just for him.

Each city street was his personal shooting gallery.

But he was careful. Very, very careful. He never killed twice in the same city. He switched weapons. He never used a car more than once. He never wore the same clothes twice on a shoot. Even the shoes would be discarded; he wore a fresh pair for each target run. And, usually, he was never seen at all.

He thought of it as a sport.

A game.

A run.

A vocation.

A skill.

But never murder.

His name was Jimmie Prescott and he was thirty-one years of age. Five foot ten. Slight build. Platform shoes could add three inches and body-pillows up to fifty pounds. He had thinning brown hair framing a bland, unmemorable face and shaved twice daily – but the case of wigs, beards and moustaches he always carried easily disguised the shape of his mouth, chin and skull. Sometimes he would wear a skin-colored fleshcap for baldness, or use heavy glasses – though his sight was perfect. Once, for a lark, he had worn a black eye patch. He would walk in a crouch, or stride with a sailor's swagger, or assume a limp. Each disguise amused him, helped make life more challenging. Each was a small work of art, flawlessly executed.

Jimmie was a perfectionist.

And he was clean: no police record. Never arrested. No set of his prints on file, no dossier.

He had a great deal of money (inherited) with no need or inclination to earn more. He had spent his lifetime honing his considerable skills: he was an expert on weaponry, car theft, body-combat, police procedures; he made it a strict rule to memorize the street system of each city he entered before embarking on a shoot. And once his target was down he knew exactly how to leave the area. The proper escape route was essential.

Jimmie was a knowledgeable historian in his field: he had made a thorough study of snipers, and held them all in cold contempt. Not a worthwhile one in the lot. They *deserved* to be caught; they were fools and idiots and blunderers, often acting out of neurotic impulse or psychotic emotion. Even the hired professionals drew Jimmie's ire – since these were men who espoused political causes or who worked for government money. Jimmie had no cause, nor would he ever allow himself to be bought like a pig on the market.

He considered himself quite sane. Lacking moral conscience, he did not suffer from a guilt complex. Nor did he operate from a basic hatred of humankind, as did so many of the warped criminals he had studied.

Basically, Jimmie liked people, got alone fine with them on a casual basis. He hated no one. (Except his parents, but they were long dead and something he did not think about any more.) He was incapable of love or friendship, but felt no need for either. Jimmie depended only on himself; he had learned to do that from childhood. He was, therefore, a loner by choice, and made it a rule (Jimmie had many rules) never to date the same female twice, no matter how sexually appealing she might be. Man-woman relationships were a weakness, a form of dangerous self-indulgence he carefully avoided.

In sum, Jimmie Prescott didn't need anyone. He had himself, his skills, his weapons and his targets. More than enough for a full, rich life. He did not drink or smoke. (Oh, a bit of vintage wine in a good restaurant was always welcome, but he had never been drunk in his life. You savor good wine; you don't *wallow* in it.) He jogged each day, morning and evening, and worked out twice a week in the local gym in whatever city he was visiting. A trim, healthy body was an absolute necessity in his specialized career. Jimmie left nothing to chance. He was not a gambler and took no joy in risk.

A few times things had been close: a roof door which had jammed shut in Detroit after a kill, forcing him to make a perilous between-buildings leap . . . an engine that died during a police chase in Portland, causing him to abandon his car and win the pursuit on foot . . . an intense struggle with an off-duty patrolman in Kansas City who'd witnessed a shot. The fellow had been tough and dispatching him was physically difficult; Jimmie finally snapped his neck – but it had been close.

He kept a neat, handwritten record of each shoot in his tooled-leather notebook: state, city, name of street, weather, time of day, sex, age and skin color of target. Under "Comments," he would add pertinent facts, including the make and year of the stolen car he had driven, and the type of disguise he had utilized. Each item of clothing worn was listed. And if he experienced any problem in exiting the target area this would also be noted. Thus, each shoot was critically analyzed upon completion – as a football coach might dissect a game after it had been played.

The only random factor was the target. Pre-selection spoiled the freshness, the *purity* of the act. Jimmie liked to surprise himself. Which shall it be: that young girl in red, laughing up at her boyfriend? The old newsman on the corner? The school kid skipping homeward with books under his arm? Or, perhaps, the beefy, bored truckdriver, sitting idly in his cab, waiting for the light to change?

Selection was always a big part of the challenge.

And *this* time . . .

A male. Strong looking. Well dressed. Businessman with a briefcase, in his late forties. Hair beginning to silver at the temples. He'd just left the drug store; probably stopped there to pick up something for his wife. Maybe she'd called to remind him at lunch.

Moving toward the corner. Walking briskly.

Yes, this one. By all means, this one.

Range: three hundred yards.

Adjust sight focus.

Rifle stock tight against right shoulder.

Finger inside guard, poised at trigger.

Cheek firm against wooden gunstock; eye to rubber scopepiece.

Line crosshairs on target.

Steady breathing.

Tighten trigger finger slowly.

Fire!

The man dropped forward to the walk like a clubbed animal, dead before he struck the pavement. Someone screamed. A child began to cry. A man shouted.

Pleasant, familiar sounds to Jimmie Prescott.

Calmly, he took apart his weapon, cased it, then carefully dusted his trousers. (Rooftops were often grimy, and although he would soon discard the trousers he liked to present a neat, well-tailored appearance – but only when the disguise called for it. What a marvelous, ill-smelling bum he had become in New Orleans; he smiled thinly, thinking about how truly offensive he was on that occasion.)

He walked through the roof exit to the elevator.

Within ten minutes he had cleared central Baltimore – and booked the next flight to the west coast.

Aboard the jet, he relaxed. In the soft, warm, humming interior of the airliner, he grew drowsy . . . closed his eyes.

And had The Dream again.

The Dream was the only disturbing element in Jimmie Prescott's life. He invariably thought of it that way: The Dream. Never as *a* dream. Always about a large metropolitan city where chaos reigned – with buses running over babies in the street, and people falling down sewer holes and through plate glass store windows . . . violent and disturbing. He was never threatened in The Dream, never personally involved in the chaos around him. Merely a mute witness to it.

He would tell himself, this is only *fantasy*, a thing deep inside his sleeping mind; it would go away once he awakened and then he could ignore it, put it out of his conscious thoughts, bury it as he had buried the hatred for his father and mother.

Perhaps he had *other* dreams. Surely he did. But The Dream was the one he woke to, again and again, emerging from the chaos of the city with sweat on his cheeks and forehead, his breath tight and shallow in his chest, his heart thudding wildly.

"Are you all right?" a passenger across the aisle was asking him. "Shall I call somebody?"

"I'm fine," said Jimmie, sitting up straight. "No problem."

"You look kinda shaky."

"No, I'm fine. But thank you for your concern."

And he put The Dream away once again, as a gun is put away in its case.

In Los Angeles, having studied the city quite thoroughly, Jimmie took a cab directly into Hollywood. The fare was steep, but money was never an issue in Jimmie's life; he paid well for services rendered, with no regrets.

He got off at Highland, on Hollywood Boulevard, and walked toward the Chinese Theater.

He wanted two things: food and sexual satisfaction.

First, he would select an attractive female, take her to dinner and then to his motel room (he'd booked one from the airport) where he would have sex. Jimmie never called it lovemaking, a *silly* word. It was always just sex, plain and simple and quickly over. He was capable of arousing a woman if he chose to do so, of bringing her to full passion and release, but he seldom bothered. His performance was always an act; the ritual bored him. Only the result counted.

He disliked prostitutes and seldom selected one. Too jaded. Too worldly. And never to be trusted. Given time, and his natural charm, he was usually able to pick up an out-of-town girl, impress her with an excellent and very expensive meal at a posh restaurant, and guide her firmly into bed.

This night, in Hollywood, the seduction was easily accomplished.

Jimmie spotted a supple, soft-faced girl in the forecourt of the Chinese. She was wandering from one celebrity footprint to another, leaning to examine a particular signature in the cement.

As she bent forward, her breasts flowed full, pressing against the soft

linen dress she wore – and Jimmie told himself, she's the one for tonight.
A young, awe-struck out-of-towner. Perfect.

He moved toward her.

"I just *love* European food," said Janet.

"That's good," said Jimmie Prescott. "I rather fancy it myself."

She smiled at him across the table, a glowing all-American girl from Ohio
named Janet Louise Lakeley. They were sitting in a small, very chic French
restaurant off La Cienega, with soft lighting and open-country decor.

"I can't read a word of this," Janet said when the menu was handed to
her. "I thought they always had the food listed in English, too, like movie
subtitles."

"Some places don't," said Jimmie quietly. "I'll order for us both. You'll
be pleased. The sole is excellent here."

"Oh, I love fish," she said. "I could eat a ton of fish."

He pressed her hand. "That's nice."

"My head is swimming. I shouldn't have had that Scotch on an empty
stomach," she said. "Are we having wine with dinner?"

"Of course," said Jimmie.

"I don't know anything about wine," she told him, "but I love champagne.
That's wine, isn't it?"

He smiled with a faint upcurve of his thin lips.

"Trust me," he said. "You'll enjoy what I select."

"I'm sure I will."

The food was ordered and served – and Jimmie was pleased to see that
his tastes had, once again, proven sound. The meal was superb, the wine
was bracing and the girl was sexually stimulating. Essentially brainless, but
that really didn't matter to Jimmie. She was what he wanted.

Then she began to talk about the sniper killings.

"Forty people in just a year and two months," she said. "And
all gunned down by the same madman. Aren't they *ever* going to
catch him?"

"The actual target figure is forty-one," he corrected her. "And what
makes you so sure the sniper is a male. Could be a woman."

She shook her head. "Whoever heard of a woman sniper?"

"There have been many," said Jimmie. "In Russia today there are
several hundred trained female snipers. Some European governments
have traditionally utilized females in this capacity."

"I don't mean women *soldiers*," she said. "I mean your nutso shoot-'em-
in-the-street sniper. Always guys. Every time. Like that kid in Texas that
shot all the people from the tower."

"Apparently you've never heard of Francine Stearn."

"Nope. Who was she?"

"Probably the most famous female sniper. Killed a dozen schoolchildren in Pittsburg one weekend in late July, 1970. One shot each. To the head. She was a very accurate shootist."

"Never heard of her."

"After she was captured, *Esquire* did a rather probing psychological profile on her."

"Well, I really don't read a lot," she admitted. "Except Gothic romances. I just can't get *enough* of those." She giggled. "Guess you could say I'm addicted."

"I'm not familiar with the genre."

"Anyway," she continued. "I know this sniper is a guy."

"*How* do you know?"

"Female intuition. I trust it. It never fails me. And it tells me that the Phantom Sniper is a man."

He was amused. "What else does it tell you?"

"That he's probably messed up in the head. Maybe beaten as a kid. Something like that. He's *got* to be a nutcase."

"You could be wrong there, too," Jimmie told her. "Not all lawbreakers are mentally unbalanced."

"This 'Deathmaster' guy is, and I'm convinced of it."

"You're a strongly-opinionated young woman."

"Mom always said that." She sipped her wine, nodded. "Yeah, I guess I am." She frowned, turning the glass slowly in her long-fingered hand. "Do you think they'll ever catch him?"

"I somehow doubt it," Jimmie declared. "No one seems to have a clear description of him. And he always seems to elude the police. Leaves no clues. Apparently selects his subjects at random. No motive to tie him to. No consistent MO."

"What's that?"

"Method of operation. Most criminals tend to repeat the same basic pattern in their crimes. But not this fellow. He keeps surprising people. Never know where he'll pop up next, or who his target will be. Tough to catch a man like that."

"You call them 'subjects' and 'targets' – but they're *people!* Innocent men and women and children. You make them sound like . . . like cutouts at a shooting gallery!"

"Perhaps I do," he admitted, smiling. "It's simply that we have different modes of expression."

"I say they'll get him eventually. He can't go on just butchering innocent people forever."

"No one goes on forever," said Jimmie Prescott.

She put down her wine glass, leaned toward him. "Know what bothers me most about the sniper?"

"What."

"The fact that his kind of act attracts copycats. Other sickos with a screw loose who read about him and want to imitate him. Arson is like that. One big fire in the papers and suddenly all the other wacko firebugs start their *own* fires. It gets 'em going. The sniper is like that."

"If some mentally-disturbed individual is motivated to kill stupidly and without thought or preparation by something he or she reads in a newspaper then the sniper himself cannot be blamed for such abnormal behavior."

"You call what *he* does normal?"

"I . . . uh . . . didn't say that. I was simply refuting your theory."

She frowned. "Then who *is* to blame? I think that guy should be caught and – "

"And what?" Jimmie fixed his cool gray eyes on her. "What would you do if you suddenly discovered who he was . . . where to find him?"

"Call the police, naturally. Like anybody."

"Wouldn't you be curious about him, about the kind of person he is? Wouldn't you *question* him first, try to understand him?"

"You don't question an animal who kills! Which is what he is. I'd like to see him gassed or hanged . . . You don't *talk* to a twisted creep like that!"

She had made him angry. His lips tightened. He was no longer amused with this conversation; the word game had turned sour. This girl was gross and stupid and insensitive. Take her to bed and be done with it. Use her body – but no words. No more words. He'd had quite enough of those from her.

"Check, please," he said to the waiter.

It was at his motel, after sex, that Jimmie decided to kill her. Her insulting tirade echoed and re-echoed in his mind. She must be punished for it.

In this special case he felt justified in breaking one of his rules: never pre-select a target. She told him that she had a job in Hollywood, that she worked the afternoon shift at a clothing store on Vine. And he knew where she lived, a few blocks from work. She walked to the store each afternoon.

He would take her home and return the next day. When she left her apartment building he would dispatch her from a roof across the street. Once this plan had settled into place in the mind of Jimmie Prescott he relaxed, allowing the tension of the evening to drain away.

By tomorrow night he'd be in Tucson, and Janet Lakeley would be dead.

Warm sun.

A summer afternoon.

The sniper emerged from the roof door, walking easily, carrying a custom-leather guncase.

Opened the case.

Assembled the weapon.

Loaded it.

Sighted the street below.

Adjusted the focus.

Waited.

Target now exiting.

Walking along street toward corner.

Adjust sight focus.

Finger on trigger.

Cheek against stock.

Eye to scope.

Crosshairs direct on target.

Fire!

Jimmie felt something like a fist strike his stomach. A sudden, shocking blow. Winded, he looked down in amazement at the blood pulsing steadily from his shirtfront.

I'm hit! Someone has actually –

Another blow – but this one stopped all thought, taking his head apart. No more shock. No more amazement.

No more Jimmie.

She put away the weapon, annoyed at herself. *Two* shots! The Phantom Sniper, whoever he was, never fired more than once. But *he* was exceptional. She got goosebumps, just thinking about him.

Well, maybe next time she could drop her target in one. Anybody can mis-calculate a shot. Nobody's perfect.

She left the roof area, walking calmly, took the elevator down to the garage, stowed her guncase in the trunk of the stolen Mustang and drove away from the motel.

Poor Jimmie, she thought. It was just his bad luck to meet *me*. But that's the way it goes.

Janet Lakeley had a rule, and she never broke it: when you bed down a guy in a new town you always target him the next day. She sighed. Usually it didn't bother her. Most of them were bastards. But not Jimmie. She'd enjoyed talking to him, playing her word games with him . . . bedding him. Too bad he had to die.

He seemed like a real nice guy.

STACKED DECK

Bill Pronzini

1

FROM WHERE HE stood in the shadow of a split-bole Douglas fir, Deighan had a clear view of the cabin down below. Big harvest moon tonight, and only a few streaky clouds scudding past now and then to dim its hard yellow shine. The hard yellow glistened off the surface of Lake Tahoe beyond, softened into a long silverish stripe out toward the middle. The rest of the water shone like polished black metal. All of it was empty as far as he could see, except for the red-and-green running lights of a boat well away to the south, pointed toward the neon shimmer that marked the South Shore gambling casinos.

The cabin was big, made of cut pine logs and red-wood shakes. It had a railed redwood deck that overlooked the lake, mostly invisible from where Deighan was. A flat concrete pier jutted out into the moonstruck water, a pair of short wooden floats making a T at its outer end. The boat tied up there was a thirty-foot Chris-Craft with sleeping accommodations for four. Nothing but the finer things for the Shooter.

Deighan watched the cabin. He'd been watching it for three hours now, from this same vantage point. His legs bothered him a little, standing around like this, and his eyes hurt from squinting. Time was, he'd had the night vision of an owl. Not anymore. What he had now, that he hadn't had when he was younger, was patience. He'd learned that in the last three years, along with a lot of other things – patience most of all.

On all sides the cabin was dark, but that was because they'd put the blackout curtains up. The six of them been inside for better than two hours now, the same five-man nucleus as on every Thursday night except during the winter months, plus the one newcomer. The Shooter went to

Hawaii when it started to snow. Or Florida or the Bahamas – someplace warm. Mannlicher and Brandt stayed home in the winter. Deighan didn't know what the others did, and he didn't care.

A match flared in the darkness between the carport, where the Shooter's Caddy Eldorado was slotted, and the parking area back among the trees. That was the lookout – Mannlicher's boy. Some lookout: he smoked a cigarette every five minutes, like clockwork, so you always knew where he was. Deighan watched him smoke this one. When he was done, he threw the butt away in a shower of sparks, and then seemed to remember that he was surrounded by dry timber and went after it and stamped it out with his shoe. *Some* lookout.

Deighan held his watch up close to his eyes, pushed the little button that lighted its dial. Ten-nineteen. Just about time. The lookout was moving again, down toward the lake. Pretty soon he would walk out on the pier and smoke another cigarette and admire the view for a few minutes. He apparently did that at least twice every Thursday night – that had been his pattern on each of the last two – and he hadn't gone through the ritual yet tonight. He was bored, that was the thing. He'd been at his job a long time and it was always the same; there wasn't anything for him to do except walk around and smoke cigarettes and look at three hundred square miles of lake. Nothing ever happened. In three years nothing had ever happened.

Tonight something was going to happen.

Deighan took the gun out of the clamshell holster at his belt. It was a Smith & Wesson .38, light-weight, compact – a good piece, one of the best he'd ever owned. He held it in his hand, watching as the lookout performed as if on cue – walked to the pier, stopped, then moved out along its flat surface. When the guy had gone halfway, Deighan came out of the shadows and went down the slope at an angle across the driveway, to the rear of the cabin. His shoes made little sliding sounds on the needled ground, but they weren't sounds that carried.

He'd been over this ground three times before, dry runs the last two Thursday nights and once during the day when nobody was around; he knew just where and how to go. The lookout was lighting up again, his back to the cabin, when Deighan reached the rear wall. He eased along it to the spare-bedroom window. The sash went up easily, noiselessly. He could hear them then, in the rec room – voices, ice against glass, the click and rattle of the chips. He got the ski mask from his jacket pocket, slipped it over his head, snugged it down. Then he climbed through the window, put his penlight on just long enough to orient himself, went straight across to the door that led into the rec room.

It didn't make a sound, either, when he opened it. He went in with the revolver extended, elbow locked. Sturgess saw him first. He said, "Jesus Christ!" and his body went as stiff as if he were suffering a stroke. The others turned in their chairs, gawking. The Shooter started up out of his.

Deighan said, fast and hard, "Sit still if you don't want to die. Hands on the table where I can see them – all of you. Do it!"

They weren't stupid; they did what they were told. Deighan watched them through a thin haze of tobacco smoke. Six men around the hexagonal poker table, hands flat on its green baize, heads lifted or twisted to stare at him. He knew five of them. Mannlicher, the fat owner of the Nevornia Club; he had Family ties, even though he was a Prussian, because he'd once done some favors for an east-coast *capo*. Brandt, Mannlicher's cousin and private enforcer, who doubled as the Nevornia's floor boss. Bellah, the quasi-legitimate real-estate developer and high roller. Sturgess, the bankroll behind the Jackpot Lounge up at North Shore. And the Shooter – hired muscle, hired gun, part-time coke runner, whose real name was Dennis D'Allesandro. The sixth man was the pigeon they'd lured in for this particular game, a lean guy in his fifties with Texas oil money written all over him and his fancy clothes – Donley or Donavan, something like that.

Mannlicher was the bank tonight; the table behind his chair was covered with stacks of dead presidents – fifties and hundreds, mostly. Deighan took out the folded-up flour sack, tossed it on top of the poker chips that littered the baize in front of Mannlicher. "All right. Fill it."

The fat man didn't move. He was no pushover; he was hard, tough, mean. And he didn't like being ripped off. Veins bulged in his neck, throbbed in his temples. The violence in him was close to the surface now, held thinly in check.

"You know who we are?" he said. "Who I am?"

"Fill it."

"You dumb bastard. You'll never live to spend it."

"Fill the sack. *Now*."

Deighan's eyes, more than his gun, made up Mannlicher's mind for him. He picked up the sack, pushed around in his chair, began to savagely feed in the stacks of bills.

"The rest of you," Deighan said, "put your wallets, watches, jewelry on the table. Everything of value. Hurry it up."

The Texan said, "Listen heah – " and Deighan pointed the .38 at his head and said, "One more word, you're a dead man." The Texan made an effort to stare him down, but it was just to save face; after two or three seconds he lowered his gaze and began stripping the rings off his fingers.

The rest of them didn't make any fuss. Bellah was sweating; he kept swiping it out of his eyes, his hands moving in little jerks and twitches. Brandt's eyes were like dull knives, cutting away at Deighan's masked face. D'Allesandro showed no emotion of any kind. That was his trademark; he was your original iceman. They might have called him that, maybe, if he'd been like one of those old-timers who used an ice pick or a blade. As it was, with his preferences, the Shooter was the right name for him.

Mannlicher had the sack full now. The platinum ring on his left hand, with its circle of fat diamonds, made little gleams and glints in the shine from the low-hanging droplight. The idea of losing that bothered him even more than losing his money; he kept running the fingers of his other hand over the stones.

"The ring," Deighan said to him. "Take it off."

"Go to hell."

"Take it off or I'll put a third eye in the middle of your forehead. Your choice."

Mannlicher hesitated, tried to stare him down, didn't have any better luck at it than the Texan. There was a tense moment; then, because he didn't want to die over a piece of jewelry, he yanked the ring off, slammed it down hard in the middle of the table.

Deighan said, "Put it in the sack. The wallets and the rest of the stuff too."

This time Mannlicher didn't hesitate. He did as he'd been told.

"All right," Deighan said. "Now get up and go over by the bar. Lie down on the floor on your belly."

Mannlicher got up slowly, his jaw set and his teeth clenched as if to keep the violence from spewing out like vomit. He lay down on the floor. Deighan gestured at Brandt, said, "You next. Then the rest of you, one at a time."

When they were all on the floor he moved to the table, caught up the sack. "Stay where you are for ten minutes," he told them. "You move before that, or call to the guy outside, I'll blow the place up. I got a grenade in my pocket, the fragmentation kind. Anybody doubt it?"

None of them said anything.

Deighan backed up into the spare bedroom, leaving the door open so he could watch them all the way to the window. He put his head out, saw no sign of the look-out. Still down by the lake somewhere. The whole thing had taken just a few minutes.

He swung out through the window, hurried away in the shadows – but in the opposite direction from the driveway and the road above. On the far side of the cabin there was a path that angled through the pine forest to the north; he found it, followed it at a trot. Enough moonlight penetrated through the branches overhead to let him see where he was going.

He was almost to the lakefront when the commotion started back there: voices, angry and pulsing in the night, Mannlicher's the loudest of them. They hadn't waited the full ten minutes, but then he hadn't expected them to. It didn't matter. The Shooter's cabin was invisible from here, cut off by a wooded finger of land a hundred yards wide. And they wouldn't be looking for him along the water, anyway. They'd be up on the road, combing that area; they'd figure automatically that his transportation was a car.

The hard yellow-and-black gleam of the lake was just ahead, the rushes and ferns where he'd tied up the rented Beachcraft inboard. He moved across the sandy strip of beach, waded out to his calves, dropped the loaded flour sack into the boat, then eased the craft free of the rushes before he lifted himself over the gunwale. The engine caught with a quiet rumble the first time he turned the key.

They were still making noise back at the cabin, blundering around like fools, as he eased away into the night.

2

The motel was called the Whispering Pines. It was back off Highway 28 below Crystal Bay, a good half mile from the lake, tucked up in a grove of pines and Douglas fir. Deighan's cabin was the farthest from the office, detached from its nearest neighbor by thirty feet of open ground.

Inside he sat in darkness except for flickering light from the television. The set was an old one; the picture was riddled with snow and kept jumping every few seconds. But he didn't care; he wasn't watching it. Or listening to it: he had the sound turned off. It was on only because he didn't like waiting in the dark.

It had been after midnight when he came in – too late to make the ritual call to Fran, even though he'd felt a compulsion to do so. She went to bed at eleven-thirty; she didn't like the phone to ring after that. How could he blame her? When he was home and she was away at Sheila's or her sister's, he never wanted it to ring that late either.

It was one-ten now. He was tired, but not too tired. The evening was still in his blood, warming him, like liquor or drugs that hadn't quite worn off yet. Mannlicher's face . . . that was an image he'd never forget. The Shooter's, too, and Brandt's, but especially Mannlicher's.

Outside, a car's headlamps made a sweep of light across the curtained window as it swung in through the motel courtyard. When it stopped nearby and the lights went out, Deighan thought: It's about time.

Footsteps made faint crunching sounds on gravel. Soft knock on the door. Soft voice following: "Prince? You in there?"

"Door's open."

A wedge of moonlight widened across the floor, not quite reaching to where Deighan sat in the lone chair with the .38 in his hand. The man who stood silhouetted in the opening made a perfect target – just a damned airhead, any way you looked at him.

"Prince?"

"I'm over here. Come on in, shut the door."

"Why don't you turn on a light?"

"There's a switch by the door."

The man entered, shut the door. There was a click and the ceiling globe came on. Deighan stayed where he was, but reached over with his left hand to turn off the TV.

Bellah stood blinking at him, running his palms along the sides of his expensive cashmere jacket. He said nervously, "For God's sake, put the gun away. What's the idea?"

"I'm the cautious type."

"Well, put it away. I don't like it."

Deighan got to his feet, slid the revolver into his belt holster. "How'd it go?"

"Hairy, damned hairy. Mannlicher was like a madman." Bellah took a handkerchief out of his pocket, wiped his forehead. His angular face was pale, shiny-damp. "I didn't think he'd take it this hard. Christ."

That's the trouble with people like you, Deighan thought. You never think. He pinched a cigarette out of his shirt pocket, lit it with the Zippo Fran had given him fifteen years ago. Fifteen years, and it still worked. Like their marriage, even with all the trouble. How long was it now? Twenty-two years in May? Twenty-three?

Bellah said, "He started screaming at D'Allesandro. I thought he was going to choke him."

"Who? Mannlicher?"

"Yeah. About the window in the spare bedroom."

"What'd D'Allesandro say?"

"He said he always keeps it locked, you must have jimmied it some way that didn't leave any traces. Mannlicher didn't believe him. He thinks D'Allesandro forgot to lock it."

"Nobody got the idea it was an inside job?"

"No."

"Okay then. Relax, Mr Bellah. You're in the clear."

Bellah wiped his face again. "Where's the money?"

"Other side of the bed. On the floor."

"You count it?"

"No. I figured you'd want to do that."

Bellah went over there, picked up the flour sack, emptied it on the bed. His eyes were bright and hot as he looked at all the loose green. Then he frowned, gnawed at his lower lip, and poked at Mannlicher's diamond ring. "What'd you take this for? Mannlicher is more pissed about the ring than anything else. He said his mother gave it to him. It's worth ten thousand."

"That's why I took it," Deighan said. "Fifteen percent of the cash isn't a hell of a lot."

Bellah stiffened. "I set it all up, didn't I? Why shouldn't I get the lion's share?"

"I'm not arguing, Mr Bellah. We agreed on a price; okay, that's the way it is. I'm only saying I got a right to a little something extra."

"All right, all right." Bellah was looking at the money again. "Must be at least two hundred thousand," he said. "That Texan, Donley, brought fifty grand alone."

"Plenty in his wallet too, then."

"Yeah."

Deighan smoked and watched Bellah count the loose bills and what was in the wallets and billfolds. There was an expression on the developer's face like a man has when he's fondling a naked woman. Greed, pure and simple. Greed was what drove Lawrence Bellah; money was his best friend, his lover, his god. He didn't have enough ready cash to buy the lakefront property down near Emerald Bay – property he stood to make three to four million on, with a string of condos – and he couldn't raise it fast enough any legitimate way; so he'd arranged to get it by knocking over his own weekly poker game, even if it meant crossing some hard people. He had balls, you had to give him that. He was stupid as hell, and one of these days he was liable to end up in pieces at the bottom of the lake, but he did have balls.

He was also lucky, at least for the time being, because the man he'd picked to do his strong-arm work was Bob Prince. He had no idea the name was a phony, no idea the whole package on Bob Prince was the result of three years of careful manipulation. All he knew was that Prince had a reputation as dependable, easy to work with, not too smart or money-hungry, and that he was willing to do any kind of muscle work. Bellah didn't have an inkling of what he'd really done by hiring Bob Prince. If he kept on being lucky, he never would.

Bellah was sweating by the time he finished adding up the take. "Two hundred and thirty-three thousand and change," he said. "More than we figured on."

"My cut's thirty-five thousand," Deighan said.

"You divide fast." Bellah counted out two stacks, hundreds and fifties, to one side of the flowered bed-spread. Then he said, "Count it? Or do you trust me?"

Deighan grinned. He rubbed out his cigarette, went to the bed, and took his time shuffling through the stacks. "On the nose," he said when he was done.

Bellah stuffed the rest of the cash back into the flour sack, leaving the watches and jewelry where they lay. He was still nervous, still sweating; he wasn't going to sleep much tonight, Deighan thought.

"That's it, then," Bellah said. "You going back to Chicago tomorrow?"

"Not right away. Thought I'd do a little gambling first."

"Around here? Christ, Prince . . ."

"No. Reno, maybe. I might even go down to Vegas."

"Just get away from Tahoe."

"Sure," Deighan said. "First thing in the morning."

Bellah went to the door. He paused there to tuck the flour sack under his jacket; it made him look as if he had a tumor on his left side. "Don't do anything with that jewelry in Nevada. Wait until you get back to Chicago."

"Whatever you say, Mr Bellah."

"Maybe I'll need you again sometime," Bellah said. "You'll hear from me if I do."

"Any time. Any old time."

When Bellah was gone, Deighan put five thousand dollars into his suitcase and the other thirty thousand into a knapsack he'd bought two days before at a South Shore sporting goods store. Mannlicher's diamond ring went into the knapsack, too, along with the better pieces among the rest of the jewelry. The watches and the other stuff were no good to him; he bundled those up in a hand towel from the bathroom, stuffed the bundle into the pocket of his down jacket. Then he had one more cigarette, set his portable alarm clock for six a.m., double-locked the door, and went to bed on the left side, with the revolver under the pillow near his right hand.

3

In the dawn light the lake was like smoky blue glass, empty except for a few optimistic fishermen anchored close to the eastern shoreline. The morning was cold, autumn-crisp, but there was no wind. The sun was just beginning to rise, painting the sky and its scattered cloudstreaks in pinks and golds. There was old snow on the upper reaches of Mount Tallac, on some of the other Sierra peaks that ringed the lake.

Deighan took the Beachcraft out half a mile before he dropped the bundle of watches and worthless jewelry overboard. Then he cut off at a long diagonal to the north that brought him to within a few hundred yards of the Shooter's cabin. He had his fishing gear out by then, fiddling with the glass rod and tackle – just another angler looking for rainbow, Mackinaw, and cutthroat trout.

There wasn't anybody out and around at the Shooter's place. Deighan glided past at two knots, angled into shore a couple of hundred yards beyond, where there were rushes and some heavy brush and trees overhanging the water. From there he had a pretty good view of the cabin, its front entrance, the Shooter's Caddy parked inside the carport.

It was eight o'clock, and the sun was all the way up, when he switched off the engine and tied up at the bole of the collapsed pine. It was a few minutes past nine-thirty when D'Allesandro came out and walked around to the Caddy. He was alone. No chippies from the casino this morning, not after what had gone down last night. He might be going to the store for cigarettes, groceries, or to a café somewhere for breakfast. He might be going to see somebody, do some business. The important thing was, how long would he be gone?

Deighan watched him back his Caddy out of the carport, drive it away and out of sight on the road above. He stayed where he was, fishing, waiting. At the end of an hour, when the Shooter still hadn't come back, he started the boat's engine and took his time maneuvering around the wooded finger of land to the north and then into the cove where he'd anchored last night. He nosed the boat into the reeds and ferns, swung overboard, and pushed it farther in, out of sight. Then he caught up the knapsack and set off through the woods to the Shooter's cabin.

He made a slow half circle of the place, keeping to the trees. The carport was still empty. Nothing moved anywhere within the range of his vision. Finally he made his way down to the rear wall, around it and along the side until he reached the front door. He didn't like standing out here for even a little while because there was no cover; but this door was the only one into the house, except for sliding doors on the terrace and a porch on the other side, and you couldn't jimmy sliding doors easily and without leaving marks. The same was true of windows. The Shooter would have made sure they were all secure anyway.

Deighan had one pocket of the knapsack open, the pick gun in his hand, when he reached the door. He'd got the pick gun from a housebreaker named Caldwell, an old-timer who was retired now; he'd also got some other tools and lessons in how to use them on the various kinds of locks. The lock on the Shooter's door was a flush-mounted, five-pin cylinder lock, with a steel lip on the door frame to protect the bolt and strike plate. That meant it was a lock you couldn't loid with a piece of plastic or a shim. It also meant that with a pick gun you could probably have it open in a couple of minutes.

Bending, squinting, he slid the gun into the lock. Set it, working the little knob on top to adjust the spring tension. Then he pulled the trigger – and all the pins bounced free at once and the door opened under his hand.

He slipped inside, nudged the door shut behind him, put the pick gun away inside the knapsack, and drew on a pair of thin plastic gloves. The place smelled of stale tobacco smoke and stale liquor. They hadn't been doing all that much drinking last night; maybe the Shooter had nibbled a few too many after the rest of them finally left. He didn't like losing money and valuables any more than Mannlicher did.

Deighan went through the front room. Somebody'd decorated the place for D'Allesandro: leather furniture, deer and antelope heads on the walls, Indian rugs on the floors, tasteful paintings. Cocaine deals had paid for part of it; contract work, including two hits on greedy Oakland and San Francisco drug dealers, had paid for the rest. But the Shooter was still small-time. He wasn't bright enough to be anything else. Cards and dice and whores-in-training were all he really cared about.

The front room was no good; Deighan prowled quickly through the other rooms. D'Allesandro wasn't the kind to have an office or a den, but there was a big old-fashioned rolltop desk in a room with a TV set and one of those big movie-type screens. None of the desk drawers were locked. Deighan pulled out the biggest one, saw that it was loaded with Danish porn magazines, took the magazines out and set them on the floor. He opened the knapsack and transferred the thirty thousand dollars into the back of the drawer. He put Mannlicher's ring in there, too, along with the other rings and a couple of gold chains the Texan had been wearing. Then he stuffed the porn magazines in at the front and pushed the drawer shut.

On his way back to the front room he rolled the knapsack tight around the pick gun and stuffed them into his jacket pocket. He opened the door, stepped out. He'd just finished resetting the lock when he heard the car approaching on the road above.

He froze for a second, looking up there. He couldn't see the car because of a screen of trees; but then he heard its automatic transmission gear down as it slowed for the turn into the Shooter's driveway. He pulled the door shut and ran toward the lake, the only direction he could go. Fifty feet away the log-railed terrace began, raised up off the sloping ground on redwood pillars. Deighan caught one of the railings, hauled himself up and half rolled through the gap between them. The sound of the oncoming car was loud in his ears as he landed, off balance, on the deck.

He went to one knee, came up again. The only way to tell if he'd been seen was to stop and look, but that was a fool's move. Instead he ran across the deck, climbed through the railing on the other side, dropped down, and tried to keep from making noise as he plunged into the woods. He stopped moving after thirty yards, where ferns and a deadfall formed a thick concealing wall. From behind it, with the .38 in his hand, he watched the house and the deck, catching his breath, waiting.

Nobody came up or out on the deck. Nobody showed himself anywhere. The car's engine had been shut off sometime during his flight; it was quiet now, except for birds and the faint hum of a powerboat out on the lake.

Deighan waited ten minutes. When there was still nothing to see or hear, he transcribed a slow curl through the trees to where he could see the front of the cabin. The Shooter's Caddy was back inside the carport, no sign of haste in the way it had been neatly slotted. The cabin door was shut. The whole area seemed deserted.

But he waited another ten minutes before he was satisfied. Even then, he didn't holster his weapon until he'd made his way around to the cove where the Beachcraft was hidden. And he didn't relax until he was well out on the lake, headed back toward Crystal Bay.

4

The Nevornia was one of South Shore's older clubs, but it had undergone some recent modernizing. Outside, it had been given a glass and gaudy-neon face-lift. Inside, they'd used more glass, some cut crystal, and a wine-red decor that included carpeting, upholstery, and gaming tables.

When Deighan walked in a few minutes before two, the banks of slots and the blackjack tables were getting moderately heavy play. That was because it was Friday; some of the small-time gamblers liked to get a jump on the weekend crowds. The craps and roulette layouts were quiet. The high rollers were like vampires: they couldn't stand the daylight, so they only came out after dark.

Deighan bought a roll of quarters at one of the change booths. There were a couple of dozen rows of slots in the main casino – flashy new ones, mostly, with a few of the old scrolled nickel-plated jobs mixed in for the sake of nostalgia. He stopped at one of the old quarter machines, fed in three dollars' worth. Lemons and oranges. He couldn't even line up two cherries for a three-coin drop. He smiled crookedly to himself, went away from the slots and into the long concourse that connected the main casino with the new, smaller addition at the rear.

There were telephone booths along one side of the concourse. Deighan shut himself inside one of them, put a quarter in the slot, pushed 0 and then the digits of his home number in San Francisco. When the operator came on he said it was a collect call; that was to save himself the trouble of having to feed in a handful of quarters. He let the circuit make exactly five burrs in his ear before he hung up. If Fran was home, she'd know now that he was all right. If she wasn't home, then she'd know it later when he made another five-ring call. He always tried to call at least twice a day, at different times, because sometimes she went out shopping or to a movie or to visit with Sheila and the kids.

It'd be easier if she just answered the phone, talked to him, but she never did when he was away. Never. Sheila or anybody else wanted to get hold of her, they had to call one of the neighbors or come over in person. She didn't want anything to do with him when he was away, didn't want to know what he was doing or even when he'd be back. "Suppose I picked up the phone and it wasn't you?" she'd said. "Suppose it was somebody telling me you were dead? I couldn't stand that." That part of it didn't make sense to him. If he were dead, somebody'd come by and tell it to her face; dead was dead, and what difference did it make how she got the news? But he didn't argue with her. He didn't like to argue with her, and it didn't cost him anything to do it her way.

He slotted the quarter again and called the Shooter's number. Four rings, five, and D'Allesandro's voice said, "Yeah?"

"Mr Carson?"

"Who?"

"Isn't this Paul Carson?"

"No. You got the wrong number."

"Oh, sorry," Deighan said, and rang off.

Another quarter in the slot. This time the number he punched out was the Nevornia's business line. A woman's voice answered, crisp and professional. He said, "Mr Mannlicher. Tell him it's urgent."

"Whom shall I say is calling?"

"Never mind that. Just tell him it's about what happened last night."

"Sir, I'm afraid I can't – "

"Tell him last night's poker game, damn it. He'll talk to me."

There was a click and some canned music began to play in his ear. He lit a cigarette. He was on his fourth drag when the canned music quit and the fat man's voice said, "Frank Mannlicher. Who's this?"

"No names. Is it all right to talk on this line?"

"Go ahead, talk."

"I'm the guy who hit your game last night."

Silence for four or five seconds. Then Mannlicher said, "Is that so?" in a flat, wary voice.

"Ski mask, Smith & Wesson .38, grenade in my jacket pocket. The take was better than two hundred thousand. I got your ring – platinum with a circle of diamonds."

Another pause, shorter this time. "So why call me today?"

"How'd you like to get it all back – the money and the ring?"

"How?"

"Go pick it up. I'll tell you where."

"Yeah? Why should you do me a favor?"

"I didn't know who you were last night. I wasn't told. If I had been, I wouldn't of gone through with it. I don't mess with people like you, people with your connections."

"Somebody hired you, that it?"

"That's it."

"Who?"

"D'Allesandro."

"What?"

"The Shooter. D'Allesandro."

". . . Bullshit."

"You don't have to believe me. But I'm telling you – he's the one. He didn't tell me who'd be at the game, and now he's trying to screw me on the money. He says there was less than a hundred and fifty thousand in the sack; I know better."

"So now you want to screw him."

"That's right. Besides, I don't like the idea of you pushing to find out who I am, maybe sending somebody to pay me a visit someday. I figure if I give you the Shooter, you'll lose interest in me."

More silence. "Why'd he do it?" Mannlicher said in a different voice – harder, with the edge of violence it had held last night. "Hit the game like that?"

"He needs some big money, fast. He's into some kind of scam back east; he wouldn't say what it is."

"Where's the money and the rest of the stuff?"

"At his cabin. We had a drop arranged in the woods; I put the sack there last night, he picked it up this morning when nobody was around. The money's in his desk – the big rolltop. Your ring, too. That's where it was an hour ago, anyhow, when I walked out."

Mannlicher said, "In his desk," as if he were biting the words off something bitter.

"Go out there, see for yourself."

"If you're telling this straight, you got nothing to worry about from me. Maybe I'll fix you up with a reward or something. Where can I get in touch?"

"You can't," Deighan said. "I'm long gone as soon as I hang up this phone."

"I'll make it five thousand. Just tell me where you – "

Deighan broke the connection.

His cigarette had burned down to the filter; he dropped it on the floor, put his shoe on it before he left the booth. On his way out of the casino he paused long enough to push another quarter into the same slot machine he'd played before. More lemons and oranges. This time he didn't smile as he moved away.

5

Narrow and twisty, hemmed in by trees, Old Lake Road branched off Highway 50 on the Nevada side and took two miles to get all the way to the lake. But it wasn't a dead-end; another road picked it up at the lakefront and looped back out to the highway. There were several nice homes hidden away in the area – it was called Pine Acres – with plenty of space between them. The Shooter's cabin was a mile and a half from the highway, off an even narrower lane called Little Cove Road. The only other cabin within five hundred yards was a summer place that the owners had already closed up for the year.

Deighan drove past the intersection with Little Cove, went two-tenths of a mile, parked on the turnout at that point. There wasn't anybody else around when he got out, nothing to see except trees and little winks of blue that marked the nearness of the lake. If anybody came along they wouldn't pay any attention to the car. For one thing, it was a '75 Ford Galaxy with nothing distinctive about it except the antenna for the GTE mobile phone. It was his – he'd driven it up from San Francisco – but the papers on it said it belonged to Bob Prince. For another thing, Old Lake Road was only a hundred yards or so from the water here, and there was a path through the trees to a strip of rocky beach. Local kids used it in the summer; he'd found that out from Bellah. Kids might have decided to stop here on a sunny autumn day as well. No reason for anybody to think otherwise.

He found the path, went along it a short way to where it crossed a little creek, dry now and so narrow it was nothing more than a natural drainage ditch. He followed the creek to the north, on a course he'd taken three days ago. It led him to a shelflike overhang topped by two chunks of granite outcrop that leaned against each other like a pair of old drunks. Below the shelf, the land fell away sharply to the Shooter's driveway some sixty yards distant. Off to the right, where the incline wasn't so steep and the trees grew in a pack, was the split-bole Douglas fir where he'd stood waiting last night. The trees were fewer and more widely spaced apart between here and the cabin, so that from behind the two outcrops you had a good look at the Shooter's property, Little Cove Road, the concrete pier, and the lake shimmering under the late afternoon sun.

The Caddy Eldorado was still slotted inside the carport. It was the only car in sight. Deighan knelt behind where the outcrops came together to form a notch, rubbed tension out of his neck and shoulders while he waited.

He didn't have to wait long. Less than ten minutes had passed when the car appeared on Little Cove Road, slowed, turned down the Shooter's driveway. It wasn't Mannlicher's fancy limo; it was a two-year-old Chrysler – Brandt's, maybe. Brandt was driving it: Deighan had a clear view of him through the side window as the Chrysler pulled up and stopped near the cabin's front door. He could also see that the lone passenger was Mannlicher.

Brandt got out, opened the passenger door for the fat man, and the two of them went to the cabin. It took D'Allesandro ten seconds to answer Brandt's knock. There was some talk, not much; then Mannlicher and Brandt went in, and the door shut behind them.

All right, Deighan thought. He'd stacked the deck as well as he could; pretty soon he'd know how the hand – and the game – played out.

Nothing happened for maybe five minutes. Then he thought he heard some muffled sounds down there, loud voices that went on for a while, something that might have been a bang, but the distance was too great for him to be sure that he wasn't imagining them. Another four or five minutes went by. And then the door opened and Brandt came out alone, looked around, called something back inside that Deighan didn't understand. If there was an answer, it wasn't audible. Brandt shut the door, hurried down to the lake, went out onto the pier. The ChrisCraft was still tied up there. Brandt climbed on board, disappeared for thirty seconds or so, reappeared carrying a square of something gray and heavy. Tarpaulin, Deighan saw when Brandt came back up the driveway. Big piece of it – big enough for a shroud.

The Shooter's hand had been folded. That left three of them still in the game.

When Brandt had gone back inside with the tarp, Deighan stood and half ran along the creek and through the trees to where he'd left the Ford. Old Lake Road was deserted. He yanked open the passenger door, leaned in, caught up the mobile phone, and punched out the emergency number for the county sheriff's office. An efficient-sounding male voice answered.

"Something's going on on Little Cove Road," Deighan said, making himself sound excited. "That's in Pine Acres, you know? It's the cabin at the end, down on the lake. I heard shots – people shooting at each other down there. It sounds like a war."

"What's the address?"

"I don't know the address, it's the cabin right on the lake. People *shooting* at each other. You better get right out there."

"Your name, sir?"

"I don't want to get involved. Just hurry, will you?"

Deighan put the receiver down, shut the car door, ran back along the path and along the creek to the shelf. Mannlicher and Brandt were still inside the cabin. He went to one knee again behind the outcrops, drew the .38, held it on his thigh.

It was another two minutes before the door opened down there. Brandt came out, looked around as he had before, went back inside – and then he and Mannlicher both appeared, one at each end of a big, tarp-wrapped bundle. They started to carry it down the driveway toward the lake. Going to put it on the boat, Deighan thought, take it out now or later on, when it's dark. Lake Tahoe was sixteen hundred feet deep in the middle. The bundle wouldn't have been the first somebody'd dumped out there.

He let them get clear of the Chrysler, partway down the drive, before he poked the gun into the notch, sighted, and fired twice. The shots went where he'd intended them to, wide by ten feet and into the roadbed so they kicked up gravel. Mannlicher and Brandt froze for an instant, confused. Deighan fired a third round, putting the slug closer this time, and that one panicked them: they let go of the bundle and began scrambling.

There was no cover anywhere close by; they both ran for the Chrysler. Brandt had a gun in his hand when he reached it, and he dropped down behind the rear deck, trying to locate Deighan's position. Mannlicher kept on scrambling around to the passenger door, pulled it open, pushed himself across the seat inside.

Deighan blew out the Chrysler's near front tire. Sighted, and blew out the rear tire. Brandt threw an answering shot his way, but it wasn't even close. The Chrysler was tilting in Deighan's direction as the tires flattened. Mannlicher pushed himself out of the car, tried to make a run for the cabin door with his arms flailing, his fat jiggling. Deighan put a bullet into the wall beside the door. Mannlicher reversed himself, fell in his frantic haste, crawled back behind the Chrysler.

Reloading the .38, Deighan could hear the sound of cars coming up fast on Little Cove Road. No sirens, but revolving lights made faint blood-red flashes through the trees.

From behind the Chrysler Brandt fired again, wildly. Beyond him, on the driveway, one corner of the tarpwrapped bundle had come loose and was flapping in the wind off the lake.

A county sheriff's cruiser, its roof light slashing the air, made the turn off Little Cove onto the driveway. Another one was right behind it. In his panic, Brandt straightened up when he saw them and fired once, blindly, at the first in line.

Deighan was on his feet by then, hurrying away from the outcrops, holstering his weapon. Behind him he heard brakes squeal, another shot, voices yelling, two more shots. All the sounds faded as he neared the turn-out and the Ford. By the time he pulled out onto the deserted road, there was nothing to hear but the sound of his engine, the screeching of a jay somewhere nearby.

Brandt had thrown in his hand by now; so had Mannlicher.

This pot belonged to him.

6

Fran was in the back yard, weeding her garden, when he got home late the following afternoon. He called to her from the doorway, and she glanced around and then got up, unsmiling, and came over to him. She was wearing jeans and one of his old shirts and a pair of gardening gloves, and her hair was tied in a long ponytail. Used to be a light, silky brown, her hair; now it was mostly gray. His fault. She was only forty-six. A woman of forty-six shouldn't be so gray.

She said, "So you're back." She didn't sound glad to see him, didn't kiss him or touch him at all. But her eyes were gentle on his face.

"I'm back."

"You all right? You look tired."

"Long drive. I'm fine; it was a good trip."

She didn't say anything. She didn't want to hear about it, not any of it. She just didn't want to know.

"How about you?" he asked. "Everything been okay?"

"Sheila's pregnant again."

"Christ. What's the matter with her? Why don't she get herself fixed? Or get Hank fixed?"

"She likes kids."

"I like kids too, but four's too many at her age. She's only twenty-seven."

"She wants eight."

"She's crazy," Deighan said. "What's she want to bring all those kids into a world like this for?"

There was an awkward moment. It was always awkward at first when he came back. Then Fran said, "You hungry?"

"You know me. I can always eat." Fact was, he was starved. He hadn't eaten much up in Nevada, never did when he was away. And he hadn't had anything today except an English muffin and some coffee for breakfast in Truckee.

"Come into the kitchen," Fran said. "I'll fix you something."

They went inside. He got a beer out of the refrigerator; she waited and then took out some covered dishes, some vegetables. He wanted to say something to her, talk a little, but he couldn't think of anything. His mind was blank at times like this. He carried his beer into the living room.

The goddamn trophy case was the first thing he saw. He hated that trophy case; but Fran wouldn't get rid of it, no matter what he said. For her it was like some kind of shrine to the dead past. All the mementoes of his years on the force – twenty-two years, from beat patrolman in North Beach all the way up to inspector on the narcotics squad. The certificate he'd won in marksmanship competition at the police academy, the two citations from the mayor for bravery, other crap like that. Bones, that's all they were to him. Pieces of a rotting skeleton. What was the sense in keeping them around, reminding both of them of what he'd been, what he'd lost.

His fault he'd lost it, sure. But it was their fault too, goddamn them. The laws, the lawyers, the judges, the *system*. No convictions on half of all the arrests he'd ever made – half! Turning the ones like Mannlicher and Brandt and D'Allesandro loose, putting them right back on the street, letting them make their deals and their hits, letting them screw up innocent lives. Sheila's kids, his grandkids – lives like that. How could they blame him for being bitter? How could they blame him for taking too many drinks now and then?

He sat down on the couch, drank some of his beer, lit a cigarette. Ah Christ, he thought, it's not them. You know it wasn't them. It was *you*, you dumb bastard. They warned you twice about drinking on duty. And you kept on doing it, you were hog-drunk the night you plowed the departmental sedan into that vanload of teenagers. What if one of *those* kids had died? You were lucky, by God. You got off easy.

Sure, he thought. Sure. But he'd been a good cop, damn it, a cop inside and out; it was all he knew how to be. What was he supposed to do after they threw him off the force? Live on his half-pension? Get a job as a part-time security guard? Forty-four years old, no skills, no friends outside the department – what the hell was he supposed to do?

He'd invented Bob Prince, that was what he'd done. He'd gone into business for himself.

Fran didn't understand. "You'll get killed one of these days," she'd said in the beginning. "It's vigilante justice," she'd said. "You think you're Rambo, is that it?" she'd said. She just didn't understand. To him it was the same job he'd always done, the only one he was any good at, only now *he* made up some of the rules. He was no Rambo, one man up against thousands, a mindless killing machine; he hated that kind of phony flag-waving crap. It wasn't real. What he was doing, that was real. It meant something. But a hero? No. Hell, no. He was a sniper, that was all, picking off a weak or vulnerable enemy here and there, now and then. Snipers weren't heroes, for Christ's sake. Snipers were snipers, just like cops were cops.

He finished his beer and his cigarette, got up, went into Fran's sewing room. The five thousand he'd held out of the poker-game take was in his pocket – money he felt he was entitled to because his expenses ran high sometimes, and they had to eat, they had to live. He put the roll into her sewing cabinet, where he always put whatever money he made as Bob Prince. She'd spend it when she had to, parcel it out, but she'd never mention it to him or anyone else. She'd told Sheila once that he had a sales job, he got paid in cash a lot, that was why he was away from home for such long periods of time.

When he walked back into the kitchen she was at the sink, peeling potatoes. He went over and touched her shoulder, kissed the top of her head. She didn't look at him; stood there stiffly until he moved away from her. But she'd be all right in a day or two. She'd be fine until the next time Bob Prince made the right kind of connection.

He wished it didn't have to be this way. He wished he could roll back the clock three years, do things differently, take the gray out of her hair and the pain out of her eyes. But he couldn't. It was just too late.

You had to play the cards you were dealt, no matter how lousy they were. The only thing that made it tolerable was that sometimes, on certain hands, you could find ways to stack the damn deck.

SO YOUNG,
SO FAIR, SO DEAD

John Lutz

YOU CAN LIVE your life through and try hard to be a decent sort, but trouble might still come to you. That's the way it seems to have been with me. My trouble was never the direct result of what I did, but the product of others. Neighbours especially. My advice is, don't ever get too friendly with your neighbors. I had to learn that the hard way.

Adelaide and I finished moving into our new house on a Sunday. That Monday I managed to stay away from the office and helped her sort the contents of cardboard boxes and move furniture about. We were both very happy that day, for we'd worked and saved for a long time to be able to afford our own home built here in the beautiful rolling hills south of the smoke-palled city. Here the air was clear as crystal and the view was the best nature had to offer.

And the house itself was what we'd always wanted. Though not large, it was well built with excellent materials and designed with a tasteful touch of miniature elegance. Adelaide and I took a walk around our green property before dark that evening and admired the way the wood shingled house seemed to blend so well with the forest-like setting.

Of course the best thing about the house and the property was that it was ours. I'd worked hard to build up my own mail order business, Smathers Enterprises, and Mr and Mrs Will Smathers were comparatively well heeled for a couple in their early thirties who'd started married life on practically nothing.

Adelaide stopped strolling and gazed down the narrow blacktop road that fronted our property. I stood off and admired her delicate features and shining blonde hair, the weight of her lithe, graceful body resting on one slender leg. Adelaide, too, blended well with the natural surroundings. She was a natural beauty, the type makeup couldn't improve.

"I wonder about our neighbor," she said.

I moved next to her, slipping my arm about her waist. From where we stood we could see the nearest home through a break in the heavy green of the trees. A large brick home with a swimming pool behind it, it was the only house within a mile of us in either direction. I could just see the top of a small beach house near the pool. Within plain view near the attached two car garage was a long, expensive blue convertible.

"Whoever our neighbor is," I said, "he has money."

"It certainly looks that way."

"On the other hand, he may be mortgaged up to his neck."

We stood for a moment longer looking down at the big house before going back inside. I say looking down because our home was situated high on one of the hills, and the blacktop road snaked sharply downward for the next two or three miles as it meandered like a still tributary to the Red Fox River.

I suppose I had no business saying anything about how our neighbor might have his property mortgaged. We'd gone into debt heavily to buy our own home. But the business was going well, and promised to continue to do so, and there was no reason we shouldn't be happy now and pay as we went along.

And in a way owing on the house could be a good thing. Once we were in it I knew we'd never give it up unless we absolutely had to, and it might serve as a spur to help make me work even harder.

But all the house motivated me to do that day was leave the office early so I could get home to enjoy living there with Adelaide. As I drove up the winding driveway I wondered when I'd get over the feeling that this was someone else's charming home I was approaching and not my own.

Adelaide knew I was coming home early and had dinner in the oven. She fixed us each a drink while we were waiting and we sat in the disarranged living room.

"I don't know when we'll ever get things the way we want them," Adelaide said, glancing around at the mess.

I grinned at her and took a sip of my Scotch and water, admiring her fresh good looks in the plain housedress she did so much for. "There's plenty of time."

"I suppose so." She sighed with contentment and settled back in her chair. "I saw our neighbor today," she said.

"Did he drop by to introduce himself?"

"No, but you can see the house from our bedroom window upstairs. When I looked out this afternoon I noticed a man swimming in the pool. He had a guest, a girl in a purple bikini who stayed there most of the day, then drove away in a little sports car."

I had to laugh. If Adelaide had any faults at all, one of them would be that she was a trifle nosy. "Are you going to start a dossier on them?" I asked jokingly.

"Not yet," she said with a smile. "And it's not 'them', it's 'him'. The man seems to live there alone."

"Big house for a single man," I remarked, "though it sounds like he has his fun there."

A timer bell sounded in the kitchen and Adelaide put down her drink and stood. I walked behind her as she hurried into the kitchen to check on the dinner.

"You keep an eye on him and keep me posted," I said, rubbing the back of my hand playfully up the nape of her neck. She didn't answer and I kept quiet. Experience had taught me to joke only so far about Adelaide's feminine curiosity.

Though without any prompting she had another tidbit of information for me the next evening when I returned home.

"Our neighbor seems to be something of a swinger," she said. "There was a girl in a red bikini there today."

"Same girl, different bikini," I speculated.

Adelaide shook her head. "The first one was a tall brunette. Today it was a short blonde."

I smiled and shrugged. "His sister?"

"I doubt it," Adelaide said, and drew a miniature bronze rooster from the carton.

"I'm sure we'll find out more about him," I said. "He'll probably turn up at our door one of these days soon to introduce himself. Could be he doesn't even realize there's anybody living here yet." Silently I wondered if he'd plant a shade tree between us and his pool when he did find out. Then for the next few hours I was busy helping Adelaide finish the job of unpacking and thought about little else.

But that night my own curiosity about our neighbor was aroused when I walked across the bedroom to close the drapes.

As my hand reached for the pull cord my eye caught the flash of a revolving red light in the distance. I leaned forward and squinted into the darkness, and I saw that a police car was parked in our neighbor's driveway beside his long blue convertible.

As I watched another car pulled up behind that one. In the reflection of its headlights I could see that it was a plain gray sedan. Two men got out of it and went into the house without knocking.

A hand touched my shoulder and Adelaide was standing beside me.

"Now who's nosy?" she asked.

I didn't answer, and we stood there for a while and watched shadows cross the distant draped windows. Then the two men and a uniformed policeman came out of the house. They got into their respective cars, the red light on the patrol car was turned off, and both cars left together. A few minutes later the windows of the house went black and Adelaide and I were staring at nothing.

"What do you think?" Adelaide asked as we turned away from the window.

"It could have been a lot of things," I said. "Maybe the police were called because somebody was sick. Maybe the two men in the plain car were doctors. Maybe our neighbor thought he saw a prowler. I guess if we really wanted to find out the thing to do would be to ask him."

The next evening I got in the car and drove down the road to do just that.

"It's because I'm a burglar," our neighbor answered me amiably.

I stood there and blinked, twice. I'd introduced myself when he'd answered the door, and he'd introduced himself as Jack Hogan and invited me inside and offered me a drink. After a few minutes' exploratory conversation with the tanned and handsome man, I'd gotten around to asking him about the commotion at his house we'd witnessed last night, offering our help if anything was wrong.

"The police were here to harass me," Jack Hogan went on. "Lieutenant Faber and his friends. I humor the lieutenant because I understand he acts out of frustration."

"But if you're innocent – " I said in a rather dumbfounded way.

"But I'm not innocent," Hogan said freely, his gray eyes as sincere as his voice. "Though if you tell anyone I said so I'll deny it. Lieutenant Faber knows I'm guilty, but he can't do anything about it because I'm too smart for him. That's the fun of it."

I didn't know if Hogan was joking or not. When I took a sip of my drink some of it spilled on my hand.

"A burglary was committed a few nights ago," Hogan said, offering me his neatly folded handkerchief to dry my fingers. "They know I did it but they don't know how, or what I did with the loot. Oh, they come and search here every now and then, but we both know they won't find anything. And if a young lady is prepared to testify that I spent the time of the robbery in her presence, where does it all leave poor Lieutenant Faber?"

"Where I am, I suppose," I said. "Confused."

"Well, no need to be confused. I say what's the sense of getting away with something if nobody knows about it? Surely you can understand that. Then too, there's the profit. Burglary is a thriving business. How else could I afford all this, living alone in a ten-room house with a pool, nights on the town, flashy women, flashy cars? A wonderful life. I admit to you, I need all that."

"Then, in a way, it's all a game," I said slowly.

"Of course it's a game. Everybody plays his own game. I just admit mine because I'm good enough to get by with it even though it is illegal."

"But it's wrong," I said, trying to bat down his clearly stated logic.

"Sure, it's wrong," Hogan said, "but so's cheating on your income tax, overcharging the public if you're a big corporation, leaving a penny for a paper when you don't have a dime. To tell you the truth, I don't worry about right or wrong."

"I guess you don't."

"You see," Hogan explained earnestly, "it's the challenge. I like nice things; I indulge myself. When I see something of value I take it. I guess I have to take it."

"Kleptomania on a grand scale, huh?"

"Hey, you might say that!" He raised his glass and grinned.

I finished my drink and got up to leave. Hogan walked with me to the door. On the porch I noticed that the long blue convertible was gone, replaced by an even longer and more expensive tan convertible. Hogan saw me looking at the car.

"Don't worry," he said. "It's not stolen and it doesn't belong to a girl I have hidden in the house. You didn't interrupt anything and I can afford to trade cars any time I feel like it. Say," he said, pointing at the long car, "how do you like it?"

"Beautiful," I said.

"Sure, and it cost a hunk of cash. Well, drop by again, why don't you? Bring the wife and we'll take a dip in the pool."

I walked down the driveway to where my car was parked. I didn't know what to think of our new neighbor. I was sure he wasn't joking, and I must admit I reacted as a lot of people would react. There was a sense of resentment in me that the things I worked so hard for, this man simply went out and took. And yet I found that I couldn't really dislike Jack Hogan. I waved to him as I started the engine and drove away.

When I told Adelaide about the visit she didn't believe me. I didn't blame her.

"You'd have to talk to him to understand how he thinks," I told her. "You might describe him as an honest crook."

"An honest crook?"

"Well, honest about being crooked, anyway."

That confused Adelaide almost as much as I was confused, so I had a snack, went over some work I'd brought home then went to bed.

Neither Adelaide or myself mentioned our neighbor for a while as we busied ourselves about our new home. Though I noticed that Adelaide kept a pair of binoculars in the bedroom now, and she often left the house to drive past the Hogan residence and look more closely at it, I suppose to check for bikini clad guests and sports cars. Still, I don't think she really completely believed what I'd told her about Jack Hogan until Lieutenant Faber called on us one Saturday afternoon.

Adelaide and I were working in the garden she'd planted when the lieutenant drove up in his gray sedan. I stood leaning on my hoe and watched him approach. He was a harried looking man who appeared to be in his mid-forties. His straight graying hair was combed to the side over his forehead and the breeze mussed it as his lined face broke into its emotionless, professional smile. Even before he introduced himself I knew who he was.

"I hope we haven't done anything wrong," Adelaide said, returning the bland smile with one that shone.

"Wrong? No," Lieutenant Faber said. "Actually I'm a city detective and have no authority out here in the county anyway."

"And yet you drove out here to talk to us," I said thoughtfully.

"I don't speak officially, Mr Smathers," Faber said in his tired, hoarse voice. "Anything I say to you folks is off the record." He got out a cigar and lit it expertly against the breeze. "How you getting along with your neighbor down the road?"

"You mean the burglar?" I'd decided it was time to stop circling.

"You said it, not me," Lieutenant Faber said.

"Actually Mr Hogan said it. He didn't seem to mind admitting that fact to me at all."

"Oh, he admits it, all right," the lieutenant said in a voice suddenly filled with frustration, "but not to anybody who can do anything about it or prove he even said it. I could tell you some things about your neighbor that would really surprise you."

"You mean he really *is* a burglar?" Adelaide asked suddenly.

"Ask him," Lieutenant Faber said. "He'll tell you. Not that we can get anything on him. We know but we can't prove."

"He told me he was clever," I said.

Lieutenant Faber nodded bitterly. "He's been clever enough so far. We know exactly how he operates – in fact, he always seems to go to some trouble to let us know he's the one who pulled his jobs, but pinning him down's another thing. He gets rid of the loot so fast and secretly we can't get him there, and usually he knows where to find big sums of cash that can't be traced. As far as alibis are concerned, there's always some girl who's willing to testify that he was with her at his house or her apartment or some motel. We can't watch him twenty-four hours a day." The lieutenant added with an undeniable touch of envy, "He seems to have an endless supply of girls."

"He is rather handsome," Adelaide said, and when we looked at her she blushed slightly. "I mean, he would be to a certain type of woman."

"The type he's handsome to will lie for him," Faber said, "that's for sure. He must have something working for him."

"Money," I said. "If used properly money will buy almost anything, and Hogan strikes me as the kind who knows how to use his wealth."

"That'd be okay," Lieutenant Faber said, "only it's other people's wealth. Just last week we know – off the record, of course – that he burglarized over three thousand in cash and five thousand in loot from the home of J. Grestom, president of Grestom Chemical."

"Isn't that the plant about four miles from here?" Adelaide asked. "The one that dumps all that sludge into the Red Fox River?"

"The same," Lieutenant Faber said, "one of the biggest operations of its kind in the state."

"Sounds like Robin Hood," I remarked.

"Yeah," the lieutenant said without amusement, "Hogan steals from the rich, only he doesn't give to anybody."

"From talking to him," I said, "my impression is that it's all a big game to him."

"A game where other people get hurt, and a game I'm tired of playing. Hogan's a crook like all crooks. He's one of the world's takers. He's a kid and the world's one big candy shop with a dumb proprietor."

I thought good manners dictated me not pointing out who that dumb proprieter must be in Hogan's mind.

"Do you think you ever will catch him?" Adelaide asked.

Lieutenant Faber nodded. "We always do in the end. He'll make a mistake, and we'll be there to notice when he does."

"He seemed awfully confident," I said.

"Confident?" Faber snorted with disgust. "Confident's not the word. Brass is more like it! About six months ago he burglarized the payroll office of a company downtown when their safe was full – "

"You mean he's a safe-cracker too?" I interrupted.

"No, he stole the whole blasted safe. It was one of those little boxes that should have been bolted to the floor from the inside but wasn't. The worst thing is that two nights later the safe turned up empty in the middle of a place that manufactures burglar alarms – bolted to the floor!"

"It really is a game with him, isn't it?" I said.

Adelaide was laughing quietly. "You must admit he's good at his game."

"And we're good at ours!" The lieutenant's face was flushed.

"I'm sure you didn't drive up here just to inform us that we're living next to a police character," I said. By that time I was certain I'd figured out the reason for Lieutenant Faber's visit. I was right.

"What I'd like," he said, "is for you to sort of keep an eye on Hogan's house. Not spy, mind you, just keep an eye on." He drew on his cigar and awaited an answer.

I took a lazy swat at the earth with the edge of the hoe blade. "I don't see anything wrong with us telling you if anything odd goes on there," I said, "under the circumstances."

Faber exhaled smoke and handed me a white card with his name and telephone extension number. "Hogan's not used to having neighbors," he said. "That's why he bought the house he's in. He might forget about you and make a slip. Do you have a pair of binoculars or a telescope?"

I looked at Adelaide and winked so the lieutenant couldn't see me. "I think I have an old pair somewhere." That somewhere was on the edge of Adelaide's dresser, where the powerful field glasses could be used by her at a moment's notice.

"Well, it's been nice to meet you folks," Lieutenant Faber said, "and it's good of you to help. Your police department thanks you." Again he shot us his mechanical smile then turned and walked toward his car.

Adelaide and I stood and watched until he'd turned from the driveway and was gone from sight.

"Now you can really play Mata Hari," I said, going back to my hoeing.

Adelaide didn't answer as she bent down and applied the spade to the broken ground.

I left the spying – as I'd come to think of it – pretty much up to Adelaide. She spent a lot of time sitting at the bedroom window, her elbows resting on the sill as she peered intently through the field glasses. But at the end of two weeks she hadn't noticed anything really noteworthy, just the comings and goings of a high living young bachelor of wealth.

She was sitting concentrating through the glasses one afternoon when the doorbell chimed. I rose from where I was lying on the bed reading and went downstairs to answer it.

When the door swung open there was Jack Hogan, dressed in swimming trunks and smiling, with a brightly colored striped towel slung about his neck.

"How about taking me up on that swimming invitation now?" he asked. "The temperature's over ninety, so I thought it'd be a good time."

I was a little surprised to see him, a little off balance. "Uh, sure, if it's okay with Adelaide." I stepped back. "Come on in and I'll ask her."

When I went upstairs Adelaide was still at the window with her eyes pressed to the binoculars.

"Jack Hogan's downstairs," I said. "He wants to know if we'll go swimming with him in his pool."

Adelaide turned abruptly and looked up at me, her eyes wide and appearing even wider due to the red circles about them left by the binoculars. "But I thought he was in his beach house! I've been waiting for him to come out!"

"You'll wait a long time, darling. He's in our living room. Do you want to go?"

"Swimming? Do you?"

"I don't see why we shouldn't. It is a hot day." I changed quickly into my swimming trunks and went downstairs to tell Jack Hogan we'd be ready to go as soon as Adelaide had changed.

Adelaide had on her skimpiest black bikini when she came downstairs. I saw Hogan look with something like momentary shock at her tanned and shapely body.

This was the first time they'd met, at least close up. After introductions we drove to Hogan's house in his long tan convertible. Seated beside him was an amply proportioned blonde who looked as if she might have been used to model the car on TV. He introduced her as Prudence, which I didn't think fitted, and we were on our way.

As we splashed around, drank highballs and got better acquainted, I found that I liked Jack Hogan, though I must still admit to some jealousy and distaste that he could come by all he had so easily while I worked so hard for less. What surprised me was that Adelaide seemed to like Hogan too. Adelaide had had a father who'd deserted her, who'd been much like Hogan, free spending and dishonest. She had hated him until the day he died, perhaps still hated his memory. And yet from time to time I could see some of her father in Adelaide, under the surface of the careful, thrifty and loving woman she really was. I saw some of that wildness and daring now as she stood on Hogan's tanned shoulders and let him flip her out and into the deep water.

When we got out of the pool and went inside for snacks I noticed an expensive looking, lewd silver statuette of Bacchus on a low table in the entrance hall. It could hardly escape my attention because Jack Hogan flicked it with his finger as we walked past.

"I stole that earlier this year," he said, "or rather one just like it. The stolen one had the owner's name engraved on the bottom, so I sold it and used the proceeds to buy this exact duplicate. Lieutenant Faber really thought he had me when he discovered that statue sitting there, but when we checked for the owner's engraving it wasn't there, and I could hardly have removed it without any trace. It drove the lieutenant almost wild." Hogan chuckled as he led us into the large kitchen with an attached dining area.

"I don't think I've ever met anyone like you," Adelaide said to Hogan with a bewildered little laugh.

Prudence, the busty blonde, popped a potato chip with cheese dip into her mouth. "Oh, there isn't anyone else like Jackie!"

I could only agree as I mixed myself another highball.

From the time of the little impromptu swimming party on, I began to notice things. It seemed to me that Adelaide spent more and more time spying from the window for Lieutenant Faber. And she found excuses to drive into the city more and more often. And on occasions when I came home from work I noticed that her hair near the base of her skull appeared damp. Did I only imagine the faint scent of chlorine those evenings as she served dinner?

It seemed, too, that Adelaide and I were caught up in more and more domestic quarrels, and we'd seldom quarreled before. She accused me of having ignored her through the years, spending all my free time and weekends working.

It didn't take long for me to be ninety percent sure that Adelaide and Jack Hogan were conducting an affair behind my back. But would I ever be more than ninety percent sure? Hogan managed his love life as he did his burglaries, with such practiced skill that the victims of his callousness could only suspect but never prove, maybe not even to themselves. For a long time I deliberated before taking any action.

There was never any doubt in my mind that I would take some sort of action. I couldn't allow things to go on as they were, and I felt confident that I could do something about them. A man who's hard to best in business is hard to best in any other phase of life.

What I finally did was go to see Lieutenant Faber.

The lieutenant's office was small, littered and dirty. There were no windows, and dented gray file cabinets stood behind the cluttered desk where Lieutenant Faber sat. As I entered he glanced up with his uneasy, weary look – then managed to smile at me.

"Have a seat, Mr Smathers," he said, motioning toward a chair with a tooth-marked yellow pencil. "I take it you've come here because you know something about Jack Hogan." I couldn't help but notice the hope in his voice.

"In a way that's why I'm here," I said, and watched the wariness creep into the lieutenant's narrow eyes as he settled back in his desk chair.

"What is it that you observed?" he asked.

"Nothing that really pertains to his burglaries, Lieutenant. In fact, nothing of use to you at all."

Faber let the pencil drop onto the desk top with a resonant little clatter. "Why don't we talk straight to each other, Mr Smathers? Save time, yours as well as mine."

"All right, I came here to ask you for a favor."

"Favor?" His gray eyebrows rose slowly.

"Yes," I said, "I wonder if you could arrange for me to have some infra red binoculars. I think most of what goes on at Hogan's house happens after dark, and it would help if I could see through that darkness."

Lieutenant Faber rolled his tongue to one side of his mouth and looked thoughtful. "Seems like a good idea," he said. "I can get you the field glasses within a few days."

"Fine. Should I pick them up here?"

"If you'd like." Lieutenant Faber looked even more thoughtful. "What is it you think you're going to see at night?" he asked.

I shrugged. "Who knows? That's why I want the infra red binoculars."
I stood to leave.

"I'll give you a telephone call when you can pick them up," the lieutenant
said, standing behind his desk.

"Call me at my office," I told him, "anytime during the day."

"Why not your home?"

"Because my office would be more convenient."

He came from around the desk and walked with me to the door.
"Mr Smathers," he said in a confidential voice, "I want Jack Hogan any
way I can get him. Do you understand?"

"I thought you wanted him that badly," I said as I went out.

That very evening, when I awoke after dozing off while watching television,
I found a gold cigarette lighter beneath the sofa cushions. During my sleep
my hand had gotten itself wedged between the cushions, and when I freed
it my fingertips had just brushed the hard, smooth surface.

When I rolled back the cushion I saw the lighter, with the initials J. H.
engraved on it. I knew it would also have J. H.'s fingerprints on it, so I
lifted it gently by the corners and slipped it into my breast pocket before
Adelaide came into the room.

Lieutenant Faber telephoned my office in the middle of the week to say
I could drop by headquarters and pick up the infra red binoculars. So
I wouldn't waste any valuable working time, I drove to see him on my
lunch hour.

The binoculars were in a small case sitting on the edge of his desk. I sat
down and examined them and he shoved a receipt across the desk top for
me to sign.

"You suspect Jack Hogan is seeing your wife, don't you?" he said in a
testing voice.

I didn't look at him as I hastily scrawled my signature on the pink receipt.
"Yes, and I want to know for sure."

"And what happens if you do find out they're seeing each other?"

I handed the receipt back to him and rested the binoculars in my lap.
"What would happen if a burglary was committed and evidence pointing
to Hogan was found at the scene?"

"Then all we'd have to worry about would be breaking down his
customary alibi."

"And if he had no alibi? If he was actually home alone at the time of
the burglary but couldn't prove it because of a witness's testimony that he
saw him leave then return?"

Lieutenant Faber ran his tongue over his dry lips. "That's what
I've been waiting for, only Hogan has never dropped a clue in his
life."

Gingerly I reached into my pocket and dropped the gold cigarette lighter with Jack Hogan's initials onto Faber's desk. As he reached for it I grabbed his hand.

"I think you'll find it has Hogan's fingerprints on it."

Lieutenant Faber leaned back away from the cigarette lighter as if it were something that might explode. I saw his glance dart to his office door to make sure it was closed, and at that moment I was very sure of him.

"Where did you get it?" he asked.

"Under the sofa cushions in my home."

"And you're giving it to me?"

I nodded. "And I don't require a receipt."

Lieutenant Faber slowly unwrapped the cellophane wrapper from one of his cigars. As he held a match to the cigar he looked at me over the rising and falling flame. Then he·flattened the cellophane wrapper, slid it deftly beneath the gold lighter and placed both lighter and cellophane in his desk drawer.

"For the next three weekends," I said, "I plan to tell my wife I have to leave town on business from Thursday evening until Monday morning. Instead I'll stay at a motel outside of town, and I'll spend my nights on a hillside watching Hogan's house."

"From Thursday night to Monday morning," Lieutenant Faber repeated slowly.

"When you find the right burglary case, call me at the motel, and I'll tell you if Hogan was home alone that night. Then you 'discover' the lighter at the scene of the crime and I testify that I saw Hogan drive away and that he was gone during the time the robbery was committed."

"One thing," Lieutenant Faber said. "What if . . .?"

"That's possible," I told him, "but Adelaide will hardly be in a position to say she was at Hogan's house all night, will she? Especially considering the fact that she knows he's a burglar anyway and deserves to be caught. She can't afford to be like his swinging single alibis."

Lieutenant Faber nodded and I stood and carefully tucked the binocular case beneath my arm.

"I'll let you know what motel I'll be staying at," I said to him as I started to leave.

"Smathers." He stopped me. "I want you to know I'm doing this because of what I think of Hogan. He's a – "

And the lieutenant told me in the purplest language I'd ever heard just what he thought of Jack Hogan.

I will say Adelaide put on a good act. When I told her about my upcoming business trips she acted convincingly upset by the idea of being left alone. She even stood in the doorway and waved wistfully after me as I got into a cab for the drive to the airport.

Only I didn't go to the airport. I had the cabbie drive me to a car rental agency where I rented a compact sedan. Then I drove to Sleepy Dan's

Motel and checked in. If I worked it right, I could write all this off as business expenses. And I was smart enough to have set up a plan that would require me to miss only three days, Fridays, in three weeks at the office. I could even sneak in and do some work on Sunday when no one was there if need be. I congratulated myself on my cleverness as I lay down to get a little sleep before sunset.

The spot I'd picked was perfect, a small clearing on the side of a hill from where I could look directly down at Hogan's large house and grounds. The powerful binoculars brought everything near to me, and the infra red lenses eliminated the darkness as a problem. The night was warm, and I unbuttoned my shirt and settled back to watch until morning.

There were no results that first week. Lieutenant Faber sounded disappointed when I told him on the phone of Jack Hogan's activities. A burglary had been committed that would have been perfect for our purposes, but I had to tell him that at the time Hogan wasn't home and I didn't know where he'd gone. Lieutenant Faber suggested hopefully that he might have gone to my house, but I quickly told him he could rule that out. My house was in view from where I watched also. We decided to wait for an opportunity we could be absolutely sure of.

The second week that I stationed myself on the hillside something did happen. My wife's affair with Jack Hogan was confirmed beyond even the slightest doubt.

It was about midnight when I saw the headlights turn from the road into Hogan's driveway. As I pressed the binoculars to my eyes and adjusted the focus dial, I saw that it was Adelaide's car that had pulled into Hogan's big double garage to park alongside his convertible. He stepped out onto the porch and met her, and they kissed for an embarrassingly long time before going inside. A few hours later I saw them emerge from the house and go for a late night swim. I didn't want to watch that, so I lowered the binoculars and sat feeling the numbness in me give way to a smoldering rage.

The next night nothing happened. Hogan spent the entire night alone, going to bed about ten o'clock. I suppose he was tired.

That afternoon Lieutenant Faber called me at the motel. A residence in the west end had been burglarized the night before, smoothly and professionally. There were no clues of any kind.

I told him that Hogan had spent the night home alone. The burglary had to have taken place during the early morning hours, so we agreed that I would say I saw Hogan leave in his convertible at two thirty a.m. and return at five. Tomorrow morning, when Lieutenant Faber returned to question the victim and re-examine the scene of the crime, he would "find" the gold lighter, and the frame around Jack Hogan would be complete.

There was really no reason to go back that third night, but the silent rage had grown in me along with my curiosity. And I suppose it gave me some small sense of power, to be able to watch them without them knowing. It kept me from being a complete fool, and while Hogan didn't know it, he had only one more night of freedom.

All that dark, hot night Adelaide didn't arrive at Hogan's home. The windows of the big ranch house were dark, the grounds silent. Around me the crickets chirped madly as if protesting the heat as I sat staring intently through the binoculars.

Then a light came on in one of the windows, the window I knew to be Jack Hogan's bedroom. After a while a downstairs light came on too, and both lights stayed on. I looked at my watch. Four-thirty.

He must have telephoned her. At twenty to five Adelaide turned her car into Hogan's driveway. This time after she pulled her car into the garage Hogan came out and lowered the door, for the sun would soon rise. I watched as he put his arm around her and they went into the house.

The sun came up amid orange streaks on the horizon, turning the heat of night into an even more intense heat.

Then I heard a door slam off in the distance, and I scanned, then focused the binoculars on Adelaide in her skimpy black bikini. Hogan was beside her with a towel draped over his shoulder. He flicked her playfully with the towel and she laughed and dived into the pool, and he laughed and jumped in after her.

I watched them for about twenty minutes before I came to my decision.

Jack Hogan had always freely admitted being a burglar. Now I intended to play his game, to tell him openly what was going to happen to him, so that he'd know he'd been outsmarted. Let the knowledge that he couldn't prove his innocence torment him. Let him suffer as he'd made Lieutenant Faber suffer, as he'd made his burglary victims suffer. As he'd made me suffer. I placed the binoculars in their case, stood and clambered down the hillside to where the car was parked.

Then it occurred to me that Hogan might give me a rough time once he realized he was cornered, so I drove by my house first and got my forty-five caliber revolver from my dresser drawer.

They were sitting in lounge chairs alongside the pool when I approached, Adelaide leaning forward and Hogan rubbing suntan lotion onto her back.

"How's the water?" I asked calmly.

They whirled, surprised, then Hogan smiled. "It's great," he said jauntily. "I've invited Adelaide over here before for an early morning swim, but this is the first time she's come."

"I know better," I said, watching Adelaide trying to control the fear and guilt that marked her features. At last she managed a facsimile of a poker face.

"Know better?" Hogan was still playing innocent.

"Yes, and now there are a few things I want you to know. There was a burglary committed night before last in the west end. No clues yet."

Hogan appeared puzzled. "So what? I was home in bed all that night."

"For the last several week-ends I've been spying on you from that hillside," I said. "Lieutenant Faber gave me infra red binoculars to use at night. I'm going to swear that I saw you leave and return at the time that burglary took place."

"You can't!" Adelaide said in a high voice.

"Quiet, dear." I looked again at Hogan. He was grinning.

"Your word against mine, old pal. I've beat that one before."

"I believe you lost your initialed gold cigarette lighter," I said. "It has your fingerprints on it and it's going to be found at the scene of the crime."

Now anger showed on Hogan's handsome face. "By Lieutenant Faber, would be my guess."

"Your guess is correct. We're framing you and sending you to prison, to put it plainly."

"As I've always put it, huh?"

I nodded and couldn't help a faint, gloating smile. Hogan's game and he was getting beat at it. "Lieutenant Faber told me you were one of the world's takers," I said. "Well, I'm one of the world's keepers. I don't give up what I have easily."

"Faber was right about that," Hogan said frankly. "I'm a taker. I can't see something of value without taking it."

"Something like Adelaide?"

"Exactly."

"Your mistake," I said tauntingly, "was in trying to take something from me. I'll think of you from time to time when you're in prison." I turned to go home, leaving Adelaide to return when she felt like it.

"It won't work," her voice said behind me.

I turned around and saw that the fear and surprise had left Adelaide's face completely to be replaced by a look of determination.

"And why won't it work?" I asked.

"Because I'll swear in court that I spent that entire night with Jack."

I started to laugh incredulously at her, but the laugh wouldn't come out. "But you were at home."

"Alone," Adelaide said. "You could never prove it. I'll swear I was here instead."

"You'd swear to that in a courtroom, under oath?" I stared at her, feeling the sun on the back of my moist shirt. "But why?"

"I don't think you'd understand."

"Now listen!"

"Nothing more to listen to, or say," Adelaide said, and as a pretense for getting away from me she turned and walked toward the diving board.

Hogan lowered himself into the shallow water with an infuriating smile.

"Nothing more to say, old pal. Sorry." And he actually looked as if he might be sorry, the gracious winner.

The sun seemed to grow hotter, unbearably hot, sending beads of sweat darting down my flesh inside my shirt. I looked up and saw Adelaide poised gracefully on the end of the diving board, tanned and beautiful in her tiny swimming suit as she carefully avoided a glance in my direction.

How the revolver got from my pocket into my hand I honestly don't know. I have no recollection of it, a magician's trick. And I don't remember pulling the trigger.

Adelaide was raising her arms, preparing to dive, when the gun roared in my hand as if of its own will. I saw Adelaide's body jerk, saw the spray of blood, heard the scream as she half fell-half jumped awkwardly from the diving board, arms and legs thrashing as she struck the water. Then there was a choking sound and she stopped thrashing and floated motionless face up.

Hogan stroked toward the ladder, a look not of shock or horror on his face, but an expression that suggested he might be very sick. "Oh, God, Smathers!" he said as he started to climb the chrome ladder. I let him get to the second step before blasting him back into the pool.

I stood there then, pulling the trigger automatically, emptying the revolver into their bodies.

Considering how large the pool was, it was amazing how quickly all the water turned red.

So now I'm sitting here awaiting trial, writing this to kill time, though I'm sure the hour will come when I'll pray I had this time back. There isn't any doubt in my mind that I'll be convicted. They have my full confession, and now they'll have this.

What concerns me is that all my life I've tried to be a decent sort of man, hard working, industrious. I'm not very religious, but I have tried to live by the ten commandments, breaking them every now and then, of course, like everybody else. And yet if you went back and read over this again you could put your finger on spot after spot until you'd realize that between the four of us, me, Adelaide, Jack Hogan and Lieutenant Faber, in one way or another we've broken every single commandment.

Evil spreads, I suppose, like the red through the water in Hogan's swimming pool.

EFFECTIVE MEDICINE

B. Traven

1

ONE AFTERNOON, ON coming home from the cotton field where I had worked all day long, I noted, outside the barbed wire fence of the bungalow I was living in, a Mexican peasant squatting on the bare ground. I did not know him because, as I learned later in the evening, he was from another village six or seven miles away. He was very poor and all in rags.

Having greeted me he waited patiently until I had dismounted from the burro I had been riding home on. When I had taken off the saddle and the burro had gone its way looking for cornstalks in the yard, the Mexican entered the front yard, came close and began talking.

He talked rapidly and in a confused manner. For a moment I thought him to be on the high – that is to say, that he might have smoked more marijuana than he could digest. However, though he was now telling the end of his story, now the beginning, now the middle, all in confusion, I soon noticed that he was neither drunk nor doped, only very ignorant and evidently suffering from a nervous breakdown – as far as this can happen to a Mexican of his kind.

It was difficult for me to make sense of his story and for a long while I was unable to see which part of his story was the end and which the beginning or the middle. The farther he came in his story the more was he swept away by his emotion until he only blubbered or shouted absolutely incoherent phrases. Never once did he fully end his tale. Whenever I thought him close to the end and I was trying to catch up with the full meaning, I realized that he was already telling his story from the middle backwards to the start again. In this confused way he told me his story more than a dozen times and always with the same words, out of a vocabulary which barely consisted of more than three hundred different words. His mood changed constantly. Each time he started as if he were telling the story of somebody else, yet invariably he ended up crying almost hysterically.

"Look here, señor doctor, that old hussy and tramp that she is and always was, she is gone. She is gone with that ugly cabron and dirty son of a heathenish dog, that thief Pánfilo, you know him, señor, the one I mean, that would steal the horns of the devil if they were not grown on, you know that housebreaker, and if you don't know him, so much the better for you because he steals barbed wire and cuts telegraph poles and the telegraph wire also and no hog is safe if he is around. I wish him the smallpox all over his face and the most terrible disease extra to make it worse for him. I come home. I come home from my work in the bush. In the bush I had to cut down hard trees for making charcoal; you see. I sell the wood and the charcoal if I have any to the agents – who are thieves, too. I come home tired and hungry. Home in my jacalito. I'm hungry more than a dog, that's what I am, from hard work in the bush. No tortillas ready. No frijoles in the pot. Nothing. I tell you the truth, señor doctor, nothing. I call my woman, that old hussy. My *mujer* I mean. No answer. I look around. She isn't at home, my woman isn't. Her sack with her dress in it, and her shirt and her torn stockings, which are in that same sack also, are all gone. The sack used to hang on a peg. My *mujer* has ran away. She doesn't ever return. Never, such what I say. And she is so full of lice too, my woman is. I've no tortillas for me to eat. Nor black beans for my empty belly. Off she went like the stinking hussy that she is. If I only knew who she ran off with, that useless old nag. I'll get *him*. And I'll learn him how to steal decent and honest women that belong to other men. He is a *mil* times worse than any dirty cabron." (*Mil* means thousand; to his kind, though, *mil* means anything between one hundred and one thousand billions.) "Now, I ask you, mister doctor señor, who will make tortillas for me? That's what I want you to tell me right now."

So he asked, but he did not wait for my answer and he went on with his story, hardly stopping to catch a full breath.

"Nobody is going to make me tortillas now. That's what it is, I tell you. She has ran away. I'll catch *him* and he won't live to tell who done it. I come home in my *choza*. I come home from the hot bush. Hungry and dying of thirst. I don't mind the thirst. I come home and no tortillas. No frijoles. She is gone. She has taken her sack with her dress and her stockings along with her."

At this point of his sad story he cried so bitterly that for the next three minutes it was difficult to understand what he was saying now because it was all blubbering. Slowly he calmed down once more. Yet, crying or not crying, he talked on and on like a cracked phonograph record.

"I come home. From the bush I come home and I've worked all day long under that blistering sun and no – "

"Now wait a minute, *manito*," I interrupted him before he went into his speech again and made it impossible for me to stop him before he reached that part of his story where he would have to cry for a few minutes. "Let's talk this over quietly. You've told me your heartbreaking experience fifteen times by now. I admit it is heartbreaking. But I can't listen to it a *mil* times because I've got other things to attend to. All I can say is that your *mujer* is not here in my jacal. Step in and look around and make sure."

"I know, señor mister, that she isn't in your house. A fine educated doctor like you would never even touch such a filthy one like her, and so full of lice that sometimes you might think the wind is in her hair, so fast it moves from all the lice in it."

The lice seemed to remind him once more of his loss and he started telling the story again. The whole thing began to bore me and I said: "Why, for hell's sake, do you have to tell all that just to me? Go to the alcalde – the mayor, I mean – and tell him your story. He is the proper person to attend to such matters. I'm just a simple doctor here without any political influence and no disputado backing me up. I've no power and so I can do nothing for you. Nothing, do you hear? Nothing at all. Go to the alcalde. He'll catch your *mujer*. It's his duty, because he is the authority in this place."

"That alcalde, you mean, señor? I can tell you right now and here that he is the biggest ass under heaven. That's why he was elected alcalde. And he is a thief too, and also a woman-raper. Just for his meanness and his stupidity it was that he got elected because no decent and no honest person had any word in that election, see? You ought to know that, señor."

"Anyway, amigo," I said, "he has to look after your troubles. And as I said before, I've no power, no power at all, to do anything for you. Get this in your mind, friend. I've no power."

"But you're wrong, mister caballero. You've got all the powers in the world. We know this very well. And no mistake. You can pull bullets out of the bodies of killed bandits with fishing hooks and make them live again. I mean the boys with federal bullets in their bellies and legs. You understand what I want to say and what I know and what the *federales* would be so very eager to know also. Because you have all the powers to do anything under heaven. That's why you know where my woman is at this hour. Tell her that I'm hungry and that I've come home from the bush after much hard work. She has to make tortillas and cook frijoles for me. I'm very hungry now."

"Now look here, friend. Let's be calm about it." I spoke to him as I would have to a little boy. "See here, I've not seen your woman go away. Since I've not seen where she went I can't tell you where she is at present. I can't even imagine where she perhaps might be. In fact, I know nothing, nothing at all. I don't even know her face or what she looks like. Please, amigo, do understand, I know nothing of her. And that'll be all. Thank you for paying me such a delightful visit. Now I'm busy. Good-bye. Adiós."

He stared at me with his brown dreamy eyes as if in wonder. His belief in the infallibility of a white, and particularly in the immaculate perfection of a Norte-americano had been shaken profoundly. At the same time, though, he seemed to recall something which had evidently been hammered into his head since he could speak his first words, and that was something which, in his opinion, was forever connected with the Americanos, as is the color green with young grass.

So he said: "I'm not rich, señor. No, I'm not. I can't pay you much. I've only two pesos and forty-six centavitos. That's all I have in the world. But this whole fortune of mine I'll give you for your work and for your medicine so that I can find my woman and get her back to my side, that hussy, because I am very hungry."

"I don't want your money. Even if you would give me *mil* gold pesos I could not get your woman back. I don't know where she is and therefore I can't tell her that you must have your tortillas and your frijoles. Can't you understand, man, that I don't know where your woman is?"

Suspicion was in his eyes when he looked at me after I had finished. He was quite evidently not certain whether it was the little money he could offer me which kept me from helping him or that in fact I might really not know the whereabouts of his spouse.

Gazing for a few minutes at me in this manner he finally shook his head as if full of doubts about something of which he had thought himself very sure before. Honoring me once more with that suspicious glance, he left my place but not until I had told him several times more that I had to cook my dinner and could no longer stand idly around and listen to his troubles, for which I had no remedies.

As I learned a few days later, he visited practically all the huts of the village, where he told his story and reported also that this white medicine-man of whom they talked so highly was but a poor faker, ignorant of the simplest things of everyday life.

This low opinion of his was taken by the villagers for a grave insult upon themselves, since I was the pride of the whole community, who considered me one of the wisest and greatest medicine-men that have ever walked the earth. I do not know, but I can fairly well guess, what the villagers recommended him to do so as to make my mysterious powers work in his favor.

2

Shortly after sunrise next day he returned to my place, placed himself outside by the barbed-wire fence, and waited there peacefully until I noticed his presence and came out to speak to him.

The moment he saw me feeding corn to my burro he called me. "Just for a very, very little short moment, señor mister, please. Please, come here close to the fence and listen what I've got to tell you. And you'd better listen terribly carefully because I'm serious. As a plain matter of fact I'm extremely serious this morning, because I haven't slept very much."

On stepping up to the fence I noted that while I was approaching he picked up from the ground a long machete which as I could see easily had been sharpened with utmost care. It must have taken him hours to give that heavy sword-like bushknife such an almost razorlike edge.

Nonchalantly, though meaningfully, he moved this machete up and down before my eyes while he was talking again. Occasionally, just as nonchalantly, he examined the edge with his wetted thumb, and now and then pulling a hair out of his thick black scalp and cutting his hair softly, practically by only touching it with the edge. Whenever he did so he looked at me as if to make sure that I was observing how sharp that machete really was.

"So you won't tell me where my *esposa* is, señor?"

"It seems," I answered with dignity, "that you have a very good and very excellent machete. Looks like well-tempered steel to me."

"And good steel it is. And it has been made in your country. There you may be assured that it is the finest and the best steel we can buy down here. You'd better not make the mistake thinking that it might be German made, because a German made is no good, you cannot even cut cheese with it; if you try that the edge is gone for good. But they are very cheap. Only you cannot cut trees with them, not the sort we have got here in the bush. But the one I have got here will do anything I want it to do."

"Let me have a close look at it," I pleaded.

He put it through the fence but held the haft fast in his hand.

"This won't do at all. I must get a swing at it to see how good it is. I know something about steel."

"Oh no, señor mister, I won't let you have it. This excellent machete won't leave my hands, not before I know where my woman is. Just touch the edge. See. Now I think you'll understand that with one single stroke I could chop off the head of a burro from its trunk like cutting through wet mud. But should it be the head of a man, even that of a gringo, instead of that of a poor burro, I tell you, señor, I wouldn't need to make half so hard a stroke as I would have to use for a burro, with a machete having an edge like this one, and made in your own country, where the best steel comes from. What do you think, señor?"

"Since you ask me, friend, I think a bullet is even quicker than a machete, and more certain too."

"Maybe. Surely it is. But a bullet, without a gun to fire it, is not much to compare with such a good American-made machete. Everybody here in the village knows very well that you haven't got a gun, not even an old Spanish muzzler. I know this or I wouldn't perhaps bring my fine machete along with me. Understand, caballero mister?"

"I understand all right, manito. I see you want to cut my fence-posts and carry them away. But you won't do that. You know that would be plain robbery. The *federales* would shoot you for banditry as soon as they come to this village again. It won't be long now and they will be on their way here once more looking for bandits."

"I don't need your fence posts. I wouldn't take them, not even for a gift. They're all termite-eaten anyhow and no good. I can get them better in the bush."

"Then what do you want? I've to get breakfast ready because I got to ride to my field and look after my tomatoes. I mean that I've got to go now, see, right now while the day is still cool and fresh."

"*Mil* times I have told you, señor mister, what I want. That's why I sharpened my machete. I want my woman back. You will now tell me where she is so that I can catch her and give her a terrific thrashing before I'll let her cook frijoles for me."

"And *mil* times I've told you that I don't know where your *mujer* is."

"So you still insist on telling me that you can't find her for me?"

"That's what I'm saying all the time and I don't know what to say any more. So what are you going to do about it?"

"Maybe you don't know where she is. What I know for sure is that you can find her if you wish to. I can't give you *mil* gold pesos for I haven't any. I suppose I've got to speak frankly with you, señor. In other words, if you don't tell me right away where my woman is I will be very sorry, and sorry for *you*. I mean, because in such a case I am desperate and I must chop off one head. I won't promise whose head it might be which is to be chopped off, and I can't promise either that it might not be your head which is going to be cut off with one single stroke and with that fine American-made machete too. Perhaps it will be done by mistake, so to say. In other words, señor mister, it will be your head, and no mistake about that, I am sure."

He raised his machete high up and swung it round above his head as a drunken pirate would his cutlass. It looked dangerous enough. I was cornered. I might, of course, try to escape into my bungalow. Sooner or later, though, I would have to come out and there he would be waiting for me. I had to get to my field to look after the crop, but he'd sneak up on me from behind or lay in ambush somewhere. His kind is patient. They will wait for days and weeks until they get their man. What does he care about killing somebody? He hides in the jungle. If he should finally be caught and fusilladed he will consider it his fate, which was his since he was born and from which he, in his opinion, could not have escaped nor avoided. Right now he is desperate. Without thinking of any of all the consequences which his murder will have afterwards, he, like a stubborn child, wants his wish come true immediately.

Again I told him the same thing I had told him twenty times the afternoon before. "I haven't seen the way your woman went. Therefore I don't know where she is now."

But my answer had lost its power. When he had told the villagers what sort of answer I had given him the day before, they had suggested what he ought to say if I were to tell him again that I had not seen his woman go away. He himself alone would never have come upon the answer he had in stock now, for his mind was not developed highly enough for such mental exercise. I was sure that the whole village was as much interested in the kind of medicine I would give him as he himself was.

At that hour I did not know that he had talked to the villagers about our discussion the previous afternoon. But from the way he now presented his answer, I knew immediately that it could not be his own, but that he had memorized it after being taught what to say, because he not only used words entirely new to him, but also spoke up like a bad amateur actor.

"Listen here, señor," he said, "if I'd seen the way my *mujer* went when she left I would have no need to trouble you, for in that case I could do well and perhaps better still alone, than with the help of a medicine-man. All people in the village here have told me that you are a far-seer. They have told me that you have two little black tubes sewn together to make them appear like one. They say, because they know, that if you look through these tubes you can see any man or woman or dog or burro which might walk on that faraway hill yonder, and you can see an eagle perching on a high tree a hundred miles away. You have told the folks in this village that there are people living on some of the stars, because this earth we live on is also but a star only we can't see it as a star since we are on it. All people here have watched you often when, by night, you look with your black tubes up to the sky so as to see the people on the stars and what they were doing at that time of night and how they lived there and how many cattle they had."

I remembered I had said something to this effect to a few of the younger men of the community.

"You've also told here that wise men in your country to the north have another black tube, by which they can look straight into the inside of any man or woman to see if there is a bullet there and where it is located, so that these medicine-men of yours can get the bullet out without cutting open the wrong part of the body. More you have said. You have said that white men can talk to other white men who are *mil* and more *mil* miles away and they can talk to one another without shouting just the way as I talk to you now, and that they don't even need a copper wire on which their words run along, as do telegraph-wires in our country. I want you to talk right now and before my eyes to my woman, and tell her that I am hungry and that I've no tortillas and no frijoles to eat. And I want you to tell her to come right home, and that she has to come home on one of those air-wagons you have said your people ride on when they are in a hurry. And I am in an awful hurry now."

Having finished his speech with the difficulty an urchin has saying his catechism at Sunday school he began again swinging his machete pirate-fashion, obviously with the intention of making his demands more imperative.

What was I to do? If I got the better of him and clubbed him down, everybody in the village would accuse me of having killed a poor, ignorant, but honest Mexican peasant, who had done me no harm and had never meant to do me any, and who had not even insulted me, but had only come, a very humble human, to another human, asking for help which no good Christian would have denied him.

I had to do something to get me out of the hole I was in, and in which I did not feel very comfortable. As I was considered one of the greatest medicine-men, there remained nothing else for me to do but to rely on medicine. The only question was, what sort of medicine I was to use to cure myself of his desperation, and of his machete which, as he demonstrated over and over again, would cut a hair as if by magic. The medicine to be served had to be of a special kind – that is, it had to be effective enough to save both of us at the same time.

At this precious moment, when I was thinking which of the gods I might call upon for a good idea and a better medicine, there flashed through my tortured mind a mental picture of two black tubes sewn together in such a way that they might look like one.

"With your kind permission and just one minute," I said to him and went into my bungalow.

Out I came, carrying in my hands my modest fieldglass. I carried it before me with a great solemnity, as if it were the holiest object under heaven.

I stepped close to the fence where the Mexican stood, high expectancy in his eyes.

In a mumbled voice I now spoke to the glass, moving it at the same time around over my head, now to the left, now to the right, also moving it towards the man who was watching me with an ever-growing bewilderment.

Now I pressed the glass firmly to my eyes. I bent down and searched the ground while walking round and round, slowly lifting up the glass until it was at a level with the far horizon. For many minutes I scanned the horizon, searching every part of it while moving round in a circle. And I said, loud enough so that he would understand it: "*Donde estás, mujer?* Where are you, woman? Answer, or I'll make you by hell's or heaven's force!"

Another idea came to my mind at this minute. I whispered to him: "Where's the village you come from?"

He tried to answer. His excitement did not allow him to speak, though he had his mouth wide open. He swallowed several times and then pointed, with one arm only slightly raised towards north.

So I knew that I had to find his woman towards south to make my medicine work properly for his benefit and mine.

Now, all of a sudden, I yelled: "I see her. *Ya la veo.* I see her. There she is now, at last. Poor woman. Oh, that poor, poor woman. A man beats her terribly. He has a black moustache, that man who beats her has. I don't know who he is. I am sure I've seen him once or twice in this village here. Oh, that devil of a man, how he beats that poor woman. And she cries out loud: '*Ay mi hombre,* my dear husband, come, come quick and help me; fetch me away from that brute who has taken me by force and without my will; I want to come home and cook frijoles for you because I know you must be hungry after so much hard work in the bush; help me, help me, come quick!' That's what she cries. Oh, I can't stand it any longer; it's too terrible."

I was breathing heavily, as if entirely exhausted from the trance I had been in.

No sooner had I stopped and taken the glass off my eyes than the man, sweat all over his face, shouted as if going mad! "Didn't I tell you, señor? I knew all the time that it must be that dirty dog Pánfilo who has raped her. He has got a black moustache. I knew it all the time. He was after her since we came to this part. Always after her and always around the house whenever I was working in the bush. All the neighbors knew it because they told me so. I haven't sharpened my machete just for the fun of it. I knew that I would need a sharp edge somehow, somewhere and for someone, to cut off his stinking head. Now I'll have to hurry to get her and get at the same time that Pánfilo cabron. Where is she, señor, quick, quick, pronto, pronto, say it. Ask her. Tell her that I'm on my way already."

I looked through my glass once more and mumbled something as if asking someone a few questions. Now I said: "She is *mil* miles away from here, your woman is. The man with the black moustache has carried her far away, I think with an air-wagon, perhaps. She says that she is in Naranjitos. That's way down in that direction." I pointed towards south-east. "It is only *mil* miles from here and along a trail not so very hard to go by."

"Well, then, señor mister, excuse me, but now I have got to hurry to fetch her and leave my marks on that Pánfilo dog."

He picked up his *moral,* a little bag, from the ground. It contained all he possessed on earth, a fact which made his life and his goings so easy, and it would have made him a truly happy man had it not been for women who would never be satisfied with such a little *bast* bag instead of some solid furniture or an electric refrigerator.

He became extremely restless now, so I thought it a good opportunity to give him another shot of the medicine. "Hustle, amigo, hurry up, or, dear God in heaven, you will miss her. And don't you dare stop on your way. You know it's more than *mil* days to walk. That rascal with the black moustache is likely to carry her farther away still. You'd better go right now, this very minute."

"This certainly I will do, señor, since you say so. This very second I shall go. In fact, I'm running already." His feet were dancing about as if the ground consisted of embers. I knew that something still held him back, or he would have been a quarter of a mile off already.

It was his courtesy, the courtesy of the primitive man, that kept him still here. After a few wrong starts which seemed not to satisfy him, he at last found the right words. "Many, many thanks, señor, *mil, mil gracias* for your magnificent medicine." The word *magnifica* appeared to be one of the new words he had heard last night from the villagers, for he stumbled on it, although he would not lose the opportunity to use it for me. "The people in the village," he continued, "are right about you. Truly and verily you are a great medicine-man. You know all the hidden secrets of the world. You found her so quickly, much sooner than I could ever have expected. Of course, the two pesos and forty-six centavitos I promised you for your medicine, señor, I cannot pay now. I am very sorry for that. But you are a great doctor, surely you are, therefore you will understand that I cannot pay for the medicine now. You'll have to be satisfied with my thanks, which are honest by all means. You see, señor mister, the money I need for my trip. That's why I cannot part with my money and pay you off. You surely will understand this easily since you're such a very wise man. Adiós, señor, adiós, and again *mil, mil gracias*."

And he was off like a hunted deer, without looking back. One minute later the bush had swallowed him up.

Never have I cheated a Mexican. I did not cheat that man either. The medicine I gave him is the best he could ever get. No other doctor would have prescribed him such a good medicine.

The village I named is about five hundred miles from here. He is without funds, save these two pesos and forty-six centavos. So he will have to walk the whole way. No hitch-hiking for him, because there is no highway. As there is no highway there cannot be motor-cars. Even if there were motor-cars none would pick him up. Latin-Americans are not dumb enough to pick up strangers parked along the highways.

It is an excellent medicine for him and for me. It saves me from the surprise of finding myself with my head chopped off. He is a strong and healthy fellow, and he is used to hard work. He won't go fifty miles, and he will find some work or a job. Or he will steal a stray cow and sell it to a butcher in one of the villages through which he passes. In the meantime, and more than a half dozen times, he will have had his belly filled with tortillas, frijoles, and green chile. His belly satisfactorily full, he will forget his grief. Once he has found some work, he will stay on in a village in the end. Once there, it won't be one week before a woman will believe herself fairly lucky if allowed to cook frijoles and toast tortillas for him, and also hang her basket, or a sugar sack with her Sunday dress in it, at a peg inside the jacalito he will eventually, and quite predictably, occupy.

KILLING BERNSTEIN

Harlan Ellison

IF GOD (or Whoever's in charge) had wanted Dr Netta Bernstein to continue living, He (or She) wouldn't have made it so easy for me to kill her.

The night before, she had said again, do it again, we can do it once more, can't we; and her thick, auburn hair smelled fresh and clean and it flowed across the pillows like the sunsets we get these days. The kind that burn the eyes they're so beautiful. Our grandparents never saw such wonders of melting copper, flickering at the edges, sliding into darkness at the horizon. Exquisite beyond belief, created by pollution. Smog produces that kind of gorgeous sunset. Grandeur, created by imminent destruction. Her hair burned and slid into darkness and I buried my face in it and we made love and I didn't make any mistakes.

And the next day she acted as if she didn't know me.

Talked to me as though I were one of the test children she had in for her perception analyses. I felt waves of actual dislike coming from her. "Netta," I said, "what's the matter? Did I say something?"

She looked back at me with the expression of someone who has been asked for her driver's license or other identification at a bank where she has had an account for sixteen years. I was a troublesome new teller, a trainee, an upstart stealing her time, impertinent and callow. "Duncaster," she said, calling me by my last name, "I have work to do. Why don't you go on about your business." The night before she had called me Jimmy a hundred times in a minute.

She pretended not to know what I was talking about. I tried to be polite referring to what had happened between us. I didn't want to use the wrong words, but there were *no words* she responded to. It was as if that bed, and the two of us on it, had never existed.

I couldn't believe she could be that brutal. I left the office early that day.

And the next day she hung me out to dry. It was even more brutal than the day before. The day before, it had only been obvious dislike, go on about your business, Duncaster. But the next day we were mortal enemies. Like ancient antagonists from some primordial swamp, she was after me, and I knew it. I can't explain *how* I knew, I simply understood somewhere deep in the blood and bones that this woman was determined to rip out my throat.

Or perhaps I *can* explain it.

Take the film they made of *Jaws*. That is a terrifying film. It collapses entire audiences, and not merely because of the cinematic tricks. People in the middle of Kansas, people who've never even *seen* an ocean or a shark, go into cardiac arrest. Why should that be? There are terrors much closer to us – muggers on the streets, a positive biopsy report, being smashed to pudding in a freeway accident – terrors that *can* reach us; why should we be so petrified by that shark? I reject abstractions: the *vagina dentatus*, that paranoid hobgoblin of Freudian shadow-myth; the simplicity of our recoiling from something filled with teeth, an eating machine. I have another theory.

The shark is one of the few life forms that has come down to the present virtually unchanged from the Devonian. So few: the cockroach, the horseshoe crab, the nautilus, the coelecanth – probably older than the dinosaurs. The shark.

When we were still aquatic creatures . . . there was the shark. And even today, in the blood that boils through us, the blood whose constituency is the same as sea water, in the blood and somewhere deep in our racial memory, there is still the remembrance of the shark. Of swimming away from that inexorable eating machine, of crawling up onto the land to be safe from it, of vowing never to return to the warm seas where the teeth can reach us.

When we see the shark, we understand that *that* is one of the dreadful furies that drove us to become human beings. Natural enemy from beyond the curtain of time, from beneath the killing darkness. Natural enemies.

Perhaps I *can* explain how I knew, that next day, that Netta Bernstein and I were blood enemies.

The moment I walked into the conference room and saw her sitting next to Sloan – a clipboard fat with charts lying on the table in front of her – I knew she was lying in wait for me. The teeth, the warm seas, the eating machines that had followed us onto the land. And in that instant, I now realize, I first decided to kill her.

You have to understand how it is with a major toy company, how it works in the corporate way; otherwise it doesn't make sense . . . the killing of Netta Bernstein.

Fighting my way to the top at the MyToy Corporation had been the commitment of ten years of my life. It wouldn't have been any different at Mattel or Marx or Fisher-Price or Ideal or Hasbro or Kenner or Mego or Playskool or even Creative Playthings. The race is always to make The Big Breakthrough, to come up with the new toy that sweeps the field before the competition can work up a knockoff imitation. Barbie, G. I. Joe, Hot Wheels, they made millions for one man and one company because they were The Big Breakthroughs. In an industry where sixty percent of each year's product is brand-new, *has to be* brand-new because the kids have a saturation/boredom threshold that is not to be believed, it is the guy with The Big Breakthrough who gets to be Vice President of Product Planning, at $50,000 a year.

I was Director of Marketing Research. Gumball, Destruction Derby, Change-A-Face, those had been my weapons in the fight toward the $50,000 plateau. MyToy was one of the big five and I'd been on the rise for ten years.

But the last four ideas I'd hawked to top management had either been rejected or been put into production and bombed. The fashion-doll line had been too sophisticated – and the recession had hit; there was backlash against opulence, conspicuous consumption; and the feminist movement had come out strong against what they called "training little girls to be empty-headed clotheshorses." Dinosaur had been too impractical to produce at a reasonable per-unit cost. Pretesting had shown that kids rejected Peggy Puffin as being "ugly," even though parents found the packaging attractive; they'd buy it, but the kids wouldn't play with it. And the lousy sales reports on Mother's Helper had verified a negative transference; old learning habits had generally inhibited learning new techniques. It was what the president of MyToy, Sloan, had called "disastrously counterproductive." And I'd begun to smell the ambivalence about me. Then the doubts. Then the veiled antagonisms. The dismissals, the offhand rejections of trial balloons I'd floated. And now there was even open hostility. I was at the crunch point.

Everything was tied up in the two new projects I'd worked out with R&D. The Can-Do Chipper and the Little Miss Goodie Two-Shoes doll. Research & Development had gotten the approval to put them into preliminary design, both aimed at pre-school development markets, and Netta Bernstein had tested them in the MyToy play therapy facilities.

MyToy was the only major toy company in America to maintain a full-time staff of child and research psychologists. Netta headed the team. The prototypes had been sent to her for live evaluation with test kids. The reports filled that clipboard. Fifty thou filled that clipboard. And I knew she was out to get me.

Sloan wouldn't look at me. I went down the length of the conference table, took an empty seat between Dixon and Schwann; I was bracketed by cost accountants, a pair of minor sales potential vassals. The seat on the right hand of Brian Sloan, God of My Toy, the seat I'd held for almost ten years, was occupied by Ostlander, the hungry little turncoat from Ideal who'd come over, bringing with him design secrets worth a fortune. Not The Big Breakthrough, but enough knockoff data to pay his way to the other side.

And on the left hand of God sat Netta Bernstein.

My future lay before her fastened tight in the clipboard. Her tests with the kids would make or break me. And the night before last she had said she loved me. And the day before she had told me to go away. And today I smelled the killing darkness of the Devonian seas.

The first hour was marking time. Sales reports, prospectus for third-quarter production, a presentation about the proposed Lexington, Kentucky, plant site, odds and ends. Then Sloan said we'd hear Netta's test results on the new designs. She never looked at me.

"I'll begin with the big dolls for preschoolers," she said, releasing the clip and removing the first batch of reports. "They all reach or exceed the expectations projected by prelim. They have the 'kid appeal' Mr Sloan discussed last Thursday, with one small modification on the shopper doll. The mother model. I found, in giving the dolls to six selected groups of test children – eight in each group – that the pocket on the apron was ignored completely. The children had no use for it, and I think it can be eliminated to the advantage of the item."

Sloan looked at me. "Jimmy," he said, "what would that mean in terms of lowering the per-unit cost of the mother shopper?"

I already had my calculator out and was running the figures. "Uh, that would be . . . three cents per unit on a projected run of – " I looked at Schwann; he scribbled *3 mil* on his pad. "A run of three million units: ninety thousand dollars." It had been a most ordinary question, and an ordinary answer.

Netta Bernstein, without looking at me, said to Sloan, "I believe that figure is incorrect. The per-unit saving would be closer to 4.6 cents, for a total of one hundred and thirty-eight thousand dollars."

Sloan didn't answer. He just looked at Schwann and Dixon. They both nodded rapidly, like a pair of those Woolworth's cork birds that dip their beaks into a glass of water and then sit upright again. It would have been pointless to say the three-cents-per-unit figure had been given to me by prelim the week before and that Netta had obviously gotten more up-to-date stats on the project. It would have been pointless, not only because Sloan didn't like to hear excuses, but because Netta had clearly set out to mousetrap me. Cost stats were not her area, never had been, never should be; yet she had them. Chance? I doubted it. Either way, I looked like a doughnut.

There was a hefty chunk of silence, and then Netta went on to the test results of three other proposals, none of them mine. On one of them the changes would have been impractical, on the second the kids simply didn't like the toy, and on the third the changes would have been too expensive.

Then she was down to the last two sheafs of notes, and I smelled the warm Devonian seas again.

How I killed her was slovenly, sloppily, untidily, random, and rumpled. As she reached into the clothes closet for her bathrobe I pushed her inside and tried to strangle her. She fought me off and started to come out and I pushed her back. The clothes rack bar fell out of its brackets and we were lying in a heap on the floor. I hit her a couple of times and she hit me back, even harder than I'd hit her. Finally, I grabbed the plastic clothing bag from a dress fresh from the dry cleaners, and suffocated her with it. Then I went into her bathroom and vomited up the prime rib and spinach.

I could feel Sloan's eyes on me as she launched into the recitation of the problems inherent in producing the Can-Do Chipper. The toy was a preschool game that flipped a group of colored chips into the air when the child stomped on a foot pedal. The chips came in four distinct shapes and colors, four of each, with decals on them of bees, birds, fishes, and flowers. The object was for the child to grab as many of his designated decal chips as possible. Some of the squares were yellow with bees, some of the circles were red with flowers, some of the triangles were blue with birds, some of the stars were green with fishes. But some stars had bees on them, some circles had birds on them . . . and so forth. So a child had to identify in that instant the chips were in the air not only its proper decal, but its shape and its color as well.

Netta had given the game to ten groups of four kids each, for "can-do" testing. She had left them alone in the big playroom on the third floor of the Research & Development wing. One needed a yellow color-coded badge to get *onto* the third floor, and a top-clearance red dot in the center of the yellow badge to get into that *wing*.

The children had not responded to the game as I'd indicated they would. They ignored the decals entirely, set up the rules the way *they* wanted to play it, and simply caught shapes or colors. The cost analysis people said we'd save twenty-five thousand dollars by omitting the decals, and I thought I was home free; but Netta added what I thought was a gratuitous observation: "I think the sales potential of this item is drastically reduced by the loss of the decals. There won't be any ready-to-hand advertising lures. In fact, when we gave each child a list of toys they could have for participating in the tests, and this was when we first brought them in, the Can-Do Chipper was in the lowest percentile of choice. And after we observed them through the one-way mirrors playing with the game, and after we showed them the cartoons and the commercials and then told them we'd made an error on the forms and they should *now* pick their prizes, it was the least wanted item on the list."

They scrubbed the project. I was two down for the day.

She went on to the Little Miss Goodie Two-Shoes doll, my Big Breakthrough. It was the last sheaf of test notes, and I harbored the foolish hope that Netta had been playing some kind of deadly stupid lovers' game with me, that she had saved my hottest project for last, so she could recommend it highly. She hung me out to dry.

"This is one of the most dangerous toys I've ever tested," she began. "To refresh your memory, it is a baby doll that contains a voice-activated tape loop. When you say to the doll, 'Good dolly, you're a good dolly,' or similar affectionate phrase, the doll goes *mmmmmm*. When you say, 'Bad dolly, you've been a bad dolly,' or similar hostile phrase, the dolly whimpers. Unfortunately, my tests with a large group of children – " and she looked directly at me, "– which I've cross-checked through our independent testing group at Harvard, clearly show that not only the tape loop is activated by hostile phrases. This toy activates aggression in children, triggering the worst in them and *feeding* it. They were brutal with the dolls, tormenting them, savaging them, tearing them apart when merely spanking them and throwing them against the walls failed to satisfy their need to hear the whimpering."

I was, on the spot, in an instant, a pariah.

I was the despoiler of the children's crusade.

I was the lurking child molester.

I was the lizard piper of Hamelin.

I was, with the good offices of Netta Bernstein, at the end of an auspicious career with the MyToy Corporation.

And the next day she kissed me, surreptitiously, in the elevator; and asked me if I was free to have dinner at her apartment that night.

I left the body in the clothes closet, shoved back in a fetal position under the mound of wrinkled dresses and pants suits. I went out and wandered around the marina till morning, playing the messy murder of Netta Bernstein over and over again. Then I went to work.

I walked past Sloan's office, toward my own, expecting the door to burst open and Sloan to be standing there with a couple of cops. "That's him, officers. The one who wanted us to sell a demon doll. And he killed our research psychologist, a beautiful woman named Netta Bernstein. Take his yellow color-coded badge with the red dot in the center, and get him the hell out of here."

But nothing of the kind happened. Sloan's door stayed closed, I walked past and headed for my office. As I came abreast of Netta's glass-walled office, I glanced in as casually as I had every day and saw Netta poring over a large graph on her desk.

I once visited the Olympic peninsula of Washington state. I thought it was very beautiful, very peaceful. Up beyond the Seattle–Tacoma vicinity. Virgin wilderness. Douglas fir and alder with whitish bark and brownish-red at the tops of the leaves. It's flat, but you can see the Olympic range and the Cascades and Mt Rainier when the mist and fog and rain aren't obscuring the view. And even the mist and fog and rain seem peaceful, comfortable; cold, but somehow sanctified. A person could live there, fast and hard away from Los Angeles and the freeway stranglehold. But there was no $50,000 plateau on the Olympic peninsula.

I couldn't accept it. I don't think I even broke stride. I just walked past, well down the corridor, leaned against the wall for a moment, and breathed deeply. Staff walked past and Nisbett stopped to ask me if I was all right; I said I was fine, just heartburn, and he said, "Ain't it the truth," and he walked away. I could feel my heart turning to anthracite in my chest. I thought I would die. And then I realized I'd been hallucinating, projecting my guilt, having a delayed reaction to what had happened the night before, to what lay huddled in that clothes closet till I could figure out how to dispose of it.

I got myself under control, swallowing several times to force down the lump, breathing through my mouth to clear the dark fog that had begun to swirl in like the fog of the Olympic peninsula.

And then I turned back, walked slowly to Netta's office, and looked through the window-wall. She was talking to one of her assistants, a young woman who had worked with Madeline Hunter at UCLA, or had it been Iris Mink at UCLA Neuropsychiatric . . . *what the hell was I thinking!*

I had killed Bernstein the night before, had seen her eyes start from her head and her tongue go fat in her mouth and her skin turn dark blue with cyanosis when the strangling failed and the suffocation succeeded. She was meat, dead meat, lying under a pile of coat hangers. She could not possibly be in there talking to her assistant.

I opened the door and walked in.

They both looked up and the assistant stopped talking. Netta looked at me with annoyance and said, "Yes?"

"I, uh, the report, I, uh . . ."

She waited. They both waited. I moved my hands in random patterns. The assistant said, "I'll check it again, Netta, and show it to you after lunch; will that be all right?"

Netta Bernstein nodded it would be all right, and the assistant took the graph and slipped past me, giving me a security guard's look; when was the last time I'd seen a look like that?

When she was gone, Netta turned to me and said, "Well, what is it, Duncaster?"

Netta Bernstein was thirty-seven. I had checked. Her dossier in personnel said she had attended the University of Washington, had obtained her degree in psychology, and had majored in child therapy. She had been married at the age of eighteen, while still an undergraduate to one of her professors, who had soon after their marriage left the academy for a job with Merck Sharp & Dohme, the drug company, in New Jersey. She had remained with him until he had received a federal grant for a research project (unspecified, probably defense-oriented), and they had moved to a remote part of the Olympic peninsula of Washington state, where they had remained for the next sixteen years. Grays Harbor County. The husband had died three years before, and Netta Bernstein had gone to work in Houston, at the Baylor Medical School, department of biochemistry. Research on the RNA messenger molecules; something related to autistic children. She had left Baylor and come to MyToy, for a startling salary, only thirteen months before. She was beautiful, with thick auburn hair and the most penetrating cobalt-colored eyes I had ever seen. Eyes that were wide and dead in a clothes closet near the marina. Before I had killed her, she looked no more than nineteen years old, still as young and beautiful as she must have been when she was an undergraduate at the University of Washington. When I left her she looked like nothing human, certainly nothing living.

I stared at her. She looked nineteen again. There were no black bruises on her throat, her color was fresh and youthful, her cobalt-colored eyes staring at me.

"*Well*, Duncaster?"

I ran away. I hid in my office, waiting for the cops to come. But they never did. I went crazy, waiting. I had all the terrors and the guilt of knowing she would turn me in, that she was playing cobra-at-the-mongoose-rally with me. She hadn't died. Somehow she had still been breathing. I'd *thought* she was dead, but she wasn't dead; she was alive. Down the hall, waiting for me to throw myself out a window or run shrieking through the corridors screaming my confession. Well, I wouldn't do it! I'd outsmart her, I'd make sure she never told anyone about the night before.

I left the building by the service elevator, went to her apartment, and used the key I'd stolen the night before in anticipation of returning to dispose of the body. The first thing I did was check the clothes closet.

It was empty. The clothes were hung neatly. The dress with the plastic clothing bag from the dry cleaner was hanging among the others. There was no sign I'd even been there, that we had had dinner together, that we'd made love, that we'd argued over her performance in the conference room, that she'd denied meaning me any harm, that she had professed her love . . . and no sign I had killed her.

The apartment was silent and had never been the scene of a battlefield engagement for possession of the $50,000 plateau. I thought I might, indeed, be going crazy.

But when she got home, I killed Bernstein. Again.

I used a wooden cooking mallet intended to soften meat. I crushed her skull and wrapped her in the shower curtain and tied up her feet and torso with baling twine from under the sink. I attached a typewriter to the end of the cord, an IBM Selectric, and I carried her out to the marina at three a.m. and threw her in.

And the next day, Netta Bernstein was in her office, and she paid no attention to me, and I thought I'd go crazy, perhaps I'd *already* gone crazy. And that night I killed her with a tire iron and buried her body in the remotest part of Topanga Canyon. And the next day . . .

She didn't come to work.

They told me she had taken a leave of absence, had gone to Washington state on family business.

I ransacked the dossier and found the location. I flew up from LA International to the Sea-Tac Airport and rented a car. West from Olympia toward Aberdeen. North on Highway 101. Twenty miles north. I turned west and drove for fifteen miles, and came to the high wire fence.

I could see the long, low structure of the research facility where Netta Bernstein had lived with her husband for sixteen years. I got in. I don't remember how. I got in, that's all.

I circled the building, looking for a way inside, and when a crack of lightning flashed down the slate of the sky I saw my reflection in a window, wild-eyed and more than a little crazy. It was terribly cold, and I could smell the rain coming.

I found a set of doors and they were open. I went into the building. I went looking, wanting only one thing: to find Netta Bernstein, to kill her once again, finally, completely, thoroughly, without room for argument or return.

There was music coming from somewhere far off in the building. Electronic music. I followed the sound and passed through research facilities, laboratories whose purpose I could not identify, and came, at last, to the living quarters at the rear of the building.

They were waiting for me.

Seven of them.

Netta times seven.

The husband had been a geneticist. Fallen in love with an eighteen-year-old, auburn-haired, cobalt-colored-eyed undergraduate he met at a lecture. He had cloned her. Had taken the cutting and run off nine copies that had been raised from infancy, that had grown up quickly as she aged so slowly, so beautifully. Netta times ten. And when they had raised their children, there, far away from all eyes and all interference, he had died and left the mother with her offspring; left the woman with her sisters; left the thirty-four-year-old original with her sixteen-year-old duplicates. And Netta had had to go out into the world to make a living, to the drug company, to Baylor, to MyToy.

But when she wanted to return to see herself in the mirrors of their lives, she would call one or two or another of the Nettas to come do her work at MyToy.

And one of them had fallen in love with me.

Killing Bernstein was impossible. Killing Netta, because love had made me crazy, was beyond anyone's power, beyond even madness and hatred.

And one of them had fallen in love with me.

I sat down and they watched me. They had removed the body of their sister from the closet, and they had brought her back home for burial. And soon they would return to Los Angeles and drive up into wild Topanga Canyon and dig up another. And the third they would never see again.

And one of them had fallen in love with me.

Here on the Olympic peninsula, the fog and the mist and the rain are cool and almost sanctified. There is music, and they don't harm me, and some day they may let me leave. They don't bind me, they don't keep me from going out into the night; but this is where I'll stay.

And perhaps some day, when they clone again, perhaps I'll get lucky again.

And perhaps one of them will fall in love with me.

THE SECOND COMING

Joe Gores

"But fix thy eyes upon the valley: for the river of blood draws nigh,
in which boils every one who by violence injures other."

Canto XII, 46–48,
The Inferno of Dante Alighieri

I'VE THOUGHT ABOUT it a lot, man; like why Victor and I made
that terrible scene out there at San Quentin, putting ourselves on
that it was just for kicks. Victor was hung up on kicks; they were
a thing with him. He was a sharp dark-haired cat with bright eyes,
built lean and hard like a French skin-diver. His old man dug only
money, so he'd always had plenty of bread. We got this idea out at
his pad on Potrero Hill – a penthouse, of course – one afternoon
when we were lying around on the sun-porch in swim trunks and
drinking gin.

"You know, man," he said, "I have made about every scene in the world.
I have balled all the chicks, red and yellow and black and white, and I have
gotten high on muggles, bluejays, redbirds and mescaline. I have even tried
the white stuff a time or two. But – "

"You're a goddam tiger, dad."

"– but there is one kick I've never had, man."

When he didn't go on I rolled my head off the quart gin bottle I was
using for a pillow and looked at him. He was giving me a shot with those
hot, wild eyes of his.

"So like what is it?"

"I've never watched an execution."

I thought about it a minute, drowsily. The sun was so hot it was like nailing me right to the air mattress. Watching an execution. Seeing a man go through the wall. A groovy idea for an artist.

"Too much," I murmured. "I'm with you, dad."

The next day, of course, I was back at work on some abstracts for my first one-man show and had forgotten all about it; but that night Victor called me up.

"Did you write to the warden up at San Quentin today, man? He has to contact the San Francisco police chief and make sure you don't have a record and aren't a psycho and are useful to the community."

So I went ahead and wrote the letter, because even sober it still seemed a cool idea for some kicks; I knew they always need twelve witnesses to make sure that the accused isn't sneaked out the back door or something at the last minute like an old Jimmy Cagney movie. Even so, I lay dead for two months before the letter came. The star of our show would be a stud who'd broken into a house trailer near Fort Ord to rape this Army lieutenant's wife, only right in the middle of it she'd started screaming so he'd put a pillow over her face to keep her quiet until he could finish. But she'd quit breathing. There were eight chicks on the jury and I think like three of them got broken ankles in the rush to send him to the gas chamber. Not that I cared. Kicks, man.

Victor picked me up at seven-thirty in the morning, an hour before we were supposed to report to San Quentin. He was wearing this really hip Italian import, and fifty-dollar shoes, and a narrow-brim hat with a little feather in it, so all he needed was a briefcase to be Chairman of the Board. The top was down on the Mercedes, cold as it was, and when he saw my black suit and hand-knit tie he flashed this crazy white-toothed grin you'd never see in any Director's meeting.

"*Too much*, killer! If you'd like comb your hair you could pass for an undertaker coming after the body."

Since I am a very long, thin cat with black hair always hanging in my eyes, who fully dressed weighs as much as a medium-size collie, I guess he wasn't too far off. I put a pint of Jose Cuervo in the side pocket of the car and we split. We were both really turned on: I mean this senseless, breathless hilarity as if we'd just heard the world's funniest joke. Or were just going to.

It was one of those chilly California brights with blue sky and cold sunshine and here and there a cloud like Mr Big was popping Himself a cap down beyond the horizon. I dug it all: the sail of a lone early yacht out in the Bay like a tossed-away paper cup; the whitecaps flipping around out by Angel Island like they were stoned out of their minds; the top down on the 300-SL so we could smell salt and feel the icy bite of the wind. But beyond the tunnel on US 101, coming down towards Marin City, I felt a sudden sharp chill as if a cloud has passed between me and the sun, but none had; and then I dug for the first time what I was actually doing.

Victor felt it, too, for he turned to me and said, "Must maintain cool, dad."

"I'm with it."

San Quentin Prison, out on the end of its peninsula, looked like a sprawled ugly dragon sunning itself on a rock; we pulled up near the East Gate and there were not even any birds singing. Just a bunch of quiet cats in black, Quakers or Mennonites or something, protesting capital punishment by their silent presence as they'd done ever since Chessman had gotten his out there. I felt dark frightened things move around inside me when I saw them.

"Let's fall out right here, dad," I said in a momentary sort of panic, "and catch the matinee next week."

But Victor was in kicksville, like desperate to put on all those squares in the black suits. When they looked over at us he jumped up on the back of the bucket seat and spread his arms wide like the Sermon on the Mount. With his tortoise-shell shades and his flashing teeth and that suit which had cost three yards, he looked like Christ on his way to Hollywood.

"Whatsoever ye do unto the least of these, my brethren, ye do unto me," he cried in this ringing apocalyptic voice.

I grabbed his arm and dragged him back down off the seat. "For Christ sake, man, cool it!"

But he went into high laughter and punched my arm with feverish exuberance, and then jerked a tiny American flag from his inside jacket pocket and began waving it around above the windshield. I could see the sweat on his forehead.

"It's worth it to live in this country!" he yelled at them.

He put the car in gear and we went on. I looked back and saw one of those cats crossing himself. It put things back in perspective: they were from nowhere. The Middle Ages. Not that I judged them: that was their scene, man. Unto every cat what he digs the most.

The guard on the gate directed us to a small wooden building set against the outside wall, where we found five other witnesses. Three of them were reporters, one was a fat cat smoking a .45-calibre stogy like a politician from Sacramento, and the last was an Army type in lieutenant's bars, his belt buckle and insignia looking as if he'd been up all night with a can of *Brasso*.

A guard came in and told us to surrender everything in our pockets and get a receipt for it. We had to remove our shoes, too; they were too heavy for the fluoroscope. Then they put us through this groovy little room one-by-one to x-ray us for cameras and so on; they don't want anyone making the Kodak scene while they're busy dropping the pellets. We ended up inside the prison with our shoes back on and with our noses full of that old prison detergent-disinfectant stink.

The politician type, who had these cold slitted eyes like a Sherman tank, started coming on with rank jokes: but everyone put him down, hard, even the reporters. I guess nobody but fuzz ever gets used to executions. The Army stud was at parade rest with a face so pale his freckles looked like a charge of shot. He had reddish hair.

After a while five guards came in to make up the twelve required witnesses. They looked rank, as fuzz always do, and got off in a corner in a little huddle, laughing and gassing together like a bunch of kids kicking a dog. Victor and I sidled over to hear what they were saying.

"Who's sniffing the eggs this morning?" asked one.

"I don't know, I haven't been reading the papers." He yawned when he answered.

"Don't you remember?" urged another, "it's the guy who smothered the woman in the house trailer. Down in the Valley by Salinas."

"Yeah. Soldier's wife; he was raping her and . . ."

Like dogs hearing the plate rattle, they turned in unison toward the Army lieutenant; but just then more fuzz came in to march us to the observation room. We went in a column of twos with a guard beside each one, everyone unconsciously in step as if following a cadence call. I caught myself listening for measured mournful drum rolls.

The observation room was built right around the gas chamber, with rising tiers of benches for extras in case business was brisk. The chamber itself was hexagonal; the three walls in our room were of plate glass with a waist-high brass rail around the outside like the rail in an old-time saloon. The other three walls were steel plate, with a heavy door, rivet-studded, in the center one, and a small observation window in each of the others.

Inside the chamber were just these two massive chairs, probably oak, facing the rear walls side-by-side; their backs were high enough to come to the nape of the neck of anyone sitting in them. Under each was like a bucket that I knew contained hydrochloric acid. At a signal the executioner would drop sodium cyanide pellets into a chute; the pellets would roll down into the bucket; hydrocyanic acid gas would form; and the cat in the chair would be wasted.

The politician type, who had this rich fruity baritone like Burl Ives, asked why they had two chairs.

"That's in case there's a double-header, dad," I said.

"You're kidding." But by his voice the idea pleased him. Then he wheezed plaintively: "I don't see why they turn the chairs away – we can't even watch his face while it's happening to him."

He was a true rank genuine creep, right out from under a rock with the slime barely dry on his scales; but I wouldn't have wanted his dreams. I think he was one of those guys who tastes the big draught many times before he swallows it.

We milled around like cattle around the chute, when they smell the blood from inside and know they're somehow involved; then we heard sounds and saw the door in the back of the chamber swing open. A uniformed guard appeared to stand at attention, followed by a priest dressed all in black like Zorro, with his face hanging down to his belly button. He must have been a new man, because he had trouble maintaining his cool: just standing there beside the guard he dropped his little black book on the floor like three times in a row.

The Army cat said to me, as if he'd wig out unless he broke the silence: "They . . . have it arranged like a stage play, don't they?"

"But no encores," said Victor hollowly.

Another guard showed up in the doorway and they walked in the condemned man. He was like sort of a shock. You expect a stud to *act* like a murderer: I mean, cringe at the sight of the chair because he knows this is it, there's finally no place to go, no appeal to make, or else bound in there full of cheap bravado and go-to-hell. But he just seemed mildly interested, nothing more.

He wore a white shirt with the sleeves rolled up, suntans that looked Army issue, and no tie. Under thirty, brown crewcut hair – the terrible thing is that I cannot even remember the features on his face, man. The closest I could come to a description would be that he resembled the Army cat right there beside me with his nose to the glass.

The one thing I'll never forget is that stud's hands. He'd been on Death Row all these months, and here his hands were still red and chapped and knobby, as if he'd still been out picking turnips in the San Joaquin Valley. Then I realized: I was thinking of him in the past tense.

Two fuzz began strapping him down in the chair. A broad leather strap across the chest, narrower belts on the arms and legs. God they were careful about strapping him in. I mean they wanted to make sure he was comfortable. And all the time he was talking with them. Not that we could hear it, but I suppose it went *that's fine, fellows, no, that strap isn't too tight, gee, I hope I'm not making you late for lunch*.

That's what bugged me, he was so damned *apologetic*! While they were fastening him down over that little bucket of oblivion, that poor dead lonely son of a bitch twisted around to look over his shoulder at us, and he *smiled*. I mean if he'd had an arm free he might have *waved*! One of the fuzz, who had white hair and these sad gentle eyes like he was wearing a hair shirt, patted him on the head on the way out. No personal animosity, son, just doing my job.

After that the tempo increased, like your heart beat when you're on a black street at three a.m. and the echo of your own footsteps begins to sound like someone following you. The warden was at one observation window, the priest and the doctor at the other. The blackrobe made the sign of the cross, having a last go at the condemned, but he was digging only Ben Casey. Here was this MD cat who'd taken the Hippocratean Oath to preserve life, waving his arms around like a tv director to show that stud the easiest way to die.

Hold your breath, then breathe deeply: you won't feel a thing. Of course hydrocyanic acid gas melts your guts into a red-hot soup and burns out every fibre in the lining of your lungs, but you won't be really feeling it as you jerk around: that'll just be raw nerve endings.

Like they should have called *his* the Hypocritical Oath.

So there we were, three yards and half an inch of plate glass apart, with us staring at him and him by just turning his head able to stare right back: but there were a million light years between the two sides of the glass. He didn't turn. He was shrived and strapped in and briefed on how to die, and he was ready for the fumes. I found out afterwards that he had even willed his body to medical research.

I did a quick take around.

Victor was sweating profusely, his eyes glued to the window.

The politician was pop-eyed, nose pressed flat and belly indented by the brass rail, pudgy fingers like plump garlic sausages smearing the glass on either side of his head. A look on his face, already, like that of a stud making it with a chick.

The reporters seemed ashamed, as if someone had caught them peeking over the transom into the ladies' john.

The Army cat just looked sick.

Only the fuzz were unchanged, expending no more emotion on this than on their targets after rapid-fire exercises at the range.

On no face was there hatred.

Suddenly, for the first time in my life, I was part of it. I wanted to yell out *STOP!* We were about to gas this stud and *none of us wanted him to die!* We've created this society and we're all responsible for what it does, but none of us as individuals is willing to take that responsibility. We're like that Nazi cat at Nuremberg who said that everything would have been all right if they'd only given him more ovens.

The warden signalled. I heard gas whoosh up around the chair.

The condemned man didn't move. He was following doctor's orders. Then he took the huge gulping breath the MD had pantomimed. All of a sudden he threw this tremendous convulsion, his body straining up against the straps, his head slewed around so I could see his eyes were tight shut and his lips were pulled back from his teeth. Then he started panting like a baby in an oxygen tent, swiftly and shallowly. Only it wasn't oxygen his lungs were trying to work on.

The lieutenant stepped back smartly from the window, blinked, and puked on the glass. His vomit hung there for an instant like a phosphorus bomb burst in a bunker; then two fuzz were supporting him from the room and we were all jerking back from the mess. All except the politician. He hadn't even noticed: he was in Henry Millerville, getting his sex kicks the easy way.

I guess the stud in there had never dug that he was supposed to be gone in two seconds without pain, because his body was still arched up in that terrible bow, and his hands were still claws. I could see the muscles standing out along the sides of his jaws like marbles. Finally he flopped back and just hung there in his straps like a machine-gunned paratrooper.

But that wasn't the end. He took another huge gasp, so I could see his ribs pressing out against his white shirt. After that one, twenty seconds. We decided that he had cut out.

Then another gasp. Then nothing. Half a minute nothing.

Another of those final terrible shuddering racking gasps. At last: all through. All used up. Making it with the angels.

But then he did it *again*. Every fibre of that dead wasted comic thrown-away body strained for air on this one. No air: only hydrocyanic acid gas. Just nerves, like the fish twitching after you whack it on the skull with the back edge of the skinning knife. Except that it wasn't a fish we were seeing die.

His head flopped sideways and his tongue came out slyly like the tongue of a dead deer. Then this gunk ran out of his mouth.

It was just saliva – they said it couldn't be anything else – but it reminded me of the residue after light-line resistors have been melted in an electrical fire. That kind of black. That kind of scorched.

Very softly, almost to himself, Victor murmured: "Later, dad."

That was it. Dig you in the hereafter, dad. Ten little minutes and you're through the wall. Mistah Kurtz, he dead. Mistah Kurtz, he very very goddamn dead.

I believed it. Looking at what was left of that cat was like looking at a chick who's gotten herself bombed on the heavy, so when you hold a match in front of her eyes the pupils don't react and there's no one home, man. No one. Nowhere. End of the lineville.

We split.

But on the way out I kept thinking of that Army stud, and wondering what had made him sick. Was it because the cat in the chair had been the last to enter, no matter how violently, the body of his beloved, and now even that febrile connection had been severed? Whatever the reason, his body had known what perhaps his mind had refused to accept: this ending was no new beginning, this death would not restore his dead chick to him. This death, no matter how just in his eyes, had generated only nausea.

Victor and I sat in the Mercedes for a long time with the top down, looking out over that bright beautiful empty peninsula, not named, as you might think, after a saint, but after some poor dumb Indian they had hanged there a hundred years or so before. Trees and clouds and blue water, and still no birds making the scene. Even the cats in the black suits had vanished, but now I understood why they'd been there. In their silent censure, they had been sounding the right gong, man. *We* were the ones from the Middle Ages.

Victor took a deep shuddering breath as if he could never get enough air. Then he said in a barely audible voice: "How did you dig that action, man?"

I gave a little shrug and, being myself, said the only thing I could say. "It was a gas, dad."

"I dig, man. I'm hip. A gas."

Something was wrong with the way he said it, but I broke the seal on the tequila and we killed it in fifteen minutes, without even a lime to suck in between. Then he started the car and we cut out, and I realized what was wrong. Watching that cat in the gas chamber, Victor had realized for the very first time that life is far, far more than just kicks. We were both partially responsible for what had happened in there, and we had been ineluctably diminished by it.

On US 101 he coked the Mercedes up to 104 mph through the traffic, and held it there. It was wild: it was the end: but I didn't sound. I was alone without my Guide by the boiling river of blood. When the Highway Patrol finally got us stopped, Victor was coming on so strong and I was coming on so mild that they surrounded us with their holsters' flaps unbuckled, and checked our veins for needle marks.

I didn't say a word to them, man, not one. Not even my name. Like they had to look in my wallet to see who I was. And while they were doing that, Victor blew his cool entirely. You know, biting, foaming at the mouth, the whole bit – he gave a very good show until they hit him on the back of the head with a gun butt. I just watched.

They lifted his license for a year, nothing else, because his old man spent a lot of bread on a shrinker who testified that Victor had temporarily wigged out, and who had him put away in the zoo for a time. He's back now, but he still sees that wig picker, three times a week at forty clams a shot.

He needs it. A few days ago I saw him on Upper Grant, stalking lithely through a grey raw February day with the fog in, wearing just a t-shirt and jeans – and no shoes. He seemed agitated, pressed, confined within his own concerns, but I stopped him for a minute.

"Ah . . . how you making it, man? Like, ah, what's the gig?"

He shook his head cautiously. "They will not let us get away with it, you know. Like to them, man, just living is a crime."

"Why no strollers, dad?"

"I cannot wear shoes." He moved closer and glanced up and down the street, and said with tragic earnestness: "I can hear only with the soles of my feet, man."

Then he nodded and padded away through the crowds on silent naked soles like a puzzled panther, drifting through the fruiters and drunken teen-agers and fuzz trying to bust some cat for possession who have inherited North Beach from the true swingers. I guess all Victor wants to listen to now is Mother Earth: all he wants to hear is the comforting sound of the worms, chewing away.

Chewing away, and waiting for Victor; and maybe for the Second Coming.

HIBISCUS AND HOMICIDE

William Campbell Gault

1 They say – "Dolly Dead."

HONOLULU IS RARELY hot – at least in the shade. That's not just a boast because I live there. But it was hot this day, even in my office with the fan going and the shades down and a Tom Collins in my hand.

My office is on Hotel Street above a bookstore and across the hall from Dr Ray Nakamura – Dentist (Painless) – or so the lettering on his door and window says.

I was nursing the drink, relishing it in my sodden way and hoping no one would drop in, when someone did.

He was wearing cocoa-brown tropical-weight trousers that fitted the ankles very snugly and billowed above (zoot), some sort of lavender sport shirt with an open collar and a sport coat of some colors I'd never met before. The shoes were white buck and immaculate. The height was around five feet.

He was a Filipino and he was very grave standing there in the doorway in that ridiculous outfit. He had the face of a man who had lost too many fights.

I didn't get up but pointed to the chair on the other side of my desk.

"Drink?" I asked.

He shook his head. "You Sandy McKane?" He was walking toward the chair and he sat in it as he finished the sentence.

"Right."

"Detective?"

"Hmmm – hmmm. Girl trouble?"

He nodded eagerly. "How you know? You know me?"

With Filipinos it was always girl trouble. "I know you," I said. "Juan

Mira. I saw you fight Billy Chun, Art Gutzdorf, Young Silva and . . ." I tapped my brow with my free hand, thinking.

"Val Yaguchi?" he suggested hopefully.

"That's it," I said. "You knocked him out in the third."

He nodded, sighing. "Him I can beat. Not many but him."

"You always try," I consoled him. "You always give them their money's worth. That's all a man's expected to give, his best."

"Yeah," he said. "Sure." But he didn't look consoled.

"And now your girl," I said.

He nodded dolefully and took a kingsize cigarette out of an enameled case.

"Missing." He lighted the cigarette with a silver lighter. "A week ago. Left me."

I coughed in my genteel way. "You – ah – were – I mean, she lived near you?"

"Next room," he said. "Door between and – "

"Hmmm – hmmm," I said quickly. "You mean you both live in a hotel?"

He nodded. "Kealia Hotel. I pay her rent and buy her clothes and feed her good and give her jewelry and leave her drive my car. We get along."

Until a week ago. "Local girl?" I asked.

He nodded.

"Filipino?"

He shook his battle-scarred head. "Chinese – Portuguese. Little Hawaiian maybe. You know, mixed."

How well I knew. "She didn't work?"

"Sometimes she sing, dance a little, make a little money. Why she work? She got Juan."

But Juan no got her now. Juan got heartache. What the boys in the ring couldn't do this girl could – hurt him, put him down.

"She's got a family?"

"In Wahiawa, I think. She no go there. No talk to them."

Or they to her, probably. Sing a little, dance a little, take Juan for a ride a little. No girl to be proud of surely – no daughter to show off to the local swains and their families.

"Juan," I said, "I don't think you want me. Maybe the Police Department, the Missing Persons Bureau or maybe Dorothy Dix. But not me. I cost money."

"Money I got. Don't worry about Juan."

"Sure. But you don't want to spend it for this. She left you, didn't she? You had a little squabble and she ran out on you?"

"No squabble. She no run out. I keep her happy. She leave no note, she say nothing. She not in town. I look all over town. I got friends. I ask them. They look. No Dolly, not in town."

"And the Police?"

"I don't want no Police in my business. You don't want to work for me?"

"It's my business," I said, "but I want you to understand that I can't patch up a quarrel. That's not my business. And you're not at all sure, are you, that she didn't just leave you?"

He shrugged, and opened both hands, palms up and out. "She loves me. I treat her fine. She treat me fine. Why she leave?" He stood up. "If she no love me, she get some one else. She no disappear."

"Maybe she went over to the big island. Maybe her boy friend, her new one, doesn't live on Oahu."

"Okay. So you find out. I pay you." He had a billfold out and he was looking down at me. "How much you want?"

"Twenty a day and expenses."

The bill he handed me was a century note. "For five days. Expenses I pay later."

For a man who lost all his fights the billfold was thick. He didn't make it betting on himself, that's for sure. Maybe – oh, well.

He reached into an inner pocket and brought out a studio portrait of the girl. "Dolly Valdez her name."

"And some of the places she worked?"

He told me and I wrote it all down, neat and businesslike.

"And her family address?"

"Kam Highway, in Wahiawa, but I don't know exactly. Block after the bridge, I think."

"Okay, Juan," I said and stood up. "I'll work on it. You still staying at the Kealia?"

He nodded.

"I'll get in touch with you," I told him and he left.

I sat down again and finished my drink slowly. My door was open and I saw a young Jap come out of the dentist's office, and I heard for a moment the sound of his drill. I heard the traffic in the street outside and my own conscience telling me not to have another drink, not to be slothful, to get to work.

So I mixed another one. I have a small, efficient second-hand mechanical ice chest. Honolulu isn't usually hot, but it does get warm, sort of.

Well, I had some business and I retired to my chair, sipping and turning it over in my keen mind and studying the picture of the girl, Dolly Valdez.

She had dark hair, dark eyes and merry, with a slant to them. Faintly round face, full lips, high cheekbones not so noticeable. Dolly Valdez who walked out on Juan Mira, maybe.

Folks in Wahiawa – danced a little and sang a little at – let's see. At the Hula Hut and Jerome's and the Kealia Pikaki Room. Drove his car and ate his food and shared his moods and probably watched him fight. Maybe that last was why she left him.

It was now two-thirty, and Wahiawa is about twenty-odd miles. And the other places were in town. Wahiawa was for now, the others later.

Gulping the rest of my drink and belching in my high-bred way, the belch tasting of gin – going out in my wrinkled Palm Beach suit and no hat and climbing into my little convertible, which was an oven right now, an oven with a canvas top.

I drove out King Street to Dillingham Boulevard and out the Boulevard to Kam Highway past the Hickman Field gate and Pearl Harbor and out past the cane fields and a few pineapple patches. Then the winding uphill climb to Wahiawa in the shadows of the Waianae Range – Aiea, Waimalu, Pearl City, sounding foreign but looking like California.

Past Wheeler Field, an intersection, and there was the bridge Juan spoke of.

The right side of the road was lined with shops – a tavern, a hair dressing studio, a novelty store, a barber shop. On the left side there were four very decrepit shacks in the first short block beyond the bridge.

I swung the convertible in a U-turn. Eeney, I said to myself, and meeny and miney moe. I went to miney.

It was no better than the others and no worse. Up the rickety steps to the sagging porch and a knocking of the knuckles on wood.

There was a little window in the door with one dirty mesh curtain in this window and presently the curtain moved to one side and some old and tired Oriental eyes in an old and unwrinkled Oriental feminine face looked out and the door opened.

She wore one of those long-sleeved, ankle-length sheaths that the older members of the race cling to and her voice was pleasantly soft.

"Good afternoon."

"Good afternoon. I'm looking for some people named Valdez."

She inclined her head. "Next door."

Which would be moe. "Thank you," I said. "Hot isn't it?"

She agreed it was.

The moe house had a bedraggled banana tree in the front yard and a small patch of periwinkle and pikaki near the porch but otherwise it was miney's twin – perhaps a little more slope to the porch.

It had a glass window in the front door but no curtain. A face there, like before, but a broad face, dark as oil rubbed mahogany, the wide, cheerful face of an Hawaiian matron.

"Aloha, good afternoon." She showed white teeth in a generous smile. "Mrs Valdez?"

The smile a laugh now, and the big body shaking slightly. "No, no, no. Mrs Valdez in town, shopping."

Some joke to her, that she should marry Valdez.

For Valdez was sitting there, a small and overalled Portuguese with some glasses on the table in front of him and a bottle and a cheap glass ash tray filled with cigarette stubs.

"I am Mr Valdez."

"And I," I told him, "am Sandy McKane." I gave him my card.

He looked from it up to me and asked, "What is it you want?"

Well, what did I want? His daughter? "I'm investigating your daughter's whereabouts," I said. "Her fiancé – "

"We do not speak of her in this house," he said and the house was the ancestral home, the castle, with the tone he put into that. "We have no information about her. We do not talk about her."

"You haven't seen her recently? This past week?"

"We have not seen her for two years. We do not care to see her."

The Hawaiian woman said nothing, watching him, then me, sorrow on her placid face, concern in those moist brown eyes. All heart, the Hawaiian. But Valdez –

He had no more for me. I went to the door. The Hawaiian woman said, "Wait. I go with you."

We went out together and down the rickety stairs. She was barefoot but the printed cotton dress she wore was spotless. She laid a big brown hand on my arm. "Dolly is dead."

I stared at her. She put a hand on her bosom. "I feel in here. Three nights ago I dream of her in the coffin, covered with hibiscus. I know then she is dead."

"I have to be sure," I said. "I can't tell my client that."

She shrugged. "You will find her dead."

"Look," I said, "Mr Valdez doesn't seem to care but – "

"Him," she said, making it sound like a curse, "Pouf! That little rooster."

We belonged to the same lodge on that. "But, Mrs Valdez," I continued, "couldn't we look her up? The shopping district isn't very big here in Wahiawa and – "

"I go with you," she said and we walked to the car.

The springs settled a little as she climbed in and I went round to get behind the wheel. Business of making another U-turn, and heading toward the heart of town.

An open market, fruit and an open market, meat and around the corner and up. California Avenue and my stout friend said, "There, there, stop the car – " and I stopped it.

A short, stout and dark woman was moving along the walk here, carrying a basket. The dress was white and the complexion was Hawaiian but the eyes were Oriental.

"Mis' Kaipapu," Mrs Valdez said, "Hullo."

Miss, or Mrs, Kaipapu left the car and whispered for a moment in consultation with Mrs Valdez. Then they both came back to the car.

"You look for my daughter?"

I nodded.

"I no see her. Mis' Kaipapu say she dead. I believe."

"Okay," I said. "I'm going back your way if you want a lift."

They did and they settled in, neat and cozy and U-turn McKane went through his act again and we stopped in front of the first of the four houses. This was cency, the abode of the Lady Kaipapu, and they both wanted to get out there for some reason of their own. They did.

"Goodby," Kaipapu said and "Goodby," Mrs Valdez said and Sandy McKane said, "You're sure there's nothing you want to tell me?"

Two heads shaking in the sunlight, two pairs of brown eyes candidly on my face but looking beyond me a little as though thinking of that lovely coffin with the hibiscus.

I moved off, saying, "Goodby," and thinking that sixty cents should cover the gas on this trip, which meant sixty cents on the expense account for Juan Mira, the often defeated.

And, I thought, there's a lot of hibiscus in Hawaii, all colors – excepting one, which I've forgotten.

2 "Meat" for Dinner

Downhill, most of the way, going back – and I needled the little convertible. But it was nearly five when I reached town and I was hungry. I thought it might be smart to eat, considering.

The Pikaki Room should have something edible. The Kealia Hotel was out in Waikiki but about a block inland from the beach. I drove out Kalakaua Avenue, past all the bathers' parked cars, past the proud arrogance of the Royal Hawaiian, all the exclusive little shops (for women), past the Moana and turned there on Kaiulani.

This Kealia was small compared to the Royal Hawaiian or the Moana but no less snooty, despite its lack of a beach – entirely too snooty to think of serving dinner at the ungodly hour of five.

Was the manager in? It wouldn't matter – I couldn't get dinner at five o'clock. The tanned blonde hostess was sure of that.

Business of flashing a badge and looking official. Was he in?

Well, she'd see, but she didn't think so. She was royalty, in white gabardine. She came back, nodded coolly and gestured with one proud hand toward a doorway.

This doorway opened into a little room, sort of a storeroom and office combined and a thin gray man in a seersucker suit was in there going over some bills at the desk. Gray eyebrows and gray hair, slim and tall, and the look he gave me was weary. Business must be bad.

No, he didn't know where Dolly Valdez was now. Yes, he had employed her at one time for a short engagement because of the – well, the insistence, almost, of one of the guests.

The guest would be Juan, the zoot boy, and how did he rate this elegant establishment on the loser's end of every purse?

There was nothing here. Going out again, I said thank you to the Princess Gabardine but her eyes were on the middle distance. Maybe, if they had a beach, things would be better. Or if they started dinner a little earlier for the proletariat.

Jerome's was out here, too – on Kalakaua but closer to town. Red front door with a big brass knocker in the middle of it for effect only. I went in.

Neat and pleasant inside – maroon and ivory the motif. Maroon bar, and maroon carpeting in the dining room but rubbertile floor in the bar.

A man in flawless white stood behind the bar, a man with a flat nose and not too much height and one of those perpetually tied bow ties. Charley – let's see – Charley Wright and a fair welter in his day.

"Sandy," he said. "Your thirst bring you in? Or your nose?"

"A little of both," I said, "though I'm on the snoop."

"What'll it be?"

"Surprise me," I said. "I can drink anything. Boss around?"

He shook his head and reached for various bottles. "Fishing. And there'll be poker after that."

I asked him about Dolly Valdez.

He wrinkled his brow. "Chubby? Bouncy?"

"Could be." I showed him the photograph.

He nodded. "Sure, sure. Used to work here. Went over, too, but Mira put his foot down. Mira's girl, huh?"

"Guess so. He likes to think so."

He was still pulling out bottles for my surprise. I bring out the artist in him.

"She missing?" he said.

"She's missing from Mira. Of course she probably isn't anti-social. A friendly type, probably, and – "

"Sure, sure," he said. "I haven't heard a word about her since she left here and the boss don't hear nothing I don't hear."

He set the drink in front of me and I took a good healthy gulp.

The maroon merged with the ivory and Charley's questioning face started to revolve. It became a pinwheel and burst and order was restored. "Good, huh?" Charley said.

"Good," I murmured hoarsely. "Very effective." Charley had finally split the atom. He'd been working on it a long time. Sensitive, he is, so I finished it slowly and paid him and chatted of this and that and left.

Which left me only the Hula Hut, which was not in exclusive Waikiki, but in non-exclusive Honolulu, on Hotel Street, not far from my office. And I knew they had steaks.

It was a basement place and it was run by Vic Malis, who also ran other things in his efficient way.

Vic had his own ideas about decoration and none of them were good. There were fish nets on the walls and some cheap Hawaiian color prints. There was a mural behind the bar of a girl, not Hawaiian, coming out of the ocean dressed in a reflective look.

The waiters wore leis, artificial and slightly worn, and the music, though Island, had a faintly commercial twang.

At the door end of the bar, Vic's righthand man was lounging and he should be worth a paragraph. His name was "Meat" Kozak, the Meat referring, no doubt, to the size of him, which was impressive. He was about six feet four inches and fifty pounds past the two hundred mark. Cauliflowered ears and a flat nose were souvenirs of the days Vic had thought this boy of his might bring him riches with his gloves. This boy hadn't. There hadn't been the proper coordination between his big body and his small brain.

Meat was wearing sport shirt and slacks and sandals and a smile he thought genial which managed to stop just this side of grotesque.

"Evening, copper," he said.

I'm only six feet high, so I had to look up at him and, looking up, I couldn't put the proper contempt in my voice.

"Hello, Meat," I said, looking around the place. "Vic in?"

"Not yet." Meat was cleaning his teeth with his tongue. "You got some trouble for him?"

I'd had some trouble for Vic Malis once before. "No," I said, "I don't think so. Just a little information if he's got it."

"I could answer any questions," Meat said.

"What's the plural of alumnus?" I said, obliging him.

"Fresh," he said, "ain't you?"

"Fresh and clean," I admitted. "It's so difficult, in this climate."

Meat worried that one, in his slow mind and chewed his lower lip in his thoughtful way and tugged at one battered ear.

Before he came out of it I said, "What I really wanted was a steak and this is the place to come for it."

The air of geniality struggled to get back to that broad face.

"Sure," he said. "We got some good ones, too."

Which they had. I took a table in the dining room near the barroom and ate one large porterhouse, rare. I had some coffee and a quarter of a head of lettuce with French dressing and some French fried and rye rolls and more coffee.

I was enjoying the second cup in company with a cigarette when the orchestra came in and began to play in their dispirited way. About five minutes after that there was a man in tan silk gabardine coming from an office behind the bandstand and walking toward my table.

Vic Malis had black hair and broad shoulders and very dark, very sharp eyes. He was about an inch under six feet. The suit, I saw on closer inspection, was beautifully tailored.

"Trouble again, Sandy?" he asked, sitting down in the chair across from me.

I shook my head. "Just routine. Checking on a girl that used to work here, a girl named Dolly Valdez."

I thought maybe there was a flicker in the dark, sharp eyes. "Private case?"

Meat was standing near, in the archway, and Meat wasn't missing a word. "Private," I admitted. Occasionally, I worked with the Police.

He was thoughtful as though considering his next question. Then, "Juan Mira looking for her?"

"Maybe. What makes you think so?"

"His girl, isn't she? He sure squealed plenty when she did work here. Always in here, every night, making trouble. She's got a lot to sell, that girl, but Juan thinks he's got a lease on it."

"Love," I said. "It does things to people."

"It didn't get him down to the License Bureau."

Who am I to judge? I am not Snow White. I asked, "Last time you saw her was when?"

"About four – five days ago. Came in for a job. I told her when she ditched the pocket-sized Dempsey we'd do business. I can use her, all right. She's – okay."

"Good voice?"

He gestured noncommittally with a well-manicured hand. "Just ordinary. Personality – I don't know what you call it. Some of them had it and some wish they had it."

"She had it?"

"Yup. And she could deliver it."

Well, I thought, you dark-haired, dark-eyed gent of infinite smoothness, you will tell me nothing you don't want me to know – if you know it. I kept remembering the flicker when Dolly's name was first broached.

"Nothing more?" I asked.

"That's all, Sandy." There was only a shadow of hesitation before he said that. Maybe he was remembering the last time I'd gone up against him. And maybe he was honestly searching his mind. But it was the first glimmer I'd had that day.

"What's good to drink?" I asked. "What's new?"

He relaxed into his urbane host characterization then and smiled pleasantly. "The Ladies' Aid is quite a number." He rose, and left me to my thoughts, such as they were.

The Ladies' Aid came in a tall frosted glass, very thin and dainty. There was a sprig of mint in it and the color was somewhere between pink and amber but the hues changed from time to time, so I couldn't be sure.

I sipped it tentatively and it was all right – it was fine. It brought out the poet in me. The place was beginning to fill up – and not with the wrong people completely. Vic had good food.

I was on my second edition of Ladies' Aid, when the girl came over to my table. She was in white linen with jet black hair and eyes as blue as the Waikiki sky and slim and with breeding. To *my* table.

I managed to get up without knocking it over.

"You've forgotten me, Saunders McKane," she said.

Saunders had been my name back in the days before I had to earn my daily bread, before Dad . . . but that's another story.

"How could I?" I lied gallantly, ransacking my mind and trying to look suave.

"You have. Don't you remember? You were fourteen and it was my first party and you didn't like girls much then and – "

Linda Ramsey – her family wasn't one of the Big Five but if it had been the Big Six they would be included.

"Linda Ramsay," I said, "and you weren't as beautiful then or my judgment wasn't as good."

"I had braces on my teeth," she said, "and some freckles."

I looked around the room. "You're with someone, of course?"

"N-no. I was waiting for someone. But I don't want to – "

I never did find out what she didn't want to do. I went around and pulled out a chair.

"We must talk," I said, "about the braces and Miss Devanty's School Of The Dance and Tommy Rice and the Kelton twins."

She sat down without further protest and I ordered her a rum and coke, which she said she liked. I ate her up with my eyes and said, "Start right after that first party and tell me all about it up to now."

She was pulling a cigarette out of a case and I snapped my lighter for her.

"What's there to tell?" she asked. "Ward-Belmont and then Columbia. I've been in the States most of the time since I left eighth grade. I just came back here last summer."

"And Tommy Rice?"

"He's in California, working in a law office in Los Angeles, and doing very well, I hear."

So that was ended, I thought. Even back when she was fourteen it had been Tommy Rice. But there wasn't any regret in the voice, none I could notice. Just a simple stating of the facts, that last sentence, with perhaps too much monotone in the voice.

"The Keltons?"

"Dick was killed in France. Sue married some man from New York, a man named Manchester."

Which brought us to Miss Devanty's School Of The Dance, which would always be painful to me, and the braces, which wouldn't be tactful.

So I just sighed and looked at her. The orchestra seemed to be in tune, on this one.

"Dance?" I suggested.

She crushed her cigarette out in the ashtray in the center of the table and we rose and danced – slowly, and with grace, of course, and with excellent rhythm. Close, and not talking, naturally, and it was a pleasure to both of us especially me. Hadn't we both been trained by Miss Devanty?

Some more dancing followed and some more talk and some more of the things out of bottles and wasn't this friend of hers ever going to show up? I hoped not. He did though.

He was a tall slim lad with a shadow of a mustache, blond – both the mustache and his curly hair – and he was tanned and in Palm Beach, not wrinkled like mine. His name, I heard dimly, was Jefferson Raleigh but I could call him Jeff – any time.

The reason I heard it dimly was because my mind was beginning to cloud over a little and I couldn't understand that. Liquor does things to me but I hadn't had enough.

Jeff and Linda danced. I tried to watch them and decided from what I could see that *Sandy* and Linda danced together with more skill.

Somebody brought another drink I hadn't remembered ordering. Perhaps Jefferson, called Jeff, had. I drank it at any rate.

They came back to the table, and their outlines weren't at all clear. "I think I need some air," I said.

Concern showed in Linda's face, maybe even in Jefferson's. Linda said, "We'll go with you. If you're ill – "

"I can't be drunk," I said. "It must be something else."

They went out with me. That much I remember. And I think I remember the voice of the man they later claimed took me home. He was supposed to have said, "Sandy's a friend of mine. I always take him home when he gets like this." The lying so-and-so.

That's all I remember about that.

Dreams, sure – I was with Linda in a cloud castle high above Diamond Head and she was trying to take the braces off *my* teeth. And Jefferson Raleigh was dancing all by himself while kids threw pennies at him.

There were some other dreams, mixed and ugly, and the smell of something like ether and I fought to open my eyes because it seemed important at the time. The ceiling I saw above me was papered in blue,

blue with silver stars. I could make that out in the dim light. My head was full of fog and the stars above began to move.

I wanted to close my eyes. Perhaps, if I did, the whirling in my head would go away and the sickness in my stomach. I was about one eighth of an inch away from active nausea. I wanted to close my eyes.

I kept them open. I was on a bed, soft with silken coverings, a double bed. My eyes moved down from the ceiling and I saw that the wall paper on the walls was blue and silver too but these were stripes, not silver stars in the blue background.

This wasn't my bedroom, I realized. There was a night lamp on the table to my right but it wasn't on. The light came from some wall brackets – cream colored.

I swung my feet off the bed and saw I was in pajamas. I swung them to the floor and started to get up, and I was a sixteenth of an inch away from active nausea and knew I'd never find the bathroom in a strange house.

But there was the window, open, and I stumbled toward that and hung my head out of it and most of my upper body and let nature take its course.

My knees were rubber and my head was full of gravel and my tongue was just an old bar rag. I got up from the window and swayed a moment, holding the wall. Then I turned slowly.

I hadn't been sleeping alone though I had been the only one just sleeping. There was a girl in the bed, not covered, wearing a robe of silk, white silk, which afforded no coverage at the moment. I didn't need the photograph to see it was Dolly Valdez despite her mottled, purplish face.

I didn't need a stethoscope to know she was dead. She had a flower in her hand, a five petaled flower which is bred in all the colors excepting one, a hibiscus.

3 Corpse with Hibiscus

Framed like an Old Master – framed like a drying curtain. Only I was Saunders McKane of an old Honolulu family now extinct, and the Police knew me from way back and we were friends and we would laugh over this ridiculous situation.

Only with murder you don't laugh. And old friendships dissolve like the morning dew and lots of men go to bed with lots of girls and drink too much and quarrel.

I could leave this place and look up an alibi. I could get the heck out of here, and quickly. Or I could call the Police.

Sick, seemingly drunk, in pajamas – what kind of a story would that be? Only a fool would call the Police.

I went to look for the phone. I found it in the hall off the bedroom and I called the Police Station number, which I knew, and somebody put a hand on my arm.

I probably jumped a couple of feet but I don't remember now. I turned, and looked into the face of Dan Arliss. Faded blue eyes under that upstanding white thatch of hair, the thin face and the high forehead of this medium high slim man. Head of all the detectives in town. Dan Arliss of the Force.

"We're here, Sandy. You don't need to phone."

"You were here all the – "

"We came a half hour ago but we waited. You were about ready to wake up and we wanted your reaction. That was important, you understand?"

That's why the lights had been on in the bedroom. I was glad now I'd been so noble and full of character and had gone to the phone.

Another figure came out of the darkness of what must have been the living room – Gus Lemke, foil for Dan, errand runner and muscle man and looking like what he was, all detective. Broad and pugnacious.

Dan said, "You know her, Sandy?"

"From her picture. Dolly Valdez, sings and dances at times. Her folks live in Wahiawa."

"You know quite a lot about her."

"I was looking for her for a client."

"Who's the client?"

I shook my head. "Oh, no. Not just yet. I'm a private detective."

Gus Lemke growled, and seemed to move toward me but Dan lifted a restraining hand. "This is murder, Sandy."

"I've seen it before. I've cleaned some cases up before." I felt dizzy again and I put a hand on the wall. "I've worked with you, Dan, before."

He considered this, the pale eyes thoughtful, and then he smiled a little. "All right. I won't throw any law at you right now. You look sick."

"I am sick."

"Maybe he doesn't remember what happened," Lemke said.

I told them all I did remember and I gave them Jefferson Raleigh's name, but not Linda's. Gallantry, you know.

"Where do her folks live?" Dan wanted to know.

"On Kam Highway," I said, "in Wahiawa. There's a bridge right after that road that goes up to Schofield Barracks and they live in the first house across the bridge."

He took it all down.

"And while you're there," I suggested, "you might go to the last house and ask for a lady named Kiapapu. She told me this afternoon that she dreamed Dolly was dead. And that she was in a coffin, covered with hibiscus."

There were men in the bedroom now, including Doc McGuire and his internes and a couple of reporters and a photographer.

Had they all waited until I opened my sleepy eyes? Evidently.

My stomach was uneasy. I told Dan, "If I don't hit the hay pretty soon you can bury me with her."

"Okay," he said. "Your car's outside and you're on Seaside, right next to the Canal."

I looked at him strangely. Seaside, right near the Canal, is where I lived.

I dressed and went out and saw that I was about four houses from home. The car was in front of this house, so whoever had brought me here had probably used that.

It was four o'clock and there was no moon and maybe my unknown and unseen enemies would strike again tonight. But I didn't care. I was very, very tired. I fell asleep as soon as I hit the bed.

Saunders McKane, eminent criminologist, student of human nature, lover of women and mixed drinks, sat in his tastefully furnished office feeling like a freighter's keel.

I'd had a good full breakfast and a good small drink. I had walked three time around the block like a fighter in training and I had the window open and was taking deep breaths of the fresh air, hoping it would do me some good. It didn't.

Outside a truck driver was swearing in hearty pidgin but the sound of Dr Ray Nakamura's drill was blessedly silent. There was a sale on books downstairs, so a lot of women were buying items they wouldn't read or for gifts to friends, so the friends could ignore them.

It was afternoon and not as hot as the day before, though the sun was shining. It was raining a little, a Hawaiian phenomenon. Liquid sunshine, it's called, and very annoying if you're wearing something cottony.

Well, there was Vic Malis. A logical suspect. In his place I'd been drugged. Right outside of his place I'd been picked up. Vic and I would go round and round, getting nowhere.

I went to the window, just for the exercise. Across the street, looking as inconspicuous as he could and probably watching my office, was the mountain who moved like a man, Meat Kozak. He was almost as inconspicuous as the statue of Kamehameha up in Palace Square.

The phone rang and I answered it and it was Linda.

"I read the papers this morning," she said. "The *Advertiser*."

"Yes? Interesting, wasn't it?"

"You didn't mention my name, I see, Saunders."

"Call me Sandy, won't you? I like it better."

"All right, all right. But I wanted to thank you. Couldn't you come out for dinner tonight? I'd like to see you and Dad would, too. You needn't dress."

"Not even in a towel?" I asked.

"I mean – oh, you know what I mean. I remember, you always teased me. But you will come, won't you?"

"Definitely. About eight?"

"Eight will be fine." A pause. "And Sandy – "

"Yes."

"I know you're innocent."

Click of her phone and a dead line and I looked up to meet the gaze of Juan Mira, standing in the doorway. He wore white flannels today, with a fingertip length coat and peg-top trousers. With a blue shirt and a whitish, figured tie and a leghorn hat with a brim big enough for a motorcycle race-track.

I studied his eyes and there was hate in them but not for me, I thought.

"You read the paper this morning?" I said.

He came on into the room. "I read. You know who did this?"

I shook my head. "They tried to frame me for it. That's the way it was but it might not look like a frame to people who didn't know me."

He nodded. "I know. Juan not so dumb."

Well, maybe not.

"I owe you some money," I said, "seventy-nine dollars and forty cents. One day's work at twenty slugs per diem and sixty cents worth of gasoline."

He shook his head. "No. You will work for me for a while? Here." He reached into his inner breast pocket and pulled out his wallet. From it he extracted three hundred-dollar bills. "This is for you, too. I want to know who killed my Dolly."

"I don't know now."

"You will find out. My friends tell me about you."

I motioned him over to the window, and pointed at Meat Kozak. "Is that one of your friends?" I asked him.

The leghorn hat shook negatively. "He used to fight?"

"More or less. Not in any way you'd be likely to remember."

He shrugged. "He's a big man."

I said, "One thing more. It wasn't in the paper but there was a hibiscus in her hand."

He looked like a small, bronze statue for a moment. There was no breath going through his lungs and not a muscle in his body quivered. His eyes were on my face, staring.

He expelled his breath at the same time he said, "Hibiscus?"

"Uh-huh. Spell something to you?"

He shook his head but to clear it, not as an answer to my question. "In the seat of my car I find hibiscus. In my room, one night, on the dresser. Now – "

"A warning?" I said. "Isn't it?"

He nodded like a robot. "Maybe, maybe."

"What's your business, Juan? Not losing fights. That wouldn't even pay for your clothes."

"It is a business others might want. It is something I no tell you. No one can take this from me. My friends are loyal."

"It may help me to find who killed Dolly Valdez."

He was firm on that. "I no tell you."

Okay, he no tell me. He left and I went back to sitting in my chair and wondering if my stomach would stand up under lunch. I'd been putting it off since noon because of the late breakfast and the stomach.

On a sudden whimsical impulse I went to the window and shouted, "Hey, Meat!" and waved for him to come up.

He stood on the curb a moment, staring up in his stupid way, and then he crossed the street, threading through traffic. Downstairs, I could see, women were still coming out, carrying books – literary town, Honolulu.

Meat just about filled the doorway. "You called me?" he asked.

"Sure. If you're going to keep an eye on me you may as well be comfortable. You can sit down up here."

"I wasn't watching you, shamus," he said. "I was waiting for a friend of mine who was buying a book."

"Don't put on airs," I said. "Your friends can't read."

He started to ball one big fist.

"And don't try to scare me. I've seen you fight."

"You're smart," he said. "You're awful smart."

"Only comparatively," I told him. "But this you might as well know. If I'm smart enough to find out who slipped me that Mickey last night there's going to be blood in the streets. There's going to be all kinds of action, all unpleasant. You can carry that back to your well-tailored boss. And buy yourself a clean sport shirt. That one stinks."

He started to move toward me and I made a motion toward my shoulder as they do in the movies. He stopped.

"Be very careful with me," he said and turned and went out the door.

It was quiet in the office. I wondered what would have happened if he'd kept on coming toward me. All I had on under my jacket was my shirt and under that the lithe, muscular me.

Oh, well, I could have hit him. I could have broken a hand and he could have hit me and broken some other part of me or all the parts of me. I'm so tough and hard bitten – a private detective. I must indulge my whimsies.

Bethel and Merchant is near the docks, and as I stood there a little later, fat Hawaiian ladies were hurrying past, loaded down with leis. That meant a boat was coming in. The odor of the flowers was heavy in the afternoon sun and the rays slanted across the building in front of me. This was the Police Station.

My convertible was parked at the curb and, about six cars back, a Packard convertible was parked, and Meat Kozak sat in that. Which gives you a truer picture of the wages of sin. Mine is no Packard.

Dan Arliss was in his office, smoking one of the brown cigarette-sized cigars he likes for some reason and gazing off into the smoke he was creating. Weary, he looked, and old. I heard the hoot of a tug and the clickety-clack of the typewriter in the next office.

"What's cooking?" I asked.

"She was strangled, of course, neck darn near broken. She and some unknown skinny gent rented the house about a month ago and the owner thought they were man and wife."

"Sure," I said. "He worried about it. He couldn't sleep nights."

"Well, anyway, his name is Walters and he's got an office out on Beretania near the Academy. I was with him for an hour and that's about all I could get out of him."

"You find out anything about those pajamas they draped me in?"

"Nothing yet. Lemke's out on it now. The rest of the clothes were hers. We've got more prints than the FBI have in their files and they'll probably all turn out to be the iceman's. We've got pictures, about enough for a one man showing, and we've got one suspect."

"One?"

"Sure – You. That is, they all have but me. I know you and your kind, gentle ways and your love for butterflies, so that isn't my guess. It's just the rest of the Force and the newspapermen who think that way."

"Well, well," I said. "Hmmmm." Looking profound.

The shock of white hair, wreathed in smoke. The faded eyes looked up at mine. "Want to tell me about your client now?"

"He's paying three hundred dollars to have me find out who killed her. If he gets to him first you'll have another killing."

"Is it ethics or just cussedness that you won't tell me his name?"

"It's privacy. It's what I sell."

"Okay. All right." A weary gesture with the hand. "You're a good boy, Sandy. Someday maybe you too will be strangled and half of my life's burden will be removed." He stomped out the small cigar in an ash tray. "It isn't important anyway. I could always operate an elevator or something."

"Things are tough all over," I said consolingly.

"Beat it," he said. "Go and get drunk, go fishing, go relax on the beach at Waikiki."

"Aloha," I said and left.

Outside, in the Packard, Meat made a ritual of lighting a cigarette. For this he cupped his hands in front of his face and thus I couldn't see him. He wasn't so dumb – no dumber than a young ape.

I drove out to Waikiki and home – to my little one story stucco job near the canal, needing only a heap of living and the feminine touch to make it truly home.

4 The Second Corpse

In this place of unparalleled elegance I prepared for my social evening. I looked out the living room window first and Meat was nowhere in sight.

I went back into my kitchen and made a cheese sandwich and some coffee. I ate and drank this and took a shower, hot, and a shower, cold, and then I relaxed on the bed a while, smoking and thinking. But the thinking led up nothing but blind alleys. I set the alarm for seven and took a nap.

At seven-thirty I was dressed and at seventy-forty I was outside. I thought I saw a light in the house that had held the body of Dolly Valdez. But it didn't appear again and I figured I must have been wrong.

The Ramsay home was on the Diamond Head Road, or just off of it. As I drove up Kalakaua past the beach I could see the bright new moon on the water and the swimmers and, far out, silhouetted, a surfboard rider coming in. Like a picture postcard. A nice, romantic night.

The Ramsay home was flat and white and rambling with a red-tile roof and the broad low front of it was *makai*, as they say, or towards the sea. The rear was towards the mountains or *mauka*. (Little bits of knowledge about our happy Polynesian neighbors.) The entire broad front backed the open flagstone lanai and, it seemed, was composed of glass, two stories high, affording a view of all that part of the Pacific.

I drove up the back drive, a road of crushed lava between slanting palms and a hibiscus hedge which walled in a section of the rear lawn. Then I was swinging around the front of the house within sight of the sea.

From the lanai I could see into the two-story living room and Linda was standing there in the middle of that impressive expanse of glass. She waved away a maid who was coming to answer the door and came herself.

She had her hair high and was wearing a nifty white-and-flowered dress and had a flower in her hair, a gardenia. With the moon it was almost too much.

"I see you didn't wear the towel," she said.

In white linen upper I was, and cocoa-brown congo-cloth lower, with white shirt and garish tie. Who cares?

"Golly, you're beautiful," I said.

"Hmph," she said, "what are you selling?"

Into a reception room with tiled floor I was led and from there into the living room and I wondered if the architect hadn't forgotten the ticket windows and the PA system and the information desk. There were Sarouks on the floor in here, the only old note in the modern air of the place.

Curtis Ramsay, of the Ramsay Sugar interests but more noted as the father of Linda, was here in this room, getting up from a mammoth white leather chair to shake my capable hand.

A very ordinary looking man, except for the eyes, which had Linda's depth and blueness. Medium height and medium width and medium coloring and maybe a little more than medium sharp. More than a little maybe.

A lot of needlework and inspired cutting had gone into the blue suit he wore but it was wasted for some reason.

We talked of old times and old faces and future hopes. Then dinner was served and we went into the dining room. A Kerman was on the floor in here and a large family must have sweated a good part of its lives away on that baby. It was almost as large as the dining room.

It was about halfway through the meal when I asked Linda. "What'd that lad look like who drove me away last night?"

Her eyes went a little wide. "Don't you know him? He said it was something he'd done before and I thought – "

"At the risk of boring you with my virtues," I said, "I don't get drunk and rarely get sick, so the man was lying. I drink but don't get drunk for some reason. Last night I was drugged."

"I hoped so," Linda said.

Which didn't make sense at first, and then it did and I gave her my warm, secret, we-share-a-future smile.

"He was short," she told me. "Shorter than I am at any rate. And he was round, a regular roly-poly, and he had the kindest, roundest, merriest face you can imagine."

"Make a good Santa Claus around Christmas time," I said, "and save his strangling for the rest of the year."

"Sandy," she said, "you don't think he – "

"No," I told her, "I don't think one way or the other on him. Excepting that he was in it, as one of the stooges probably. How about this Jefferson Raleigh?"

Curtis (sugar magnate) Ramsay answered that one. "He works for me," he said. "Fine lad."

Linda nodded in agreement. "A nice boy." Looking at me. "What made you think of him?"

"My jealous nature probably," I said and I was probably right.

We were finishing dinner when Mr Ramsay got the phone call, which seemed to be urgent, because he asked to be excused, and he did hope I wouldn't think him rude.

Which left me alone with Linda. And that certainly couldn't be construed as rudeness even in my own highly correct gold book of social behavior.

"Would you like to go for a swim?" Linda suggested. "There are some trunks upstairs I'm sure you could wear."

It seemed like a good idea and she called the maid and had her bring the trunks and show me where to dress. This was the guest room in the back and I could see the road from here and it looked to me as if there was a big man sitting in the Packard convertible parked out there on the road. But there are lots of Packard convertibles on the island and quite a few big men.

Linda wore a white, pure-white, swimming suit. She was slim, all right, but not in any of the wrong places.

She could swim like a porpoise. The water is always warm so there's no danger of cramps but there is an undertow along this section of private beach. It didn't bother her and I started swimming when I was three, so we swam way out.

Then we swam back and sat on the sand and smoked and looked out at the moon on the water and watched the breakers rolling in. To the west we could see the lights of Waikiki and the public beach but they seemed far away.

"What happened to Tommy Rice?" I asked her.

The blue eyes were startled as they had a right to be. "Nothing," she said finally. "That's a strange question."

"Tactless, too," I said, "but I was wondering, because – " And I said no more.

She was laughing, now, quietly. "No broken heart if that's what you mean. We grew up together and then outgrew each other."

"Like that, huh?"

"Like that." Looking up at me, faintly wondering.

And I was looking down at her and wondering too. Her lips parted a little, the moon was in her eyes and I kissed her. There was some slight response, no denial anyway.

"Well," I said.

"Well?"

"Nothing," I said. "Just me, Sandy McKane, private eye at twenty a day when I get it, and a windfall here and there, and Linda Ramsay. Different leagues and it doesn't matter that you're as important to me as either or both of my arms."

"You talk too much," she said, "but if it helps you think go ahead."

The moon, looking down, was laughing.

"How about you?" I asked.

"Before that first party and since," she said. "Always in my mind like a tune you can't forget, Saunders McKane."

"Called Sandy."

"So called."

I kissed her again and the response was more than slight this time. I'll bet the moon stopped laughing.

"It's ridiculous," I said. "It's impossible, of course."

"Naturally," she said, "there wouldn't be movies if it weren't."

I said nothing.

"Linda McKane," she said. "That sounds all right don't you think."

"It sounds," I said, "a lot better than it would be."

Philosopher in borrowed trunks on the beach, looking stern.

At twelve the moon was still shining and I was driving slowly down the crushed lava road between the palms. There was no Packard parked there now, on the highway.

Down Kalakaua to Seaside and down Seaside. There was a light on in that house for sure this time – in the back, where the bedroom was. I drove past and pulled in to my own drive and walked back. There was a light on in the front room now and, very visible from the street, the short squat figure of Juan Mira.

I went up and rang the bell, and Juan came to the door. "You're taking a big chance," I told him, "coming around here. There's probably a cop watching us right now."

"I want to see this place," Juan said. "I want to see how she live."

"She lived here at least part of the time for at least a month," I said. "You told me she'd only been missing a week."

"For two weeks, two Saturdays I am in Hilo, two fights. When I come back she is there at the hotel. Juan no suspect."

"And something else," I said. "When she worked at the Hula Hut and Jerome's you kicked. But you practically made them give her that job at the Pikaki Room. Why?"

"Long time ago, Pikaki Room. She no love Juan then. I make play, get her job. Later she love Juan. Sabe now?"

"Okay," I said, "but get out of here quick. The police are just looking for a number-two boy, and you'd do."

He looked around the living room sadly and backed toward the bedroom. "You catch him soon, I hope," he said angrily.

"I'm no closer than I was this morning," I said, "and no brighter."

Only a little more in love, I thought, and perhaps a little more unhappy, though I hadn't been exactly joyous this morning.

I slept fairly well that night – because of the swim, no doubt.

I was at the office bright and early and the sound of Dr Ray Nakamura's drill was muffled but busy. A little Jap boy came along the hall, holding on to his mother's hand. Maybe it wasn't his mother. He looked scared and sick and the woman was worried.

They disappeared into the office of Dr Ray.

There was a kid in the doorway then, older than the one who was going to the dentist. This lad was about seventeen and he was barefoot. He was the captain of my own stalwart crew, the Barefoot Boys.

You'll find them all around town, on all the downtown corners – and in the pool halls, and in trouble, generally. Barefoot, all of them. The police call them "juvenile delinquents" and the papers "young hoodlums" but I just call them the Barefoot Boys. Pollyanna Sandy McKane, incipient secretary, YMCA.

This one in my office was about as close to pure Hawaiian as they come. He was a good lad over a pool table and he made a fine figure on a surf board. Out at the Waialae golf course he caddied for me occasionally and gave me a few pointers.

"I'm glad you dropped in," I said. "I've got a job for the gang, I think."

His black face split in a toothy grin and he rubbed his thumb against his forefinger.

"How much?"

"Later," I said and went to work, composing the list and looking up addresses, business and home.

When I was finished I handed it to him. "All you can get on all of them," I said.

"Pay now?"

I shook my head. "I did that once, remember? Pay later."

He went quietly out and down the hall. From the dentist's office came the sound of the drill and a whimper. The drill stopped a moment, then continued. I had a wisdom tooth that really needed pulling. But it could wait. I was too busy.

I went to the window and looked out. The big man was not in sight but there was a Packard parked across the street, a Packard convertible.

I studied my nails and hummed a little and went over to the ice chest and my little cupboard. Lots of powdered sugar left, plenty of gin – I made a Tom Collins. I phoned Dan Arliss, and asked him if Lemke had turned up anything on the pajamas. Lemke hadn't.

"How about that guy who drove me over there? Get any leads on that?"

"This town," Dan said caustically, "is loaded with little, skinny men who wear caps. It might take some time if you don't mind?"

I hung up slowly, trying to figure that one out, and there was only one way to figure it. I went to the phone book again. But if he was a working-man – Well, I'd try.

Jefferson Raleigh lived on Beretania near the Academy of Arts and near the realty office of the man named Walters. Walters' first name was Bruce and his office and home were combined.

I drove past to the apartment house where Jefferson Raleigh lived. In the hall of this small apartment building there were four mailboxes and four bell buttons.

I pressed the button belonging to Raleigh's apartment.

There was no answer.

A Japanese woman came through the door above, carrying a pail and a mop. Did she, I asked, have keys for all the apartments?

She nodded, looking at me doubtfully. I pulled the quick flash with my badge and tried to sound like a headquarters man.

"I have to get in there immediately. Lead the way."

It worked. She didn't even hesitate but hurried ahead of me through the door and up the stairs to the apartment on the right. She unlocked the door wordlessly and stepped aside for me to enter.

It was a furnished apartment, cheaply furnished. There was a pull-up chair, unoccupied, and a faded overstuffed chair, which was occupied.

The occupant had curly blond hair and a blond mustache and there was the handle of a knife protruding from his throat. Jefferson Raleigh was quite dead.

In his right hand, he held a hibiscus, of the color called apricot, which is one of the many.

5 Roly-Poly Man

The Japanese woman made some strangled sound in her throat and I turned to her swiftly.

"Get the manager. *Wikiwiki*." Which means hastily.

She left and I went to the phone and called the Station. Then I went over the place as thoroughly as I could in a hurry but found nothing that would do me any good.

Dan Arliss was the first one there though Lemke wasn't far behind. And Doc McGuire. They got there even before the manager, who came in looking sick.

Dan said something unprintable, looking from me to the body of Raleigh and back again. The manager was chattering something incoherent and Lemke was looking more pugnacious than ever.

It was a pleasant little tableau and it looked as if they had me picked for the heavy. I told them the way it was.

"Why'd you come here?" Dan asked.

"Because he told you the man who picked me up was thin. And I had it on better authority that he was fat. And I wanted to know why he lied."

"Sure. So he didn't answer the bell but you're in here."

"I thought there might be something here that would give me a tip-off, and I got the maid to let me in. I was going to give it a once-over lightly and – "

"That's breaking and entering. We throw guys in the can for that. You know that, huh?"

"I'm on a murder case," I said evenly. "The ethics of the thing, maybe didn't bother me as they should."

"You're on a murder case," Dan said, "and I'm on a merry-go-round – *because* you're on a murder case."

"Why argue with the guy, Dan?" Lemke questioned. "Let's throw him in the jug."

"Sure," I said, "why not? Put Lemke on it. He's bright."

"You don't want no trouble with me," Lemke said. "Stay in line, boy."

"You haven't got any trouble for me," I said. "Any time you think you have, for money, marbles or chalk, I'm ready."

Lemke sized me up and thought of something to say and then changed his mind. I'd had about enough from him to last me a long time.

"Any time you think you've got troubles, you could try it alone, like I'm doing, without the monthly check, and without the pension," I told Dan. "And if you want to put me in the can, either as a material witness or as a suspect, do it. Don't just talk about it. I don't give the tiniest hoot either way."

"All right." Dan's voice was weary. "I'll think it over. Hang around. Hang around out in the hall."

I stayed out there while Doc McGuire finished his job and they took the body out, while Dan quizzed the manager, while the print man and the photographer and the newspapermen handled their part of it. All alone, out in the hallway, I was alone with my thoughts.

Dan and Lemke came out finally. On a hunch, I said, "Why not take this Walters, this realtor, down to look at Raleigh's body?"

Dan looked at me quizzically. "You think, maybe he's the guy that Valdez dame was – "

"Maybe," I said. "Just a guess." Just an unreasonable tie-up in my mind. I could have said it was because of the proximity of this apartment to the realty office.

Dan was looking thoughtful. "All right. How about this hibiscus? You got any ideas on that?"

"Looks like a warning, doesn't it? Unless the killer is crazy. The only sensible answer is that it's a warning."

"Which would bring in the rackets," Dan said. "Some kind of racket."

I nodded.

"And your client."

"You're guessing," I told him. "We're not going to start that all over again, are we?"

Lemke was saying nothing, which was a blessing. Dan studied the floor and looked back into the apartment and back to me.

"I'll see you later. Drop in this afternoon."

"Sure," I said – and, "Who phoned the other night and tipped you off to Dolly Valdez' death?"

Dan shrugged. "Some man. He didn't leave a name. We tried to check up but we couldn't."

He left then and I left. I drove slowly back to the office. Dan's car, I saw as I was going past, was parked in front of the realtor's office – the man named Walters who had thought they were man and wife, Dolly and her new friend.

Back to Hotel Street and the snug confines of my home away from home. Back to make another drink and to call up Juan Mira on the phone.

I told him about the death of Jefferson Raleigh, and the hibiscus in his hand.

"Want to come down and talk to me about it?" I asked.

"Why I come down? I no know him."

Why, indeed? "I thought perhaps you could have some information that would help."

He didn't have.

"Your name hasn't come into this," I told him, "and I'll try to see that it doesn't. But the Police aren't happy about my being such a gentleman."

"I no want the Police in my business."

Nor me, evidently. I had no more words for him. I didn't seem to be earning the three hundred dollars. I surely wouldn't earn it sitting around here. I went out and walked down Hotel Street to the Hula Hut.

The same girl was coming out of the water in the mural behind the bar. She still wore the same reflective look. Whether or not it was the same bartender I didn't know. So I asked him.

He nodded. "Sure. Why?"

"Somebody slipped me a Mickey."

"Not me," he said. "What were you drinking?"

"Ladies' Aid."

"That could do it."

"Not to me," I said.

He shrugged. "You're wasting your time."

"I'd like to talk to Vic," I said.

"What's your name?"

"McKane, Sandy McKane."

He walked the length of the bar and came out from behind it, walked through the deserted dining room to the deserted bandstand and around that to the office behind it.

In less than a minute he was on his way back. "Vic'll see you," he said. "His office is behind the stage."

"Thank you," I said. "Thank you kindly."

He said nothing – nothing I could hear anyway. The office was small, paneled in koa wood. Vic was sitting behind a green steel desk and he didn't get up as I entered.

"Trouble?" he asked.

"Jefferson Raleigh was killed. The police just found his body. Or rather I did."

Interest showed in the face all right. The name spelled something. "What's your angle, Sandy?"

"A case. A piece of business. You seem to be getting in the way. I come here, get drugged. Get picked up outside and darn near framed. Your big boy with the little mind is haunting me." I was building myself up to a peeve. "You wouldn't expect me to steer clear of you after all that, would you?"

"Lots do," he said.

"Maybe you frighten them."

"Maybe." He studied a paper on his desk. He looked up. "I'm no scoutmaster. It's no secret to you that I might even be outside the law."

"Well?"

"Lots of people in this town outside the law. Some of them I get along with and some I don't."

"I'm still listening."

He lighted up a cigar, studied the end for a moment and then went on, "You're working for Juan or you were the other night when you came in. Maybe you've switched over to the Police by now, in which case I could clam up. But there are some things I want you to understand."

I lit a cigarette without studying the end.

"I didn't drug you or have you drugged," he explained. "I didn't have you picked up or framed. You can believe that or not – this time it happens to be true. Somebody would like to have it look like I'm doing these things. Maybe Mira, though we've got no reason to fight. There's plenty of business for both of us."

"And the big boy who's living in my hair?"

"I'll call him off."

"Sure. But why is he haunting me now?"

He waited too long to answer. He waited long enough to make up an answer.

"I thought you were nosing into something else. I found out you're not."

A random thought hit me and made sense but I didn't give it a voice. "Jefferson Raleigh worked for you, didn't he?" I asked.

He took a little time on that one, too. "No," he answered.

Which was a lie, of course, or he wouldn't have taken any time.

"Maybe Juan's business is being cut into," I said.

"Not by me. I've got all I can handle. All my protection will cover."

That protection sentence was a phony, to scare me, to get the upper hand. All his protection came in holsters.

But he didn't scare me. And it was a sure thing I didn't scare him enough to be noticeable.

I went to the door. "I hope we don't have to tangle," I said.

"I hope so too," he said, but his voice was flat. He wasn't going to lose any sleep about that.

Outside, traffic was going by and a little brown kid was trying to sell a shoe shine to a round and roly-poly kind of man who was lounging near the awning over Vic's cellar entrance. This man had the merriest, kindest face you can imagine. I was in a bad mood.

I went over to stand about an inch away from him and I put my ugliest scowl on my face.

"Strangle anybody lately, junior?" I asked. "Take any drunks home?"

There was honest and startled surprise in the roly-poly face of the roly-poly man. "I, sir," he said, "am a full professor of botany at the University of Hawaii. Is there anything I can do for you?"

I took a big gulp of air and closed my eyes. I opened them. I said meekly, "Could you tell me the color hibiscus *don't* come in."

"Blue, of course," he said, "though many able men are working on that, too. It might not be long before we have blue hibiscus."

I could hardly wait. I thanked him gently and walked quietly away. Three thousand varieties of hibiscus – but no blue.

It wasn't afternoon yet but I drove over to the Police Station, and Dan was there in the office, making smoke.

"Well?" I said.

"Dolly's pal," he admitted. "Walters was sure about that. For a chubby little Filipino she did all right, didn't she?"

"Yup." He wasn't watching me. "Still hot?" I said.

He turned around in his chair and his quiet tired eyes came up to meet mine. "Nobody likes to get told off in front of subordinates. No cop likes to get told off by a citizen. But maybe I had it coming. Next time be a little more respectful."

"Right. I was a little unnerved."

There was a question in his eyes but he didn't want to voice it. I said, "If I don't crack this thing in forty-eight hours, you can have my client. I won't only give you his name, I'll drag him in here and sit him in your lap. I'm getting a little fed up with him myself."

"Okay." Then. "You've got your boys working again, haven't you? Your young hoodlums?"

"Maybe," I said and laughed.

"People are complaining. One old lady found one of them in the back of her car when she came back from marketing and she passed right out."

"They're active," I admitted. "I'll tone them down." Just words, to make sound in a quiet place. Then. "Anything else you'd like me to know now that we're friends again?"

"Nothing. And we're not exactly holding hands yet. Remember that. You get a lot of freedom around this town, Sandy."

"That's what I like about it," I said. "That and the remarkable efficiency of this alert, progressive Department."

"Beat it," he said. "Go some place where they like you."

"All doors are open to me," I told him, "because of my charming nature."

"Find one," he said. "Go find one *Wikiwiki*." Which means quickly as I've told you before.

One place I'm always welcome because of my promptness with the rent is my office. So I went there.

I considered mixing a drink but if I mixed many more today I would be well on the path to becoming a lush. So I resisted the temptation. I sat and thought of Linda but that didn't get me anywhere either. So I stopped thinking about Linda. I tried anyway.

I picked up the phone and called Juan. He was in and I told him that the man who had been killed this morning was the man who had shared the house with his Dolly.

There was a long silence on the other end of the line. Finally his voice came matter-of-factly. "I glad he dead. You kill him?"

"No."

"Well, I glad he dead."

Which was about all he had to say this sunny day. Glib, articulate Juan Mira, always talking, always chattering away.

I went back to thinking about Linda – about her hair and the cool firm slimness of her and her lack of pose and her straightness. I thought of her wearing a blue apron and standing in the doorway of my little stucco castle. First in a yellow apron, then in a green one, but none of them looked natural to me. They looked like something out of a woman's magazine.

I put together what I had. Linda I'd met at Vic's place. And Raleigh was working for Mr Ramsay and probably for Vic. Juan was being warned but two murders had gone into that and why hadn't they just had one murder, Juan's? It would have served the same purpose.

One reason I could think of – Juan was popular with the Filipinos, a sort of minor god. If anything happened to him personally this town would rock. Well, that was one. Another was that Juan had customers, a customer list or a customer loyalty, and they needed that.

If it was customers I could guess at the product. It's quite a business with our population.

Which brought me back to the Ramsays, father and daughter, and what was papa's part in this? In it he was by what little I had so far. Maybe, later, he'd be cleared – I hoped.

The phone rang and I answered it and it was Dan Arliss' dry voice. "I just got a tip you were jealous of this Raleigh guy. Anything in it?" A sort of chuckle but without humor.

"Sure," I said, "that's why I bumped him. Who was responsible for the information?"

"I wouldn't tell you if I knew," Dan said. "I've got to protect our citizens."

He hung up. I wasn't doing any good here. I went down to the little convertible.

6 Red Hibiscus

Mr Ramsay's offices were out on Dillingham Boulevard but Curtis Ramsay wasn't there this morning. He was out at the house his secretary told me – which was where I didn't want to go.

It was close to noon so I stopped in Waikiki to eat, and I took my time. Getting to the Ramsay house at lunchtime would maybe put me at a disadvantage.

Then I was driving slowly up the Diamond Head Road and turning slowly in at the drive. When I got to the front of the house I could see a figure in a white bathing suit, down at the beach and I think she was looking my way, but I didn't wave.

A maid came to the door and I gave her my name and told her my desire. She went back to see if Mr Curtis Ramsay cared to see me this morning.

He evidently did and she ushered me into the glass-fronted room a little later.

Curtis Ramsay was wearing gray this morning and this suit had about the same effect the blue one had had, which was none. He was sitting in the same white leather chair and he rose as he had the evening before. The same mechanical smile was on his face.

I asked, "Any of the servants likely to be within hearing distance?"

He was motionless a moment and then he shook his head. He pulled up another chair, close to the leather one, and I sat in that.

"One of your employees was murdered," I opened. "Man named Jefferson Raleigh."

His eyes were on my face with nothing in them. "Well?"

"He also worked for Vic Malis. You know Vic?"

He nodded. "I know who he is."

"He work for you too?"

No anger came to the face but he was very watchful. He was being very careful.

"What are you getting at?"

"I don't know myself," I said. "Somebody called the police this morning and told them I was jealous of Jefferson Raleigh. I said that here last night in jest."

He tried to put some indignation into his voice but it was phony. "What is the purpose of this ridiculous conversation?"

"That's what I'm trying to find out. I came up here for information but maybe you haven't got any. Or any you want to give me."

I rose, ready to leave. He was looking at me and he thought for a moment of stopping me. Of that I was sure. But he didn't. His eyes were still on me and they were thoughtful. I turned and went out and I could feel them on my back until I left the room.

Linda was out there, on the flagstone lanai. She was in the white swimming suit. "Hey, snob, who do you think you're ignoring?" she asked.

"Whom," I corrected her.

She wrinkled her nose.

I said, "I'm sure your dad doesn't want you to talk to me. Go in and see."

I went down to the car, got in and started the motor and drove away. When I turned the corner she was still standing on the lanai, staring.

I drove down the Diamond Head Road to where it joined Kalakaua. There's a little jog here and I parked so I could watch the traffic both ways.

All kinds of traffic went by – cars, big and little, driven by people of both sexes – of Chinese ancestry and Korean and Japanese and Filipino, of Portuguese, white and black and *haole* – which is white – and *hapahaole* – which is half white. There was all kinds of other hapas, and all kinds of mixtures, the arithmetical possibility of the current strains being 127 if you're interested.

Then a black Lincoln convertible with the top down went by, making time. Vic Malis was behind the wheel.

I started my car and drove slowly back to the office. There I mixed a good strong drink and sat in my chair, sulking.

It was quiet in the office with no sound of the drill. From outside came a little traffic noise but it was muffled up here as though from far away. I heard heavy feet coming down the hall and they turned in at my door. I looked up to see the bulk of Meat Kozak filling the doorway.

He came all the way in and closed the door behind him and locked it. He had a clean sport shirt on today. He walked right over to me, and stood there on the other side of the desk.

"Why don't you leave Vic alone?"

I started to get up and one big hand came over to sit me down again. It was a casual gesture but it jarred me. My shoulder hurt.

"Vic ain't bothering you and there's no reason you should be bothering him, see? You gonna lay off?"

I shook my head. His big hand came around with surprising speed and slapped me out of my chair. My ear was ringing when I got up off the floor.

He was standing over me and started a right hand. I put all I had into a right to beat him to it. I was flat-footed and I had my weight in it and it connected. I could feel pain all the way up to my shoulder. His own right landed somewhere along my jaw and the roof fell in . . .

When my eyes opened again, my door was open and Dr Ray Nakamura, in starchy white, was bending over me. In the doorway a little Japanese boy stood with a white towel fastened as a bib.

"Shall I call the Police?" Nakamura wanted to know. I shook my head.

"Private battle," I said. It hurt to talk.

He went out, looking doubtful, taking his curious customer with him. I straightened my upset chair and sat in it, rubbing my jaw. My right hand was swelling up but I didn't think anything was broken.

I sat there a long time, feeling sorry for myself and not thinking of anything much that was coherent.

Some time later the phone rang. It was Linda's voice and would I be in the office all afternoon? I said I would. She would be down as quickly as she could get here.

I sat, waiting, rubbing my jaw and watching my hand, which was dark now between the first two knuckles but which had stopped swelling. I was faintly sick to my stomach. I didn't want a drink.

Linda wore kelly-green shantung, which did things for her. And to me. I got up and motioned to a chair. She took it.

"Why were you up at the house this morning, Sandy?" she asked.

"To see your dad."

"He's in trouble, isn't he?"

"What makes you think so?"

"A little while after you left Vic Malis came up to the house and Dad took him back to his study in the rear."

I smiled. "You listened."

Her blue eyes widened. "How do you know?"

"Didn't you?"

"I did. I couldn't hear all of it, just enough to know that Vic and Dad must have been in business together. Dad said he was through, that Vic could have the whole filthy mess. What did he mean by that, Sandy?"

"He means that they aren't going to be partners any more. I can't be sure about the business."

"Is it that liquor – ?"

One of the by-products of the Ramsay sugar interests was liquor from cane. Excellent stuff for removing the enamel from your teeth. Some people even drink it. Filipinos even relish it.

"No," I said, "it isn't the liquor. That's a crime but not illegal. Only against reason and taste."

"You're not being flippant, are you?" she said.

"Maybe I was. I'm sorry, Linda. What I'm on is a murder case. Maybe your dad's mixed up in it, and maybe he isn't. That's all I've got right now."

"Is this going to make any difference between us?"

I shook my head. "The only thing that would change that situation would be my coming into a couple million dollars. The possibilities of that are very remote."

She rose, her face frozen. She said, "It would be your decision," and left.

I could hear her heels clicking down the hallway. I went to the window and saw her leave the building entrance. Across the street a little fat man was lounging. When Linda came out he turned his back and pretended to be absorbed in the show window behind him. When she was out of sight he turned around again.

I couldn't see from here whether he had the roundest, kindest face, imaginable or not. I could see it wasn't the full professor of botany. Maybe it was an assistant professor but I didn't think so.

I took my .38 out of the drawer and put it in the pocket of my Palm Beach suit, wrinkled. I went down the stairs and outside and looked across the street. He was gone.

I went back up, feeling faintly foolish. But I took off my jacket and put on my shoulder harness and put the .38 in that.

I sat there for a while, hating the world and wondered what time my barefoot boy would show up. I mixed a drink finally and drank it, not worrying if I was becoming a lush or not.

My phone rang some aeons later and I answered it. It was Linda again and she said, "I found a red hibiscus in the seat of my car. What does it mean, Sandy?"

"It means you shouldn't go anywhere without a cop. You had better phone them right away, right now."

When I put the phone back on the cradle I was sweating but I wasn't hot. A kid was selling papers down below and I waved for him to come up and bought one.

The new hibiscus murder was all over page one and the hibiscus angle was given lots of ink, but Sandy McKane was not mentioned by name. Jefferson Raleigh, the paper said, had held a responsible position in Ramsay Sugar and there was no known motive for his death.

Which meant that the police had soft-pedaled the house-sharing angle or the papers had. None of it made sense. Maybe it was Dan's idea.

I spent some more time feeling owly. I went to the window but the lounger's heaven was vacant. I went out to supper.

7 Dead in the Night

After supper I came back to the office and my boy was there, holding a handful of notes written in pencil and looking greedy.

"How much?" he said.

"Let's see them."

He handed them over and I looked through them hastily.

Then I said, "How much?"

"Twenty," he said.

I gave him two fives and a ten. "See that the other boys get a cut for a change," I said. "I don't want them heckling me."

"Sure," he said. "Of course." At the doorway he turned and said, "Aloha," and then I heard the pad of his feet in the hall.

There was something here. There was a farm Juan had gone to that afternoon and the name of an importer Vic had gone to and an address Meat had gone to and lots of things that weren't any help at all.

The farm, I decided, could wait until tomorrow. I went downstairs and climbed into my busy little car.

I went down King, going north, and the smell of fish from the markets blanketed the air. Across from the markets, there were some ramshackle buildings. One of them was called the T. Y. Young Importing Company and the door was open. I pushed in.

The place was lofty and piled high with merchandise. It smelled of tea and camphor and perfume and dust. Toward the back there was a light coming from the glass doorway of a little walled-in corner office. I went back to the door and knocked.

There was a Chinese in there, round and placid, wearing a black silk, or silky, suit and a jade ring I could see from the doorway. He was sitting at a desk and he beckoned me in.

I came in and told him who I was and went through the business of flashing my badge, hoping it would frighten him. His smooth face didn't lose any of its placidity. His eyes were dreamy, out of this world, and I thought I detected a sweetish odor among the others.

"You do business through Vic Malis, don't you?" I asked.

His hands were folded over his big middle, the jade ring very much in evidence. "Maybe," he said.

"Cocaine? Heroin? Opium?"

His head moved slowly in the negative. "Fish."

"Vic doesn't sell fish," I said.

"Doesn't he?" Not that he was interested, his face said.

"You've been reading too many stories about the enigmatic, shrewd Oriental," I told him. "The heat's on and you won't find the clink any more pleasant just because you're not talkative."

"What do you want?" he asked. "You want to buy something?"

"I want some co-operation," I said.

"Why? Who are you? Sandy McKane with the big nose. You are not the Police. With the Police I co-operate."

"Okay," I said. "I'll call them." And I reached for the phone on his desk.

He didn't move at first. I called the Police Station number and his hand gestured and, when they answered, I asked if it was the Bishop National Bank. It wasn't and I put the phone back.

"All right," I said, "I imagine that movement of your hand meant something."

"What do you want?" he said.

"I want to know if Vic's the only one you work for. I don't give a hoot about your business. I can guess it by your eyes. But has anybody been trying to sell you something else?"

He nodded. "A little round man, used to work for Vic."

"What'd he try to sell you?"

"In the same line. A cheap product."

"He doesn't work for Vic any more?"

The negative movement, slow.

"You know his name?"

"No. I never knew it, even before."

"Is it what Juan Mira sells?" I asked.

His big shoulders moved slightly. "Might be."

I left him to his dreams then and went through the big room of many smells and out to the fish smell.

I had another address not far from here and I went over there. I parked about a block away and walked the rest. There was a rooming house here, an unpainted wooden structure that called itself the Queen Hotel but hadn't been that for a long time. The fish odor carried over there.

There was a slovenly hapa-Hawaiian woman in what had once been the lobby but was now her quarters. I asked her if she had as a tenant the rolypoly man. She thought she had but he wasn't in.

I went out again and, in the yard of the house next door, there was a hibiscus shrub with red hibiscus blooming on the shrub. No one seemed to be around. I sneaked over and broke off a blossom.

I went back to the rooming house, and gave it to the landlady. "Give this to him when he comes in," I said. "It's just a joke but he'll understand. He'll appreciate it."

She looked puzzled and then she began to look a little scared. She probably read the papers. But she assured me he would get it.

I went back and brought the car a little closer, and turned on the radio and waited. A sailor went by, drunk, and a sailor went by, sober. Both of them turned into the rooming house. Your guess as to why is as good as mine.

Some other assorted characters turned into the rooming house, but none of them stayed much more than ten minutes, including the sailors. This was just like River Street.

Somebody was strumming a guitar somewhere and singing something about not finding another Kanaka like him. Maybe she didn't want to.

In about a half hour a car stopped in front of the rooming house, a Chevvy coupé, and a little round man got out of it and went up the walk and disappeared through the door. I cut off the radio and waited.

The little round man came out, moving hurriedly, and climbed into the Chevvy. I kicked my car into life. The Chevvy started with a shudder, batting over toward King. I wasn't far behind. Just far enough not to be noticeable.

Up King I trailed him to Bethel, and up Bethel to Hotel and down Hotel to the Hula Hut. Here he parked and went in. I parked not too far behind and waited. I waited a long time and nothing happened. Some customers went in and a few customers came out – but not the round man.

I felt the weight of my .38 under my jacket and the heft of it was reassuring. I got out of the car and over to the entrance of the Hula Hut. I went down the stairs and in.

At a table not too far from the bar Curtis Ramsay and Vic Malis were in earnest and quiet conversation. There was no sign of the rolypoly man.

I ordered a drink and looked the place over carefully and considered asking the bartender some questions. But he wasn't too agreeable a type.

I went out and up the stairs again and the Chevvy was gone. I cursed quietly and with some fluency and went back to the car and waited.

Some time later, Curtis Ramsay came out alone and I blew the horn and opened the door of my car. He walked over.

"Feeling like talking any more now?" I asked him.

His shoulders sagged, and the face he lifted to mine was heavy with fatigue. He was a beaten man. "Where?" he asked.

"In my office. It's right up the street."

He climbed into the car without saying a word. I drove the few blocks to my office. He took the chair on the other side of the desk and asked me, "What do you want to know?"

"About Raleigh and Dolly Valdez."

"I wish I knew. My daughter got one of those hibiscus today. Did you know that?"

I nodded.

"It's my fault I suppose – getting myself into the mess I have but I didn't think she would ever – " He broke off, and ran a tired hand over his face. He looked about ready for a collapse.

"Sugar business bad?" I asked him.

"You know what income taxes are," he asked me, "for a man in my income bracket?"

"I can guess."

"Terrific," he said. "I'm not trying to blame anybody but myself, but there wasn't enough left, not enough for all I wanted. And there was this easy way to make it with a market crying for stuff, according to Vic, and all he needed was a little money. Not a lot to start with, though we went into bigger money later. None of it I would need to declare."

"Dope," I said. "Opium."

"I'm not saying," he told me.

"Raleigh?"

"Worked for us, knew the markets, handled the women."

"You let your daughter go with him."

"No. She met him at the house one day and he did the rest. I told her I didn't favor it, and she didn't care for him particularly. So there wasn't much danger, there."

"How about this little round man, the rolypoly one? Do you know who he is?"

He shook his head wearily. I couldn't feel any particular sympathy for him. Not for anyone who made money out of the drug racket.

"Do you think Linda is in serious danger?" he asked me.

"I suppose she is. You have some protection up at the house?"

He nodded. "Police."

He had no more answers that would do me any good – excepting that he hadn't told the police I might be jealous of Raleigh. After he left I sat for awhile in the office, thinking of nothing much. My jaw was all right and the swelling in my hand had gone down. The bruise between the first and second knuckles was still evident though.

I went to bed early and tossed for a long time. It was a bad night.

In the morning paper I read that Curtis Ramsay of the Ramsay sugar interests had died in the night. He had taken (by mistake, the paper said) an overdose of sleeping tablets.

8 Long Enough

I ate at home and went directly out to this farm the next morning. It was out beyond Waipahu, off the Farrington Highway, and I would know it, the note said, by an enormous banyan tree in the front yard.

I found it and turned up the rutted drive. There were two or three small houses here and some Filipino kids playing in the strip of lawn between the houses. The house facing the road must be the one Juan Mira had gone to the day before because the banyan tree was directly in front of it.

I knocked on the front door.

There was some conversation inside in one of the Filipino dialects and then a thin, sallow Filipino woman opened the door. "I'm a friend of Juan's," I said, "and he sent me out to look the place over."

The woman looked doubtful and I didn't blame her. She called something in the language to the man in the room with her and he came to the door. He looked more than doubtful – he looked suspicious.

"What is your name?"

"McKane," I said. "Sandy McKane."

The suspicion melted a little, I thought. "Juan speak of you."

"He's been trying to sell me an interest," I lied, "but I like to see what I'm buying. Can't blame me for that, can you?"

He smiled doubtfully, not at all sure. "What did you want to see?"

"The crop."

The woman said something in the dialect to him and her voice was shrill. His answering voice was harsh and then he came out and closed the door.

"Women," he said, and beckoned for me to follow.

There was a field back of the houses and some weeds, high and thick, surrounding the field. What was growing in the field was some kind of five-leafed plant which I didn't recognize, but I took a guess.

"Hemp?" I asked.

He nodded. "There are some other fields over a ways."

"It looks good to me," I said.

He nodded. "Good money crop."

Good marihuana crop, I thought, and, if it's Indian hemp, good hashish. "A cheap product," the Chinese had said, "in the same line." Cheap enough for high school kids and the poor who couldn't afford the more expensive lines of forgetfulness and degeneration.

He walked back to the car with me.

"Juan sent you, all right?" he asked.

I just looked at him. I started the motor and drove away. I rolled, going back to town. They couldn't kill Juan because he controlled the source of supply. Maybe they had a little of their own but not in the quantities Juan had it. And with reefers selling for about a quarter apiece quantity was necessary in this business.

I drove over to the Kealia Hotel when I got back to town. The desk clerk was sure Mr Mira was still in bed and wouldn't want to be disturbed.

"Give him a buzz anyway," I told him, "and tell him Sandy McKane has to see him, right away."

Which, after some hemming and a little hawing, he agreed to do.

Juan would see me. I went up in the elevator and down the hall and he had the door open when I got there. He was dressed in lavender silk pajamas and a purple silk robe and patent leather slippers.

After I was in and he'd closed the door I said, "I've just been out to the farm."

"Farm?" Nothing showed in the face.

"Your farm or one of them."

Something showed in the face now – anger. "You in Juan's business?"

"Not for a million dollars. But if you'd told me what it was when you first came to see me I might have had more luck. Or I might have turned you down, depending on my morals that day."

"I no like this," he said.

"Nor me. There's a little fat roly-poly man who seems to be in the same business. A competitor, you might call him. Know him?"

He was looking thoughtful.

"Used to work for Vic Malis," I prompted him.

"Garcia, Joe Garcia. Round man?"

"Round man."

He nodded emphatically. "Joe Garcia. He kill my Dolly?"

"Maybe. He was trying to sell T. Y. Young some reefers but T. Y. works through Vic alone."

"T. Y. Young? I no know him."

"You've got your own agents, your own organization?"

"I have my friends." He put a hand on my arm. "You know who kill Dolly?"

"Just about," I said. "I've got a very good hunch but I wouldn't want to name any names yet. I'm not that sure."

He nodded, looking through me. He had nothing more to say.

From there I drove back to town and down to the fish market district again. They were doing a big business this morning but the odor was no stronger, I felt certain. There are limits.

I drove over to the rooming house which was formerly the Queen Hotel and the semi-Hawaiian lady wasn't up but there was a girl in a sleazy black kimono who was. She told me Joe Garcia lived in the front room on the right side of the second floor and I could go up myself and see if he was home.

I went carefully up the stairs and down the hall to the front. I put my .38 in the pocket of my coat and kept my hand on it while I knocked on the door with my left hand. No answer.

I knocked again without result. Then I tried the knob and the door was open. I kicked it open the rest of the way and stepped in quickly.

It was empty. But there was a closet door, closed. That too was empty. I opened some drawers, and found nothing. The bed had been slept in and there were enough clothes in the closet to make me certain he hadn't changed addresses.

There was a tablet of cheap note paper on top of the dresser. I wrote a note in pencil:

> *Joe,*
>   *It is very important that I see you in my office this afternoon, very important to you.*
>
> *Sandy McKane*

From there I drove over to the Hula Hut. I kept my .38 in the pocket of my jacket. The front door was closed, locked. But that was just for business. I rattled it and in a couple of minutes Vic Malis was coming along the narrow barroom. He didn't look glad to see me. I stepped in and he closed the door again.

"Come back to the office," he said.

I shook my head. "Just a couple of questions."

"I can't guarantee the answers," he said.

"Joe Garcia still working for you?" I asked him.

"No. He's too ambitious. I tied a can to him a couple of months ago. That's a straight answer."

"He's trying to sell your customers."

No answer to that.

"T. Y. Young, for one."

No answer.

"You really didn't have Meat shadowing me, did you? You were just covering for him the other day."

No answer.

"I figured you a little smarter," I told him. "After you get yourself a nice clean profitable business it wouldn't be smart to get it all smashed up because one of your boys goes in for a little personal murder on the side.

"But if you want to take the rap for him, okay. Maybe the police will begin to wonder why Ramsay took so many sleeping tablets. Maybe they'll tie it up with the hibiscus Joe Garcia put in his daughter's car. Maybe they'll get the whole story."

"From you?"

"All I want to know is – did you have Meat shadow me the other day? And Garcia."

He hesitated. Between loyalty, maybe, and his nice business. Though I really shouldn't accuse him of loyalty, not this boy.

"I didn't."

"Meat's getting ambitious?"

"With what you tell me, maybe."

"Raleigh, how about him? Did you send him to spy on this Valdez girl? Did he make a play for her to get the dope on Juan?"

"I don't think so. He just liked women. I didn't send him anyway. There's no money in Juan's business, not the kind of money I want and not the kind of customers."

"Okay," I said. "I'll be seeing you. I'll be in for a steak."

I went out and he locked the door behind me again. I went over to the office and read the morning paper. There was nothing in it about the hibiscus Linda had received, so the papers didn't know. If they had, that and her father's death would have been too good a story for them to kill. I mixed a drink, my first of the day.

I thought about Linda and tried to stop thinking about her. I felt hungry and irritable and nervous.

At noon I went out to lunch. I ate quickly and came right back to the office. Nothing happened. Nothing happened in the office, that is. Around the island it might have been raining and in other spots not raining. People were probably making love and making biscuits and making marihuana from hemp.

Kids were studying in school and other kids were hanging around corners and in pool halls, studying life. Out at Waikiki on the sand and in the cane fields and the pineapple fields day laborers would be putting in their day of labor. But nothing happened in my office excepting that I began to fidget.

I mixed another drink and thought about Linda and tried to stop thinking about Linda.

About three the phone rang, and a carefully guarded voice came over the wire. "I just got your note. You want to see me?"

"That's right, Joe."

"What about?"

"About saving your life."

"You crazy or something?"

"You want to come over and find out?"

Hesitation, then, "Okay. In about ten minutes."

In about eight he was there and I didn't think he had such a kind face. It was round and not wrinkled but his eyes were hard.

He closed the door behind him, and kept his hand in his pocket. He had a wrinkled linen suit on and no hat and dirty white-and-black shoes.

"What's your story?" he said.

"The Police," I lied, "are trying to nail you for the death of Dolly Valdez and Jefferson Raleigh."

"Those weren't mine."

"I know they weren't. They were Meat Kozak's. But you were the man who drove me out there to Dolly's. Your prints are on the bed out there and they want somebody in a hurry. You'll do. You'll be a lamb they can throw to the lions."

He shook his head. "Never."

"Vic knows you're working against him and that Meat is. Vic's gunning for both of you."

"You don't make sense," he said. "You're talking to the wrong man."

"Maybe I am," I said. "I've got two boys who saw Meat go into Raleigh's apartment and leave it at the time Raleigh was killed. That should do it but if you want to take the rap it won't matter to me. My client will be satisfied and I've already got my money."

He said nothing.

"Raleigh left some information behind, too," I told him. "This is a hard island to get off of, if the police want you, Joe, and too small for hiding in very long."

The door behind him opened and closed. There was a big man standing in the office now, a man named Meat Kozak. He too had his hand in his pocket.

Garcia turned and I looked up and Meat said, "You were lying about those boys of yours, huh?"

I shook my head.

"Why should I kill Raleigh?"

"Because he saw you kill Dolly Valdez. He was hiding in the house when you strangled her and he tried to blackmail you later. So you killed him too. You wanted Juan's business or a part of it.

"It wasn't big enough for Vic but it would do for you and you used that hibiscus gag as a warning. You sent them to Juan so he'd get the tie-up and you killed Juan's girl friend. You couldn't touch him personally without getting into more trouble than you could handle. And without losing your intended source of supply."

"Sounds good," he said. "Only you're guessing."

I shook my head. "I've still got my two boys."

Garcia looked frightened now – but not Meat. Meat just looked thoughtful and ugly. He took his hand out of his pocket. The gun was in it. Maybe he meant to kill me. I never found out. Because, for the third time, the door opened.

Meat whirled swiftly and saw who was there. He tried a shot, a fast shot, and it looked as if it missed for it went crashing into the door and through it.

Garcia and I hit the floor as flame and racket erupted near the doorway.

Meat turned around once, slowly, like a slow-motion picture. Then he crashed. I saw for a moment the short, dapper figure of Juan Mira. Then he toppled too. Meat's shot hadn't missed. It had gone through Mira and then through the door. It was the final count, the last round, for Mira, the often defeated . . .

Meat lived long enough to confess. Garcia lived long enough to be killed about a week later by a person or persons unknown. Linda no longer lives in the big house by the sea. She lives in the little house by the canal, and her last name is McKane, and we're doing very well, thank you.

HELL ON WHEELS

Thomas S. Roche

THE CAR SHOULD have spelled it out for me, early on. She drove a '56 Mercury Medalist, the 292 bored out to a 312 with a stock Holly Haystack carb and one fuck of a hot cam. Hell on wheels. It was the radials that really made the difference, though, they stuck to the road like bad news to an ex-con. She'd glued a plastic Jesus on the dash and hung a St Christopher medal from the rear-view, presumably in case the radials gave out.

Those goddamn radials. Not even a hint of scratch, just nothing but grip from the second you laid it down. That fucker could haul ass, go from zero to ninety in the time it took you to shit your pants and it didn't stop there while you pissed them, too. The 312 never even worked up a sweat.

Lady drives a car like that, she just ain't safe.

Then I should have known to back off when she said to meet her at the Hammerhead. A rich lady hangs out at the Hammerhead, something's wrong with her, she's got a thing for danger, or maybe a death wish. The Hammerhead is down by the water, out on the Delta. It's by the freeway so there's a weird mix there of bikers, killer truckers, freaks, and college kids. But not your normal college kids, it's kids buying speed, looking for trouble, that sort of thing. And not your average truckers – the kind of guys you figure are shipping human heads to some factory upstate. Or something. And freeway hookers looking for tricks. It's a nasty place, nasty things happen there. I saw this guy get cut up in there, seems someone didn't like his colors so they did that beer bottle trick you always see in movies but never seems to happen much in real life. Turned out later the biker who did the cutting had a knife in his back pocket, he just liked the idea of grinding that shattered beer bottle into the guy's face. He was laughing as the cops led him away. Still gives me bad dreams sometimes, on my bad days.

Me, I don't wear colors. Roxanne Ketchum, she wears black.

I don't expect her to show up, but sure enough the lady is a tramp. Ha ha ha. She slides into the bar, real cool, like she belongs there, clearing a path through the crowd of Angels. Whistles go up as she passes, and she ignores them. She's changed into a tight black skirt and a white T-shirt that shows just what it needs to show. She doesn't look anything like that bored, rich woman who had her Medalist fixed at my garage today, the one who was bossing me around, the one who gave me a goddamn *tip*, for Chrissake. She could even be a local trailer-park whore or something – only thing that gives her away are those boots, pointy-toed, black patent leather, knee-high, buckled. The sort you just can't get in a small town. That's City stuff – Haight-Ashbury, Nordstrom's.

Ketchum's up close to me in a second, against the bar, like she doesn't even need to know me to come on to me.

She leans up hard against me and asks what I'm drinking. *Jack and Ginger. That's a kid's drink*, she tells me, orders her Jack straight up.

We make some small talk, about cars mostly. She knows more about engines than any lady I've ever known. I tell her a thing or two about Mercs, but there isn't a lot she doesn't know. I tell her about the bored out 312 and the power transfer down the drive shaft. She seems impressed. Go figure. She tells me she's thinking of going home early, doesn't like to be out late and get a hangover. She wants to hit the sack by midnight. Now it's my turn to be impressed.

"You're a Mrs for a reason, right – *Mrs* Ketchum?" I say.

"Everything that happens has a reason," she tells me, and gets down off the barstool, tossing a bill on the counter.

Five minutes after that we're in the Merc. My hand's on her thigh, and she isn't wearing anything under that skirt. But I don't get to find out what she does have under it – not yet, anyway, because before I know it she's got the Merc in gear and the radials grabbing pavement, not a hint of scratch, out of the parking lot, then slams the pedal down up the ramp, thirty, forty, forty-five, like it was nothing. She's going north on 99 and I watch the dial hit fifty, sixty, sixty-five. She lights a cigarette. Her hands are steady. Then, not seeming to think too much about it, she wriggles in the seat and pulls her skirt down as we level off at eighty. I did the right things with the Merc this afternoon. She's running like a dream, not a hint of rough stuff in the carb, listen to that engine, it's like a whisper on the edge of a growl.

I laugh and light up a Pall Mall, blowing the smoke out the window. She drives like a dream, like smooth velvet across flesh. She lets her right foot sink down a little bit, pretty soon we're doing 95 on the straightaway, inching toward 100 before we hit the curve near the Cuervo billboard. But I can't resist busting her balls. "Mrs Ketchum, you drive like a city girl."

Ketchum draws deep on her cig, an expensive European brand, a Gitanes or something. She says coolly, "Oh yeah? Well, you kiss like a fucking redneck."

The mansion out on the delta has a big lawn and a remote-control iron gate outside, razorwire at the top.

She brakes hard into the turnabout, drops the keys on the car floor, pushes herself across the gearshift, crawls on top of me, pulls the door handle, shoves me out of the car. The two of us come down hard and roll onto the manicured lawn. The car door stays open as she rubs hard against me. Right there on the front lawn. Then her tongue's in my mouth and she's kneeling over me, getting my pants open.

She comes down harder than ever against me, if I didn't know better I'd say she was trying to kill me. We do it on the front lawn and it's like I can't stop myself, Roxanne Ketchum has totally taken me over, all I want to do is make it with her in front of the whole world, the hot Central-Valley night blowing over us.

After, we just lay there on the expensive lawn and breathe hard for a while.

Finally, she gets up, gathers her clothes in a ball, walks to the front door fumbling with her keys. She's standing there at the door, stark naked in the security lights, except for the boots. She turns and looks back at me, her skin all unnaturally blue-white, like she doesn't give a damn what the neighbors see, which in this part of the state is more guts than most chicks have, but then why does that surprise me? She cocks her head at me.

"There's beer in the fridge, right through the first hallway," she says as she goes in. "Bedroom's at the top of the stairs, turn right."

Everything's packed in boxes from expensive stores. Roxy told me at the garage earlier today that they're just moving in. Seems weird to be fooling around in such a brand-new, empty house, with her fine China sealed in boxes.

She's waiting for me on the four-poster bed, boots off this time. Sprawled out like she owns the world. I take a plug from the bottle of Anchor Steam and join her.

Mr Ketchum's off on business in New York until Tuesday. According to Roxy, that means balling young whores in skirts too short to properly be called garments. He has a recent taste for blondes. Roxy's hair is black, just inching toward grey.

*   *   *

"I heard some rumors about you," she tells me.

We're under the canopy in her four-poster bed, and it's four in the morning. She's tangled me up in black satin sheets and scattered dead rose petals around me. Candles fill the room, the light flickering and scattering through the white lace curtain.

I take a long pull off the warm Anchor. "Something bad?"

"Something real bad." No expression on her face.

"Worse than adultery?"

"You tell me."

"You're a big girl – you don't think it's that easy to find out a man's secrets, do you? Look, maybe I did something and maybe I didn't. What the fuck business is it of yours?"

"Maybe it is my business."

"You better have a good reason for asking, then."

Roxy presses against me and nuzzles my throat. Then she starts kissing me.

I almost forget what we were talking about by the time she tells me, long minutes later, "I got a reason. If you did it once, you'd do it again."

Sunday morning, Roxy and I miss church, I'll have to remember to mention it to my priest next time I go to confession, ha ha. We sit out on the balcony watching the smog settle in the Central Valley. Roxy's sent all the servants home so she cooks me breakfast. She pours out her whole sad story over Eggs Benedict, sautéd vegetables, fresh-squeezed juice, coffee. She's one hell of a cook. She tells me all her problems, and what she wants to do about them.

Sweet Roxy's horny hubby Roger Ketchum won't give her a divorce, not the kind she wants. And she's sick and tired of his habit of coming home with a different perfume every night. There's other shit, too, I guess he doesn't treat her so good. Roxy has scars across her back and a couple of bruises on her shoulder, old ones, at least a week, so they must have been pretty bad. Nothing makes me sicker than a guy who slaps his woman around like he owns her.

But it seems Roger and Roxy had a pre-nuptial agreement, so even though he's hitting the sack with nineteen-year-old cocktail waitresses, Roxy won't get a dime if she leaves her old man. Of course, while he's doing younger chicks she's making it with ex-con garage mechanics, but that's strictly a moral dilemma and way the fuck out of my territory. What's in my territory, is fifty grand, cash, small bills, non-consecutive serial numbers.

I get to thinking about old Luis Reyes as I lay there with Roxy Ketchum wrapped around me, sleeping restlessly. Reyes was a smartass college fuck, young and cocky, always talking shit. A little too smart for his own good, talking how he had money waiting for him in Frisco soon as he finished up at the State College. Liked to talk about rednecks and scumbags. Thought he was hot shit, some sort of business major, weekend saucier, wanted to go to chef school and open up a restaurant. One day he fucked with me a little, just a little, and it was the wrong day. I was pissed off and high on a little speed. I must have beat him pretty bad. Didn't mean to, but he had it coming. I did some time but it was my hometown and he was half spic, even if he was raised in Marin fucking County. I had this girlfriend, Annie, she had a little money, her nephew's college fund. She got me a slick City lawyer and I plea bargained down to manslaughter. I figure Annie'd wait for me, but fourteen months into my time in the joint she finds some other guy, and she hits the road with him. His name was Carver, ha ha. Poor Annie, she never did have the best judgement. She ended up face down in the Delta. Carver got off scot-free 'cause all the evidence is circumstantial and it's a capital offense. Explain that one to me. He was smart enough not to leave prints, smarter than me, I guess. It made the papers. Seems Carver was the wrong guy for poor Annie to run away with. Annie never did have any taste in men except for me.

It wasn't fair, that was for sure. The serial killer sex criminal weirdo never gets convicted. But I go up the river for teaching a college asshole some manners, which is why Carver could kill Annie, because if I'd been around he wouldn't have gotten near her. I never would have hurt Annie, even though I was pretty pissed when she stopped visiting me. I loved Annie like I loved nothing else in this world, except maybe that 289 I dropped into the Fairlane I had when I was 17. So I took care of things after I got out. Found Carver coming out of his house, just off of 99 by the interchange. I was on parole so I couldn't carry a gun. Bummer for Carver, he took a long time to die with that 2 × 4.

Just my luck that just as I finish him off a patrol car comes to pick the bastard up. Seems they've had complaints from PG & E linemen about the smell.

This time it was clearly self-defense. I should have been a damn hero, especially when they found that shit in the guy's basement. Fuck! It still weirds me out to think about it. The cops should have gotten on their knees and sucked my dick for what I did. Carver would have convinced a court his mama made him wear panties or something, and would have been living in a trailer park in Fresno in six years, carving up someone else's daughters and girlfriends.

But the pigs didn't see it that way, and this time I didn't have Annie's money, so I got a lousy Public Defender, the guy couldn't give a rat's ass whether I got the gas chamber or a room at the Ritz. He bargained me down to aggravated assault or something and I got two more years in the joint – hard time. That's where I learned about piano wire.

Reyes was just a stuck-up bastard, he deserved what he got. Carver was the fucking Devil's right hand as far as I'm concerned, the fucker still gives me nightmares when I think about that basement of his with that heater-pipe. The Governor should have given me a medal for killing the bastard. Manslaughter my ass. Aggravated assault my ass. Way I figure it I was the only guy around who was sane, both times.

I'm not asking you to scare him," she tells me, her legs twined with mine. "I don't want you to beat him up or anything. I don't want a divorce – not now. I'm not trying to get rid of him. I tried to reason with him . . ."

He calls her from the car phone. She tells him she's sorry for the things she said, that she wants to show him how sorry she was. I sit there smoking a Pall Mall as she tells him all the things she's going to do to him, to make up for their fight.

Roxy lays down on the black velvet divan in the living room. Leaves the front curtains open, with the room lights down and candles lit behind her. So he'll see her right when he pulls up in the Jag.

When he comes in he isn't seeing anything except Roxy. He doesn't look behind the curtains on the side of the window.

He doesn't see much for long.

I take the Medalist out on 99, heading south. It's a crime to drive the thing at 65. But I can't take any chances. Even holding back like that, the thing's a dream, it makes me want to cry just hearing that 312 whisper-growl. It's a fucking beauty, it's like the chariot of the gods. I pull off down by the old power plant, near the drainage system, where they used to dump the toxic waste. I pop the trunk and get started. No one'll come here in a million years.

I learned things, in the joint. Besides cars. Of course, nothing's for sure – it never is. But if I did everything right, the cops won't find a thing. There isn't much left to find anyway. The only thing that spooks me is, he's not dead when I get him out of the trunk of the Medalist. All I can grab on short notice is the tire iron. I guess I didn't learn that first part right. I'll have to practice with the piano wire.

It kind of freaks me out, you know? I mean, don't get me wrong, I'm not getting religious on you. I just don't like it when you have to see their eyes. I'm not saying he didn't deserve it. I just don't like seeing his eyes.

Out on 99 again, Christ, now I can really lay it down. Clean. Smooth. Lush. The feeling of total power under my right foot. Driving with the window down, one hand on the wheel, blowing Pall Mall smoke – it's like a dream come true. I get it up to 95 in the straightaway, then push it just a little. One hundred. Beautiful.

*　　*　　*

Roxy's waiting for me in the bedroom. She has a bottle of champagne on ice. She's stretched out on the four-poster bed.

"Did you do it?" she asks, her voice a whisper on the edge of a growl. Her lips are painted red. She brushes her hair out of her face.

"Don't ask that," I tell her.

She looks me right in the eye. "I want to know everything," she says.

I don't like it at first, but I guess I don't take much convincing. And Roxy's a good talker. She wants to know it all.

Wants to know what he looked like when I opened the trunk. What kind of a knife I used to carve him up. Where I tossed the knife and the wire so the pigs wouldn't find them. She wants to know whether it made me hard when I did him. It didn't. She seems disappointed.

People watch too much TV these days. Turns them into fucking weirdos.

I don't like to think this, but it's gotta be pretty obvious by now. Roxy's some kind of a sex-kill freak, a weirdo like Carver. She wants me to tie her up and then she struggles, pulling hard against the ropes. Makes me tell her over and over again how I killed her husband, makes me give her every detail. Then she wants me to call her names.

I've never done this to a chick before. But it turns me on pretty hardcore, which freaks me out. I do her like there's nothing else either of us wants in the world, and she and I both come more times than I can count.

After, smoking a cigarette, I don't feel so good about what I did. Not the killing, that's OK. I mean what Roxy and me did. It seems too close to something I've seen before, something I see every night lately, something that hits me right where I live, in my nightmares.

I'd never kill a chick, that'd be fucking demented, but Roxy wants me to pretend like I would, and I do it better than I want to. I'm not sure I like that.

But I do what she wants me to do. It makes me kind of nauseous, but I do it. This chick is fucking scary.

Way I figure it, it's like she's slamming me right up face to face with my dark side or something, my evil twin serial killer. Making me become someone like Carver. Making me touch my own darkness. People see too many sex crime serial-killer movies these days on late-night cable and video. Makes them unable to deal with reality, as far as I'm concerned. Makes them crave violence like it was some sort of candy.

The Merc should have tipped me off. Woman drives a car like that, she's fucking slow dynamite, fuse in your mouth, gonna blow your head off. That's what I think.

It's definitely not right for a chick to get into a killing like this, any more than it was right for Carver. How long 'till Roxy decides she wants another corpse to hear about? Just for laughs?

How long till that's what I want? That's what really fucking bugs me about it.

By the time both of us fall asleep I've figured out that this is going to have to be a short-lived affair.

"Wake up," says Roxy softly.

Roxy's legs are spread around my torso and she has a pistol in my face. It's a revolver – looks like a .357. Those things'll blow your head open like a melon. I try to stay calm.

"Jesus, Roxy, what the – "

"I called the cops. I'm just holding you till they get here. I called them from downstairs. They know everything."

"What the fuck?" I start to get up. Roxy's hand tightens on the gun, and I freeze. She's got her knees wedged on my wrists, holding me down. Maybe I could throw her off, take her down, get the gun away from her. But if I try that she just might do me. She lets the short barrel of the revolver creep closer to my face, until it almost touches my lips. I cross my eyes looking to see if it's loaded. It is. Six shells in six cylinders. Hell on wheels.

"Roxy," I say calmly. "When did you call the cops?"

"Just a few minutes ago," she tells me.

"There's still time to get away. We can get away together. We'll take some cash and run like hell, all right? Mexico or something. I've got a friend who grows weed down there, he's got connections."

Roxy looks me right in the eye.

"You ever make it down to Frisco?" She says it without emotion. She's flipping out, I figure. Reverting to childhood or something.

"Look, Roxy, you're hysterical – we've got to get out of here – "

"I asked you a question."

"No," I say, fighting hard not to lose my calm. I don't want to set her off. "I don't get to Frisco much. Been there a couple times. What the fuck is wrong with you?"

"Me and Luis wanted to open up a restaurant on Valencia. You know, around Twenty-fourth Street? A breakfast place. He made a hell of an omelet. Roger was going to finance it, before he found out about the affair I was having with Luis. I was slipping him money so he could do his time at the Culinary Academy. When Roger found out he pulled the rug on me. Kept track of all my cash. Threatened to have Luis killed. I couldn't give him money any more. So Luis had to transfer to the state school."

I hear the sirens in the distance.

"You are one crazy bitch," I say flatly.

I look into her eyes, and see him. See the memory, something she has held onto, kept close to her heart for three years, kept close and hard and tight, through years of her marriage – loveless, bru-tal, cruel.

"You're a three time loser. This time it's Murder One with extenuating circumstances. You know what that means, in California?"

I've got to kill some time so I can get my hand free, get the gun out of her hand. So I ask her a question I don't give a shit about. "Why not just kill me?"

I think I can get my hand out from under her knee.

"It wouldn't be right," she tells me. "That wouldn't be *justice*."

I'm playing her, getting her to talk to me so she won't notice I'm getting my wrist angled just right to pull it free. The barrel of the revolver is against my lips, I can taste the metal. Drool is running down the side of my face. "I'll tell the cops everything – "

"Tell 'em. Let's see who they believe. I put the fifty grand in the furnace. You did my man so you could have me to yourself. Sound reasonable?"

"Sounds like a Matlock episode, for Chrissake."

But I can see her wrists have raw, bloody, bruised lines where the ropes cut into her skin. "You even took Polaroids, you sick bastard. You're going straight to the gas chamber, and if the cops find out about the fifty grand, make it conspiracy to murder, that's one more count for you and maybe they haul me in too – you'll *still* get the chamber and I'll be out on parole in less than ten years. Your friendly Public Defender is going to plea bargain your three-time-loser ass up to mass murder and treason and conspiracy to sell the H-Bomb to Canada. Three strikes, asshole. You're out."

There's no emotion in her voice, and I know she's going to kill me if I don't do it right. But I move faster than she does. I yank my hand out from under her knee, grab the lamp off the nightstand before she can pull the trigger. I hit her hard with the base of the lamp, as hard as I can. It shatters across her skull, blood splattering into my eyes. The revolver smashes my lip, cutting it. Footsteps on the stairs. I wrestle the gun to the side and then everything's thunder, my ears explode and I can't hear a thing but this high-pitched whine, and everything's filmed in a white light. The side of my face burns like fuck and one eye seems seared shut. Feathers scatter about us, clogging my mouth, from where the bullet slammed into the satin feather pillow.

I twist, hard, with both hands, slamming the heel of my hand into her wrist so that I hear it cracking. But still Roxy doesn't let go. The barrel of the .357 is hovering in front of my face, ready to take me out. I try to peel her fingers back. I get hold of two of them and bend them back, fighting to keep the muzzle of the gun out of my face. I pull hard until I hear a crack. She rolls, screaming in pain, but still both her hands are wrapped around the butt of the gun. I get her off the bed and she hits the floor, hard, but she doesn't let go of the gun even after I land on her chest with my knee, all my weight in her solar plexus. Her face goes white and her eyes bulge, there's a weird puking sound deep in her throat, her eyes flood with red. I can hear her ribs crack. I get my hand around her wrist but even with her ribs and two fingers broken she's got a death-grip on the butt of the revolver. I hear the door splintering. She's got one finger, must be her middle, under the trigger guard of the .357. Everything opens up in a blaze of flame and heat. First bullet. Wall. Powder burning in my hair. Second bullet. Ceiling. Every breath burns.

Third bullet. Throat.

Blood covers both our faces in a fine spray. Roxy probably figures she can plea-bargain this one down to unlawful discharge.

I hit the floor trying to scream, not having much luck. Roxy's body is pressed up against me; her face is filmed with blood, her teeth pink. The cops are screaming at her to put the gun down. Sounds like there's a million of them. Roxy puts the Ladysmith under my chin.

ORDO

Donald E. Westlake

1

MY NAME IS Ordo Tupikos, and I was born in North Flat, Wyoming on November 9th, 1936. My father was part Greek and part Swede and part American Indian, while my mother was half Irish and half Italian. Both had been born in this country, so I am one hundred per cent American.

My father, whose first name was Samos, joined the United States Navy on February 17th, 1942, and he was drowned in the Coral Sea on May 15th, 1943. At that time we were living in West Bowl, Oklahoma, my mother and my two sisters and my brother and I, and on October 12th of that year my mother married a man named Eustace St Claude, who claimed to be half Spanish and half French but who later turned out to be half Negro and half Mexican and passing for white. After the divorce, my mother moved the family to San Itari, California. She never remarried, but she did maintain a long-term relationship with an air conditioner repairman named Smith, whose background I don't know.

On July 12th, 1955, I followed my father's footsteps by joining the United States Navy. I was married for the first time in San Diego, California on March 11th, 1958, when I was twenty-one, to a girl named Estelle Anlic, whose background was German and Welsh and Polish. She put on the wedding license that she was nineteen, having told me the same, but when her mother found us in September of the same year it turned out she was only sixteen. Her mother arranged the annulment, and it looked as though I might be in some trouble, but the Navy transferred me to a ship and that was the end of that.

By the time I left the Navy, on June 17, 1959, my mother and my half brother, Jacques St Claude, had moved from California to Deep Mine,

Pennsylvania, following the air conditioner repairman named Smith, who had moved back east at his father's death in order to take over the family hardware store. Neither Smith nor Jacques was happy to have me around, and I'd by then lost touch with my two sisters and my brother, so in September of that year I moved to Old Coral, Florida, where I worked as a carpenter (non-union) and where, on January 7th, 1960, I married my second wife, Sally Fowler, who was older than me and employed as a waitress in a diner on the highway toward Fort Lauderdale.

Sally, however, was not happy tied to one man, and so we were divorced on April 12th, 1960, just three months after the marriage. I did some drinking and trouble-making around that time, and lost my job, and a Night Court judge suggested I might be better off if I rejoined the Navy, which I did on November 4th, 1960, five days before my twenty-fourth birthday.

From then on, my life settled down. I became a career man in the Navy, got into no more marriages, and except for my annual Christmas letter from my mother in Pennsylvania I had no more dealings with the past. Until October 7th, 1974, when an event occurred that knocked me right over.

I was assigned at that time to a Naval Repair Station near New London, Connecticut, and my rank was Seaman First Class. It was good weather for October in that latitude, sunny, clean air, not very cold, and some of us took our afternoon break out on the main dock. Norm and Stan and Pat and I were sitting in one group, on some stacks of two by fours, Norm and Stan talking football and Pat reading one of his magazines and me looking out over Long Island Sound. Then Pat looked up from his magazine and said, "Hey, Orry."

I turned my head and looked at him. My eyes were half-blinded from looking at the sun reflected off the water. I said, "What?"

"You never said you were married to Dawn Devayne."

Dawn Devayne was a movie star. I'd seen a couple of her movies, and once or twice I saw her talking on television. I said, "Sure."

He gave me a dirty grin and said, "You shouldn't of let that go, boy."

With Pat, you play along with the joke and then go do something else, because otherwise he won't give you any peace. So I grinned back at him and said, "I guess I shouldn't," and then I turned to look some more at the water.

But this time he didn't quit. Instead, he raised his voice and he said, "Goddamit, Orry, it's right here in this goddam magazine."

I faced him again. I said, "Come on, Pat."

By now, Norm and Stan were listening too, and Norm said, "What's in the magazine, Pat?"

Pat said, "That Orry was married to Dawn Devayne."

Norm and Stan both grinned, and Stan said, "Oh, *that*."

"Goddamit!" Pat jumped to his feet and stormed over and shoved the magazine in Stan's face. "You look at that!" he shouted. "You just look at that!"

I saw Stan look, and start to frown, and I couldn't figure out what was going on. Had they set this up ahead of time? But not Stan; Norm sometimes went along with Pat's gags, but Stan always brushed them away like mosquitoes. And now Stan frowned at the magazine, and he said, "Son of a bitch."

"Now, look," I said, "a joke's a joke."

But nobody was acting like it was a joke. Norm was looking over Stan's shoulder, and he too was frowning. And Stan, shaking his head, looked at me and said, "Why try to hide it, for Christ's sake? Brother, if *I'd* been married to Dawn Devayne, I'd tell the world about it."

"But I wasn't," I said. "I swear to God, I never was."

Norm said, "How many guys you know named Ordo Tupikos?"

"It's a mistake," I said. "It's got to be a mistake."

Norm seemed to be reading aloud from the magazine. He said, "Married in San Diego, California, in 1958, to a sailor named Ordo Tu – "

"Wait a minute," I said. "I was married then to, uh, Estelle – "

"Anlic," Pat said, and nodded his head at me. "Estelle Anlic, right?"

I stared at him. I said, "How'd you know that name?"

"Because that's Dawn Devayne, dummy! That's her real name!" Pat grabbed the magazine out of Norm's hands and rushed over to jab it at me. "Is that you, or isn't it?"

There was a small black-and-white photo on the page, surrounded by printing. I hadn't seen that picture in years.

It was Estelle and me, on our wedding day, a picture taken outside City Hall by a street photographer. There I was in my whites – you don't wear winter blues in San Diego – and there was Estelle. She was wearing her big shapeless black sweater and that tight tight gray skirt down to below her knees that I liked in those days. We were both squinting in the sunlight, and Estelle's short dark hair was in little curls all around her head.

"That's not Dawn Devayne," I said. "Dawn Devayne has blonde hair."

Pat said something scornful about people dyeing their hair, but I didn't listen. I'd seen the words under the picture and I was reading them. They said: "Dawn and her first husband, Navy man Ordo Tupikos. Mama had the marriage annulled six months later."

Norm and Stan had both come over with Pat, and now Stan looked at me and said, "You didn't even know it."

"I never saw her again." I made a kind of movement with the magazine, and I said, "When her mother took her away. The Navy put me on a ship, I never saw her after that."

Norm said, "Well, I'll be a son of a bitch."

Pat laughed, slapping himself on the hip. He said:

"You're married to a movie star!"

I got to my feet and went between them and walked away along the dock toward the repair sheds. The guys shouted after me, wanting to know where I was going, and Pat yelled, "That's my magazine!"

"I'll bring it back," I said. "I want to borrow it." I don't know if they heard.

I went to the Admin Building and into the head and closed myself in a stall and sat on the toilet and started in to read about Dawn Devayne.

The magazine was called *True Man*, and the picture on the cover was a foreign sports car with a girl lying on the hood. Down the left side of the cover was lettering that read:

*WILL THE
ENERGY CRISIS
KILL LE MANS?*

. . . .

*DAWN DEVAYNE:
THE WORLD'S NEXT
SEX GODDESS*

. . . .

*WHAT SLOPE?
CONFESSIONS OF A
GIRL SKI BUM*

Inside the magazine, the article was titled, *Is Dawn Devayne The World's New Sex Queen?* by Abbie Lancaster. And under the title in smaller letters was another question, with an answer:

"Where did all the bombshells go? Dawn Devayne is ready to burst on the scene."

Then the article didn't start out to be about Dawn Devayne at all, but about all the movie stars that had ever been considered big sex symbols, like Jean Harlow and Marilyn Monroe and Rita Hayworth and Jayne Mansfield. Then it said there hadn't been any major sex star for a long time, which was probably because of Women's Lib and television and X-rated movies and looser sexual codes. "You don't need a fantasy bedwarmer," the article said, "if you've got a real-life bedwarmer of your own."

Then the article said there were a bunch of movie stars who were all set to take the crown as the next sex queen if the job ever opened up again. It mentioned Raquel Welch and Ann-Margret and Goldie Hawn and Julie Christie. But then it said Dawn Devayne was the likeliest of them all to make it, because she had that wonderful indescribable quality of being all things to all men.

Then there was a biography. It said Dawn Devayne was born Estelle Anlic in Big Meadow, Nebraska on May 19th, 1942, and her father died in the Korean conflict in 1955, and she and her mother moved to Los Angeles in 1956 because her mother had joined a religious cult that was based in Los Angeles. It said her mother was a bus driver in that period, and Dawn Devayne grew up without supervision and hung around with boys a lot. It didn't exactly say she was the neighborhood lay, but it almost said it.

Then it came to me. It said Dawn Devayne ran away from home a lot of times in her teens, and one time when she was sixteen she ran away to San Diego and married me until her mother took her home again and turned her over to the juvenile authorities, who put her in a kind of reformatory for wayward girls. It called me a "stock figure." What it said was:

". . . a sailor named Ordo Tupikos, a stock figure, the San Diego sailor in every sex star's childhood."

I didn't much care for that, but what I was mostly interested in was where Estelle Anlic became Dawn Devayne, so I kept reading. The article said that after the reformatory Estelle got a job as a carhop in a drive-in restaurant in Los Angeles, and it was there she got her first crack at movie stardom, when an associate producer with Farber International Pictures met her and got her a small role in a B-movie called *Tramp Killer*. She played a prostitute who was murdered. That was in 1960, when she was eighteen. There was a black-and-white still photo from that movie, showing her cowering back from a man with a meat cleaver, and she still looked like Estelle Anlic then, except her hair was dyed platinum blonde. Her stage name for that movie was Honey White.

Then nothing more happened in the movies for a while, and Estelle went to San Francisco and was a cashier in a movie theater. The article quoted her as saying, "When 'Tramp Killer' came through, I sold tickets to myself." She had other jobs too for the next three years, and then when she was twenty-one, in 1963, a man named Les Moore, who was the director of *Tramp Killer*, met her at a party in San Francisco and remembered her and told her to come back to Los Angeles and he would give her a big part in the movie he was just starting to work on.

(The article then had a paragraph in parentheses that said Les Moore had become a very important new director in the three years since *Tramp Killer*, which had only been his second feature, and that the movie he wanted Dawn Devayne to come back to Los Angeles for was *Bubbletop*, the first of the zany comedies that had made Les Moore the Preston Sturges of the sixties.)

So Dawn Devayne – or Estelle, because her name wasn't Dawn Devayne yet and she'd quit calling herself Honey White – went back to Los Angeles and Les Moore introduced her to a star-making agent named Byron Cartwright, who signed her to exclusive representation and who changed her name to Dawn Devayne. And *Bubbletop* went on to become a smash hit and Dawn Devayne got rave notices, and she'd been a movie star ever since, with fifteen movies in the last eleven years, and her price for one movie now was seven hundred fifty thousand dollars. The article said she was one of the very few stars who had never had a box-office flop.

About her private life, the article said she was "between marriages." I thought that would mean she was engaged to somebody, but so far as I could see from the rest of the article she wasn't. So I guess that's just a phrase they use for people like movie stars when they aren't married.

Anyway, the marriages she was between were numbers four and five. After me in 1958, her next marriage was in 1963, to a movie star named Rick Tandem. Then in 1964 there was a fight in a nightclub where a producer named Josh Weinstein knocked Rick Tandem down and Rick Tandem later sued for divorce and said John Weinstein had come between him and Dawn Devayne. The article didn't quite say that Rick Tandem was in reality queer, but it got the point across.

Then marriage number three, in 1966, was to another movie actor, Ken Forrest, who was an older man, a contemporary of Gable and Tracy who was still making movies but wasn't quite the power he used to be. That marriage ended in 1968 when Forrest shot himself on a yacht off the coast of Spain; Dawn Devayne was in London making a picture when it happened.

And the fourth marriage, in 1970, was to a Dallas businessman with interests in computers and airlines and oil. His name was Ralph Chucklin, and that marriage had ended with a quiet divorce in 1973. "Dawn is dating now," the article said, "but no one in particular tops her list. 'I'm still looking for the right guy,' she says."

Then the article got to talking about her age, and the person who wrote the article raised the question as to whether a thirty-two year old woman was young enough to still make it as the next Sex Goddess of the World. "Dawn is more beautiful every year," the article said, and then it went back to all the business about Women's Lib and television and X-rated movies and looser sexual codes, and it said the next Superstar Sex Symbol wasn't likely to be another girl-child type like the ones before, but would be more of an adult woman, who could bring brains and experience to sex. "Far from the dumb blondes of yesteryear," the article said, "Dawn Devayne is a bright blonde, who combines with good old-fashioned lust the more modern feminine virtues of intelligence and independence. A Jane Fonda who doesn't nag." And the article finished by saying maybe the changed social conditions meant there wouldn't be any more Blonde Bombshells or Sexpot Movie Queens, which would make the world a colder and a drabber place, but the writer sure hoped there would be more, and the best bet right now to bring sex back to the world was Dawn Devayne.

There were photographs with the article, full page color pictures of Dawn Devayne with her clothes off, and when I finished reading I sat there on the toilet a while longer looking at the pictures and trying to remember Estelle. Nothing. The face, the eyes, the smile, all different. The stomach and legs were different. Even the nipples didn't remind me of Estelle Anlic's nipples.

There's something wrong, I thought. I wondered if maybe this Dawn Devayne woman had a criminal record or was wanted for murder somewhere or something like that, and she'd just paid Estelle money to borrow her life story. Was that possible?

It sure didn't seem possible that *this* sexy woman was Estelle. I know it was sixteen years, but how much can one person change? I sat studying the pictures until I noticed I was beginning to get an erection, so I left the head and went back to work.

All I could think about, the next three days, was Dawn Devayne. I was once married to her, married to a sexy movie star. Me. I just couldn't get used to the idea.

And the other guys didn't help. Norm and Stan and Pat spread the word, and pretty soon all the guys were coming around, even some of the younger officers, talking and grinning and winking and all that. Nobody came right out with the direct question, but what they really wanted to know was what it was like to be in bed with Dawn Devayne.

And what could I tell them? I didn't *know* what it was like to be in bed with Dawn Devayne. I knew what it was like to be in bed with Estelle Anlic – or anyway I had a kind of vague memory, after sixteen years – but that wasn't what they wanted to know, and anyway I didn't feel like telling them. She was a teenage girl, sixteen (though she told me nineteen), and I was twenty-one, and neither of us was exactly a genius about sex, but we had fun. I remember she had very very soft arms and she liked to have her arms around my neck, and she laughed with her mouth wide open, and she always drowned her french fries in so much ketchup I used to tell her I had to eat them with ice tongs and one time in bed she finally admitted she didn't know what ice tongs were and she cried because she was sure she was stupid, and we had sex that time in order for me to tell her (a) she wasn't stupid, and (b) I loved her anyway even though she was stupid, and that's the one time in particular I have any memory of at all, which is mostly because that was the time I learned I could control myself and hold back ejaculation almost as long as I wanted, almost forever. We were both learning about things then, we were both just puppies rolling in a basket of wool, but the guys didn't want to hear anything like that, it would just depress them. And I didn't want to tell them about it either. Their favorite sex story anyway was one that Pat used to tell about being in bed with a girl with a candle in her ass. That's what they really wanted me to tell them, that Dawn Devayne had a candle in her ass.

But even though I couldn't tell them any stories that would satisfy them, they kept coming around, they kept on and on with the same subject, they couldn't seem to let it go. It fascinated them, and every time they saw me they got reminded and fascinated all over again. In fact, a couple of the guys started calling me "Devayne," as though that was going to be my new nickname, until one time I picked up a wrench and patted it into my other palm and went over to the guy and said:

"My name is Orry."

He looked surprised, and a little scared. He said:

"Sure. Sure, I know that."

I said:

"Let me hear you say it."

He said:

"Jeez, Orry, it was just a – "

"Okay, then," I said, and went back over to where I was working, and that was the last I heard of that.

But it wasn't the last I heard of Dawn Devayne. For instance, I was more or less going then with a woman in New London named Fran Skiburg, who was divorced from an Army career man and had custody of the three children. She was part Norwegian and part Belgian and her husband had been almost all German. Fran and I would go to the movies sometimes, or she'd cook me a meal, but it wasn't serious. Mostly, we didn't even go to bed together. But then somebody told her about Dawn Devayne, and the next time I saw Fran she was a different person. She kept grinning and winking all through dinner, and she hustled the kids to bed earlier than usual, and then sort of crowded me into the living room. She liked me to rub her feet sometimes, because she was standing all day at the bank, so I sat on the sofa and she kicked off her slippers and while I rubbed her feet she kept opening and closing her knees and giggling at me.

Well, I was looking up her skirt anyway, so I slid my hand up from her feet, and the next thing we were rolling around on the wall-to-wall carpet together. She was absolutely all over me, nervous and jumpy and full of loud laughter, all the time wanting to change position or do this and that. Up till then, my one complaint about Fran was that she'd just lie there; now all of a sudden she was acting like the star of an X-movie.

I couldn't figure it out, until after it was all finished and I was lying there on the carpet on my back, breathing like a diver with the bends. Then Fran, with this big wild-eyed smile, came looming over me, scratching my chest with her fingernails and saying, "What would you like to do to me? What do you *really* want to do to me?"

This was *after*. I panted at her for a second, and then I said, "What?"

And she said, "What would you do to me if I was Dawn Devayne?"

Then I understood. I sat up and said, "Who told you that?"

"What would you do? Come on, Orry, let's do something!"

"Do what? We just did everything!"

"There's *lots* more! There's *lots* more!" Then she leaned down close to my ear, where I couldn't see her face, and whispered, "You don't want me to have to *say* it."

I don't know if she had anything special in mind, but I don't think so. I think she was just excited in general, and wanted something different to happen. Anyway, I pushed her off and got to my feet and said, "I don't know anything about any Dawn Devayne or any kind of crazy sex stuff. That's no way to act."

She sat there on the green carpet with her legs curled to the side, looking something like the nude pictures in Pat's magazines except whiter and a little heavier, and she stared up at me without saying anything at all. Her mouth was open because she was looking upward so her expression seemed to be mainly surprised. I felt grumpy. I sat down on the sofa and put on my underpants.

And all at once Fran jumped up and grabbed half her clothes and ran out of the room. I finished getting dressed, and sat on the sofa a little longer, and then went out to the kitchen and ate a bowl of raisin bran. When Fran still didn't come back, I went to her bedroom and looked in through the open door, and she wasn't there. I said, "Fran?"

No answer.

The bathroom door was closed, so I knocked on it, but nothing happened. I turned the knob and the door was locked. I said, "Fran?"

A mumble sounded from in there.

"Fran? You all right?"

"Go away."

"What?"

"Go *away!*"

That was the last she said. I tried talking to her through the door, and I tried to get her to come out, and I tried to find out what the problem was, but she wouldn't say anything else. There wasn't any sound of crying or anything, she was just sitting in there by herself. After a while I said, "I have to get back to the base, Fran."

She didn't say anything to that, either. I said it once or twice more, and said some other things, and then I left and went back to the base.

I was shaving the next morning when I suddenly remembered that picture, the one in the magazine of Estelle and me on our wedding day. We were squinting there in the sunlight, the both of us, and now I was squinting again because the light bulb over the mirror was too bright. Shaving, I looked at myself, looked at my nose and my eyes and my ears, and here I was. I was still here. The same guy. Same short haircut, same eyebrows, same chin.

The same guy.

What did Fran want from me, anyway? Just because it turns out I used to be married to somebody famous, all of a sudden I'm supposed to be different? I'm not any different, I'm the same guy I always was. People don't just change, they have ways that they are, and that's what they are. That's who they are, that's what you mean by personality. The way a person is.

Then I thought: Estelle changed.

That's right. Estelle Anlic is Dawn Devayne now. She's changed, she's somebody else. There isn't any – she isn't – there isn't any Estelle Anlic any more, nowhere on the face of the earth.

But it isn't the same as if she died, because her *memories* are still there inside Dawn Devayne, she'd remember being the girl with the mother that drove the bus, and she'd remember marrying the sailor in San Diego in 1958, and even in that article I'd read there'd been a part where she was remembering being Estelle Anlic and working as a movie cashier in San Francisco. But still she was changed, she was somebody else now, she was different. Like a wooden house turning itself into a brick house. How could she . . . how could anybody do that? How could *anybody* do that?

Then I thought: Estelle Anlic is Dawn Devayne now, but I'm still me. Ordo Tupikos, the same guy. But if she was – If I'm –

It was hard even to figure out the question. If she was that back then, and if she's this now, and if I was *that* . . .

I kept on shaving. More and more of my face came out from behind the white cream, and it was the same face. Getting older, a little older every minute, but not –

Not different.

I finished shaving. I looked at that face, and then I scrubbed it with hot water and dried it on a towel. And after mess I went to Headquarters office and put in for leave. Twenty-two days, all I had saved up.

2

The first place I went was New York, on the bus, where I looked in a magazine they have there called *Cue* that tells you what movies are playing all over the city. A Dawn Devayne movie called. "The Captain's Pearls" was showing in a theater on West 86th Street, which was forty-six blocks uptown from the bus terminal, so I walked up there and sat through the second half of a western with Charles Bronson and then "The Captain's Pearls" came on.

The story was about an airline captain with two girl friends both named Pearl, one of them in Paris and one in New York. Dawn Devayne played the one in New York, and the advertising agency she works for opens an office in Paris and she goes there to head it, and the Paris girl friend is a model who gets hired by Dawn Devayne for a commercial for the captain's airline, and then the captain has to keep the two girls from finding out he's going out with both of them. It was a comedy.

This movie was made in 1967, which was only nine years after I was married to Estelle, so I should have been able to recognize her, but she just wasn't there. I stared and stared and stared at that woman on the screen, and the only person she reminded me of was Dawn Devayne. I mean, from before I knew who she was. But there wasn't anything of Estelle there. Not the voice, not the walk, not the smile, not anything.

But sexy. I saw what that article writer meant, because if you looked at Dawn Devayne your first thought was she'd be terrific in bed. And then you'd decide she'd also be terrific otherwise, to talk with or take a trip together or whatever it was. And then you'd realize since she was so all-around terrific she wouldn't have to settle for anybody but an all-around terrific guy, which would leave you out, so you'd naturally idolize her. I mean, you'd want it without any idea in your head that you could ever get it.

I was thinking all that, and then I thought, *But I've had it!* And then I tried to put together arms-around-neck ice-tongs-stupid Estelle Anlic with this terrific female creature on the screen here, and I just couldn't do it. I mean, not even with a fantasy. If I had a fantasy about going to bed with Dawn Devayne, not even in my fantasy did I see myself in bed with Estelle.

After the movie I walked back downtown toward the bus terminal, because I'd left my duffel bag in a locker there. It was only around four-thirty in the afternoon, but down around 42nd Street the whores were already out, strolling on the sidewalks and standing in the doorways of shoe stores. The sight of a Navy uniform really agitates a whore, and half a dozen of them called out to me as I walked along, but I didn't answer.

Then one of them stepped out from a doorway and stood right in my path and said, "Hello, sailor. You off a ship?"

I started to walk around her, but then I stopped dead and stared, and I said, "You look like Dawn Devayne!"

She grinned and ducked her head, looking pleased with herself. "You really think so, sailor?"

She did. She was wearing a blonde wig like Dawn Devayne's hair style, and her eyes and mouth were made up like Dawn Devayne, and she'd even fixed her eyebrows to look like Dawn Devayne's eyebrows.

Only at a second look none of it worked. The wig didn't look like real hair, and the make-up was too heavy, and the eyebrows looked like little false moustaches. And down inside all that phony stuff she was Puerto Rican or Cuban or something like that. It was all like a Halloween costume.

She was poking a finger at my arm, looking up at me sort of slantwise in imitation of a Dawn Devayne movement I'd just seen in *The Captain's Pearls*. "Come on, sailor," she said. "Wanna fuck a movie star?"

"No," I said. It was all too creepy. "No no," I said, and went around her and hurried on down the street.

And she shouted after me, "You been on that ship too long! What you want is Robert Redford!"

This was my first time in Los Angeles since 1963, when the Gulf of Tonkin incident got me transferred from a ship in the Mediterranean to a ship in the Pacific. They'd flown me with a bunch of other guys from Naples to Washington, then by surface transportation to Chicago and by air to Los Angeles and Honolulu, where I met my ship. I'd had a two-day layover in Los Angeles, and now I remembered thinking then about looking up Estelle. But I didn't do it, mostly because five years had already gone by since I'd last seen her, and also because her mother might start making trouble again if she caught me there.

The funny thing is, that was the year Estelle first became Dawn Devayne, in the movie called *Bubbletop*. Now I wondered what might have happened if I'd actually found her back then, got in touch somehow. I'd never seen *Bubbletop*, so I didn't know if by 1963 she was already this new person, this Dawn Devayne, if she'd already changed so completely that Estelle Anlic couldn't be found in there any more. If I'd met her that time, would something new have started? Would my whole life have been shifted, would I now be somebody in the movie business instead of being a sailor? I tried to see myself as that movie person; who would I be, what would I be like? Would I be *different*?

But there weren't any answers for questions like that. A person is who he is, and he can't guess who he would be if he was somebody else. The question doesn't even make sense. But I guess it's just impossible to think at all about movie stars without some fantasy or other creeping in.

My plane for Los Angeles left New York a little after seven p.m. and took five hours to get across the country, but because of the time zone differences it was only a little after nine at night when I landed, and still not ten o'clock when the taxi let me off at a motel on Cahuenga Boulevard, pretty much on the line separating Hollywood from Burbank. The taxi cost almost twenty dollars from the airport, which was kind of frightening. I'd taken two thousand dollars out of my savings, leaving just over three thousand in the account, and I was spending the money pretty fast.

The cabdriver was a leathery old guy who buzzed along the freeways like it was a stock car race, all the time telling me how much better the city had been before the freeways were built. Most people pronounce Los Angeles as though the middle is "angel," but he was one of those who pronounce it as though the middle is "angle." "Los Ang-gleez," he kept saying, and one time he said, "I'm a sight you won't see all that much. I'm your native son."

"Born here?"

"Nope. Come out in forty-eight."

The motel had a large neon sign out front and very small rooms in a low stucco building in back. It was impossible to tell what color the stucco was because green and yellow and orange and blue floodlights were aimed at it from fixtures stuck into the ivy border, but in the morning the color turned out to be a sort of dirty cream shade.

My room had pale blue walls and a heavy maroon bedspread and a paper ribbon around the toilet seat saying it had been sanitized. I unpacked my duffel and turned on the television set, but I was too restless to stay cooped up in that room forever. Also, I decided I was hungry. So I changed into civvies and went out and walked down Highland to Hollywood Boulevard, where I ate something in a fast-food place. It was like New York in that neighborhood, only skimpier. For some reason Los Angeles looks older than New York. It looks like an old old Pueblo Indian village with neon added to it by real estate people. New York doesn't look any older than Europe, but Los Angeles looks as old as sand. It looks like a place that almost had a Golden Age, a long long time ago, but nothing happened and now it's too late.

After I ate I walked around for half an hour, and then I went back to the motel and all of a sudden I was very sleepy. I had the television on, and the light, and I still wore all my clothes except my shoes, but I fell asleep anyway, lying on top of the bedspread, and when I woke up the TV was hissing and it was nearly four in the morning. I was very thirsty, and nervous for some reason. Lonely, I felt lonely. I drank water, and went out to the street again, and after a while I found an all-night supermarket called Hughes. I took a cart and went up and down the aisles.

There were some people in there, not many. I noticed something about them. They were all dressed up in suede and fancy denim, like people at a terrific party in some movie, but they were buying the cheapest of everything. Their baskets were filled as though by gnarled men and women wearing shabby pants or faded kerchiefs, but the men were all young and tanned and wearing platform shoes, and the women were all made up with false eyelashes and different-colored fingernails. Also, some of them had food stamps in their hands.

Another thing. When these people pushed their carts down the aisles they stood very straight and were sure of themselves and on top of the world, but when they lowered their heads to take something off a shelf they looked very worried.

Another thing. Every one of them was alone. They went up and down the aisles, pushing their carts past one another – from up above, they must have looked like pieces in a labyrinth game – and they never looked at one another, never smiled at one another. They were just alone in there, and from up front came the clatter of the cash register.

After a while I didn't want to be in that place any more. I bought shaving cream and a can of soda and an orange, and walked back to the motel and went to bed.

★　　★　　★

There wasn't anybody in the phone book named Byron Cartwright, who was the famous agent who had changed Estelle's name to Dawn Devayne and then guided her to stardom. In the motel office they had the five different Los Angeles phone books, and he wasn't in any of them. He also wasn't in the yellow pages under "Theatrical Agencies." Finally I found a listing for something called the Screen Actors' Guild, and I called, and spoke to a girl who said, "Byron Cartwright? He's with GLA."

"I'm sorry?"

"GLA," she repeated, and hung up.

So I went back to the phone books, hoping to find something called GLA. The day clerk, a sunken-cheeked faded-eyed man of about forty with thinning yellow hair and very tanned arms, said, "You seem to be having a lot of trouble."

"I'm looking for an actor's agent," I told him.

His expression lit up a bit. "Oh, yeah? Which one?"

"Byron Cartwright."

He was impressed. "Pretty good," he said. "He's with GLA now, right?"

"That's right. Do you know him?"

"Don't I wish I did." This time he was rueful. His face seemed to jump from expression to expression with nothing in between, as though I were seeing a series of photographs instead of a person.

"I'm trying to find the phone number," I said.

I must have seemed helpless, because his next expression showed the easy superiority of the insider. "Look under Global-Lipkin," he told me.

Global-Lipkin. I looked, among "Theatrical Agencies," and there it was: Global-Lipkin Associates. You could tell immediately it was an important organization; the phone number ended in three zeroes. "Thank you," I said.

His face now showed slightly belligerent doubt. He said, "They send for you?"

"Send for me? No."

The face was shut; rejection and disapproval. Shaking his head he said, "Forget it."

Apparently he thought I was a struggling actor. Not wanting to go through a long explanation, I just shrugged and said, "Well, I'll try it," and went back to the phone booth.

A receptionist answered. When I asked for Byron Cartwright she put me through to a secretary, who said, "Who's calling, please?"

"Ordo Tupikos."

"And the subject, Mr Tupikos?"

"Dawn Devayne."

"One moment, please."

I waited a while, and then she came back and said, "Mr Tupikos, could you tell me who you're with?"

"With? I'm sorry, I . . ."

"Which firm."

"Oh. I'm not with any firm, I'm in the Navy."

"In the Navy."

"Yes. I used to be – " But she'd gone away again.

Another wait, and then she was back. "Mr Tupikos, is this official Navy business?"

"No," I said. "I used to be married to Dawn Devayne."

There was a little silence, and then she said, "Married?"

"Yes. In San Diego."

"One moment, please."

This was a longer wait, and when she came back she said, "Mr Tupikos, is this a legal matter?"

"No, I just want to see Estelle again."

"I beg your pardon?"

"Dawn Devayne. She was named Estelle when I married her."

A male voice suddenly said, "All right, Donna, I'll take it."

"Yes, sir," and there was a click.

The male voice said, "You're Ordo Tupikos?"

"Yes, sir," I said. It wasn't sensible to call him "sir," but the girl had just done it, and in any event he had an authoritative officer-like sound in his voice, and it just slipped out.

He said, "I suppose you can prove your identity."

That surprised me. "Of course," I said. "I still look the same." *I* still look the same.

"And what is it you want?"

"To see Estelle. Dawn. Miss Devayne."

"You told my secretary you were with the Navy."

"I'm *in* the Navy."

"You're due to retire pretty soon, aren't you?"

"Two years," I said.

"Let me be blunt, Mr Tupikos," he said. "Are you looking for money?"

"Money?" I couldn't think what he was talking about. (Later, going over it in my mind, I realized what he'd been afraid of, but just at that moment I was bewildered.) "Money for what?" I asked him.

He didn't answer. Instead, he said, "Then why show up like this, after all these years?"

"There was something in a magazine. A friend showed it to me."

"Yes?"

"Well, it surprised me, that's all."

"*What* surprised you?"

"About Estelle turning into Dawn Devayne."

There was a very short silence. But it wasn't an ordinary empty silence, it was a kind of slammed-shut silence, a startled silence. Then he said, "You mean you didn't know? You just found out?"

"It was some surprise," I said.

He gave out with a long loud laugh, turning his head away from the phone so it wouldn't hurt my ears. But I could still hear it. Then he said, "God damn, Mr Tupikos, that's a new one."

I had nothing to say to that.

"All right," he said. "Where are you?"

I told him the name of the motel.

"I'll get back to you," he said. "Some time today."

"Thank you," I said.

The phone booth was out in front of the motel, and I had to go back through the office to get to the inner courtyard and my room. When I walked into the office the day clerk motioned to me. "Come here." His expression now portrayed pride.

I went over and he handed me a large black-and-white photograph; what they call a glossy. The blacks in it were very dark and solid, which made it a little bit hard to make out what was going on, but the picture seemed to have been taken in a parking garage. Two people were in the foreground. I couldn't swear to it, but it looked as though Ernest Borgnine was strangling the day clerk.

"Whadaya think of that?"

I didn't know what I thought of it. But when people hand you a picture – their wife, their girl friend, their children, their dog, their new house, their boat, their garden – what you say is *very nice*. I handed the picture back. "Very nice," I said.

Everybody knows about the movie stars' names being embedded in the sidewalks of Hollywood Boulevard, but it's always strange when you see it. There are the squares of pavement, and on every square is a gold outline of a five-pointed star, and in every other star there is the name of a movie star. Every year, fewer of those names mean anything. The idea of the names is immortality, but what they're really about is death.

I took a walk for a while after talking to Byron Cartwright, and I walked along two or three blocks of Hollywood Boulevard with some family group behind me that had a child with a loud piercing voice, and the child kept wanting to know who people were:

"Daddy, who's Vilma Banky?"

"Daddy, who's Charles Farrell?"

"Daddy, who's Dolores Costello?"

"Daddy, who's Conrad Nagel?"

The father's answers were never loud enough for me to hear, but what could he have said? "She was a movie star." "He used to be in silent movies, a long time ago." Or maybe, "I don't know. Emil Jannings? I don't know."

I didn't look back, so I have no idea what the family looked like, or even if the child was a boy or a girl, but pretty soon I hated listening to them, so I turned in at a fast-food place to have a hamburger and onion rings and a Coke. I sat at one of the red formica tables to eat, and at the table across the plastic partition from me was another family – father, mother, son, daughter – and the daughter was saying, "Why did they put those names there anyway?"

"Just to be nice," the mother said.

The son said, "Because they're buried there."

The daughter stared at him, not knowing if that was true or not. Then she said, "They are not!"

"Sure they are," the son said. "They bury them standing up, so they can all fit. And they all wear the clothes from their most famous movie. Like their cowboy hats and the long gowns and their Civil War Army uniforms."

The father, chuckling, said, "And their white telephones?"

The son gave his father a hesitant smile and a headshake, saying, "I don't get it."

"That's okay," the father said. He grinned and ruffled the son's hair, but I could see he was irritated. He was older, so his memory stretched back farther, so his jokes wouldn't always mean anything to his son, whose memories had started later – and would probably end later. The son had reminded his father that the father would some day die.

After I ate I didn't feel like walking on the stars' names any more. I went up to the next parallel street, which is called Yucca, and took that over to Highland Avenue and then on back to the motel.

When I walked into the office the day clerk said, "Got a message for you." His expression was tough and secretive, like a character in a spy movie. The hotel clerk in a spy movie who is really a part of the spy organization; this is the point where he tells the hero that the Gestapo is in his room.

"A message?"

"From GLA," he said. His face flipped to the next expression, like a digital clock moving on to the next number. This one showed make-believe comic envy used to hide real envy. I wondered if he really did feel envy or if he was just practicing being an actor by pretending to show envy. No; pretending to *hide* envy. Maybe he himself was actually feeling envy but was hiding it by pretending to be someone who was showing envy by trying to hide it. That was too confusing to think about; it made me dizzy, like looking too long off the fantail of a ship at the swirls of water directly beneath the stern. Layers and layers of twisting white foam with bottomless black underneath; but then it all organizes itself into swinging straight white lines of wake.

I said, "What did they want?"

"They'll send a car for you at three o'clock." Flip; friendliness, conspiracy. "You could do me a favor."

"I could?"

From under the counter he took out a tan manila envelope, then halfway withdrew from it another glossy photograph; I couldn't see the subject. "This," he said, and slid the photo back into the envelope. Twisting the red string on the two little round closure tabs of the envelope, he said, "Just leave it in the office, you know? Just leave it some place where they can see it."

"Oh," I said. "All right." And I took the envelope.

The car was a black Cadillac limousine with a uniformed chauffeur who held the door for me and called me, "sir." It didn't seem to matter to him that he was picking me up at a kind of seedy motel, or that I was wearing clothes that were somewhat shabby and out of date. (I wear civvies so seldom that I almost never pay any attention to what clothing I own or what condition it's in.)

I had never been in a limousine before, with or without a chauffeur. In fact, this was the first time in my life I'd ever ridden in a Cadillac. I spent the first few blocks just looking at the interior of the car, noticing that I had my own radio in the back, and power windows, and that there were separate air conditioner controls on both sides of the rear seat.

There were grooves for a glass partition between front and rear, but the glass was lowered out of sight, and when we'd driven down Highland and made a right turn onto Hollywood Boulevard, going past Grauman's Chinese theater, the chauffeur suddenly said, "You a writer?"

"What? Me? No."

"Oh," he said. "I always try to figure out what people are. They're fascinating, you know? People."

"I'm in the Navy," I said.

"That right? I did two in the Army myself."

"Ah," I said.

He nodded. He'd look at me in the rear-view mirror from time to time while he was talking. He said, "Then I pushed a hack around Houston for six years, but I figured the hell with it, you know? Who needs it. Come out here in sixty-seven, never went back."

"I guess it's all right out here."

"No place like it," he said.

I didn't have an answer for that, and he didn't seem to have anything else to say, so I opened the day clerk's envelope and looked at the photograph he wanted me to leave in Byron Cartwright's office.

Actually it was four photographs on one eight-by-ten sheet of glossy paper, showing the day clerk in four poses, with different clothing in each one. Four different characters, I guess. In the upper left, he was wearing a light plaid jacket and a pale turtleneck sweater and a medium-shade cloth cap, and he had a cigarette in the corner of his mouth and he was squinting; looking mean and tough. In the upper right he was wearing a tuxedo, and he had a big smile on his face. His head was turned toward the camera, but his body was half-twisted away and he was holding a top hat out to the side, as though he were singing a song and was about to march off-stage at the end of the music. In the bottom left, he was wearing a cowboy hat and a bandana around his neck and a plaid shirt, and he had a kind of comical-foolish expression on his face, as though somebody had just made a joke and he wasn't sure he'd understood the point. And in the bottom right he was wearing a dark suit and white shirt and pale tie, and he was leaning forward a little and smiling in a friendly way directly at the camera. I guess that was supposed to be him in his natural state, but it actually looked less like him than any of the others.

The whole back of the photograph was filled with printing. His name was at the top (MAURY DEE) and underneath was a listing of all the movies he'd been in and all the play productions, with the character he performed in each one. Down at the bottom were three or four quotes from critics about how good he was.

The driver turned left on Fairfax and went down past Selma to Sunset Boulevard, and then turned right. Then he said, "The best thing about this job is the people."

"Is that right?" I put Maury Dee's photograph away and twisted the red string around the closure tabs.

"And I'll tell you something," said the driver. "The bigger they are, the nicer they are. You'd be amazed, some of the people been sitting right where you are right now."

"I bet."

"But you know who's the best of them all? I mean, just a nice regular person, not stuck up at all."

"Who's that?"

"Dawn Devayne," he said. "She's always got a good word for you, she'll take a joke, she's just terrific."

"That's nice," I said.

"Terrific." He shook his head. "Always remembers your name. 'Hi, Harry,' she says. 'How you doing?' Just a terrific person."

"I guess she must be all right," I said.

"Terrific," he said, and turned the car in at one of the taller buildings just before the Beverly Hills line. We drove down into the basement parking garage and the driver stopped next to a bank of elevators. He hopped out and opened my door for me, and when I got out he said, "Eleventh floor."

"Thanks, Harry," I said.

3

All you could see was artificial plants. I stepped out of the elevator and there were great pots all over the place on the green rug, all with plastic plants in them with huge dark-green leaves. Beyond them, quite a ways back, expanses of plate glass showed the white sky.

I moved forward, not sure what to do next, and then I saw the receptionist's desk. With the white sky behind her, she was very hard to find. I went over to her and said, "Excuse me."

She'd been writing something on a long form, and now she looked up with a friendly smile and said, "May I help you?"

"I'm supposed to see Byron Cartwright."

"Name, please?"

"Ordo Tupikos."

She used her telephone, sounding very chipper, and then she smiled at me again, saying, "He'll be out in a minute. If you'll have a seat?"

There were easy chairs in among the plastic plants. I thanked her and went off to sit down, picking up a newspaper from a white formica table beside the chair. It was called *The Hollywood Reporter*, and it was magazine size and printed on glossy paper. I read all the short items about people signing to do this or that, and I read a nightclub review of somebody whose name I didn't recognize, and then a girl came along and said, "Mr Tupikos?"

"Yes?"

"I'm Mr Cartwright's secretary. Would you come with me?"

I put the paper down and followed her away from the plants and down a long hall with tan walls and brown carpet. We passed offices on both sides of the hall; about half were occupied, and most of the people were on the phone.

I suddenly realized I'd forgotten the day clerk's photograph. I'd left it behind in the envelope on the table with *The Hollywood Reporter*.

Well, that actually was what he'd asked me to do; leave it in the office. Maybe on the way back I should take it out of the envelope.

The girl stopped, gesturing at a door on the left. "Through here, Mr Tupikos."

Byron Cartwright was standing in the middle of the room. He had a big heavy chest and brown leathery skin and yellow-white hair brushed straight back over his balding head. He was dressed in different shades of pale blue, and there was a white line of smoke rising from a long cigar in an ashtray on the desk behind him. The room was large and so was everything in it; massive desk, long black sofa, huge windows showing the white sky, with the city of Los Angeles down the slope on the flat land to the south, pastel colors glittering in the haze; pink, peach, coral.

Byron Cartwright strode toward me, hand outstretched. He was laughing, as though remembering a wonderful time we'd once shared together. Laughter made erosion lines crisscrossing all over his face. "Well, hello, Orry," he said. "Glad to see you." He took my hand, and patted my arm with his other hand, saying, "That's right, isn't it? Orry?"

"That's right."

"Everybody calls me By. Come in, sit down."

I was already in. We sat together on the long sofa. He crossed one leg over the other, half-turning in my direction, his arm stretched out toward me along the sofa back. He had what looked like a class ring on one finger, with a dark red stone. He said, "You know where I got it from? The name 'Orry'? From Dawn." There was something almost religious about the way he said the name. It reminded me of when Jehovah's Witnesses pass out their literature; they always smile and say, "Here's good news!"

I said, "You told her about me?"

"Phoned her the first chance I got. She's on location now. You could've knocked her over with a feather, Orry, I could hear it in her voice."

"It's been a long time," I said. I wasn't sure what this conversation was about, and I was sorry to hear Dawn Devayne was "on location." It sounded as though I might not be able to get to see her.

"Sixteen years," Byron Cartwright said, and he had that reverential sound in his voice again, with the same happiness around his mouth and eyes. "Your little girl has come a long way, Orry."

"I guess so."

"It's just amazing that you never knew. Didn't any reporters ever come around, any magazine writers?"

"I never knew anything," I told him. "When the fellows told me about it, I didn't believe them. Then they showed me the magazine."

"Well, it's just astonishing." But he didn't seem to imply that I might be a liar. He kept smiling at me, and shaking his head with his astonishment.

"It sure was astonishing to me," I said.

He nodded, letting me know he understood completely. "So the first thing you thought," he said, "you had to see her again, just had to say hello. Am I right?"

"Not to begin with." It was hard talking when looking directly at him, because his face was so full of smiling eagerness. I leaned forward a little, resting my elbows on my knees, and looked across the room. There was a huge full-color blown-up photograph of a horse taking up most of the opposite wall. I said, looking at the horse, "At first I just thought it was eerie. Of course, nice for Estelle. Or Dawn, I guess. Nice for her, I was glad things worked out for her. But for me it was really strange."

"In what way *strange*, Orry?" This time he sounded like a chaplain, sympathetic and understanding.

"It took me a while to figure that out." I chanced looking at him again, and he had just a small smile going now, he looked expectant and receptive. It was easier to face him with that expression. I said, "There was a picture of Estelle and me in the magazine, from our wedding day."

"Got it!" He bounded up from the sofa and hurried over to the desk. I became aware then that most of the knick-knacks and things around on the desk and the tables and everywhere had some connection with golf; small statues of golfers, a gold golf ball on a gold tee, things like that.

Byron Cartwright came back with a small photo in a frame. He handed it to me, smiling, then sat down again and said, "That's the one, right?"

"Yes," I said, looking at it. Then I turned my face toward him, not so much to see him as to let him see me. "You can recognize me from that picture."

"I know that," he said. "I was noticing that, Orry, you're remarkable. You haven't aged a bit. I'd hate to see a picture of *me* taken sixteen years ago."

"I'm not talking about getting older," I said. "I'm talking about getting *different*. I'm not different."

"I believe you're right." He moved the class-ring hand to pat my knee, then put it back on the sofa. "Dawn told me a little about you, Orry," he said. "She told me you were the gentlest man she'd ever met. She told me she's thought about you often, she's always hoped you found happiness somewhere. I believe you're still the same good man you were then."

"The same." I pointed at Estelle in the photo. "But that isn't Dawn Devayne."

"Ha ha," he said. "I'll have to go along with you there."

I looked at him again. "How did that happen? How do people change, or not change?"

"Big questions, Orry." If a smile can be serious, his smile had turned serious. But still friendly.

"I kept thinking about it," I said. I almost told him about Fran then, and the changes all around me, but at the last second I decided not to. "So I came out to talk to her about it," I said. And then, because I suddenly realized this could be a brush-off, that Byron Cartwright might have the job of smiling at me and being friendly and telling me I wasn't going to be allowed to see Estelle, I added to that, "If she wants to see me."

"She does, Orry," he said. "Of course she does." And he acted surprised. But I could see he was *acting* surprised.

I said, "You were supposed to find out if I'd changed or not, weren't you? If I was going to be a pest or something."

Grinning, he said, "She told me you weren't stupid, Orry. But you could have been an impostor, you know, maybe some maniac or something. Dawn *wants* to see you, if you're still the Orry she used to know."

"That's the problem."

He laughed hugely, as though I'd said a joke. "She's filming up in Stockton today," he said, "but she'll be flying back when they're done. She wants you to go out to the house, and she'll meet you there."

"Her house?"

"Well, naturally." Chuckling at me, he got to his feet, saying, "You'll be driven out there now, unless you have other plans."

"No, nothing." I also stood.

"I'll phone down for the car. You came in through the parking area?"

"Yes."

"Just go straight back down. The car will be by the elevators."

"Thank you."

We shook hands again, at his prompting, and this time he held my hand in both of his and gazed at me. The religious feeling was there once more, this time as though he were an evangelist and I a cripple he was determined would walk. Total sincerity filled his eyes and his smile. "She's my little girl now, too, Orry," he said.

The envelope containing the day clerk's pictures was gone from the table out front.

"Hello, Harry," I said. He was holding the door open for me.

He gave me a kind of roguish grin, and waggled a finger at me. "You didn't tell me you were pals with Dawn Devayne."

"It was a long story," I said.

"Good thing I didn't have anything bad to say, huh?" And I could see that inside his joking he was very upset.

I didn't know what to answer. I gave him an apologetic smile and got into the car and he shut the door behind me. It wasn't until we were out on Sunset driving across the line into Beverly Hills, that I decided what to say: "I don't really know Dawn Devayne," I told him. "I haven't seen her for sixteen years. I wasn't trying to be smart with you or anything."

"Sixteen years, huh?" That seemed to make things better. Lifting his head to look at me in the rear-view mirror, he said, "Old high school pals?"

I might as well tell him the truth; he'd probably find out sooner or later anyway. "I was married to her."

The eyes in the rear-view mirror got sharper, and then fuzzier, and then he looked out at Sunset Boulevard and shifted position so I could no longer see his face in the mirror. I don't suppose he disbelieved me. I guess he didn't know what attitude to take. He didn't know what to think about me, or about what I'd told him, or about anything. He didn't say another word the whole trip.

The house was in Bel Air, way up in the hills at the very end of a curving steep street with almost no houses on it. What residences I did see were very spread out and expensive-looking, though mostly only one story high, and tucked away in folds and dimples of the slope, above or below the road. Many had flat roofs with white stones sprinkled on top for decoration. Like pound cake with confectioner's sugar on it.

At the end of the street was a driveway with a No Trespassing sign. Great huge plants surrounded the entrance to the driveway; they reminded me of the plants in Byron Cartwright's outer office, except that these were real. But the leaves were so big and shiny and green that the real ones looked just as fake as the plastic ones.

The driveway curved upward to the right and then came to a closed chain-link gate. The driver stopped next to a small box mounted on a pipe beside the driveway, and pushed a button on the box. After a minute a metallic voice spoke from the box, and the driver responded, and then the gate swung open and we drove on up, still through this forest of plastic-like plants, until we suddenly came out on a flat place where there was a white stucco house with many windows. The center section was two stories high, with tall white pillars out front, but the wings angling back on both sides were only one story, with flat roofs. These side sections were bent back at acute angles, so that they really did look like wings, so that the taller middle section would be the body of the bird. Either that, or the central part could be thought of as a ship, with the side sections as the wake.

The driver stopped before the main entrance, hopped out, and opened the door for me. "Thanks, Harry," I said.

Something about me – my eyes, my stance, something – made him soften in his attitude. He nodded as I got out, and almost smiled, and said, "Good luck."

The Filipino who let me in said his name was Wang, "Miss Dawn told me you were coming," he said. "She said you should swim."

"She did?"

"This way. No luggage? This way."

The inside was supposed to look like a Spanish mission, or maybe an old ranch house. There were shiny dark wood floors, and rough plaster walls painted white, and exposed dark beams in the ceiling, and many rough chandeliers of wood or brass, some with amber glass.

Wang led me through different rooms into a corrider in the right wing, and down the corridor to a large room at the end with bluish-green drapes hanging ceiling-to-floor on two walls, making a great L of underwater cloth through which light seemed to shimmer. A king size bed with a blue spread took up very little of the room, which had a lot of throw rugs here and there on the dark-stained random-plank floor. Wang went to one of the dressers – there were three, two with mirrors – and opened a drawer full of clothing. "Swim suit," he said. "Change of linen. Everything." Going to one of two doors in the end wall, he opened it and waved at the jackets and coats and slacks in the closet there. "Everything." He tugged the sleeve of a white terrycloth robe hanging inside the door. "Very nice robe."

"Everything's fine," I said.

"Here." He shut the closet door, opened the other one, flicked a light switch. "Bathroom," he said. "Everything here."

"Fine. Thank you."

He wasn't finished. Back by the entrance, he demonstrated the different light switches, then pointed to a lever sticking horizontally out from the wall, and raised a finger to get my complete attention. "Now this," he said. He pushed the lever down, and the drapes on the two walls silently slid open, moving from the two ends toward the right angle where the walls met.

Beyond the drapes were walls of sliding glass doors, and beyond the glass doors were two separate views. The view to the right, out the end wall, was of a neat clipped lawn sweeping out to a border of those lush green plants. The view straight ahead, of the section enclosed by the three sides of the house, was of a large oval swimming pool, with big urns and statues around it, and with a small narrow white structure on the fourth side, consisting mostly of doors; a cabana, probably, changing rooms for guests who weren't staying in rooms like this.

Wang showed me that the drapes opened when the lever was pushed down, and closed when it was pulled up. He demonstrated several times; back and forth ran the drapes, indecisively. Then he said, "You swim."

"All right."

"Miss Dawn say she be back, seven o'clock."

The digital clock on one of the dressers read three fifty-two. "All right," I said, and Wang grinned at me and left.

It was a heated pool. When I finally came out and slipped into the terrycloth robe I felt very rested and comfortable. In the room I found a small bottle of white wine, and a glass, and half a dozen different cheeses on a plate under a glass dome. I had some cheese and wine, and then I shaved, and then I looked at the clothing here.

There was a lot of it, but in all different sizes, so I really didn't have that much to choose from. Still, I found a pair of soft gray slacks, and a kind of ivory shirt with full sleeves, and a black jacket in a sort of Edwardian style, and in the mirror I almost didn't recognize myself. I looked taller, and thinner, and successful. I picked up the wine glass and stood in front of the mirror and watched myself drink. All right, I thought. Not bad at all.

I went out by the pool and walked around, wearing the clothes and carrying the wine glass. Part of the area was in late afternoon sun and part in shade. I strolled this way and that, admiring my reflections in the glass doors all around, and trying not to smile too much. I wondered if Wang was watching, and what he thought about me. I wondered if there were other servants around the place, and what kind of job it was to be a servant for a famous movie star. Like being assigned to an Admiral, I supposed. I was once on a ship with a guy who'd been an Admiral's servant for three years, and he said it was terrific duty, the best in the world. He lost his job because he started sleeping with some other officer's wife. He always claimed he'd kept strictly away from the Admiral's family and friends, but there was this Lieutenant Commander who lived in the same area near Arlington, Virginia, and whose wife kept trying to suck up to the Admiral's wife. That's how Tony met her, one time when she came over and the Admiral's wife wasn't there. According to Tony it wasn't his fault there was trouble; it was just that the Lieutenant Commander's wife kept making things so obvious, hanging around all the time, honking horns at him, calling him on the phone in the Admiral's house. "So they kicked me out," he said. (Tony wasn't very popular with the guys on the ship, which probably wasn't fair, but we couldn't help it. The rest of us had been assigned here as a normal thing, but he'd been sent to this ship as a *punishment*. If this was punishment duty, what did that say about the rest of us? Nobody particularly wanted to think about that, so Tony was generally avoided.)

Anyway, he did always claim that the job of servant to the brass was the best duty in the world, and I suppose it is. Except for *being* the brass, of course, which is probably even better duty, except who thinks that way?

After a while I went back into the room, and the digital clock said six twenty-four. I looked at myself in the mirror one more time, and all of a sudden it occurred to me I was looking at Dawn Devayne's clothes. Not my clothes. She'd come home, she wouldn't see somebody looking terrific, she'd see somebody wearing *her* clothes.

No. I changed into my own things, and went back to the living room by the main entrance. There were long low soft sofas there, in brown corduroy. I sat on one, and read more *Hollywood Reporters*, and pretty soon Wang came and asked me if I wanted a drink.

I did.

She arrived at twenty after seven, with a bunch of people. It later turned out there were only five, but at first it seemed like hundreds. To me, anyway. I didn't give them separate existences then; they were just a bunch of laughing, hand-waving, talking people surrounding a beautiful woman named Dawn Devayne.

Dawn Devayne. No question. The clear, bright, level gray eyes. The skin as smooth as a lion's coat. Those slightly sunken cheeks. (Estelle had round cheeks.) The look of intelligence, sexiness, recklessness. Of course that was Dawn Devayne; I'd seen her in the movies.

I got to my feet, looking through the wide arched doorway from the living room to the entrance hall, where they were clustered around her. That group all bunched there made me realize Dawn Devayne already had her own full life, as much as she wanted. What was I doing here? Did I think I could wedge myself into Dawn Devayne's life? How? And why?

"Wang!" she yelled. "God damn it, Wang, bring me liquor! I've been kissing a faggot all day!" Then she turned, and over someone's shoulder, past someone else's laugh, she caught a glimpse of me beyond the doorway, and she put an expression on her face that I remembered from movies; quizzical-amused. She said something, quietly, that I couldn't hear, but from the way her lips moved I thought it was just my own name: "Orry." Then she nodded at two things that were being said to her, stepped through the people as though they were grouped statues, and came through the doorway with her hand out for shaking and her mouth widely smiling. "Orry," she said. "God damn, Orry, if you don't bring it back."

Her hand was strong when I took it; I could feel the bones, as though I were holding a small wild bird in my palm. "Hello . . ." I said, stumbling because I didn't know what name to use. I couldn't call her Estelle, and I couldn't call her Dawn, and I wouldn't call her Miss Devayne.

"We'll talk later on," she said, squeezing my hand, then turned to the others, who had followed her. "This is Orry," she said. "An old friend of mine." And said the names of everybody else.

Wang arrived then, and while he took drink orders Dawn Devayne looked at me, frowning slightly at my clothing, saying, "Didn't Wang give you a room?"

"Yes. Down at the end there."

Her glance at my clothes was a bit puzzled, but then her expression cleared and she grinned at me, saying, "Yes, Orry. I'm beginning to remember you now."

"I don't remember you at all," I told her. Which was true. So far, Estelle Anlic had made no appearance in this room.

She still didn't. Dawn Devayne laughed, patting my arm, saying, "We'll talk later, after this crowd goes." She turned half away: "Wang! Get over here." Back to me: "What are you drinking?"

I tried not to drink too much, not wanting to make a fool of myself. Though Dawn Devayne had spoken about the others as though they would leave at any instant, in fact they stayed on for an hour or more, mostly gossiping about absent people involved in the movie they were currently making. Then we all got into two cars and drove down to Beverly Hills for dinner at a Chinese restaurant. I rode in the same car with Dawn Devayne, a tan-colored Mercedes Benz with the license plate WIPPER, but I didn't sit beside her. I rode in back with a grim-faced moustached man named Frank, whose job I didn't yet know, while Dawn Devayne sat beside the driver, a tall and skinny, leathery-faced, sly-smiling man named Rod, who I remembered as having played the airline pilot in *The Captain's Pearls*, and who was apparently Dawn Devayne's co-star again this time. The other three people, an actor named Wally and an unidentified man called Bobo and a heavyset girl named June, followed us in Wally's black Porsche, which also had a special license plate; BIG JR.

Phone-calling had been done before we'd left the house, and four more people joined us at the restaurant; Frank's plump wife, a tough-looking blonde girl for Wally, a grinning hippie-type guy in blue denim for June, and a willowy young man in a black jumpsuit for Rod. I realized Rod must be the faggot Dawn Devayne had been kissing all day, and the fact of his homosexuality startled me a lot less than what she had shouted in his presence.

The eleven of us filled an alcove at the rear of the restaurant. Eleven people can't possibly be quiet; we made our presence felt. There was a party atmosphere, and I saw other patrons glancing our way with envy. We were, after all, quite obviously having a wonderful time. Not only that, but at least two of us were famous. But perhaps in Beverly Hills there's more sophistication about movie fame than in most other places; no one came by the table in search of autographs.

As for the party atmosphere, that was more apparent than real. Dawn Devayne and Rod and Wally and June's hippie-type friend did a lot of loud talking, mostly anecdotes about the movie world or the record business, to which June's friend belonged, but the rest of us were no more than audience. We laughed at the right moments, and otherwise sat silent, eating one platter of Chinese food after another. Rounds of drinks kept being ordered, but I let them pile up in front of me – four glasses, eventually – while I drank tea.

Rod drove us back home. Again Dawn Devayne sat up front with him, while I shared the back seat with Rod's friend, who was called Dennis. In the dark, wearing his black jumpsuit and with his pale-skinned hands and face and wispy yellow hair, Dennis was startling to look at, almost unearthly. And when he touched the back of my hand with a fingertip, his skin was so cold that I automatically flinched away.

He ignored that; maybe people always flinched when he touched them. "I know who you are," he said, and his small head floating there had a smile on it that was very sweet and innocent, as though he were on his way to his First Communion. *My* God, I thought, *you'd last six hours on a ship. They'd shove what was left in a canvas bag.*

I said, "You do?"

"Orry," he said. "That's not a common name."

"No, I guess it isn't."

"You were in the Navy."

"I still am."

"You were married to Dawn."

"That's right," I said.

He turned his sweet smile and his wide eyes toward the two heads up front. They were talking seriously together now, Dawn Devayne and Rod, about some disagreement they were having with the director, and what they should do about it tomorrow.

Dennis, staring and smiling so hard that it was as though he wanted to burrow into their ears and live inside their brains, said, "It must have been wonderful. To know her at the very beginning of her career. If only I'd met Rod, all those years ago." When he looked at me again, his eyes were luminous. Maybe he was crying. "I keep everything that's ever written about him," he said. "I have dozens of scrapbooks, dozens. That's how I know about *you*."

"Ah."

"Do you keep scrapbooks?"

"About what?" Then I understood. "Oh, you mean Dawn Devayne."

"You don't? I'll *never* be blasé about Rod. Never."

In the house Dawn Devayne held my forearm and said, "Orry, I'm bushed. I'm sorry, baby, I can't talk tonight. Come along with me tomorrow, all right? We'll have some time together."

"All right." I was disappointed, but she did look tired. Also, my own body was still more on East Coast time, three hours later; I wouldn't mind sleeping, after such a long day. I don't know why it is, but emotions are exhausting.

"I'm going to swim for five minutes," she said, "and then hit the sack. We get up at seven around here. You ready for that?"

"I will be." And I smiled at her. God knows she wasn't Estelle, but I felt just the same as though I knew her. We were old friends in some other way, entirely different and apart from reality. I suspected that was a form of human contact she had learned to develop, as a means of dealing with all the faces a movie star has to meet. It wasn't the real thing, but that didn't matter. It was a friendly falseness, a fakery that made life smoother.

I watched her swim. She was naked, and she spent as much time diving as she did swimming, and it was the same nude body that had excited me so much in the magazine pictures, and yet my sexual feelings were thwarted, imprisoned. Maybe it was because I was being a peeping tom and felt ashamed of myself. Or maybe it was because, in accepting the counterfeit friendship of Dawn Devayne, I had lessened the existence of Estelle Anlic just that much more, and I felt guilty about *that*. Whatever it was, for as long as I looked at her I kept feeling the lust rise, and then become strangled, and then rise, and then become strangled.

I should have stopped looking, of course, but I couldn't. The most I could do was close my eyes from time to time and argue with myself. But I couldn't leave, I had to stay kneeling at a corner of the darkened room, with one edge of the drapes pulled back just far enough to peek out, during the ten minutes that Dawn Devayne spent moving, diving, swimming, the green-white underwater lights and yellow surrounding lanterns glinting and flashing off the wet sheen slickness of her flesh. Drops of water caught in her hair made tiny flashing round rainbows. Her legs were long, her body strong and sleek, a tanned thoroughbred, graceful and self-contained.

When at last she put on a white robe and walked away, I awkwardly stood, padded across the room by the dim light filtering through the drapes, and slid into the cool bed. A few seconds later, as though waiting for me to settle, the pool lights went off.

4

I must have gone to sleep almost at once, though I'd been sure I would stay awake for hours. But the pool lights ceased to shine on the blue-green drapes, darkness and silence drifted down like a collapsing tent – four white numerals floating in the black said 11:42, then 11:43 – and I closed my eyes and slept.

To awake in the same darkness, with the white numbers reading 12:12 and some fuss taking place at the edge of my consciousness. I didn't know where I was, I didn't know what that pair of twelves meant, and I couldn't understand the rustling and whooshing going on. In my bewilderment I thought I was assigned to a ship again, and we were in a storm; but the double twelve made no sense.

Then one of the twelves became thirteen, and I remembered where I was, and I understood that someone was at the glass doors leading to the pool, making a racket. Then Dawn Devayne's voice, loud and rather exasperated, said, "Orry?"

"Yes?"

"Open these damn drapes, will you?"

At the Chinese restaurant there had been a red-jacketed young man who parked the cars. He leaped into every car that came along, and whipped it away with practiced skill, as though he'd been driving *that* car all his life. At some point he must have had a first car, of course, the car in which he'd learned to drive and with which he'd gotten his first license, but if some customer of the restaurant were to drive up in that car today would the young man recognize it? Would it feel *different* to him? Since his driving technique was already perfect with any car, what special familiarity would he be able to display? It could not be by skill that he would show his particular relationship with this car; possibly it would be with a breakdown of skill, a tiny reminiscent awkwardness.

Dawn Devayne was wonderful in bed. It's true, she was what men thought she would be, she was agile and quick and lustful and friendly and funny and demanding and responsive and exhausting and exhilarating and plunging and utterly skillful. Her skill produced in me responses of invention I hadn't known I possessed. Fran Skiburg was right; there *are* other things to do. I did things with Dawn Devayne that I'd never done before, that it had never occurred to me to do but that now came spontaneously into my mind. For instance, I followed with the tip of my tongue all the creases of her body; the curving borders of her rump, the line at the inside of each elbow, the arcs below her breasts. She laughed and hugged me and gave me a great deal of pleasure, and not once did I think of Estelle Anlic, who was not there.

We'd turned the lights on for our meeting, and when she kissed my shoulder and leaned away to turn them off again the digital clock read 2:02. In the dark she kissed my mouth, bending over me, and whispered, "Welcome back, Orry."

"Mmm." I said nothing more, partly because I was tired and partly because I still hadn't fixed on a name to call her.

She rolled away, adjusting her head on the pillow next to me, settling down with a pleasant sigh, and when next I opened my eyes vague daylight pressed grayly at the drapes and the clock read 6:03, and Dawn Devayne was asleep on her back beside me, tousled but beautiful, one hand, palm up, with curled fingers, on the pillow by her ear.

How did Estelle look asleep? She was becoming harder to remember. We had lived together in off-base quarters, a two-room apartment with a used bed. Sunlight never entered the bedroom, where the sheets and clothing and the very air itself were always just slightly damp. Estelle would curl against me in her sleep, and at times I would awake to find her arm across my chest. A memory returned; Estelle once told me she'd slept with a toy panda in her childhood, and at times she would call me Panda. I hadn't thought of that in years. Panda.

Dawn Devayne's eyes opened. They focused on me at once, and she smiled, saying, "Don't frown, Orry, Dawn is here." Then she looked startled, stared toward the drapes, and cried, "My God, dawn *is* here! What time is it?"

"Six oh six," I read.

"Oh." She relaxed a little, but said, "I have to get back to my room." Then she looked at me with another of her private smiles and said, "Orry, do you know you're terrific in bed?"

"No," I said. "But you are."

"A workman is as good as his tools," she said, grinning, and reached under the covers for me. "And you've been practicing."

"So have you."

She laughed, pulling me closer, with easy ownership. "Time for a quickie," she said.

*　　*　　*

We swam together naked in the pool while the sun came up. ("If Wang *does* look," she'd answered me, "I'll blind him.") Then at last she climbed out of the pool, wet, glistening gold and orange in the fresh sunlight, saying, "Time to face the new day, baby."

"All right." I followed her up to the blue tiles.

"Orry."

"Yes?"

"Take a look in the closet," she said. "See if there's something that fits you. Wang can have your other stuff cleaned."

I knew she was laughing at me, but in a friendly way. And the problem of what to call her was solved. "Thanks, Dawn," I said. "I will."

"See you at breakfast."

I wore the gray slacks, but neither the full-sleeved shirt nor the Edwardian jacket seemed right for me, so I found instead a green shirt and a gray pullover sweater. "That's fine," Dawn said, with neutral disinterest.

A limousine took us to Burbank Airport, over the hills and across the stucco floor of the San Fernando Valley, a place that looks like an over-exposed photograph. Dawn asked me questions as we rode together, and I told her about my marriage to Sally Fowler and my years in the Navy, and even a little about Fran Skiburg, though not the part where Fran got so excited about me having once been married to Dawn Devayne. There were spaces of silence as we rode, and I could have asked her my question several times, but there didn't seem to be any way to phrase it. I tried different practice sentences in my head, but none of them were right:

"*Why aren't you Estelle Anlic any more, when I'm still Orry Tupikos?*" No. That sounded as though I was blaming her for something.

"*Who would I be, if I wasn't me?*" No. That wasn't even the right question.

"How do you stop being the person you are and become somebody entirely different? What's it like?" No. That was like a panel-show question on television, and anyway not exactly what I was trying for.

Dawn herself gave me a chance to open the subject, when she asked me what I figured to do after I retired from the Navy two years from now, but all I said was, "I haven't thought about it very much. Maybe I'll just travel around a while, and find some place, and settle down."

"Will you marry Fran?"

"That might be an idea."

At Burbank Airport we got on a private plane with the two actors, Rod and Wally, and the grim-faced man named Frank and the heavyset quiet man called Bobo, all of whom I'd met last night. Listening to conversations during the flight, I finally worked it out that Frank was a photographer whose job it was to take pictures while the movie was being made; the "stills man," he was called. Bobo's job was harder to describe; he seemed to be somewhere between servant and bodyguard, and mostly he just sat and smiled at everybody and looked alert but not very bright.

We flew from Burbank to Stockton, where another limousine took us to the movie location, which was an imitation Louisiana bayou in the San Joaquin River delta. The rest of the movie people, who were staying in nearby motels and not commuting home every night, were already there, and most of the morning was spent with the crew endlessly preparing things – setting up reflectors to catch the sunlight, laying a track for the camera to roll along, moving potted plants this way and that along the water's edge – while Dawn and Rod argued for hours with the director, a fat man with pasty jowls and an amused-angry expression and a habit of constantly taking off and putting back on his old black cardigan sweater. His name was Harvey, and when I was introduced to him he nodded without looking at me and said, "Ted, they really *are* putting that fucking dock the wrong place," and a short man with a moustache went away to do something about it.

The argument, with Dawn and Rod on one side and Harvey on the other, wasn't like anything I'd ever seen in my life. When the people I've known get into an argument, they either settle it pretty soon or they get violent; the men hit and the women throw things. Dawn and Rod and Harvey almost immediately got to the point where hitting and throwing would start, except it never happened. Dawn Devayne stood with her feet apart and her hands on her hips, as though leaning into a strong wind, and made firm logical statements of her point of view, salted with insults; for instance, "The motivation throughout the whole story, you cocksucker, is for my character to feel protective toward Jenny." Rod's style, on the other hand, was heavy sarcasm: "Since it's a *given* that you have the sensitivity of a storm drain, Harvey, why not simply accept the fact that Dawn and I have thought this over very carefully." Harvey, with his angry-amused smile, always looked as though he was either just about to say something horribly insulting or would suddenly start pounding the other two with a piece of wood, and his *manner* was very insulting-patronizing-hostile, but in fact he merely kept saying things like, "Well, I think we'll simply all be much happier if we do it my way."

Unless there's a fist fight, the person who remains the calmest usually wins most arguments, so I knew from the beginning Harvey would win this one, but it went on for hours anyway, and when it ended (Harvey won, and Dawn and Rod both sulked) they only had time before lunch to shoot one small scene with Dawn and Wally on the riverbank. It was just a scene where Dawn said, "I don't think they'll ever come back, Billy." They shot it eight times, with the camera in three different positions, and then we all had a buffet lunch brought out from Stockton by a catering service.

Dawn's dressing room was a small motor home, where she took a nap by herself after lunch, while I walked around looking at everything. Another part of the Dawn-Wally scene was shot, with just Wally visible in the picture, talking to an empty spot in space where Dawn was supposed to be, and then they set up a more complicated scene involving Dawn and Rod and some other people getting into a boat and rowing away. Dawn woke up while the crew was still preparing that one, and she and Rod groused together about Harvey, but when they went out to shoot the scene everybody was polite to everybody else, and then the day was over, and we flew back to Los Angeles.

There was a huge gift-wrapped package in the front hall at Dawn's house. It was about the size and shape of a door, all wrapped up in colorful paper and miles of ribbon and a big red bow, and a card hung from the bow reading, "Love to Dawn and Orry, from By."

Dawn frowned and said, "What's that asshole up to now?"

Rod and Wally and Frank and Bobo had come in with us, and Wally said, "It's an aircraft carrier. By gave you an aircraft carrier."

"For God's sake, open it," Rod said.

"I'm afraid to," Dawn told him. She tried to make that sound like a joke, but I could see she really was afraid to open it. I later learned that Byron Cartwright's sentimentalism was famous for causing embarrassment, but I don't think even Dawn suspected what he had chosen to send us. I know I didn't.

Finally it was Wally and Rod who pulled off the bow and the ribbon and the paper, and inside was the wedding day picture, Estelle and me in San Diego, squinting in the sunlight. The picture had been blown up to be slightly bigger than life, and it was in a wooden frame with a piece of glass in front of it, and here were these two stiff uncomfortable figures in grainy gray, staring out of some horrible painful prison of the past. Usually this picture was perfectly ordinary, neither wonderful nor awful, but blown up to life size – larger than life – it became a kind of cruelty.

Everybody stared at it. Wally said, "What the hell is *that*?"

They hadn't recognized that earlier me. Dawn wouldn't have been recognizable anyway, of course, but expanding the original photo had strained the rough quality of the negative beyond its capacity, so that I myself might not have guessed at first the white blob face was mine.

After the first shock of staring at the picture, I turned to look at Dawn, to see her with a face of stone, glaring – with hatred? rage? revulsion? bitterness? resentment? – at her own image in the photograph. She turned her head, flashed me a look of irritation that I'd been watching her, and without a word strode out of the room.

Rod, with the eager look of the born gossip, said, "I don't know what's going on here, but it looks to *me* like By's done it again."

Wally was still frowning at the picture. "What *is* that?" he said. "Who *are* those people?"

"Orry? Isn't that you?"

It was the voice of Frank, the stills man, the professional photographer, who had backed away from the giant picture, across the hall and through the doorway into the next room, until he was distant enough to see it clear. Head cocked to one side, eyes half closed, he was standing against the back of a sofa in there, studying the picture.

At first I didn't say anything. Wally turned to frown at Frank, then at me, then at the picture, then at me again. "You? That's you?"

Rod and Bobo were moving toward Frank, squinting over their shoulders at the picture as they went. I said to Wally, "Yes. It's me."

"That girl is familiar," Frank said.

I felt obscurely that Dawn would want to be protected, though I didn't see how it was going to be possible. "That's my wife," I said. "Or, she *was* my wife. That was our wedding day."

Rod and Bobo were now standing next to Frank, gazing at the picture, and Wally was moving back to join them. I was like a stage performer, and they were my audience, and the picture was used in my act. Frank said, "I know that girl. What's her name?"

Rod suddenly said, "Wait a minute, *I* know that picture! That's Dawn!"

"Yes," I said, but before I could say anything else – explain, apologize, defend – Wang came in to say, "Miss Dawn say, everybody out."

Rod, nodding at the picture and ignoring Wang, said thoughtfully, "Byron Cartwright, the avalanche that walks like a man."

Wang said to me, "You, too. Miss Dawn say, go away, eat dinner, come back."

"All right," I said.

We were joined by Frank's wife and Wally's girl and Rod's friend Dennis in an Italian restaurant that looked like something from a silent movie about Biblical times. Bronze-colored plaster statues, lots of columns, heavily-framed paintings of Roman emperors on the walls. The food was covered with too much tomato sauce.

My story was amazing but short, and when I was done Rod and Wally told stories for the rest of dinner about other disastrous gestures made by Byron Cartwright in the past. He was everyone's warmhearted uncle, except that his instincts were constantly betrayed by his inability to think through the effect of his activities. As a businessman he was considered one of the best (toughest, coldest, coolest) in his very tough business, but away from the office his affection toward his clients and other acquaintances led him to one horrible misjudgment after another.

(These acts of Byron Cartwright's were not simple goofs like sending flowers to a hay-fever victim. As with the picture to Dawn and me, each story took about five minutes to explain the characters and relationships involved, the nuances that turned Byron Cartwright's offerings into Molotov cocktails, and while some of the errors were funny, most of them produced only groans among the listeners at the table. It was Wally who finally summed it up, saying, "Most mutations don't work, and By is simply one more proof of it. You can't have an agent with a heart of gold, it isn't a viable combination.")

After dinner, Rod drove me back to Dawn's house, with Dennis a silent worshipper vibrating behind us on the back seat. As we neared the house, Rod said, "May I give you a piece of advice, Orry?"

"Sure."

"You haven't known Dawn for a long time, and she's probably changed a lot."

"Yes, she has."

"I don't think she'll ever mention that picture again," Rod told me, "and I don't think you ought to bring it up either."

"You may be right."

"If it's still there, have Wang get rid of it. If you want it yourself, tell Wang to ship it off to your home. But don't show it to Dawn, don't ask her about it. Just deal with Wang."

"Thank you," I said. "I agree with you."

We reached the house, and Rod stopped in front of the door. "Good luck," he said.

I didn't immediately leave the car. I said, "Do you mind if I ask you a question?"

"Go ahead."

"You saw how different Dawn used to be, when she was Estelle Anlic. And if you remember the picture, I haven't changed very much."

"Hardly at all. The Navy must agree with you."

"The reason I came out here," I said, "was because I had a question in my mind about that. I wanted to know how a person could change so completely into somebody different. Somebody with different looks, a different personality, a whole different kind of life. I mean, when I married Estelle, she wasn't anybody who could even *hope* to be a movie star."

Rod seemed both amused and in some hidden way upset by the question. He said, "You want to know how she did it?"

"I suppose. Not exactly. Something like that."

"She decided to," he said. He had a crinkly, masculine, self-confident smile, but at the same time he had another expression going behind the smile, an expression that told me the smile was a fake, a mask. The inner expression was also smiling, but it was more intelligent, and more truly friendly. He said, using that inner expression, "Why did you ask *me* that question, Orry?"

It was, of course, because I believed he'd somehow done the same sort of thing as Dawn, that somewhere there existed photos of him in some unimaginable other person. But it would sound like an insult to say that, and I said nothing, floundering around for an alternate answer.

He nodded. "You're right," he said.

"Then how?" I asked him. "She decided to be somebody else. How is it possible to *do* that?"

He shrugged and grinned, friendly and amiable but not really able to describe colors to a blind man. "You find somebody you'd rather be," he said. "It really is as simple as that, Orry."

I knew he was wrong. There was truth in the idea that people like Dawn and himself had found somebody else they'd rather be, but it surely couldn't be as simple as that. Everybody has fantasies, but not everybody throws away the real self and lives in the fantasy.

Still, it would have been both rude and useless to press him, so I said; "Thank you," and got out of the car.

"Hold the door," he said. Then he patted the front seat, as though calling a dog, and said, "Dennis, come on up." And Dennis, a nervous high-bred afghan hound in his fawn-colored jumpsuit, clambered gratefully into the front seat.

I was about to shut the door when Rod leaned over Dennis and said, "One more little piece of advice, Orry."

"Yes?"

"Don't ask Dawn that question."

"Oh," I said.

The picture was gone from the front hallway. My luggage from the motel was in my room, and Dawn was naked in the pool, her slender long

intricate body golden-green in the underwater lights. I opened the drapes
and stepped out to the tepid California air and said, "Shall I join you in
there?"

"Hey, baby," she called, treading water, grinning at me, sunny and
untroubled. "Come on in, the water's fine."

5

The rest of the days that week were all the same, except that no more
unfortunate presents came from Byron Cartwright. Dawn and I got up
early every morning, flew to Stockton, she worked in the movie and
napped – alone – after lunch, we flew back to Los Angeles, and then
there'd be dinner in a restaurant with several other people, a shifting
cast that usually included Rod and Wally and Dennis, plus others,
sometimes strangers and sometimes known to me. Then Dawn and
I would go back to the house and swim and go to bed and play
with one another's bodies until we slept. The sex was wonderful, and
endlessly various, but afterwards it never seemed real. I would look at
Dawn during the daytime, and I would remember this or that specific
thing we had done together the night before, and it wasn't as though
I'd actually done it with *her*. It was more as though I'd dreamed it, or
fantasized it.

Maybe that was partly because we always slept in the guest room, in
what had become my bed. Dawn never took me to her own bed, or even
brought me into her private bedroom. Until the second week I was there,
I was never actually in that wing of the house.

On the Thursday evening we stayed longer in Stockton, to see
the film shot the day before. Movie companies when they're filming
generally show the previous day's work every evening, which some
people call the *dailies* and some call the *rushes*. Its purpose is to
give the director and performers and other people involved a chance
to see how they're doing, and also so the film editor and director can
begin discussing the way the pieces of film will be organized together
to make the movie. Dawn normally stayed away from the rushes, but
on Thursday evening they would be viewing the sequence that she and
Rod had argued about with Harvey, so the whole group of us stayed
and watched.

I suppose movie people get so they can tell from the rushes whether
things are working right or not, but when I look at half a dozen
strips of film each recording the same action sequence or lines of
dialogue, over and over and over, all I get is bored. Nevertheless,
I could sense when the lights came up in the screening room that

almost everybody now believed Harvey to have been right all along. Rod wouldn't come right out and admit it, but it was clear his objections were no longer important to him. Dawn, on the other hand, had some sort of emotional commitment to her position, and all she had to say afterwards was, grumpily, "Well, I suppose the picture will survive, despite that." And off she stomped, me in her wake.

Still, by the time we reached the plane to go back to Los Angeles, she was in a cheerful mood again. Bad temper never lasted long with her.

Friday afternoon there were technical problems of some sort, delaying the shooting, so after Dawn's nap she and I sat in the parlor of her dressing room and talked together about the past. It was one of those conversations full of sentences beginning, "Do you remember when – ?" We talked about troubles we'd had with the landlord, about the time we snuck into a movie theater when we didn't have any money, things like that. She didn't seem to have any particular attitude about these memories, neither nostalgia nor revulsion; they were simply interesting anecdotes out of our shared history.

But they led me finally, despite Rod's advice, to ask her the question that had brought me out here. "You've changed an awful lot since then," I said. "How did you do that?"

She frowned at me, apparently not understanding. "What do you mean, changed?"

"Changed. Different. Somebody else."

"I'm not somebody else," she said. Now she looked and sounded annoyed, as though somebody were pestering her with stupidities. "I dyed my hair, that's all. I learned about makeup, I learned how to dress."

"Personality," I said. "Emotions. Everything about you is different."

"It is not." Her annoyance was making her almost petulant. "People change when they grow older, that's all. It's been sixteen years, Orry."

"I'm still the same."

"Yes, you are," she said. "You still plod along with those flat feet of yours."

"I suppose I do," I said.

Abruptly she shifted, shaking her head and softening her expression and saying, "I'm sorry, Orry, you didn't deserve that. You're right, you are the same man. You were wonderful then, and you're wonderful now."

"I think the flat feet was more like the truth," I said, because that is what I think.

But she shook her head, saying, "No. I loved living with you, Orry, I loved being your wife. That was the first time in my life I ever relaxed. You know what you taught me?"

"Taught you?"

"That I didn't have to just run all the time, in a panic. That I could slow down, and look around."

I wanted to ask her if that was when she realized she could become somebody else, but I understood by now that Rod had been right, it wasn't something I could ask her directly, so I changed the subject. But I remembered what the magazine article had said about me being a "stock figure, the San Diego sailor in every sex star's childhood," and I wondered if what Dawn had just said was really true, if being with me had in some way started the change that turned Estelle Anlic into Dawn Devayne. Plodding with my flat feet? Most of the Estelle Anlics in the world marry flat-footed Orry Tupikoses; what had been different with us?

Saturday we drove to Palm Springs, to the home of a famous comedian named Lennie Hacker, for a party. There were about two hundred people there, many of them famous, and maybe thirty of them staying on as house guests for the rest of the weekend. Lennie Hacker had his own movie theater on his land, and we all watched one of his movies plus some silent comedies. That was in the afternoon. In the evening, different guests who were professional entertainers performed, singing, dancing, playing the piano, telling jokes. It was too big a party for anybody to notice one face more or less, so I didn't have to explain myself to anybody. (There was only one bad moment, at the beginning, when I was introduced to the host. Lennie Hacker was a short round man with sparkly black eyes and a built-in grin on his face, and when he shook my hand he said, "Hiya, sailor." I thought that was meant to be some kind of insult joke, but later on I heard him say the same thing to different other people, so it was just a way he had of saying hello.)

I'd never been to a party like this – a famous composer sat at the piano, singing his own songs and interrupting himself to make put-down gags about the lyrics – and I just walked around with a drink in my hand, looking at everything, enjoying being a spectator. (I was wearing the Edwardian jacket and the full-sleeved shirt, no longer self-conscious about my appearance.) Dawn and I crossed one another's paths from time to time, but we didn't stay together; she had lots of friends she wanted to spend time with.

As for me, I had very few conversations. Rod and Dennis were there, and I had a few words with Rod about the silent comedies we'd seen, and I also made small talk with a few other people I'd met at different restaurant dinners over the last week. At one point, when I was standing in a corner watching two television comedians trade insult jokes in front of an audience of twenty or thirty other guests, Lennie Hacker came over to me and said, "Listen."

"Yes?"

"You look like an intelligent fella," he said. He looked out at the crowd of his guests, and made a sweeping gesture to include them all. "Tell me," he said, "who the fuck *are* all these people?"

"Movie stars," I said.

"Yeah?" He studied them, skeptical but interested. "They look like a bunch a bums," he said. "See ya." And he drifted away.

A little later I ran into Byron Cartwright, who beamed at me and took my hand in both of his and said, "How *are* you, Orry?"

"Fine," I said.

"Listen, Orry," he said. He kept my hand in one of his, and put his other arm around my shoulders, turning me a bit away from the room and the party, making ours a private conversation. "I've wanted to have a *good* talk with you," he said.

"You have?"

"I'm sorry about that picture." He looked at me with a pained smile. "The way Dawn talked about you, I thought she'd *like* that reminder."

I didn't know what to say. "I guess so," I told him.

"But things are good between *you* two, aren't they? No trouble there."

"No, we're fine."

"That's good, that's good." He thumped my back, and finally released my hand. "You two look good together, Orry," he said. "You did way back then, and you do now."

"Well, *she* looks good."

"The two of you," he insisted. "Together. When's your leave up, Orry? When do you have to go back to the Navy?"

"In two weeks."

"Do you want me to fix it?"

"Fix it?"

"We could get you an early release," he said. "Get you out of the Navy."

"I've only got two years before I collect my pension."

"We could probably work something out," he told me. "Make some arrangement with the Navy. Believe me, Orry, I know people who know people."

I said, "But I couldn't go on living at Dawn's house."

"Orry," he said, chuckling at me and patting my arm. "You were her first love, Orry. You're her man. Look how she took you right in again, the minute you showed up. Look how well you're getting along. In some little corner of that girl, Orry, you've always been her husband. She left the others, but she was taken away from you."

I stared at him. "*Marry* her? Dawn Devayne? Mr Cartwright, I don't – "

"By. Call me By. And think about it, Orry. Will you do that? Just think about it."

There was no question in the Hacker household about our belonging together, Dawn and me. We'd been initially shown by a uniformed maid to a bedroom we were to share on the second floor, overlooking Hacker's private three-hole golf course, and by one o'clock in the morning I was ready to return to it and go to sleep, although the party was still going strong. I found Dawn with a group of people singing show tunes around the piano, and I told her, "I'm going to sleep now."

"Stick around five minutes, we'll go up together."

I did – it's surprising how many old lyrics we all remember, the words to songs we no longer know we know – and then we found our way to the right bedroom, used the private bath next door, and went to bed. When I reached for Dawn, though, she laughed and said, "You must be kidding."

I was. I realized I was too sleepy to have any true interest in sex, that I'd started only out of a sense of obligation, that I'd felt it was my duty to perform at this point. "You're right," I said. "See you in the morning."

"You're a good old boy, Orry," she said, and kissed my chin, and rolled away, and I guess we both went right to sleep.

When I woke up it was still dark, but light of some sort was glittering faintly outside the window, and there were distant voices. I'd lived with Dawn Devayne less than a week, but already I was used to the rounded shapes of her asleep beside me, and already I missed the numerals of the digital clock shimmering white in the darkness. I didn't know what time it was, but it had to be very late.

I got up from bed and looked out the window, and the illumination came from floodlights over the golf course. Lennie Hacker and some of his male guests were playing golf out there. I recognized Byron Cartwright among them. Lennie Hacker's distinctive nasal voice said something, and the others laughed, and somebody drove a white ball high up out of the light, briefly out of existence before it suddenly bounced, small and white and clear, on the clipped grass of the green.

The men moved as a group, accompanied by a servant driving a golf cart filled with bags and clubs. A portable bar was mounted on the back of the cart, and they were all having drinks from it, but no one appeared drunk, or sloppy, or tired. None of them were particularly young, but none of them were in any way old.

The golf course made a wobbly triangle around an artificial pond, with the first tee and the third green forming the angle nearest the house. As the players moved away toward the first green, I looked beyond the lit triangle, seeing only black darkness, but sensing the other Palm Springs estates around us, and then the great circle of desert around that. Desert. These men – *some* men – had come out to this desert and by force of will had converted it into a royal domain. "To live like kings." That's a cliché, but here it was the truth. In high school I read that the ancient Roman emperors had ordered snow carted down from the mountain peaks to cool their palaces in summer. It has always been the prerogative of kings to make a comfortable toy of their environment. Here, where a hundred years ago they would have broiled and starved and died grindingly of thirst, these men strolled on clipped green grass under floodlights, laughing together and reaching for their drinks from the back of a golf cart.

If I married Dawn Devayne –

I shook my head, and closed my eyes, and then turned away from the window to look at the mound of her asleep in the bed. It was a good thing I'd been warned about Byron Cartwright's sentimental errors, or I might actually have started dreaming about such impossibilities, and wound up a character in another Byron Cartwright horror story: "And the poor fellow actually proposed to her!" If an Indian who had grubbed his lean and careful existence from this desert a hundred years ago were to return here now, how could he set up his tent? How could he take up his life again? He's never been *here*. I was married to Estelle Anlic once, a long time ago. I was never married to Dawn Devayne.

6

After the weekend, we went back to the old routine until Wednesday evening, when, on the plane back to Los Angeles, Dawn said, "We won't be going out to dinner tonight."

"No?"

"My mother's coming over, with her husband."

I felt a sudden nervousness. "Oh," I said.

She laughed at my expression. "Don't worry, she won't even remember you."

"She won't?"

"And if she does, she won't care. I'm not sixteen any more."

Nevertheless, it seemed to me that Dawn was also nervous, and when we got to the house she immediately started finding fault with Wang and the other servants. These servants, a staff of four or five, I almost never saw – except for the cook at breakfast – but now they were abruptly visible, cleaning, carrying things, being yelled at for no particular reason. Dawn had said her mother would arrive at eight, so I went off to my own room with today's *Hollywood Reporter* – I was getting so I recognized some of the names in the stories there – until the digital clock read 7:55. Then I went out to the living room, got a drink from Wang, and sat there waiting. Dawn was out of both sight and hearing now, probably changing her clothes.

They came in about ten after eight, two short leathery-skinned people in pastel clothing that looked all wrong. Dawn's mother had on a fuzzy pink sweater of the kind worn by young women twenty years ago, with a stiff-looking skirt and jacket in checks of pale green and white. Her shoes were white and she carried a white patent leather purse with a brass clasp. None of the parts went together, though it was understandable that they would all belong in the same wardrobe. She looked like a blind person who'd been dressed by an indifferent volunteer.

Her husband, as short as she was but considerably thinner, was dressed more consistently, in white casual shoes, pale blue slacks, white plastic belt, and white and blue short-sleeved shirt. He had a seamed and bony face, the tendons stood out on his neck, and his elbows looked like the kind of bone soothsayers once used to tell the future. With his thin black hair slicked to the side over his browned scalp, and his habit of leaning slightly forward from the waist at all times, and his surprisingly bright pale blue eyes, he looked like a finalist in some Senior Citizens' golf tournament.

I stood up when the doorbell rang, and moved tentatively forward as Wang let them both in, but I was saved from introducing (explaining) myself by Dawn's sudden arrival from the opposite direction. Striding forward in a swirl of floor-length white skirt, she held both arms straight out from the shoulder and cried, "Mother! Leo! Delighted!"

All I could do was stare. She had redone herself from top to bottom, had changed her hair, covered herself with necklaces and bracelets and rings, made up her face differently, dressed herself in a white ballgown I'd never seen before, and she was coming forward with such patently false joy that I could hardly believe I'd ever watched her do a *good* job of acting. I was suddenly reminded of that whore back in New York, and I realized that now Dawn herself was pretending to be Dawn Devayne. Some imitation Dawn Devayne, utterly impregnable and larger than life, had been wrapped around the original, and the astonishing thing was, the real Dawn Devagne was just as bad at imitating Dawn Devayne as that whore had been.

I don't mean to say that finally I saw Estelle again, tucked away inside those layers of Dawn, as I had seen the Hispanic hidden inside the whore. It was Dawn Devayne, the one I had come to know over the last week, who was inside this masquerade.

But now Dawn was introducing me, saying, "Mother, this is a friend of mine called Orry. Orry, this is my mother, Mrs Hettick, and her husband Leo."

Leo gave me a firm if bony handclasp, and a nod of his pointed jaw. "Good to know you," he said.

Dawn's mother gave me a sharp look. Inside her mismatched vacation clothing and her plump body and her expensive beauty shop hair treatment she was some kind of scrawny bird. She said, "You in pictures?"

"No, I'm not."

"Seen you someplace."

"Come along, everybody," Dawn said, swirling and swinging her arms so all her jewelry jangled, "we'll sit out by the pool for a while."

I didn't think there was anything wrong with the evening except that Dawn was so tense all the time. Her mother, whom I'd never met before except when she was yelling at me, did a lot of talking about arguments she'd had with different people in stores – "So then *I* said, so then *she* said . . ." – but she wasn't terrible about it, and she did have an amusing way of phrasing herself sometimes. Leo Hettick, who sat to my right in the formal dining room where we had our formal dinner, was an old Navy man as it turned out, who'd done a full thirty years and got out in 1972, so he and I talked about different tours we'd spent, ships we'd been on, what we thought of different ports and things like that. Meantime, Dawn mostly listened to her mother, pretending the things she said were funnier than they were.

What started the fight was when Mrs Hettick turned to me, over the parfait and coffee, and said, "You gonna be number five?"

I had to pretend I didn't know what she was talking about. "I beg pardon?"

"You're living here, aren't you?"

"I'm a houseguest," I said. "For a couple of weeks."

"I know that kind of houseguest," she said. "I've seen a lot of them."

Dawn said, "Mother, eat your parfait." Her tension had suddenly closed down in from all that sprightliness, had become very tightly knotted and quiet.

Her mother ignored her. Watching me with her quick bird eyes she said, "You can't be worse than any of the others. The first one was a child molester, you know, and the second was a faggot."

"Stop, Mother," Dawn said.

"The third was impotent," her mother said. "He couldn't get it up if the flag went by. What do you think *of that*?"

"I don't think people should talk about other people's marriages," I said.

Leo Hettick said, "Edna, let it go now."

"You stay out of this, Leo," she told him, and turned back to say to me, "The whole world talks about my daughter's marriages, why shouldn't I? If you *are* number five, you'll find your picture in newspapers you wouldn't use to wrap fish."

"I don't think I read those papers," I said.

"No, but my mother does," Dawn said. Some deep bitterness had twisted her face into someone I'd never seen before. "My mother has the instincts of a pig," she said. "Show her some mud and she can't wait to start rooting in it."

"Being *your* mother, I get plenty of mud to root in."

I said, "I was the first husband, Mrs Hettick, and I always thought *you* were the child molester."

"Oh, Orry," Dawn said; not angry but sad, as though I'd just made some terrible mistake that we both would suffer for.

Slowly, delightedly, as though receiving an unexpected extra dessert, Mrs Hettick turned to stare at me, considering me, observing me. Slowly she nodded, slowly she said, "By God, you are, aren't you? That filthy sailor."

"You treated your daughter badly, Mrs Hettick. If you'd ever – "

But she didn't care what I had to say. Turning back to her daughter, crowing, she said, "You running through the whole lot again? A triumphant return tour! Let me know when you dig up Ken Forrest, will you? At least he'll be stiff this time."

Leo Hettick said, "That's just about enough, Edna."

His wife glared at him. "What do *you* know about it?"

"I know when you're being impolite, Edna," he said. "If you remember, you made me a promise, some little time ago."

She sat there, glaring at him with a sullen stare, her body looking more than ever at odds with her clothing; the fuzzy pink sweater, most of all, seeming like some unfunny joke. While the Hetticks looked at one another, deciding who was in charge, I found myself remembering that magazine's description of me as "a stock figure," and of course here was another stock figure, the quarrelsome mother of the movie star. I thought of myself as something other than, or more than, a stock figure; was Mrs Hettick also more than she seemed? What did it mean that she had broken up her daughter's first marriage, to a sailor, and later had married a sailor herself, and wore clothing dating from the time of her daughter's marriage? What promise had she made her husband, "some little time ago"? Was *he* a stock figure? The feisty old man telling stories on the porch of the old folks' home; all the rest of us were simply characters in one of his reminiscences.

Maybe that was the truth, and he was the hero of the story after all. He was certainly the one who decided how this evening would end; he won the battle of wills with his wife, while Dawn and I both sat out of the picture, having no influence, having no part to play until Edna Hettick's face finally softened, she gave a quick awkward nod, and she said, "You're right, Leo. I get carried away." She even apologized to her daughter, to some extent, turning to Dawn and saying, "I guess I live in the past too much."

"Well, it's over and forgotten," Dawn said, and invented a smile.

After they left – not late – the smile at last fell like a dead thing from Dawn's mouth. "I have a headache," she said, not looking at me. "I don't feel like swimming tonight, I'm going to bed."

Her own bed, she meant. I went off to my room, and left the drapes partway open, and didn't go to sleep till very late, but she never came by.

It was ten forty-three by the digital clock when I awoke. I put on the white robe and wandered through the house, and found Wang in the kitchen. Nodding at me with his usual polite smile, he said, "Breakfast?"

"Is Dawn up yet?"

"Gone to work."

I couldn't understand that. Last night she'd been upset, and of course she'd wanted to be alone for a while. But why ignore me this morning? I had breakfast, and then I settled down with magazines and the television set, and waited for the evening.

By nine o'clock I understood she wasn't coming home. It had been a long long day, an empty day, but at least I'd been able to tell myself it would eventually end, Dawn would come home around seven and everything would be the same again. Now it was nine o'clock, she wasn't here, I knew she wouldn't be here tonight at all, and I didn't know what to do.

I thought of all the people I'd met in the last week and a half, Dawn's friends, and the only ones I might talk to at all were Byron Cartwright or Rod, but even if I did talk to one of them what would I say? "Dawn and her mother had a little argument, and Dawn didn't sleep with me, and she left alone this morning and hasn't come back." Rod, I was certain, would simply advise me to sit tight, wait, do nothing. As for Byron Cartwright, this was a situation tailor-made for him to do the wrong thing. So I talked to no one, I stayed where I was, I watched more television, read more magazines, and I waited for Dawn.

*   *   *

The next day, driven more by boredom than anything else, I finally explored that other wing of the house. Dawn's bedroom, directly across the pool from mine, was all done in pinks and golds, with a thick white rug on the floor. Several awkward paintings of white clapboard houses in rural settings were on the walls. They weren't signed, and I never found out who'd done them.

But a more interesting room was also over there, down a short side corridor. A small cluttered attic-like place, it was filled with luggage and old pieces of furniture and mounds of clothing. Leaning with its face to the wall was the blown-up photograph, unharmed, and atop a ratty bureau in the farthest corner slumped a small brown stuffed animal; a panda? The room had a damp smell — it reminded me of our old apartment in San Diego — and I didn't like being in there, so I went back once more to the television set.

People on game shows are very emotional.

Saturday morning I finally admitted to myself that Dawn was staying away only because I was still there. I'd been alone now for three days, except for Wang and the silent anonymous other servants — from time to time the phone would ring, but it was Wang's right to answer it, and he always assured me afterward it was nothing, nothing, unimportant — and all I'd done was sit around and think, and try to ignore the truth, and by Saturday morning I couldn't hide it from myself any more.

Dawn would not come back until I had given up and left. She couldn't throw me out of her house, but she couldn't face me either, not now or ever again. I belonged in the room with the photograph and the panda and the old clothing, the furniture, the bits and pieces of Estelle Anlic.

I knew the answer now to the question I'd brought out here. In order to create a new person to be, you have to hate the old person enough to kill it. Estelle *was* Dawn, and Dawn was happy.

She had dealt with my sudden reappearance out of the past by forcing me also to accept Dawn Devayne, to put this new person in Estelle's place in my memory, so that once more Estelle would cease to exist.

But the mother remained outside control, with her dirty knowledge; in front of her, Estelle was only pretending to be Dawn Devayne. After Wednesday night, Dawn must believe her mother had recreated Estelle also in my mind, turned Dawn back into Estelle in my eyes. No wonder she couldn't be in my presence any longer.

I put the borrowed clothes away and packed my bag and asked Wang to call a taxi. There wasn't anybody to say goodbye to.

Back on the base a week early, I explained part of the situation to the Commander and applied for a transfer, and got it. I told Fran everything — almost everything — and she moved to Norfolk to be near me at my new post (where my history with Dawn Devayne never came to light), and when I retired this year we were married.

I don't go to Dawn Devayne movies. I also don't do those things with Fran that I'd first done with Dawn. I don't have any reason not to, it's just I don't feel that way any more. And Fran's vehemence for new sexual activity was only a temporary thing anyway; she very quickly cooled back down to what she had been before. We get along very well.

Sometimes I have a dream. In the dream, I'm walking on Hollywood Boulevard, on the stars' names, and I stop at one point, and look down, and the name in the pavement is ESTELLE ANLIC. I just stand there. That's the dream. Later, when I wake up, I understand there isn't any Estelle Anlic any more; she's buried out there, on Hollywood Boulevard, underneath her name, standing up, squinting in the San Diego sun.